THE DARK OF THE SUN

AND

THE SUNBIRD

THE COURTNEYS

Birds of Prey
When the Lion Feeds
The Sound of Thunder
A Sparrow Falls
Monsoon

THE COURTNEYS OF AFRICA

The Burning Shore
Power of the Sword
Rage
A Time to Die
Golden Fox

THE BALLANTYNE NOVELS

A Falcon Flies
Men of Men
The Angels Weep
The Leopard Hunts in Darkness

also

Shout at the Devil
Gold Mine
The Diamond Hunters
Eagle in the Sky
The Eye of the Tiger
Cry Wolf
Hungry as the Sea
Wild Justice
Elephant Song
River God
The Seventh Scroll

Wilbur Smith was born in Central Africa in 1933. He was educated at Michaelhouse and Rhodes University.

He became a full-time writer in 1964 after the successful publication of *When the Lion Feeds*, and has since written twenty-six novels, all meticulously researched on his numerous expeditions worldwide. His books are now translated into twenty-six languages.

He owns a farm and game reserve and has an abiding concern for the peoples and wildlife of his native continent, an interest strongly reflected in his novels.

WILBUR SMITH

THE DARK
OF THE SUN

AND

THE SUNBIRD

PAN BOOKS

The Dark Side of the Sun published 1965 by William Heinemann Ltd.
First published in paperback by Pan Books 1965.
The Sunbird first published 1972 by William Heinemann Ltd.
First published in paperback by Pan Books 1974.

This omnibus edition published 2003 by Pan Books
an imprint of Pan Macmillan Ltd
Pan Macmillan, 20 New Wharf Road, London NI 9RR
Basingstoke and Oxford
Associated companies throughout the world
www.panmacmillan.com

ISBN 0 330 43671 6

1 3 5 7 9 8 6 4 2

A CIP catalogue record for this book is available from
the British Library.

Printed and bound in Great Britain by
Mackays of Chatham PLC, Chatham, Kent

THE DARK OF THE SUN

'I don't like the idea,' announced Wally Hendry, and belched. He moved his tongue round his mouth getting the taste of it before he went on. 'I think the whole idea stinks like a ten-day corpse.' He lay sprawled on one of the beds with a glass balanced on his naked chest and he was sweating heavily in the Congo heat.

'Unfortunately your opinion doesn't alter the fact that we are going.' Bruce Curry went on laying out his shaving tackle without looking up.

'You shoulda told them to keep it, told them we were staying here in Elisabethville – why didn't you tell them that, hey?' Hendry picked up his glass and swallowed the contents.

'Because they pay me not to argue.' Bruce spoke without interest and looked at himself in the fly-spotted mirror above the washbasin. The face that looked back was sun-darkened with a cap of close-cropped black hair; soft hair that would be unruly and inclined to curl if it were longer. Black eyebrows slanting upwards at the corners, green eyes with a heavy fringe of lashes and a mouth which could smile as readily as it could sulk. Bruce regarded his good looks without pleasure. It was a long time since he had felt that emotion, a long time since his mouth had either smiled or sulked. He did not feel the old tolerant affection for his nose, the large slightly hooked nose that rescued his face from prettiness and gave him the air of a genteel pirate.

'Jesus!' growled Wally Hendry from the bed. 'I've had just about a gutsful of this nigger army. I don't mind fighting

1

– but I don't fancy going hundreds of miles out into the bush to play nursemaid to a bunch of bloody refugees.'

'It's a hell of a life,' agreed Bruce absently and spread shaving-soap on his face. The lather was very white against his tan. Under a skin that glowed so healthily that it appeared to have been freshly oiled, the muscles of his shoulders and chest changed shape as he moved. He was in good condition, fitter than he had been for many years, but this fact gave him no more pleasure than had his face.

'Get me another drink, André.' Wally Hendry thrust his empty glass into the hand of the man who sat on the edge of the bed.

The Belgian stood up and went across to the table obediently.

'More whisky and less beer in this one,' Wally instructed, turned once more to Bruce and belched again. 'That's what I think of the idea.'

As André poured Scotch whisky into the glass and filled it with beer Wally hitched around the pistol in its webbing holster until it hung between his legs.

'When are we leaving?' he asked.

'There'll be an engine and five coaches at the goods yard first thing tomorrow morning. We'll load up and get going as soon as possible.' Bruce started to shave, drawing the razor down from temple to chin and leaving the skin smooth and brown behind it.

'After three months of fighting a bunch of greasy little Gurkhas I was looking forward to a bit of fun – I haven't even had a pretty in all that time – now the second day after the ceasefire and they ship us out again.'

'C'est la guerre,' muttered Bruce, his face twisted in the act of shaving.

'What's that mean?' demanded Wally suspiciously.

'That's war,' Bruce translated.

'Talk English, Bucko.'

It was the measure of Wally Hendry that after six months

2

in the Belgian Congo he could neither speak nor understand a single word of French.

There was silence again, broken only by the scraping of Bruce's razor and the small metallic sound as the fourth man in the hotel room stripped and cleaned his FN rifle.

'Have a drink, Haig,' Wally invited him.

'No, thanks.' Michael Haig glanced up, not trying to conceal his distaste as he looked at Wally.

'You're another snotty bastard – don't want to drink with me, hey? Even the high-class Captain Curry is drinking with me. What makes you so goddam special?'

'You know that I don't drink.' Haig turned his attention back to his weapon, handling it with easy familiarity. For all of them the ugly automatic rifles had become an extension of their own bodies. Even while shaving Bruce had only to drop his hand to reach the rifle propped against the wall, and the two men on the bed had theirs on the floor beside them.

'You don't drink!' chuckled Wally. 'Then how did you get that complexion, Bucko? How come your nose looks like a ripe plum?'

Haig's mouth tightened and the hands on his rifle stilled.

'Cut it out, Wally,' said Bruce without heat.

'Haig don't drink,' crowed Wally, and dug the little Belgian in the ribs with his thumb, 'get that, André! He's a tee-bloody-total! My old man was a teetotal also; sometimes for two, three months at a time he was teetotal, and then he'd come home one night and sock the old lady in the clock so you could hear her teeth rattle from across the street.'

His laughter choked him and he had to wait for it to clear before he went on.

'My bet is that you're that kind of teetotal, Haig. One drink and you wake up ten days later; that's it, isn't it? One drink and – pow! – the old girl gets it in the chops and the kids don't eat for a couple of weeks.'

3

Haig laid the rifle down carefully on the bed and looked at Wally with his jaws clenched, but Wally had not noticed. He went on happily.

'André, take the whisky bottle and hold it under Old Teetotal Haig's nose. Let's watch him slobber at the mouth and his eyes stand out like a pair of dog's balls.'

Haig stood up. Twice the age of Wally – a man in his middle fifties, with grey in his hair and the refinement of his features not completely obliterated by the marks that life had left upon them. He had arms like a boxer and a powerful set to his shoulders. 'It's about time you learned a few manners, Hendry. Get on your feet.'

'You wanta dance or something? I don't waltz – ask André. He'll dance with you – won't you, André?'

Haig was balanced on the balls of his feet, his hands closed and raised slightly. Bruce Curry placed his razor on the shelf above the basin, and moved quietly round the table with soap still on his face to take up a position from which he could intervene. There he waited, watching the two men.

'Get up, you filthy guttersnipe.'

'Hey, André, get that. He talks pretty, hey? He talks real pretty.'

'I'm going to smash that ugly face of yours right into the middle of the place where your brain should have been.'

'Jokes! This boy is a natural comic.' Wally laughed, but there was something wrong with the sound of it. Bruce knew then that Wally was not going to fight. Big arms and swollen chest covered with ginger hair, belly flat and hard-looking, thick-necked below the wide flat-featured face with its little Mongolian eyes; but Wally wasn't going to fight. Bruce was puzzled: he remembered the night at the road bridge and he knew that Hendry was no coward, and yet now he was not going to take up Haig's challenge.

Mike Haig moved towards the bed.

'Leave him, Mike.' André spoke for the first time, his

4

voice soft as a girl's. 'He was only joking. He didn't mean it.'

'Hendry, don't think I'm too much of a gentleman to hit you because you're on your back. Don't make that mistake.'

'Big deal,' muttered Wally. 'This boy's not only a comic, he's a bloody hero also.'

Haig stood over him and lifted his right hand with the fist, bunched like a hammer, aimed at Wally's face.

'Haig!' Bruce hadn't raised his voice but its tone checked the older man.

'That's enough,' said Bruce.

'But this filthy little—'

'Yes, I know,' said Bruce. 'Leave him!' With his fist still up Mike Haig hesitated, and there was no movement in the room. Above them the corrugated iron roof popped loudly as it expanded in the heat of the Congo midday, and the only other sound was Haig's breathing. He was panting and his face was congested with blood.

'Please, Mike,' whispered André. 'He didn't mean it.'

Slowly Haig's anger changed to disgust and he dropped his hand, turned away and picked up his rifle from the other bed.

'I can't stand the smell in this room another minute. I'll wait for you in the truck downstairs, Bruce.'

'I won't be long,' agreed Bruce as Mike went to the door.

'Don't push your luck, Haig,' Wally called after him. 'Next time you won't get off so easily.'

In the doorway Mike Haig swung quickly, but, with a hand on his shoulder, Bruce turned him again.

'Forget it, Mike,' he said, and closed the door after him.

'He's just bloody lucky that he's an old man,' growled Wally. 'Otherwise I'd have fixed him good.'

'Sure,' said Bruce. 'It was decent of you to let him go.' The soap had dried on his face and he wet his brush to lather again.

'Yeah, I couldn't hit an old bloke like that, could I?'

5

'No.' Bruce smiled a little. 'But don't worry, you frightened the hell out of him. He won't try it again.'

'He'd better not!' warned Hendry. 'Next time I'll kill the old bugger.'

No, you won't, thought Bruce, you'll back down again as you have just done, as you've done a dozen times before. Mike and I are the only ones who can make you do it; in the same way as an animal will growl at its trainer but cringe away when he cracks the whip. He began shaving again.

The heat in the room was unpleasant to breathe; it drew the perspiration out of them and the smell of their bodies blended sourly with stale cigarette smoke and liquor fumes.

'Where are you and Mike going?' André ended the long silence.

'We're going to see if we can draw the supplies for this trip. If we have any luck we'll take them down to the goods yard and have Ruffy put an armed guard on them overnight,' Bruce answered him, leaning over the basin and splashing water up into his face.

'How long will we be away?'

Bruce shrugged. 'A week – ten days'. He sat on his bed and pulled on one of his jungle boots. 'That is, if we don't have any trouble.'

'Trouble, Bruce?' asked André.

'From Msapa Junction we'll have to go two hundred miles through country crawling with Baluba.'

'But we'll be in a train,' protested André. 'They've only got bows and arrows, they can't touch us.'

'André, there are seven rivers to cross – one big one – and bridges are easily destroyed. Rails can be torn up.' Bruce began to lace the boot. 'I don't think it's going to be a Sunday school picnic.'

'Christ. I think the whole thing stinks,' repeated Wally moodily. 'Why are we going anyway?'

'Because,' Bruce began patiently, 'for the last three

months the entire population of Port Reprieve has been cut off from the rest of the world. There are women and children with them. They are fast running out of food and the other necessities of life.' Bruce paused to light a cigarette, and then went on talking as he exhaled. 'All around them the Baluba tribe is in open revolt, burning, raping and killing indiscriminately. As yet they haven't attacked the town but it won't be very long until they do. Added to which there are rumours that rebel groups of Central Congolese troops and of our own forces have formed themselves into bands of heavily-armed *shufta*. They also are running amok through the northern part of the territory. Nobody knows for certain what is happening out there, but whatever it is you can be sure it's not very pretty. We are going to fetch those people in to safety.'

'Why don't the U.N. people send out a plane?' asked André.

'No landing field.'

'Helicopters?'

'Out of range.'

'For my money the bastards can stay there,' grunted Wally. 'If the Balubas fancy a little man steak, who are we to do them out of a meal? Every man's entitled to eat and as long as it's not me they're eating, more power to their teeth, say I.' He placed his foot against André back and straightened his leg suddenly, throwing the Belgian off the bed on to his knees.

'Go and get me a pretty.'

'There aren't any, Wally. I'll get you another drink.' André scrambled to his feet and reached for Wally's empty glass, but Wally's hand dropped on to his wrist.

'I said *pretty*, André, not *drink*.'

'I don't know where to find them, Wally.' André's voice was desperate. 'I don't know what to say to them even.'

'You're being stupid, Bucko. I might have to break your arm.' Wally twisted the wrist slowly. 'You know as well as I do that the bar downstairs is full of them. You know that, don't you?'

'But what do I say to them?' André's face was contorted with the pain of his twisted wrist.

'Oh, for Christ's sake, you stupid bloody frog-eater – just go down and flash a banknote. You don't have to say a dicky bird.'

'You're hurting me, Wally.'

'No? You're kidding!' Wally smiled at him, twisting harder, his slitty eyes smoky from the liquor, and Bruce could see he was enjoying it. 'Are you going, Bucko? Make up your mind – get me a pretty or get yourself a broken arm.'

'All right, if that's what you want. I'll go. Please leave me, I'll go,' mumbled André.

'That's what I want.' Wally released him, and he straightened up massaging his wrist.

'See that she's clean and not too old. You hear me?'

'Yes, Wally. I'll get one.' André went to the door and Bruce noticed his expression. It was stricken beyond the pain of a bruised wrist. What lovely creatures they are, thought Bruce, and I am one of them and yet apart from them. I am the watcher, stirred by them as much as I would be by a bad play. André went out.

'Another drink, Bucko?' said Wally expansively. 'I'll even pour you one.'

'Thanks,' said Bruce, and started on the other boot. Wally brought the glass to him and he tasted it. It was strong, and the mustiness of the whisky was ill-matched with the sweetness of the beer, but he drank it.

'You and I,' said Wally, 'we're the shrewd ones. We drink 'cause we want to, not 'cause we have to. We live like we want to live, not like other people think we should. You and I got a lot in common, Bruce. We should be friends, you and I. I mean us being so much alike.' The drink was working in him now, blurring his speech a little.

'Of course we are friends – I count you as one of my very dearest, Wally.' Bruce spoke solemnly, no trace of sarcasm showing.

'No kidding?' Wally asked earnestly. 'How's that, hey? Christ, I always thought you didn't like me. Christ, you never can tell, isn't that right? You just never can tell,' shaking his head in wonder, suddenly sentimental with the whisky. 'That's really true? You like me. Yeah, we could be buddies. How's that, Bruce? Every guy needs a buddy. Every guy needs a back stop.'

'Sure,' said Bruce. 'We're buddies. How's that, hey?'

'That's on, Bucko!' agreed Wally with deep feeling, *and I feel nothing*, thought Bruce, *no disgust, no pity – nothing. That way you are secure; they cannot disappoint you, they cannot disgust you, they cannot sicken you, they cannot smash you up again.*

They both looked up as André ushered the girl into the room. She had a sexy little pug face, painted lips – ruby on amber.

'Well done, André,' applauded Wally, looking at the girl's body. She wore high heels and a short pink dress that flared into a skirt from her waist but did not cover her knees.

'Come here, cookie.' Wally held out his hand to her and she crossed the room without hesitation, smiling a bright professional smile. Wally drew her down beside him on to the bed.

André went on standing in the doorway. Bruce got up and shrugged into his camouflage battle-jacket, buckled on his webbing belt and adjusted the holstered pistol until it hung comfortably on his outer thigh.

'Are you going?' Wally was feeding the girl from his glass.

'Yes.' Bruce put his slouch hat on his head; the red, green and white Katangese sideflash gave him an air of artificial gaiety.

'Stay a little – come on, Bruce.'

9

'Mike is waiting for me.' Bruce picked up his rifle.

'Muck him. Stay a little, we'll have some fun.'

'No, thanks.' Bruce went to the door.

'Hey, Bruce. Take a look at this.' Wally tipped the girl backwards over the bed, he pinned her with one arm across her chest while she struggled playfully and with the other hand he swept her skirt up above her waist.

'Take a good look at this and tell me you still want to go!'

The girl was naked under the skirt, her lower body shaven so that her plump little sex pouted sulkily.

'Come on, Bruce,' laughed Wally. 'You first. Don't say I'm not your buddy.'

Bruce glanced at the girl, her legs scissored and her body wriggled as she fought with Wally. She was giggling.

'Mike and I will be back before curfew. I want this woman out of here by then,' said Bruce.

There is no desire, he thought as he looked at her, *that is all finished*. He opened the door.

'Curry!' shouted Wally. 'You're a bloody nut also. Christ, I thought you were a man. Jesus Christ! You're as bad as the others. André, the doll boy. Haig, the rummy. What's with you, Bucko? It's women with you, isn't it? You're a bloody nut-case also!'

Bruce closed the door and stood alone in the passage. The taunt had gone through a chink in his armour and he clamped his mind down on the sting of it, smothering it.

It's all over. She can't hurt me any more. He thought with determination, remembering her, the woman, not the one in the room he had just left but the other one who had been his wife.

'The bitch,' he whispered, and then quickly, almost guiltily, 'I do not hate her. There is no hatred and there is no desire.'

10

The lobby of the Hotel Grand Leopold II was crowded. There were gendarmes carrying their weapons ostentatiously, talking loudly, lolling against walls and over the bar; women with them, varying in colour from black through to pastel brown, some already drunk; a few Belgians still with the stunned disbelieving eyes of the refugee, one of the women crying as she rocked her child on her lap; other white men in civilian clothes but with the alertness about them and the quick restless eyes of the adventurer, talking quietly with Africans in business suits; a group of journalists at one table in damp shirtsleeves, waiting and watching with the patience of vultures. And everybody sweated in the heat.

Two South African charter pilots hailed Bruce from across the room.

'Hi, Bruce. How about a snort?'

'Dave. Carl.' Bruce waved. 'Big hurry now – tonight perhaps.'

'We're flying out this afternoon.' Carl Engelbrecht shook his head. 'Back next week.'

'We'll make it then,' Bruce agreed, and went out of the front door into the Avenue du Kasai. As he stopped on the sidewalk the white-washed buildings bounced the glare into his face. The naked heat made him wince and he felt fresh sweat start out of his body beneath his battle-suit. He took the dark glasses from his top pocket and put them on as he crossed the street to the Chev three-tonner in which Mike Haig waited.

'I'll drive, Mike.'

'Okay.' Mike slid across the seat and Bruce stepped up into the cab. He started the truck north down the Avenue du Kasai.

'Sorry about that scene, Bruce.'

'No harm done.'

'I shouldn't have lost my temper like that.'

Bruce did not answer, he was looking at the deserted buildings on either side. Most of them had been looted and all of them were pock-marked with shrapnel from the mortar bursts. At intervals along the sidewalk were parked the burnt out bodies of automobiles looking like the carapaces of long-dead beetles.

'I shouldn't have let him get through to me, and yet the truth hurts like hell.'

Bruce was silent but he trod down harder on the accelerator and the truck picked up speed. *I don't want to hear*, he thought, *I am not your confessor – I just don't want to hear*. He turned into the Avenue l'Etoile, headed towards the zoo.

'He was right, he had me measured to the inch,' persisted Mike.

'We've all got our troubles, otherwise we wouldn't be here.' And then, to change Mike's mood, 'We few, we happy few. We band of brothers.'

Mike grinned and his face was suddenly boyish. 'At least we have the distinction of following the second oldest profession – we, the mercenaries.'

'The oldest profession is better paid and much more fun,' said Bruce and swung the truck into the driveway of a double-storeyed residence, parked outside the front door and switched off the engine.

Not long ago the house had been the home of the chief accountant of Union Minière du Haut, now it was the billet of 'D' section, Special Striker Force, commanded by Captain Bruce Curry.

Half a dozen of his black gendarmes were sitting on the low wall of the verandah, and as Bruce came up the front steps they shouted the greeting that had become traditional since the United Nations intervention.

'U.N. – Merde!'

'Ah!' Bruce grinned at them in the sense of companionship that had grown up between them in the past months. 'The cream of the Army of Katanga!'

He offered his cigarettes around and stood chatting idly for a few minutes before asking, 'Where's Sergeant Major?' One of the gendarmes jerked a thumb at the glass doors that led into the lounge and Bruce went through with Mike behind him.

Equipment was piled haphazardly on the expensive furniture, the stone fireplace was half filled with empty bottles, a gendarme lay snoring on the Persian carpet, one of the oil paintings on the wall had been ripped by a bayonet and the frame hung askew, the imbuia-wood coffee table tilted drunkenly towards its broken leg, and the whole lounge smelled of men and cheap tobacco.

'Hello, Ruffy,' said Bruce.

'Just in time, boss.' Sergeant Major Ruffararo grinned delightedly from the armchair which he was overflowing. 'These goddam Arabs have run fresh out of folding stuff.' He gestured at the gendarmes that crowded about the table in front of him. 'Arab' was Ruffy's word of censure or contempt, and bore no relation to a man's nationality.

Ruffy's accent was always a shock to Bruce. You never expected to hear pure Americanese come rumbling out of that huge black frame. But three years previously Ruffy had returned from a scholarship tour of the United States with a command of the idiom, a diploma in land husbandry, a prodigious thirst for bottled beer (preferably Schlitz, but any other was acceptable) and a raving dose of the Old Joe.

The memory of this last, which had been a farewell gift from a high yellow sophomore of U.C.L.A., returned most painfully to Ruffararo when he was in his cups; so painfully that it could be assuaged only by throwing the nearest citizen of the United States.

Fortunately, it was only on rare occasions that an American and the necessary five or six gallons of beer were

13

assembled in the same vicinity so that Ruffy's latent race antipathy could find expression. A throwing by Ruffy was an unforgettable experience, both for the victim and the spectators. Bruce vividly recalled that night at the Hotel Lido when he had been a witness at one of Ruffy's most spectacular throwings.

The victims, three of them, were journalists representing publications of repute. As the evening wore on they talked louder; an American accent has a carry like a well-hit golf ball and Ruffy recognized it from across the terrace. He became silent, and in his silence drank the last gallon which was necessary to tip the balance. He wiped the froth from his upper lip and stood up with his eyes fastened on the party of Americans.

'Ruffy, hold it. Hey!' – Bruce might not have spoken. Ruffy started across the terrace. They saw him coming and fell into an uneasy silence.

The first was in the nature of a practice throw; besides, the man was not aerodynamically constructed and his stomach had too much wind resistance. A middling distance of twenty feet.

'Ruffy, leave them!' shouted Bruce.

On the next throw Ruffy was getting warmed up, but he put excessive loft into it. Thirty feet; the journalist cleared the terrace and landed on the lawn below with his empty glass still clutched in his hand.

'Run, you fool!' Bruce warned the third victim, but he was paralysed.

And this was Ruffy's best ever, he took a good grip – neck and seat of the pants – and put his whole weight into it. Ruffy must have known that he had executed the perfect throw, for his shout of 'Gonorrhoea!' as he launched his man had a ring of triumph to it.

Afterwards, when Bruce had soothed the three Americans, and they had recovered sufficiently to appreciate the fact that they were privileged by being party to a record throwing session, they all paced out the distances. The three journalists developed an almost proprietary affection for Ruffy and spent the rest of the evening buying him beers and boasting to every newcomer in the bar. One of them, he who had been thrown last and farthest, wanted to do an article on Ruffy – with pictures. Towards the end of the evening he was talking wildly of whipping up sufficient enthusiasm to have a man-throwing event included in the Olympic Games.

Ruffy accepted both their praise and their beer with modest gratitude; and when the third American offered to let Ruffy throw him again, he declined the offer on the grounds that he never threw the same man twice. All in all, it had been a memorable evening.

Apart from these occasional lapses, Ruffy had a more powerful body and happier mind than any man Bruce had ever known, and Bruce could not help liking him. He could not prevent himself smiling as he tried to reject Ruffy's invitation to play cards.

'We've got work to do now, Ruffy. Some other time.'

'Sit down, boss,' Ruffy repeated, and Bruce grimaced resignedly and took the chair opposite him.

'How much you going to bet?' Ruffy leaned forward.

'Un mille.' Bruce laid a thousand-franc note on the table; 'when that's gone, then we go.'

'No hurry,' Ruffy soothed him. 'We got all day.' He dealt the three cards face down. 'The old Christian monarch is in there somewhere; all you got to do is find him and it's the easiest mille you ever made.'

'In the middle,' whispered the gendarme standing beside Bruce's chair. 'That's him in the middle.'

'Take no notice of that mad Arab – he's lost five mille already this morning,' Ruffy advised.

Bruce turned over the right-hand card.

'Mis-luck,' crowed Ruffy. 'You got yourself the queen of hearts.' He picked up the banknote and stuffed it into his breast pocket. 'She'll see you wrong every time, that sweet-faced little bitch.' Grinning, he turned over the middle card to expose the jack of spades with his sly eyes and curly little moustache. 'She's been shacked up there with the jack right under the old king's nose.' He turned the king face up. 'Look you at that dozy old guy – he's not even facing in the right direction.'

Bruce stared at the three cards and he felt that sickness in his stomach again. The whole story was there; even the man's name was right, but the jack should have worn a beard and driven a red Jaguar and his queen of hearts never had such innocent eyes. Bruce spoke abruptly. 'That's it, Ruffy. I want you and ten men to come with me.'

'Where we going?'

'Down to Ordinance – we're drawing special supplies.'

Ruffy nodded and buttoned the playing cards into his top pocket while he selected the gendarmes to accompany them; then he asked Bruce, 'We might need some oil; what you think, boss?'

Bruce hesitated; they had only two cases of whisky left of the dozen they had looted in August. The purchasing power of a bottle of genuine Scotch was enormous and Bruce was loath to use them except in extraordinary circumstances. But now he realized that his chances of getting the supplies he needed were remote, unless he took along a substantial bribe for the quartermaster.

'Okay, Ruffy. Bring a case.'

Ruffy came up out of the chair and clapped his steel helmet on his head. The chin straps hung down on each side of his round black face.

'A full case?' He grinned at Bruce. 'You want to buy a battleship?'

'Almost,' agreed Bruce; 'go and get it.'

Ruffy disappeared into the back area of the house and returned almost immediately with a case of Grant's Standfast under one arm and half a dozen bottles of Simba beer held by their necks between the fingers of his other hand.

'We might get thirsty,' he explained.

The gendarmes climbed back into the back of the truck with a clatter of weapons and shouted cheerful abuse at their fellows on the verandah. Bruce, Mike and Ruffy crowded into the cab and Ruffy set the whisky on the floor and placed two large booted feet upon it.

'What's this all about, boss?' he asked as Bruce trundled the truck down the drive and turned into the Avenue l'Etoile. Bruce told him and when he had finished Ruffy grunted noncommittally and opened a bottle of beer with his big white chisel-blade teeth; the gas hissed softly and a little froth ran down the bottle and dripped onto his lap.

'My boys aren't going to like it,' he commented as he offered the open bottle to Mike Haig. Mike shook his head and Ruffy passed the bottle to Bruce.

Ruffy opened a bottle for himself and spoke again. 'They going to hate it like hell.' He shook his head. 'And there'll be even bigger trouble when we get to Port Reprieve and pick up the diamonds.'

Bruce glanced sideways at him, startled. 'What diamonds?'

'From the dredgers,' said Ruffy. 'You don't think they're sending us all that way just to bring in these other guys. They're worried about the diamonds, that's for sure!'

Suddenly, for Bruce, much which had puzzled him was explained. A half-forgotten conversation that he had held earlier in the year with an engineer from Union Minière jumped back into his memory. They had discussed the three diamond dredgers that worked the gravel from the bed of the Lufira swamps. The boats were based on Port Reprieve and clearly they would have returned there at the beginning of the emergency; they must still be there with three or four months' recovery of diamonds on board. Something like half a million sterling in uncut stones. That was the reason why the Katangese Government placed such priority on this expedition, the reason why such a powerful force was being used, the reason why no approaches had been made to the U.N. authorities to conduct the rescue.

Bruce smiled sardonically as he remembered the humanitarian arguments that had been given to him by the Minister of the Interior.

'It is our duty, Captain Curry. We cannot leave these people to the not-so-tender mercy of the tribesmen. It is our duty as civilized human beings.'

There were others cut off in remote mission stations and government outposts throughout southern Kasai and Katanga; nothing had been heard of them for months, but their welfare was secondary to that of the settlement at Port Reprieve.

Bruce lifted the bottle to his lips again, steering with one hand and squinting ahead through the windscreen as he drank. All right, we'll fetch them in and afterwards an ammunition box will be loaded on to a chartered aircraft, and later still there will be another deposit to a numbered account in Zurich. Why should I worry? They're paying me for it.

'I don't think we should mention the diamonds to my boys.' Ruffy spoke sadly. 'I don't think it would be a good idea at all.'

Bruce slowed the truck as they ran into the industrial area beyond the railway line. He watched the buildings as they passed, until he recognized the one he wanted and swung off the road to stop in front of the gate. He blew a blast on the hooter and a gendarme came out and inspected his pass minutely. Satisfied, he shouted out to someone beyond the gate and it swung open. Bruce drove the truck through into the yard and switched off the engine.

There were half a dozen other trucks parked in the yard, all emblazoned with the Katangese shield and surrounded by gendarmes in uniforms patchy with sweat. A white lieutenant leaned from the cab of one of the trucks and shouted.

'Ciao, Bruce!'

'How things, Sergio?' Bruce answered him.

'Crazy! Crazy!' Bruce smiled. For the Italian everything was crazy. Bruce remembered that in July, during the fighting at the road bridge, he had bent him over the bonnet of a Land Rover and with a bayonet dug a piece of schrapnel out of his hairy buttocks – that had also been crazy.

'See you around,' Bruce dismissed him and led Mike and Ruffy across the yard to the warehouse. There was a sign on the large double doors *Dépôt Ordinance – Armée du Katanga* and beyond them at a desk in a glass cubicle sat a major with a pair of Gandhi-type steel-rimmed spectacles perched on a face like that of a jovial black toad. He looked up at Bruce.

'Non,' he said with finality. 'Non, non.' Bruce produced his requisition form and laid it before him. The major brushed it aside contemptuously.

'We have not got these items, we are destitute. I cannot do it. No! I cannot do it. There are priorities. There are circumstances to consider. No, I am sorry.' He snatched a sheaf of papers from the side of his desk and turned his whole attention to them, ignoring Bruce.

'This requisition is signed by Monsieur le Président,' Bruce pointed out mildly, and the major laid down his papers and came round from behind the desk. He stood close to Bruce with the top of his head on a level with Bruce's chin.

'Had it been signed by the Almighty himself, it would be of no use. I am sorry, I am truly sorry.'

Bruce lifted his eyes and for a second allowed them to wander over the mountains of stores which packed the interior of the warehouse. From where he stood he could identify at least twenty items that he needed. The major noticed the gesture and his French became so excited that Bruce could only make out the repeated use of the word 'Non'. He glanced significantly at Ruffy and the sergeant major stepped forward and placed an arm soothingly about the major's shoulders; then very gently he led him, still protesting, out into the yard and across to the truck. He opened the door of the cab and the major saw the case of whisky.

A few minutes later, after Ruffy had prised open the lid with his bayonet and allowed the major to inspect the seals on the caps, they returned to the office with Ruffy carrying the case.

'Captain,' said the major as he picked up the requisition from the desk. 'I see now that I was mistaken. This is indeed signed by Monsieur le Président. It is my duty to afford you the most urgent priority.'

Bruce murmured his thanks and the major beamed at him. 'I will give you men to help you.'

'You are too kind. It would disrupt your routine. I have my own men.'

'Excellent,' agreed the major and waved a podgy hand around the warehouse. 'Take what you need.'

– 3 –

Again Bruce glanced at his wristwatch. It was still twenty minutes before the curfew ended at 06.00 hours. Until then he must fret away the time watching Wally Hendry finishing his breakfast. This was a spectacle without much appeal, for Hendry was a methodical but untidy eater.

'Why don't you keep your mouth closed?' snapped Bruce irritably, unable to stand it any longer.

'Do I ask you your business?' Hendry looked up from his plate. His jowls were covered with a ginger stubble of beard, and his eyes were inflamed and puffy from the previous evening's debauchery. Bruce looked away from him and checked his watch again.

The suicidal temptation to ignore the curfew and set off immediately for the railway station was very strong. It required an effort to resist it. The least he could expect if he followed that course was an arrest by one of the patrols and a delay of twelve hours while he cleared himself; the worst thing would be a shooting incident.

He poured himself another cup of coffee and sipped it slowly. Impatience has always been one of my weaknesses, he reflected; nearly every mistake I have ever made stems from that cause. But I have improved a little over the years – at twenty I wanted to live my whole life in a week. Now I'll settle for a year.

He finished his coffee and checked the time again. Five minutes before six, he could risk it now. It would take almost that long to get out to the truck.

'If you are ready, gentlemen.' He pushed back his chair and picked up his pack, slung it over his shoulder and led the way out.

Ruffy was waiting for them, sitting on a pile of stones in one of the corrugated iron goods sheds. His men squatted round a dozen small fires on the concrete floor cooking breakfast.

'Where's the train?'

'That's a good question, boss,' Ruffy congratulated him, and Bruce groaned.

'It should have been here long ago,' Bruce protested, and Ruffy shrugged.

'*Should have been* is a lot different from *is*.'

'Goddammit! We've still got to load up. We'll be lucky if we get away before noon,' snapped Bruce. 'I'll go up to the station master.'

'You'd better take him a present, boss. We've still got a case left.'

'No, hell!' Bruce growled. 'Come with me, Mike.'

With Mike beside him they crossed the tracks to the main platform and clambered up on to it. At the far end a group of railway officials stood chatting and Bruce fell upon them furiously.

Two hours later Bruce stood beside the coloured engine driver on the footplate and they puffed slowly down towards the goods yard.

The driver was a roly-poly little man with a skin too dark for mere sunburn and a set of teeth with bright red plastic gums.

'Monsieur, you do not wish to proceed to Port Reprieve?' he asked anxiously.

'Yes.'

'There is no way of telling the condition of the permanent way. No traffic has used it these last four months.'

'I know. You'll have to proceed with caution.'

'There is a United Nations barrier across the lines near the old aerodrome,' protested the man.

'We have a pass.' Bruce smiled to soothe him; his bad temper was abating now that he had his transport. 'Stop next to the first shed.'

With a hiss of steam brakes the train pulled up beside the concrete platform and Bruce jumped down.

'All right, Ruffy,' he shouted. 'Let's get cracking.'

Bruce had placed the three steel-sided open trucks in the van, for they were the easiest to defend. From behind the breast-high sides the Bren guns could sweep ahead and on both flanks. Then followed the two passenger coaches, to be used as store rooms and officer's quarters; also for accommodation of the refugees on the return journey. Finally, the locomotive in the rear, where it would be least vulnerable and would not spew smoke and soot back over the train.

The stores were loaded into four of the compartments, the windows shuttered and the doors locked. Then Bruce set about laying out his defences. In a low circle of sandbags on the roof of the leading coach he sited one of the Brens and made his own post. From here he could look down over the open trucks, back at the locomotive, and also command an excellent view of the surrounding country.

The other Brens he placed in the leading truck and put Hendry in command there. He had obtained from the major at Ordinance three of the new walkie-talkie sets; one he gave to the engine driver, another to Hendry up front, and the third he retained in his emplacement; and his system of communication was satisfactory.

It was almost twelve o'clock before these preparations were complete and Bruce turned to Ruffy who sat on the sandbags beside him.

'All set?'

'All set, boss.'

'How many missing?' Bruce had learned from experience never to expect his entire command to be in any one place at any one time.

'Eight, boss.'

'That's three more than yesterday; leaves us only fifty-two men. Do you think they've taken off into the bush also?' Five of his men had deserted with their weapons on the day of the ceasefire. Obviously they had gone out into the bush to join one of the bands of *shufta* that were already playing havoc along the main roads: ambushing all unprotected traffic, beating up lucky travellers and murdering those less fortunate, raping when they had the opportunity, and generally enjoying themselves.

'No, boss. I don't think so, those three are good boys. They'll be down in the cité indigène having themselves some fun; guess they just forgot the time.' Ruffy shook his head. 'Take us about half an hour to find them; all we do is go down and visit all the knock-shops. You want to try?'

'No, we haven't time to mess around if we are going to

23

make Msapa Junction before dark. We'll pick them up again when we get back.' Was there ever an army since the Boer War that treated desertion so lightly, Bruce wondered.

He turned to the radio set beside him and depressed the transmit button.

'Driver.'

'Oui, monsieur.'

'Proceed – very slowly until we approach the United Nations barrier. Stop well this side of it.'

'Oui, monsieur.'

They rolled out of the goods yard, clicking over the points; leaving the industrial quarter on their right with the Katangese guard posts on the Avenue du Cimetière intersection; out through the suburbs until ahead of them Bruce saw the U.N. positions and he felt the first stirring of anxiety. The pass he carried in the breast pocket of his jacket was signed by General Rhee Singh, but before in this war the orders of an Indian general had not been passed by a Sudanese captain to an Irish sergeant. The reception that awaited them could be exciting.

'I hope they know about us.' Mike Haig lit his cigarette with a show of nonchalance, but he peered over it anxiously at the piles of fresh earth on each side of the tracks that marked the position of emplacements.

'These boys have got bazookas, and they're Irish Arabs,' muttered Ruffy. 'I reckon it's the maddest kind of Arabs there is – Irish. How would you like a bazooka bomb up your throat, boss?'

'No, thanks, Ruffy,' Bruce declined, and pressed the button of the radio.

'Hendry!'

In the leading truck Wally Hendry picked up his set and, holding it against his chest, looked back at Bruce.

'Curry?'

'Tell your gunners to stand away from the Brens, and the rest of them to lay down their rifles.'

24

'Right.'

Bruce watched him relaying the order, pushing them back, moving among the gendarmes who crowded the forward trucks. Bruce could sense the air of tension that had fallen over the whole train, watched as his gendarmes reluctantly laid down their weapons and stood empty-handed staring sullenly ahead at the U.N. barrier.

'Driver!' Bruce spoke again into the radio. 'Slow down. Stop fifty metres this side of the barrier. But if there is any shooting open the throttle and take us straight through.'

'Oui, monsieur.'

Ahead of them there was no sign of a reception committee, only the hostile barrier of poles and petrol drums across the line.

Bruce stood upon the roof and lifted his arms above his head in a gesture of neutrality. It was a mistake; the movement changed the passive mood of the gendarmes in the trucks below him. One of them lifted his arms also, but his fists were clenched.

'U.N. – merde!' he shouted, and immediately the cry was taken up.

'U.N. – merde! U.N. – merde!' They chanted the war cry – laughing at first, but then no longer laughing, their voices rising sharply.

'Shut up, damn you,' Bruce roared and swung his open hand against the head of the gendarme beside him, but the man hardly noticed it. His eyes were glazing with the infectious hysteria to which the African is so susceptible; he had snatched up his rifle and was holding it across his chest; already his body was beginning to jerk convulsively as he chanted.

Bruce hooked his fingers under the rim of the man's steel helmet and yanked it forward over his eyes so the back of his neck was exposed; he chopped him with a judo blow and the gendarme slumped forward over the sandbags, his rifle slipping from his hands.

Bruce looked up desperately; in the trucks below him the hysteria was spreading.

'Stop them – Hendry, de Surrier! Stop them for God's sake.' But his voice was lost in the chanting.

A gendarme snatched up his rifle from where it lay at his feet; Bruce saw him elbow his way towards the side of the truck to begin firing; he was working the slide to lever a round into the breech.

'Mwembe!' Bruce shouted the gendarme's name, but his voice could not penetrate the uproar.

In two seconds the whole situation would dissolve into a pandemonium of tracer and bazooka fire.

Poised on the forward edge of the roof, Bruce checked for an instant to judge the distance, and then he jumped. He landed squarely on the gendarme's shoulders, his weight throwing the man forward so his face hit the steel edge of the truck, and they went down together on to the floor.

The gendarme's finger was resting on the trigger and the rifle fired as it spun from his hands. A complete hush followed the roar of the rifle and in it Bruce scrambled to his feet, drawing his pistol from the canvas holster on his hip.

'All right,' he panted, menacing the men around him. 'Come on, give me a chance to use this!' He picked out one of his sergeants and held his eyes. 'You! I'm waiting for you – start shooting!'

At the sight of the revolver the man relaxed slowly and the madness faded from his face. He dropped his eyes and shuffled awkwardly.

Bruce glanced up at Ruffy and Haig on the roof, and raised his voice.

'Watch them. Shoot the first one who starts it again.'

'Okay, boss.' Ruffy thrust forward the automatic rifle in his hands. 'Who's it going to be?' he asked cheerfully, looking down at them. But the mood had changed. Their attitudes of defiance gave way to sheepish embarrassment and a small buzz of conversation filled the silence.

'Mike,' Bruce yelled, urgent again. 'Call the driver, he's trying to take us through!'

The noise of their passage had risen, the driver accelerating at the sound of the shot, and now they were racing down towards the U.N. barrier.

Mike Haig grabbed the set, shouted an order into it, and immediately the brakes swooshed and the train jolted to a halt not a hundred yards short of the barrier.

Slowly Bruce clambered back on to the roof of the coach.

'Close?' asked Mike.

'My God!' Bruce shook his head, and lit a cigarette with slightly unsteady hands. 'Another fifty yards—!' Then he turned and stared coldly down at his gendarmes.

'Canaille! Next time you try to commit suicide don't take me with you.' The gendarme he had knocked down was now sitting up, fingering the ugly black swelling above his eye. 'My friend,' Bruce turned on him, 'later I will have something for your further discomfort!' Then to the other man in the emplacement beside him who was massaging his neck, 'And for you also! Take their names, Sergeant Major.'

'Sir!' growled Ruffy.

'Mike.' Bruce's voice changed, soft again. 'I'm going ahead to toss the blarney with our friends behind the bazookas. When I give you the signal bring the train through.'

'You don't want me to come with you?' asked Mike.

'No, stay here.' Bruce picked up his rifle, slung it over his shoulder, dropped down the ladder on to the path beside the tracks, and walked forward with the gravel crunching beneath his boots.

An auspicious beginning to the expedition, he decided grimly, tragedy averted by the wink of an eye before they had even passed the outskirts of the city.

At least the Mickies hadn't added a few bazooka bombs to the altercation. Bruce peered ahead, and could make out the shape of helmets behind the earthworks.

Without the breeze of the train's passage it was hot again, and Bruce felt himself starting to sweat.

'Stay where you are, Mister.' A deep brogue from the emplacement nearest the tracks; Bruce stopped, standing on the wooden crossties in the sun. Now he could see the faces of the men beneath the helmets: unfriendly, not smiling.

'What was the shooting for?' the voice questioned.

'We had an accident.'

'Don't have any more or we might have one also.'

'I'd not be wanting that, Paddy.' Bruce smiled thinly, and the Irishman's voice had an edge to it as he went on. 'What's your mission?'

'I have a pass, do you want to see it?' Bruce took the folded sheet of paper from his breast pocket.

'What's your mission?' repeated the Irishman.

'Proceed to Port Reprieve and relieve the town.'

'We know about you.' The Irishman nodded. 'Let me see the pass.'

Bruce left the tracks, climbed the earth wall and handed the pink slip to the Irishman. He wore the three pips of a captain, and he glanced briefly at the pass before speaking to the man beside him.

'Very well, Sergeant, you can be clearing the barrier now.'

'I'll call the train through?' Bruce asked, and the captain nodded again.

'But make sure there are no more accidents – we don't like hired killers.'

'Sure and begorrah now, Paddy, it's not your war you're a-fighting either,' snapped Bruce and abruptly turned his back on the man, jumped down on to the tracks and waved to Mike Haig on the roof of the coach.

The Irish sergeant and his party had cleared the tracks

28

and while the train rumbled slowly down to him Bruce struggled to control his irritation – the Irish captain's taunt had reached him. Hired killer, and of course that was what he was. Could a man sink any lower?

As the coach drew level with where he stood, Bruce caught the hand rail and swung himself aboard, waved an ironical farewell to the Irish captain and climbed up on to the roof.

'No trouble?' asked Mike.

'A bit of lip, delivered in music-hall brogue,' Bruce answered, 'but nothing serious.' He picked up the radio set.

'Driver.'

'Monsieur?'

'Do not forget my instructions.'

'I will not exceed forty kilometres the hour, and I shall at all times be prepared for an emergency stop.'

'Good!' Bruce switched off the set and sat down on the sandbags between Ruffy and Mike.

Well, he thought, here we go at last. Six hours run to Msapa Junction. That should be easy. And then – God knows, God alone knows.

The tracks curved, and Bruce looked back to see the last white-washed buildings of Elisabethville disappear among the trees. They were out into the open savannah forest.

Behind them the black smoke from the loco rolled sideways into the trees; beneath them the crossties clattered in strict rhythm, and ahead the line ran arrow straight for miles, dwindling with perspective until it merged into the olive-green mass of the forest.

Bruce lifted his eyes. Half the sky was clear and tropical blue, but in the north it was bruised with cloud, and beneath the cloud grey rain drifted down to meet the earth. The sunlight through the rain spun a rainbow, and the cloud shadow moved across the land as slowly and as darkly as a herd of grazing buffalo.

He loosened the chin strap of his helmet and laid his rifle on the roof beside him.

'You'd like a beer, boss?'

'Have you any?'

'Sure.' Ruffy called to one of the gendarmes and the man climbed down into the coach and came back with half a dozen bottles. Ruffy opened two with his teeth. Each time half the contents frothed out and splattered back along the wooden side of the coach.

'This beer's as wild as an angry woman,' he grunted as he passed a bottle to Bruce.

'It's wet anyway.' Bruce tasted it, warm and gassy and too sweet.

'Here's how!' said Ruffy.

Bruce looked down into the open trucks at the gendarmes who were settling in for the journey. Apart from the gunners at the Brens, they were lying or squatting in attitudes of complete relaxation and most of them had stripped down to their underwear. One skinny little fellow was already asleep on his back with his helmet as a pillow and the tropical sun beating full into his face.

Bruce finished his beer and threw the bottle overboard. Ruffy opened another and placed it in his hand without comment.

'Why we going so slowly, boss?'

'I told the driver to keep the speed down – give us a chance to stop if the tracks have been torn up.'

'Yeah. Them Balubas might have done that – they're mad Arabs all of them.'

The warm beer drunk in the sun was having a soothing effect on Bruce. He felt at peace, now, withdrawn from the need to make decisions, to participate in the life around him.

'Listen to that train-talk,' said Ruffy, and Bruce focused his hearing on the clickety-clack of the crossties.

'Yes, I know. You can make it say anything you want it to,' agreed Bruce.

'And it can sing,' Ruffy went on. 'It's got real music in it, like this.' He inflated the great barrel of his chest, lifted his head and let it come.

His voice was deep but with a resonance that caught the attention of the men in the open trucks below them. Those who had been sprawled in the amorphous shapes of sleep stirred and sat up. Another voice joined in humming the tune, hesitantly at first, then more confidently; then others took it up, the words were unimportant, it was the rhythm that they could not resist. They had sung together many times before and like a well-trained choir each voice found its place, the star performers leading, changing the pace, improvising, quickening until the original tune lost its identity and became one of the tribal chants. Bruce recognized it as a planting song. It was one of his favourites and he sat drinking his lukewarm beer and letting the singing wash round him, build up into the chorus like storm waves, then fall back into a tenor solo before rising once more. And the train ran on through the sunlight towards the rain clouds in the north.

Presently André came out of the coach below him and picked his way forward through the men in the trucks until he reached Hendry. The two of them stood together, André's face turned up towards the taller man and deadly earnest as he talked.

'*Doll boy*,' Hendry had called him, and it was an accurate description of the effeminately pretty face with the big toffee eyes; the steel helmet he wore seemed too large for his shoulders to carry.

I wonder how old he is; Bruce watched him laugh suddenly, his face still turned upwards to Hendry; not much over twenty and I have never seen anything less like a hired killer.

'How the hell did anyone like de Surrier get mixed up in this?' His voice echoed the thought, and beside him Mike answered.

'He was working in Elisabethville when it started, and he couldn't return to Belgium. I don't know the reason but I guess it was something personal. When it started his firm closed down. I suppose this was the only employment he could find.'

'That Irishman, the one at the barrier, he called me a hired killer.' Thinking of André's position in the scheme of things had turned Bruce's thoughts back to his own status. 'I hadn't thought about it that way before, but I suppose he's right. That is what we are.'

Mike Haig was silent for a moment, but when he spoke there was a stark quality in his voice.

'Look at these hands!' Involuntarily Bruce glanced down at them, and for the first time noticed that they were narrow with long moulded fingers, possessed of a functional beauty, the hands of an artist.

'Look at them,' Mike repeated, flexing them slightly; 'they were fashioned for a purpose, they were made to hold a scalpel, they were made to save life.' Then he relaxed them and let them drop on to the rifle across his lap, the long delicate fingers incongruous upon the blue metal. 'But look what they hold now!'

Bruce stirred irritably. He had not wanted to provoke another bout of Mike Haig's soul-searching. Damn the old fool – why must he always start this, he knew as well as anyone that in the mercenary army of Katanga there was a taboo upon the past. It did not exist.

'Ruffy,' Bruce snapped, 'aren't you going to feed your boys?'

'Right now, boss.' Ruffy opened another beer and handed it to Bruce. 'Hold that – it will keep your mind off food while I rustle it up.' He lumbered off along the roof of the coach still singing.

'Three years ago, it seems like all eternity,' Mike went on as though Bruce had not interrupted. 'Three years ago I was a surgeon and now this—' The desolation had spread to his eyes, and Bruce felt his pity for the man deep down where he kept it imprisoned with all his other emotions. 'I was good. I was one of the best. Royal College. Harley Street. Guy's.' Mike laughed without humour, with bitterness. 'Can you imagine my being driven in my Rolls to address the College on my advanced technique of cholecystectomy?'

'What happened?' The question was out before he could stop it, and Bruce realized how near to the surface he had let his pity rise. 'No, don't tell me. It's your business. I don't want to know.'

'But I'll tell you, Bruce, I want to. It helps somehow, talking about it.'

At first, thought Bruce, I wanted to talk also, to try and wash the pain away with words.

Mike was silent for a few seconds. Below them the singing rose and fell, and the train ran on through the forest.

'It had taken me ten hard years to get there, but at last I had done it. A fine practice; doing the work I loved with skill, earning the rewards I deserved. A wife that any man would have been proud of, a lovely home, many friends, too many friends perhaps; for success breeds friends the way a dirty kitchen breeds cockroaches.'

Mike pulled out a handkerchief and dried the back of his neck where the wind could not reach.

'Those sort of friends mean parties,' he went on. 'Parties when you've worked all day and you're tired; when you need the lift that you can get so easily from a bottle. You don't know if you have the weakness for the stuff until it's too late; until you have a bottle in the drawer of your desk; until suddenly your practice isn't so good any more.'

Mike twisted the handkerchief around his fingers as he

ploughed doggedly on. 'Then you know it suddenly. You know it when your hands dance in the morning and all you want for breakfast is *that*, when you can't wait until lunchtime because you have to operate and that's the only way you can keep your hands steady. But you know it finally and utterly when the knife turns in your hand and the artery starts to spurt and you watch it paralysed – you watch it hosing red over your gown and forming pools on the theatre floor.' Mike's voice dried up then and he tapped a cigarette from his pack and lit it. His shoulders were hunched forward and his eyes were full of shadows of his guilt. Then he straightened up and his voice was stronger.

'You must have read about it. I was headlines for a few days, all the papers. But my name wasn't Haig in those days. I got that name off a label on a bottle in a bar-room.

'Gladys stayed with me, of course, she was that type. We came out to Africa. I had enough saved from the wreck for a down payment on a tobacco farm in the Centenary block outside Salisbury. Two good seasons and I was off the bottle. Gladys was having our first baby, we had both wanted one so badly. It was all coming right again.'

Mike stuffed the handkerchief back in his pocket, and his voice lost its strength again, turned dry and husky.

'Then one day I took the truck into the village and on the way home I stopped at the club. I had been there often before, but this time they threw me out at closing time and when I got back to the farm I had a case of Scotch on the seat beside me.'

Bruce wanted to stop him; he knew what was coming and he didn't want to hear it.

'The first rains started that night and the rivers came down in flood. The telephone lines were knocked out and we were cut off. In the morning—' Mike stopped again and turned to Bruce.

'I suppose it was the shock of seeing me like that again, but in the morning Gladys went into labour. It was her first and she wasn't so young any more. She was still in labour the next day, but by then she was too weak to scream. I remember how peaceful it was without her screaming and pleading with me to help. You see she knew I had all the instruments I needed. She begged me to help. I can remember that; her voice through the fog of whisky. I think I hated her then. I think I remember hating her, it was all so confused, so mixed up with the screaming and the liquor. But at last she was quiet. I don't think I realized she was dead. I was simply glad she was quiet and I could have peace.'

He dropped his eyes from Bruce's face.

'I was too drunk to go to the funeral. Then I met a man in a bar-room, I can't remember how long after it was, I can't even remember where. It must have been on the Copperbelt. He was recruiting for Tshombe's army and I signed up; there didn't seem anything else to do.'

Neither of them spoke again until a gendarme brought food to them, hunks of brown bread spread with tinned butter and filled with bully beef and pickled onions. They ate in silence listening to the singing, and Bruce said at last:

'You needn't have told me.'

'I know.'

'Mike—' Bruce paused.

'Yes?'

'I'm sorry, if that's any comfort.'

'It is,' Mike said. 'It helps to have – not to be completely alone. I like you, Bruce.' He blurted out the last sentence and Bruce recoiled as though Mike had spat in his face.

You fool, he rebuked himself savagely, *you were wide open then. You nearly let one of them in again*.

Remorselessly he crushed down his sympathy, shocked at the effort it required, and when he picked up the radio the gentleness had gone from his eyes.

'Hendry,' he spoke into the set, 'don't talk so much. I put you up front to watch the tracks.'

From the leading truck Wally Hendry looked round and forked two fingers at Bruce in a casual obscenity, but he turned back and faced ahead.

'You'd better go and take over from Hendry,' Bruce told Mike. 'Send him back here.'

Mike Haig stood up and looked down at Bruce.

'What are you afraid of?' his voice softly puzzled.

'I gave you an order, Haig.'

'Yes, I'm on my way.'

— 4 —

The aircraft found them in the late afternoon. It was a Vampire jet of the Indian Air Force and it came from the north.

They heard the soft rumble of it across the sky and then saw it glint like a speck of mica in the sunlight above the storm clouds ahead of them.

'I bet you a thousand francs to a handful of dung that this Bucko don't know about us,' said Hendry with anticipation, watching the jet turn off its course towards them.

'Well, he does now,' said Bruce.

Swiftly he surveyed the rain clouds in front of them. They were close; another ten minutes' run and they would be under them, and once there they were safe from air attack for the belly of the clouds pressed close against the earth and the rain was a thick blue-grey mist that would reduce visibility to a few hundred feet. He switched on the radio.

'Driver, give us all the speed you have – get us into that rain.'

'Oui, monsieur,' came the acknowledgement and almost immediately the puffing of the loco quickened and the clatter of the crossties changed its rhythm.

'Look at him come,' growled Hendry. The jet fell fast

against the backdrop of cloud, still in sunlight, still a silver point of light, but growing.

Bruce clicked over the band selector of the radio, searching the ether for the pilot's voice. He tried four wavelengths and each time found only the crackle and drone of static, but with the fifth came the gentle sing-song of Hindustani. Bruce could not understand it, but he could hear that the tone was puzzled. There was a short silence on the radio while the pilot listened to an instruction from the Kamina base which was beyond the power of their small set to receive, then a curt affirmative.

'He's coming in for a closer look,' said Bruce, then raising his voice, 'Everybody under cover – and stay there.' He was not prepared to risk another demonstration of friendship.

The jet came cruising in towards them under half power, yet incredibly fast, leaving the sound of its engine far behind it, sharklike above the forest. Then Bruce could see the pilot's head through the canopy; now he could make out his features. His face was very brown beneath the silver crash helmet and he had a little moustache, the same as the jack of spades. He was so close that Bruce saw the exact moment that he recognized them as Katangese; his eyes showed white and his mouth puckered as he swore. Beside Bruce the radio relayed the oath with metallic harshness, and then the jet was banking away steeply, its engine howling in full throttle, rising, showing its swollen silver belly and the racks of rockets beneath its wings.

'That frightened seven years' growth out of him,' laughed Hendry. 'You should have let me blast him. He was close enough for me to hit him in the left eyeball.'

'You'll get another chance in a moment,' Bruce assured him grimly. The radio was gabbling with consternation as the jet dwindled back into the sky. Bruce switched quickly to their own channel.

'Driver, can't you get this thing moving?'

'Monsieur, never before has she moved as she does now.'

Once more he switched back to the jet's frequency and listened to the pilot's excited voice. The jet was turning in a wide circle, perhaps fifteen miles away. Bruce glanced at the piled mass of cloud and rain ahead of them; it was moving down to meet them, but with ponderous dignity.

'If he comes back,' Bruce shouted down at his gendarmes, 'we can be sure that it's not just to look at us again. Open fire as soon as he's in range. Give him everything you've got, we must try and spoil his aim.'

Their faces were turned up towards him, subdued by the awful inferiority of the earthbound to the hunter in the sky. Only André did not look at Bruce; he was staring at the aircraft with his jaws clenching nervously and his eyes too large for his face.

Again there was silence on the radio, and every head turned back to watch the jet.

'Come on, Bucko, come on!' grunted Hendry impatiently. He spat into the palm of his right hand and then wiped it down the front of his jacket. 'Come on, we want you.' With his thumb he flicked the safety catch of his rifle on and off, on and off.

Suddenly the radio spoke again. Two words, obviously acknowledging an order, and one of the words Bruce recognized. He had heard it before in circumstances that has burned it into his memory. The Hindustani word 'Attack!'

'All right,' he said and stood up. 'He's coming!'

The wind fluttered his shirt against his chest. He settled his helmet firmly and pumped a round into the chamber of his FN.

'Get down into the truck, Hendry,' he ordered.

'I can see better from here.' Hendry was standing beside him, legs planted wide to brace himself against the violent motion of the train.

'As you like,' said Bruce. 'Ruffy, you get under cover.'

'Too damn hot down there in that box,' grinned the huge Negro.

'You're a mad Arab too,' said Bruce.

'Sure, we're all mad Arabs.'

The jet wheeled sharply and stooped towards the forest, levelling, still miles out on their flank.

'This Bucko is a real apprentice. He's going to take us from the side, so we can all shoot at him. If he was half awake he'd give it to us up the bum, hit the loco and make sure that we were all shooting over the top of each other,' gloated Hendry.

Silently, swiftly it closed with them, almost touching the tops of the trees. Then suddenly the cannon fire sparkled lemon-pale on its nose and all around them the air was filled with the sound of a thousand whips. Immediately every gun on the train opened up in reply. The tracers from the Brens chased each other out to meet the plane and the rifles joined their voices in a clamour that drowned the cannon fire.

Bruce aimed carefully, the jet unsteady in his sights from the lurching of the coach; then he pressed the trigger and the rifle juddered against his shoulder. From the corner of his eye he saw the empty cartridge cases spray from the breech in a bright bronze stream, and the stench of cordite stung his nostrils.

The aircraft slewed slightly, flinching from the torrent of fire.

'He's yellow!' howled Hendry. 'The bastard's yellow!'

'Hit him!' roared Ruffy. 'Keep hitting him.'

The jet twisted, lifted its nose so that the fire from its cannons passed harmlessly over their heads. Then its nose dropped again and it fired its rockets, two from under each wing. The gunfire from the train stopped abruptly as everybody ducked for safety; only the three of them on the roof kept shooting.

Shrieking like four demons in harness, leaving parallel lines of white smoke behind them, the rockets came from about four hundred yards out and they covered the distance in the time it takes to draw a deep breath, but the pilot had dropped his nose too sharply and fired too late. The rockets exploded in the embankment of the tracks below them.

The blast threw Bruce over backwards. He fell and rolled, clutching desperately at the smooth roof, but as he went over the edge his fingers caught in the guttering and he hung there. He was dazed with the concussion, the guttering cutting into his fingers, the shoulder strap of his rifle round his neck strangling him, and the gravel of the embankment rushing past beneath him.

Ruffy reached over, caught him by the front of his jacket and lifted him back like a child.

'You going somewhere, boss?' The great round face was coated with dust from the explosions, but he was grinning happily. Bruce had a confused conviction that it would take at least a case of dynamite to make any impression on that mountain of black flesh.

Kneeling on the roof Bruce tried to rally himself. He saw that the wooden side of the coach nearest the explosions was splintered and torn and the roof was covered with earth and pebbles. Hendry was sitting beside him, shaking his head slowly from side to side; a small trickle of blood ran down from a scratch on his cheek and dripped from his chin. In the open trucks the men stood or sat with stunned expressions on their faces, but the train still raced on towards the rain storm and the dust of the explosions hung in a dense brown cloud above the forest far behind them.

Bruce scrambled to his feet, searched frantically for the aircraft and found its tiny shape far off above the mass of cloud.

The radio was undamaged, protected by the sandbags from the blast. Bruce reached for it and pressed the transmit button.

'Driver, are you all right?'

'Monsieur, I am greatly perturbed. Is there—'

'You're not alone,' Bruce assured him. 'Keep this train going.'

'Oui, monsieur.'

Then he switched to the aircraft's frequency. Although his ears were singing shrilly from the explosions, he could hear that the voice of the pilot had changed its tone. There was a slowness in it, a breathless catch on some of the words. He's frightened or he's hurt, thought Bruce, but he still has time to make another pass at us before we reach the storm front.

His mind was clearing fast now, and he became aware of the complete lack of readiness in his men.

'Ruffy!' he shouted. 'Get them on their feet. Get them ready. That plane will be back any second now.'

Ruffy jumped down into the truck and Bruce heard his palm slap against flesh as he began to bully them into activity. Bruce followed him down, then climbed over into the second truck and began the same process there.

'Haig, give me a hand, help me get the lead out of them.'

Further removed from the shock of the explosion, the men in this truck reacted readily and crowded to the side, starting to reload, checking their weapons, swearing, faces losing the dull dazed expressions.

Bruce turned and shouted back, 'Ruffy, are any of your lot hurt?'

'Couple of scratches, nothing bad.'

On the roof of the coach Hendry was standing again, watching the aircraft, blood on his face and his rifle in his hands.

'Where's André?' Bruce asked Haig as they met in the middle of the truck.

'Up front. I think he's been hit.'

Bruce went forward and found André doubled up, crouching in a corner of the truck, his rifle lying beside him and both hands covering his face. His shoulders heaved as though he were in pain.

Eyes, thought Bruce, he's been hit in the eyes. He reached him and stooped over him, pulling his hands from his face, expecting to see blood.

André was crying, his cheeks wet with tears and his eyelashes gummed together. For a second Bruce stared at him and then he caught the front of his jacket and pulled him to his feet. He picked up André's rifle and the barrel was cold, not a single shot had been fired out of it. He dragged the Belgian to the side and thrust the rifle into his hands.

'De Surrier,' he snarled, 'I'm going to be standing beside you. If you do that again I'll shoot you. Do you understand?'

'I'm sorry, Bruce.' André's lips were swollen where he had bitten them; his face was smeared with tears and slack with fear. 'I'm sorry. I couldn't help it.'

Bruce ignored him and turned his attention back to the aircraft. It was turning in for its next run.

He's going to come from the side again, Bruce thought; this time he'll get us. He can't miss twice in a row.

In silence once more they watched the jet slide down the valley between two vast white mountains of cloud and level off above the forest. Small and dainty and deadly it raced in towards them.

One of the Bren guns opened up, rattling raucously, sending out tracers like bright beads on a string.

'Too soon,' muttered Bruce. 'Much too soon; he must be all of a mile out of range.'

But the effect was instantaneous. The jet swerved, almost hit the tree tops and then over-corrected, losing its line of approach.

A howl of derision went up from the train and was immediately lost in the roar as every gun opened fire. The jet loosed its remaining rockets, blindly, hopelessly, without a chance of a hit. Then it climbed steeply, turning away into the cloud ahead of them. The sound of its engines receded, was muted by the cloud and then was gone.

Ruffy was performing a dance of triumph, waving his rifle over his head. Hendry on the roof was shouting abuse at the clouds into which the jet had vanished, one of the Brens was still firing short ecstatic bursts, someone else was chanting the Katangese war cry and others were taking it up. And then the driver in the locomotive came in with his whistle, spurting steam with each shriek.

Bruce slung his rifle over his shoulder, pushed his helmet on to the back of his head, took out a cigarette and lit it, then stood watching them sing and laugh and chatter with the relief from danger.

Next to him André leaned out and vomited over the side; a little of it came out of his nose and dribbled down the front of his battle-jacket. He wiped his mouth with the back of his hand.

'I'm sorry, Bruce. I'm sorry, truly I'm sorry,' he whispered.

And they were under the cloud, its coolness slumped over them like air from an open refrigerator. The first heavy drops stung Bruce's cheek and then rolled down heavily washing away the smell of cordite, melting the dust from Ruffy's face until it shone again like washed coal.

Bruce felt his jacket cling wetly to his back.

'Ruffy, two men at each Bren. The rest of them can get back into the covered coaches. We'll relieve every hour.' He reversed his rifle so the muzzle pointed downwards. 'De Surrier, you can go, and you as well, Hendry.'

'I'll stay with you, Bruce.'

'All right then.'

The gendarmes clambered back into the covered coaches still laughing and chattering, and Ruffy came forward with a groundsheet and handed it to Bruce.

'The radios are all covered. If you don't need me, boss, I

got some business with one of those Arabs in the coach. He's got near twenty thousand francs on him; so I'd better go and give him a couple of tricks with the cards.'

'One of these days I'm going to explain your Christian monarchs to the boys. Show them that the odds are three to one against them,' Bruce threatened.

'I wouldn't do that, boss,' Ruffy advised seriously. 'All that money isn't good for them, just gets them into trouble.'

'Off you go then. I'll call you later,' said Bruce. 'Tell them I said "well done", I'm proud of them.'

'Yeah. I'll tell them,' promised Ruffy.

Bruce lifted the tarpaulin that covered the set.

'Driver, desist before you burst the boiler!'

The abandoned flight of the train steadied to a more sedate pace, and Bruce tilted his helmet over his eyes and pulled the groundsheet up around his mouth before he leaned out over the side of the truck to inspect the rocket damage.

'All the windows blown out on this side and the woodwork torn a little,' he muttered. 'But a lucky escape all the same.'

'What a miserable comic-opera war this is,' grunted Mike Haig. 'That pilot had the right idea: why risk your life when it's none of your business.'

'He was wounded,' Bruce guessed. 'I think we hit him on his first run.'

Then they were silent, with the rain driving into their faces, slitting their eyes to peer ahead along the tracks. The men at the Brens huddled into their brown and green camouflage groundsheets, all their jubilation of ten minutes earlier completely gone. They are like cats, thought Bruce as he noticed their dejection, they can't stand being wet.

'It's half past five already.' Mike spoke at last. 'Do you think we'll make Msapa Junction before nightfall?'

'With this weather it will be dark by six.' Bruce looked up at the low cloud that was prematurely bringing on the night. 'I'm not going to risk travelling in the dark. This is the edge of Baluba country and we can't use the headlights of the loco.'

'You going to stop then?'

Bruce nodded. What a stupid bloody question, he thought irritably. Then he recognized his irritation as reaction from the danger they had just experienced, and he spoke to make amends.

'We can't be far now – if we start again at first light we'll reach Msapa before sun-up.'

'My God, it's cold,' complained Mike and he shivered briefly.

'Either too hot or too cold,' Bruce agreed; he knew that it was also reaction that was making him garrulous. But he did not attempt to stop himself. 'That's one of the things about this happy little planet of ours: nothing is in moderation. Too hot or too cold, either you are hungry or you've overeaten, you are in love or you hate the world—'

'Like you?' asked Mike.

'Dammit, Mike, you're as bad as a woman. Can't you conduct an objective discussion without introducing personalities?' Bruce demanded. He could feel his temper rising to the surface, he was cold and edgy, and he wanted a smoke.

'Objective theories must have subjective application to prove their worth,' Mike pointed out. There was just a trace of an amused smile on his broad ravaged old face.

'Let's forget it then. I don't want to talk personalities,' snapped Bruce; then immediately went on to do so. 'Humanity sickens me if I think about it too much. De Surrier puking his heart out with fear, that animal Hendry, you trying to keep off the liquor, Joan—' He stopped himself abruptly.

'Who is Joan?'

'Do I ask you your business?' Bruce flashed the standard reply to all personal questions in the mercenary army of Katanga.

'No. But I'm asking you yours – who is Joan?'

All right. I'll tell him. If he wants to know, I'll tell him. Anger had made Bruce reckless.

'Joan was the bitch I married.'

'So, that's it then!'

'Yes – that's it! Now you know. So you can leave me alone.'

'Kids?'

'Two – a boy and a girl.' The anger was gone from Bruce's voice, and the raw naked pain was back for an instant. Then he rallied and his voice was neutral once more.

'And none of it matters a damn. As far as I'm concerned the whole human race – all of it – can go and lose itself. I don't want any part of it.'

'How old are you, Bruce?'

'Leave me alone, damn you!'

'How old are you?'

'I'm thirty.'

'You talk like a teenager.'

'And I feel like an old, old man.'

The amusement was no longer on Mike's face as he asked.

'What did you do before this?'

'I slept and breathed and ate – and got trodden on.'

'What did you do for a living?'

'Law.'

'Were you successful?'

'How do you measure success? If you mean, did I make money, the answer is yes.'

I made enough to pay off the house and the car, he thought bitterly, *and to contest custody of my children, and finally to meet the divorce settlement. I had enough for that, but, of course, I had to sell my partnership.*

'Then you'll be all right,' Mike told him. 'If you've

succeeded once you'll be able to do it again when you've recovered from the shock; when you've rearranged your life and taken other people into it to make you strong again.'

'I'm strong now, Haig. I'm strong *because* there is no one in my life. That's the only way you can be secure, on your own. Completely free and on your own.'

'Strong!' Anger flared in Mike's voice for the first time. 'On your own you're *nothing*, Curry. On your own you're so weak I could piss on you and wash you away!' Then the anger evaporated and Mike went on softly, 'But you'll find out – you're one of the lucky ones. You attract people to you. You don't have to be alone.'

'Well, that's the way I'm going to be from now on.'

'We'll see,' murmured Mike.

'Yes, we'll see,' Bruce agreed, and lifted the tarpaulin over the radio.

'Driver, we are going to halt for the night. It's too dark to proceed with safety.'

– 5 –

Brazzaville Radio came through weakly on the set and the static was bad, for outside the rain still fell and thunder rolled around the sky like an unsecured cargo at sea.

' – Our Elisabethville correspondent reports that elements of the Kantangese Army in the South Kasai province today violated the ceasefire agreement by firing upon a low-flying aircraft of the United Nations command. The aircraft, a Vampire jet fighter of the Indian Air Force, returned safely to its base at Kamina airfield. The pilot, however, was wounded by small arms fire. His condition is satisfactory.

'The United Nations Commander in Katanga, General

Rhee, has lodged a strong protest with the Kantangese government—' The announcer's voice was overlaid by the electric crackle of static.

'We winged him!' rejoiced Wally Hendry. The scab on his cheek had dried black, with angry red edges.

'Shut up,' snapped Bruce, 'we're trying to hear what's happening.'

'You can't hear a bloody thing now. André, there's a bottle in my pack. Get it! I'm going to drink to that coolie with a bullet up his—'

Then the radio cleared and the announcer's voice came through loudly.

' – at Senwati Mission fifty miles from the river harbour of Port Reprieve. A spokesman for the Central Congolese Government denied that the Congolese troops were operating in this area, and it is feared that a large body of armed bandits is taking advantage of the unsettled conditions to—' Again the static drowned it out.

'Damn this set,' muttered Bruce as he tried to tune it.

' – stated today that the removal of missile equipment from the Russian bases in Cuba had been confirmed by aerial reconnaissance—'

'That's all that we are interested in.' Bruce switched off the radio. 'What a shambles! Ruffy, where is Senwati Mission?'

'Top end of the swamp, near the Rhodesian border.'

'Fifty miles from Port Reprieve,' muttered Bruce, not attempting to conceal his anxiety.

'It's more than that by road, boss, more like a hundred.'

'That should take them three or four days in this weather, with time off for looting along the way,' Bruce calculated. 'It will be cutting it fairly fine. We must get through to Port Reprieve by tomorrow evening and pull out again at dawn the next day.'

'Why not keep going tonight?' Hendry removed the

48

bottle from his lips to ask. 'Better than sitting here being eaten by mosquitoes.'

'We'll stay,' Bruce answered. 'It won't do anybody much good to derail this lot in the dark.' He turned back to Ruffy. 'Three-hour watches tonight, Sergeant Major. Lieutenant Haig will take the first, then Lieutenant Hendry, then Lieutenant de Surrier, and I'll do the dawn spell.'

'Okay, boss. I'd better make sure my boys aren't sleeping.'

He left the compartment and the broken glass from the corridor windows crunched under his boots.

'I'll be on my way also.' Mike stood up and pulled the groundsheet over his shoulders.

'Don't waste the batteries of the searchlights, Mike. Sweep every ten minutes or so.'

'Okay, Bruce.' Mike looked across at Hendry. 'I'll call you at nine o'clock.'

'Jolly good show, old fruit.' Wally exaggerated Mike's accent. 'Good hunting, what!' and then as Mike left the compartment, 'Silly old bugger, why does he have to talk like that?'

No one answered him, and he pulled up his shirt behind.

'André, what's this on my back?'

'It's a pimple.'

'Well, squeeze it then.'

Bruce woke in the night, sweating, with the mosquitoes whining about his face. Outside it was still raining and occasionally the reflected light from the searchlight on the roof of the coach lit the interior dimly.

On one of the bottom bunks Mike Haig lay on his back. His face was shining with sweat and he rolled his head from side to side on the pillow. He was grinding his teeth – a sound to which Bruce had become accustomed, and he preferred it to Hendry's snores.

'You poor old bugger,' whispered Bruce.

From the bunk opposite, André de Surrier whimpered.

49

In sleep he looked like a child with dark soft hair falling over his forehead.

– 6 –

The rain petered out in the dawn and the sun was hot before it cleared the horizon. It lifted a warm mist from the dripping forest. As they ran north the forest thickened, the trees grew closer together and the undergrowth beneath them was coarser than it had been around Elisabethville.

Through the warm misty dawn Bruce saw the water tower at Msapa Junction rising like a lighthouse above the forest, its silver paint streaked with brown rust. Then they came round the last curve in the tracks and the little settlement huddled before them.

It was small, half a dozen buildings in all, and there was about it the desolate aspect of human habitation reverting to jungle.

Beside the tracks stood the water tower and the raised concrete coal bins. Then the station buildings of wood and iron, with the large sign above the verandah:

MSAPA JUNCTION. Elevation 963m.

There was an avenue of casia flora trees with very dark green foliage and orange flowers; and beyond that, on the edge of the forest, a row of cottages.

One of the cottages had been burned, its ruins were fire blackened and tumbled; and the gardens had lost all sense of discipline with three months' neglect.

'Driver, stop beside the water tower. You have fifteen minutes to fill your boiler.'

'Thank you, monsieur.'

With a heavy sigh of steam the loco pulled up beside the tower.

'Haig, take four men and go back to give the driver a hand.'

'Okay, Bruce.'

Bruce turned once more to the radio.

'Hendry.'

'Hello there.'

'Get a patrol together, six men, and search those cottages. Then take a look at the edge of the bush, we don't want any unexpected visitors.'

Wally Hendry waved an acknowledgement from the leading truck, and Bruce went on:

'Put de Surrier on.' He watched Hendry pass the set to André. 'De Surrier, you are in charge of the leading trucks in Hendry's absence. Keep Hendry covered, but watch the bush behind you also. They could come from there.'

Bruce switched off the set and turned to Ruffy. 'Stay up here on the roof, Ruffy. I'm going to chase them up with the watering. If you see anything, don't write me a postcard, start pooping off.'

Ruffy nodded. 'Have some breakfast to take with you.' He proffered an open bottle of beer.

'Better than bacon and eggs.' Bruce accepted the bottle and climbed down on to the platform. Sipping the beer he walked back along the train and looked up at Mike and the engine driver in the tower.

'Is it empty?' he called up at them.

'Half full, enough for a bath if you want one,' answered Mike.

'Don't tempt me.' The idea was suddenly very attractive, for he could smell his own stale body odour and his eyelids were itchy and swollen from mosquito bites. 'My kingdom for a bath.' He ran his fingers over his jowls and they rasped over stiff beard.

He watched them swing the canvas hose out over the loco. The chubby little engine driver clambered up and sat astride the boiler as he fitted the hose.

A shout behind him made Bruce turn quickly, and he saw Hendry's patrol coming back from the cottages. They were dragging two small prisoners with them.

'Hiding in the first cottage,' shouted Hendry. 'They tried to leg it into the bush.' He prodded one of them with his bayonet. The child cried out and twisted in the hands of the gendarme who held her.

'Enough of that.' Bruce stopped him from using the bayonet again and went to meet them. He looked at the two children.

The girl was close to puberty with breasts like insect bites just starting to show, thin-legged with enlarged knee-caps out of proportion to her thighs and calves. She wore only a dirty piece of trade cloth drawn up between her legs and secured around her waist by a length of bark string, and the tribal tattoo marks across her chest and cheeks and forehead stood proud in ridges of scar tissue.

'Ruffy.' Bruce called him down from the coach. 'Can you speak to them?'

Ruffy picked up the boy and held him on his hip. He was younger than the girl – seven, perhaps eight years old. Very dark-skinned and completely naked, as naked as the terror on his face.

Ruffy grunted sharply and the gendarme released the girl. She stood trembling, making no attempt to escape.

Then in a soothing rumble Ruffy began talking to the boy on his hip; he smiled as he spoke and stroked the child's head. Slowly a little of the fear melted and the boy answered in a piping treble that Bruce could not understand.

'What does he say?' urged Bruce.

'He thinks we're going to eat them,' laughed Ruffy. 'Not enough here for a decent breakfast.' He patted the skinny little arm, grey with crushed filth, then he gave an order to one of the gendarmes. The man disappeared into the coach and came back with a handful of chocolate bars. Still talking, Ruffy peeled one of them and placed it in the boy's mouth. The child's eyes widened appreciatively at the taste and he chewed quickly, his eyes on Ruffy's face, his answers now muffled with chocolate.

At last Ruffy turned to Bruce.

'No trouble here, boss. They come from a small village about an hour's walk away. Just five or six families, and no war party. These kids sneaked across to have a look at the houses, pinch what they could perhaps, but that's all.'

'How many men at this village?' asked Bruce, and Ruffy turned back to the boy. In reply to the question he held up the fingers of both hands, without interrupting the chewing.

'Does he know if the line is clear through to Port Reprieve? Have they burnt the bridges or torn up the tracks?' Both children were dumb to this question. The boy swallowed the last of his chocolate and looked hungrily at Ruffy, who filled his mouth again.

'Jesus,' muttered Hendry with deep disgust. 'Is this a crèche or something. Let's all play ring around the roses.'

'Shut up,' snapped Bruce, and then to Ruffy, 'Have they seen any soldiers?'

Two heads shaken in solemn unison.

'Have they seen any war parties of their own people?'

Again solemn negative.

'All right, give them the rest of the chocolate,' instructed Bruce. That was all he could get out of them, and time was wasting. He glanced back at the tower and saw that Haig and the engine driver had finished watering. For a further second he studied the boy. His own son would be about the same age now; it was twelve months since – Bruce stopped himself hurriedly. That way lay madness.

'Hendry, take them back to the edge of the bush and turn them loose. Hurry up. We've wasted long enough.'

'You're telling me!' grunted Hendry and beckoned to the

two children. With Hendry leading and a gendarme on each side they trotted away obediently and disappeared behind the station building.

'Driver, are your preparations complete?'

'Yes, monsieur, we are ready to depart.'

'Shovel all the coal in, we've gotta keep her rolling.' Bruce smiled at him, he liked the little man and their stilted exchanges gave him pleasure.

'Pardon, monsieur.'

'It was an imbecility, a joke – forgive me.'

'Ah, a joke!' The roly-poly stomach wobbled merrily.

'Okay, Mike,' Bruce shouted, 'get your men aboard. We are—'

A burst of automatic gunfire cut his voice short. It came from behind the station buildings, and it battered into the heat-muted morning with such startling violence that for an instant Bruce stood paralysed.

'Haig,' he yelled, 'get up front and take over from de Surrier.' That was the weak point, and Mike's party ran down the train.

'You men.' Bruce stopped the six gendarmes. 'Come with me.' They fell in behind him, and with a quick glance Bruce assured himself that the train was safe. All along its length rifle barrels were poking out protectively, while on the roof Ruffy was dragging the Bren round to cover the flank. A charge by even a thousand Baluba must fail before the fire power that was ready now to receive it.

'Come on,' said Bruce and ran, with the gendarmes behind him, to the sheltering wall of the station building. There had been no shot fired since that initial burst, which could mean either that it was a false alarm or that Hendry's party had been overwhelmed by the first rush.

The door of the station master's office was locked. Bruce kicked and it crashed open with the weight of his booted foot behind it.

I've always wanted to do that, he thought happily in his excitement, ever since I saw Gable do it in *San Francisco*.

'You four – inside! Cover us from the windows.' They crowded into the room with their rifles held ready. Through the open door Bruce saw the telegraph equipment on the table by the far wall; it was clattering metallically from traffic on the Elisabethville-Jadotville line. Why is it that under the stimulus of excitement my mind always registers irrelevances? Which thought is another irrelevancy, he decided.

'Come on, you two, stay with me.' He led them down the outside wall, keeping in close to its sheltering bulk, pausing at the corner to check the load of his rifle and slip the selector on to rapid fire.

A further moment he hesitated. What will I find around this corner? A hundred naked savages crowded round the mutilated bodies of Hendry and his gendarmes, or . . . ?

Crouching, ready to jump back behind the wall, rifle held at high port across his chest, every muscle and nerve of his body cocked like a hair-trigger, Bruce stepped sideways into the open.

Hendry and the two gendarmes stood in the dusty road beyond the first cottage. They were relaxed, talking together, Hendry reloading his rifle, cramming the magazine with big red hands on which the gingery hair caught the sunlight. A cigarette dangled from his lower lip and he laughed suddenly, throwing his head back as he did so and the cigarette ash dropped down his jacket front. Bruce noticed the long dark sweat stain across his shoulders.

The two children lay in the road fifty yards farther on.

Bruce was suddenly cold, it came from inside, a cramping coldness of the guts and chest. Slowly he straightened up and began to walk towards the children. His feet fell silently in the powder dust and the only sound was his own breathing, hoarse, as though a wounded beast followed close behind him. He walked past Hendry and the two gendarmes without looking at them; but they stopped talking, watching him uneasily.

He reached the girl first and went down on one knee beside her, laying his rifle aside and turning her gently on to her back.

'This isn't true,' he whispered. 'This can't be true.'

The bullet had taken half her chest out with it, a hole the size of a coffee cup, with the blood still moving in it, but slowly, oozing, welling up into it with the viscosity of new honey.

Bruce moved across to the boy; he felt an almost dreamlike sense of unreality.

'No, this isn't true.' He spoke louder, trying to undo it with words.

Three bullets had hit the boy; one had torn his arm loose at the shoulder and the sharp white end of the bone pointed accusingly out of the wound. The other bullets had severed his trunk almost in two.

It came from far away, like the rising roar of a train along a tunnel. Bruce could feel his whole being shaken by the strength of it, he shut his eyes and listened to the roaring in his head, and with his eyes tight closed his vision was filled with the colour of blood.

'Hold on!' a tiny voice screamed in his roaring head. 'Don't let go, fight it. Fight it as you've fought before.'

And he clung like a flood victim to the straw of his sanity while the great roaring was all around him. Then the roar was muted, rumbling away, gone past, a whisper, now nothing.

The coldness came back to him, a coldness more vast than the flood had been.

He opened his eyes and breathed again, stood up and walked back to where Hendry stood with the two gendarmes.

'Corporal,' Bruce addressed one of the men beside Hendry; and with a shock he heard that his own voice was calm, without any trace of the fury that had so nearly carried him away on its flood.

'Corporal, go back to the train. Tell Lieutenant Haig and Sergeant Major Ruffararo that I want them here.'

Thankfully the man went, and Bruce spoke to Wally Hendry in the same dispassionate tone.

'I told you to turn them loose,' he said.

'So they could run home and call the whole pack down on us – is that what you wanted, Bucko?' Hendry had recovered now, he was defiant, grinning.

'So instead you murdered them?'

'Murdered! You crazy or something, Bruce? They're Balubes, aren't they? Bloody man-eating Balubes!' shouted Hendry angrily, no longer grinning. 'What's wrong with you, man? This is war, Bucko, war. C'est la guerre, like the man said, c'est la guerre!' Then suddenly his voice moderated again. 'Let's forget it. I did what was right, now let's forget it; what's two more bloody Balubes after all the killing that's been going on? Let's forget it.'

Bruce did not answer, he lit a cigarette and looked beyond Hendry for the others to come.

'How's that, Bruce? You willing we just forget it?' persisted Hendry.

'On the contrary, Hendry, I make you a sacred oath, and I call upon God to witness it.' Bruce was not looking at him, he couldn't trust himself to look at Hendry without killing him. 'This is my promise to you: I will have you hanged for this, not shot, hanged on good hemp rope. I have sent for Haig and Ruffararo so we'll have plenty of witnesses. The first thing I do once we get back to Elisabethville will be to turn you over to the proper authorities.'

'You don't mean that!'

'I have never meant anything so seriously in my life.'

'Jesus, Bruce—!'

Then Haig and Ruffy came; they came running until they saw, and they stopped suddenly and stood uncertainly in the bright sun, looking from Bruce to the two frail little corpses lying in the road.

'What happened?' asked Mike.

'Hendry shot them,' answered Bruce.

'What for?'

'Only he knows.'

'You mean he – he just killed them, just shot them down?'

'Yes.'

'My God,' said Mike, and then again, his voice dull with shock, 'my God.'

'Go and look at them, Haig. I want you to look closely so you remember.'

Haig walked across to the children.

'You too, Ruffy. You'll be a witness at the trial.'

Mike Haig and Ruffy walked side by side to where the children lay, and stood staring down at them. Hendry shuffled his feet in the dust awkwardly and then went on loading the magazine of his rifle.

'Oh, for Chrissake!' he blustered. 'What's all the fuss? They're just a couple of Balubes.'

Wheeling slowly to face him Mike Haig's face was a yellowish colour with only his cheeks and his nose still flushed with the tiny burst of veins beneath the surface of the skin, but there was no colour in his lips. Each breath he drew sobbed in his throat. He started back towards Hendry, still breathing that way, and his mouth was working as he tried to force it to speak. As he came on he unslung the rifle from his shoulder.

'Haig!' said Bruce sharply.

'This time – you – you bloody – this is the last—' mouthed Haig.

'Watch it, Bucko!' Hendry warned him. He stepped

back, clumsily trying to fit the loaded magazine on to his rifle.

Mike Haig dropped the point of his bayonet to the level of Hendry's stomach.

'Haig!' shouted Bruce, and Haig charged surprisingly fast for a man of his age, leaning forward, leading with the bayonet at Hendry's stomach, the incoherent mouthings reaching their climax in a formless bellow.

'Come on, then!' Hendry answered him and stepped forward. As they came together Hendry swept the bayonet to one side with the butt of his own rifle. The point went under his armpit and they collided chest to chest, staggering as Haig's weight carried them backwards. Hendry dropped his rifle and locked both arms round Haig's neck, forcing his head back so that his face was tilted up at the right angle.

'Look out, Mike, he's going to butt!' Bruce had recognized the move, but his warning came too late. Hendry's head jerked forward and Mike gasped as the front of Hendry's steel helmet caught him across the bridge of his nose. The rifle slipped from Mike's grip and fell into the road, he lifted his hands and covered his face with spread fingers and the redness oozed out between them.

Again Hendry's head jerked forward like a hammer and again Mike gasped as the steel smashed into his face and fingers.

'Knee him, Mike!' Bruce yelled as he tried to take up a position from which to intervene, but they were staggering in a circle, turning like a wheel and Bruce could not get in.

Hendry's legs were braced apart as he drew his head back to strike again, and Mike's knee went up between them, all the way up with power into the fork of Hendry's crotch.

Breaking from the clinch, his mouth open in a silent scream of agony, Hendry doubled up with both hands holding his lower stomach, and sagged slowly on to his knees in the dust.

Dazed, with blood running into his mouth, Mike fumbled with the canvas flap of his holster.

'I'll kill you, you murdering swine.'

The pistol came out into his right hand; short-barrelled, blue and ugly.

Bruce stepped up behind him, his thumb found the nerve centre below the elbow and as he dug in the pistol dropped from Mike's paralysed hand and dangled on its lanyard against his knee.

'Ruffy, stop him,' Bruce shouted, for Hendry was clawing painfully at the rifle that lay in the dust beside him.

'Got it, boss!' Ruffy stooped quickly over the crawling body at his feet, in one swift movement opened the flap of the holster, drew the revolver and the lanyard snapped like cotton as he jerked on it.

They stood like that: Bruce holding Haig from behind, and Hendry crouched at Ruffy's feet. The only sound for several seconds was the hoarse rasping of breath.

Bruce felt Mike relaxing in his grip as the madness left him; he unclipped his pistol from his lanyard and let it drop.

'Leave me, Bruce. I'm all right now.'

'Are you sure? I don't want to shoot you.'

'No, I'm all right.'

'If you start it again, I'll have to shoot you. Do you understand?'

'Yes, I'll be all right now. I lost my senses for a moment.'

'You certainly did,' Bruce agreed, and released him.

They formed a circle round the kneeling Hendry, and Bruce spoke.

'If either you or Haig start it again you'll answer to me, do you hear me?'

Hendry looked up, his small eyes slitted with pain. He did not answer.

'Do you hear me?' Bruce repeated the question and Hendry nodded.

'Good! From now on, Hendry, you are under open arrest.

I can't spare men to guard you, and you're welcome to escape if you'd like to try. The local gentry would certainly entertain you most handsomely, they'd probably arrange a special banquet in your honour.'

Hendry's lips drew back in a snarl that exposed teeth with green slimy stains on them.

'But remember my promise, Hendry, as soon as we get back to—'

'Wally, Wally, are you hurt?' André came running from the direction of the station. He knelt beside Hendry.

'Get away, leave me alone.' Hendry struck out at him impatiently and André recoiled.

'De Surrier, who gave you permission to leave your post? Get back to the train.'

André looked up uncertainly, and then back to Hendry.

'De Surrier, you heard me. Get going. And you also, Haig.'

He watched them disappear behind the station building before he glanced once more at the two children. There was a smear of blood and melted chocolate across the boy's cheek and his eyes were wide open in an expression of surprise. Already the flies were settling, crawling delightedly over the two small corpses.

'Ruffy, get spades. Bury them under those trees.' He pointed at the avenue of casia flora. 'But do it quickly.' He spoke brusquely so that how he felt would not show in his voice.

'Okay, boss. I'll fix it.'

'Come on, Hendry,' Bruce snapped, and Wally Hendry heaved to his feet and followed him meekly back to the train.

Slowly from Msapa Junction they travelled northwards through the forest. Each tree seemed to have been cast from the same mould, tall and graceful in itself, but when multiplied countless million times the effect was that of numbing monotony. Above them was a lane of open sky with the clouds scattered, but slowly regrouping for the next assault, and the forest shut in the moist heat so they sweated even in the wind of the train's movement.

'How is your face?' asked Bruce and Mike Haig touched the parallel swellings across his forehead where the skin was broken and discoloured.

'It will do,' he decided; then he lifted his eyes and looked across the open trucks at Wally Hendry. 'You shouldn't have stopped me, Bruce.'

Bruce did not answer, but he also watched Hendry as he leaned uncomfortably against the side of the leading truck, obviously favouring his injuries, his face turned half away from them, talking to André.

'You should have let me kill him,' Mike went on. 'A man who can shoot down two small children in cold blood and then laugh about it afterwards—!' Mike left the rest unsaid, but his hands were opening and closing in his lap.

'It's none of your business,' said Bruce, sensitive to the implied rebuke. 'What are you? One of God's avenging angels?'

'None of my business, you say?' Mike turned quickly to face Bruce. 'My God, what kind of man are you? I hope for your sake you don't mean that!'

'I'll tell you in words of one syllable what kind of man I am, Haig,' Bruce answered flatly. 'I'm the kind that minds my own bloody business, that lets other people lead their own lives. I am ready to take reasonable measures to prevent others flouting the code which society has drawn up for us, but that's all. Hendry has committed murder; this I agree is a bad thing, and when we get back to Elisabethville I will bring it to the attention of the people whose business it is. But I am not going to wave banners and quote from the Bible and froth at the mouth.'

'That's all?'

'That's all.'

'You don't feel sorry for those two kids?'

'Yes I do. But pity doesn't heal bullet wounds; all it does is distress me. So I switch off the pity – they can't use it.'

'You don't feel anger or disgust or horror at Hendry?'

'The same thing applies,' explained Bruce, starting to lose patience again. 'I could work up a sweat about it if I let myself loose on an emotional orgy, as you are doing.'

'So instead you treat something as evil as Hendry with an indifferent tolerance?' asked Mike.

'Jesus Christ!' grated Bruce. 'What the hell do you want me to do?'

'I want you to stop playing dead. I want you to be able to recognize evil and to destroy it.' Mike was starting to lose his temper also; his nerves were taut.

'That's great! Do you know where I can buy a second-hand crusader outfit and a white horse, then singlehanded I will ride out to wage war on cruelty and ignorance, lust and greed and hatred and poverty—'

'That's not what I—' Mike tried to interrupt, but Bruce overrode him, his handsome face flushed darkly with anger and the sun. 'You want me to destroy evil wherever I find it. You old fool, don't you know that it has a hundred heads and that for each one you cut off another hundred grow in its place? Don't you know that it's in you also, so to destroy it you have to destroy yourself?'

'You're a coward, Curry! The first time you burn a finger you run away and build yourself an asbestos shelter—'

'I don't like being called names, Haig. Put a leash on your tongue.'

Mike paused and his expression changed, softening into a grin.

'I'm sorry, Bruce. I was just trying to teach you—'

'Thank you,' scoffed Bruce, his voice still harsh; he had not been placated by the apology. 'You are going to teach me, thanks very much! But what are you going to teach me, Haig? What are you qualified to teach? "How to find success and happiness" by Laughing Lad Haig who worked his way down to a lieutenancy in the black army of Katanga – how's that as a title for your lecture, or do you prefer something more technical like: "The applications of alcohol to spiritual research—"'

'All right, Bruce. Drop it, I'll shut up,' and Bruce saw how deeply he had wounded Mike. He regretted it then, he would have liked to unsay it. But that's one thing you can never do.

Beside him Mike Haig was suddenly much older and more tired looking, the pouched wrinkles below his eyes seemed to have deepened in the last few seconds, and a little more of the twinkle had gone from his eyes. His short laughter had a bitter humourless ring to it.

'When you put it that way it's really quite funny.'

'I punched a little low,' admitted Bruce, and then, 'perhaps I should let you shoot Hendry. A waste of ammunition really, but seeing that you want to so badly,' Bruce drew his pistol and offered it to Mike butt first, 'use mine.' He grinned disarmingly at Mike and his grin was almost impossible to resist; Mike started to laugh. It wasn't a very good joke, but somehow it caught fire between them and suddenly they were laughing together.

Mike Haig's battered features spread like warm butter and twenty years dropped from his face. Bruce leaned back against the sandbags with his mouth wide open, the pistol still in his hand and his long lean body throbbing uncontrollably with laughter.

There was something feverish in it, as though they were trying with laughter to gargle away the taste of blood and hatred. It was the laughter of despair.

Below them the men in the trucks turned to watch them, puzzled at first, and then beginning to chuckle in sympathy, not recognizing the sickness of that sound.

'Hey, boss,' called Ruffy. 'First time I ever seen you laugh like you meant it.'

And the epidemic spread, everyone was laughing, even André de Surrier was smiling.

Only Wally Hendry was untouched by it, silent and sullen, watching them with small expressionless eyes.

They came to the bridge over the Cheke in the middle of the afternoon. Both the road and the railway crossed it side by side, but after this brief meeting they diverged and the road twisted away to the left. The river was padded on each bank by dense dark green bush; three hundred yards thick, a matted tangle of thorn and tree fern with the big trees growing up through it and bursting into flower as they reached the sunlight.

'Good place for an ambush,' muttered Mike Haig, eyeing the solid green walls of vegetation on each side of the lines.

'Charming, isn't it,' agreed Bruce, and by the uneasy air of alertness that had settled on his gendarmes it was clear that they agreed with him.

The train nosed its way carefully into the river bush like a steel snake along a rabbit run, and they came to the river. Bruce switched on the set.

'Driver, stop this side of the bridge. I wish to inspect it before entrusting our precious cargo to it.'

'Oui, monsieur.'

The Cheke river at this point was fifty yards wide, deep, quick-flowing and angry with flood water which had almost covered the white sand beaches along each bank. Its bottle-green colour was smoked with mud and there were whirlpools round the stone columns of the bridge.

'Looks all right,' Haig gave his opinion. 'How far are we from Port Reprieve now?'

Bruce spread his field map on the roof of the coach between his legs and found the brackets that straddled the convoluted ribbon of the river.

'Here we are.' He touched it and then ran his finger along the stitched line of the railway until it reached the red circle that marked Port Reprieve. 'About thirty miles to go, another hour's run. We'll be there before dark.'

'Those are the Lufira hills.' Mike Haig pointed to the blue smudge that only just showed above the forest ahead of them.

'We'll be able to see the town from the top,' agreed Bruce. 'The river runs parallel to them on the other side, and the swamp is off to the right, the swamp is the source of the river.'

He rolled the map and passed it back to Ruffy who slid it into the plastic map case.

'Ruffy, Lieutenant Haig and I are going ahead to have a look at the bridge. Keep an eye on the bush.'

'Okay, boss. You want a beer to take with you?'

'Thanks.' Bruce was thirsty and he emptied half the bottle before climbing down to join Mike on the gravel embankment. Rifles unslung, watching the bush on each side uneasily, they hurried forward and with relief reached the bridge and went out into the centre of it.

'Seems solid enough,' commented Mike. 'No one has tampered with it.'

'It's wood.' Bruce stamped on the heavy wild mahogany timbers. They were three feet thick and stained with a dark chemical to inhibit rotting.

'So, it's wood?' enquired Mike.

'Wood burns,' explained Bruce. 'It would be easy to burn

it down.' He leaned his elbows on the guard rail, drained the beer bottle and dropped it to the surface of the river twenty feet below. There was a thoughtful expression on his face.

'Very probably there are Baluba in the bush' – he pointed at the banks – 'watching us at this moment. They might get the same idea. I wonder if I should leave a guard here?'

Mike leaned on the rail beside him and they both stared out to where the river took a bend two hundred yards downstream; in the crook of the bend grew a tree twice as tall as any of its neighbours. The trunk was straight and covered with smooth silvery bark and its foliage piled to a high green steeple against the clouds. It was the natural point of focus for their eyes as they weighed the problem.

'I wonder what kind of tree that is. I've never seen one like it before.' Bruce was momentarily diverted by the grandeur of it. 'It looks like a giant blue gum.'

'It's quite a sight,' Mike concurred. 'I'd like to go down and have a closer—'

Then suddenly he stiffened and there was an edge of alarm in his voice as he pointed.

'Bruce, there! What's that in the lower branches?'

'Where?'

'Just above the first fork, on the left—' Mike was pointing and suddenly Bruce saw it. For a second he thought it was a leopard, then he realized it was too dark and long.

'It's a man,' exclaimed Mike.

'Baluba,' snapped Bruce; he could see the shape now and the sheen of naked black flesh, the kilt of animal tails and the headdress of feathers. A long bow stood up behind the man's shoulder as he balanced on the branch and steadied himself with one hand against the trunk. He was watching them.

Bruce glanced round at the train. Hendry had noticed their agitation and, following the direction of Mike's raised arm, he had spotted the Baluba. Bruce realized what Hendry was going to do and he opened his mouth to shout, but before he could do so Hendry had snatched his rifle off his shoulder, swung it up and fired a long, rushing, hammering burst.

'The trigger-happy idiot,' snarled Bruce and looked back at the tree. Slabs of white bark were flying from the trunk and the bullets reaped leaves that fluttered down like crippled insects, but the Baluba had disappeared.

The gunfire ceased abruptly and in its place Hendry was shouting with hoarse excitement.

'I got him, I got the bastard.'

'Hendry!' Bruce's voice was also hoarse, but with anger, 'Who ordered you to fire?'

'He was a bloody Baluba, a mucking big bloody Baluba. Didn't you see him, hey? Didn't you see him, man?'

'Come here, Hendry.'

'I got the bastard,' rejoiced Hendry.

'Are you deaf? Come here!'

While Hendry climbed down from the truck and came towards them Bruce asked Haig:

'Did he hit him?'

'I'm not sure. I don't think so, I think he jumped. If he had been hit he'd have been thrown backwards, you know how it knocks them over.'

'Yes,' said Bruce, 'I know.' A .300 bullet from an FN struck with a force of well over a ton. When you hit a man there was no doubt about it. All right, so the Baluba was still in there.

Hendry came up, swaggering, laughing with excitement.

'So you killed, hey?' Bruce asked.

'Stone dead, stone bloody dead!'

'Can you see him?'

'No, he's down in the bush.'

'Do you want to go and have a look at him, Hendry? Do you want to go and get his ears?'

Ears are the best trophy you can take from a man, not as

good as the skin of a black-maned lion or the great bossed horns of a buffalo, but better than the scalp. The woolly cap of an African scalp is a drab thing, messy to take and difficult to cure. You have to salt it and stretch it inside out over a helmet; even then it smells badly. Ears are much less trouble and Hendry was an avid collector. He was not the only one in the army of Katanga; the taking of ears was common practice.

'Yeah, I want them.' Hendry detached the bayonet from the muzzle of his rifle. 'I'll nip down and get them.'

'You can't let anyone go in there, Bruce. Not even him,' protested Haig quietly.

'Why not? He deserves it, he worked hard for it.'

'Only take a minute.' Hendry ran his thumb along the bayonet to test the edge. My God! He really means it, thought Bruce; he'd go into that tangled stuff for a pair of ears – he's not brave, he's just stupendously lacking in imagination.

'Wait for me, Bruce, it won't take long.' Hendry started back.

'You're not serious, Bruce?' Mike asked.

'No,' agreed Bruce, 'I'm not serious,' and his voice was cold and hard as he caught hold of Hendry's shoulder and stopped him.

'Listen to me! You have no more chances – that was it. I'm waiting for you now, Hendry. Just once more, that's all. Just once more.'

Hendry's face turned sullen again.

'Don't push me, Bucko.'

'Get back to the train and bring it across,' said Bruce contemptuously and turned to Haig.

'Now we'll have to leave a guard here. They know we've gone across and they'll burn it for a certainty, especially after that little fiasco.'

'Who are you going to leave?'

'Ten men, say, under a sergeant. We'll be back by

69

nightfall or tomorrow morning at the latest. They should be safe enough. I doubt there is a big war party here, a few strays perhaps, but the main force will be closer to the town.'

'I hope you're right.'

'So do I,' said Bruce absently, his mind busy with the problem of defending the bridge. 'We'll strip all the sandbags off the coaches and build an emplacement here in the middle of the roadway, leave two of the battery-operated searchlights and a case of flares with them, one of the Brens and a couple of cases of grenades. Food and water for a week. No, they'll be all right.'

The train was rolling down slowly towards them – and a single arrow rose from the edge of the jungle. Slowly it rose, curving in flight and falling towards the train, dropping faster now, silently into the mass of men in the leading truck.

So Hendry had missed and the Baluba had come up stream through the thick bush to launch his arrow in retaliation. Bruce sprang to the guard rail and, using it as a rest for his rifle, opened up in short bursts, searching the green mass and seeing it tremble with his bullets. Haig was shooting also, hunting the area from which the arrow had come.

The train was up to them now and Bruce slung his rifle over his shoulder and scrambled up the side of the truck. He pushed his way to the radio set.

'Driver, stop the covered coaches in the middle of the bridge,' he snapped, and then he switched it off and looked for Ruffy.

'Sergeant Major, get all those sandbags off the roof into the roadway.' While they worked, the gendarmes would be protected from further arrows by the body of the train.

'Okay, boss.'

'Kanaki.' Bruce picked his most reliable sergeant. 'I am leaving you here with ten men to hold the bridge for us.

Take one of the Brens, and two of the lights—' Quickly Bruce issued his orders and then he had time to ask André:

'What happened to that arrow? Was anyone hit?'

'No, missed by a few inches. Here it is.'

'That was a bit of luck.' Bruce took the arrow from André and inspected it quickly. A light reed, crudely fletched with green leaves and with the iron head bound into it with a strip of rawhide. It looked fragile and ineffectual, but the barbs of the head were smeared thickly with a dark paste that had dried like toffee.

'Pleasant,' murmured Bruce, and then he shuddered slightly. He could imagine it embedded in his body with the poison purple-staining the flesh beneath the skin. He had heard that it was not a comfortable death, and the iron-tipped reed was suddenly malignant and repulsive. He snapped it in half and threw it out over the side of the bridge before he jumped down from the truck to supervise the building of the guard post.

'Not enough sandbags, boss.'

'Take the mattresses off all the bunks, Ruffy.' Bruce solved that quickly. The leather-covered coir pallets would stop an arrow with ease.

Fifteen minutes later the post was completed, a shoulder-high ring of sandbags and mattresses large enough to accommodate ten men and their equipment, with embrasures sited to command both ends of the bridge.

'We'll be back early tomorrow, Kanaki. Let none of your men leave this post for any purpose; the gaps between the timbers are sufficient for purposes of sanitation.'

'We shall enjoy enviable comfort, Captain. But we will lack that which soothes.' Kanaki grinned meaningly at Bruce.

'Ruffy, leave them a case of beer.'

'A whole case?' Ruffy made no attempt to hide his shocked disapproval of such a prodigal order.

'Is my credit not good?'

'You credit is okay, boss,' and then he changed to French to make his protest formal. 'My concern is the replacement of such a valuable commodity.'

'You're wasting time, Ruffy!'

– 8 –

From the bridge it was thirty miles to Port Reprieve. They met the road again six miles outside the town; it crossed under them and disappeared into the forest again to circle out round the high ground taking the easier route into Port Reprieve. But the railroad climbed up the hills in a series of traverses and came out at the top six hundred feet above the town. On the stony slopes the forest found meagre purchase and the vegetation was sparser; it did not obscure the view.

Standing on the roof Bruce looked out across the Lufira swamps to the north, a vastness of poisonous green swamp grass and open water, disappearing into the blue heat haze without any sign of ending. From its southern extremity it was drained by the Lufira river. The river was half a mile wide, deep olive-green, ruffled darker by eddies of wind across its surface, fenced into the very edge of the water by a solid barrier of dense river bush. In the angle formed by the swamp and the river was a headland which protected the natural harbour of Port Reprieve. The town was on a spit of land, the harbour on one side and a smaller swamp on the other. The road came round the right-hand side of the hills, crossed a causeway over the swamp and entered the single street of the town from the far side.

There were three large buildings in the centre of the town opposite the railway yard, their iron roofs bright beacons in the sunlight; and clustered round them were perhaps fifty smaller thatched dwellings.

Down on the edge of the harbour was a long shed,

obviously a workshop, and two jetties ran into the water. The diamond dredgers were moored alongside; three of them, ungainly black hulks with high superstructures and blunt ends.

It was a place of heat and fever and swamp smells, an ugly little village by a green reptile river.

'Nice place to retire,' Mike Haig grunted.

'Or open a health resort,' said Bruce.

Beyond the causeway, on the main headland, there was another cluster of buildings, just the tops were showing above the forest. Among them rose the copper-clad spire of a church.

'Mission station,' guessed Bruce.

'St Augustine's,' agreed Ruffy. 'My first wife's little brudder got himself educated there. He's an attaché to the ministry of something or other in Elisabethville now, doing damn good for himself.' Boasting a little.

'Bully for him,' said Bruce.

The train had started angling down the hills towards the town.

'Well, I reckon we've made it, boss.'

'I reckon also; all we have to do is get back again.'

'Yessir, I reckon that's all.'

And they ran into the town.

There were more than forty people in the crowd that lined the platform to welcome them.

We'll have a heavy load on the way home, thought Bruce as he ran his eye over them. He saw the bright spots of women's dresses in the throng. Bruce counted four of them. That's another complication; one day I hope I find something in this life that turns out exactly as expected, something that will run smoothly and evenly through to its right and logical conclusion. Some hope, he decided, some bloody hope.

The joy and relief of the men and women on the platform was pathetically apparent in their greetings. Most of the women were crying and the men ran beside the train like small boys as it slid in along the raised concrete platform. All of them were of mixed blood, Bruce noted. They varied in colour from creamy yellow to charcoal. The Belgians had certainly left much to be remembered by.

Standing back from the throng, a little aloof from the general jollification, was a half-blooded Belgian. There was an air of authority about him that was unmistakable. On one side of him stood a large bosomy woman of his own advanced age, darker skinned than he was; but Bruce saw immediately that she was his wife. At his other hand stood a figure dressed in a white open-necked shirt and blue jeans that Bruce at first thought was a boy, until the head turned and he saw the long plume of dark hair that hung down her back, and the unmanly double pressure beneath the white shirt.

The train stopped and Bruce jumped down on to the platform and laughingly pushed his way through the crowds towards the Belgian. Despite a year in the Congo, Bruce had not grown accustomed to being kissed by someone who had not shaved for two or three days and who smelled strongly of garlic and cheap tobacco. This atrocity was committed upon him a dozen times or more before he arrived before the Belgian.

'The Good Lord bless you for coming to our aid, Monsieur Captain.' The Belgian recognized the twin bars on the front of Bruce's helmet and held out his hand. Bruce had expected another kiss, so he accepted the handshake with relief.

'I am only glad that we are in time,' he answered.

'May I introduce myself – Martin Boussier, district manager of Union Miniére Corporation, and this is my wife, Madame Boussier.' He was a tall man, but unlike his wife, sparsely fleshed. His hair was completely silver and his skin folded, toughened and browned by a life under the equatorial sun. Bruce took an instant liking to him. Madame

Boussier pressed her bulk against Bruce and kissed him heartily. Her moustache was too soft to cause him discomfort and she smelled of toilet soap, which was a distinct improvement, decided Bruce.

'May I also present Madame Cartier,' and for the first time Bruce looked squarely at the girl. A number of things registered in his mind simultaneously: the paleness of her skin which was not unhealthy but had an opaque coolness which he wanted to touch, the size of her eyes which seemed to fill half her face, the unconscious provocation of her lips, and the use of the word *Madame* before her name.

'Captain Curry – of the Katanga Army,' said Bruce. She's too young to be married, can't be more than seventeen. She's still got that little girl freshness about her and I bet she smells like an unweaned puppy.

'Thank you for coming, monsieur.' She had a throatiness in her voice as though she were just about to laugh or to make love, and Bruce added three years to his estimate of her age. That was not a little girl's voice, nor were those little girl's legs in the jeans, and little girls had less under their shirt fronts.

His eyes came back to her face and he saw that there was colour in her cheeks now and sparks of annoyance in her eyes.

My God, he thought, I'm ogling her like a matelot on shore leave. He hurriedly transferred his attention back to Boussier, but his throat felt constricted as he asked:

'How many are you?'

'There are forty-two of us, of which five are women and two are children.'

Bruce nodded, it was what he had expected. The women could ride in one of the covered coaches. He turned and surveyed the railway yard.

'Is there a turntable on which we can revolve the locomotive?' he asked Boussier.

'No, Captain.'

They would have to reverse all the way back to Msapa Junction, another complication. It would be more difficult to keep a watch on the tracks ahead, and it would mean a sooty and uncomfortable journey.

'What precautions have you taken against attack, monsieur?'

'They are inadequate, Captain,' Boussier admitted. 'I have not sufficient men to defend the town – most of the population left before the emergency. Instead I have posted sentries on all the approaches and I have fortified the hotel to the best of my ability. It was there we intended to stand in the event of attack.'

Bruce nodded again and glanced up at the sun. It was already reddening as it dropped towards the horizon, perhaps another hour or two of daylight.

'Monsieur, it is too late to entrain all your people and leave before nightfall. I intend to load their possessions this evening. We will stay overnight and leave in the early morning.'

'We are all anxious to be away from this place; we have twice seen large parties of Baluba on the edge of the jungle.'

'I understand,' said Bruce. 'But the dangers of travelling by night exceed those of waiting another twelve hours.'

'The decision is yours,' Boussier agreed. 'What do you wish us to do now?'

'Please see to the embarkation of your people. I regret that only the most essential possessions may be entertained. We will be almost a hundred persons.'

'I shall see to that myself,' Boussier assured him, 'and then?'

'Is that the hotel?' Bruce pointed across the street at one of the large double-storeyed buildings. It was only two hundred yards from where they stood.

'Yes, Captain.'

'Good,' said Bruce. 'It is close enough. Your people can

spend the night there in more comfort than aboard the train.'

He looked at the girl again; she was watching him with a small smile on her face. It was a smile of almost maternal amusement, as though she were watching a little boy playing at soldiers. Now it was Bruce's turn to feel annoyed. He was suddenly embarrassed by his uniform and epaulettes, by the pistol at his hip, the automatic rifle across his shoulder and the heavy helmet on his head.

'I will require someone who is familiar with the area to accompany me, I want to inspect your defences,' he said to Boussier.

'Madame Cartier could show you,' suggested Boussier's wife artlessly. I wonder if she noticed our little exchange, thought Bruce. Of course she did. All women have a most sensitive nose for that sort of thing.

'Will you go with the captain, Shermaine?' asked Madame Boussier.

'As the captain wishes.' She was still smiling.

'That is settled then,' said Bruce gruffly. 'I will meet you at the hotel in ten minutes, after I have made arrangements here.' He turned back to Boussier. 'You may proceed with the embarkation, monsieur.' Bruce left them and went back to the train.

'Hendry,' he shouted, 'you and de Surrier will stay on board. We are not leaving until the morning but these people are going to load their stuff now. In the meantime rig the searchlights to sweep both sides of the track and make sure the Brens are properly sited.'

Hendry grunted an acknowledgement without looking at Bruce.

'Mike, take ten men with you and go to the hotel. I want you there in case of trouble during the night.'

'Okay, Bruce.'

'Ruffy.'

'Sa!'

'Take a gang and help the driver refuel.'

'Okay, boss. Hey, boss!'

'Yes.' Bruce turned to him.

'When you go to the hotel, have a look-see maybe they got some beer up there. We're just about fresh out.'

'I'll keep it in mind.'

'Thanks, boss.' Ruffy looked relieved. 'I'd hate like hell to die of thirst in this hole.'

The townsfolk were streaming back towards the hotel. The girl Shermaine walked with the Boussiers, and Bruce heard Hendry's voice above him.

'Jesus, look what that pretty has got in her pants. What ever it is, one thing is sure: it's round and it's in two pieces, and those pieces move like they don't belong to each other.'

'You haven't any work to do Hendry?' Bruce asked harshly.

'What's wrong, Curry?' Hendry jeered down at him. 'You got plans yourself? Is that it, Bucko?'

'She's married,' said Bruce, and immediately was surprised that he had said it.

'Sure,' laughed Hendry. 'All the best ones are married; that don't mean a thing, not a bloody thing.'

'Get on with your work,' snapped Bruce, and then to Haig, 'Are you ready? Come with me then.'

– 9 –

When they reached the hotel Boussier was waiting for them on the open verandah. He led Bruce aside and spoke quietly.

'Monsieur, I don't wish to be an alarmist but I have received some most disturbing news. There are brigands armed with modern weapons raiding down from the north.

78

The last reports state that they had sacked Senwati Mission about three hundred kilometres north of here.'

'Yes,' Bruce nodded, 'I know about them. We heard on the radio.'

'Then you will have realized that they can be expected to arrive here very soon.'

'I don't see them arriving before tomorrow afternoon; by then we should be well on our way to Msapa Junction.'

'I hope you are right, Monsieur. The atrocities committed by this General Moses at Senwati are beyond the conception of any normal mind. He appears to bear an almost pathological hatred for all people of European descent.' Boussier hesitated before going on. 'There were a dozen white nuns at Senwati. I have heard that they—'

'Yes,' Bruce interrupted him quickly; he did not want to listen to it. 'I can imagine. Try and prevent these stories circulating amongst your people. I don't want to have them panic.'

'Of course,' Boussier nodded.

'Do you know what force this General Moses commands?'

'It is not more than a hundred men but, as I have said, they are all armed with modern weapons. I have even heard that they have with them a cannon of some description, though I think this unlikely. They are travelling in a convoy of stolen vehicles and at Senwati they captured a gasoline tanker belonging to the commercial oil companies.'

'I see,' mused Bruce. 'But it doesn't alter my decision to remain here overnight. However, we must leave at first light tomorrow.'

'As you wish, Captain.'

'Now, monsieur,' Bruce changed the subject, 'I require some form of transport. Is that car in running order?' He pointed at a pale green Ford Ranchero station wagon parked beside the verandah wall.

'It is. It belongs to my company.' Boussier took a key ring

from his pocket and handed it to Bruce. 'Here are the keys. The tank is full of gasoline.'

'Good,' said Bruce. 'Now if we can find Madame Cartier—'

She was waiting in the hotel lounge and she stood up as Bruce and Boussier came in.

'Are you ready, madame?'

'I await your pleasure,' she answered, and Bruce looked at her sharply. Just a trace of a twinkle in her dark blue eyes suggested that she was aware of the double meaning.

They walked out to the Ford and Bruce opened the door for her.

'You are gracious, monsieur.' She thanked him and slid into the seat. Bruce went round to the driver's side and climbed in beside her.

'It's nearly dark,' he said.

'Turn right on to the Msapa Junction road, there is one post there.'

Bruce drove out along the dirt road through the town until they came to the last house before the causeway. 'Here,' said the girl and Bruce stopped the car. There were two men there, both armed with sporting rifles. Bruce spoke to them. They had seen no sign of Baluba, but they were both very nervous. Bruce made a decision.

'I want you to go back to the hotel. The Baluba will have seen the train arrive; they won't attack in force, we'll be safe tonight. But they may try and cut a few throats if we leave you out here.'

The two half-breeds gathered together their belongings and set off towards the centre of town, obviously with lighter hearts.

'Where are the others?' Bruce asked the girl.

'The next post is at the pumping station down by the river, there are three men there.'

Bruce followed her directions. Once or twice as he drove

80

he glanced surreptitiously at her. She sat in her corner of the seat with her legs drawn up sideways under her. She sat very still, Bruce noticed. I like a woman who doesn't fidget; it's soothing. Then she smiled; this one isn't soothing. She is as disturbing as hell! She turned suddenly and caught him looking again, but this time she smiled.

'You are English, aren't you, Captain?'

'No, I am a Rhodesian,' Bruce answered.

'It's the same,' said the girl. 'You speak French so very badly that you had to be English.'

Bruce laughed. 'Perhaps your English is better than my French,' he challenged her.

'It couldn't be much worse,' she answered him in his own language. 'You are different when you laugh, not so grim, not so heroic. Take the next road to your right.'

Bruce turned the Ford down towards the harbour.

'You are very frank,' he said. 'Also your English is excellent.'

'Do you smoke?' she asked, and when he nodded she lit two cigarettes and passed one to him.

'You are also very young to smoke, and very young to be married.'

She stopped smiling and swung her legs off the seat.

'Here is the pumping station,' she said.

'I beg your pardon. I shouldn't have said that.'

'It's of no importance.'

'It was an impertinence,' Bruce demurred.

'It doesn't matter.'

Bruce stopped the car and opened his door. He walked out on to the wooden jetty towards the pump house, and the boards rang dully under his boots. There was a mist coming up out of the reeds round the harbour and the frogs were piping in fifty different keys. He spoke to the men in the single room of the pump station.

'You can get back to the hotel by dark if you hurry.'

'Oui, monsieur,' they agreed. Bruce watched them set off up the road before they went to the car. He spun the starter motor and above the noise of it the girl asked:

'What is your given name, Captain Curry?'

'Bruce.'

She repeated it, pronouncing it 'Bruise', and then asked:

'Why are you a soldier?'

'For many reasons.' His tone was flippant.

'You do not look like a soldier, for all your badges and your guns, for all the grimness and the frequent giving of orders.'

'Perhaps I am not a very good soldier.' He smiled at her.

'You are very efficient and very grim except when you laugh. But I am glad you do not look like one,' she said.

'Where is the next post?'

'On the railway line. There are two men there. Turn to your right again at the top, Bruce.'

'You are also very efficient, Shermaine.' They were silent again, having used each other's names. Bruce could feel it between them, a good feeling, warm like new bread. But what of her husband, he thought, I wonder where he is, and what he is like. Why isn't he here with her?

'He is dead,' she said quietly. 'He died four months ago of malaria.'

With the shock of it, Shermaine answering his unspoken question and also the answer itself, Bruce could say nothing for the moment, then:

'I'm sorry.'

'There is the post,' she said, 'in the cottage with the thatched roof.'

Bruce stopped the car and switched off the engine. In the silence she spoke again.

'He was a good man, so very gentle. I only knew him for a few months but he was a good man.'

She looked very small sitting beside him in the gathering dark with the sadness on her, and Bruce felt a great wave of tenderness wash over him. He wanted to put his arm round her and hold her, to shield her from the sadness. He searched for the words, but before he found them, she roused herself and spoke in a matter-of-fact tone.

'We must hurry, it's dark already.'

At the hotel the lounge was filled with Boussier's employees; Haig had mounted a Bren in one of the upstairs windows to cover the main street and posted two men in the kitchens to cover the back. The civilians were in little groups, talking quietly, and their expressions of complete doglike trust as they looked at Bruce disconcerted him.

'Everything under control, Mike?' he asked brusquely.

'Yes, Bruce. We should be able to hold this building against a sneak attack. De Surrier and Hendry, down at the station yard, shouldn't have any trouble either.'

'Have these people,' Bruce pointed at the civilians, 'loaded their luggage?'

'Yes, it's all aboard. I have told Ruffy to issue them with food from our stores.'

'Good.' Bruce felt relief; no further complications so far.

'Where is old man Boussier?'

'He is across at his office.'

'I'm going to have a chat with him.'

Unbidden, Shermaine fell in beside Bruce as he walked out into the street, but he liked having her there.

Boussier looked up as Bruce and Shermaine walked into his office. The merciless glare of the petromax lamp accentuated the lines at the corners of his eyes and mouth, and showed up the streaks of pink scalp beneath his neatly combed hair.

'Martin, you are not still working!' exclaimed Shermaine, and he smiled at her, the calm smile of his years.

'Not really, my dear, just tidying up a few things. Please be seated, Captain.'

He came round and cleared a pile of heavy leatherbound

ledgers off the chair and packed them into a wooden case on the floor, went back to his own chair, opened a drawer in the desk, brought out a box of cheroots and offered one to Bruce.

'I cannot tell you how relieved I am that you are here, Captain. These last few months have been very trying. The doubt. The anxiety.' He struck a match and held it out to Bruce who leaned forward across the desk and lit his cheroot. 'But now it is all at an end; I feel as though a great weight has been lifted from my shoulders.' Then his voice sharpened. 'But you were not too soon. I have heard within the last hour that this General Moses and his column have left Senwati and are on the road south, only two hundred kilometres north of here. They will arrive tomorrow at their present rate of advance.'

'Where did you hear this?' Bruce demanded.

'From one of my men, and do not ask me how he knows. There is a system of communication in this country which even after all these years I do not understand. Perhaps it is the drums, I heard them this evening, I do not know. However, their information is usually reliable.'

'I had not placed them so close,' muttered Bruce. 'Had I known this I might have risked travelling tonight, at least as far as the bridge.'

'I think your decision to stay over the night was correct. General Moses will not travel during darkness – none of his men would risk that – and the condition of the road from Senwati after three months neglect is such that he will need ten or twelve hours to cover the distance.'

'I hope you're right.' Bruce was worried. 'I'm not sure that we shouldn't pull out now.'

'That involves a risk also, Captain,' Boussier pointed out. 'We know there are tribesmen in close proximity to the town. They have been seen. They must be aware of your arrival, and might easily have wrecked the lines to prevent our departure. I think your original decision is still good.'

'I know.' Bruce was hunched forward in his chair, frowning, sucking on the cheroot. At last he sat back and the frown evaporated. 'I can't risk it. I'll place a guard on the causeway, and if this Moses gentleman arrives we can hold him there long enough to embark your people.'

'That is probably the best course,' agreed Boussier. He paused, glanced towards the open windows and lowered his voice. 'There is another point, Captain, which I wish to bring to your attention.'

'Yes?'

'As you know, the activity of my company in Port Reprieve is centred on the recovery of diamonds from the Lufira swamps.'

Bruce nodded.

'I have in my safe' – Boussier jerked his thumb at the heavy steel door built into the wall behind his desk – 'nine and a half thousand carats of gem-quality diamonds and some twenty-six thousand carats of industrial diamonds.'

'I had expected that.' Bruce kept his tone non-committal.

'It may be as well if we could agree on the disposition and handling of these stones.'

'How are they packaged?' asked Bruce.

'A single wooden case.'

'Of what size and weight?'

'I will show you.'

Boussier went to the safe, turned his back to them and they heard the tumblers whirr and click. While he waited Bruce realized suddenly that Shermaine had not spoken since her initial greeting to Boussier. He glanced at her now and she smiled at him. I like a woman who knows when to keep her mouth shut.

Boussier swung the door of the safe open and carried a small wooden case across to the desk.

'There,' he said.

Bruce examined it. Eighteen inches long, nine deep and twelve wide. He lifted it experimentally.

'About twenty pounds weight,' he decided. 'The lid is sealed.'

'Yes,' agreed Boussier, touching the four wax imprints.

'Good,' Bruce nodded. 'I don't want to draw unnecessary attention to it by placing a guard upon it.'

'No, I agree.'

Bruce studied the case a few seconds longer and then he asked:

'What is the value of these stones?'

Boussier shrugged. 'Possibly five hundred million francs.' And Bruce was impressed; half a million sterling. Worth stealing, worth killing for.

'I suggest, monsieur, that you secrete this case in your luggage. In your blankets, say. I doubt there will be any danger of theft until we reach Msapa Junction. A thief will have no avenue of escape. Once we reach Msapa Junction I will make other arrangements for its safety.'

'Very well, Captain.'

Bruce stood up and glanced at his watch. 'Seven o'clock, as near as dammit. I will leave you and see to the guard on the causeway. Please make sure that your people are ready to entrain before dawn tomorrow morning.'

'Of course.'

Bruce looked at Shermaine and she stood up quickly. Bruce held the door open for her and was just about to follow her when a thought struck him.

'That mission station – St Augustine's, is it? I suppose it's deserted now?'

'No, it's not.' Boussier looked a little shamefaced. 'Father Ignatius is still there, and of course the patients at the hospital.'

'Thanks for telling me.' Bruce was bitter.

'I'm sorry, Captain. It slipped my mind, there are so many things to think of.'

'Do you know the road out to the mission?' he snapped at Shermaine. *She* should have told him.

'Yes, Bruce.'

'Well, perhaps you'd be good enough to direct me.'

'Of course.' She also looked guilty.

Bruce slammed the door of Boussier's office and strode off towards the hotel with Shermaine trotting to keep pace with him. You can't rely on anyone, he thought, not anybody!

And then he saw Ruffy coming up from the station, looking like a big bear in the dusk. With a few exceptions, Bruce corrected himself.

'Sergeant Major.'

'Hello, boss.'

'This General Moses is closer to us than we reckoned. He's reported two hundred kilometres north of here on the Senwati road.'

Ruffy whistled through his teeth. 'Are you going to take off now, Boss?'

'No, I want a machine-gun post on this end of the causeway. If they come we can hold them there long enough to get away. I want you to take command.'

'I'll see to it now.'

'I'm going out to the mission – there's a white priest there. Lieutenant Haig is in command while I'm away.'

'Okay, boss.'

– 10 –

'I'm sorry, Bruce. I should have told you.' Shermaine sat small and repentant at her end of the Ranchero.

'Don't worry about it,' said Bruce, not meaning it.

'We have tried to make Father Ignatius come in to town. Martin has spoken to him many times, but he refuses to move.'

Bruce did not answer. He took the car down on to the causeway, driving carefully. There were shreds of mist lifting out of the swamp and drifting across the concrete ramp. Small insects, bright as tracer in the headlights, zoomed in to squash against the windscreen. The froggy chorus from the swamp honked and clinked and boomed deafeningly.

'I have apologized,' she murmured.

'Yes, I heard you,' said Bruce. 'You don't have to do it again.'

She was silent, and then:

'Are you always so bad-tempered?' she asked in English.

'*Always*,' snapped Bruce, 'is one of the words which should be eliminated from the language.'

'Since it has not been, I will continue to use it. You haven't answered my question: are you always so bad-tempered?'

'I just don't like balls-ups.'

'What is *balls-up*, please?'

'What has just happened: a mistake, a situation precipitated by inefficiency, or by somebody not using his head.'

'You never make balls-up, Bruce?'

'It is not a polite expression, Shermaine. Young ladies of refinement do not use it.' Bruce changed into French.

'You never make mistakes?' she corrected herself. Bruce did not answer. That's quite funny, he thought – never make mistakes! Bruce Curry, the original balls-up.

Shermaine held one hand across her middle and sat up straight.

'Bonaparte,' she said. 'Cold, silent, efficient.'

'I didn't say that—' Bruce started to defend himself. Then in the glow from the dash light he saw her impish expression and he could not stop himself; he had to grin.

'All right, I'm acting like a child.'

'You would like a cigarette?' she asked.

'Yes, please.'

She lit it and passed it to him.

'You do not like—' she hesitated, 'mistakes. Is there anything you do like?'

'Many things,' said Bruce.

'Tell me some.'

They bumped off the end of the causeway and Bruce accelerated up the far bank.

'I like being on a mountain when the wind blows, and the taste of the sea. I like Sinatra, crayfish thermidor, the weight and balance of a Purdey Royal, and the sound of a little girl's laughter. I like the first draw of a cigarette lit from a wood fire, the scent of jasmine, the feel of silk; I also enjoy sleeping late in the morning, and the thrill of forking a queen with my knight. Shadows on the floor of a forest please me. And, of course, money. But especially I like women who do not ask too many questions.'

'Is that all?'

'No, but it's a start.'

'And apart from – mistakes, what are the things you do not like.'

'Women who ask too many questions,' and he saw her smile. 'Selfishness except my own, turnip soup, politics, blond pubic hairs, Scotch whisky, classical music and hangovers.'

'I'm sure that is not all.'

'No, not nearly.'

'You are very sensual. All these things are of the senses.'

'Agreed.'

'You do not mention other people. Why?'

'Is this the turn-off to the mission?'

'Yes, go slowly, the road is bad. Why do you not mention your relationship to other people?'

'Why do you ask so many questions? Perhaps I'll tell you some day.'

She was silent a while and then softly:

'And what do you want from life – just those things you have spoken of? Is that all you want?'

'No. Not even them. I want nothing, expect nothing; that way I cannot be disappointed.'

Suddenly she was angry. 'You not only act like a child, you talk like one.'

'Another thing I don't like: criticism.'

'You are young. You have brains, good looks—'

'Thank you, that's better.'

' – and you are a fool.'

'That's not so good. But don't fret about it.'

'I won't, don't worry,' she flamed at him. 'You can—' she searched for something devastating. 'You can go jump out of the lake.'

'Don't you mean into?'

'Into, out of, backwards, sideways. I don't care!'

'Good, I'm glad we've got that settled. There's the mission, I can see a light.'

She did not answer but sat in her corner, breathing heavily, drawing so hard on her cigarette that the glowing tip lit the interior of the Ford.

The church was in darkness, but beyond it and to one side was a long low building. Bruce saw a shadow move across one of the windows.

'Is that the hospital?'

'Yes.' Abruptly.

Bruce stopped the Ford beside the small front verandah and switched off the headlights and the ignition.

'Are you coming in?'

'No.'

'I'd like you to present me to Father Ignatius.'

For a moment she did not move, then she threw open her door and marched up the steps of the verandah without looking back at Bruce.

He followed her through the front office, down the passage, past the clinic and small operating theatre, into the ward.

'Ah, Madame Cartier.' Father Ignatius left the bed over which he was stooping and came towards her.

90

'I heard that the relief train had arrived at Port Reprieve. I thought you would have left by now.'

'Not yet, Father. Tomorrow morning.'

Ignatius was tall, six foot three or four, Bruce estimated, and thin. The sleeve of his brown cassock had been cut short as a concession to the climate and his exposed arms appeared to be all bone, hairless, with the veins blue and prominent. Big bony hands, and big bony feet in brown open sandals.

Like most tall, thin men he was round-shouldered. His face was not one that you would remember, an ordinary face with steel-rimmed spectacles perched on a rather shapeless nose, neither young nor old, nondescript hair without grey in it, but there was about him that unhurried serenity you often find in a man of God. He turned his attention to Bruce, scrutinizing him gently through his spectacles.

'Good evening, my son.'

'Good evening, Father.' Bruce felt uncomfortable; they always made him feel that way. If only, he wished with envy, I could be as certain of one thing in my life as this man is certain of everything in his.

'Father, this is Captain Curry.' Shermaine's tone was cold, and then suddenly she smiled again. 'He does not care for people, that is why he has come to take you to safety.'

Father Ignatius held out his hand and Bruce found the skin was cool and dry, making him conscious of the moistness of his own.

'That is most thoughtful of you,' he said smiling, sensing the tension between them. 'I don't want to seem ungrateful, but I regret I cannot accept your offer.'

'We have received reports that a column of armed bandits are only two hundred kilometres or so north of here. They will arrive within a day or two. You are in great danger, these people are completely merciless,' Bruce urged him.

'Yes,' Father Ignatius nodded. 'I have also heard, and I am taking the steps I consider necessary. I shall take all my staff and patients into the bush.'

'They'll follow you,' said Bruce.

'I think not.' Ignatius shook his head. 'They will not waste their time. They are after loot, not sick people.'

'They'll burn your mission.'

'If they do, then we shall have to rebuild it when they leave.'

'The bush is crawling with Baluba, you'll end up in the cooking pot.' Bruce tried another approach.

'No.' Ignatius shook his head. 'Nearly every member of the tribe has at one time or another been a patient in this hospital. I have nothing to fear there, they are my friends.'

'Look here, Father. Don't let us argue. My orders are to bring you back to Elisabethville. I must insist.'

'And my orders are to stay here. You do agree that mine come from a higher authority than yours?' Ignatius smiled mildly. Bruce opened his mouth to argue further; then, instead, he laughed.

'No, I won't dispute that. Is there anything you need that I might be able to supply?'

'Medicines?' asked Ignatius.

'Acriflavine, morphia, field dressings, not much I'm afraid.'

'They would help, and food?'

'Yes, I will let you have as much as I can spare,' promised Bruce.

One of the patients, a woman at the end of the ward, screamed so suddenly that Bruce started.

'She will be dead before morning,' Ignatius explained softly. 'There is nothing I can do.'

'What's wrong with her?'

'She has been in labour these past two days; there is some complication.'

'Can't you operate?'

'I am not a doctor, my son. We had one here before the trouble began, but he is here no longer – he has gone back to Elisabethville. No,' his voice seemed to carry helpless regret for all the suffering of mankind, 'No, she will die.'

'Haig!' said Bruce.

'Pardon?'

'Father, you have a theatre here. Is it fully equipped?'

'Yes, I believe so.'

'Anaesthetic?'

'We have chloroform and pentothal.'

'Good,' said Bruce. 'I'll get you a doctor. Come on, Shermaine.'

– 11 –

'This heat, this stinking heat!' Wally Hendry mopped at his face with a grubby handkerchief and threw himself down on the green leather bunk. 'You notice how Curry leaves me and you here on the train while he puts Haig up at the hotel and he goes off with that little French bit. It doesn't matter that me and you must cook in this box, long as he and his buddy Haig are all right. You notice that, hey?'

'Somebody's got to stay aboard, Wally,' André said.

'Yeah, but you notice who it is? Always you and me – those high society boys stick together, you've got to give them that, they look after each other.' He transferred his attention back to the open window of the compartment. 'Sun's down already, and still hot enough to boil eggs. I could use a drink.' He unlaced his jungle boots, peeled off his socks and regarded his large white feet with distaste. 'This stinking heat got my athlete's foot going again.'

He separated two of his toes and picked at the loose scaly skin between. 'You got any of that ointment left, André?'

'Yes, I'll get it for you.' André opened the flap of his pack, took out the tube and crossed to Wally's bunk.

'Put it on,' instructed Wally and lay back offering his feet. André took them in his lap as he sat down on the bunk and went to work. Wally lit a cigarette and blew smoke towards the roof, watching it disperse.

'Hell, I could use a drink. A beer with dew on the glass and a head that thick.' He held up four fingers, then he lifted himself on one elbow and studied André as he spread ointment between the long prehensile toes.

'How's it going?'

'Nearly finished, Wally.'

'Is it bad?'

'Not as bad as last time, it hasn't started weeping yet.'

'It itches like you wouldn't believe it,' said Wally.

André did not answer and Wally kicked him in the ribs with the flat of his free foot.

'Did you hear what I said?'

'Yes, you said it itches.'

'Well, answer me when I talk to you. I ain't talking to myself.'

'I'm sorry, Wally.'

Wally grunted and was silent a while, then:

'Do you like me, André?'

'You know I do, Wally.'

'We're friends, aren't we, André?'

'Of course, you know that, Wally.'

An expression of cunning had replaced Wally's boredom.

'You don't mind when I ask you to do things for me, like putting stuff on my feet?'

'I don't mind – it's a pleasure, Wally.'

'It's a pleasure, is it?' There was an edge in Wally's voice now. 'You like doing it?'

André looked up at him apprehensively. 'I don't mind it.' His molten toffee eyes clung to the narrow Mongolian ones in Wally's face.

94

'You like touching me, André?'

André stopped working with the ointment and nervously wiped his fingers on his towel.

'I said, do you like touching me, André? Do you sometimes wish I'd touch you?'

André tried to stand up, but Wally's right arm shot out and his hand fastened on André's neck, forcing him down on to the bunk.

'Answer me, damn you, do you like it?'

'You're hurting me, Wally,' whispered André.

'Shame, now ain't that a shame!'

Wally was grinning. He shifted his grip to the ridge of muscle above André's collar bone and dug his fingers in until they almost met through the flesh.

'Please, Wally, please,' whimpered André, wriggling face down on the bunk.

'You love it, don't you? Come on, answer me.'

'Yes, all right, yes. Please don't hurt me, Wally.'

'Now, tell me truly, doll boy, have you ever had it before? I mean for real.' Wally put his knee in the small of André's back, bearing down with all his weight.

'No!' shrieked André. 'I haven't. Please, Wally, don't hurt me.'

'You're lying to me, André. Don't do it.'

'All right. I was lying.' André tried to twist his head round, but Wally pushed his face into the bunk.

'Tell me all about it – come on, doll boy.'

'It was only once, in Brussels.'

'Who was this beef bandit?'

'My employer. I worked for him. He had an export agency.'

'Did he throw you out, doll boy? Did he throw you out when he was tired of you?'

'No, you don't understand!' André denied with sudden vehemence. 'You don't understand. He looked after me. I had my own apartment, my own car, everything. He wouldn't have abandoned me if it hadn't been for – for what happened. He couldn't help it, he was true to me. I swear to you – he loved me!'

Wally snorted with laughter, he was enjoying himself now.

'Loved you! Jesus wept!' He threw his head back, for the laughter was almost strangling him, and it was ten seconds before he could ask: 'Then what happened between you and your true blue lover? Why didn't you get married and settle down to raise a family, hey?' At the improbability of his own sense of humour Wally convulsed with laughter once more.

'There was an investigation. The police – ooh! you're hurting me, Wally.'

'Keep talking, mamselle!'

'The police – he had no alternative. He was a man of position, he couldn't afford the scandal. There was no other way out – there never is for us. It's hopeless, there is no happiness.'

'Cut the crap, doll boy. Just give me the story.'

'He arranged employment for me in Elisabethville, gave me money, paid for my air fare, everything. He did everything, he looked after me, he still writes to me.'

'That's beautiful, real true love. You make me want to cry.'

Then Wally's laughter changed its tone, harsher now. 'Well, get this, doll boy, and get it good. I don't like queers!' He dug his fingers in again and André squealed.

'I'll tell you a story. When I was in reform school there was a queer there that tried to touch me up. One day I got him in the shower rooms with a razor, just an ordinary Gillette razor. There were twenty guys singing and shouting in the other cubicles. He screamed just like they were all screaming when the cold water hit them. No one took any notice of him. He wanted to be a woman, so I helped him.' Hendry's voice went hoarse and gloating with the memory.

'Jesus!' he whispered. 'Jesus, the blood!' André was sobbing now, his whole body shaking.

'I won't – please, Wally, I can't help it. It was just that one time. Please leave me.'

'How would you like me to help you, André?'

'No,' shrieked André. And Hendry lost interest; he released him, left him lying on the bunk and reached for his socks.

'I'm going to find me a beer.' He laced on his boots and stood up.

'Just you remember,' he said darkly, standing over the boy on the bunk. 'Don't get any ideas with me, Bucko.' He picked up his rifle and went out into the corridor.

Wally found Boussier on the verandah of the hotel talking with a group of his men.

'Where's Captain Curry?' he demanded.

'He has gone out to the mission station.'

'When did he leave?'

'About ten minutes ago.'

'Good,' said Wally. 'Who's got the key to the bar?'

Boussier hesitated.

'The captain has ordered that the bar is to remain locked.'

Wally unslung his rifle.

'Don't give me a hard time, friend.'

'I regret, monsieur, that I must obey the captain's instructions.'

For a minute they stared at each other, and there was no sign of weakening in the older man.

'Have it your way, then,' said Wally and swaggered through the lounge to the bar-room door. He put his foot against the lock and the flimsy mechanism yielded to the pressure. The door flew open and Wally marched across to the counter, laid his rifle on it and reached underneath to the shelves loaded with Simba beer.

The first bottle he emptied without taking it from his

lips. He belched luxuriously and reached for the second, hooked the cap off with the opener and inspected the bubble of froth that appeared at its mouth.

'Hendry!' Wally looked up at Mike Haig in the doorway.

'Hello, Mike.' He grinned.

'What do you think you're doing?' Mike demanded.

'What does it look like?' Wally raised the bottle in salutation and then sipped delicately at the froth.

'Bruce has given strict orders that no one is allowed in here.'

'Oh, for Chrissake, Haig. Stop acting like an old woman.'

'Out you get, Hendry. I'm in charge here.'

'Mike,' Wally grinned at him, 'you want me to die of thirst or something?' He leaned his elbows on the counter. 'Give me a couple more minutes. Let me finish my drink.'

Mike Haig glanced behind him into the lounge and saw the interested group of civilians who were craning to see into the bar-room. He closed the door and walked across to stand opposite Hendry.

'Two minutes, Hendry,' he agreed in an unfriendly tone, 'then out with you.'

'You're not a bad guy, Mike. You and I rubbed each other up wrong. I tell you something, I'm sorry about us.'

'Drink up!' said Mike. Without turning Wally reached backwards and took a bottle of Remy Martin cognac off the shelf. He pulled the cork with his teeth, selected a brandy balloon with his free hand and poured a little of the oily amber fluid into it.

'Keep me company, Mike,' he said and slid the glass across the counter towards Haig. First without expression, and then with his face seeming to crumble, Mike Haig stared at the glass. He moistened his lips, again older and tired-looking. With a physical wrench he pulled his eyes away from the glass.

'Damn you, Hendry.' His voice unnaturally low. 'God

damn you to hell.' He hit out at the glass, spinning it off the counter to shatter against the far wall.

'Did I do something wrong, Mike?' asked Hendry softly. 'Just offered you a drink, that's all.'

The smell of spilt brandy arose, sharp, fruity with the warmth of the grape, and Mike moistened his lips again. The saliva jetting from under his tongue, and the deep yearning aching want in his stomach spreading outwards slowly, numbing him.

'Damn you,' he whispered. 'Oh, damn you, damn you,' pleading now as Hendry filled another glass.

'How long has it been, Mike? A year, two years? Try a little, just a mouthful. Remember the lift it gives you. Come on, boy. You're tired, you've worked hard. Just one – there you are. Just have this one with me.'

Mike wiped his mouth with the back of his hand, sweating now across the forehead and on his upper lip, tiny jewels of sweat squeezed out of the skin by the craving of his body.

'Come on, boy.' Wally's voice hoarse with excitement; teasing, wheedling, tempting.

Mike's hand closed round the tumbler, moving of its own volition, lifting it towards lips that were suddenly slack and trembling, his eyes filled with mingled loathing and desire.

'Just this one,' whispered Hendry. 'Just this one.'

Mike gulped it with a sudden savage flick of his arm, one swallow and the glass was empty. He held it with both hands, his head bowed over it.

'I hate you. My God, I hate you.' He spoke to Hendry, and to himself, and to the empty glass.

'That's my boy!' crowed Wally. 'That's the lad! Come on, let me fill you up.'

99

B ruce went in through the front door of the hotel with Shermaine trying to keep pace with him. There were a dozen or so people in the lobby, and an air of tension amongst them. Boussier was one of them and he came quickly to Bruce.

'I'm sorry, Captain, I could not stop them. That one, that one with the red hair, he was violent. He had his gun and I think he was ready to use it.'

'What are you talking about?' Bruce asked him, but before Boussier could answer there was the bellow of Hendry's laughter from behind the door at the far end of the lobby; the door to the bar-room.

'They are in there,' Boussier told him. 'They have been there for the past hour.'

'Goddam it to hell,' swore Bruce. 'Now of all times. Oh, goddam that bloody animal.'

He almost ran across the room and threw open the double doors. Hendry was standing against the far wall with a tumbler in one hand and his rifle in the other. He was holding the rifle by the pistol grip and waving vague circles in the air with it.

Mike Haig was building a pyramid of glasses on the bar counter. He was just placing the final glass on the pile.

'Hello, Bruce, old cock, old man, old fruit,' he greeted Bruce, and waved in an exaggerated manner. 'Just in time, you can have a couple of shots as well. But Wally's first, he gets first shot. Must abide by the rules, no cheating, strictly democratic affair, everyone has equal rights. Rank doesn't count. That's right, isn't it Wally?' Haig's features had blurred; it was as though he were melting, losing his shape. His lips were loose and flabby, his jowls hung pendulously as an old woman's breasts, and his eyes were moist.

He picked up a glass from beside the pyramid, but this

glass was nearly full and a bottle of Remy Martin cognac stood beside it.

'A very fine old brandy, absolutely exquisite.' The last two words didn't come out right, so he repeated them carefully. Then he grinned loosely at Bruce and his eyes weren't quite in focus.

'Get out of the way, Mike,' said Hendry, and raised the rifle one-handed, aiming at the pile of glasses.

'Every time she bucks, she bounces,' hooted Haig, 'and every time she bounces you win a coconut. Let her rip, old fruit.'

'Hendry, stop that,' snapped Bruce.

'Go and get mucked,' answered Hendry and fired. The rifle kicked back over his shoulder and he fell against the wall. The pyramid of glasses exploded in a shower of fragments and the room was filled with the roar of the rifle.

'Give the gentleman a coconut!' crowed Mike.

Bruce crossed the room with three quick strides and pulled the rifle out of Hendry's hand.

'All right, you drunken ape. That's enough.'

'Go and muck yourself,' growled Hendry. He was massaging his wrist; the rifle had twisted it.

'Captain Curry,' said Haig from behind the bar, 'you heard what my friend said. You go and muck yourself sideways to sleep.'

'Shut up, Haig.'

'This time I'll fix you, Curry,' Hendry growled. 'You've been on my back too long – now I'm going to shake you off!'

'Kindly descend from my friend's back, Captain Curry,' chimed in Mike Haig. 'He's not a howdah elephant, he's my blood brother. I will not allow you to persecute him.'

'Come on, Curry. Come on then!' said Wally.

'That's it, Wally. Muck him up.' Haig filled his glass again as he spoke. 'Don't let him ride you.'

'Come on then, Curry.'

'You're drunk,' said Bruce.

'Come on then; don't talk, man. Or do I have to start it?'

'No, you don't have to start it,' Bruce assured him, and lifted the rifle butt-first under his chin, swinging it up hard. Hendry's head jerked and he staggered back against the wall. Bruce looked at his eyes; they were glazed over. That will hold him, he decided; that's taken the fight out of him. He caught Hendry by the shoulder and threw him into one of the chairs. I must get to Haig before he absorbs any more of that liquor, he thought, I can't waste time sending for Ruffy and I can't leave this thing behind me while I work on Haig.

'Shermaine,' he called. She was standing in the doorway and she came to his side. 'Can you use a pistol?'

She nodded. Bruce unclipped his Smith & Wesson from its lanyard and handed it to her.

'Shoot this man if he tries to leave that chair. Stand here where he cannot reach you.'

'Bruce—' she started.

'He is a dangerous animal. Yesterday he murdered two small children and, if you let him, he'll do the same to you. You must keep him here while I get the other one.'

She lifted the pistol, holding it with both hands and her face was even paler than was usual.

'Can you do it?' Bruce asked.

'Now I can,' she said and cocked the action.

'Hear me, Hendry.' Bruce took a handful of his hair and twisted his face up. 'She'll kill you if you leave this chair. Do you understand? She'll shoot you.'

'Muck you and your little French whore, muck you both. I bet that's what you two have been doing all evening in that car – playing "hide the sausage" down by the riverside.'

Anger flashed through Bruce so violently that it startled him. He twisted Hendry's hair until he could feel it coming away in his hand. Hendry squirmed with pain.

'Shut that foul mouth – or I'll kill you.'

He meant it, and suddenly Hendry knew he meant it.

'Okay, for Chrissake, okay. Just leave me.'

Bruce loosened his grip and straightened up.

'I'm sorry, Shermaine,' he said.

'That's all right – go to the other one.'

Bruce went to the bar counter, and Haig watched him come.

'What do you want, Bruce? Have a drink.' He was nervous. 'Have a drink, we are all having a little drink. All good clean fun, Bruce. Don't get excited.'

'You're not having any more; in fact, just the opposite,' Bruce told him as he came round the counter. Haig backed away in front of him.

'What are you going to do?'

'I'll show you,' said Bruce and caught him by the wrist, turning him quickly and lifting his arm up between his shoulder-blades.

'Hey, Bruce. Cut it out, you've made me spill my drink.'

'Good,' said Bruce and slapped the empty glass out of his hand. Haig started to struggle. He was still a powerful man but the liquor had weakened him and Bruce lifted his wrist higher, forcing him on to his toes.

'Come along, buddy boy,' instructed Bruce and marched him towards the back door of the bar-room. He reached round Haig with his free hand, turned the key in the lock and opened the door.

'Through here,' he said and pushed Mike into the kitchens. He kicked the door shut behind him and went to the sink, dragging Haig with him.

'All right, Haig, let's have it up,' he said and changed his grip quickly, thrusting Haig's head down over the sink. There was a dishtowel hanging beside it which Bruce screwed into a ball; then he used his thumbs to open Haig's jaws and wedged the towel between his back teeth.

'Let's have all of it.' He probed his finger down into Haig's throat. It came up hot and gushing over his hand,

and he fought down his own nausea as he worked. When he had finished he turned on the cold tap and held Haig's head under it, washing his face and his own hand.

'Now, I've got a little job for you, Haig.'

'Leave me alone, damn you,' groaned Haig, his voice indistinct beneath the rushing tap. Bruce pulled him up and held him against the wall.

'There's a woman in childbirth at the mission. She's going to die, Haig. She's going to die if you don't do something about it.'

'No,' whispered Haig. 'No, not that. Not that again.'

'I'm taking you there.'

'No, please not that. I can't – don't you see that I can't.' The little red and purple veins in his nose and cheeks stood out in vivid contrast to his pallor. Bruce hit him open-handed across the face and the water flew in drops from his hair at the shock.

'No,' he mumbled, 'please Bruce, please.'

Bruce hit him twice more, hard. Watching him carefully, and at last he saw the first flickering of anger.

'Damn you, Bruce Curry, damn you to hell.'

'You'll do,' rejoiced Bruce. 'Thank God for that.'

He hustled Haig back through the bar-room. Shermaine still stood over Hendry, holding the pistol.

'Come on, Shermaine. You can leave that thing now. I'll attend to him when we get back.'

As they crossed the lobby Bruce asked Shermaine. 'Can you drive the Ford?'

'Yes.'

'Good,' said Bruce. 'Here are the keys. I'll sit with Haig in the back. Take us out to the mission.'

Haig lost his balance on the front steps of the hotel and nearly fell, but Bruce caught him and half carried him to the car. He pushed him into the back seat and climbed in beside him. Shermaine slid in behind the wheel, started the engine and U-turned neatly across the street.

'You can't force me to do this, Bruce. I can't, I just can't,' Haig pleaded.

'We'll see,' said Bruce.

'You don't know what it's like. You can't know. She'll die on the table.' He held out his hands palms down. 'Look at that, look at them. How can I do it with these?' His hands were trembling violently.

'She's going to die anyway,' said Bruce, his voice hard. 'So you might as well do it for her quickly and get it over with.'

Haig brought his hands up to his mouth and wiped his lips.

'Can I have a drink, Bruce? That'll help. I'll try then, if you give me a drink.'

'No,' said Bruce, and Haig began to swear. The filth poured from his lips and his face twisted with the effort. He cursed Bruce, he cursed himself, and God in a torrent of the most obscene language that Bruce had ever heard. Then suddenly he snatched at the door handle and tried to twist it open. Bruce had been waiting for this and he caught the back of Haig's collar, pulled him backwards across the seat and held him there. Haig's struggles ceased abruptly and he began to sob softly.

Shermaine drove fast; across the causeway, up the slope and into the side road. The headlights cut into the darkness and the wind drummed softly round the car. Haig was still sobbing on the back seat.

Then the lights of the mission were ahead of them through the trees and Shermaine slowed the car, turned in past the church and pulled up next to the hospital block.

Bruce helped Haig out of the car, and while he was doing so the side door of the building opened and Father Ignatius came out with a petromax lantern in his hand. The harsh white glare of the lantern lit them all and threw grotesque shadows behind them. It fell with special cruelty on Haig's face.

'Here's your doctor, Father,' Bruce announced.

Ignatius lifted the lantern and peered through his spectacles at Haig.

'Is he sick?'

'No, Father,' said Bruce. 'He's drunk.'

'Drunk? Then he can't operate?'

'Yes, he damn well can!'

Bruce took Haig through the door and along the passage to the little theatre. Ignatius and Shermaine followed them.

'Shermaine, go with Father and help him bring the woman,' Bruce ordered, and they went; then he turned his attention back to Haig.

'Are you so far down there in the slime that you can't understand me?'

'I can't do it, Bruce. It's no good.'

'Then she'll die. But this much is certain: you are going to make the attempt.'

'I've got to have a drink, Bruce.' Haig licked his lips. 'It's burning me up inside, you've got to give me one.'

'Finish the job and I'll give you a whole case.'

'I've got to have one now.'

'No.' Bruce spoke with finality. 'Have a look at what they've got here in the way of instruments. Can you do it with these?' Bruce crossed to the sterilizer and lifted the lid, the steam came up out of it in a cloud. Haig looked in also.

'That's all I need, but there's not enough light in here, and I need a drink.'

'I'll get you more light. Start cleaning up.'

'Bruce, please let me—'

'Shut up,' snarled Bruce. 'There's the basin. Start getting ready.'

Haig crossed to the handbasin; he was more steady on his feet and his features had firmed a little. You poor old bastard, thought Bruce, I hope you can do it. My God, how much I hope you can.

'Get a move on, Haig, we haven't got all night.'

Bruce left the room and went quickly down the passage to the ward. The windows of the theatre were fixed and Haig could escape only into the passage. Bruce knew that he could catch him if he tried to run for it.

He looked into the ward. Shermaine and Ignatius, with the help of an African orderly, had lifted the woman on to the theatre trolley.

'Father, we need more light.'

'I can get you another lantern, that's all.'

'Good, do that then. I'll take the woman through.'

Father Ignatius disappeared with the orderly and Bruce helped Shermaine manoeuvre the trolley down the length of the ward and into the passage. The woman was whimpering with pain, and her face was grey, waxy grey. They only go like that when they are very frightened, or when they are dying.

'She hasn't much longer,' he said.

'I know,' agreed Shermaine. 'We must hurry.'

The woman moved restlessly on the trolley and gabbled a few words; then she sighed so that the great blanket-covered mound of her belly rose and fell, and she started to whimper again.

Haig was still in the theatre. He had stripped off his battle-jacket and, in his vest, he stooped over the basin washing. He did not look round as they wheeled the woman in.

'Get her on the table,' he said, working the soap into suds up to his elbows.

The trolley was of a height with the table and, using the blanket to lift her, it was easy to slide the woman across.

'She's ready, Haig,' said Bruce. Haig dried his arms on a clean towel and turned. He came to the woman and stood over her. She did not know he was there; her eyes were open but unseeing. Haig drew a breath; he was sweating a little across his forehead and the stubble of beard on the lower part of his face was stippled with grey.

He pulled back the blanket. The woman wore a short white jacket, open-fronted, that did not cover her stomach. Her stomach was swollen out, hard-looking, with the navel inverted. Knees raised slightly and the thick peasant's thighs spread wide in the act of labour. As Bruce watched, her whole body arched in another contraction. He saw the stress of the muscles beneath the dark greyish skin as they struggled to expel the trapped foetus.

'Hurry, Mike!' Bruce was appalled by the anguish of birth. I didn't know it was like this; in sorrow thou shalt bring forth children – but this! Through the woman's dry grey swollen lips burst another of those moaning little cries, and Bruce swung towards Mike Haig.

'Hurry, goddam you!'

And Mike Haig began his examination, his hands very pale as they groped over the dark skin. At last he was satisfied and he stood back from the table.

Ignatius and the orderly came in with two more lanterns. Ignatius started to say something, but instantly he sensed the tension in the room and he fell silent. They all watched Mike Haig's face.

His eyes were tight closed, and his face was hard angles and harsh planes in the lantern light. His breathing was shallow and laboured.

I must not push him now, Bruce knew instinctively, I have dragged him to the lip of the precipice and now I must let him go over the edge on his own.

Mike opened his eyes again, and he spoke.

'Caesarian section,' he said, as though he had pronounced his own death sentence. Then his breathing stopped. They waited, and at last the breath came out of him in a sigh.

'I'll do it,' he said.

'Gowns and gloves?' Bruce fired the question at Ignatius.

'In the cupboard.'

'Get them!'

'You'll have to help me, Bruce. And you also Shermaine.'

'Yes, show me.'

Quickly they scrubbed and dressed. Ignatius held the pale green theatre gowns while they dived into them and flapped and struggled through.

'That tray, bring it here,' Mike ordered as he opened the sterilizer. With a pair of long-nosed forceps he lifted the instruments out of the steaming box and laid them on the tray naming each one as he did so.

'Scalpel, retractors, clamps.'

In the meantime the orderly was swabbing the woman's belly with alcohol and arranging the sheets.

Mike filled the syringe with pentothal and held it up to the light. He was an unfamiliar figure now; his face masked, the green skull cap covering his hair, and the flowing gown falling to his ankles. He pressed the plunger and a few drops of the pale fluid dribbled down the needle.

He looked at Bruce, only his haunted eyes showing above the mask.

'Ready?'

'Yes,' Bruce nodded. Mike stooped over the woman, took her arm and sent the needle searching under the soft black skin on the inside of her elbow. The fluid in the syringe was suddenly discoloured with drawn blood as Mike tested for the vein, and then the plunger slid slowly down the glass barrel.

The woman stopped whimpering, the tension went out of her body and her breathing slowed and became deep and unhurried.

'Come here.' Mike ordered Shermaine to the head of the table, and she took up the chloroform mask and soaked the gauze that filled the cone.

'Wait until I tell you.'

She nodded. Christ, what lovely eyes she has, thought Bruce, before he turned back to the job in hand.

'Scalpel,' said Mike from across the table, pointing to it on the tray, and Bruce handed it to him.

109

Afterwards the details were confused and lacking reality in Bruce's mind.

The wound opening behind the knife, the tight stretched skin parting and the tiny blood vessels starting to squirt.

Pink muscle laced with white; butter-yellow layers of subcutaneous fat, and then through to the massed bluish coils of the gut. Human tissue, soft and pulsing, glistening in the flat glare of the petromax.

Clamps and retractors, like silver insects crowding into the wound as though it were a flower.

Mike's hands, inhuman in yellow rubber, moving in the open pit of the belly. Swabbing, cutting, clamping, tying off.

Then the swollen purple bag of the womb, suddenly unzipped by the knife.

And at last, unbelievably, the child curled in a dark grey ball of legs and tiny arms, head too big for its size, and the fat pink snake of the placenta enfolding it.

Lifted out, the infant hung by its heels from Mike's hand like a small grey bat, still joined to its mother.

Scissors snipped and it was free. Mike worked a little longer, and the infant cried.

It cried with minute fury, indignant and alive. From the head of the table Shermaine laughed with spontaneous delight, and clapped her hands like a child at a Punch and Judy show. Suddenly Bruce was laughing also. It was a laugh from long ago, coming out from deep inside him.

'Take it,' said Haig and Shermaine cradled it, wet and feebly wriggling in her arms. She stood with it while Haig sewed up. Watching her face and the way she stood, Bruce suddenly and unaccountably felt the laughter snag his throat, and he wanted to cry.

Haig closed the womb, stitching the complicated pattern of knots like a skilled seamstress, then the external sutures laid neatly across the fat lips of the wound, and at last the white tape hiding it all. He covered the woman, jerked the mask from his face and looked up at Shermaine.

'You can help me clean it up,' he said, and his voice was strong again and proud. The two of them crossed to the basin.

Bruce threw off his gown and left the room, went down the passage and out into the night. He leaned against the bonnet of the Ford and lit a cigarette.

Tonight I laughed again, he told himself with wonder, and then I nearly cried. And all because of a woman and a child. It is finished now, the pretence. The withdrawal. The big act. There was more than one birth in there tonight. I laughed again, I had the need to laugh again, and the desire to cry. A woman and a child, the whole meaning of life. The abscess had burst, the poison drained, and he was ready to heal.

'Bruce, Bruce, where are you?' She came out through the door; he did not answer her for she had seen the glow of his cigarette and she came to him. Standing close in the darkness.

'Shermaine—' Bruce said, then he stopped himself. He wanted to hold her, just hold her tightly.

'Yes, Bruce.' Her face was a pale round in the darkness, very close to him.

'Shermaine, I want—' said Bruce and stopped again.

'Yes, me too,' she whispered and then, drawing away, 'come, let's go and see what your doctor is doing now.' She took his hand and led him back into the building. Her hand was cool and dry with long tapered fingers in his.

Mike Haig and Father Ignatius were leaning over the cradle that now stood next to the table on which lay the blanket-covered body of the Baluba woman. The woman was breathing softly, and the expression on her face was of deep peace.

'Bruce, come and have a look. It's a beauty,' called Haig.

Still holding hands Bruce and Shermaine crossed to the cradle.

'He'll go all of eight pounds,' announced Haig proudly. Bruce looked at the infant; newborn black babies are more handsome than ours – they have not got that half-boiled look.

'Pity he's not a trout,' murmured Bruce. 'That would be a national record.' Haig stared blankly at him for a second, then he threw back his head and laughed; it was a good sound. There was a different quality in Haig now, a new confidence in the way he held his head, a feeling of completeness about him.

'How about that drink I promised you, Mike?' Bruce tested him.

'You have it for me, Bruce, I'll duck this one.' He isn't just saying it either, thought Bruce, as he looked at his face; he really doesn't need it now.

'I'll make it a double as soon as we get back to town.' Bruce glanced at his watch. 'It's past ten, we'd better get going.'

'I'll have to stay until she comes out from the anaesthetic,' demurred Haig. 'You can come back for me in the morning.'

Bruce hesitated. 'All right then. Come on, Shermaine.'

They drove back to Port Reprieve, sitting close together in the intimate darkness of the car. They did not speak until after they had reached the causeway, then Shermaine said:

'He is a good man, your doctor. He is like Paul.'

'Who is Paul?'

'Paul was my husband.'

'Oh.' Bruce was embarrassed. The mention of that name snapped the silken thread of his mood. Shermaine went on, speaking softly and staring down the path of the headlights.

'Paul was of the same age. Old enough to have learned understanding – young men are so cruel.'

'You loved him.' Bruce spoke flatly, trying to keep any trace of jealousy from his voice.

'Love has many shapes,' she answered. Then, 'Yes, I had begun to love him. Very soon I would have loved him enough to—' She stopped.

'To what?' Bruce's voice had gone rough as a wood rasp. *Now it starts*, he thought, *once again I am vulnerable*.

'We were only married four months before he – before the fever.'

'So?' Still harsh, his eyes on the road ahead.

'I want you to know something. I must explain it all to you. It is very important. Will you be patient with me while I tell you?' There was a pleading in her voice that he could not resist and his expression softened.

'Shermaine, you don't have to tell me.'

'I must. I want you to know.' She hesitated a moment, and when she spoke again her voice had steadied. 'I am an orphan, Bruce. Both my Mama and Papa were killed by the Germans, in the bombing. I was only a few months old when it happened, and I do not remember them. I do not remember anything, not one little thing about them; there is not even a photograph.' For a second her voice had gone shaky but again it firmed. 'The nuns took me, and they were my family. But somehow that is different, not really your own. I have never had anything that has truly belonged to me, something of my very own.'

Bruce reached out and took her hand; it lay very still in his grasp. You have now, he thought, you have me for your very own.

'Then when the time came the nuns made the arrangements with Paul Cartier. He was an engineer with Union Minière du Haut here in the Congo, a man of position, a suitable man for one of their girls.

113

'He flew to Brussels and we were married. I was not unhappy, for although he was old – as old as Doctor Mike – yet he was very gentle and kind, of great understanding. He did not—' She stopped and turned suddenly to Bruce, gripping his hand with both of hers, leaning towards him with her face serious and pale in the half-darkness, the plume of dark hair falling forward over her shoulder and her voice full of appeal. 'Bruce, do you understand what I am trying to tell you?'

Bruce stopped the car in front of the hotel, deliberately he switched off the ignition and deliberately he spoke.

'Yes, I think so.'

'Thank you,' and she flung the door open and went out of it and up the steps of the hotel with her long jeaned legs flying and her hair bouncing on her back.

Bruce watched her go through the double doors. Then he pressed the lighter on the dashboard and fished a cigarette from his pack. He lit it, exhaled a jet of smoke against the windscreen, and suddenly he was happy. He wanted to laugh again.

He threw the cigarette away only a quarter finished and climbed out of the Ford. He looked at his wristwatch; it was after midnight. My God, I'm tired. Too much has happened today; rebirth is a severe emotional strain. And he laughed out loud, savouring the sensation, letting it come slowly shaking up his throat from his chest.

Boussier was waiting for him in the lounge. He wore a towelling dressing-gown, and the creases of sleep were on his face.

'Are all your preparations complete, monsieur?'

'Yes,' the old man answered. 'The women and the two children are asleep upstairs. Madame Cartier has just gone up.'

'I know,' said Bruce, and Boussier went on, 'As you see, I have all the men here.' He gestured at the sleeping bodies that covered the floor of the lounge and bar-room.

114

'Good,' said Bruce. 'We'll leave as soon as it's light tomorrow.' He yawned, then rubbed his eyes, massaging them with his finger tips.

'Where is my officer, the one with the red hair?'

'He has gone back to the train, very drunk. We had more trouble with him after you had left.' Boussier hesitated delicately. 'He wanted to go upstairs, to the women.'

'Damn him.' Bruce felt his anger coming again. 'What happened?'

'Your sergeant major, the big one, dissuaded him and took him away.'

'Thank God for Ruffy.'

'I have reserved a place for you to sleep.' Boussier pointed to a comfortable leather armchair. 'You must be exhausted.'

'That is kind of you,' Bruce thanked him. 'But first I must inspect our defences.'

– 13 –

Bruce woke with Shermaine leaning over the chair and tickling his nose. He was fully dressed with his helmet and rifle on the floor beside him and only his boots unlaced.

'You do not snore, Bruce,' she congratulated him, laughing her small husky laugh. 'That is a good thing.'

He struggled up, dopey with sleep.

'What time is it?'

'Nearly five o'clock. I have breakfast for you in the kitchen.'

'Where is Boussier?'

'He is dressing; then he will start moving them down to the train.'

'My mouth tastes as though a goat slept in it.' Bruce moved his tongue across his teeth, feeling the fur on them.

'Then I shall not kiss you good morning, mon capitaine.'

She straightened up with the laughter still in her eyes. 'But your toilet requisites are in the kitchen. I sent one of your gendarmes to fetch them from the train. You can wash in the sink.'

Bruce laced up his boots and followed her through into the kitchen, stepping over sleeping bodies on the way.

'There is no hot water,' Shermaine apologized.

'That is the least of my worries.' Bruce crossed to the table and opened his small personal pack, taking out his razor and soap and comb.

'I raided the chicken coop for you,' Shermaine confessed. 'There were only two eggs. How shall I cook them?'

'Soft boiled, one minute.' Bruce stripped off his jacket and shirt, went to the sink and filled it. He sluiced his face and lifted handfuls of water over his head, snorting with pleasure.

Then he propped his shaving mirror above the taps and spread soap on his face. Shermaine came to sit on the draining board beside him and watched with frank interest.

'I will be sorry to see the beard go,' she said. 'It looked like the pelt of an otter, I liked it.'

'Perhaps I will grow it for you one day.' Bruce smiled at her. 'Your eyes are blue, Shermaine.'

'It has taken you a long time to find that out,' she said and pouted dramatically. Her skin was silky and cool-looking, lips pale pink without make-up. Her dark hair, drawn back, emphasized the high cheek bones and the size of her eyes.

'In India "sher" means "tiger",' Bruce told her, watching her from the corner of his eye. Immediately she abandoned the pout and drew her lips up into a snarl. Her teeth were small and very white and only slightly uneven. Her eyes rolled wide and then crossed at an alarming angle. She growled. Taken by surprise, Bruce laughed and nearly cut himself.

'I cannot abide a woman who clowns before breakfast. It ruins my digestion,' he laughed at her.

'Breakfast!' said Shermaine and uncrossed her eyes, jumped off the draining board and ran to the stove.

'Only just in time.' She checked her watch. 'One minute and twenty seconds, will you forgive me?'

'This once only, never again.' Bruce washed the soap off his face, dried and combed his hair and came to the table. She had a chair ready for him.

'How much sugar in your coffee?'

'Three, please.' Bruce chopped the top off his egg, and she brought the mug and placed it in front of him.

'I like making breakfast for you.' Bruce didn't answer her. This was dangerous talk. She sat down opposite him, leaned forward on her elbows with her chin in her hands.

'You eat too fast,' she announced and Bruce raised an eyebrow. 'But at least you keep your mouth closed.'

Bruce started on his second egg.

'How old are you?'

'Thirty,' said Bruce.

'I'm twenty – nearly twenty-one.'

'A ripe old age.'

'What do you do?'

'I'm a soldier,' he answered.

'No, you're not.'

'All right, I'm a lawyer.'

'You must be clever,' she said solemnly.

'A genius, that's why I'm here.'

'Are you married?'

'No – I was. What is this, a formal interrogation?'

'Is she dead?'

'No.' He prevented the hurt from showing in his face, it was easier to do now.

'Oh!' said Shermaine. She picked up the teaspoon and concentrated on stirring his coffee.

117

'Is she pretty?'

'No – yes, I suppose so.'

'Where is she?' Then quickly, 'I'm sorry it's none of my business.'

Bruce took the coffee from her and drank it. Then he looked at his watch.

'It's nearly five fifteen. I must go out and get Mike Haig.'

Shermaine stood up quickly.

'I'm ready.'

'I know the way – you had better get down to the station.'

'I want to come with you.'

'Why?'

'Just because, that's why.' Searching for a reason. 'I want to see the baby again.'

'You win.' Bruce picked up his pack and they went through into the lounge. Boussier was there, dressed and efficient. His men were nearly ready to move.

'Madame Cartier and I are going out to the mission to fetch the doctor. We will be back in half an hour or so. I want all your people aboard by then.'

'Very well, Captain.'

Bruce called to Ruffy who was standing on the verandah. 'Did you load those supplies for the mission?'

'They're in the back of the Ford, boss.'

'Good. Bring all your sentries in and take them down to the station. Tell the engine driver to get steam up and keep his hand on the throttle. We'll shove off as soon as I get back with Lieutenant Haig.'

'Okay, boss.'

Bruce handed him his pack. 'Take this down for me, Ruffy.' Then his eyes fell on the large heap of cardboard cartons at Ruffy's feet. 'What's that?'

Ruffy looked a little embarrassed. 'Coupla bottles of beer, boss. Thought we might get thirsty going home.'

'Good for you!' grinned Bruce. 'Put them in a safe place and don't drink them all before I get back.'

'I'll save you one or two,' promised Ruffy.

'Come along, tiger girl,' and Bruce led Shermaine out to the Ford. She sat closer to him than the previous day, but with her legs curled up under her, as before. As they crossed the causeway she lit two cigarettes and passed one to him.

'I'll be glad to leave this place,' she said, looking out across the swamp with the mist lifting sluggishly off it in the dawn, hanging in grey shreds from the fluffy tops of the papyrus grass.

'I've hated it here since Paul died. I hate the swamp and the mosquitoes and the jungle all around. I'm glad we're going.'

'Where will you go?' Bruce asked.

'I haven't thought about it. Back to Belgium, I suppose. Anywhere away from the Congo. Away from this heat to a country where you can breathe. Away from the disease and the fear. Somewhere so that I know tomorrow I will not have to run. Where human life has meaning, away from the killing and the burning and the rape.' She drew on her cigarette almost fiercely, staring ahead at the green wall of the forest.

'I was born in Africa,' said Bruce. 'In the time when the judge's gavel was not the butt of an FN rifle, before you registered your vote with a burst of gunfire.' He spoke softly with regret. 'In the time before the hatred. But now I don't know. I haven't thought much about the future either.'

He was silent for a while. They reached the turn-off to the mission and he swung the Ford into it.

'It has all changed so quickly; I hadn't realized how quickly until I came here to the Congo.'

'Are you going to stay here, Bruce? I mean, stay here in the Congo?'

'No,' he said, 'I've had enough. I don't even know what I'm fighting for.'

He threw the butt of his cigarette out of the window.

Ahead of them were the mission buildings.

Bruce parked the car outside the hospital buildings and they sat together quietly.

'There must be some other land,' he whispered, 'and if there is I'll find it.'

He opened the door and stepped out. Shermaine slid across the seat under the wheel and joined him. They walked side by side to the hospital; her hand brushed his and he caught it, held it and felt the pressure of his fingers returned by hers. She was taller than his shoulder, but not much.

Mike Haig and Father Ignatius were together in the women's ward, too engrossed to hear the Ford arrive.

'Good morning, Michael,' called Bruce. 'What's the fancy dress for?'

Mike Haig looked up and grinned. 'Morning, Bruce. Hello, Shermaine.' Then he looked down at the faded brown cassock he wore.

'Borrowed it from Ignatius. A bit long in the leg and tight round the waist, but less out of place in a sick ward than the accoutrements of war.'

'It suits you, Doctor Mike,' said Shermaine.

'Nice to hear someone call me that again.' The smile spread all over Haig's face. 'I suppose you want to see your baby, Shermaine?'

'Is he well?'

'Mother and child both doing fine,' he assured her and led Shermaine down between the row of beds, each with a black woolly head on the pillow and big curious eyes following their progress.

'May I pick him up?'

'He's asleep, Shermaine.'

'Oh, please!'

'I doubt it will kill him. Very well, then.'

'Bruce, come and look. Isn't he a darling?' She held the tiny black body to her chest and the child snuffled, its mouth automatically starting to search. Bruce leaned forward to peer at it.

'Very nice,' he said and turned to Ignatius. 'I have those supplies I promised you. Will you send an orderly to get them out of the car?' Then to Mike Haig, 'You'd better get changed, Mike. We're all ready to leave.'

Not looking at Bruce, fiddling with the stethoscope round his neck, Mike shook his head. 'I don't think I'll be going with you, Bruce.'

Surprised, Bruce faced him.

'What?'

'I think I'll stay on here with Ignatius. He has offered me a job.'

'You must be mad, Mike.'

'Perhaps,' agreed Haig and took the infant from Shermaine, placed it back in the cradle beside its mother and tucked the sheet in round its tiny body, 'and then again, perhaps not.' He straightened up and waved a hand down the rows of occupied beds. 'There's plenty to do here, that you must admit.'

Bruce stared helplessly at him and then appealed to Shermaine.

'Talk him out of it. Perhaps you can make him see the futility of it.'

Shermaine shook her head. 'No, Bruce, I will not.'

'Mike, listen to reason, for God's sake. You can't stay here in this disease-ridden backwater, you can't—'

'I'll walk out to the car with you, Bruce. I know you're in a hurry—'

He led them out through the side door and stood by the driver's window of the Ford while they climbed in. Bruce extended his hand and Mike took it, gripping hard.

'Cheerio, Bruce. Thanks for everything.'

'Cheerio, Mike. I suppose you'll be taking orders and having yourself made into a fully licensed dispenser of salvation?'

'I don't know about that, Bruce. I doubt it. I just want another chance to do the only work I know. I just want a last-minute rally to reduce the formidable score that's been chalked up against me so far.'

'I'll report you "missing, believed killed" – throw your uniform in the river,' said Bruce.

'I'll do that.' Mike stepped back. 'Look after each other, you two.'

'I don't know what you mean,' Shermaine informed him primly, trying not to smile.

'I'm an old dog, not easy to fool,' said Mike. 'Go to it with a will.'

Bruce let out the clutch and the Ford slid forward.

'God speed, my children.' That smile spread all over Mike's face as he waved.

'Au revoir, Doctor Michael.'

'So long, Mike.'

Bruce watched him in the rear-view mirror, tall in his ill-fitting cassock, something proud and worthwhile in his stance. He waved once more and then turned and hurried back into the hospital.

Neither of them spoke until they had almost reached the main road. Shermaine nestled softly against Bruce, smiling to herself, looking ahead down the tree-lined passage of the road.

'He's a good man, Bruce.'

'Light me a cigarette, please, Shermaine.' He didn't want to talk about it. It was one of those things that can only be made grubby by words.

Slowing for the intersection, Bruce dropped her into second gear, automatically glancing to his left to make sure the main road was clear before turning into it.

'Oh my God!' he gasped.

'What is it, Bruce?' Shermaine looked up with alarm from the cigarette she was lighting.

'Look!'

A hundred yards up the road, parked close to the edge of the forest, was a convoy of six large vehicles. The first five were heavy canvas-canopied lorries painted dull military olive, the sixth was a gasoline tanker in bright yellow and red with the Shell Company insignia on the barrel-shaped body. Hitched behind the leading lorry was a squat, rubber-tyred 25-pounder anti-tank gun with its long barrel pointed jauntily skywards. Round the vehicles, dressed in an assortment of uniforms and different styled helmets, were at least sixty men. They were all armed, some with automatic weapons and others with obsolete bolt-action rifles. Most of them were urinating carelessly into the grass that lined the road, while the others were standing in small groups smoking and talking.

'General Moses!' said Shermaine, her voice small with the shock.

'Get down,' ordered Bruce and with his free hand thrust her on to the floor. He rammed the accelerator flat and the Ford roared out into the main road, swerving violently, the back end floating free in the loose dust as he held the wheel over. Correcting the skid, meeting it and straightening out, Bruce glanced at the rear-view mirror. Behind them the men had dissolved into a confused pattern of movement; he heard their shouts high and thin above the racing engine of the Ford. Bruce looked ahead; it was another hundred yards to the bend in the road that would hide them and take them down to the causeway across the swamp.

Shermaine was on her knees pulling herself up to look over the back of the seat.

'Keep on the floor, damn you!' shouted Bruce and pushed her head down roughly.

As he spoke the roadside next to them erupted in a rapid series of leaping dust fountains and he heard the high hysterical beat of machine-gun fire.

The bend in the road rushed towards them, just a few more seconds. Then with a succession of jarring crashes that shook the whole body of the car a burst of fire hit them from behind. The windscreen starred into a sheet of opaque diamond lacework, the dashboard clock exploded powdering Shermaine's hair with particles of glass, two bullets tore through the seat ripping out the stuffing like the entrails of a wounded animal.

'Close your eyes,' shouted Bruce and punched his fist through the windscreen. Slitting his own eyes against the chips of flying glass, he could just see through the hole his fist had made. The corner was right on top of them and he dragged the steering-wheel over, skidding into it, his off-side wheels bumping into the verge, grass and leaves brushing the side of the car.

Then they were through the corner and racing down towards the causeway.

'Are you all right, Shermaine?'

'Yes, are you?' She emerged from under the dashboard, a smear of blood across one cheek where the glass had scratched her, and her eyes bigger than ever with fright.

'I only pray that Boussier and Hendry are ready to pull out. Those bastards won't be five minutes behind us.'

They went across the causeway with the needle of the speedometer touching eighty, up the far side and into the main street of Port Reprieve. Bruce thrust his hand down on the hooter ring, blowing urgent warning blasts.

'Please God, let them be ready,' he muttered. With relief he saw that the street was empty and the hotel seemed deserted. He kept blowing the horn as they roared down towards the station, a great billowing cloud of dust rising behind them. Braking the Ford hard, he turned it in past the station buildings and on to the platform.

Most of Boussier's people were standing next to the train. Boussier himself was beside the last truck with his wife and the small group of women around him. Bruce shouted at them through the open window.

'Get those women into the train, the *shufta* are right behind us, we're leaving immediately.'

Without question or argument old Boussier gathered them together and hurried them up the steel ladder into the truck. Bruce drove down the station platform shouting as he went.

'Get in! For Chrissake, hurry up! They're coming!'

He braked to a standstill next to the cab of the locomotive and shouted up at the bald head of the driver.

'Get going. Don't waste a second. Give her everything she's got. There's a bunch of *shufta* not five minutes behind us.'

The driver's head disappeared into the cab without even the usual polite, 'Oui monsieur.'

'Come on, Shermaine.' Bruce grabbed her hand and dragged her from the car. Together they ran to one of the covered coaches and Bruce pushed her half way up the steel steps.

At that moment the train jerked forward so violently that she lost her grip on the handrails and tumbled backwards on top of Bruce. He was caught off balance and they fell together in a heap on the dusty platform. Above them the train gathered speed, pulling away. He remembered this nightmare from his childhood, running after a train and never catching it. He had to fight down his panic as he and Shermaine scrambled up, both of them panting, clinging to each other, the coaches clackety-clacking past them, the rhythm of their wheels mounting.

'Run!' he gasped, 'Run!' and with the panic weakening their legs he just managed to catch the handrail of the second coach. He clung to it, stumbling along beside the train, one arm round Shermaine's waist. Sergeant Major

Ruffararo leaned out, took Shermaine by the scruff of her neck and lifted her in like a lost kitten. Then he reached down for Bruce.

'Boss, some day we going to lose you if you go on playing around like that.'

'I'm sorry, Bruce,' she panted, leaning against him.

'No damage done.' He could grin at her. 'Now I want you to get into that compartment and stay there until I tell you to come out. Do you understand?'

'Yes, Bruce.'

'Off you go.' He turned from her to Ruffy. 'Up on to the roof, Sergeant Major! We're going to have fireworks. Those *shufta* have got a field gun with them and we'll be in full view of the town right up to the top of the hills.'

By the time they reached the roof of the train it had pulled out of Port Reprieve and was making its first angling turn up the slope of the hills. The sun was up now, well clear of the horizon, and the mist from the swamp had lifted so that they could see the whole village spread out beneath them.

General Moses's column had crossed the causeway and was into the main street. As Bruce watched, the leading truck swung sharply across the road and stopped. Men boiled out from under the canopy and swarmed over the field gun, unhitching it, manhandling it into position.

'I hope those Arabs haven't had any drill on that piece,' grunted Ruffy.

'We'll soon find out,' Bruce assured him grimly and looked back along the train. In the last truck Boussier stood protectively over the small group of four women and their children, like an old white-haired collie with its sheep. Crouched against the steel side of the truck, André de Surrier and half a dozen gendarmes were swinging and sighting the two Bren guns. In the second truck also the gendarmes were preparing to open fire.

'What are you waiting for?' roared Ruffy. 'Get me that field gun – start shooting.'

They fired a ragged volley, then the Bren guns joined in. With every burst André's helmet slipped forward over his eyes and he had to stop and push it back. Lying on the roof of the leading coach, Wally Hendry was firing short businesslike bursts.

The *shufta* round the field gun scattered, leaving one of their number lying in the road, but there were men behind the armour shield – Bruce could see the tops of their helmets.

Suddenly there was a long gush of white smoke from the barrel, and the shell rushed over the top of the train, with a noise like the wings of a giant pheasant.

'Over!' said Ruffy.

'Under!' to the next shot as it ploughed into the trees below them.

'And the third one right up the throat,' said Bruce. But it hit the rear of the train. They were using armour-piercing projectiles, not high explosive, for there was not the burst of yellow cordite fumes but only the crash and jolt as it struck.

Anxiously Bruce tried to assess the damage. The men and women in the rear trucks looked shaken but unharmed and he started a sigh of relief, which changed quickly to a gasp of horror as he realized what had happened.

'They've hit the coupling,' he said. 'They've sheared the coupling on the last truck.'

Already the gap was widening, as the rear truck started to roll back down the hill, cut off like the tail of a lizard.

'Jump,' screamed Bruce, cupping his hands round his mouth. 'Jump before you gather speed.'

Perhaps they did not hear him, perhaps they were too stunned to obey, but no one moved. The truck rolled back, faster and faster as gravity took it, down the hill towards the village and the waiting army of General Moses.

'What can we do, boss?'

'Nothing,' said Bruce.

The firing round Bruce had petered out into silence as every man, even Wally Hendry, stared down the slope at the receding truck. With a constriction of his throat Bruce saw old Boussier stoop and lift his wife to her feet, hold her close to his side and the two of them looking back at Bruce on the roof of the departing train. Boussier raised his right hand in a gesture of farewell and then he dropped it again and stood very still. Behind him, André de Surrier had left the Bren gun and removed his helmet. He also was looking back at Bruce, but he did not wave.

At intervals the field gun in the village punctuated the stillness with its deep boom and gush of smoke, but Bruce hardly heard it. He was watching the *shufta* running down towards the station yard to welcome the truck. Losing speed it ran into the platform and halted abruptly as it hit the buffers at the end of the line. The *shufta* swarmed over it like little black ants over the body of a beetle and faintly Bruce heard the pop, pop, pop of their rifles, saw the low sun glint on their bayonets. He turned away.

They had almost reached the crest of the hills; he could feel the train increasing speed under him. But he felt no relief, only the prickling at the corners of his eyes and the ache of it trapped in his throat.

'The poor bastards,' growled Ruffy beside him. 'The poor bastards.' And then there was another crashing jolt against the train, another hit from the field gun. This time up forward, on the locomotive. Shriek of escaping steam, the train checking its pace, losing power. But they were over the crest of the hills, the village was out of sight and gradually the train speeded up again as they started down the back slope. But steam spouted out of it, hissing white jets of it, and Bruce knew they had received a mortal wound. He switched on the radio.

'Driver, can you hear me? How bad is it?'

128

'I cannot see, Captain. There is too much steam. But the pressure on the gauge is dropping swiftly.'

'Use all you can to take us down the hill. It is imperative that we pass the level crossing before we halt. It is absolutely imperative – if we stop this side of the level crossing they will be able to reach us with their lorries.'

'I will try, Captain.'

They rocketed down the hills but as soon as they reached the level ground their speed began to fall off. Peering through the dwindling clouds of steam Bruce saw the pale brown ribbon of road ahead of them, and they were still travelling at a healthy thirty miles an hour as they passed it. When finally the train trickled to a standstill Bruce estimated that they were three or four miles beyond the level crossing, safely walled in by the forest and hidden from the road by three bends.

'I doubt they'll find us here, but if they do they'll have to come down the line from the level crossing to get at us. We'll go back a mile and lay an ambush in the forest on each side of the line,' said Bruce.

'Those Arabs won't be following us, boss. They've got themselves women and a whole barful of liquor. Be two or three days before old General Moses can sober them up enough to move them on.'

'You're probably right, Ruffy. But we'll take no chances. Get that ambush laid and then we'll try and think up some idea for getting home.'

Suddenly a thought occurred to him: Martin Boussier had the diamonds with him. They would not be too pleased about that in Elisabethville.

Almost immediately Bruce was disgusted with himself. The diamonds were by far the least important thing that they had left behind in Port Reprieve.

14

André de Surrier held his steel helmet against his chest the way a man holds his hat at a funeral, the wind blew cool and caressing through his dark sweat-damp hair. His hearing was dulled by the strike of the shell that had cut the truck loose from the rear of the train, he could hear one of the children crying and the crooning, gentling voice of its mother. He stared back up the railway line at the train, saw the great bulk of Ruffy beside Bruce Curry on the roof of the second coach.

'They can't help us now.' Boussier spoke softly. 'There's nothing they can do.' He lifted his hand stiffly in almost a military salute and then dropped it to his side. 'Be brave, ma chère,' he said to his wife. 'Please be brave,' and she clung to him.

André let the helmet drop from his hands. It clanged on to the metal floor of the truck. He wiped the sweat from his face with nervous fluttering hands and then turned slowly to look down at the village.

'I don't want to die,' he whispered. 'Not like this, not now, please not now.' One of his gendarmes laughed, a sound without mirth, and stepped across to the Bren. He pushed André away from it and started firing at the tiny running figures of the men in the station yard.

'No,' shrilled André. 'Don't do that, no, don't antagonize them. They'll kill us if you do that—'

'They'll kill us anyway,' laughed the gendarme and emptied the magazine in one long despairing burst. André started towards him, perhaps to pull him away from the gun, but his resolve did not carry him that far. His hands dropped to his sides, clenching and unclenching. His lips quivered and then opened to spill out his terror.

'No!' he screamed. 'Please, no! No! Oh, God have mercy.

Oh, save me, don't let this happen to me, please, God. Oh, my God.'

He stumbled to the side of the truck and clambered on to it. The truck was slowing as it ran into the platform. He could see men coming with rifles in their hands, shouting as they ran, black men in dirty tattered uniforms, their faces working with excitement, pink shouting mouths, baying like hounds in a pack.

André jumped and the dusty concrete of the platform grazed his cheek and knocked the wind out of him. He crawled to his knees, clutching his stomach and trying to scream. A rifle butt hit him between the shoulder-blades and he collapsed. Above him a voice shouted in French.

'He is white, keep him for the general. Don't kill him.' And again the rifle butt hit him, this time across the side of the head. He lay in the dust, dazed, with the taste of blood in his mouth and watched them drag the others from the truck.

They shot the black gendarmes on the platform, without ceremony, laughing as they competed with each other to use their bayonets on the corpses. The two children died quickly torn from their mothers, held by the feet and swung head first against the steel side of the truck.

Old Boussier tried to prevent them stripping his wife and was bayoneted from behind in anger, and then shot twice with a pistol held to his head as he lay on the platform.

All this happened in the first few minutes before the officers arrived to control them; by that time André and the four women were the only occupants of the truck left alive.

André lay where he had fallen, watching in fascinated skin-crawling horror as they tore the clothing off the women and with a man to each arm and each leg held them down on the platform as though they were calves to be branded, hooting with laughter at their struggling naked bodies, bickering for position, already unbuckling belts, pushing each other, arguing, some of them with fresh blood on their clothing.

But then two men, who by their air of authority and the red sashes across their chests were clearly officers, joined the crowd. One of them fired his pistol in the air to gain their attention and both of them started a harangue that slowly had effect. The women were dragged up and herded off towards the hotel.

One of the officers came across to where André lay, stooped over him and lifted his head by taking a handful of hair.

'Welcome, mon ami. The general will be very pleased to see you. It is a pity that your other white friends have left us, but then, one is better than nothing.'

He pulled André into a sitting position, peered into his face and then spat into his eyes with sudden violence. 'Bring him! The general will talk to him later.'

They tied André to one of the columns on the front verandah of the hotel and left him there. He could have twisted his head and looked through the large windows into the lounge at what they were doing to the women, but he did not. He could hear what was happening; by noon the screams had become groans and sobbing; by mid-afternoon the women were making no sound at all. But the queue of *shufta* was still out of the front door of the lounge. Some of them had been to the head of the line and back to the tail three or four times.

All of them were drunk now. One jovial fellow carried a bottle of Parfait Amour liqueur in one hand and a bottle of Harpers whisky in the other. Every time he came back to join the queue again he stopped in front of André.

'Will you drink with me, little white boy?' he asked. 'Certainly you will,' he answered himself, filled his mouth from one of the bottles and spat it into André's face. Each time it got a big laugh from the others waiting in the line. Occasionally one of the other *shufta* would stop in front of

André, unsling his rifle, back away a few paces, sight along the bayonet at André's face and then charge forward, at the last moment twisting the point aside so that it grazed his cheek. Each time André could not suppress his shriek of terror, and the waiting men nearly collapsed with merriment.

Towards evening they started to burn the houses on the outskirts of town. One group, sad with liquor and rape, sat together at the end of the verandah and started to sing. Their deep beautiful voices carrying all the melancholy savagery of Africa, they kept on singing while an argument between two *shufta* developed into a knife fight in the road outside the hotel.

The sweet bass lilt of singing covered the coarse breathing of the two circling, bare-chested knife fighters and the shuffle, shuffle, quick shuffle of their feet in the dust. When finally they locked together for the kill, the singing rose still deep and strong but with a triumphant note to it. One man stepped back with his rigid right arm holding the knife buried deep in the other's belly and as the loser sank down, sliding slowly off the knife, the singing sank with him, plaintive, regretful and lamenting into silence.

They came for André after dark. Four of them less drunk than the others. They led him down the street to the Union Minière offices. General Moses was there, sitting alone at the desk in the front office.

There was nothing sinister about him; he looked like an elderly clerk, a small man with the short woollen cap of hair grizzled to grey above the ears and a pair of horn-rimmed spectacles. On his chest he wore three rows of full-dress medals; each of his fingers was encased in rings to the second joint, diamonds, emeralds and the occasional red glow of a ruby; most of them had been designed for women, but the metal had been cut to enlarge them for his stubby black fingers. The face was almost kindly, except the eyes. There was a blankness of expression in them, the lifeless eyes of a madman. On the desk in front of him was a small wooden case made of unvarnished deal which bore the seal of the Union Minière Company stencilled in black upon its side. The lid was open, and as André came in through the door with his escort General Moses lifted a white canvas bag from the case, loosened the drawstring and poured a pile of dark grey industrial diamonds on to the blotter in front of him.

He prodded them thoughtfully with his finger, stirring them so they glittered dully in the harsh light of the petromax.

'Was this the only case in the truck?' he asked without looking up.

'Oui, mon général. There was only one,' answered one of André's escorts.

'You are certain?'

'Oui, mon général. I myself have searched thoroughly.'

General Moses took another of the canvas bags from the case and emptied it on to the blotter. He grunted with disappointment as he saw the drab little stones. He reached for another bag, and another, his anger mounting steadily as each yielded only dirty grey and black industrial diamonds. Soon the pile on the blotter would have filled a pint jug.

'Did you open the case?' he snarled.

'Non, mon général. It was sealed. The seal was not broken, you saw that.'

General Moses grunted again, his dark chocolate face set hard with frustration. Once more he dipped his hand into the wooden case and suddenly he smiled.

'Ah!' he said pleasantly. 'Yes! yes! what is this?' He brought out a cigar box, with the gaudy wrappers still on the cedarwood. A thumbnail prised the lid back and he beamed happily. In a nest of cotton wool, sparkling, breaking the white light of the petromax into all the rainbow colours of the spectrum, were the gem stones. General Moses picked one up and held it between thumb and forefinger.

'Pretty,' he murmured. 'Pretty, so pretty.' He swept the industrial stones to one side and laid the gem in the centre of the blotter. Then one by one he took the others from the cigar box, fondling each and laying it on the blotter, counting them, smiling, once chuckling softly, touching them, arranging them in patterns.

'Pretty,' he kept whispering. 'Bon – forty-one, forty-two. Pretty! My darlings! Forty-three.'

Then suddenly he scooped them up and poured them into one of the canvas bags, tightened the drawstring, dropped it into his breast pocket above the medals and buttoned the flap.

He laid his black, bejewelled hands on the desk in front of him and looked up at André.

His eyes were smoky yellow with black centres behind his spectacles. They had an opaque, dreamlike quality.

'Take off his clothes,' he said in a voice that was as expressionless as the eyes.

They stripped André with rough dispatch and General Moses looked at his body.

'So white,' he murmured. 'Why so white?' Suddenly his jaws began chewing nervously and there was a faint shine of sweat on his forehead. He came round from behind the desk, a small man, yet with an intensity about him that doubled his size.

'White like the maggots that feed in the living body of the elephant.' He brought his face close to André's. 'You should be fatter, my maggot, having fed so long and so well. You should be much fatter.'

He touched André's body, running his hands down his flanks in a caress.

'But now it is too late, little white maggot,' he said, and

André cringed from his touch and from his voice. 'For the elephant has shaken you from the wound, shaken you out on to the ground, shaken you out beneath his feet – and will you pop when he crushes you?'

His voice was still soft though the sweat oozed in oily lines down his cheeks and the dreaminess of his eyes had been replaced by a burning black brightness.

'We shall see,' he said and drew back. 'We shall see, my maggot,' he repeated, and brought his knee up into André's crotch with a force that jerked his whole frame and flung his shoulders back.

The agony flared through André's lower body, fierce as the touch of heated steel. It clamped in on his stomach, contracting it in a spasm like childbirth, it rippled up across the muscles of his chest into his head and burst beneath the roof of his skull in a whiteness that blinded him.

'Hold him,' commanded General Moses, his voice suddenly shrill. The two guards took André by the elbows and forced him to his knees, so that his genitals and lower belly were easily accessible to the general's boots. They had done this often.

'For the times you gaoled me!' And General Moses swung his booted foot into André's body. The pain blended with the other pain, and it was too strong for André to scream.

'This, for the insults,' and André could feel his testicles crush beneath it. Still it was too strong – he could not use his voice.

'This, for the times I have grovelled.' The pain had passed its zenith, this time he could scream with it. He opened his mouth and filled his empty lungs.

'This, for the times I have hungered.' Now he must scream. Now he must – the pain, oh, sweet Christ, I must, please let me scream.

'This, for your white man's justice.' Why can't I, please let me. Oh, no! No – please. Oh, God, oh, please.

'This, for your prisons and your Kiboko!'

The kicks so fast now, like the beat of an insane drummer, like rain on a tin roof. In his stomach he felt something tear.

'And this, and this, and this.'

The face before him filled the whole field of his vision. The voice and the sound of the boot into him filled his ears.

'This, and this, and this.' The voice high-pitched and within him the sudden warm flood of internal bleeding.

The pain was fading now as his body closed it out in defence, and he had not screamed. The leap of elation as he knew it. *This last thing I can do well, I can die now WITHOUT SCREAMING.* He tried to stand up, but they held him down and his legs were not his own, they were on the other side of the great numb warmth of his belly. He lifted his head and looked at the man who was killing him.

'This for the white filth that bore you, and this, and this—'

The blows were not a part of reality, he could feel the shock of them as though he stood close to a man who was cutting down a tree with an axe. And André smiled.

He was still smiling when they let him fall forward to the floor.

'I think he is dead,' said one of the guards. General Moses turned away and walked back to his seat at the desk. He was shaking as though he had run a long way, and his breathing was deep and fast. The jacket of his uniform was soaked with sweat. He sank into the chair and his body seemed to crumple; slowly the brightness faded from his eyes until once more they were filmed over, opaque and dreamy. The two guards squatted down quickly on each side of André's body; they knew it would be a long wait.

Through the open window there came an occasional shout of drunken laughter, and the red flicker and leap of flames.

15

B ruce stood in the centre of the tracks and searched the floor of the forest critically. At last he could make out the muzzle of the Bren protruding a few inches from the patch of elephant grass. Despite the fact that he knew exactly where to look for it, it had taken him a full two minutes to find it.

'That'll do, Ruffy,' he decided. 'We can't get it much better than that.'

'I reckon not, boss.'

Bruce raised his voice. 'Can you hear me?' There were muffled affirmatives from the bush on each side, and Bruce continued.

'If they come you must let them reach this spot before you open fire. I will mark it for you.' He went to a small shrub beside the line, broke off a branch and dropped it on the tracks.

'Can you see that?'

Again the affirmatives from the men in ambush. 'You will be relieved before darkness – until then stay where you are.'

The train was hidden beyond a bend in the line, half a mile ahead, and Bruce walked back with Ruffy.

The engine driver was waiting for them, talking with Wally Hendry beside the rear truck.

'Any luck?' Bruce asked him.

'I regret, mon capitaine, that she is irreparably damaged. The boiler is punctured in two places and there is considerable disruption of the copper tubing.'

'Thank you,' Bruce nodded. He was neither surprised nor disappointed. It was precisely what his own judgement had told him after a brief examination of the locomotive.

'Where is Madame Cartier?' he asked Wally.

'*Madame* is preparing the luncheon, *monsir*,' Wally told

him with heavy sarcasm. 'Why do you ask, Bucko? Are you feeling randy again so soon, hey? You feel like a slice of veal for lunch, is that it?'

Bruce snuffed out the quick flare of his temper and walked past him. He found Shermaine with four gendarmes in the cab of the locomotive. They had scraped the coals from the furnace into a glowing heap on the steel floor and were chopping potatoes and onions into the five gallon pots.

The gendarmes were all laughing at something Shermaine had said. Her usually pale cheeks were flushed with the heat; there was a sooty smudge on her forehead. She wielded the big knife with professional dexterity. She looked up and saw Bruce, her face lighting instantly and her lips parting.

'We're having a Hungarian goulash for lunch – bully beef, potatoes and onions.'

'As of now I am rating you acting second cook without pay.'

'You are too kind,' and she put her tongue out at him. It was a pink pointed little tongue like a cat's. Bruce felt the old familiar tightening of his legs and the dryness in his throat as he looked at it.

'Shermaine, the locomotive is damaged beyond repair. It is of no further use.' He spoke in English.

'It makes a passable kitchen,' she demurred.

'Be serious.' Bruce's anxiety made him irritable. 'We're stranded here until we think of something.'

'But, Bruce, you are the genius. I have complete faith in you. I'm sure you'll think of some truly beautiful idea.' Her face was solemn but she couldn't keep the banter out of her eyes. 'Why don't you go and ask General Moses to lend you his transportation?'

Bruce's eyes narrowed in thought and the black inverted curves of his eyebrows nearly touched above the bridge of his nose.

'The food better be good or I'll break you to third cook,' he warned, clambered down from the cab to the ground and hurried back along the train.

'Hendry, Sergeant Major, come here, please. I want to discuss something with you.'

They came to join him and he led the way up the ladder into one of the covered coaches. Hendry dropped on to the bunk and placed his feet on the washbasin.

'That was a quick one,' he grinned through the coppery stubble of his beard.

'You're the most uncouth, filthy-mouthed son of a bitch I have ever met, Hendry,' said Bruce coldly. 'When I get you back to Elisabethville I'm going to beat you to pulp before I hand you over to the military authority for murder.'

'My, my,' laughed Hendry. 'Big talker, hey? Curry, big, big talker.'

'Don't make me kill you now – don't do that, please. I still need you.'

'What's with you and that Frenchy, hey? You love it or something? You love it, or you just fancy a bit of that fat little arse? It can't be her titties – she ain't got much there, not even a handful each side.'

Bruce started for him, then changed his mind and swung round to stare out of the window. His voice was strangled when he spoke.

'I'll make a bargain with you, Hendry. Until we get out of this you keep off my back and I'll keep off yours. When we reach Msapa Junction the truce is off. You can do and say whatever you like and, if I don't kill you for it, I'll try my level best to see you hanged for murder.'

'I'm making no bargain with you or nobody, Curry. I play along until it suits me, and I won't give you no warning when it doesn't suit me to play along any more. And let me tell you now, Bucko, I don't need you and I don't need nobody. Not Haig or you, with your fancy too-good-to-kiss-my-arse talk; when the time comes I'm going to trim you

140

down to size – just remember that, Curry. And don't say I didn't warn you.' Hendry was leaning forward, hands on his knees, body braced and his whole face twisting and contorted with the vehemence of his speech.

'Let's make it now, Hendry.' Bruce wheeled away from the window, crouching slightly, his hands stiffening into the flat hard blades of the judo fighter.

Sergeant Major Ruffararo stood up from the opposite bunk with surprising grace and speed for such a big man. He interposed his great body.

'You wanted to tell us something, boss?'

Slowly Bruce straightened out of his crouch, his hands relaxing. Irritably he brushed at the damp lock of dark hair that had fallen on to his forehead, as if to brush Wally Hendry out of his mind with the same movement.

'Yes,' controlling his voice with an effort, 'I wanted to discuss our next move.' He fished the cigarette pack from his top pocket and lit one, sucking the smoke down deep. Then he perched on the lid of the washbasin and studied the ash on the tip of the cigarette. When he spoke again his voice was normal.

'There is no hope of repairing this locomotive, so we have to find alternative transport out of here. Either we can walk two hundred miles back to Msapa Junction with our friends the Baluba ready to dispute our passage, or we can ride back in General Moses's trucks!' He paused to let it sink in.

'You going to pinch those trucks off him?' asked Ruffy. 'That's going to take some doing, boss.'

'No, Ruffy, I don't think we have any chance of getting them out from under his nose. What we will have to do is attack the town and wipe him out.'

'You're bloody crazy,' exclaimed Wally. 'You're raving bloody mad.'

Bruce ignored him. 'I estimate that Moses has about sixty men. With Kanaki and nine men on the bridge, Haig and de Surrier and six others gone, we have thirty-four men left. Correct, Sergeant Major?'

'That's right, boss.'

'Very well,' Bruce nodded. 'We'll have to leave at least ten men here to man that ambush in case Moses sends a patrol after us, or in case of an attack by the Baluba. It's not enough, I know, but we will just have to risk it.'

'Most of these civilians got arms with them, shotguns and sports rifles,' said Ruffy.

'Yes,' agreed Bruce. 'They should be able to look after themselves. So that leaves twenty-four men to carry out the attack, something like three to one.'

'Those *shufta* will be so full of liquor, half of them won't be able to stand up.'

'That's what I am banking on: drunkenness and surprise. We'll hit them and try and finish it before they know what's happened. I don't think they will have realized how badly we were hit; they probably expect us to be a hundred miles away by now.'

'When do you want to leave, boss?'

'We are about twelve miles from Port Reprieve – say, six hours' march in the dark. I want to attack in the early hours of tomorrow morning, but I'd like to be in position around midnight. We'll leave here at six o'clock, just before dark.'

'I'd better go and start sorting the boys out.'

'Okay, Ruffy. Issue an extra hundred rounds to each man and ten grenades. I'll want four extra haversacks of grenades also.' Bruce turned to Hendry and looked at him for the first time. 'Go with the sergeant major, Hendry, and give him a hand.'

'Jesus, this is going to be a ball,' grinned Wally in anticipation. 'With any luck I'll get me a sackful of ears.' He disappeared down the corridor behind Ruffy, and Bruce lay back on the seat and took off his helmet. He closed his eyes and once again he saw Boussier and his wife standing together in the truck as it rolled back down the hill, he saw the huddle of frightened women, and André standing bareheaded staring back at him with big brown gentle eyes. He groaned softly. 'Why is it always the good ones, the harmless, the weak?'

A tap on the door roused him and he sat up quickly.

'Yes?'

'Hello, Bruce.' Shermaine came in with a multiple-decked metal canteen in one hand and two mugs in the other. 'It's lunchtime.'

'Already!' Bruce checked his watch. 'Good Lord, it's after one.'

'Are you hungry?'

'Breakfast was a century ago.'

'Good,' she said, lowered the collapsible table and began serving the food.

'Smells good.'

'I am a chef Cordon Bleu. My bully beef goulash is demanded by the crowned heads of Europe.'

They ate in silence for both of them were hungry. Once they looked at each other and smiled but returned to the food.

'That was good,' sighed Bruce at last.

'Coffee, Bruce?'

'Please.'

As she poured it she asked, 'So, what happens now?'

'Do you mean what happens now we are alone?'

'You are forward, monsieur. I meant how do we get out of here?'

'I am adopting your suggestion: borrowing General Moses's transportation.'

'You make jokes, Bruce!'

'No,' he said, and explained briefly.

'It will be very dangerous, will it not? You may be hurt?'

'Only the good die young.'

'That is why I worry. Please do not get hurt – I am starting to think I would not like that.' Her face was very serious and pale. Bruce crossed quickly and stooped over her, lifting her to her feet.

'Shermaine, I—'

'No, Bruce. Don't talk. Don't say anything.' Her eyes were closed with thick black lashes interlaced, her chin lifted exposing the long smooth swell of her neck. He touched it with his lips and she made a soft noise in her throat so he could feel the skin vibrate. Her body flattened against his and her fingers closed in the hair at the back of his head.

'Oh, Bruce. My Bruce, please do not get hurt. Do not let them hurt you.'

Wanting now, urgently, his mouth hunted upwards and hers came to meet it, willing prey. Her lips were pink and not greased with make-up, they parted to the pressure of his tongue, he felt the tip of her nose cool upon his cheek and his hand moved up her back and closed round the nape of her neck, slender neck with silky down behind her ears.

'Oh, Bruce—' she said into his mouth. His other hand went down on to the proud, round, deeply divided thrust of her buttocks, he pulled her lower body against his and she gasped as she felt him – the arrogant maleness through cloth.

'No,' she gasped and tried to pull away, but he held her until she relaxed against him once more. She shook her head, 'Non, non,' but her mouth was open still and her tongue fluttered against his. Down came his hand from her neck and twitched her shirt tails loose from under her belt, then up again along her back, touching the deep lateral depression of her spine so that she shuddered, clinging to him. Stroking velvet skin stretched tight over rubber-hard flesh, finding the outline of her shoulder blades, tracing them upwards then back to the armpits, silky-haired armpits that maddened him with excitement, quickly past them to her breasts, small breasts with soft tips hardening to his touch.

Now she struggled in earnest, her fists beating on his shoulders and her mouth breaking from his, and he stopped himself, dropped the hand away to encircle her waist. Holding her loosely within his arms.

'That was not good, Bruce. You get naughty very quick.' Her cheeks flamed with colour and her blue eyes had darkened to royal, her lips still wet from his, and her voice was unsteady, as unsteady as his when he answered.

'I'm sorry, Shermaine. I don't know what happened then, I did not mean to frighten you.'

'You are very strong, Bruce. But you do not frighten me, only a little bit. Your eyes frighten me when they look at me but do not see.'

You really made a hash of that one, he rebuked himself. Bruce Curry, the gentle sophisticated lover. Bruce Curry, the heavyweight, catch-as-catch-can, two-fisted rape artist.

He felt shaky, his legs wobbly, and there was something seriously wrong with his breathing.

'You do not wear a brassière,' he said without thinking, and immediately regretted it, but she chuckled, soft and husky.

'Do you think I need to, Bruce?'

'No, I didn't mean that,' he protested quickly, remembering the saucy tilt of that small breast. He was silent then, marshalling his words, trying to control his breathing, fighting down the madness of desire.

She studied his eyes. 'You can see again now – perhaps I will let you kiss me.'

'Please,' he said and she came back to him.

Gently now, Bruce me boy.

The door of the compartment flew back with a crash and they jumped apart. Wally Hendry stood on the threshold.

'Well, well, well.' His shrewd little eyes took it all in. 'That's nice!'

Shermaine was hurriedly tucking in her shirt tail and trying to smooth her hair at the same time.

Wally grinned. 'Nothing like it after a meal, I always say. Gets the digestion going.'

'What do you want?' snapped Bruce.

'There's no doubt what you want,' said Wally. 'Looks like you're getting it too.' He let his eyes travel up from Shermaine's waist, slowly over her body to her face.

Bruce stepped out into the corridor, pushing Hendry back and slammed the door.

'What do you want?' he repeated.

'Ruffy wants you to check his arrangements, but I'll tell him you're busy. We can put the attack off until tomorrow night if you like.'

Bruce scowled at him. 'Tell him I'll be with him in two minutes.'

Wally leaned against the door. 'Okay, I'll tell him.'

'What are you waiting for?'

'Nothing, just nothing,' grinned Wally.

'Well, bugger off then,' snarled Bruce.

'Okay, okay, don't get your knickers in a knot, Bucko.'

He sauntered off down the corridor.

Shermaine was standing where Bruce had left her, but with her eyes bright with tears of anger.

'He is a pig, that one. A filthy, filthy pig.'

'He's not worth worrying about.' Bruce tried to take her in his arms again, but she shrugged him off.

'I hate him. He makes everything seem so cheap, so dirty.'

'Nothing between you and I could be cheap and dirty,' said Bruce, and instantly her fury abated.

'I know, my Bruce. But he can make it seem that way.' They kissed gently.

'I must go. They want me.' For a second she clung to him.

'Be careful. Promise me you'll be careful.'

'I promise,' said Bruce and she let him go.

16

They left before dark, but the clouds had come up during the afternoon and now they hung low over the forest, trapping the heat beneath them.

Bruce led, with Ruffy in the middle of the line and Hendry in the rear.

By the time they reached the level crossing the night was on them and it had started to rain, soft fat drops weeping like a woman exhausted with grief, warm rain in the darkness. And the darkness was complete. Once Bruce touched the top of his nose with his open palm, but he could not see his hand.

He used a staff to keep contact with the steel rail that ran beside him, tapping along it like a blind man, and at each step the gravel of the embankment crunched beneath his feet. The hand of the man behind him was on his shoulder, and he could sense the presence of the others that followed him like the body of a serpent, could hear the crunch of their steps and the muted squeak and rattle of their equipment. A man's voice was raised in protest and immediately quenched by Ruffy's deep rumble.

They crossed the road and the gradient changed beneath Bruce's feet so that he had to lean forward against it. They were starting up the Lufira hills.

I will rest them at the top, he thought, and from there we will be able to see the lights of the town.

The rain stopped abruptly, and the quietness after it was surprising. Now he could distinctly hear the breathing of the man behind him above the small sounds of their advance, and in the forest nearby a tree frog clinked as though steel pellets were being dropped into a crystal glass. It was a sound of great purity and beauty.

All Bruce's senses were enhanced to compensate for his lack of sight; his hearing; his sense of smell, so that he could catch the over-sweet perfume of a jungle-flower and the heaviness of decaying wet vegetation; his sense of touch, so that he could feel the raindrops on his face and the texture of his clothing against his body; then the other animal sense of danger told him with sickening, stomach-tripping certainty that there was something ahead of him in the darkness.

He stopped, and the man following him bumped into him throwing him off balance. All along the line there was a ripple of confusion and then silence. They all waited.

Bruce strained his hearing, half crouched with his rifle held ready. There was something there, he could almost feel it.

Please God, let them not have a machine-gun set up here, he thought; they could cut us into a shambles.

He turned cautiously and felt for the head of the man behind him, found it and drew it towards him until his mouth was an inch from the ear.

'Lie down very quietly. Tell the one behind you that he may pass it back.'

Bruce waited poised, listening and trying to see ahead into the utter blackness. He felt a gentle tap on his ankle from the gendarme at his feet. They were all down.

'All right, let's go take a look.' Bruce detached one of the grenades from his webbing belt. He drew the pin and dropped it into the breast pocket of his jacket. Then feeling for the crossties of the rails with each foot he started forward. Ten paces and he stopped again. Then he heard it, the tiny click of two pebbles just ahead of him. His throat closed so he could not breathe and his stomach was very heavy.

I'm right on top of them. My God, if they open up now—

Inch by inch he drew back the hand that held the grenade.

I'll have to lob short and get down fast. Five-second fuse – too long, they'll hear it and start shooting.

His hand was right back, he bent his legs and sank slowly on to his knees.

Here we go, he thought, and at that instant sheet lightning fluttered across the sky and Bruce could see. The hills were outlined black below the pale grey belly of the clouds, and the steel rails glinted in the sudden light. The forest was dark and high at each hand, and – a leopard, a big golden and black leopard, stood facing Bruce. In that brief second they stared at each other and then the night closed down again.

The leopard coughed explosively in the darkness, and Bruce tried desperately to bring his rifle up, but it was in his left hand and his other arm was held back ready to throw.

This time for sure, he thought, this time they lower the boom on you.

It was with a feeling of disbelief that he heard the leopard crash sideways into the undergrowth, and the scrambling rush of its run dwindle into the bush.

He subsided on to his backside, with the primed grenade in his hand, the hysterical laughter of relief coming up into his throat.

'You okay, boss?' Ruffy's voice lifted anxiously.

'It was a leopard,' answered Bruce, and was surprised at the squeakiness of his own voice.

There was a buzz of voices from the gendarmes and a rattle and clatter as they started to stand up. Someone laughed.

'That's enough noise,' snapped Bruce and climbed to his feet; he found the pin in his pocket and fitted it back into the grenade. He groped his way back, picked up the staff from where he had dropped it, and took his position at the head of the column again.

'Let's go,' he said.

His mouth was dry, his breathing too quick and he could feel the heat beneath the skin of his cheeks from the shock of the leopard.

I truly squirted myself full of adrenalin that time, Bruce grinned precariously in the dark, I'm as windy as hell. And before tonight is over I shall find fear again.

They moved on up the incline of the hills, a serpent of twenty-six men, and the tension was in all of them. Bruce could hear it in the footsteps behind him, feel it in the grip of the hand upon his shoulder and catch it in the occasional whiffs of body smell that came forward to him, the smell of nervous sweat like acid on metal.

Ahead of them the clouds that had crouched low upon the hills lifted slowly, and Bruce could see the silhouette of the crests. It was no longer utterly dark for there was a glow on the belly of the clouds now. A faint orange glow of reflected light that grew in strength, then faded and grew again. It puzzled Bruce for a while, and thinking about it gave his nerves a chance to settle. He plodded steadily on watching the fluctuations of the light. The ground tilted more sharply upwards beneath his feet and he leaned forward against it, slogging up the last half mile to the pass between the peaks, and at last came out on the top.

'Good God,' Bruce spoke aloud, for from here he could see the reason for that glow on the clouds. They were burning Port Reprieve. The flames were well established in the buildings along the wharf, and as Bruce watched one of the roofs collapsed slowly in upon itself in a storm of sparks leaving the walls naked and erect, the wooden sills of the windows burning fiercely. The railway buildings were also on fire, and there was fire in the residential area beyond the Union Minière offices and the hotel. Quickly Bruce looked towards St Augustine's. It was dark, no flames there, no light even, and he felt a small lift of relief.

'Perhaps they have overlooked it, perhaps they're too busy looting,' and as he looked back at Port Reprieve, his mouth hardened. 'The senseless wanton bastards!' His anger started as he watched the meaningless destruction of the town.

'What can they possibly hope to gain by this?' There were new fires nearer the hotel. Bruce turned to the man behind him.

'We will rest here, but there will be no smoking and no talking.'

He heard the order passed back along the line and the careful sounds of equipment being lowered and men settling gratefully down upon the gravel embankment. Bruce unslung the case that contained his binoculars. He focused them on the burning town.

It was bright with the light of fires and through the glasses he could almost discern the features of the men in the streets. They moved in packs, heavily armed and restless. Many carried bottles and already the gait of some of them was unsteady. Bruce tried to estimate their numbers but it was impossible, men kept disappearing into buildings and reappearing, groups met and mingled and dispersed.

He dropped his glasses on to his chest to rest his eyes, and heard movement beside him in the dark. He glanced sideways. It was Ruffy, his bulk exaggerated by the load he carried; his rifle across one shoulder, on the other a full case of ammunition, and round his neck half a dozen haversacks full of grenades.

'Looks like they're having fun, hey, boss?'

'Fifth of November,' agreed Bruce. 'Aren't you going to take a breather?'

'Why not?' Ruffy set down the ammunition case and lowered his great backside on to it. 'Can you see any of those folks we left behind?' he asked.

Bruce lifted the glasses again and searched the area beyond the station buildings. It was darker there but he made out the square shape of the truck standing among the moving shadows.

'The truck's still there,' he murmured, 'but I can't see—'

At that moment the thatched roof of one of the houses exploded upwards in a column of flame, lighting the railway yard, and the truck stood out sharply.

'Yes,' said Bruce, 'I can see them now.' They were littered untidily across the yard, still lying where they had died. Small and fragile, unwanted as broken toys.

'Dead?' asked Ruffy.

'Dead,' confirmed Bruce.

'The women?'

'It's hard to tell.' Bruce strained his eyes. 'I don't think so.'

'No.' Ruffy's voice was soft and very deep. 'They wouldn't waste the women. I'd guess they've got them up at the hotel, taking it in turn to give them the business. Four women only – they won't last till morning. Those bastards down there could shag an elephant to death.' He spat thoughtfully into the gravel at his feet. 'What you going to do, boss?'

Bruce did not answer for a minute; he swung the glasses slowly back across the town. The field gun was still standing where he had last seen it, its barrel pointing accusingly up towards him. The transports were parked before the Union Minière offices; he could see the brilliant yellow and red paint and the Shell sign on the tanker. I hope it's full, Bruce thought, we'll need plenty of gasoline to get us back to Elisabethville.

'Ruffy, you'd better tell your boys to keep their bullets away from that tanker, otherwise it'll be a long walk home.'

'I'll tell them,' grunted Ruffy. 'But you know these mad Arabs – once they start shooting they don't stop till they're out of bullets, and they not too fussy where those bullets go.'

'We'll split into two groups when we get to the bottom of the hill. You and I will take our lot through the edge of the swamp and cross to the far side of the town. Tell

Lieutenant Hendry to come here.' Bruce waited until Wally came forward to join them, and when the three of them crouched together he went on.

'Hendry, I want you to spread your men out at the top of the main street – there in the darkness on this side of the station. Ruffy and I are going to cross the edge of the swamp to the causeway and lay out on the far side. For God's sake keep your boys quiet until Ruffy and I hit them – all we need is for your lot to start pooping off before we are ready and we won't need those lorries, we'll need coffins for the rest of our journey. Do you understand me?'

'Okay, okay, I know what I'm doing,' muttered Wally.

'I hope so,' said Bruce, and then went on. 'We'll hit them at four o'clock tomorrow morning, just before first light. Ruffy and I will go into the town and bomb the hotel – that's where most of them will be sleeping. The grenades should force the survivors into the street and as soon as that happens you can open up – but not before. Wait until you get them in the open. Is that clear?'

'Jesus,' growled Hendry. 'Do you think I'm a bloody fool, do you think I can't understand English?'

'The crossfire from the two groups should wipe most of them out.' Bruce ignored Wally's outburst. 'But we mustn't give the remainder a chance to organize. Hit them hard and as soon as they take cover again you must follow them in – close with them and finish them off. If we can't get it over in five to ten minutes then we are going to be in trouble. They outnumber us three to one, so we have to exploit the element of surprise to the full.'

'Exploit the element of surprise to the full!' mimicked Wally. 'What for all the fancy talk – why not just murder the bastards?'

Bruce grinned lightly in the dark. 'All right, murder the bastards,' he agreed. 'But do it as quickly as bloody possible.' He stood up and inclined the luminous dial of his wrist-watch to catch the light. 'It's half past ten now – we'll move

153

down on them. Come with me, Hendry, and we'll sort them into two groups.'

Bruce and Wally moved back along the line and talked to each man in turn.

'You will go with Lieutenant Hendry.'

'You come with me.'

Making sure that the two English-speaking corporals were with Wally, they took ten minutes to divide them into two units and to redistribute the haversacks of grenades. Then they moved on down the slope, still in Indian file.

'This is where we leave you, Hendry,' whispered Bruce. 'Don't go jumping the gun – wait until you hear my grenades.'

'Yeah, okay – I know all about it.'

'Good luck,' said Bruce.

'Your bum in a barrel, Captain Curry,' rejoined Wally and moved away.

'Come on, Ruffy.' Bruce led his men off the embankment down into the swamp. Almost immediately the mud and slime was knee-deep and as they worked their way out to the right it rose to their waists and then to their armpits, sucking and gurgling sullenly as they stirred it with their passage, belching little evil-smelling gusts of swamp gas.

The mosquitoes closed round Bruce's face in a cloud so dense that he breathed them into his mouth and had to blink them out of his eyes. Sweat dribbled down from under his helmet and clung heavily in his eyebrows and the matted stems of the papyrus grass dragged at his feet. Their progress was tortuously slow and for fifteen minutes at a time Bruce lost sight of the lights of the village through the wall of papyrus; he steered by the glow of the fires and the occasional column of sparks.

It was an hour before they had half completed their circuit of Port Reprieve. Bruce stopped to rest, still waist-deep in swamp ooze and with his arms aching numb from holding his rifle above his head.

'I could use a smoke now, boss,' grunted Ruffy.

'Me too,' answered Bruce, and he wiped his face on the sleeve of his jacket. The mosquito bites on his forehead and round his eyes burnt like fire.

'What a way to make a living,' he whispered.

'You go on living and you'll be one of the lucky ones,' answered Ruffy. 'My guess is there'll be some dying before tomorrow.'

But the fear of death was submerged by physical discomfort. Bruce had almost forgotten that they were going into battle; right now he was more worried that the leeches which had worked their way through the openings in his anklets and were busily boring into his lower legs might find their way up to his crotch. There was a lot to be said in favour of a zip fly, he decided.

'Let's get out of this,' he whispered. 'Come on, Ruffy. Tell your boys to keep it quiet.'

He worked in closer to the shore and the level fell to their knees once more. Progress was more noisy now as their legs broke the surface with each step and the papyrus rustled and brushed against them.

It was almost two o'clock when they reached the causeway. Bruce left his men crouched in the papyrus while he made a stealthy reconnaissance along the side of the concrete bridge, keeping in its shadow, moving doubled up until he came to dry land on the edge of the village. There were no sentries posted and except for the crackle of the flames the town was quiet, sunk into a drunken stupor, satiated. Bruce went back to call his men up.

He spread them in pairs along the outskirts of the village. He had learned very early in this campaign not to let his men act singly; nothing drains an African of courage more than to be on his own, especially in the night when the ghosts are on the walk-about.

To each couple he gave minute instructions.

'When you hear the grenades you shoot at anybody in

the streets or at the windows. When the street is empty move in close beside that building there. Use your own grenades on every house and watch out for Lieutenant Hendry's men coming through from the other side. Do you understand?'

'It is understood.'

'Shoot carefully. Aim each shot – not like you did at the road bridge, and in the name of God do not hit the gasoline tanker. We need that to get us home.'

Now it was three o'clock, Bruce saw by the luminous figures on his wristwatch. Eight hours since they had left the train, and twenty-two hours since Bruce had last slept. But he was not tired, although his body ached and there was that gritty feeling under his eyelids, yet his mind was clear and bright as a flame.

He lay beside Ruffy under a low bush on the outskirts of Port Reprieve and the night wind drifted the smoke from the burning town down upon them, and Bruce was not tired. For I am going to another rendezvous with fear.

Fear is a woman, he thought, with all the myriad faces and voices of a woman. Because she is a woman and because I am a man I must keep going back to her. Only this time the appointment is one that I cannot avoid, this time I am not deliberately seeking her out.

I know she is evil, I know that after I have possessed her I will feel sick and shaken. I will say, 'That was the last time, never again.'

But just as certainly I know I will go back to her again, hating her, dreading her, but also needing her.

I have gone to find her on a mountain – on Dutoits Kloof Frontal, on Turret Towers, on the Wailing Wall, and the Devil's Tooth.

And she was there, dressed in a flowing robe of rock, a robe that fell sheer two thousand feet to the scree slope below. And she shrieked with the voice of the wind along the exposed face. Then her voice was soft, tinkling like cooling glass in the Berg ice underfoot, whispering like nylon rope running free, grating as the rotten rock moved in my hand.

I have followed her into the Jessie bush on the banks of the Sabi and the Luangwa, and she was there, waiting, wounded, in a robe of buffalo hide with the blood dripping from her mouth. And her smell was the sour-acid smell of my own sweat, and her taste was like rotten tomatoes in the back of my throat.

I have looked for her beyond the reef in the deep water with the demand valve of a scuba repeating my breathing with metallic hoarseness. And she was there with rows of white teeth in the semicircle of her mouth, a tall fin on her back, dressed this time in shagreen, and her touch was cold as the ocean, and her taste was salt and the taint of dying things.

I have looked for her on the highway with my foot pressed to the floorboards and she was there with her cold arm draped round my shoulders, her voice the whine of rubber on tarmac and the throaty hum of the motor.

With Colin Butler at the helm (a man who treated fear not as a lover, but with tolerant contempt as though she were his little sister) I went to find her in a small boat. She was dressed in green with plumes of spray and she wore a necklace of sharp black rock. And her voice was the roar of water breaking on water.

We met in darkness at the road bridge and her eyes glinted like bayonets. But that was an enforced meeting not of my choosing, as tonight will be.

I hate her, he thought, but she is a woman and I am a man.

Bruce lifted his arm and turned his wrist to catch the light of the fires.

'Fifteen minutes to four, Ruffy. Let's go and take a look.'

'That's a good idea, boss.' Ruffy grinned with a show of white teeth in the darkness.

'Are you afraid, Ruffy?' he asked suddenly, wanting to know, for his own heart beat like a war drum and there was no saliva in his mouth.

'Boss, some questions you don't ask a man.' Ruffy rose slowly into a crouch. 'Let's go take a look around.'

So they moved quickly together into the town, along the street, hugging the hedges and the buildings, trying to keep in shadow, their eyes moving everywhere, breathing quick and shallow, nerves screwed up tight until they reached the hotel.

There were no lights in the windows and it seemed deserted until Bruce made out the untidy mass of humanity strewn in sleep upon the front verandah.

'How many there, Ruffy?'

'Dunno – perhaps ten, fifteen.' Ruffy breathed an answer. 'Rest of them will be inside.'

'Where are the women – be careful of them.'

'They're dead long ago, you can believe me.'

'All right then, let's get round the back.' Bruce took a deep breath and then moved quickly across the twenty yards of open firelit street to the corner of the hotel. He stopped in the shadow and felt Ruffy close beside him. 'I want to take a look into the main lounge, my guess is that most of them will be in there,' he whispered.

'There's only four bedrooms,' agreed Ruffy. 'Say the officers upstairs and the rest in the lounge.'

Now Bruce moved quickly round the corner and stumbled over something soft. He felt it move against his foot.

'Ruffy!' he whispered urgently as he teetered off balance. He had trodden on a man, a man sleeping in the dust beside the wall. He could see the firelight on his bare torso and the glint of the bottle clutched in one outflung hand. The man sat up, muttering, and then began to cough, hacking painfully, swearing as he wiped his mouth with his free hand. Bruce regained his balance and swung his rifle up to use the bayonet, but Ruffy was quicker. He put one foot on the man's chest and trod him flat on to his back once more, then standing over him he used his bayoneted rifle the way a gardener uses a spade to lift potatoes, leaning his weight on it suddenly and the blade vanished into the man's throat.

The body stiffened convulsively, legs thrust out straight and arms rigid, there was a puffing of breath from the severed windpipe and then the slow melting relaxation of death. Still with his foot on the chest, Ruffy withdrew the bayonet and stepped over the corpse.

That was very close, thought Bruce, stifling the qualm of horror he felt at the execution. The man's eyes were fixed open in almost comic surprise, the bottle still in his hand, his chest bare, the front of his trousers unbuttoned and stiff with dried blood – not his blood, guessed Bruce angrily.

They moved on past the kitchens. Bruce looked in and saw that they were empty with the white enamel tiles reflecting the vague light and piles of used plates and pots cluttering the tables and the sink. Then they reached the bar-room and there was a hurricane lamp on the counter diffusing a yellow glow; the stench of liquor poured out through the half-open window, the shelves were bare of bottles and men were asleep upon the counter, men lay curled together upon the floor like a pack of dogs, broken glass and rifles and shattered furniture littered about them. Someone had vomited out of the window leaving a yellow streak down the whitewashed wall.

'Stand here,' breathed Bruce into Ruffy's ear. 'I will go round to the front where I can throw on to the verandah and also into the lounge. Wait until you hear my first grenade blow.'

Ruffy nodded and leaned his rifle against the wall; he took a grenade in each fist and pulled the pins.

Bruce slipped quickly round the corner and along the side wall. He reached the windows of the lounge. They were tightly closed and he peered in over the sill. A little of the

159

light from the lamp in the bar-room came through the open doors and showed up the interior. Here again there were men covering the floor and piled upon the sofas along the far wall. Twenty of them at least, he estimated by the volume of their snoring, and he grinned without humour. My God, what a shambles it is going to be.

Then something at the foot of the stairs caught his eye and the grin on his face became fixed, baring his teeth and narrowing his eyes to slits. It was the mound of nude flesh formed by the bodies of the four women; they had been discarded once they had served their purpose, dragged to one side to clear the floor for sleeping space, lying upon each other in a jumble of naked arms and legs and cascading hair.

No mercy now, thought Bruce with hatred replacing his fear as he looked at the women and saw by the attitudes in which they lay that there was no life left in them. *No mercy now!*

He slung his rifle over his left shoulder and filled his hand with grenades, pulled the pins and moved quickly to the corner so that he could look down the length of the covered verandah. He rolled both grenades down among the sleeping figures, hearing clearly the click of the priming and the metallic rattle against the concrete floor. Quickly he ducked back to the lounge window, snatching two more grenades from his haversack and pulling the pins, he hurled them through the closed windows. The crash of breaking glass blended with the double thunder of the explosions on the verandah.

Someone shouted in the room, a cry of surprise and alarm, then the windows above Bruce blew outwards, showering him with broken glass and the noise half deafening him as he tossed two more grenades through the gaping hole of the window. They were screaming and groaning in the lounge. Ruffy's grenades roared in the bar-room bursting through the double doors, then Bruce's grenades snuffed out the sounds of life in the lounge with violent white flame and thunder. Bruce tossed in two more grenades and ran back to the corner of the verandah unslinging his rifle.

A man with his hands over his eyes and blood streaming through his fingers fell over the low verandah wall and crawled to his knees. Bruce shot him from so close that the shaft of gun flame joined the muzzle of his rifle and the man's chest, punching him over backwards, throwing him spreadeagled on to the earth.

He looked beyond and saw two more in the road, but before he could raise his rifle the fire from his own gendarmes found them, knocking them down amid spurts of dust.

Bruce hurdled the verandah wall. He shouted, a sound without form or meaning. Exulting, unafraid, eager to get into the building, to get amongst them. He stumbled over the dead men on the verandah. A burst of gunfire from down the street rushed past him, so close he could feel the wind on his face. Fire from his own men.

'You stupid bastards!' Shouting without anger, without fear, with only the need to shout, he burst into the lounge through the main doors. It was half dark but he could see through the darkness and the haze of plaster dust.

A man on the stairs, the bloom of gunfire and the sting of the bullet across Bruce's thigh, fire in return, without aiming from the hip, miss and the man gone up and round the head of the stairs, yelling as he ran.

A grenade in Bruce's right hand, throw it high, watch it hit the wall and bounce sideways round the angle of the stairs. The explosion shocking in the confined space and the flash of it lighting the building and outlining the body of the man as it blew him back into the lounge, lifting him clear of the banisters, shredded and broken by the blast, falling heavily into the room below.

Up the stairs three at a time and into the bedroom

passage, another man naked and bewildered staggering through a doorway still drunk or half asleep, chop him down with a single shot in the stomach, jump over him and throw a grenade through the glass skylight of the second bedroom, another through the third and kick open the door of the last room in the bellow and flash of the explosions.

A man was waiting for Bruce across the room with a pistol in his hand, and both of them fired simultaneously, the clang of the bullet glancing off the steel of Bruce's helmet, jerking his head back savagely, throwing him sideways against the wall, but he fired again, rapid fire, hitting with every bullet, so that the man seemed to dance, a jerky grotesque twitching jig, pinned against the far wall by the bullets.

On his knees now Bruce was stunned, ears singing like a million mad mosquitoes, hands clumsy and slow on the reload, back on his feet, legs rubbery but the loaded rifle in his hands making a man of him.

Out into the passage, another one right on top of him, a vast dark shape in the darkness – kill him! kill him!

'Don't shoot, boss!'

Ruffy, thank God, Ruffy.

'Are there any more?'

'All finished, boss – you cleaned them out good.'

'How many?' Bruce shouted above the singing in his ears.

'Forty or so. Jesus, what a mess! There's blood all over the place. Those grenades—'

'There must be more.'

'Yes, but not in here, boss. Let's go and give the boys outside a hand.'

They ran back down the passage, down the stairs, and the floor of the lounge was sodden and sticky, dead men everywhere; it smelt like an abattoir – blood and ripped bowels. One still on his hands and knees, creepy-crawling towards the door. Ruffy shot him twice, flattening him.

'Not the front door, boss. Our boys will get you for sure. Go out the window.'

Bruce dived through the window head first, rolled over behind the cover of the verandah wall and came to his knees in one movement. He felt strong and invulnerable. Ruffy was beside him.

'Here come our boys,' said Ruffy, and Bruce could see them coming down the street, running forward in short bursts, stopping to fire, to throw a grenade, then coming again.

'And there are Lieutenant Hendry's lot.' From the opposite direction but with the same dodging, checking run, Bruce could see Wally with them. He was holding his rifle across his hip when he fired, his whole body shaking with the juddering of the gun.

Like a bird rising in front of the beaters one of the *shufta* broke from the cover of the grocery store and ran into the street unarmed, his head down and his arms pumping in time with his legs. Bruce was close enough to see the panic in his face. He seemed to be moving in slow motion, and the flames lit him harshly, throwing a distorted shadow in front of him. When the bullets hit him he stayed on his feet, staggering in a circle, thrashing at the air with his hands as though he were beating off a swarm of bees, the bullets slapping loudly against his body and lifting little puffs of dust from his clothing. Beside Bruce, Ruffy aimed carefully and shot him in the head, ending it.

'There must be more,' protested Bruce. 'Where are they hiding?'

'In the offices, I'd say.'

And Bruce turned his attention quickly to the block of Union Minière offices. The windows were in darkness and as he stared he thought he saw movement. He glanced quickly back at Wally's men and saw that four of them had bunched up close behind Wally as they ran.

'Hendry, watch out!' he shouted with all his strength. 'On your right, from the offices!'

But it was too late, gunfire sparkled in the dark windows and the little group of running men disintegrated.

Bruce and Ruffy fired together, raking the windows, emptying their automatic rifles into them. As he reloaded Bruce glanced back at where Wally's men had been hit. With disbelief he saw that Wally was the only one still on his feet; crossing the road, sprinting through an area of bullet-churned earth towards them, he reached the verandah and fell over the low wall.

'Are you wounded?' Bruce asked.

'Not a touch – those bastards couldn't shoot their way out of a French letter,' Wally shouted defiantly, and his voice carried clearly in the sudden hush. He snatched the empty magazine off the bottom of his rifle, threw it aside and clipped on a fresh one. 'Move over,' he growled, 'let me get a crack at those bastards.' He lifted his rifle and rested the stock on top of the wall, knelt behind it, cuddled the butt into his shoulder and began firing short bursts into the windows of the office block.

'This is what I was afraid of.' Bruce lifted his voice above the clamour of the guns. 'Now we've got a pocket of resistance right in the centre of the town. There must be fifteen or twenty of them in there – it might take us days to winkle them out.' He cast a longing look at the canvas-covered trucks lined up outside the station yard. 'They can cover the lorries from here, and as soon as they guess what we're after, as soon as we try and move them, they'll knock out that tanker and destroy the trucks.'

The firelight flickered on the shiny yellow and red paint of the tanker. It looked so big and vulnerable standing there in the open. It needed just one bullet out of the many hundred that had already been fired to end its charmed existence.

We've got to rush them now, he decided. Beyond the office block the remains of Wally's group had taken cover

164

and were keeping up a heated fire. Bruce's group straggled up to the hotel and found positions at the windows.

'Ruffy.' Bruce caught him by the shoulder. 'We'll take four men with us and go round the back of the offices. From that building there we've got only twenty yards or so of open ground to cover. Once we get up against the wall they won't be able to touch us and we can toss grenades in amongst them.'

'That twenty yards looks like twenty miles from here,' rumbled Ruffy, but picked up his sack of grenades and crawled back from the verandah wall.

'Go and pick four men to come with us,' ordered Bruce.

'Okay, boss. We'll wait for you in the kitchen.'

'Hendry. Listen to me.'

'Yeah. What is it?'

'When I reach that corner over there I'll give you a wave. We'll be ready to go then. I want you to give us all the cover you can – keep their heads down.'

'Okay,' agreed Wally and fired another short burst.

'Try not to hit us when we close in.'

Wally turned to look at Bruce and he grinned wickedly.

'Mistakes happen, you know. I can't promise anything. You'd look real grand in my sights.'

'Don't joke,' said Bruce.

'Who's joking?' grinned Wally and Bruce left him. He found Ruffy and four gendarmes waiting in the kitchen.

'Come on,' he said and led them out across the kitchen yard, down the sanitary lane with the steel doors for the buckets behind the outhouses and the smell of them thick and fetid, round the corner and across the road to the buildings beyond the office block. They stopped there and crowded together, as though to draw courage and comfort from each other. Bruce measured the distance with his eye.

'It's not far,' he announced.

'Depends on how you look at it,' grunted Ruffy.

'There are only two windows opening out on to this side.'

'Two's enough – how many do you want?'

'Remember, Ruffy, you can only die once.'

'Once is enough,' said Ruffy. 'Let's cut out the talking, boss. Too much talk gets you in the guts.'

Bruce moved across to the corner of the building out of the shadows. He waved towards the hotel and imagined that he saw an acknowledgement from the end of the verandah.

'All together,' he said, sucked in a deep breath, held it a second and then launched himself into the open. He felt small now, no longer brave and invulnerable, and his legs moved so slowly that he seemed to be standing still. The black windows gaped at him.

Now, he thought, now you die.

Where, he thought, not in the stomach, please God, not in the stomach.

And his legs moved stiffly under him, carrying him half way across.

Only ten more paces, he thought, one more river, just one more river to Jordan. But not in the stomach, please God, not in my stomach. And his flesh cringed in anticipation, his stomach drawn in hard as he ran.

Suddenly the black windows were brightly lit, bright white oblongs in the dark buildings, and the glass sprayed out of them like untidy spittle from an old man's mouth. Then they were dark again, dark with smoke billowing from them and the memory of the explosion echoing in his ears.

'A grenade!' Bruce was bewildered. 'Someone let off a grenade in there!'

He reached the back door without stopping and it burst open before his rush. He was into the room, shooting, coughing in the fumes, firing wildly at the small movements of dying men.

In the half darkness something long and white lay against

166

the far wall. A body, a white man's naked body. He crossed to it and looked down.

'André,' he said, 'it's André – he threw the grenade.' And he knelt beside him.

– 17 –

Curled naked upon the concrete floor, André was alive but dying as the haemorrhage within him leaked his life away. His mind was alive and he heard the crump, crump of Bruce's grenades, then the gunfire in the street, and the sound of running men. The shouts in the night and then the guns very close, they were in the room in which he lay.

He opened his eyes. There were men at each of the windows, crouched below the sills, and the room was thick with cordite fumes and the clamour of the guns as they fired out into the night.

André was cold, the coldness was all through him. Even his hands drawn up against his chest were cold and heavy. His stomach only was warm, warm and immensely bloated.

It was an effort to think, for his mind also was cold and the noise of the guns confused him.

He watched the men at the windows with a detached disinterest, and slowly his body lost its weight. He seemed to float clear of the floor and look down upon the room from the roof. His eyelids sagged and he dragged them up again, and struggled down towards his own body.

There was suddenly a rushing sound in the room and plaster sprayed from the wall above André's head, filling the air with pale floating dust. One of the men at the windows fell backwards, his weapon ringing loudly on the floor as it dropped from his hands; he flopped over twice and lay still, face down within arm's length of André.

Ponderously André's mind analysed the sights his eyes

were recording. Someone was firing on the building from outside. The man beside him was dead and from his head wound the blood spread slowly across the floor towards him. André closed his eyes again, he was very tired and very cold.

There was a lull in the sound of gunfire, one of those freak silences in the midst of battle. And in the lull André heard a voice far off, shouting. He could not hear the words but he recognized the voice and his eyelids flew open. There was an excitement in him, a new force, for it was Wally's voice he had heard.

He moved slightly, clenching his hands and his brain started to sing.

Wally has come back for me – he has come to save me. He rolled his head slowly, painfully, and the blood gurgled in his stomach.

I must help him, I must not let him endanger himself – these men are trying to kill him. I must stop them. I mustn't let them kill Wally.

And then he saw the grenades hanging on the belt of the man that lay beside him. He fastened his eyes on the round polished metal bulbs and he began to pray silently.

'Hail, Mary, full of grace, the Lord is with thee.'

He moved again, straightening his body.

'Blessed art thou among women, and blessed is the fruit of thy womb, Jesus.'

His hand crept out into the pool of blood, and the sound of the guns filled his head so he could not hear himself pray. Walking on its fingers, his hand crawled through the blood as slowly as a fly through a saucer of treacle.

'Blessed is the fruit of thy womb, Jesus. Oh, Jesus. Pray for me now, and at the hour. Full of grace.'

He touched the smooth, deeply segmented steel of the grenade.

'Us sinners – at the day, at the hour. This day – this day our daily bread.'

He fumbled at the clip, fingers stiff and cold.

'Hallowed be thy – Hallowed be thy—'

The clip clicked open and he held the grenade, curling his fingers round it.

'Hail, Mary, full of grace.'

He drew the grenade to him and held it with both hands against his chest. He lifted it to his mouth and took the pin between his teeth.

'Pray for us sinners,' he whispered, and pulled the pin.

'Now and at the hour of our death.'

And he tried to throw it. It rolled from his hand and bumped across the floor. The firing handle flew off and rattled against the wall. General Moses turned from the window and saw it – his lips opened and his spectacles glinted above the rose-pink cave of his mouth. The grenade lay at his feet. Then everything was gone in the flash and roar of the explosion.

Afterwards in the acrid swirl of fumes, in the patter of falling plaster, in the tinkle and crunch of broken glass, in the small scrabbling noises and the murmur and moan of dying men, André was still alive. The body of the man beside him had shielded his head and chest from the full force of the blast.

There was still enough life in him to recognize Bruce Curry's face close to his, though he could not feel the hands that touched him.

'André!' said Bruce. 'It's André – he threw the grenade!'

'Tell him—' whispered André and stopped.

'Yes, André—?' said Bruce.

'I didn't, this day and at the hour. I had to – not this time.' He could feel it going out in him like a candle in a high wind and he tried to cup his hands around it.

'What is it, André? What must I tell him?' Bruce's voice, but so far away.

'Because of him – this time – not of it, I didn't.' He

169

stopped again and gathered all of what was left. His lips quivered as he tried so hard to say it.

'Like a man!' he whispered and the candle went out.

'Yes,' said Bruce softly, holding him. 'This time like a man.'

He lowered André gently until his head touched the floor again; then he stood upright and looked down at the terribly mutilated body. He felt empty inside, a hollowness, the same feeling as after love.

He moved across to the desk near the far wall. Outside the gunfire dwindled like half-hearted applause, flared up again and then ceased. Around him Ruffy and the four gendarmes moved excitedly, inspecting the dead, exclaiming, laughing the awkward embarrassed laughter of men freshly released from mortal danger.

Loosening the chin straps of his helmet with slow steady fingers, Bruce stared across the room at André's body.

'Yes,' he whispered again. 'This time like a man. All the other times are wiped out, the score is levelled.'

His cigarettes were damp from the swamp, but he took one from the centre of the pack and straightened it with calm nerveless fingers. He found his lighter and flicked it open – then, without warning, his hands started to shake. The flame of the lighter fluttered and he had to hold it steady with both hands. There was blood on his hands, new sticky blood. He snapped the lighter closed and breathed in the smoke. It tasted bitter and the saliva flooded into his mouth. He swallowed it down, nausea in his stomach, and his breathing quickened.

It was not like this before, he remembered, even that night at the road bridge when they broke through on the flank and we met them with bayonets in the dark. Before it had no meaning, but now I can feel again. Once more I'm alive.

Suddenly he had to be alone; he stood up.

'Ruffy.'

'Yes, boss?'

'Clean up here. Get blankets from the hotel for de Surrier and the women, also those men down in the station yard.' It was someone else speaking; he could hear the voice as though it were a long way off.

'You okay, boss?'

'Yes.'

'Your head?'

Bruce lifted his hand and touched the long dent in his helmet.

'It's nothing,' he said.

'Your leg?'

'Just a touch, get on with it.'

'Okay, boss. What shall we do with these others?'

'Throw them in the river,' said Bruce and walked out into the street. Hendry and his gendarmes were still on the verandah of the hotel, but they had started on the corpses there, using their bayonets like butchers' knives, taking the ears, laughing also the strained nervous laughter.

Bruce crossed the street to the station yard. The dawn was coming, drawing out across the sky like a sheet of steel rolled from the mill, purple and lilac at first, then red as it spread above the forest.

The Ford Ranchero stood on the station platform where he had left it. He opened the door, slid in behind the wheel, and watched the dawn become day.

– 18 –

'Captain, the sergeant major asks you to come. There is something he wants to show you.'

Bruce lifted his head from where it was resting on the steering wheel. He had not heard the gendarme approach.

'I'll come,' he said, picked up his helmet and his rifle

171

from the seat beside him and followed the man back to the office block.

His gendarmes were loading a dead man into one of the trucks, swinging him by his arms and legs.

'Un, deux, trois,' and a shout of laughter as the limp body flew over the tailboard on to the gruesome pile already there.

Sergeant Jacque came out of the office dragging a man by his heels. The head bumped loosely down the steps and there was a wet brown drag mark left on the cement verandah.

'Like pork,' Jacque called cheerily. The corpse was that of a small grey-headed man, skinny, with the marks of spectacles on the bridge of his nose and a double row of decorations on his tunic. Bruce noted that one of them was the purple and white ribbon of the military cross – strange loot for the Congo. Jacque dropped the man's heels, drew his bayonet and stooped over the man. He took one of the ears that lay flat against the grizzled skull, pulled it forward and freed it with a single stroke of the knife. The opened flesh was pink with the dark hole of the eardrum in the centre.

Bruce walked on into the office and his nostrils flared at the abattoir stench.

'Have a look at this lot, boss.' Ruffy stood by the desk.

'Enough to buy you a ranch in Hyde Park,' grinned Hendry beside him. In his hand he held a pencil. Threaded on to it like a kebab were a dozen human ears.

'Yes,' said Bruce as he looked at the pile of industrial and gem diamonds on the blotter. 'I know about those. Better count them, Ruffy, then put them back in the bags.'

'You're not going to turn them in?' protested Hendry. 'Jesus, if we share this lot three ways – you, Ruffy and I – there's enough to make us all rich.'

'Or put us against a wall,' said Bruce grimly. 'What makes

172

you think the gentlemen in Elisabethville don't know about them?' He turned his attention back to Ruffy. 'Count them and pack them. You're in charge of them. Don't lose any.'

Bruce looked across the room at the blanket-wrapped bundle that was André de Surrier.

'Have you detailed a burial squad?'

'Yes, boss. Six of the boys are out back digging.'

'Good,' Bruce nodded. 'Hendry, come with me. We'll go and have a look at the trucks.'

Half an hour later Bruce closed the bonnet of the last vehicle. 'This is the only one that won't run. The carburettor's smashed. We'll take the tyres off it for spares.' He wiped his greasy hands on the sides of his trousers. 'Thank God, the tanker is untouched. We've got six hundred gallons there, more than enough for the return trip.'

'You going to take the Ford?' asked Hendry.

'Yes, it may come in useful.'

'And it will be more comfortable for you and your little French thing.' Heavy sarcasm in Hendry's voice.

'That's right,' Bruce answered evenly. 'Can you drive?'

'What you think? You think I'm a bloody fool?'

'Everyone is always trying to get at you, aren't they? You can't trust anyone, can you?' Bruce asked softly.

'You're so bloody right!' agreed Hendry.

Bruce changed the subject. 'André had a message for you before he died.'

'Old doll boy!'

'He threw that grenade. Did you know that?'

'Yeah. I knew it.'

'Don't you want to hear what he said?'

'Once a queer, always a queer, and the only good queer is a dead queer.'

'All right.' Bruce frowned. 'Get a couple of men to help you. Fill the trucks with gas. We've wasted enough time already.'

They buried their dead in a communal grave, packing them in quickly and covering them just as quickly. Then they stood embarrassed and silent round the mound.

'You going to say anything, boss?' Ruffy asked, and they all looked at Bruce.

'No.' Bruce turned away and started for the trucks.

What the hell can you say, he thought angrily. Death is not someone to make conversation with. All you can say is, 'These were men; weak and strong, evil and good, and a lot in between. But now they're dead – like pork.'

He looked back over his shoulder.

'All right, let's move out.'

The convoy ground slowly over the causeway. Bruce led in the Ford and the air blowing in through the shattered windscreen was too humid and steamy to give relief from the rising heat.

The sun stood high above the forest as they passed the turn-off to the mission.

Bruce looked along it, and he wanted to signal the convoy to continue while he went up to St Augustine's. He wanted to see Mike Haig and Father Ignatius, make sure that they were safe.

Then he put aside the temptation. If there is more horror up there at St Augustine's, if the *shufta* have found them and there are raped women and dead men there, then there is nothing I can do and I don't want to know about it.

It is better to believe that they are safely hidden in the jungle. It is better to believe that out of all this will remain something good.

He led the convoy resolutely past the turn-off and over the hills towards the level crossing.

Suddenly another idea came to him and he thought about it, turning it over with pleasure.

Four men came to Port Reprieve, men without hope, men abandoned by God.

And they learned that it was not too late, perhaps it is never too late.

For one of them found the strength to die like a man, although he had lived his whole life with weakness.

Another rediscovered the self-respect he had lost along the way, and with it the chance to start again.

The third found – he hesitated – yes, the third found love.

And the fourth? Bruce's smile faded as he thought of Wally Hendry. It was a neat little parable, except for Wally Hendry. What had he found? A dozen human ears threaded on a pencil?

– 19 –

'Can't you get up enough steam to move us back to the crossing – only a few miles.'

'I am desolate, m'sieur. She will not hold even a belch, to say nothing of a head of steam.' The engine driver spread his pudgy little hands in a gesture of helplessness. Bruce studied the rent in the boiler. The metal was torn open like the petals of a flower. He knew it had been a forlorn request.

'Very well. Thank you.' He turned to Ruffy. 'We'll have to carry everything back to the convoy. Another day wasted.'

'It's a long walk,' Ruffy agreed. 'Better get started.'

'How much food have we?'

'Not too much. We've been feeding a lot of extra mouths, and we sent a lot out to the mission.'

'How much?'

'About two more days.'

'That should get us to Elisabethville.'

'Boss, you want to carry everything to the lorries? Searchlights, ammunition, blankets – all of it?'

175

Bruce paused for a moment. 'I think so. We may need it.'

'It's going to take the rest of the day.'

'Yes,' agreed Bruce. Ruffy walked back along the train but Bruce called after him.

'Ruffy!'

'Boss?'

'Don't forget the beer.'

Ruffy's black moon of a face split laterally into a grin.

'You think we should take it?'

'Why not?' Bruce laughed.

'Man, you talked me right into it!'

And the night was almost on them before the last of the equipment had been carried back from the abandoned train to the convoy and loaded into the trucks.

Time is a slippery thing, even more so than wealth. No bank vault can hold it for you, this precious stuff which we spend in such prodigal fashion on the trivialities. By the time we have slept and eaten and moved from one place to the next there is such a small percentage left for the real business of living.

Bruce felt futile resentment as he always did when he thought about it. And if you discount the time spent at an office desk, then how much is there left? Half of one day a week, that's how much the average man lives! That's how far short of our potential is the actuality of existence.

Take it further than that: we are capable of using only a fraction of our physical and mental strength. Only under hypnosis are we able to exert more than a tenth of what is in us. So divide that half of one day a week by ten, and the rest is waste! Sickening waste!

'Ruffy, have you detailed sentries for tonight?' Bruce barked at him.

'Not yet. I was just—'

'Well, do it, and do it quickly.'

Ruffy looked at Bruce in speculation and through his anger Bruce felt a qualm of regret that he had selected that mountain of energy on which to vent his frustration.

'Where the hell is Hendry?' he snapped.

Without speaking Ruffy pointed to a group of men round one of the trucks at the rear of the convoy and Bruce left him.

Suddenly consumed with impatience Bruce fell upon his men. Shouting at them, scattering them to a dozen different tasks. He walked along the convoy making sure that his instructions were being carried out to the letter; checking the siting of the Brens and the searchlights, making sure that the single small cooking fire was screened from Baluba eyes, stopping to watch the refuelling of the trucks and the running maintenance he had ordered. Men avoided catching his eye and bent to their tasks with studied application. There were no raised voices or sounds of laughter in the camp.

Again Bruce had decided against a night journey. The temptation itched within him, but the exhaustion of those gendarmes who had not slept since the previous morning and the danger of travelling in the dark he could not ignore.

'We'll leave as soon as it's light tomorrow,' Bruce told Ruffy.

'Okay, boss,' Ruffy nodded, and then soothingly, 'you're tired. Food's nearly ready, then you get some sleep.'

Bruce glared at him, opening his mouth to snarl a retort, and then closed it again. He turned and strode out of the camp into the forest.

He found a fallen log, sat down and lit a cigarette. It was dark now and there were only a few stars among the rain clouds that blackened the sky. He could hear the faint sounds from the camp but there were no lights – the way he had ordered it.

The fact that his anger had no focal point inflamed it rather than quenched it. It ranged restlessly until at last it found a target – himself.

He recognized the brooding undirected depression that was descending upon him. It was a thing he had not experienced for a long time, nearly two years. Not since the wreck of his marriage and the loss of his children. Not since he had stifled all emotion and trained himself not to participate in the life around him.

But now his barrier was gone, there was no sheltered harbour from the storm surf and he would have to ride it out. Furl all canvas and rig a sea anchor.

The anger was gone now. At least anger had heat but this other thing was cold; icy waves of it broke over him, and he was small and insignificant in the grip of it.

His mind turned to his children and the loneliness howled round him like a winter wind from the south. He closed his eyes and pressed his fingers against the lids. Their faces formed in the eye of his mind.

Christine with pink fat legs under her frilly skirt, and the face of a thoughtful cherub below soft hair cropped like a page boy.

'I love you best of all,' said with much seriousness, holding his face with small hands only a little sticky with ice cream.

Simon, a miniature reproduction of Bruce even to the nose. Scabs on the knees and dirt on the face. No demonstrations of affection from him, but in its place something much better, a companionship far beyond his six years. Long discussions on everything from religion, 'Why didn't Jesus used to shave?' to politics, 'When are you going to be prime minister, Dad?'

And the loneliness was a tangible thing now, like the coils of a reptile squeezing his chest. Bruce ground out the cigarette beneath his heel and tried to find refuge in his hatred for the woman who had been his wife. The woman who had taken them from him.

But his hatred was a cold thing also, dead ash with a stale taste. For he knew that the blame was not all hers. It was another of his failures; perhaps if I had tried harder, perhaps if I had left some of the cruel things unsaid, perhaps – yes, it might have been, and perhaps and maybe. But it was not. It was over and finished and now I am alone. There is no worse condition; no state beyond loneliness. It is the waste land and the desolation.

Something moved near him in the night, a soft rustle of grass, a presence felt rather than seen. And Bruce stiffened. His right hand closed over his rifle. He brought it up slowly, his eyes straining into the darkness.

The movement again, closer now. A twig popped under-foot. Bruce slowly trained his rifle round to cover it, pressure on the trigger and his thumb on the safety. Stupid to have wandered away from the camp; asking for it, and now he had got it. Baluba tribesmen! He could see the figure now in the dimness of starlight, stealthily moving across his front. How many of them, he wondered. If I hit this one, there could be a dozen others with him. Have to take a chance. One quick burst and then run for it. A hundred yards to the camp, about an even chance. The figure was stationary now, standing listening. Bruce could see the outline of the head – no helmet, can't be one of us. He raised the rifle and pointed it. Too dark to see the sights, but at that range he couldn't miss. Bruce drew his breath softly, filling his lungs, ready to shoot and run.

'Bruce?' Shermaine's voice, frightened, almost a whisper. He threw up the rifle barrel. God, that was close. He had nearly killed her.

'Yes, I'm here.' His own voice was scratchy with the shock of realization.

'Oh, there you are.'

'What the hell are you doing out of the camp?' he demanded furiously as anger replaced his shock.

'I'm sorry, Bruce, I came to see if you were all right. You were gone such a long time.'

'Well, get back to the camp, and don't try any more tricks like that.'

There was a long silence, and then she spoke softly, unable to keep the hurt out of her tone.

'I brought you something to eat. I thought you'd be hungry. I'm sorry if I did wrong.'

She came to him, stooped and placed something on the ground in front of him. Then she turned and was gone.

'Shermaine.' He wanted her back, but the only reply was the fading rustle of the grass and then silence. He was alone again.

He picked up the plate of food.

You fool, he thought. You stupid, ignorant, thoughtless fool. You'll lose her, and you'll have deserved it. You deserve everything you've had, and more.

You never learn, do you, Curry? You never learn that there is a penalty for selfishness and for thoughtlessness.

He looked down at the plate in his hands. Bully beef and sliced onion, bread and cheese.

Yes, I have learned, he answered himself with sudden determination. I will not spoil this, this thing that is between this girl and me. That was the last time; now I am a man I will put away childish things, like temper and self-pity.

He ate the food, suddenly aware of his hunger. He ate quickly, wolfing it. Then he stood up and walked back to the camp.

A sentry challenged him on the perimeter and Bruce answered with alacrity. At night his gendarmes were very quick on the trigger; the challenge was an unusual courtesy.

'It is unwise to go alone into the forest in the darkness,' the sentry reprimanded him.

'Why?' Bruce felt his mood changing. The depression evaporated.

'It is unwise,' repeated the man vaguely.

'The spirits?' Bruce teased him delicately.

'An aunt of my sister's husband disappeared not a short throw of a spear from my hut. There was no trace, no shout, nothing. I was there. It is not a matter for doubt,' said the man with dignity.

'A lion perhaps?' Bruce prodded him.

'If you say so, then it is so. I know what I know. But I say only that there is no wisdom in defying the custom of the land.'

Suddenly touched by the man's concern for him, Bruce dropped a hand on to his shoulder and gripped it in the old expression of affection.

'I will remember. I did it without thinking.'

He walked into the camp. The incident had confirmed something he had vaguely suspected, but in which previously he had felt no interest. The men liked him. A hundred similar indications of this fact he had only half noted, not caring one way or the other. But now it gave him intense pleasure, fully compensating for the loneliness he had just experienced.

He walked past the little group of men round the cooking fire to where the Ford stood at the head of the convoy. Peering through the side window he could make out Shermaine's blanket-wrapped form on the back seat. He tapped on the glass and she sat up and rolled down the window.

'Yes?' she asked coolly.

'Thank you for the food.'

'It is nothing.' The slightest hint of warmth in her voice.

'Shermaine, sometimes I say things I do not mean. You startled me. I nearly shot you.'

'It was my fault. I should not have followed you.'

'I was rude,' he persisted.

'Yes.' She laughed now. That husky little chuckle. 'You were rude but with good reason. We shall forget it.' She placed her hand on his arm. 'You must rest, you haven't slept for two days.'

'Will you ride in the Ford with me tomorrow to show that I am forgiven?'

'Of course,' she nodded.

'Good night, Shermaine.'

'Good night, Bruce,'

No, Bruce decided as he spread his blankets beside the fire, I am not alone. Not any more.

– 20 –

'What about breakfast, boss?'

'They can eat on the road. Give them a tin of bully each – we've wasted enough time on this trip.'

The sky was paling and pinking above the forest. It was light enough to read the dial of his wristwatch. Twenty minutes to five.

'Get them moving, Ruffy. If we make Msapa Junction before dark we can drive through the night. Home for breakfast tomorrow.'

'Now you're talking, boss.' Ruffy clapped his helmet on to his head and went off to rouse the men who lay in the road beside the trucks.

Shermaine was asleep. Bruce leaned into the window of the Ford and studied her face. A wisp of hair lay over her mouth, rising and falling with her breathing. It tickled her nose and in her sleep it twitched like a rabbit.

Bruce felt an almost unbearable pang of tenderness towards her. With one finger he lifted the hair off her face. Then he smiled at himself.

If you can feel like this before breakfast, then you've got it in a bad way, he told himself.

Do you know something, he retorted. I like the feeling.

'Hey, you lazy wench!' He pulled the lobe of her ear. 'Time to wake up.'

It was almost half past five before the convoy got under way. It had taken that long to bully and cajole the sleep out of sixty men and get them into the lorries. This morning Bruce did not find the delay unbearable. He had managed to find time for four hours' sleep during the night. Four hours was not nearly enough to make up for the previous two days.

Now he felt light-headed, a certain unreal quality of gaiety overlaying his exhaustion, a carnival spirit. There was no longer the same urgency, for the road to Elisabethville was clear and not too long. Home for breakfast tomorrow!

'We'll be at the bridge in a little under an hour.' He glanced sideways at Shermaine.

'You've left a guard on it?'

'Ten men,' answered Bruce. 'We'll pick them up almost without stopping, and then the next stop, room 201, Grand Hotel Leopold II, Avenue du Kasai.' He grinned in anticipation. 'A bath so deep it will slop over on to the floor, so hot it will take five minutes to get into it. Clean clothes. A steak that thick, with French salad and a bottle of Liebfraumilch.'

'For breakfast!' protested Shermaine.

'For breakfast,' Bruce agreed happily. He was silent for a while, savouring the idea. The road ahead of him was tiger-striped with the shadows of the trees thrown by the low sun. The air that blew in through the missing windscreen was cool and clean-smelling. He felt good. The responsibility of command lay lightly on his shoulders this morning; a pretty girl beside him, a golden morning, the horror of the last few days half-forgotten – they might have been going on a picnic.

'What are you thinking?' he asked suddenly. She was very quiet beside him.

'I was wondering about the future,' she answered softly. 'There is no one I know in Elisabethville, and I do not wish to stay there.'

'Will you return to Brussels?' he asked. The question was without significance, for Bruce Curry had very definite plans for the immediate future, and these included Shermaine.

'Yes, I think so. There is nowhere else.'

'You have relatives there?'

'An aunt.'

'Are you close?'

Shermaine laughed, but there was bitterness in the husky chuckle. 'Oh, very close. She came to see me once at the orphanage. Once in all those years. She brought me a comic book of a religious nature and told me to clean my teeth and brush my hair a hundred strokes a day.'

'There is no one else?' asked Bruce.

'No.'

'Then why go back?'

'What else is there to do?' she asked. 'Where else is there to go?'

'There's a life to live, and the rest of the world to visit.'

'Is that what you are going to do?'

'That is exactly what I'm going to do, starting with a hot bath.'

Bruce could feel it between them. They both knew it was there, but it was too soon to talk about it. I have only kissed her once, but that was enough. So what will happen? Marriage? His mind shied away from that word with startling violence, then came hesitantly back to examine it. Stalking it as though it were a dangerous beast, ready to take flight again as soon as it showed its teeth.

For some people it is a good thing. It can stiffen the spineless; ease the lonely; give direction to the wanderers; spur those without ambition – and, of course, there was the final unassailable argument in its favour. Children.

But there are some who can only sicken and shrivel in the colourless cell of matrimony. With no space to fly, your wings must weaken with disuse; turned inwards, your eyes become short-sighted; when all your communication with the rest of the world is through the glass windows of the cell, then your contact is limited.

And I already have children. I have a daughter and I have a son.

Bruce turned his eyes from the road and studied the girl beside him. There is no fault I can find. She is beautiful in the delicate, almost fragile way that is so much better and longer-lived than blond hair and big bosoms. She is unspoilt; hardship has long been her travelling companion and from it she has learned kindness and humility.

She is mature, knowing the ways of this world; knowing death and fear, the evilness of men and their goodness. I do not believe she has ever lived in the fairy-tale cocoon that most young girls spin about themselves.

And yet she has not forgotten how to laugh.

Perhaps, he thought, perhaps. But it is too soon to talk about it.

'You are very grim.' Shermaine broke the silence, but the laughter shivered just below the surface of her voice. 'Again you are Bonaparte. And when you are grim your nose is too big and cruel. It is a nose of great brutality and it does not fit the rest of your face. I think that when they had finished you they had only one nose left in stock. "It is too big," they said, "but it is the only nose left, and when he smiles it will not look too bad." So they took a chance and stuck it on anyway.'

'Were you never taught that it is bad manners to poke fun at a man's weakness?' Bruce fingered his nose ruefully.

'Your nose is many things, but not weak. Never weak.' She laughed now and moved a little closer to him.

'You know you can attack me from behind your own perfect nose, and I cannot retaliate.'

'Never trust a man who makes pretty speeches so easily, because he surely makes them to every girl he meets.' She slid an inch further across the seat until they were almost touching. 'You waste your talents, mon capitaine. I am immune to your charm.'

'In just one minute I will stop this car and—'

'You cannot.' Shermaine jerked her head to indicate the two gendarmes in the seat behind them. 'What would they think, Bonaparte? It would be very bad for discipline.'

'Discipline or no discipline, in just one minute I will stop this car and spank you soundly before I kiss you.'

'One threat does not frighten me, but because of the other I will leave your poor nose.' She moved away a little and once more Bruce studied her face. Beneath the frank scrutiny she fidgeted and started to blush.

'Do you mind! Were you never taught that it is bad manners to stare?'

So now I am in love again, thought Bruce. This is only the third time, an average of once every ten years or so. It frightens me a little because there is always pain with it. The exquisite pain of loving and the agony of losing.

It starts in the loins and it is very deceptive because you think it is only the old thing, the tightness and tension that any well-rounded stern or cheeky pair of breasts will give you. Scratch it, you think, it's just a small itch. Spread a little of the warm salve on it and it will be gone in no time.

But suddenly it spreads, upwards and downwards, all through you. The pit of your stomach feels hot, then the flutters round the heart. It's dangerous now; once it gets this far it's incurable and you can scratch and scratch but all you do is inflame it.

Then the last stages, when it attacks the brain. No pain

there, that's the worst sign. A heightening of the senses; your eyes are sharper, your blood runs too fast, food tastes good, your mouth wants to shout and legs want to run. Then the delusions of grandeur: you are the cleverest, strongest, most masculine male in the universe, and you stand ten feet tall in your socks.

How tall are you now, Curry, he asked himself. About nine feet six and I weigh twenty stone, he answered, and almost laughed aloud.

And how does it end? It ends with words. Words can kill anything. It ends with cold words; words like fire that stick in the structure and take hold and lick it up, blackening and charring it, bringing it down in smoking ruins.

It ends in suspicion of things not done, and in the certainty of things done and remembered. It ends with selfishness and carelessness, and words, always words.

It ends with pain and greyness, and it leaves scar tissue and damage that will never heal.

Or it ends without fuss and fury. It just crumbles and blows away like dust on the wind. But there is still the agony of loss.

Both these endings I know well, for I have loved twice, and now I love again.

Perhaps this time it does not have to be that way. Perhaps this time it will last. Nothing is for ever, he thought. Nothing is for ever, not even life, and perhaps this time if I cherish it and tend it carefully it will last that long, as long as life.

'We are nearly at the bridge,' said Shermaine beside him, and Bruce started. The miles had dropped unseen behind them and now the forest was thickening. It crouched closer to the earth, greener and darker along the river.

Bruce slowed the Ford and the forest became dense bush around them, the road a tunnel through it. They came round one last bend in the track and out of the tunnel of green vegetation into the clearing where the road met the railway line and ran beside it on to the heavy timber platform of the bridge.

Bruce stopped the Ranchero, switched off the engine and they all sat silently, staring out at the solid jungle on the far bank with its screen of creepers and monkey-ropes hanging down, trailing the surface of the deep green swift-flowing river. They stared at the stumps of the bridge thrusting out from each bank towards each other like the arms of parted lovers; at the wide gap between with the timbers still smouldering and the smoke drifting away downstream over the green water.

'It's gone,' said Shermaine. 'It's been burnt.'

'Oh, no,' groaned Bruce. 'Oh, God, no!'

With an effort he pulled his eyes from the charred remains of the bridge and turned them on to the jungle about them, a hundred feet away, ringing them in. Hostile, silent. 'Don't get out of the car,' he snapped as Shermaine reached for the door handle. 'Roll your window up, quickly.'

She obeyed.

'They're waiting in there.' He pointed at the edge of the jungle.

Behind them the first of the convoy came round the bend into the clearing. Bruce jumped from the Ford and ran back towards the leading truck.

'Don't get out, stay inside,' he shouted and ran on down the line, repeating the instruction to each of them as he passed. When he reached Ruffy's cab he jumped on to the running board, jerked the door open, slipped in on to the seat and slammed the door.

'They've burnt the bridge.'

'What's happened to the boys we left to guard it?'

'I don't know but we'll find out. Pull up alongside the others so that I can talk to them.'

Through the half-open window he issued his orders to each of the drivers and within ten minutes all the vehicles had been manoeuvred into the tight defensive circle of the laager, a formation Bruce's ancestors had used a hundred years before.

'Ruffy, get out those tarpaulins and spread them over the top to form a roof. We don't want them dropping arrows in amongst us.'

Ruffy selected half a dozen gendarmes and they went to work, dragging out the heavy folded canvas.

'Hendry, put a couple of men under each truck. Set up the Brens in case they try to rush us.'

In the infectious urgency of defence, Wally did not make his usual retort, but gathered his men. They wriggled on their stomachs under the vehicles, rifles pointed out towards the silent jungle.

'I want the extinguishers here in the middle so we can get them in a hurry. They might use fire again.'

Two gendarmes ran to each of the cabs and unclipped the fire-extinguishers from the dashboards.

'What can I do?' Shermaine was standing beside Bruce.

'Keep quiet and stay out of the way,' said Bruce as he turned and hurried across to help Ruffy's gang with the tarpaulins.

It took them half an hour of desperate endeavour before they completed the fortifications to Bruce's satisfaction.

'That should hold them.' Bruce stood with Ruffy and Hendry in the centre of the laager and surveyed the green canvas roof above them and the closely packed vehicles around them. The Ford was parked beside the tanker, not included in the outer ring for its comparative size would have made it a weak point in the defence.

'It's going to be bloody hot and crowded in here,' grumbled Hendry.

'Yes, I know.' Bruce looked at him. 'Would you like to relieve the congestion by waiting outside?'

'Funny boy, big laugh,' answered Wally.

'What now, boss?' Ruffy put into words the question Bruce had been asking himself.

'You and I will go and take a look at the bridge,' he said.

'You'll look a rare old sight with an arrow sticking out of your jack,' grinned Wally. 'Boy, that's going to kill me!'

'Ruffy, get us half a dozen gas capes each. I doubt their arrows will go through them at a range of a hundred feet, and of course we'll wear helmets.'

'Okay, boss.'

It was like being in a sauna bath beneath the six layers of rubberized canvas. Bruce could feel the sweat squirting from his pores with each pace, and rivulets of it coursing down his back and flanks as he and Ruffy left the laager and walked up the road to the bridge.

Beside him Ruffy's bulk was so enhanced by the gas capes that he reminded Bruce of a prehistoric monster reaching the end of its gestation period.

'Warm enough, Ruffy?' he asked, feeling the need for humour. The ring of jungle made him nervous. Perhaps he had underestimated the carry of a Baluba arrow – despite the light reed shaft, they used iron heads, barbed viciously and ground to a needle point, and poison smeared thickly between the barbs.

'Man, look at me shiver,' grunted Ruffy and the sweat greased down his jowls and dripped from his chin.

Long before they reached the access to the bridge the stench of putrefaction crept out to meet them. In Bruce's mind every smell had its own colour, and this one was green, the same green as the sheen of putrefaction on rotting meat. The stench was so heavy he could almost feel it bearing down on them, choking in his throat and coating his tongue and the roof of his mouth with the oily over-sweetness.

'No doubt what that is!' Ruffy spat, trying to get the taste out of his mouth.

'Where are they?' gagged Bruce, starting to pant from the heat and the effort of breathing the fouled air.

They reached the bank and Bruce's question was answered as they looked down on to the narrow beach.

There were the black remains of a dozen cooking fires along the water's edge, and closer to the high bank were two crude structures of poles. For a moment their purpose puzzled Bruce and then he realized what they were. He had seen those crosspieces suspended between two uprights often before in hunting camps throughout Africa. They were paunching racks! At intervals along the crosspieces were the bark ropes that had been used to string up the game, heels first, with head and forelegs dangling and belly bulging forward so that at the long abdominal stroke of the knife the viscera would drop out easily.

But the game they had butchered on *these* racks were men, his men. He counted the hanging ropes. There were ten of them, so no one had escaped.

'Cover me, Ruffy. I'm going down to have a look.' It was a penance Bruce was imposing upon himself. They were his men, and he had left them there.

'Okay, boss.'

Bruce clambered down the well-defined path to the beach. Now the smell was almost unbearable and he found the source of it. Between the racks lay a dark shapeless mass. It moved with flies; its surface moved, trembled, crawled with flies. Suddenly, humming, they lifted in a cloud from the pile of human debris, and then settled once more upon it.

A single fly buzzed round Bruce's head and then settled on his hand. Metallic blue body, wings cocked back, it crouched on his skin and gleefully rubbed its front legs together. Bruce's throat and stomach convulsed as he began to retch. He struck at the fly and it darted away.

There were bones scattered round the cooking fires and a skull lay near his feet, split open to yield its contents.

Another spasm took Bruce and this time the vomit came

up into his mouth, acid and warm. He swallowed it, turned away and scrambled up the bank to where Ruffy waited. He stood there gasping, suppressing his nausea until at last he could speak.

'All right, that's all I wanted to know,' and he led the way back to the circle of vehicles.

Bruce sat on the bonnet of the Ranchero and sucked hard on his cigarette, trying to get the taste of death from his mouth.

'They probably swam downstream during the night and climbed the supports of the bridge. Kanaki and his boys wouldn't have known anything about it until they came over the sides.' He drew on the cigarette again and trickled the smoke out of his nostrils, fumigating the back of his throat and his nasal passages. 'I should have thought of that. I should have warned Kanaki of that.'

'You mean they ate all ten of them – Jesus!' even Wally Hendry was impressed. 'I'd like to have a look at that beach. It must be quite something.'

'Good!' Bruce's voice was suddenly harsh. 'I'll put you in charge of the burial squad. You can go down there and clean it up before we start work on the bridge.' And Wally did not argue.

'You want me to do it now?' he asked.

'No,' snapped Bruce. 'You and Ruffy are going to take two of the trucks back to Port Reprieve and fetch the materials we need to repair the bridge.'

They both looked at Bruce with rising delight.

'I never thought of that,' said Wally.

'There's plenty of roofing timber in the hotel and the office block,' grinned Ruffy.

'Nails,' said Wally as though he were making a major contribution. 'We'll need nails.'

Bruce cut through their comments. 'It's two o'clock

now. You can get back to Port Reprieve by nightfall, collect the material tomorrow morning and return here by the evening. Take those two trucks there — check to see they're full of gas and you'll need about fifteen men. Say, five gendarmes, in case of trouble, and ten of those civilians.'

'That should be enough,' agreed Ruffy.

'Bring a couple of dozen sheets of corrugated iron back with you. We'll use them to make a shield to protect us from arrows while we're working.'

'Yeah, that's a good idea.'

They settled the details, picked men to go back, loaded the trucks, worked them out of the laager, and Bruce watched them disappear down the road towards Port Reprieve. An ache started deep behind his eyes and suddenly he was very tired, drained of energy by too little sleep, by the heat and by the emotional pace of the last four days. He made one last circuit of the laager, checking the defences, chatting for a few minutes with his gendarmes and then he stumbled to the Ford, slid on to the front seat, laid his helmet and rifle aside, lowered his head on to his arms and was instantly asleep.

– 21 –

Shermaine woke him after dark with food unheated from the cans and a bottle of Ruffy's beer.

'I'm sorry, Bruce, we have no fire to cook upon. It is very unappetizing and the beer is warm.'

Bruce sat up and rubbed his eyes. Six hours' sleep had helped; they were less swollen and inflamed. The headache was still there.

'I'm not really hungry, thank you. It's this heat.'

'You must eat, Bruce. Try just a little,' and then she smiled. 'At least you are more gallant after having rested. It

193

is "Thank you" now, instead of "Keep quiet and stay out of the way".'

Ruefully Bruce grimaced. 'You are one of those women with a built-in recording unit; every word remembered and used in evidence against a man later.' Then he touched her hand. 'I'm sorry.'

'I'm sorry,' she repeated. 'I like your apologies, mon capitaine. They are like the rest of you, completely masculine. There is nothing about you which is not male, sometimes almost overpoweringly so.' Impishly she watched his eyes; he knew she was talking about the little scene on the train that Wally Hendry had interrupted.

'Let's try this food,' he said, and then a little later, 'not bad – you are an excellent cook.'

'This time the credit must go to M. Heinz and his fifty-seven children. But one day I shall make for you one of my tournedos au Prince. It is my special.'

'Speciality,' Bruce corrected her automatically.

The murmur of voices within the laager was punctuated occasionally by a burst of laughter. There was a feeling of relaxation. The canvas roof and the wall of vehicles gave security to them all. Men lay in dark huddles of sleep or talked quietly in small groups.

Bruce scraped the metal plate and filled his mouth with the last of the food.

'Now I must check the defences again.'

'Oh, Bonaparte. It is always duty.' Shermaine sighed with resignation.

'I will not be long.'

'And I'll wait here for you.'

Bruce picked up his rifle and helmet, and was half-way out of the Ford when out in the jungle the drum started.

'Bruce!' whispered Shermaine and clutched his arm. The voices round them froze into a fearful silence, and the drum beat in the night. It had a depth and resonance that you could feel; the warm sluggish air quivered with it. Not fixed in space but filling it, beating monotonously, insistently, like the pulse of all creation.

'Bruce!' whispered Shermaine again; she was trembling and the fingers on his arm dug into his flesh with the strength of terror. It steadied his own leap of fear.

'Baby, baby,' he soothed her, taking her to his chest and holding her there. 'It's only the sound of two pieces of wood being knocked together by a naked savage. They can't touch us here, you know that.'

'Oh, Bruce, it's horrible – it's like bells, funeral bells.'

'That's silly talk.' Bruce held her at arm's length. 'Come with me. Help me calm down these others, they'll be terrified. You'll have to help me.'

And he pulled her gently across the seat out of the Ford, and with one arm round her waist walked her into the centre of the laager.

What will counteract the stupefying influence of the drum, the hypnotic beat of it, he asked himself. Noise, our own noise.

'Joseph, M'pophu—' he shouted cheerfully picking out the two best singers amongst his men. 'I regret the drumming is of a low standard, but the Baluba are monkeys with no understanding of music. Let us show them how a Bambala can sing.'

They stirred; he could feel the tension diminish.

'Come, Joseph—' He filled his lungs and shouted the opening chorus of one of the planting songs, purposely off-key, singing so badly that it must sting them.

Someone laughed, then Joseph's voice hesitantly starting the chorus, gathering strength. M'pophu coming in with the bass to give a solid foundation to the vibrant, sweet-ringing tenor. Half-beat to the drum, hands clapped in the dark; around him Bruce could feel the rhythmic swinging of bodies begin.

Shermaine was no longer trembling; he squeezed her waist and felt her body cling to him.

Now we need light, thought Bruce. A night lamp for my children who fear the darkness and the drum.

With Shermaine beside him he crossed the laager.

'Sergeant Jacque.'

'Captain?'

'You can start sweeping with the searchlights.'

'Oui, Captain.' The answer was less subdued. There were two spare batteries for each light, Bruce knew. Eight hours' life in each, so they would last tonight and tomorrow night.

From each side of the laager the beams leapt out, solid white shafts through the darkness; they played along the edge of the jungle and reflected back, lighting the interior of the laager sufficiently to make out the features of each man. Bruce looked at their faces. They're all right now, he decided, the ghosts have gone away.

'Bravo, Bonaparte,' said Shermaine, and Bruce became aware of the grins on the faces of his men as they saw him embracing her. He was about to drop his arm, then stopped himself. The hell with it, he decided, give them something else to think about. He led her back to the Ford.

'Tired?' he asked.

'A little,' she nodded.

'I'll fold down the seat for you. A blanket over the windows will give you privacy.'

'You'll stay close?' she asked quickly.

'I'll be right outside.' He unbuckled the webbing belt that carried his pistol. 'You'd better wear this from now on.'

Even at its minimum adjustment the belt was too large for her and the pistol hung down almost to her knee.

'The Maid of Orleans.' Bruce revenged himself. She pulled a face at him and crawled into the back of the station wagon.

A long while later she called softly above the singing and the throb of the drum.

'Bruce.'

'Yes?'

'I wanted to make sure you were there. Good night.'

'Good night, Shermaine.'

Bruce lay on a single blanket and sweated. The singing had long ago ceased but the drum went on and on, never faltering, throb-throb-throbbing out of the jungle. The searchlights swept regularly back and forth, at times lighting the laager clearly and at others leaving it in shadow. Bruce could hear around him the soft sounds of sleep, the sawing of breath, a muted cough, a gabbled sentence, the stirring of dreamers.

But Bruce could not sleep. He lay on his back with one hand under his head, smoking, staring up at the canvas. The events of the preceding four days ran through his mind: snatches of conversation, André dying. Boussier standing with his wife, the bursting of grenades, blood sticky on his hands, the smell of death, the violence and the horror.

He moved restlessly, flicked away his cigarette and covered his eyes with his hands as though to shut out the memories. But they went on flickering through his mind like the images of a gigantic movie projector, confused now, losing all meaning but retaining the horror.

He remembered the fly upon his arm, grinning at him, rubbing its legs together, gloating, repulsive. He rolled his head from side to side on the blanket.

I'm going mad, he thought, I must stop this.

He sat up quickly hugging his knees to his chest and the memories faded. But now he was sad, and alone. So terribly alone, so lost, so without purpose.

He sat alone on the blanket and he felt himself shrinking, becoming small and frightened.

I'm going to cry, he thought, I can feel it there heavy in my throat. And like a hurt child crawling into its mother's lap, Bruce Curry groped his way over the tailboard of the station wagon to Shermaine.

'Shermaine!' he whispered, blindly, searching for her.

'Bruce, what is it?' She sat up quickly. She had not been sleeping either.

'Where are you?' There was panic in Bruce's voice.

'Here I am – what's the matter?'

And he found her; clumsily he caught her to him.

'Hold me, Shermaine, please hold me.'

'Darling.' She was anxious. 'What is it? Tell me, my darling.'

'Just hold me, Shermaine. Don't talk.' He clung to her, pressing his face into her neck. 'I need you so much – oh, God! How I need you!'

'Bruce.' She understood, and her fingers were at the nape of his neck, stroking, soothing.

'My Bruce,' she said and held him. Instinctively her body began to rock, gentling him as though he were her child.

Slowly his body relaxed, and he sighed against her – a gusty broken sound.

'My Bruce, my Bruce.' She lifted the thin cotton vest that was all she wore and, instinctively in the ageless ritual of comfort, she gave him her breasts. Holding his mouth to them with both her arms clasped around his neck, her head bowed protectively over his, her hair falling forward and covering them both.

With the hard length of his body against hers, with the soft tugging at her bosom, and in the knowledge that she was giving strength to the man she loved, she realized she had never known happiness before this moment. Then his body was no longer quiescent; she felt her own mood change, a new urgency.

'Oh yes, Bruce, yes!' Speaking up into his mouth, his hungry hunting mouth and he above her, no longer child, but full man again.

'So beautiful, so warm.' His voice was strangely husky, she shuddered with the intensity of her own need.

'Quickly, Bruce, oh, Bruce.' His cruel loving hands, seeking, finding.

'Oh, Bruce – quickly,' and she reached up for him with her hips.

'I'll hurt you.'

'No – yes, I want the pain.' She felt the resistance to him within her and cried out impatiently against it.

'Go through!' and then, 'Ah! It burns.'

'I'll stop.'

'No, No!'

'Darling. It's too much.'

'Yes – I can't – oh, Bruce. My heart – you've touched my heart.'

Her clenched fists drumming on his back. And in to press against the taut, reluctantly yielding springiness, away, then back, away, and back to touch the core of all existence, leave it, and come long gliding back to it, nuzzle it, feel it tilt, then come away, then back once more. Welling slowly upwards scalding, no longer to be contained, with pain almost – and gone, and gone, and gone.

'I'm falling. Oh, Bruce! Bruce! Bruce!'

Into the gulf together – gone, all gone. Nothing left, no time, no space, no bottom to the gulf.

Nothing and everything. Complete.

Out in the jungle the drum kept beating.

Afterwards, long afterwards, she slept with her head on his arm and her face against his chest. And he unsleeping listened to her sleep. The sound of it was soft, so gentle breathing soft that you could not hear it unless you listened very carefully – or unless you loved her, he thought.

Yes. I think I love this woman – but I must be certain. In fairness to her and to myself I must be entirely certain, for I cannot live through another time like the last, and because I love her I don't want her to take the terrible wounding of a bad marriage. Better, much better to leave it now, unless it has the strength to endure.

Bruce rolled his head slowly until his face was in her hair, and the girl nuzzled his chest in her sleep.

But it is so hard to tell, he thought. It is so hard to tell at the beginning. It is so easy to confuse pity or loneliness with love, but I cannot afford to do that now. So I must try to think clearly about my marriage to Joan. It will be difficult, but I must try.

Was it like this with Joan in the beginning? It was so long ago, seven years, that I do not know, he answered truthfully. All I have left from those days are the pictures of places and the small heaps of words that have struck where the wind and the pain could not blow them away.

A beach with the sea mist coming in across it, a whole tree of driftwood half buried in the sand and bleached white with the salt, a basket of strawberries bought along the road, so that when I kissed her I could taste the sweet tartness of the fruit on her lips.

I remember a tune that we sang together, 'The mission bells told me that I mustn't stay, South of the border, down Mexico way.' I have forgotten most of the words.

And I remember vaguely how her body was, and the shape of her breasts before the children were born.

But that is all I have left from the good times.

The other memories are clear, stinging, whiplash clear. Each ugly word, and the tone in which it was said. The sound of sobbing in the night, the way it dragged itself on for three long grey years after it was mortally wounded, and both of us using all our strength to keep it moving because of the children.

The children! Oh, God, I mustn't think about them now. It hurts too much. Without the children to complicate it, I must think about her for the last time; I must end this woman Joan. So now finally and for all to end this woman who made me cry. I do not hate her for the man with whom she went away. She deserved another try for happiness. But I hate her for my children and for making shabby the love that I could have given Shermaine as a new thing. Also, I pity her for her inability to find the happiness for which she hunts so fiercely. I pity her for her coldness of body and of mind, I pity her for her prettiness that is now almost gone (it goes round her eyes first, cracking like oil paint) and I pity her for her consuming selfishness which will lose her the love of her children.

My children – not hers! My children!

That is all, that is an end to Joan, and now I have Shermaine who is none of the things that Joan was. I also deserve another try.

'Shermaine,' he whispered and turned her head slightly to kiss her. 'Shermaine, wake up.'

She stirred and murmured against him.

'Wake up.' He took the lobe of her ear between his teeth and bit it gently. Her eyes opened.

'Bon matin, madame.' He smiled at her.

'Bonjour, monsieur,' she answered and closed her eyes to press her face once more against his chest.

'Wake up. I have something to tell you.'

'I am awake, but tell me first if I am still dreaming. I have a certainty that this cannot be reality.'

'You are not dreaming.'

She sighed softly, and held him closer.

'Now tell me the other thing.'

'I love you,' he said.

'No. Now I am dreaming.'

'In truth,' he said.

'No, do not wake me. I could not bear to wake now.'

'And you?' he asked.

'You know it—' she answered. 'I do not have to tell you.'

'It is almost morning,' he said. 'There is only a little time.'

'Then I will fill that little time with saying it—' He held her and listened to her whispering it to him.

No, he thought, now I am certain. I could not be that wrong. This is my woman.

– 22 –

The drum stopped with the dawn. And after it the silence was very heavy, and it was no relief.

They had grown accustomed to that broken rhythm and now in some strange way they missed it.

As Bruce moved around the laager he could sense the uneasiness in his men. There was a feeling of dread anticipation on them all. They moved with restraint, as though they did not want to draw attention to themselves. The laughter with which they acknowledged his jokes was nervous, quickly cut off, as though they had laughed in a cathedral. And their eyes kept darting back towards the ring of jungle.

Bruce found himself wishing for an attack. His own nerves were rubbed sensitive by contact with the fear all around him.

If only they would come, he told himself. If only they would show themselves and we could see men not phantoms.

But the jungle was silent. It seemed to wait, it watched them. They could feel the gaze of hidden eyes. Its malignant presence pressed closer as the heat built up.

Bruce walked across the laager to the south side, trying to move casually. He smiled at Sergeant Jacque, squatted beside him and peered from under the truck across open ground at the remains of the bridge.

'Trucks will be back soon,' he said. 'Won't take long to repair that.'

Jacque did not answer. There was a worried frown on his high intelligent forehead and his face was shiny with perspiration.

'It's the waiting, Captain. It softens the stomach.'

'They will be back soon,' repeated Bruce. If this one is worried, and he is the best of them, then the others must be almost in a jelly of dread.

Bruce looked at the face of the man on the other side of Jacque. Its expression shrieked with fear.

If they attack now, God knows how it will turn out. An African can think himself to death, they just lie down and die. They are getting to that stage now; if an attack comes they will either go berserk or curl up and wail with fear. You can never tell.

Be honest with yourself – you're not entirely happy either, are you? No, Bruce agreed, it's the waiting does it.

It came from the edge of the clearing on the far side of the laager. A high-pitched inhuman sound, angry, savage.

Bruce felt his heart trip and he spun round to face it. For a second the whole laager seemed to cringe from it.

It came again. Like a whip across aching nerves. Immediately it was lost in the roar of twenty rifles.

Bruce laughed. Threw his head back and let it come from the belly.

The gunfire stammered into silence and others were laughing also. The men who had fired grinned sheepishly and made a show of reloading.

It was not the first time that Bruce had been startled by the cry of a yellow hornbill. But now he recognized his laughter and the laughter of the men around him, a mild form of hysteria.

'Did you want the feathers for your hat?' someone shouted and the laughter swept round the laager.

The tension relaxed as the banter was tossed back and forth. Bruce stood up and brought his own laughter under control.

No harm done, he decided. For the price of fifty rounds of ammunition, a purchase of an hour's escape from tension. A good bargain.

He walked across to Shermaine. She was smiling also.

'How is the catering section?' He grinned at her. 'What miracle of the culinary art is there for lunch?'

'Bully beef.'

'And onions?'

'No, just bully beef. The onions are finished.'

Bruce stopped smiling.

'How much is left?' he asked.

'One case – enough to last till lunchtime tomorrow.'

It would take at least two days to complete the repairs to the bridge; another day's travel after that.

'Well,' he said, 'we should all have healthy appetites by the time we get home. You'll have to try and spread it out. Half rations from now on.'

He was so engrossed in the study of this new complication that he did not notice the faint hum from outside the laager.

'Captain,' called Jacques. 'Can you hear it?'

Bruce inclined his head and listened.

'The trucks!' His voice was loud with relief, and instantly there was an excited murmur round the laager.

The waiting was over.

They came growling out of the bush into the clearing. Heavily loaded, timber and sheet-iron protruding backwards from under the canopies, sitting low on their suspensions.

Ruffy leaned from the cab of the leading truck and shouted.

'Hello boss. Where shall we dump?'

'Take it up to the bridge. Hang on a second and I'll come with you.'

Bruce slipped out of the laager and crossed quickly to Ruffy's truck. He could feel his back tingling while he was in the open and he slammed the door behind him with relief.

'I don't relish stopping an arrow,' he said.

'You have any trouble while we were gone?'

'No,' Bruce told him. 'But they're here. They were drumming in the jungle all night.'

'Calling up their buddies,' grunted Ruffy and let out the clutch. 'We'll have some fun before we finish this bridge. Most probably take them a day or two to get brave, but in the end they'll have a go at us.'

'Pull over to the side of the bridge, Ruffy,' Bruce instructed and rolled down his window. 'I'll signal Hendry to pull in beside us. We'll off-load into the space between the two trucks and start building the corrugated iron shield there.'

While Hendry manoeuvred his truck alongside, Bruce forced himself to look down on the carnage of the beach.

'Crocodiles,' he exclaimed with relief. The paunching racks still stood as he had last seen them, but the reeking pile of human remains was gone. The smell and the flies, however, still lingered.

'During the night,' agreed Ruffy as he surveyed the long slither marks in the sand of the beach.

'Thank God for that.'

'Yeah, it wouldn't have made my boys too joyful having to clean up that lot.'

'We'll send someone down to tear out those racks. I don't want to look at them while we work.'

'No, they're not very pretty.' Ruffy ran his eyes over the two sets of gallows.

Bruce climbed down into the space between the trucks.

'Hendry.'

'That's my name.' Wally leaned out of the window.

'Sorry to disappoint you, but the crocs have done the chore for you.'

'I can see. I'm not blind.'

'Very well then. On the assumption that you are neither blind nor paralysed, how about getting your trucks unloaded?'

205

'Big deal,' muttered Hendry, but he climbed down and began shouting at the men under the canvas canopy.

'Get the lead out there, you lot. Start jumping about!'

'What were the thickest timbers you could find?' Bruce turned to Ruffy.

'Nine by threes, but we got plenty of them.'

'They'll do,' decided Bruce. 'We can lash a dozen of them together for each of the main supports.' Frowning with concentration, Bruce began the task of organizing the repairs.

'Hendry, I want the timber stacked by sizes. Put the sheet-iron over there.' He brushed the flies from his face. 'Ruffy, how many hammers have we got?'

'Ten, boss, and I found a couple of handsaws.'

'Good. What about nails and rope?'

'We got plenty. I got a barrel of six-inch and—'

Preoccupied, Bruce did not notice one of the coloured civilians leave the shelter of the trucks. He walked a dozen paces towards the bridge and stopped. Then unhurriedly he began to unbutton his trousers and Bruce looked up.

'What the hell are you doing?' he shouted and the man started guiltily. He did not understand the English words, but Bruce's tone was sufficiently clear.

'Monsieur,' he explained, 'I wish to—'

'Get back here!' roared Bruce. The man hesitated in confusion and then he began closing his fly.

'Hurry up – you bloody fool.'

Obediently the man hastened the closing of his trousers. Everyone had stopped work and they were all watching him. His face was dark with embarrassment and he fumbled clumsily.

'Leave that.' Bruce was frantic. 'Get back here.'

The first arrow rose lazily out of the undergrowth along the river in a silent parabola. Gathering speed in its descent, hissing softly, it dropped into the ground at the man's feet and stuck up jauntily. A thin reed, fletched with green leaves, it looked harmless as a child's plaything.

'Run,' screamed Bruce. The man stood and stared with detached disbelief at the arrow.

Bruce started forward to fetch him, but Ruffy's huge black hand closed on his arm and he was helpless in its grip. He struck out at Ruffy, struggling to free himself but he could not break that hold.

A swarm of them like locusts on the move, high arching, fluting softly, dropping all around the man as he started to run.

Bruce stopped struggling and watched. He heard the metal heads clanking on the bonnet of the truck, saw them falling wide of the man, some of the frail shafts snapping as they hit the ground.

Then between the shoulders, like a perfectly placed banderilla, one hit him. It flapped against his back as he ran and he twisted his arms behind him, vainly trying to reach it, his face twisted in horror and in pain.

'Hold him down,' shouted Bruce as the coloured man ran into the shelter. Two gendarmes jumped forward, took his arms and forced him face downwards on to the ground.

He was gabbling incoherently with horror as Bruce straddled his back and gripped the shaft. Only half the barbed head had buried itself – a penetration of less than an inch – but when Bruce pulled the shaft it snapped off in his hand leaving the steel twitching in the flesh.

'Knife,' shouted Bruce and someone thrust a bayonet into his hand.

'Watch those barbs, boss. Don't cut yourself on them.'

'Ruffy, get your boys ready to repel them if they rush us,' snapped Bruce and ripped away the shirt. For a moment he stared at the crudely hand-beaten iron arrowhead. The poison coated it thickly, packed in behind the barbs, looking like sticky black toffee.

'He's dead,' said Ruffy from where he leaned over the bonnet of the truck. 'He just ain't stopped breathing yet.'

The man screamed and twisted under Bruce as he made the first incision, cutting in deep beside the arrowhead with the point of the bayonet.

'Hendry, get those pliers out of the tool kit.'

'Here they are.'

Bruce gripped the arrow-head with the steel jaws and pulled. The flesh clung to it stubbornly, lifting in a pyramid. Bruce hacked at it with the bayonet, feeling it tear. It was like trying to get the hook out of the rubbery mouth of a cat-fish.

'You're wasting your time, boss!' grunted Ruffy with all the calm African acceptance of violent death. 'This boy's a goner. That's no horse! That's snake juice in him, fresh mixed. He's finished.'

'Are you sure, Ruffy?' Bruce looked up, 'Are you sure it's snake venom?'

'That's what they use. They mix it with kassava meal.'

'Hendry, where's the snake bite outfit?'

'It's in the medicine box back at the camp.'

Bruce tugged once more at the arrowhead and it came away, leaving a deep black hole between the man's shoulder blades.

'Everybody into the trucks, we've got to get him back. Every second is vital.'

'Look at his eyes,' grunted Ruffy. 'That injection stuff ain't going to help him much.'

The pupils had contracted to the size of match heads and he was shaking uncontrollably as the poison spread through his body.

'Get him into the truck.'

They lifted him into the cab and everybody scrambled aboard. Ruffy started the engine, slammed into reverse and the motor roared as he shot backwards over the intervening thirty yards to the laager.

'Get him out,' instructed Bruce. 'Bring him into the shelter.'

The man was blubbering through slack lips and he had started to sweat. Little rivulets of it coursed down his face and naked upper body. There was hardly any blood from the wound, just a trickle of brownish fluid. The poison must be a coagulant, Bruce decided.

'Bruce, are you all right?' Shermaine ran to meet him.

'Nothing wrong with me.' Bruce remembered to check his tongue this time. 'But one of them has been hit.'

'Can I help you?'

'No, I don't want you to watch.' And he turned from her. 'Hendry, where's that bloody snake bite outfit?' he shouted.

They had dragged the man into the laager and laid him on a blanket in the shade. Bruce went to him and knelt beside him. He took the scarlet tin that Hendry handed him and opened it.

'Ruffy, get those two trucks worked into the circle and make sure your boys are on their toes. With this success they may get brave sooner than you expected.'

Bruce fitted the hypodermic needle on to the syringe as he spoke.

'Hendry, get them to rig some sort of screen round us. You can use blankets.'

With his thumb he snapped the top off the ampoule and filled the syringe with the pale yellow serum.

'Hold him,' he said to the two gendarmes, lifted a pinch of skin close beside the wound and ran the needle under it. The man's skin felt like that of a frog, damp and clammy.

As he expelled the serum Bruce was trying to calculate the time that had elapsed since the arrow had hit. Possibly seven or eight minutes; mamba venom kills in fourteen minutes.

'Roll him over,' he said.

The man's head lolled sideways, his breathing was quick

and shallow and the saliva poured from the corners of his mouth, running down his cheeks.

'Get a load of that!' breathed Wally Hendry, and Bruce glanced up at his face. His expression was a glow of deep sensual pleasure and his breathing was as quick and shallow as that of the dying man.

'Go and help Ruffy,' snapped Bruce as his stomach heaved with disgust.

'Not on your Nelly. This I'm not going to miss.'

Bruce had no time to argue. He lifted the skin of the man's stomach and ran the needle in again. There was an explosive spitting sound as the bowels started to vent involuntarily.

'Jesus,' whispered Hendry.

'Get away,' snarled Bruce. 'Can't you let him die without gloating over it?'

Hopelessly he injected again, under the skin of the chest above the heart. As he emptied the syringe the man's body twisted violently in the first seizure and the needle snapped off under the skin.

'There he goes,' whispered Hendry, 'there he goes. Just look at him, man. That's really something.'

Bruce's hands were trembling and slowly a curtain descended across his mind.

'You filthy swine,' he screamed and hit Hendry across the face with his open hand, knocking him back against the side of the gasoline tanker. Then he went for his throat and found it with both hands. The windpipe was ropey and elastic under his thumbs.

'Is nothing sacred to you, you unclean animal?' he yelled into Hendry's face. 'Can't you let a man die without—'

Then Ruffy was there, effortlessly plucking Bruce's hands from the throat, interposing the bulk of his body, holding them away from each other.

'Let it stand, boss.'

210

'For that—' gasped Hendry as he massaged his throat. 'For that I'm going to make you pay.'

Bruce turned away, sick and ashamed, to the man on the blanket.

'Cover him up.' His voice was shaky. 'Put him in the back of one of the trucks. We'll bury him tomorrow.'

– 23 –

Before nightfall they had completed the corrugated iron screen. It was a simple four-walled structure with no roof to it. One end of it was detachable and all four walls were pierced at regular intervals with small loop-holes for defence.

Long enough to accommodate a dozen men in comfort, high enough to reach above the heads of the tallest, and exactly the width of the bridge, it was not a thing of beauty.

'How you going to move it, boss?' Ruffy eyed the screen dubiously.

'I'll show you. We'll move it back to the camp now, so that in the morning we can commute to work in it.'

Bruce selected twelve men and they crowded through the open end into the shelter, and closed it behind them.

'Okay, Ruffy. Take the trucks away.'

Hendry and Ruffy reversed the two trucks back to the laager, leaving the shelter standing at the head of the bridge like a small Nissen hut. Inside it Bruce stationed his men at intervals along the walls.

'Use the bottom timber of the frame to lift on,' he shouted. 'Are you all ready? All right, lift!'

The shelter swayed and rose six inches above the ground. From the laager they could see only the boots of the men inside.

'All together,' ordered Bruce. 'Walk!'

Rocking and creaking over the uneven ground the structure moved ponderously back towards the laager. Below it the feet moved like those of a caterpillar.

The men in the laager started to cheer, and from inside the shelter they answered with whoops of laughter. It was fun. They were enjoying themselves enormously, completely distracted from the horror of poison arrows and the lurking phantoms in the jungle around them.

They reached the camp and lowered the shelter. Then one at a time the gendarmes slipped across the few feet of open ground into the safety of the laager to be met with laughter, and back-slapping and mutual congratulation.

'Well, it works, boss,' Ruffy greeted Bruce in the uproar.

'Yes.' Then he lifted his voice. 'That's enough. Quiet down all of you. Get back to your posts.'

The laughter subsided and the confusion became order again. Bruce walked to the centre of the laager and looked about him. There was complete quiet now. They were all watching him. I have read about this so often, he grinned inwardly, the heroic speech to the men on the eve of battle. Let's pray I don't make a hash of it.

'Are you hungry?' he asked loudly in French and received a chorus of hearty affirmatives.

'There is bully beef for dinner.' This time humorous groans.

'And bully beef for breakfast tomorrow,' he paused, 'and then it's finished.'

They were silent now.

'So you are going to be truly hungry by the time we cross this river. The sooner we repair the bridge the sooner you'll get your bellies filled again.'

I might as well rub it in, decided Bruce.

'You all saw what happened to the person who went into the open today, so I don't have to tell you to keep under cover. The sergeant major is making arrangements for

212

sanitation – five-gallon drums. They won't be very comfortable, so you won't be tempted to sit too long.'

They laughed a little at that.

'Remember this. As long as you stay in the laager or the shelter they can't touch you. There is absolutely nothing to fear. They can beat their drums and wait as long as they like, but they can't harm us.'

A murmur of agreement.

'And the sooner we finish the bridge the sooner we will be on our way.'

Bruce looked round the circle of faces and was satisfied with what he saw. The completion of the shelter had given their morale a boost.

'All right, Sergeant Jacque. You can start sweeping with the searchlights as soon as it's dark.'

Bruce finished and went across to join Shermaine beside the Ford. He loosed the straps of his helmet and lifted it off his head. His hair was damp with perspiration and he ran his fingers through it.

'You are tired,' Shermaine said softly, examining the dark hollows under his eyes and the puckered marks of strain at the corners of his mouth.

'No. I'm all right,' he denied, but every muscle in his body ached with fatigue and nervous tension.

'Tonight you must sleep all night,' she ordered him. 'I will make the bed in the back of the car.'

Bruce looked at her quickly. 'With you?' he asked.

'Yes.'

'You do not mind that everyone should know?'

'I am not ashamed of us.' There was a fierceness in her tone.

'I know, but—'

'You said once that nothing between you and I could ever be dirty.'

'No, of course it couldn't be dirty. I just thought—'

213

'Well then, I love you and from now on we have only one bed between us.' She spoke with finality.

Yesterday she was a virgin, he thought with amazement, and now – well, now it's no holds barred. Once she is roused a woman is more reckless of consequences than any man. They are such wholesale creatures. But she's right, of course. She's my woman and she belongs in my bed. The hell with the rest of the world and what it thinks!

'Make the bed, wench.' He smiled at her tenderly.

Two hours after dark the drum started again. They lay together, holding close, and listened to it. It held no terror now, for they were warm and secure in the afterglow of passion. It was like lying and listening to the impotent fury of a rainstorm on the roof at night.

– 24 –

They went out to the bridge at sunrise, the shelter moving across the open ground like the carapace of a multi-legged metallic turtle. The men chattered and joked loudly inside, still elated by the novelty of it.

'All right, everybody. That's enough talking,' Bruce shouted them down. 'There's work to do now.'

And they began.

Within an hour the sun had turned the metal box into an oven. They stripped to the waist and the sweat dripped from them as they worked. They worked in a frenzy, gripped by a new urgency, oblivious of everything but the rough-sawed timber that drove white splinters into their skin at the touch. They worked in the confined heat, amidst the racket of hammers and in the piney smell of sawdust. The labour fell into its own pattern with only an occasional grunted order from Bruce or Ruffy to direct it.

By midday the four main trusses that would span the gap in the bridge had been made up. Bruce tested their rigidity by propping one at both ends and standing all his men on the middle of it. It gave an inch under their combined weight.

'What do you think, boss?' Ruffy asked without conviction.

'Four of them might just do it. We'll put in king-posts underneath,' Bruce answered.

'Man, I don't know. That tanker weights plenty.'

'It's no flyweight,' Bruce agreed. 'But we'll have to take the chance. We'll bring the Ford across first, then the trucks and the tanker last.'

Ruffy nodded and wiped his face on his forearm; the muscles below his armpits knotted as he moved and there was no flabbiness in the powerful bulge of his belly above his belt.

'Phew!' He blew his lips out. 'I got the feeling for a beer now. This thirst is really stalking me.'

'You've got some with you?' Bruce asked as he passed his thumbs across his eyebrows and squeezed the moisture from them so it ran down his cheeks.

'Two things I never travel without, my trousers and a stock of the brown and bubbly.' Ruffy picked up the small pack from the corner of the shelter and it clinked coyly. 'You hear that sound, boss?'

'I hear it, and it sounds like music,' grinned Bruce. 'All right, everybody.' He raised his voice. 'Take ten minutes.'

Ruffy opened the bottles and passed them out, issuing one to be shared between three gendarmes. 'These Arabs don't properly appreciate this stuff,' he explained to Bruce. 'It'd just be a waste.'

The liquor was lukewarm and gassy; it merely aggravated Bruce's thirst. He drained the bottle and tossed it out of the shelter.

'All right.' He stood up. 'Let's get these trusses into position.'

'That's the shortest ten minutes I ever lived,' commented Ruffy.

'Your watch is slow,' said Bruce.

Carrying the trusses within it, the shelter lumbered out on to the bridge. There was no laughter now, only laboured breathing and curses.

'Fix the ropes!' commanded Bruce. He tested the knots personally, then looked up at Ruffy and nodded.

'That'll do.'

'Come on, you mad bastards,' Ruffy growled. 'Lift it.'

The first truss rose to the perpendicular and swayed there like a grotesque maypole with the ropes hanging from its top.

'Two men on each rope,' ordered Bruce. 'Let it down gently.' He glanced round to ensure that they were all ready.

'Drop it over the edge, and I'll throw you bastards in after it,' warned Ruffy.

'Lower away!' shouted Bruce.

The truss leaned out over the gap towards the fire-blackened stump of bridge on the far side slowly at first, then faster as gravity took it.

'Hold it, damn you. Hold it!' roared Ruffy with the muscles in his shoulders humped out under the strain. They lay back against the ropes, but the weight of the truss dragged them forward as it fell.

It crashed down across the gap, lifted a cloud of dead wood ash as it struck, and lay there quivering.

'Man, I thought we'd lost that one for sure,' growled Ruffy, then turned savagely on his men.

'You bastards better be sharper with the next one – if you don't want to swim this river.'

They repeated the process with the second truss, and again they could not hold its falling length, but this time they were not so lucky. The end of the truss hit the far side, bounced and slid sideways.

'It's going! Pull, you bastards, pull!' shouted Ruffy.

The truss toppled slowly sideways and over the edge. It hit the river below them with a splash, disappeared under the surface, then bobbed up and floated away downstream until checked by the ropes.

Both Bruce and Ruffy fumed and swore during the lengthy exasperating business of dragging it back against the current and manhandling its awkward bulk back on to the bridge. Half a dozen times it slipped at the crucial moment and splashed back into the river.

Despite his other virtues, Ruffy's vocabulary of cursing words was limited and it added to his frustration that he had to keep repeating himself. Bruce did much better – he remembered things that he had heard and he made up a few.

When finally they had the dripping baulk of timber back on the bridge and were resting, Ruffy turned to Bruce with honest admiration.

'You swear pretty good,' he said. 'Never heard you before, but no doubt about it, you're good! What's that one about the cow again?'

Bruce repeated it for him a little self-consciously.

'You make that up yourself?' asked Ruffy.

'Spur of the moment,' laughed Bruce.

'That's 'bout the dirtiest I ever heard.' Ruffy could not conceal his envy. 'Man, you should write a book.'

'Let's get this bridge finished first,' said Bruce. 'Then I'll think about it.'

Now the truss was almost servile in its efforts to please. It dropped neatly across the gap and lay beside its twin.

'You curse something good enough, and it works every time,' Ruffy announced sagely. 'I think your one about the cow made all the difference, boss.'

With two trusses in position they had broken the back of the project. They carried the shelter out and set it on the trusses, straddling the gap. The third and fourth trusses were dragged into position and secured with ropes and nails before nightfall.

When the shelter waddled wearily back to the laager at dusk, the men within it were exhausted. Their hands were bleeding and bristled with wood splinters, but they were also mightily pleased with themselves.

'Sergeant Jacque, keep one of your searchlights trained on the bridge all night. We don't want our friends to come out and set fire to it again.'

'There are only a few hours' life left in each of the batteries.' Jacque kept his voice low.

'Use them one at a time then.' Bruce spoke without hesitation. 'We must have that bridge lit up all night.

'You think you could spare a beer for each of the boys that worked on the bridge today?'

'A whole one each!' Ruffy was shocked. 'I only got a couple cases left.'

Bruce fixed him with a stern eye and Ruffy grinned.

'Okay, boss. Guess they've earned it.'

Bruce transferred his attention to Wally Hendry who sat on the running-board of one of the trucks cleaning his nails with the point of his bayonet.

'Everything under control here, Hendry?' he asked coolly.

'Sure, what'd you think would happen? We'd have a visit from the archbishop? The sky'd fall in? Your French thing'd have twins or something?' He looked up from his nails at Bruce. 'When are you jokers going to get that bridge finished, instead of wandering around asking damn-fool questions?'

Bruce was too tired to feel annoyed. 'You've got the night watch, Hendry,' he said, 'from now until dawn.'

'Is that right, hey? And you? What're you going to do all night, or does that question make you blush?'

'I'm going to sleep, that's what I'm going to do. I haven't been lolling round camp all day.'

Hendry pegged the bayonet into the earth between his feet and snorted.

'Well, give her a little bit of sleep for me too, Bucko.'

Bruce left him and crossed to the Ford.

'Hello, Bruce. How did it go today? I missed you,' Shermaine greeted him, and her face lit up as she looked at him. It is a good feeling to be loved, and some of Bruce's fatigue lifted.

'About half finished, another day's work.' Then he smiled back at her. 'I won't lie and say I missed you – I've been too damn busy.'

'Your hands!' she said with quick concern and lifted them to examine them. 'They're in a terrible state.'

'Not very pretty, are they?'

'Let me get a needle from my case. I'll get the splinters out.'

From across the laager Wally Hendry caught Bruce's eye and with one hand made a suggestive sign below his waist. Then, at Bruce's frown of anger, he threw back his head and laughed with huge delight.

– 25 –

Bruce's stomach grumbled with hunger as he stood with Ruffy and Hendry beside the cooking fire. In the early morning light he could just make out the dark shape of the bridge at the end of the clearing. That drum was still beating in the jungle, but they hardly noticed it now. It was taken for granted like the mosquitoes. 'The batteries are finished,' grunted Ruffy. The feeble yellow beam of the searchlight reached out tiredly towards the bridge.

'Only just lasted the night,' agreed Bruce.

'Christ, I'm hungry,' complained Hendry. 'What could I do to a couple of fried eggs and a porterhouse steak.'

At the mention of food Bruce's mouth flooded with saliva. He shut his mind against the picture that Wally's words had evoked in his imagination.

'We won't be able to finish the bridge and get the trucks across today,' he said, and Ruffy agreed.

'There's a full day's work left on her, boss.'

'This is what we'll do then,' Bruce went on. 'I'll take the work party out to the bridge. Hendry, you will stay here in the laager and cover us the same as yesterday. And Ruffy, you take one of the trucks and a dozen of your boys. Go back ten miles or so to where the forest is open and they won't be able to creep up on you. Then cut us a mountain of firewood; thick logs that will burn all night. We will set a ring of watch fires round the camp tonight.'

'That makes sense,' Ruffy nodded. 'But what about the bridge?'

'We'll have to put a guard on it,' said Bruce, and the expressions on their faces changed as they thought about this.

'More pork chops for the boys in the bushes,' growled Hendry. 'You won't catch me sitting out on the bridge all night.'

'No one's asking you to,' snapped Bruce. 'All right, Ruffy. Go and fetch the wood, and plenty of it.'

Bruce completed the repairs to the bridge in the late afternoon. The most anxious period was in the middle of the day when he and four men had to leave the shelter and clamber down on to the supports a few feet above the surface of the river to set the king-posts in place. Here they were exposed at random range to arrows from the undergrowth along the banks. But no arrows came and they finished the job and climbed back to safety again with something of a sense of anticlimax.

They nailed the crossties over the trusses and then roped everything into a compact mass.

Bruce stood back and surveyed the fruit of two full days' labour.

'Functional,' he decided, speaking aloud. 'But we certainly aren't going to win any prizes for aesthetic beauty or engineering design.'

He picked up his jacket and thrust his arms into the sleeves; his sweaty upper body was cold now that the sun was almost down.

'Home, gentlemen,' he said, and his gendarmes scattered to their positions inside the shelter.

The metal shelter circled the laager, squatting every twenty or thirty paces like an old woman preparing to relieve herself. When it lifted and moved on it left a log fire behind it. The ring of fires was completed by dark and the shelter returned to the laager.

'Are you ready, Ruffy?' From inside the shelter Bruce called across to where Ruffy waited.

'All set, boss.'

Followed by six heavily armed gendarmes, Ruffy crossed quickly to join Bruce and they set off to begin their all-night vigil on the bridge.

Before midnight it was cold in the corrugated iron shelter, for the wind blew down the river and they were completely exposed to it, and there was no cloud cover to hold the day's warmth against the earth.

The men in the shelter huddled under their gas capes and waited. Bruce and Ruffy leaned together against the corrugated iron wall, their shoulders almost touching, and there was sufficient light from the stars to light the interior of the shelter and allow them to make out the guard rails of the bridge through the open ends.

'Moon will be up in an hour,' murmured Ruffy.

'Only a quarter of it, but it will give us a little more

light,' Bruce concurred, and peered down into the black hole between his feet where he had prised up one of the newly laid planks.

'How about taking a shine with the torch?' suggested Ruffy.

'No.' Bruce shook his head, and passed the flashlight into his other hand. 'Not until I hear them.'

'You might not hear them.'

'If they swim downstream and climb up the piles, which is what I expect, then we'll hear them all right. They'll be dripping water all over the place,' said Bruce.

'Kanaki and his boys didn't hear them,' Ruffy pointed out.

'Kanaki and his boys weren't listening for it,' said Bruce.

They were silent then for a while. One of the gendarmes started to snore softly and Ruffy shot out a huge booted foot that landed in the small of his back. The man cried out and scrambled to his knees, looking wildly about him.

'You have nice dreams?' Ruffy asked pleasantly.

'I wasn't sleeping,' the man protested. 'I was thinking.'

'Well, don't think so loudly,' Ruffy advised him. 'Sounds though you sawing through the bridge with a cross cut.'

Another half hour dragged itself by like a cripple.

'Fires are burning well,' commented Ruffy, and Bruce turned his head and glanced through the loophole in the corrugated iron behind him at the little garden of orange flame-flowers in the darkness.

'Yes, they should last till morning.'

Silence again, with only the singing of the mosquitoes and the rustle of the river as it flowed by the piles of the bridge. Shermaine has my pistol, Bruce remembered with a small trip in his pulse, I should have taken it back from her. He unclipped the bayonet from the muzzle of his rifle, tested the edge of the blade with his thumb, and slid it into the scabbard on his web-belt. Could easily lose the rifle if we start mixing it in the dark, he decided.

'Christ, I'm hungry,' grunted Ruffy beside him.

'You're too fat,' said Bruce. 'The diet will do you good.' And they waited.

Bruce stared down into the hole in the floorboards. His eyes began weaving fantasies out of the darkness, he could see vague shapes that moved, like things seen below the surface of the sea. His stomach tightened and he fought the impulse to shine his flashlight into the hole. He closed his eyes to rest them. I will count slowly to ten, he decided, and then look again.

Ruffy's hand closed on his upper arm; the pressure of his fingers transmitted alarm like a current of electricity. Bruce's eyelids flew open.

'Listen,' breathed Ruffy.

Bruce heard it. The stealthy drip of water on water below them. Then something bumped the bridge, but so softly that he felt rather than heard the jar.

'Yes,' Bruce whispered back. He reached out and tapped the shoulder of the gendarme beside him and the man's body stiffened at his touch.

With his breath scratching his dry throat, Bruce waited until he was sure the warning had been passed to all his men. Then he shifted the weight of his rifle from across his knees and aimed down into the hole.

He drew in a deep breath and switched on the flashlight. The beam shot down and he looked along it over his rifle barrel.

The square aperture in the floorboards formed a frame for the picture that flashed into his eyes. Black bodies, naked, glossy with wetness, weird patterns of tattoo marks, a face staring up at him, broad sloped forehead above startlingly white eyes and flat nose. The long gleaming blade of a panga. Clusters of humanity clinging to the wooden piles like ticks on the legs of a beast. Legs and arms and shiny trunks merged into a single organism, horrible as some slimy sea-creature.

Bruce fired into it. His rifle shuddered against his shoulder and the long orange spurts from its muzzle gave the picture a new flickering horror. The mass of bodies heaved, and struggled like a pack of rats trapped in a dry well. They dropped splashing into the river, swarmed up the timber piles, twisting and writhing as the bullets hit them, screaming, babbling over the sound of the rifle.

Bruce's weapon clicked empty and he groped for a new magazine. Ruffy and his gendarmes were hanging over the guard rails of the bridge, firing downwards, sweeping the piles below them with long bursts, the flashes lighting their faces and outlining their bodies against the sky.

'They're still coming!' roared Ruffy. 'Don't let them get over the side.'

Out of the hole at Bruce's feet thrust the head and naked upper body of a man. There was a panga in his hand; he slashed at Bruce's legs, his eyes glazed in the beam of the flashlight.

Bruce jumped back and the knife missed his knees by inches. The man wormed his way out of the hole towards Bruce. He was screaming shrilly, a high meaningless sound of fury.

Bruce lunged with the barrel of his empty rifle at the contorted black face. All his weight was behind that thrust and the muzzle went into the Baluba's eye. The foresight and four inches of the barrel disappeared into his head, stopping only when it hit bone. Colourless fluid from the burst eyeball gushed from round the protruding steel.

Tugging and twisting, Bruce tried to free the rifle, but the foresight had buried itself like the barb of a fish hook. The Baluba had dropped his panga and was clinging to the rifle barrel with both hands. He was wailing and rolling on his back upon the floorboards, his head jerking every time Bruce tried to pull the muzzle out of his head.

Beyond him the head and shoulders of another Baluba appeared through the aperture.

Bruce dropped his rifle and gathered up the fallen panga; he jumped over the writhing body of the first Baluba and lifted the heavy knife above his head with both hands.

The man was jammed in the hole, powerless to protect himself. He looked up at Bruce and his mouth fell open.

Two-handed, as though he were chopping wood, Bruce swung his whole body into the stroke. The shock jarred his shoulders and he felt blood splatter his legs. The untempered blade snapped off at the hilt and stayed imbedded in the Baluba's skull.

Panting heavily, Bruce straightened up and looked wildly about him. Baluba were swarming over the guard rail on one side of the bridge. The starlight glinted on their wet skins. One of his gendarmes was lying in a dark huddle, his head twisted back and his rifle still in his hands. Ruffy and the other gendarmes were still firing down over the far side.

'Ruffy!' shouted Bruce. 'Behind you! They're coming over!' and he dropped the handle of the panga and ran towards the body of the gendarme. He needed that rifle.

Before he could reach it the naked body of a Baluba rushed at him. Bruce ducked under the sweep of the panga and grappled with him. They fell locked together, the man's body slippery and sinuous against him, and the smell of him fetid as rancid butter.

Bruce found the pressure point below the elbow of his knife arm and dug in with his thumb. The Baluba yelled and his panga clattered on the floorboards. Bruce wrapped his arm round the man's neck while with his free hand he reached for his bayonet.

The Baluba was clawing for Bruce's eyes with his fingers, his nails scored the side of Bruce's nose, but Bruce had his bayonet out now. He placed the point against the man's chest and pressed it in. He felt the steel scrape against the bone of a rib and the man redoubled his struggles at the sting of it. Bruce twisted the blade, working it in with his wrist, forcing the man's head backwards with his other arm.

The point of the bayonet scraped over the bone and found the gap between. Like taking a virgin, suddenly the resistance to its entrance was gone and it slid home full length. The Baluba's body jerked mechanically and the bayonet twitched in Bruce's fist.

Bruce did not even wait for the man to die. He pulled the blade out against the sucking reluctance of tissue that clung to it and scrambled to his feet in time to see Ruffy pick another Baluba from his feet and hurl him bodily over the guard rail.

Bruce snatched the rifle from the gendarme's dead hands and stepped to the guard rail. They were coming over the side, those below shouting and pushing at the ones above.

Like shooting a row of sparrows from a fence with a shotgun, thought Bruce grimly, and with one long burst he cleared the rail. Then he leaned out and sprayed the piles below the bridge. The rifle was empty. He reloaded with a magazine from his pocket. But it was all over. They were dropping back into the river, the piles below the bridge were clear of men, their heads bobbed away downstream.

Bruce lowered his rifle and looked about him. Three of his gendarmes were killing the man that Bruce had wounded, standing over him and grunting as they thrust down with their bayonets. The man was still wailing.

Bruce looked away.

One horn of the crescent moon showed above the trees; it had a gauzy halo about it.

Bruce lit a cigarette and behind him those gruesome noises ceased.

'Are you okay, boss?'

'Yes, I'm fine. How about you, Ruffy?'

'I got me a terrible thirst now. Hope nobody trod on my pack.'

About four minutes from the first shot to the last, Bruce guessed. That's the way of war, seven hours of waiting and

226

boredom, then four minutes of frantic endeavour. Not only of war either, he thought. The whole of life is like that.

Then he felt the trembling in his thighs and the first spasm of nausea as the reaction started.

'What's happening?' A shout floated across from the laager. Bruce recognized Hendry's voice. 'Is everything all right?'

'We've beaten them off,' Bruce shouted back. 'Everything under control. You can go to sleep again.'

And now I have got to sit down quickly, he told himself.

Except for the tattoos upon his cheeks and forehead the dead Baluba's features were little different from those of the Bambala and Bakuba men who made up the bulk of Bruce's command.

Bruce played the flashlight over the corpse. The arms and legs were thin but stringy with muscle, and the belly bulged out from years of malnutrition. It was an ugly body, gnarled and crabbed. With distaste Bruce moved the light back to the features. The bone of the skull formed harsh angular planes beneath the skin, the nose was flattened and the thick lips had about them a repellent brutality. They were drawn back slightly to reveal the teeth which had been filed to sharp points like those of a shark.

'This is the last one, boss. I'll toss him overboard.' Ruffy spoke in the darkness beside Bruce.

'Good.'

Ruffy heaved and grunted, the corpse splashed below them and Ruffy wiped his hands on the guard rail, then came to sit beside Bruce.

'Goddam apes.' Ruffy's voice was full of the bitter tribal antagonism of Africa. 'When we get shot of these U.N. people there'll be a bit of sorting out to do. They've got a few things to learn, these bloody Baluba.'

And so it goes, thought Bruce, Jew and Gentile, Catholic and Protestant, black and white, Bambala and Baluba.

He checked the time, another two hours to dawn. His nervous reaction from physical violence had abated now; the hand that held the cigarette no longer trembled.

'They won't come again,' said Ruffy. 'You can get some sleep now if you want. I'll keep an eye open, boss.'

'No, thanks. I'll wait with you.' His nerves had not settled down enough for sleep.

'How's it for a beer?'

'Thanks.'

Bruce sipped the beer and stared out at the watch fires round the laager. They had burned down to puddles of red ash but Bruce knew that Ruffy was right. The Baluba would not attack again that night.

'So how do you like freedom?'

'How's that, boss?' The question puzzled Ruffy and he turned to Bruce questioningly.

'How do you like it now the Belgians have gone?'

'It's pretty good, I reckon.'

'And if Tshombe has to give in to the Central Government?'

'Those mad Arabs!' snarled Ruffy. 'All they want is our copper. They're going to have to get up early in the morning to take it. We're in the saddle here.'

The great jousting tournament of the African continent. I'm in the saddle, try to unhorse me! As in all matters of survival it was not a question of ethics and political doctrine (except to the spectators in Whitehall, Moscow, Washington and Peking). There were big days coming, thought Bruce. My own country, when she blows, is going to make Algiers look like an old ladies' sewing circle.

26

T he sun was up, throwing long shadows out into the clearing, and Bruce stood beside the Ford and looked across the bridge at the corrugated iron shelter on the far bank.

He relaxed for a second and let his mind run unhurriedly over his preparations for the crossing. Was there something left undone, some disposition which could make it more secure?

Hendry and a dozen men were in the shelter across the bridge, ready to meet any attack on that side.

Shermaine would take the Ford across first. Then the lorries would follow her. They would cross empty to minimize the danger of the bridge collapsing, or being weakened for the passage of the tanker. After each lorry had crossed, Hendry would shuttle its load and passengers over in the shelter and deposit them under the safety of the canvas canopy.

The last lorry would go over fully loaded. That was regrettable but unavoidable.

Finally Bruce himself would drive the tanker across. Not as an act of heroism, although it was the most dangerous business of the morning, but because he would trust no one else to do it, not even Ruffy. The five hundred gallons of fuel it contained was their safe-conduct home. Bruce had taken the precaution of filling all the gasoline tanks in the convoy in case of accidents, but they would need replenishing before they reached Msapa Junction.

He looked down at Shermaine in the driver's seat of the Ford.

'Keep it in low gear, take her over slowly but steadily. Whatever else you do, don't stop.'

She nodded. She was composed and she smiled at him. Bruce felt a stirring of pride as he looked at her, so small and lovely, but today she was doing man's work. He went on. 'As soon as you are over, I will send one of the trucks after you. Hendry will put six of his men into it and then come back for the others.'

'Oui, Monsieur Bonaparte.'

'You'll pay for that tonight,' he threatened her. 'Off you go.'

Shermaine let out the clutch and the Ford bounced over rough ground to the road, accelerated smoothly out on to the bridge.

Bruce held his breath, but there was only a slight check and sway as it crossed the repaired section.

'Thank God for that,' Bruce let out his breath and watched while Shermaine drew up alongside the shelter.

'Allez,' Bruce shouted at the coloured engine driver who was ready at the wheel of the first truck. The man smiled his cheerful chubby-faced smile, waved, and the truck rolled forward.

Watching anxiously as it went on to the bridge, Bruce saw the new timbers give perceptibly beneath the weight of the truck, and he heard them creak loudly in protest.

'Not so good,' he muttered.

'No—' agreed Ruffy. 'Boss, why don't you let someone else take the tanker over?'

'We've been over that already,' Bruce answered him without turning his head. Across the river Hendry was transferring his men from the shelter to the back of the truck. Then the shelter started its tedious way back towards them.

Bruce fretted impatiently during the four hours that it took to get four trucks across. The long business was the shuttling back and forth of the corrugated iron shelter, at least ten minutes for each trip.

Finally there was only the fifth truck and the tanker left on the north bank. Bruce started the engine of the tanker and put her into auxiliary low, then he blew a single blast on the horn. The driver of the truck ahead of him waved an acknowledgement and pulled forward.

The truck reached the bridge and went out into the middle. It was fully loaded, twenty men aboard. It came to the repaired section and slowed down, almost stopping.

'Go on! Keep it going, damn you,' Bruce shouted in impotent anger. The fool of a driver was forgetting his orders. He crawled forward and the bridge gave alarmingly under the full weight, the high canopied roof rocked crazily, and even above the rumble of his own engine Bruce could hear the protesting groan of the bridge timbers.

'The fool, oh, the bloody fool,' whispered Bruce to himself. Suddenly he felt very much alone and unprotected here on the north bank with the bridge being mutilated by the incompetence of the truck driver. He started the tanker moving.

Ahead of him the other driver had panicked. He was racing his engine, the rear wheels spun viciously, blue smoke of scorched tyres, and one of the floorboards tore loose. Then the truck lurched forward and roared up the south bank.

Bruce hesitated, applying the brakes and bringing the tanker to a standstill on the threshold of the bridge.

He thought quickly. The sensible thing would be to repair the damage to the bridge before chancing it with the weight of the tanker. But that would mean another day's delay. None of them had eaten since the previous morning. Was he justified in gambling against even odds, for that's what they were? A fifty-fifty chance, heads you get across, tails you dump the tanker in the middle of the river.

Then unexpectedly the decision was made for him.

From across the river a Bren gun started firing. Bruce jumped in his seat and looked up. Then a dozen other guns joined in and the tracer flew past the tanker. They were firing across towards him, close on each side of him. Bruce struggled to drag from his uncomprehending brain an explanation of this new development. Suddenly everything was moving too swiftly. Everything was confusion and chaos.

Movement in the rear-view mirror of the tanker caught his eye. He stared at it blankly. Then he twisted quickly in his seat and looked back.

'Christ!' he swore with fright.

From the edge of the jungle on both sides of the clearing Baluba were swarming into the open. Hundreds of them running towards him, the animal-skin kilts swirling about their legs, feather headdresses fluttering, sun bright on the long blades of their pangas. An arrow rang dully against the metal body of the tanker.

Bruce revved the engine, gripped the wheel hard with both hands and took the tanker out on to the bridge. Above the sound of the guns he could hear the shrill ululation, the excited squealing of two hundred Baluba. It sounded very close, and he snatched a quick look in the mirror. What he saw nearly made him lose his head and give the tanker full throttle. The nearest Baluba, screened from the guns on the south bank by the tanker's bulk, was only ten paces away. So close that Bruce could see the tattoo marks on his face and chest.

With an effort Bruce restrained his right foot from pressing down too hard, and instead he bore down on the repaired section of the bridge at a sedate twenty miles an hour. He tried to close his mind to the squealing behind him and the thunder of gunfire ahead of him.

The front wheels hit the new timbers, and above the other sounds he heard them groan loudly, and felt them sag under him.

The tanker rolled on and the rear wheels brought their weight to bear. The groan of wood became a cracking, rending sound. The tanker slowed as the bridge subsided, its wheels spun without purchase, it tilted sideways, no longer moving forward.

A sharp report, as one of the main trusses broke, and Bruce felt the tanker drop sharply at the rear; its nose pointed upwards and it started to slide back.

'Get out!' his brain shrieked at him. 'Get out, it's falling!' He reached for the door handle beside him, but at that moment the bridge collapsed completely. The tanker rolled off the edge.

Bruce was hurled across the cab with a force that stunned him, his legs wedged under the passenger seat and his arms tangled in the strap of his rifle. The tanker fell free and Bruce felt his stomach swoop up and press against his chest as though he rode a giant roller coaster.

The sickening drop lasted only an instant, and then the tanker hit the river. Immediately the sounds of gunfire and the screaming of Baluba were drowned out as the tanker disappeared below the surface. Through the windscreen Bruce saw now the cool cloudy green of water, as though he looked into the windows of an aquarium. With a gentle rocking motion the tanker sank down through the green water.

'Oh, my God, not this!' He spoke aloud as he struggled up from the floor of the cab. His ears were filled with the hiss and belch of escaping air bubbles; they rose in silver clouds past the windows.

The truck was still sinking, and Bruce felt the pain in his eardrums as the pressure built up inside the cab. He opened his mouth and swallowed convulsively, and his eardrums squeaked as the pressure equalized and the pain abated. Water was squirting in through the floor of the cab and jets of it spurted out of the instrument panel of the dashboard. The cab was flooding.

Bruce twisted the handle of the door beside him and hit it with his shoulder. It would not budge an inch. He flung all his weight against it, anchoring his feet on the dashboard and straining until he felt his eyeballs starting out of their sockets. It was jammed solid by the immense pressure of water on the outside.

'The windscreen,' he shouted aloud. 'Break the windscreen.' He groped for his rifle. The cab had flooded to his waist as he sat in the passenger's seat. He found the rifle and brought it dripping to his shoulder. He touched the muzzle to the windscreen and almost fired. But his good sense warned him.

Clearly he saw the danger of firing. The concussion in the confined cab would burst his eardrums, and the avalanche of broken glass that would be thrown into his face by the water pressure outside would certainly blind and maim him.

He lowered the rifle despondently. He felt his panic being slowly replaced by the cold certainty of defeat. He was trapped fifty feet below the surface of the river. There was no way out.

He thought of turning the rifle on himself, ending the inevitable, but he rejected the idea almost as soon as it had formed. Not that way, never that way!

He flogged his mind, driving it out of the cold lethargic clutch of certain death. There must be something. Think! Damn you, think!

The tanker was still rocking; it had not yet settled into the ooze of the river bottom. How long had he been under? About twenty seconds. Surely it should have hit the bottom long ago.

Unless! Bruce felt hope surge into new life within him. The tank! By God, that was it.

The great, almost empty tank behind him! The five-thousand-gallon tank which now contained only four hundred gallons of gasoline – it would have a displacement of nearly eighteen tons! It would float.

As if in confirmation of his hope, he felt his eardrums creak and pop. The pressure was falling! He was rising.

Bruce stared out at green water through the glass. The silver clouds of bubbles no longer streamed upwards; they seemed to hang outside the cab. The tanker had overcome the initial impetus that had driven it far below the surface, and now it was floating upwards at the same rate of ascent as its bubbles.

The dark green of deep water paled slowly to the colour of Chartreuse. And Bruce laughed. It was a gasping hysterical giggle and the sound of it shocked him. He cut it off abruptly.

The tanker bobbed out on to the surface, water streamed from the windscreen and through it Bruce caught a misty distorted glimpse of the south bank.

He twisted the door handle and this time the door burst open readily, water poured into the cab and Bruce floundered out against its rush.

With one quick glance he took in his position. The tanker had floated down twenty yards below the bridge, the guns on the south bank had fallen silent, and he could see no Baluba on the north bank. They must have disappeared back into the jungle.

Bruce plunged into the river and struck out for the south bank. Vaguely he heard the thin high shouts of encouragement from his gendarmes.

Within a dozen strokes he knew he was in difficulties. The drag of his boots and his sodden uniform was enormous. Treading water he tore off his steel helmet and let it sink. Then he tried to struggle out of his battle-jacket. It clung to his arms and chest and he disappeared under the surface four times before he finally got rid of it. He had breathed water into his lungs and his legs were tired and heavy.

The south bank was too far away. He would never make it. Coughing painfully he changed his objective and struck upstream against the current towards the bridge.

He felt himself settling lower in the water; he had to force his arms to lift and fall forward into each stroke.

Something plopped into the water close beside him. He paid no attention to it; suddenly a sense of disinterest had come over him, the first stage of drowning. He mistimed a breath and sucked in more water. The pain of it goaded him into a fresh burst of coughing. He hung in the water, gasping and hacking painfully.

Again something plopped close by, and this time he lifted his head. An arrow floated past him – then they began dropping steadily about him.

Baluba hidden in the thick bush above the beach were shooting at him; a gentle pattering rain of arrows splashed around his head. Bruce started swimming again, clawing his way frantically upstream. He swam until he could no longer lift his arms clear of the surface and the weight of his boots dragged his feet down.

Again he lifted his head. The bridge was close, not thirty feet away, but he knew that those thirty feet were as good as thirty miles. He could not make it.

The arrows that fell about him were no longer a source of terror. He thought of them only with mild irritation.

Why the hell can't they leave me alone? I don't want to play any more. I just want to relax. I'm so tired, so terribly tired.

He stopped moving and felt the water rise up coolly over his mouth and nose.

'Hold on, boss. I'm coming.' The shout penetrated through the grey fog of Bruce's drowning brain. He kicked and his head rose once more above the surface. He looked up at the bridge.

Stark naked, big belly swinging with each pace, thick legs flying, the great dangling bunch of his genitals bouncing merrily, black as a charging hippopotamus, Sergeant Major Ruffararo galloped out along the bridge.

He reached the fallen section and hauled himself up on to the guard rail. The arrows were falling around him, hissing down like angry insects. One glanced off his shoulder without penetrating and Ruffy shrugged at it, then launched himself up and out, falling in an ungainly heap of arms and legs to hit the water with a splash.

'Where the hell are you, boss?'

Bruce croaked a water-strangled reply and Ruffy came ploughing down towards him with clumsy overarm strokes.

He reached Bruce.

'Always playing around,' he grunted. 'Guess some guys never learn!' His fist closed on a handful of Bruce's hair.

Struggling unavailingly Bruce felt his head tucked firmly under Ruffy's arm and he was dragged through the water. Occasionally his face came out long enough to suck a breath but mostly he was under water. Consciousness receded and he felt himself going, going.

His head bumped against something hard but he was too weak to reach out his hand.

'Wake up, boss. You can have a sleep later.' Ruffy's voice bellowed in his ear. He opened his eyes and saw beside him the pile of the bridge.

'Come on. I can't carry you up here.'

Ruffy had worked round the side of the pile, shielding them from arrows, but the current was strong here, tugging at their bodies. Without the strength to prevent it Bruce's head rolled sideways and his face flopped forward into the water.

'Come on, wake up.' With a stinging slap Ruffy's open hand hit Bruce across the cheek. The shock roused him, he coughed and a mixture of water and vomit shot up his throat and out of his mouth and nose. Then he blenched painfully and retched again.

'How's it feel now?' Ruffy demanded.

Bruce lifted a hand from the water and wiped his mouth. He felt much better.

'Okay? Can you make it?'

Bruce nodded.

'Let's go then.'

With Ruffy dragging and pushing him, he worked his way up the pile. Water poured from his clothing as his body emerged, his hair was plastered across his forehead and he could feel each breath gurgle in his lungs.

'Listen boss. When we get to the top we'll be in the open again. There'll be more arrows – not time to sit around and chat. We're going over the rail fast and then run like hell, okay?'

Bruce nodded again. Above him were the floorboards of the bridge. With one hand he reached up and caught an upright of the guard rail, and he hung there without strength to pull himself the rest of the way.

'Hold it there,' grunted Ruffy and wriggled his shiny wet bulk up and over.

The arrows started falling again; one pegged into the wood six inches from Bruce's face and stood there quivering. Slowly Bruce's grip relaxed. I can't hold on, he thought, I'm going.

Then Ruffy's hand closed on his wrist, he felt himself dragged up, his legs dangled. He hung suspended by one arm and the water swirled smoothly past twenty feet below.

Slowly he was drawn upwards, his chest scraped over the guard rail, tearing his shirt, then he tumbled over it into an untidy heap on the bridge.

Vaguely he heard the guns firing on the south bank, the flit and thump of the arrows, and Ruffy's voice.

'Come on, boss. Get up.'

He felt himself being lifted and dragged along. With his legs boneless soft under him, he staggered beside Ruffy. Then there were no more arrows; the timbers of the bridge became solid earth under his feet. Voices and hands on him. He was being lifted, then lowered face down on to the wooden floor of a truck. The rhythmic pressure on his chest as someone started artificial respiration above him, the warm gush of water up his throat, and Shermaine's voice. He could not understand what she was saying, but just the sound of it was enough to make him realize he was safe. Darkly through the fog he became aware that her voice was the most important sound in his life.

He vomited again.

Hesitantly at first, and then swiftly, Bruce came back from the edge of oblivion.

'That's enough,' he mumbled and rolled out from under Sergeant Jacque who was administering the artificial respiration. The movement started a fresh paroxysm of coughing and he felt Shermaine's hands on his shoulders restraining him.

'Bruce, you must rest.'

'No.' He struggled into a sitting position. 'We've got to get out into the open,' he gasped.

'No hurry, boss. We've left all the Balubes on the other bank. There's a river between us.'

'How do you know?' Bruce challenged him.

'Well—'

'You don't!' Bruce told him flatly. 'There could easily be another few hundred on this side.' He coughed again painfully and then went on. 'We're leaving in five minutes, get them ready.'

'Okay.' Ruffy turned to leave.

'Ruffy!'

'Boss?' He turned back expectantly.

'Thank you.'

Ruffy grinned self-consciously. "At's all right. I needed a wash anyway.'

'I'll buy you a drink when we get home.'

'I won't forget,' Ruffy warned him, and climbed down out of the truck. Bruce heard him shouting to his boys.

'I thought I'd lost you.' Shermaine's arm was still round his shoulders and Bruce looked at her for the first time.

'My sweet girl, you won't get rid of me that easily,' he assured her. He was feeling much better now.

'Bruce, I want to – I can't explain—' Unable to find the

words she leaned forward instead and kissed him, full on the mouth.

When they drew apart, Sergeant Jacque and the two gendarmes with him were grinning delightedly.

'There is nothing wrong with you now, Captain.'

'No, there isn't,' Bruce agreed. 'Make your preparations for departure.'

From the passenger seat of the Ford Bruce took one last look at the bridge.

The repaired section hung like a broken drawbridge into the water. Beyond it on the far bank were scattered a few dead Baluba, like celluloid dolls in the sunlight. Far downstream the gasoline tanker had been washed by the current against the beach. It lay on its side, half-submerged in the shallows and the white Shell insignia showed clearly.

And the river flowed on, green and inscrutable, with the jungle pressing close along its banks.

'Let's get away from here,' said Bruce.

Shermaine started the engine and the convoy of trucks followed them along the track through the belt of thick river bush and into the open forest again.

Bruce looked at his watch. The inside of the glass was dewed with moisture and he lifted it to his ear.

'Damn thing has stopped. What's your time?'

'Twenty minutes to one.'

'Half the day wasted,' Bruce grumbled.

'Will we reach Msapa Junction before dark?'

'No, we won't. For two good reasons. Firstly, it's too far, and secondly, we haven't enough gas.'

'What are you going to do?' Her voice was unruffled, already she had complete faith in him. I wonder how long it will last, he mused cynically. At first you're a god. You have not a single human weakness. They set a standard for you, and the standard is perfection. Then the first time you fall short of it, their whole world blows up.

'We'll think of something,' he assured her.

'I'm sure you will,' she agreed complacently and Bruce grinned. The big joke, of course, was that when she said it he also believed it. Damned if being in love doesn't make you feel one hell of a man.

He changed to English so as to exclude the two gendarmes in the back seat from the conversation.

'You are the best thing that has happened to me in thirty years.'

'Oh, Bruce.' She turned her face towards him and the expression of trusting love in it and the intensity of his own emotion struck Bruce like a physical blow.

I will keep this thing alive, he vowed. I must nourish it with care and protect it from the dangers of selfishness and familiarity.

'Oh, Bruce, I do love you so terribly much. This morning when – when I thought I had lost you, when I saw the tanker go over into the river—' She swallowed and now her eyes were full of tears. 'It was as though the light had gone – it was so dark, so dark and cold without you.'

Absorbed with him so that she had forgotten about the road, Shermaine let the Ford veer and the offside wheels pumped into the rough verge.

'Hey, watch it!' Bruce cautioned her. 'Dearly as I love you also, I have to admit that you're a lousy driver. Let me take her.'

'Do you feel up to it?'

'Yes, pull into the side.'

Slowly, held to the speed of the lumbering vehicles behind them, they drove on through the afternoon. Twice they passed deserted Baluba villages beside the road, the grass huts disintegrating and the small cultivated lands about them thickly overgrown.

'My God, I'm hungry. I've got a headache from it and my belly feels as though it's full of warm water,' complained Bruce.

'Don't think you're the only one. This is the strictest diet I've ever been on, must have lost two kilos! But I always lose in the wrong place, never on my bottom.'

'Good,' Bruce said. 'I like it just the way it is, never shed an ounce there.' He looked over his shoulder at the two gendarmes. 'Are you hungry?' he asked in French.

'Mon Dieu!' exclaimed the fat one. 'I will not be able to sleep tonight, if I must lie on an empty stomach.'

'Perhaps it will not be necessary.' Bruce let his eyes wander off the road into the surrounding bush. The character of the country had changed in the last hundred miles. 'This looks like game country. I've noticed plenty of spoor on the road. Keep your eyes open.'

The trees were tall and widely spaced with grass growing beneath them. Their branches did not interlock so that the sky showed through. At intervals there were open glades filled with green swamp grass and thickets of bamboo and ivory palms.

'We've got another half hour of daylight. We might run into something before then.'

In the rear-view mirror he watched the lumbering column of transports for a moment. They must be almost out of gasoline by now, hardly enough for another half hour's driving. There were compensations however; at least they were in open country now and only eighty miles from Msapa Junction.

He glanced at the petrol gauge – half the tank. The Ranchero still had sufficient to get through even if the trucks were almost dry.

Of course! That was the answer. Find a good camp, leave the convoy, and go on in the Ford to find help. Without the trucks to slow him down he could get through to Msapa Junction in two hours. There was a telegraph in the station office, even if the junction was still deserted.

'We'll stop on the other side of this stream,' said Bruce and slowed the Ford, changed into second gear and let it idle down the steep bank.

The stream was shallow. The water hardly reached the hubcaps as they bumped across the rocky bottom. Bruce gunned the Ford up the far bank into the forest again.

'There!' shouted one of the gendarmes from the back seat and Bruce followed the direction of his arm.

Standing with humped shoulders, close beside the road, bunched together with mournfully drooping horns, heads held low beneath the massive bosses, bodies very big and black, were two old buffalo bulls.

Bruce hit the brakes, skidding the Ranchero to a stop, reaching for his rifle at the same instant. He twisted the door handle, hit the door with his shoulder and tumbled out on to his feet.

With a snort and a toss of their ungainly heads the buffalo started to run.

Bruce picked the leader and aimed for the neck in front of the plunging black shoulder. Leaning forward against the recoil of the rifle he fired and heard the bullet strike with a meaty thump. The bull slowed, breaking his run. The stubby forelegs settled and he slid forward on his nose, rolling as he fell, dust and legs kicking.

Turning smoothly without taking the butt from his shoulder, swinging with the run of the second bull, Bruce fired again, and again the thump of bullet striking.

The buffalo stumbled, giving in the legs, then he steadied and galloped on like a grotesque rocking horse, patches of baldness grey on his flanks, big-bellied, running heavily.

Bruce shifted the bead of the foresight on to his shoulder and fired twice in quick succession, aiming low for the heart, hitting each time, the bull so close he could see the bullet wounds appear on the dark skin.

The gallop broke into a trot, with head swinging low, mouth open, legs beginning to fold. Aiming carefully for the head Bruce fired again. The bull bellowed – a sad lonely sound – and collapsed into the grass.

The lorries had stopped in a line behind the Ford, and now from each of them swarmed black men. Jabbering happily, racing each other, they streamed past Bruce to where the buffalo had fallen in the grass beside the road.

'Nice shooting, boss,' applauded Ruffy. 'I'm going to have me a piece of tripe the size of a blanket.'

'Let's make camp first.' Bruce's ears were still singing with gunfire. 'Get the lorries into a ring.'

'I'll see to it.'

Bruce walked up to the nearest buffalo and watched for a while as a dozen men strained to roll it on to its back and begin butchering it. There were clusters of grape-blue ticks in the folds of skin between the legs and body.

A good head, he noted mechanically, forty inches at least.

'Plenty of meat, Captain. Tonight we eat thick!' grinned one of his gendarmes as he bent over the huge body to begin flensing.

'Plenty,' agreed Bruce and turned back to the Ranchero. In the heat of the kill it was a good feeling: the rifle's kick and your stomach screwed up with excitement. But afterwards you felt a little bit dirtied; sad and guilty as you do after lying with a woman you do not love.

He climbed into the car and Shermaine sat away from him, withdrawn.

'They were so big and ugly – beautiful,' she said softly.

'We needed the meat. I didn't kill them for fun.' But he thought with a little shame, I have killed many others for fun.

'Yes,' she agreed. 'We needed the meat.'

He turned the car off the road and signalled to the truck drivers to pull in behind him.

27

Later it was all right again. The meat-rich smoke from a dozen cooking fires drifted across the camp. The dark tree tops silhouetted against a sky full of stars, the friendly glow of the fires, and laughter, men's voices raised, someone singing, the night noises of the bush – insects and frogs in the nearby stream – a plate piled high with grilled fillets and slabs of liver, a bottle of beer from Ruffy's hoard, the air at last cooler, a small breeze to keep the mosquitoes away, and Shermaine sitting beside him on the blankets.

Ruffy drifted across to them, in one hand a stick loaded with meat from which the juice dripped and in the other hand a bottle held by the throat.

'How's it for another beer, boss?'

'Enough.' Bruce held up his hand. 'I'm full to the back teeth.'

'You're getting old, that's for sure. Me and the boys going to finish them buffalo or burst trying.' He squatted on his great haunches and his tone changed. 'The trucks are flat, boss. Reckon there's not a bucketful of gas in the lot of them.'

'I want you to drain all the tanks, Ruffy, and pour it into the Ford.'

Ruffy nodded and bit a hunk of meat off the end of the stick.

'Then first thing tomorrow morning you and I will go on to Msapa in the Ranchero and leave everyone else here. Lieutenant Hendry will be in charge.'

'You talking about me?' Wally came from one of the fires.

'Yes, I'm going to leave you in charge here while Ruffy and I go on to Msapa Junction to fetch help.' Bruce did not look at Hendry and he had difficulty keeping the loathing out of his voice. 'Ruffy, fetch the map will you?'

They spread it on the earth and huddled round it. Ruffy held the flashlight.

'I'd say we are about here.' Bruce touched the tiny black vein of the road. 'About seventy, eighty miles to Msapa.' He ran his finger along it. 'It will take us about five hours there and back. However, if the telegraph isn't working we might have to go on until we meet a patrol or find some other way of getting a message back to Elisabethville.'

Almost parallel to the road and only two inches from it on the large-scale map ran the thick red line that marked the Northern Rhodesian border. Wally Hendry's slitty eyes narrowed even further as he looked at it.

'Why not leave Ruffy here, and I'll go with you.' Hendry looked up at Bruce.

'I want Ruffy with me to translate if we meet any Africans along the way.' Also, thought Bruce, I don't want to be left on the side of the road with a bullet in my head while you drive on to Elisabethville.

'Suits me,' grunted Hendry. He dropped his eyes to the map. About forty miles to the border. A hard day's walk.

Bruce changed to French and spoke swiftly. 'Ruffy, hide the diamonds behind the dashboard of your truck. That way we are certain they will send a rescue party, even if we have to go Elisabethville.'

'Talk English, Bucko,' growled Hendry, but Ruffy nodded and answered, also in French.

'I will leave Sergeant Jacque to guard them.'

'NO!' said Bruce. 'Tell no one.'

'Cut it out!' rasped Hendry. 'Anything you say I want to hear.'

'We'll leave at dawn tomorrow,' Bruce reverted to English.

'May I go with you?' Shermaine spoke for the first time.

'I don't see why not.' Bruce smiled quickly at her, but Ruffy coughed awkwardly.

'Reckon that's not such a good idea, boss.'

'Why?' Bruce turned on him with his temper starting to rise.

'Well, boss,' Ruffy hesitated, and then went on, 'you, me and the lady all shoving off towards Elisabethville might not look so good to the boys. They might get ideas, think we're not coming back or something.'

Bruce was silent, considering it.

'That's right,' Hendry cut in. 'You might just take it into your head to keep going. Let her stay, sort of guarantee for the rest of us.'

'I don't mind, Bruce. I didn't think about it that way. I'll stay.'

'She'll have forty good boys looking after her, she'll be all right,' Ruffy assured Bruce.

'All right then, that's settled. It won't be for long, Shermaine.'

'I'll go and see about draining the trucks.' Ruffy stood up. 'See you in the morning, boss.'

'I'm going to get some more of that meat.' Wally picked up the map carelessly. 'Try and get some sleep tonight, Curry. Not too much grumble and grunt.'

In his exasperation, Bruce did not notice that Hendry had taken the map.

– 28 –

It rained in the early hours before the dawn and Bruce lay in the back of the Ranchero and listened to it drum on the metal roof. It was a lulling sound and a good feeling to lie warmly listening to the rain with the woman you love in your arms.

He felt her waking against him, the change in her breathing and the first slow movements of her body.

There were buffalo steaks for breakfast, but no coffee. They ate swiftly and then Bruce called across to Ruffy.

'Okay, Ruffy?'

'Let's go, boss.' They climbed into the Ford and Ruffy filled most of the seat beside Bruce. His helmet perched on the back of his head, rifle sticking out through the space where the windscreen should have been, and two large feet planted securely on top of the case of beer on the floor.

Bruce twisted the key and the engine fired. He warmed it at a fast idle and turned to Hendry who leaned against the roof of the Ford and peered through the window.

'We'll be back this afternoon. Don't let anybody wander away from camp.'

'Okay.' Hendry breathed his morning breath full into Bruce's face.

'Keep them busy, otherwise they'll get bored and start fighting.'

Before he answered Hendry let his eyes search the interior of the Ford carefully and then he stood back.

'Okay,' he said again. 'On your way!'

Bruce looked beyond him to where Shermaine sat on the tailboard of a truck and smiled at her.

'Bon voyage!' she called and Bruce let out the clutch. They bumped out on to the road amid a chorus of cheerful farewells from the gendarmes round the cooking fires and Bruce settled down to drive. In the rear-view mirror he watched the camp disappear round the curve in the road. There were puddles of rainwater in the road, but above them the clouds had broken up and scattered across the sky.

'How's it for a beer, boss?'

'Instead of coffee?' asked Bruce.

'Nothing like it for the bowels,' grunted Ruffy and reached down to open the case.

Wally Hendry lifted his helmet and scratched his scalp. His short red hair felt stiff and wiry with dried sweat and there was a spot above his right ear that itched. He fingered it tenderly.

The Ranchero disappeared round a bend in the road, the trees screening it abruptly, and the hum of its motor faded.

Okay, so they haven't taken the diamonds with them. I had a bloody good look around. I guessed they'd leave them. The girl knows where they are like as not. Perhaps – no, she'd squeal like a stuck pig if I asked.

Hendry looked sideways at Shermaine; she was staring after the Ranchero.

Silly bitch! Getting all broody now that Curry's giving her the rod. Funny how these educated Johnnies like their women to have small tits – nice piece of arse though. Wouldn't mind a bit of that myself. Jesus, that would really get to Mr High Class Bloody Curry, me giving his pretty the business. Not a chance though. These niggers think he's a god or something. They'd tear me to pieces if I touched her. Forget about it! Let's get the diamonds and take off for the border.

Hendry settled his helmet back on to his head and strolled casually across to the truck that Ruffy had been driving the day before.

Got a map, compass, coupla spare clips of ammo – now all we need is the glass.

He climbed into the cab and opened the cubby hole.

Bet a pound to a pinch of dung that they've hidden them somewhere in this truck. They're not worried – think they've got me tied up here. Never occurred to them that old Uncle Wally might up and walk away. Thought I'd just sit here and wait for them to come back and fetch me –

take me in and hand me over to a bunch of nigger police aching to get their hands on a white man.

Well, I got news for you, Mr Fancy-talking Curry!

He rummaged in the cubbyhole and then slammed it shut.

Okay, they're not there. Let's try under the seats. The border is not guarded, might take me three or four days to get through to Fort Rosebery, but when I do I'll have me a pocket full of diamonds and there's a direct air service out to Ndola and the rest of the world. Then we start living!

There was nothing under the seats except a greasy dust-coated jack and wheel spanner. Hendry turned his attention to the floorboards.

Pity I'll have to leave that bastard Curry. I had plans for him. There's a guy who really gets to me. So goddam cocksure of himself. One of them. Makes you feel you're shit — fancy talk, pretty face, soft hands. Christ, I hate him.

Viciously he tore the rubber mats off the floor and the dust made him cough.

Been to university, makes him think he's something special. The bastard. I should have fixed him long ago — that night at the road bridge I nearly gave it to him in the dark. Nobody would have known, just a mistake. I shoulda done it then. I shoulda done it at Port Reprieve when he ran out across the road to the office block. Big bloody hero. Big lover. Bet he had everything he ever wanted, bet his Daddy gave him all the money he could use. And he looks at you like that, like you crawled out of rotting meat.

Hendry straightened up and gripped the steering wheel, his jaws chewing with the strength of his hatred. He stared out of the windscreen.

Shermaine Cartier walked past the front of the truck. She had a towel and a pink plastic toilet bag in her hand; the pistol swung against her leg as she moved.

Sergeant Jacque stood up from the cooking fire and

moved to intercept her. They talked, arguing, then Shermaine touched the pistol at her side and laughed. A worried frown creased Jacque's black face and he shook his head dubiously. Shermaine laughed again, turned from him and set off down the road towards the stream. Her hair, caught carelessly at her neck with a ribbon, hung down her back on to the rose-coloured shirt she wore and the heavy canvas holster emphasized the unconsciously provocative swing of her hips. She went out of sight down the steep bank of the stream.

Wally Hendry chuckled and then licked his lips with the quick-darting tip of his tongue.

'This is going to make it perfect,' he whispered. 'They couldn't have done things to suit me better if they'd spent a week working it out.'

Eagerly he turned back to his search for the diamonds. Leaning forward he thrust his hand up behind the dashboard of the truck and it brushed against the bunch of canvas bags that hung from the mass of concealed wires.

'Come to Uncle Wally.' He jerked them loose and, holding them in his lap, began checking their contents. The third bag he opened contained the gem stones.

'Lovely, lovely grub,' he whispered at the dull glint and sparkle in the depths of the bag. Then he closed the drawstring, stuffed the bag into the pocket of his battle-jacket and buttoned the flap. He dropped the bags of industrial diamonds on to the floor and kicked them under the seat, picked up his rifle and stepped down out of the truck.

Three or four gendarmes looked up curiously at him as he passed the cooking fires. Hendry rubbed his stomach and pulled a face.

'Too much meat last night!'

The gendarme who understood English laughed and translated into French. They all laughed and one of them called something in a dialect that Hendry did not understand. They watched him walk away among the trees.

As soon as he was out of sight of the camp Hendry started to run, circling back towards the stream.

'This is going to be a pleasure!' He laughed aloud.

– 29 –

Fifty yards below the drift where the road crossed the stream Shermaine found a shallow pool. There were reeds with fluffy heads around it and a small beach of white river sand, black boulders, polished round and glossy smooth, the water almost blood warm and so clear that she could see a shoal of fingerlings nibbling at the green algae that coated the boulders beneath the surface.

She stood barefooted in the sand and looked around carefully, but the reeds screened her, and she had asked Jacque not to let any of his men come down to the river while she was there.

She undressed, dropped her clothes across one of the black boulders and with a cake of soap in her hand waded out into the pool and lowered herself until she sat with the water up to her neck and the sand pleasantly rough under her naked behind.

She washed her hair first and then lay stretched out with the water moving gently over her, soft as the caress of silk. Growing bold the tiny fish darted in and nibbled at her skin, tickling, so that she gasped and splashed at them.

At last she ducked her head under the surface and, with the water streaming out of her hair into her eyes, she groped her way back to the bank.

As she stooped, still half blinded, for her towel Wally Hendry's hand closed over her mouth and his other arm circled her waist from behind.

'One squeak out of you and I'll wring your bloody neck.' He spoke hoarsely into her ear. She could smell his breath, warm and sour in her face. 'Just pretend I'm old Bruce – then both of us will enjoy it.' And he chuckled.

Sliding quickly over her hip his hand moved downwards and the shock of it galvanized her into frantic struggles. Holding her easily Hendry kept on chuckling.

She opened her mouth suddenly and one of his fingers went in between her teeth. She bit with all her strength and felt the skin break and tasted blood in her mouth.

'You bitch!' Hendry jerked his hand away and she opened her mouth to scream, but the hand swung back, clenched, into the side of her face, knocking her head across. The scream never reached her lips for he hit her again and she felt herself falling.

Stunned by the blows, lying in the sand, she could not believe it was happening, until she felt his weight upon her and his knee forced cruelly between hers.

Then she started to struggle again, trying to twist away from his mouth and the smell of his breath.

'No, no, no.' She repeated it over and over, her eyes shut tightly so she did not have to see that face above her, and her head rolling from side to side in the sand. He was so strong, so immensely powerful.

'No,' she said, and then, 'Ooah!' at the pain, the tearing stinging pain within, and the thrusting heaviness above.

And through the pounding, grunting, thrusting nightmare she could smell him and feel the sweat drip from him and splash into her upturned unprotected face.

It lasted forever, and then suddenly the weight was gone and she opened her eyes.

He stood over her, fumbling with his clothing, and there was a dullness in his expression. He wiped his mouth with the back of his hand and she saw the fingers were trembling. His voice when he spoke was tired and disinterested.

'I've had better.'

Swiftly Shermaine rolled over and reached for the pistol

that lay on top of her clothes. Hendry stepped forward with all his weight on her wrist and she felt the bones bend under his boot and she moaned. But through pain she whispered. 'You pig, you filthy pig,' and he hit her again, flat-handed across the face, knocking her on to her back once more.

He picked up the pistol and opened it, spilling the cartridges into the sand, then he unclipped the lanyard and threw the pistol far out into the reed bed.

'Tell Curry I say he can have my share of you,' he said and walked quickly away among the reeds.

The white sand coated her damp body like icing sugar. She sat up slowly holding her wrist, the side of her face inflamed and starting to swell where he had hit her.

She started to cry, shaking silently, and the tears squeezed out between her eyelids and matted her long dark lashes.

– 30 –

Ruffy held up the brown bottle and inspected it ruefully.

'Seems like one mouthful and it's empty.' He threw the bottle out of the side window. It hit a tree and burst with a small pop.

'We can always find our way back by following the empties,' smiled Bruce, once more marvelling at the man's capacity. But there was plenty of storage space. He watched Ruffy's stomach spread on to his lap as he reached down to the beer crate.

'How we doing, boss?'

Bruce glanced at the milometer.

'We've come eighty-seven miles,' and Ruffy nodded.

'Not bad going. Be there pretty soon now.'

They were silent. The wind blew in on to them through

the open front. The grass that grew between the tracks brushed the bottom of the chassis with a continuous rushing sound.

'Boss—' Ruffy spoke at last.

'Yes?'

'Lieutenant Hendry – those diamonds. You reckon we did a good thing leaving him there?'

'He's stranded in the middle of the bush. Even if he did find them they wouldn't do him much good.'

'Suppose that's right.' Ruffy lifted the beer bottle to his lips and when he lowered it he went on. 'Mind you, that's one guy you can never be sure of.' He tapped his head with a finger as thick and as black as a blood-sausage. 'Something wrong with him – he's one of the maddest Arabs I've found in a long time of looking.'

Bruce grunted grimly.

'You want to be careful there, boss,' observed Ruffy. 'Any time now he's going to try for you. I've seen it coming. He's working himself up to it. He's a mad Arab.'

'I'll watch him,' said Bruce.

'Yeah, you do that.'

Again they were silent in the steady swish of the wind and the drone of the motor.

'There's a railway.' Ruffy pointed to the blue-gravelled embankment through the trees.

'Nearly there,' said Bruce.

They came out into another open glade and beyond it the water tank of Msapa Junction stuck up above the forest.

'Here we are,' said Ruffy and drained the bottle in his hand.

'Just say a prayer that the telegraph lines are still up and that there's an operator on the Elisabethville end.'

Bruce slowed the Ford past the row of cottages. They were exactly as he remembered them, deserted and forlorn. The corners of his mouth were compressed into a hard angle as he looked at the two small mounds of earth beneath the casia flora trees. Ruffy looked at them also but neither of them spoke.

Bruce stopped the Ford outside the station building and they climbed out stiffly and walked together on to the verandah. The wooden flooring echoed dully under their boots as they made for the door of the office.

Bruce pushed the door open and looked in. The walls were painted a depressing utility green, loose paper was scattered on the floor, the drawers of the single desk hung open, and a thin grey skin of dust coated everything.

'There she is,' said Ruffy and pointed to the brass and varnished wood complexity of the telegraph on a table against the far wall.

'Looks all right,' said Bruce. 'As long as the lines haven't been cut.'

As if to reassure him, the telegraph began to clatter like a typewriter.

'Thank God for that,' sighed Bruce.

They walked across to the table.

'You know how to work this thing?' asked Ruffy.

'Sort of,' Bruce answered and set his rifle against the wall. He was relieved to see a Morse table stuck with adhesive tape to the wall above the apparatus. It was a long time since he had memorized it as a boy scout.

He laid his hand on the transmission key and studied the table. The call sign for Elisabethville was 'EE'.

He tapped it out clumsily and then waited. Almost immediately the set clattered back at him, much too fast to be intelligible and the roll of paper in the repeater was exhausted. Bruce took off his helmet and laboriously spelled out, 'Transmit slower.'

It was a long business with requests for repetition. 'Not understood' was made nearly every second signal, but finally Bruce got the operator to understand that he had an urgent message for Colonel Franklyn of President Tshombe's staff.

'Wait,' came back the laconic signal.

And they waited. They waited an hour, then two.

'That mad bastard's forgotten about us,' grumbled Ruffy and went to the Ford to fetch the beer crate. Bruce fidgeted restlessly on the unpadded chair beside the telegraph table. He reconsidered anxiously all his previous arguments for leaving Wally Hendry in charge of the camp, but once again decided that it was safe. He couldn't do much harm. Unless, unless, Shermaine! No, it was impossible. Not with forty loyal gendarmes to protect her.

He started to think about Shermaine and the future. There was a year's mercenary captain's pay accumulated in the Crédit Banque Suisse at Zurich. He made the conversion from francs to pounds – about two and a half thousand. Two years' operating capital, so they could have a holiday before he started working again. They could take a chalet up in the mountains, there should be good snow this time of the year.

Bruce grinned. Snow that crunched like sugar, and a twelve-inch-thick eiderdown on the bed at night.

Life had purpose and direction again.

'What you're laughing at, boss?' asked Ruffy.

'I was thinking about a bed.'

'Yeah? That's a good thing to think about. You start there, you're born there, you spend most of your life in it, you have plenty of fun in it, and if you're lucky you die there. How's it for a beer?'

The telegraph came to life at Bruce's elbow. He turned to it quickly.

'Curry – Franklyn,' it clattered. Bruce could imagine the wiry, red-faced little man at the other end. Ex-major in the third brigade of the Legion. A prime mover in the O.A.S., with a sizeable price still on his head from the De Gaulle assassination attempt.

'Franklyn – Curry,' Bruce tapped back. 'Train unserviceable. Motorized transport stranded without fuel. Port

Reprieve road. Map reference approx—' He read the numbers off the sheet on which he had noted them.

There was a long pause, then:

'Is U.M.C. property in your hands?' The question was delicately phrased.

'Affirmative,' Bruce assured him.

'Await air-drop at your position soonest. Out.'

'Message understood. Out.' Bruce straightened from the telegraph and sighed with relief.

'That's that, Ruffy. They'll drop gas to us from one of the Dakotas. Probably tomorrow morning.' He looked at his wristwatch. 'Twenty to one, let's get back.'

Bruce hummed softly, watching the double tracks ahead of him, guiding the Ford with a light touch on the wheel.

He was contented. It was all over. Tomorrow the fuel would drop from the Dakota under those yellow parachutes. (He must lay out the smudge signals this evening.) And ten hours later they would be back in Elisabethville.

A few words with Carl Engelbrecht would fix seats for Shermaine and himself on one of the outward-bound Daks. Then Switzerland, and the chalet with icicles hanging from the eaves. A long rest while he decided where to start again. Louisiana was under Roman-Dutch Law, or was it Code Napoléon? He might even have to rewrite his bar examinations, but the prospect pleased rather than dismayed him. It was fun again.

'Never seen you so happy,' grunted Ruffy.

'Never had so much cause,' Bruce agreed.

'She's a swell lady. Young still – you can teach her.'

Bruce felt his hackles rise, and then he thought better of it and laughed.

'You going to sign her up, boss?'

'I might.'

Ruffy nodded wisely. 'Man should have plenty wives – I got three. Need a couple more.'

'One I could only just handle.'

'One's difficult. Two's easier. Three, you can relax. Four, they're so busy with each other they don't give you no trouble at all.'

'I might try it.'

'Yeah, you do that.'

And ahead of them through the trees they saw the ring of trucks.

'We're home,' grunted Ruffy, then he stirred uncomfortably in his seat. 'Something going on.'

Men stood in small groups. There was something in their attitude: strain, apprehension. Two men ran up the road to meet them. Bruce could see their mouths working, but could not hear the words.

Dread, heavy and cold, pushed down on the pit of Bruce's gut.

Gabbled, incoherent, Sergeant Jacque was trying to tell him something as he ran beside the Ford.

'Tenente Hendry – the river – the madame – gone.' French words like driftwood in the torrent of dialect.

'Your girl,' translated Ruffy. 'Hendry's done her.'

'Dead?' The question dropped from Bruce's mouth.

'No. He's hurt her. He's – you know!'

'Where's she?'

'They've got her in the back of the truck.'

Bruce climbed heavily out of the car. Now they were silent, grouped together, not looking at him, faces impassive, waiting.

Bruce walked slowly to the truck. He felt cold and numb. His legs moved automatically beneath him. He drew back the canvas and pulled himself up into the interior. It was an effort to move forward, to focus his eyes in the gloom.

Wrapped in a blanket she lay small and still.

'Shermaine.' It stuck in his throat.

'Shermaine,' he said again and knelt beside her. A great

259

livid swelling distorted the side of her face. She did not turn her head to him, but lay staring up at the canvas roof.

He touched her face and the skin was cold, cold as the dread that gripped his stomach. The coldness of it shocked him so he jerked his hand away.

'Shermaine.' This time it was a sob. The eyes, her big haunted eyes, turned unseeing towards him and he felt the lift of escape from the certainty of her death.

'Oh, God,' he cried and took her to him, holding the unresisting frailty of her to his chest. He could feel the slow even thump of her heart beneath his hand. He drew back the blanket and there was no blood.

'Darling, are you hurt? Tell me, are you hurt?' She did not answer. She lay quietly in his arms, not seeing him.

'Shock,' he whispered. 'It's only shock,' and he opened her clothing. With tenderness he examined the smoothly pale body; the skin was clammy and damp, but there was no damage.

He wrapped her again and laid her gently back on to the floor.

He stood and the thing within him changed shape. Cold still, but now burning cold as dry ice.

Ruffy and Jacque were waiting for him beside the tailboard.

'Where is he?' asked Bruce softly.

'He is gone.'

'Where?'

'That way.' Jacque pointed towards the south-east. 'I followed the spoor a short distance.'

Bruce walked to the Ford and picked up his rifle from the floor. He opened the cubby hole and took two spare clips of ammunition from it.

Ruffy followed him. 'He's got the diamonds, boss.'

'Yes,' said Bruce and checked the load of his rifle. The diamonds were of no importance.

'Are you going after him, boss?'

260

Bruce did not answer. Instead he looked up at the sky. The sun was half way towards the horizon and there were clouds thickly massed around it.

'Ruffy, stay with her,' he said softly. 'Keep her warm.'

Ruffy nodded.

'Who is the best tracker we've got?'

'Jacque. Worked for a safari outfit before the war as a tracker boy.'

Bruce turned to Jacque. The thing was still icy cold inside him, with tentacles that spread out to every extremity of his body and his mind.

'When did this happen?'

'About an hour after you left,' answered Jacque.

Eight hours start. It was a long lead.

'Take the spoor,' said Bruce softly.

– 31 –

The earth was soft from the night's rain and the spoor deep trodden, the heels had bitten in under Hendry's weight, so they followed fast.

Watching Sergeant Jacque work, Bruce felt his anxiety abating, for although the footprints were so easy to follow in these early stages that it was no test of his ability, yet from the way he moved swiftly along – half-crouched and wholly absorbed, occasionally glancing ahead to pick up the run of the spoor, stooping now and then to touch the earth and determine its texture – Bruce could tell that this man knew his business.

Through the open forest with tufted grass below, holding steadily south by east, Hendry led them straight towards the Rhodesian border. And after the first two hours Bruce knew they had not gained upon him. Hendry was still eight hours ahead, and at the pace he was setting eight hours' start was something like thirty miles in distance.

261

Bruce looked over his shoulder at the sun where it lay wedged between two vast piles of cumulonimbus. There in the sky were the two elements which could defeat him.

Time. There were perhaps two more hours of daylight. With the onset of night they would be forced to halt.

Rain. The clouds were swollen and dark blue round the edges. As Bruce watched, the lightning lit them internally, and at a count of ten the thunder grumbled suddenly. If it rained again before morning there would be no spoor to follow.

'We must move faster,' said Bruce.

Sergeant Jacque straightened up and looked at Bruce as though he were a stranger. He had forgotten his existence.

'The earth hardens.' Jacque pointed at the spoor and Bruce saw that in the last half hour the soil had become gritty and compacted. Hendry's heels no longer broke the crust. 'It is unwise to run on such a lean trail.'

Again Bruce looked back at the menace of gathering clouds.

'We must take the chance,' he decided.

'As you wish,' grunted Jacque, and transferred his rifle to his other shoulder, hitched up his belt and settled the steel helmet more firmly on his head.

'Allez!'

They trotted on through the forest towards the south-east. Within a mile Bruce's body had settled into the automatic rhythm of his run, leaving his mind free.

He thought about Wally Hendry, saw again the little eyes and round them the puffy folded skin, and the mouth below, thin and merciless, the obscene ginger stubble of beard. He could almost smell him. His nostrils flared at the memory of the rank red-head's body odour. Unclean, he thought, unclean mind and unclean body.

His hatred of Wally Hendry was a tangible thing. He could feel it sitting heavily at the base of his throat, tingling in his fingertips and giving strength to his legs.

And yet there was something else. Suddenly Bruce grinned: a wolfish baring of his teeth. That tingling in his fingertips was not all hatred, a little of it was excitement.

What a complex thing is a man, he thought. He can never hold one emotion – always there are others to confuse it. Here I am hunting the thing that I most loathe and hate, and I am enjoying it. Completely unrelated to the hatred is the thrill of hunting the most dangerous and cunning game of all, man.

I have always enjoyed the chase, he thought. It has been bred into me, for my blood is that of the men who hunted and fought with Africa as the prize.

The hunting of this man will give me pleasure. If ever a man deserved to die, it is Wally Hendry. I am the plaintiff, the judge and the executioner.

Sergeant Jacque stopped so suddenly that Bruce ran into him and they nearly fell.

'What is it?' panted Bruce, coming back to reality.

'Look!'

The earth ahead of them was churned and broken.

'Zebra,' groaned Bruce, recognizing the round uncloven hoof prints. 'God damn it to hell – of all the filthy luck!'

'A big herd,' Jacque agreed. 'Spread out. Feeding.'

As far ahead as they could see through the forest the herd had wiped out Hendry's tracks.

'We'll have to cast forward.' Bruce's voice was agonized by his impatience. He turned to the nearest tree and hacked at it with his bayonet, blazing it to mark the end of the trail, swearing softly, venting his disappointment on the trunk.

'Only another hour to sunset,' he whispered. 'Please let us pick him up again before dark.'

Sergeant Jacque was already moving forward, following the approximate line of Hendry's travel, trying vainly to recognize a single footprint through the havoc created there by the passage of thousands of hooves. Bruce hurried to join him and then moved out on his flank. They zigzagged slowly ahead, almost meeting on the inward leg of each tack and then separating again to a distance of a hundred yards.

There it was! Bruce dropped to his knees to make sure. Just the outline of the toecap showing from under the spoor of an old zebra stallion. Bruce whistled, a windy sound through his dry lips, and Jacque came quickly. One quick look, then:

'Yes, he is holding more to the right now.' He raised his eyes and squinted ahead, marking a tree which was directly in line with the run of the spoor. They went forward.

'There's the herd.' Bruce pointed at the flicker of a grey body through the trees.

'They've got our wind.'

A zebra snorted and then there was a rumbling, a low blurred drumming of hooves as the herd ran. Through the trees Bruce caught glimpses of the animals on the near side of the herd. Too far off to show the stripes, looking like fat grey ponies as they galloped, ears up, black-maned heads nodding. Then they were gone and the sound of their flight dwindled.

'At least they haven't run along the spoor,' muttered Bruce, and then bitterly: 'Damn them, the stupid little donkeys! They've cost us an hour. A whole priceless hour.'

Desperately searching, wild with haste, they worked back and forth. The sun was below the trees; already the air was cooling in the short African dusk. Another fifteen minutes and it would be dark.

Then abruptly the forest ended and they came out on the edge of a vlei. Open as wheatland, pastured with green waist-high grass, hemmed in by the forest, it stretched ahead of them for nearly two miles. Dotted along it were clumps of ivory palms with each graceful stem ending in an untidy cluster of leaves. Troops of guinea-fowls were scratching and chirruping along the edge of the clearing, and near the far end a herd of buffalo formed a dark mass as they grazed beneath a canopy of white egrets.

In the forest beyond the clearing, rising perhaps three hundred feet out of it, stood a kopje of tumbled granite. The great slabs of rock with their sheer sides and square tops looked like a ruined castle. The low sun struck it and gave the rock an orange warmth.

But Bruce had no time to admire the scene; his eyes were on the earth, searching for the prints of Hendry's jungle boots.

Out on his left Sergeant Jacque whistled sharply and Bruce felt the leap of excitement in his chest. He ran across to the crouching gendarme.

'It has come away.' Jacque pointed at the spoor that was strung ahead of them like beads on a string, skirting the edge of the vlei, each depression filled with shadow and standing out clearly on the sandy grey earth.

'Too late,' groaned Bruce. 'Damn those bloody zebra.' The light was fading so swiftly it seemed as though it were a stage effect.

'Follow it.' Bruce's voice was sharp with helpless frustration. 'Follow it as long as you can.'

It was not a quarter of a mile farther on that Jacque rose out of his crouch and only the white of his teeth showed in the darkness as he spoke.

'We will lose it again if we go on.'

'All right.' Bruce unslung his rifle with weary resignation. He knew that Wally Hendry was at least forty miles ahead of them; more if he kept travelling after dark. The spoor was cold. If this had been an ordinary hunt he would long ago have broken off the chase.

He looked up at the sky. In the north the stars were fat and yellow, but above them and to the south it was black with cloud.

'Don't let it rain,' he whispered. 'Please God, don't let it rain.'

The night was long. Bruce slept once for perhaps two hours and then the strength of his hatred woke him. He lay flat upon his back and stared up at the sky. It was all dark with clouds; only occasionally they opened and let the stars shine briefly through.

'It must not rain. It must not rain.' He repeated it like a prayer, staring up at the dark sky, concentrating upon it as though by the force of his mind he could control the elements.

There were lions hunting in the forest. He heard the male roaring, moving up from the south, and once his two lionesses answered him. They killed a little before dawn and Bruce lay on the hard earth and listened to their jubilation over the kill. Then there was silence as they began to feed.

That I might have success as well, he thought. I do not often ask for favours, Lord, but grant me this one. I ask it not only for myself but for Shermaine and the others.

In his mind he saw again the two children lying where Hendry had shot them. The smear of mingled blood and chocolate across the boy's cheek.

He deserves to die, prayed Bruce, so please don't let it rain.

As long as the night had been, that quickly came the dawn. A grey dawn, gloomy with low cloud.

'Will it go?' Bruce asked for the twentieth time, and this time Jacque looked up from where he knelt beside the spoor.

'We can try now.'

They moved off slowly with Jacque leading, doubled over to peer short-sightedly at the earth and Bruce close behind him, bedevilled by his impatience and anxiety, lifting his head every dozen paces to the dirty grey roof of cloud.

The light strengthened and the circle of their vision opened from six feet to as many yards, to a hundred, so they could make out the tops of the ivory palms, shaggy against the grey cloud.

Jacque broke into a trot and ahead of them was the end of the clearing and the beginning of the forest. Two hundred yards beyond rose the massive pile of the kopje, in the early light looking more than ever like a castle, turreted and sheer. There was something formidable in its outline. It seemed to brood above them and Bruce looked away from it uneasily.

Cold and with enough weight behind it to sting, the first raindrop splashed against Bruce's cheek.

'Oh, no!' he protested, and stopped. Jacque straightened up from the spoor and he too looked at the sky.

'It is finished. In five minutes there will be nothing to follow.'

Another drop hit Bruce's upturned face and he blinked back the tears of anger and frustration that pricked the rims of his eyelids.

Faster now, tapping on his helmet, plopping on to his shoulders and face, the rain fell.

'Quickly,' cried Bruce. 'Follow as long as you can.'

Jacque opened his mouth to speak, but before a word came out he was flung backwards, punched over as though by an invisible fist, his helmet flying from his head as he fell and his rifle clattering on the earth.

Simultaneously Bruce felt the bullet pass him, disrupting the air, so the wind of it flattened his shirt against his chest, cracking viciously in his ears, leaving him dazedly looking down at Sergeant Jacque's body.

It lay with arms thrown wide, the jaw and the side of the head below the ear torn away; white bone and blood bubbling over it. The trunk twitched convulsively and the hands fluttered like trapped birds. Then flat-sounding through the rain he heard the report of the rifle.

The kopje, screamed Bruce's brain, *he's lying in the kopje!*

And Bruce moved, twisting sideways, starting to run.

Wally Hendry lay on his stomach on the flat top of the turret. His body was stiff and chilled from the cold of the night and the rock was harsh under him, but the discomfort hardly penetrated the fringe of his mind. He had built a low parapet with loose flakes of granite, and he had screened the front of it with the thick bushy stems of broom bush.

His rifle was propped on the parapet in front of him and at his elbow were the spare ammunition clips.

He had lain in this ambush for a long time now – since early the preceding afternoon. Now it was dawn and the darkness was drawing back; in a few minutes he would be able to see the whole of the clearing below him.

I coulda been across the river already, he thought, *coulda been fifty miles away*. He did not attempt to analyse the impulse that had made him lie here unmoving for almost twenty hours.

Man, I knew old Curry would have to come. I knew he would only bring one nigger tracker with him. These educated Johnnies got their own rules – man to man stuff, and he chuckled as he remembered the two minute figures that he had seen come out of the forest in the fading light of the previous evening.

The bastard spent the night down there in the clearing. Saw him light a match and have hisself a smoke in the night – well, I hope he enjoyed it, his last.

Wally peered anxiously out into the gradually gathering dawn.

They'll be moving now, coming up the clearing. Must get them before they reach the trees again. Below him the clearing showed as a paleness, a leprous blotch, on the dark forest.

The bastard! Without preliminaries Hendry's hatred

returned to him. *This time he don't get to make no fancy speeches. This time he don't get no chance to be hoity-toity.*

The light was stronger now. He could see the clumps of ivory palms against the pale brown grass of the clearing.

'Ha!' Hendry exclaimed.

There they were, like two little ants, dark specks moving up the middle of the clearing. The tip of Hendry's tongue slipped out between his lips and he flattened down behind his rifle.

Man, I've waited for this. Six months now I've thought about this, and when it's finished I'll go down and take his ears. He slipped the safety catch; it made a satisfying mechanical click.

Nigger's leading, that's Curry behind him. Have to wait till they turn, don't want the nigger to get it first. Curry first, then the nigger.

He picked them up in his sights, breathing quicker now, the thrill of it so intense that he had to swallow and it caught in his throat like dry bread.

A raindrop hit the back of his neck. It startled him. He looked up quickly at the sky and saw it coming.

'Goddam it,' he groaned, and looked back at the clearing. Curry and nigger were standing together, a single dark blob in the half-light. There was no chance of separating them. The rain fell faster, and suddenly Hendry was overwhelmed by the old familiar feeling of inferiority; of knowing that everything, even the elements, conspired against him; the knowledge that he could never win, not even this once.

They, God and the rest of the world.

The ones who had given him a drunk for a father.

A squalid cottage for a home and a mother with cancer of the throat.

The ones who had sent him to reform school, had fired him from two dozen jobs, had pushed him, laughed at him, gaoled him twice – They, all of them (and Bruce Curry who

269

was their figurehead), they were going to win again. Not even this once, not even ever.

'Goddam it,' he cursed in hopeless, wordless anger against them all.

'Goddam it, goddam it to hell,' and he fired at the dark blob in his sights.

– 33 –

As he ran Bruce looked across a hundred yards of open ground to the edge of the forest.

He felt the wind of the next bullet as it cracked past him.

If he uses rapid fire he'll get me even at three hundred yards.

And Bruce jinked his run like a jack-rabbit. The blood roaring in his ears, fear driving his feet.

Then all around him the air burst asunder, buffeting him so he staggered; the vicious whip-whip-whip of bullets filled his head.

I can't make it.

Seventy yards to the shelter of the trees. Seventy yards of open meadowland, and above him the commanding mass of the kopje.

The next burst is for me – it must come, now!

And he flung himself to one side so violently that he nearly fell. Again the air was ripping to tatters close beside him.

I can't last! He must get me!

In his path was an ant-heap, a low pile of clay, a pimple on the open expanse of earth. Bruce dived for it, hitting the ground so hard that the wind was forced from his lungs out through his open mouth.

The next burst of gunfire kicked lumps of clay from the top of the ant-heap, showering Bruce's back.

He lay with his face pressed into the earth, wheezing

with the agony of empty lungs, flattening his body behind the tiny heap of clay.

Will it cover me? Is there enough of it?

And the next hail of bullets thumped into the ant-heap, throwing fountains of earth, but leaving Bruce untouched.

I'm safe. The realization came with a surge that washed away his fear.

But I'm helpless, answered his hatred. *Pinned to the earth for as long as Hendry wants to keep me here.*

The rain fell on his back. Soaking through his jacket, coldly caressing the nape of his neck and dribbling down over his jaws.

He rolled his head sideways, not daring to lift it an inch, and the rain beat on to the side of his face.

The rain! Falling faster. Thickening. Hanging from the clouds like the skirts of a woman's dress.

Curtains of rain. Greying out the edge of the forest, leaving no solid shapes in the mist of falling liquid mother-of-pearl.

Still gasping but with the pain slowly receding, Bruce lifted his head.

The kopje was a vague blue-green shape ahead of him, then it was gone, swallowed by the eddying columns of rain.

Bruce pushed himself up on to his knees and the pain in his chest made him dizzy.

Now! he thought. *Now, before it thins*, and he lumbered clumsily to his feet.

For a moment he stood clutching his chest, sucking for breath in the haze of water-filled air, and then he staggered towards the edge of the forest.

His feet steadied under him, his breathing eased, and he was into the trees.

They closed round him protectively. He leaned against the rough bark of one of them and wiped the rain from his face with the palm of his hand. The strength came back to him and with it his hatred and his excitement.

He unslung the rifle from his shoulder and stood away from the tree with his feet planted wide apart.

'Now, my friend,' he whispered, 'we fight on equal terms.' He pumped a round into the chamber of the FN and moved towards the kopje, stepping daintily, the weight of the rifle in his hands, his mind suddenly sharp and clear, vision enhanced, feeling his strength and the absence of fear like a song within him, a battle hymn.

He made out the loom of the kopje through the dripping rain-heavy trees and he circled out to the right. There is plenty of time, he thought. I can afford to case the joint thoroughly. He completed his circuit of the rock pile.

The kopje, he found, was the shape of a galleon sinking by the head. At one end the high double castles of the poop, from which the main deck canted steeply forward as though the prow were already under water. This slope was scattered with boulders and densely covered with dwarf scrub, an interwoven mass of shoulder-high branches and leaves.

Bruce squatted on his haunches with the rifle in his lap and looked up the ramp at the twin turrets of the kopje. The rain had slackened to a drizzle.

Hendry was on top. Bruce knew he would go to the highest point. Strange how height makes a man feel invulnerable, makes him think he is a god.

And since he had fired upon them he must be in the turret nearest the vlei, which was slightly the higher of the two, its summit crowned by a patch of stunted broom bush.

So now I know exactly where he is and I will wait half an hour. He may become impatient and move; if he does I will get a shot at him from here.

Bruce narrowed his eyes, judging the distance.

'About two hundred yards.'

He adjusted the rear-sight of the FN and then checked the load, felt in the side pocket of his jacket to make sure the two extra clips of ammunition were handy, and settled back comfortably to wait.

'Curry, you sonofabitch, where are you?' Hendry's shout floated down through the drizzling rain and Bruce stiffened.

I was right – he's on top of the left-hand turret.

'Come on, Bucko. I've been waiting for you since yesterday afternoon.'

Bruce lifted the rifle and sighted experimentally at a dark patch on the wall of the rock. It would be difficult shooting in the rain, the rifle slippery with wet, the fine drizzle clinging to his eyebrows and dewing the sights of the rifle with little beads of moisture.

'Hey, Curry, how's your little French piece of pussy? Man, she's hot, that thing, isn't she?'

Bruce's hands tightened on the rifle.

'Did she tell you how I gave her the old business? Did she tell you how she loved it? You should have heard her panting like a steam engine. I'm telling you, Curry, she just couldn't get enough!'

Bruce felt himself start to tremble. He clenched his jaws, biting down until his teeth ached.

Steady, Bruce my boy, that's what he wants you to do.

The trees dripped steadily in the silence and a gust of wind stirred the scrub on the slope of the kopje. Bruce waited, straining his eyes for the first hint of movement on the left-hand turret.

'You yellow or something, Curry? You scared to come on up here? Is that what it is?'

Bruce shifted his position slightly, ready for a snap shot.

'Okay, Bucko. I can wait, I've got all day. I'll just sit here thinking about how I mucked your little bit of French. I'm telling you it was something to remember. Up and down, in and out, man it was something!'

Bruce came carefully up on to his feet behind the trunk of the tree and once more studied the layout of the kopje.

If I can move up the slope, keeping well over to the side, until I reach the right-hand turret, there's a ledge there that will take me to the top. I'll be twenty or thirty feet from him, and at that range it will all be over in a few seconds.

He drew a deep breath and left the shelter of the tree.

Wally Hendry spotted the movement in the forest below him; it was a flash of brown quickly gone, too fast to get a bead on it.

He wiped the rain off his face and wriggled a foot closer to the edge.

'Come on, Curry. Let's stop buggering about,' he shouted, and cuddled the butt of his rifle into his shoulder. The tip of his tongue kept darting out and touching his lips.

At the foot of the slope he saw a branch move slightly, stirring when there was no wind. He grinned and snuggled his hips down on to the rock. *Here he comes*, he gloated, *he's crawling up, under the scrub.*

'I know you're sitting down there. Okay, Curry, I can wait also.'

Half-way up the slope the top leaves of another bush swayed gently, parting and closing.

'Yes!' whispered Wally, 'Yes!' and he clicked off the safety catch of the rifle. His tongue came out and moved slowly from one corner of his mouth to the other.

I've got him, for sure! There – he'll have to cross that piece of open ground. A couple a yards, that's all. But it'll be enough.

He moved again, wriggling a few inches to one side, settling his aim into the gap between two large grey boulders; he pushed the rate-of-fire selector on to rapid and his forefinger rested lightly on the trigger.

'Hey, Curry, I'm getting bored. If you are not going to come up, how about singing to me or cracking a few jokes?'

Bruce Curry crouched behind a large grey boulder. In front of him were three yards of open ground and then the shelter of another rock. He was almost at the top of the slope and Hendry had not spotted him. Across the patch of open ground was good cover to the foot of the right-hand turret.

It would take him two seconds to cross and the chances were that Hendry would be watching the forest at the foot of the slope.

He gathered himself like a sprinter on the starting blocks.

'Go!' he whispered and dived into the opening, and into a hell storm of bullets. One struck his rifle, tearing it out of his hand with such force that his arm was paralysed to the shoulder, another stung his chest, and then he was across. He lay behind the far boulder, gasping with the shock, and listened to Hendry's voice roaring triumphantly.

'Fooled you, you stupid bastard! Been watching you all the way up from the bottom.'

Bruce held his left arm against his stomach; the use of it was returning as the numbness subsided, but with it came the ache. The top joint of his thumb had caught in the trigger guard and been torn off; now the blood welled out of the stump thickly and slowly, dark blood the colour of apple jelly. With his right hand he groped for his handkerchief.

'Hey, Curry, your rifle's lying there in the open. You might need it in a few minutes. Why don't you go out and fetch it?'

Bruce bound the handkerchief tightly round the stump of his thumb and the bleeding slowed. Then he looked at the rifle where it lay ten feet away. The foresight had been knocked off, and the same bullet that had amputated his thumb had smashed into the breech, buckled the loading handle and the slide. He knew that it was damaged beyond repair.

'Think I'll have me a little target practice,' shouted Hendry from above, and again there was a burst of automatic fire. Bruce's rifle disappeared in a cloud of dust and flying rock fragments and when it cleared the woodwork of the rifle was splintered and torn and there was further damage to the action.

Well, that's that, thought Bruce, *rifle's wrecked, Shermaine has the pistol, and I have only one good hand. This is going to be interesting.*

He unbuttoned the front of his jacket and examined the welt that the bullet had raised across his chest. It looked like a rope burn, painful and red, but not serious. He rebuttoned his jacket.

'Okay, Bruce Baby, the time for games is over. I'm coming down to get you.' Hendry's voice was harsh and loud, filled with confidence.

Bruce rallied under the goading of it. He looked round quickly. *Which way to go? Climb high so he must come up to get at you. Take the right-hand turret, work round the side of it and wait for him on the top.*

In haste now, spurred by the dread of being the hunted, he scrambled to his feet and dodged away up the slope, keeping his head down using the thick screen of rock and vegetation.

He reached the wall of the right-hand turret and followed it round, found the spiral ledge that he had seen from below and went on to it, up along it like a fly on a wall, completely exposed, keeping his back to the cliff of granite, shuffling sideways up the eighteen-inch ledge with the drop below him growing deeper with each step.

Now he was three hundred feet above the forest and could look out across the dark green land to another row of kopjes on the horizon. The rain had ceased but the cloud was unbroken, covering the sky.

The ledge widened, became a platform and Bruce hurried across it round the far shoulder and came to a dead end. The ledge had petered out and there was only the drop below. He had trapped himself on the side of the turret – the summit was unattainable. If Hendry descended to the forest floor and circled the kopje he would find Bruce completely at his mercy, for there was no cover on the narrow ledge. Hendry could have a little more target practice.

Bruce leaned against the rock and struggled to control his breathing. His throat was clogged with the thick saliva of exhaustion and fear. He felt tired and helpless, his thumb throbbed painfully and he lifted it to examine it once more. Despite the tourniquet it was bleeding slowly, a wine-red drop at a time.

Bleeding! Bruce swallowed the thick gluey stuff in his throat and looked back along the way he had come. On the grey rock the bright red splashes stood out clearly. He had laid a blood spoor for Hendry to follow.

All right then, perhaps it is best this way. At least I may be able to come to grips with him. If I wait behind this shoulder until he starts to cross the platform, there's a three hundred foot drop on one side, I may be able to rush him and throw him off.

Bruce leaned against the shoulder of granite, hidden from the platform, and tuned his ears to catch the first sound of Hendry's approach.

The clouds parted in the eastern sector of the sky and the sun shone through, slanting across the side of the kopje.

It will be better to die in the sun, thought Bruce, *a sacrifice to the Sun god thrown from the roof of the temple*, and he grinned without mirth, waiting with patience and with pain.

The minutes fell like drops into the pool of time, slowly measuring out the ration of life that had been allotted to him. The pulse in his ears counted also, and his breath that he drew and held and gently exhaled – how many more would there be?

I should pray, he thought, *but after this morning when I prayed that it should not rain, and the rains came and saved me, I will not presume again to tell the Old Man how to run things. Perhaps he knows best after all.*

Thy will be done, he thought instead, and suddenly his

nerves jerked tight as a line hit by a marlin. The sound he had heard was that of cloth brushing against rough rock.

He held his breath and listened, but all he could discern was the pulse in his ears and the wind in the trees of the forest below. The wind was a lonely sound.

Thy will be done, he repeated without breathing, and heard Hendry breathe close behind the shoulder of rock.

He stood away from the wall and waited. Then he saw Hendry's shadow thrown by the early morning sun along the ledge. A great distorted shadow on the grey rock.

Thy will be done. And he went round the shoulder fast, his good hand held like a blade and the weight of his body behind it.

Hendry was three feet away, the rifle at high port across his chest, standing close in against the cliff, the cup-shaped steel helmet pulled low over the slitty eyes and little beads of sweat clinging in the red-gold stubble of his beard. He tried to drop the muzzle of the rifle but Bruce was too close.

Bruce lunged with stiff fingers at his throat and he felt the crackle and give of cartilage. Then his weight carried him on and Hendry sprawled backwards on to the stone platform with Bruce on top of him.

The rifle slithered across the rock and dropped over the edge, and they lay chest to chest with legs locked together in a horrible parody of the love act. But in *this* act we do not procreate, we destroy!

Hendry's face was purple and swollen above his damaged throat, his mouth open as he struggled for air, and his breath smelt old and sour in Bruce's face.

With a twist towards the thumb Bruce freed his right wrist from Hendry's grip and, lifting it like an axe, brought it down across the bridge of Hendry's nose. Twin jets of blood spouted from the nostrils and gushed into his open mouth.

With a wet strangling sound in his throat Hendry's body

arched violently upwards and Bruce was thrown back against the side of the cliff with such force that for a second he lay there.

Wally was on his knees, facing Bruce, his eyes glazed and sightless, and the strangling rattling sound spraying from his throat in a pink cloud of blood. With both hands he was fumbling his pistol out of its canvas holster.

Bruce drew his knees up on to his chest, then straightened his legs in a mule kick. His feet landed together in the centre of Hendry's stomach, throwing him backwards off the platform. Hendry made that strangled bellow all the way to the bottom, but at the end it was cut off abruptly, and afterwards there was only the sound of the wind in the forest below.

For a long time, drained of strength and the power to think, Bruce sat on the ledge with his back against the rock.

Above him the clouds had rolled aside and half the sky was blue. He looked out across the land and the forest was lush and clean from the rain. *And I am still alive.* The realization warmed Bruce's mind as comfortably as the early sun was warming his body. He wanted to shout it out across the forest. *I am still alive!*

At last he stood up, crossed to the edge of the cliff and looked down at the tiny crumpled figure on the rocks below. Then he turned away and dragged his beaten body down the side of the turret.

It took him twenty minutes to find Wally Hendry in the chaos of broken rock and scrub below the turret. He lay on his side with his legs drawn up as though he slept. Bruce knelt beside him and drew his pistol from the olive-green canvas holster; then he unbuttoned the flap of Hendry's bulging breast pocket and took out the white canvas bag.

He stood up, opened the mouth of the bag and stirred the diamonds with his forefinger. Satisfied, he jerked the drawstring closed and dropped them into his own pocket.

In death he is even more repulsive than he was alive, thought Bruce without regret as he looked down at the corpse.

The flies were crawling into the bloody nostrils and clustering round the eyes.

Then he spoke aloud.

'So Mike Haig was right and I was wrong – you can destroy it.'

Without looking back he walked away. The tiredness left him.

– 34 –

Carl Engelbrecht came through the doorway from the cockpit into the main cabin of the Dakota.

'Are you two happy?' he asked above the deep drone of the engines, and then grinning with his big brown face, 'I can see you are!'

Bruce grinned back at him and tightened his arm around Shermaine's shoulders.

'Go away! Can't you see we're busy?'

'You've got lots of cheek for a hitch-hiker – bloody good mind to make you get out and walk,' he grumbled as he sat down beside them on the bench that ran the full length of the fuselage. 'I've brought you some coffee and sandwiches.'

'Good. Good. I'm starving.' Shermaine sat up and reached for the thermos flask and the greaseproof paper packet. The bruise on her cheek had faded to a shadow with yellow edges – it was almost ten days old. With his mouth full of chicken sandwich Bruce kicked one of the wooden cases that were roped securely to the floor of the aircraft.

'What have you got in these, Carl?'

'Dunno,' said Carl and poured coffee into the three plastic mugs. 'In this game you don't ask questions. You fly out, take your money, and let it go.' He drained his mug and stood up. 'Well, I'll leave you two alone now. We'll be in Nairobi in a couple of hours, so you can sleep or something!' He winked. 'You'll have to stay aboard while we refuel. But we'll be airborne again in an hour or so, and the day after tomorrow, God and the weather permitting, we'll set you down in Zurich.'

'Thanks, old cock.'

'Think nothing of it – all in the day's work.'

He went forward and disappeared into the cockpit, closing the door behind him.

Shermaine turned back to Bruce, studied him for a moment and then laughed.

'You look so different – now you look like a lawyer!'

Self-consciously Bruce tightened the knot of his Old Michaelhouse tie.

'I must admit it feels strange to wear a suit and tie again.' He looked down at the well-cut blue suit – the only one he had left – and then up again at Shermaine.

'And in a dress I hardly recognize you either.' She was wearing a lime-green cotton frock, cool and crisp looking, white high-heel shoes and just a little make-up to cover the bruise. A damn fine woman, Bruce decided with pleasure.

'How does your thumb feel?' she asked, and Bruce held up the stump with its neat little turban of adhesive tape.

'I had almost forgotten about it.'

Suddenly Shermaine's expression changed, and she pointed excitedly out of the perspex window behind Bruce's shoulder.

'Look, there's the sea!' It lay far below them, shaded from blue to pale green in the shallows, with a round of white beach and the wave formation moving across it like ripples on a pond.

'That's Lake Tanganyika.' Bruce laughed. 'We've left the Congo behind.'

'Forever?' she asked.

'Forever!' he assured her.

The aircraft banked slightly, throwing them closer together, as Carl picked out his landmarks and altered course towards the north-east.

Four thousand feet below them the dark insect that was their shadow flitted and hopped across the surface of the water.

THE SUNBIRD

For my wife, Danielle

PART I

I t cut across the darkened projection room and exploded silently against the screen – and I did not recognize it. I had waited fifteen years for it, and when it came I did not recognize it. The image was swirled and vague, and it made no sense to me for I had expected a photograph of some small object; a skull perhaps, or pottery, or an artefact, a piece of gold work, beads – certainly not this surrealistic pattern of grey and white and black.

Louren's voice, tight with excitement, gave me the clue I needed. 'Taken at thirty-six thou. at six forty-seven on the fourth of Sept,' that was eight days ago, 'exposed in a 35 mm. Leica.'

An aerial photograph then. My eyes and brain adjusted, and almost instantly I felt the first tickle of my own excitement begin as Louren went on in the same crisp tone.

'I've got a charter company running an aerial survey over all my concession areas. The idea is to pick the strike and run of geographical formations. This photograph is only one of a couple of hundred thousand of the area – the navigator did not even know what he was photographing. However, the people in analysis spotted it, and passed it on to me.'

His face turned towards me, pale and solemn in the glare of the projector.

'You can see it, can't you, Ben? Just off centre. Top right quarter.'

I opened my mouth to reply, but my voice caught in my throat and I had to turn the sound I made into a cough. With surprise I found I was trembling, and my guts seethed with an amalgam of hope and dread.

3

'It's classic! Acropolis, double enclosure and the "phallic towers".' He was exaggerating, they were faint outlines, indistinct and in places disappearing, but the general shape and configuration were right.

'North,' I blurted. 'Where is north?'

'Top of picture – he's right, Ben. Facing north. Could the towers be sun-orientated?'

I did not speak again. The reaction was coming swiftly now. Nothing in my life had been this easy, therefore this was suspect and I searched for the flaws.

'Stratification,' I said. 'Probably limestone in contact with the country granite. Throwing surface patterns.'

'Oh bull!' Louren cut in, the excitement still bubbling in his voice. He jumped up and strode to the screen, picked up an ebony pointer from the lectern and used it to spot the cell-like stippling around the outline of what he was pleased to presume was the main enclosure. 'You tell me where you've ever seen geographical patterns like that.'

I didn't want to accept it. I didn't want to make myself vulnerable again with hope.

'Perhaps,' I said.

'Damn you.' He laughed now, and the sound was good for he did not often laugh these days. 'I should have known you'd fight it. You are without doubt the most miserable bloody pessimist in Africa.'

'It could be anything, Lo,' I protested. 'A trick of light, of shape and shade. Even conceding that it is man-made – it could be recent gardens or agriculture—'

'A hundred miles from the nearest surface water? Forget it, Ben! You know as well as I do that this is the—'

'Don't say it,' I almost shouted, and was out of the padded leather chair, across the projection room and had hold of his arm before I realized I had moved.

'Don't say it,' I repeated. 'It's – it's bad luck.' I always stutter when I am excited, but it is the least of my physical disabilities and I have long ago ceased worrying about it.

Louren laughed again, but with the trace of uneasiness he shows whenever I move quickly or unleash the strength of my arms. He stooped over me now, and eased my fingers that were sunk into the flesh of his forearm.

'Sorry – did I hurt you?' I released the grip.

'No.' But he massaged his arm as he moved to the control panel and doused the projector, then turned the wall switch and we stood blinking at each other in the light.

'My little Yiddish leprechaun,' he smiled. 'You cannot fool me. You are wetting yourself.'

I looked up at him, ashamed of my outburst now, but still excited.

'Where is it, Lo? Where did you find it?'

'I want you to admit it first. I want you to go out on a limb for once in your life. I want you to say it – before I'll tell you another thing,' he teased.

'All right.' I looked away and picked my words. 'It looks, at first glance, quite interesting.'

And he threw back that great golden head and bellowed with bull laughter.

'You're going to have to do a lot better than that. Let's try again.'

His laughter I cannot resist, and my own followed immediately. I was aware of its birdlike quality against his.

'It looks to me,' I wheezed, 'as though you may have found – it.'

'You beauty!' he shouted. 'You little beauty.'

It was years since I had seen him like this. The solemn banker's mask stripped away, the cares of the Sturvesant financial empire forgotten in this moment of promise and achievement.

'Now tell me,' I pleaded. 'Where did you find it?'

'Come,' he said, serious again, and we went to the long table against the wall. There was a chart spread and pinned on the green baize. It was a high table, and I scrambled quickly onto a chair and leaned across it. Now I was almost on equal terms with Louren who stood beside me. We pored over the chart.

'Aeronautical Series A. Southern Africa. Chart 5. Botswana and Western Rhodesia.'

I searched it quickly, looking for some indication – a cross, or pencil mark perhaps.

'Where?' I said. 'Where?'

'You know that I've got twenty-five thousand square miles of mineral concession down here south of Maun—'

'Come *on*, Lo. Don't try and sell me shares in Sturvesant Minerals. Where the hell is it?'

'We've put a landing-strip in here that will take the Lear jet. Just finished it.'

'It can't be that far south of the gold series.'

'It isn't,' Louren reassured me. 'Throttle back, you'll rupture something.' He was enjoying himself tormenting me.

His finger moved across the chart, and stopped suddenly – my heart seemed to stop with it. It was looking better and better. The latitude was perfect, all the clues I had so painstakingly gathered over the years pointed to this general area.

'Here,' he said. 'Two hundred and twelve miles southeast of Maun, fifty-six miles from the south-western beacon of the Wankie game reserve, tucked below a curve of low hills, lost in a wilderness of rock and dry land scrub.'

'When can we leave?' I asked.

'Wow!' Louren shook his head. 'You do believe it. You really do!'

'Someone else could stumble on it.'

'It's been lying there for a thousand years – another week won't—'

'Another week!' I cried in anguish.

'Ben, I can't get away before then. I've got the Annual

6

General Meeting of Anglo-Sturvesant on Friday, and on Saturday I have business in Zürich – but I'll cut it short, especially for you.'

'Cut it altogether,' I begged. 'Send one of your bright young men.'

'When somebody lends you twenty-five million, it's only polite to go fetch the cheque yourself, not send the office boy.'

'Christ, Lo. It's only money – this is really important.'

For a moment Louren stared at me, the pale blue eyes bemused and reflective.

'Twenty-five million is only money?' He shook his head slowly and then wonderingly as though he had heard a new truth spoken. 'I suppose you are right.' He smiled, gently now, the smile of affection for a well-loved friend. 'Sorry, Ben. Tuesday. We'll fly at dawn, I promise you. We'll recce from the air. Then land at Maun. Peter Larkin – you know him?'

'Yes, very well.' Peter ran a big safari business out of Maun. Twice I'd used him on my Kalahari expeditions.

'Good. I've been on to him already. He will service the expedition. We will go in light and fast – one Land-Rover and a pair of three-ton Unimogs. I can only spare five days – and that's a squeeze – but I'll get a charter helicopter to fetch me out, and I'll leave you to scratch around—' As he talked Louren led me out of the projection room into the long gallery.

Sunlight spilled in through the high windows, giving good light to the paintings and sculptures that decorated the gallery. Here works of the leading South African artists mingled easily with those of the great internationals living and dead. Louren Sturvesant, and his ancestors before him, had spent money wisely. Even now in the urgency of the moment, my eyes were tugged aside by the soft fleshy glow of a Renoir nude.

Louren paced easily over the sound-deadening pile of Oriental carpets, and I matched stride for stride. My legs are as long as his and as powerful.

'If you turn up what we are both hoping for, then you can go in full-scale. A permanent camp, airstrip, assistants of your choice, a full crew, and any equipment you call for.'

'Please God, let it happen,' I said softly and at the head of the staircase we paused. Louren and I grinned at each other like conspirators.

'You know what it could cost?' I asked. 'We might be digging for five or six years.'

'I hope so,' he agreed.

'It could run into – a couple of hundred thousand.'

'It's only money, like the man said.' And again that great bull laugh started me off. We went down the staircase roaring and tittering, each in his own way. Elated and hyper-tense, we faced each other in the hall.

'I'll be back at seven-thirty Monday evening. Can you meet me at the airport, Alitalia flight 310 from Zürich? In the meantime you get your end arranged.'

'I'll need a copy of that photograph.'

'I've already had an enlargement delivered by hand to the Institute. You have got a week to gloat over it.' He glanced at the gold Piaget on his wrist. 'Damn. I'm late.'

He turned to the doorway at the moment that Hilary Sturvesant came through it from the patio. She wore a short white tennis dress, and her legs were long and achingly beautiful. A tall girl with gold-brown hair hanging shiny and soft to her shoulders.

'Darling, you aren't going?'

'I'm sorry, Hil. I meant to tell you I wouldn't be staying for lunch, but Ben will need somebody to hold him down.'

'You've shown him?' She turned and came to me, stooped to kiss me on the lips easily and naturally, with not the least sign of revulsion, and then she stepped back

8

and smiled full into my eyes. Every time she does that she makes me her slave for another hundred years.

'What do you think of it, Ben? Is it possible?' But before I could answer Louren had slipped his arm about her waist and they both smiled down at me.

'He's doing his nut. He's frothing at the mouth and doing back flips. He wants to rush into the desert now, this minute.' Then he pulled Hilary to him and kissed her. For a long minute they were oblivious of my presence as they embraced. They are, for me, the epitome of beautiful woman and manhood, both of them tall and strong and well-favoured. Hilary is younger than he is by twelve years, his fourth wife and the mother of only the youngest of his seven children. In her middle twenties she has the maturity and poise of a much older woman.

'Give Ben some lunch, my darling. I'll be home late.' Louren pulled away from the embrace.

'I'll miss you,' Hilary said.

'And I you. I'll see you Monday, Ben. Cable Larkin if you think of anything special we will need. So long, partner.' And he was gone.

Hilary took my hand and led me out on to the wide flagged patio. Five acres of lawn and dazzling flowerbeds sloped gently down to the stream and artificial lake. Both tennis courts were occupied and a shrieking mob of small near-naked bodies thrashed the water of the swimming-pool to a sun-sparkled white. Two uniformed servants were laying out a cold buffet on the long patio trestle-table, and with a small squirming twinge of dread I saw a half-dozen young matrons in tennis dress sprawled in the lounging chairs beside the outside bar. They were flushed with exertion, perspiration dampened the crisp white dresses and they sipped at long dewy, fruit-laden glasses of Pimms No. 1.

'Come,' said Hilary, and led me towards them. I steeled

myself, trying to draw myself up to an extra inch of height as we moved towards the group.

'Girls – we've got a man to keep us company. I want you to meet Dr Benjamin Kazin, Dr Kazin is the Director of the Institute of African Anthropology and Prehistory. Ben, this is Marjory Phelps.'

I turned to each of them as she spoke their names, and I acknowledged the slightly over-effusive greetings, giving each my eyes and voice, they are my good things. It was as difficult for them as it was for me. You do not expect your hostess to spring a hunchback on you with the pre-lunch drinks.

The children rescued me. Bobby spotted me and came at a run, shrieking, 'Uncle Ben! Uncle Ben!' She flung her cold wet arms around my neck and pressed her sopping bathing-costume to my new suit, before dragging me away to become overwhelmed by the rest of the Sturvesant brood and their hordes of young friends. I find it easier with children; they either do not seem to notice or they come straight out with it. 'Why do you walk all bent over like that?'

For once I was not very good value, I was too preoccupied to give them my full attention – and soon they drifted away, all but Bobby – for she is ever loyal. Then Hilary took over from her stepdaughter and I was returned to the league of young mothers where I made a better impression. I cannot resist pretty women, once the first awkwardness wears off. It was three o'clock before I left for the Institute.

Bobby Sturvesant pours Glen Grant malt whisky with the same heavy thirteen-year-old hand she uses to pour Coca-Cola. Consequently I floated into the Institute feeling very good indeed.

The envelope was on my desk marked 'Private and Confidential' with a note pinned to one corner, 'This came for you at lunch-time. Looks exciting! Sal.'

With a quick stab of jealousy I inspected the seal of the

envelope. It was unbroken. Sally hadn't been into it – but I knew it must have taken all her self-control for she has an almost neurotic curiosity. She calls it a fine inquiring scientific mind.

I guessed she would arrive within the next five minutes so I found the packet of Three X peppermints in my top drawer and slipped one into my mouth to smother the whisky fumes before I opened the envelope and drew out the glossy twelve-by-twelve enlargement, switched on the desk light and adjusted it and the magnifying table lens over the print. Then I looked around at the hosts of the past that crowd my office. All four walls are lined with shelves, and from floor to shoulder height – my shoulder height – these are filled with books: the tools of my trade, all bound in brown and green calf-skin, and titled in gold leaf. It is a big room, and there are many thousands of volumes. The shelves above the books carry the plaster busts of all the creatures that preceded man. Head and shoulders only. Australopithecus, Proconsul, Robusta, Rhodesian Man, Peking – all of them up to Neanderthal and finally Cro-Magnon himself – *Homo sapiens sapiens* in all his glory and infamy. The shelves to the right of my desk are laden with busts of all the typical ethnic types found in Africa, Hamites, Arabs, pygmies, the negroids, Boskops, bushmen, Griqua, Hottentot and all the others. They watched me attentively with their bulging glass eyes as I addressed them.

'Gentlemen,' I said, 'I think we are on to something good.' I only speak aloud to them when I am excited or drunk, and now I was more than a little of each.

'Who are you talking to?' asked Sally from the doorway, making me leap in my seat. It was a rhetorical question, she knew damn well who I was talking to. She lounged against the jamb, her hands thrust deeply into the pockets of her grubby white dust-coat. Dark hair drawn back with a ribbon from the deep bulging forehead, large green eyes well spaced beside the pert nose. High cheek-bones, wide sensual smiling mouth. A big girl with long well-muscled legs in the tight-fitting blue jeans. Why do I always like them big?

'Good lunch?' she asked, starting the slow sliding approach across the carpet towards my desk that would put her in position to check what was going on. She can read documents upside-down, as I have proved to my cost.

'Great,' I answered, deliberately covering the photograph with the envelope. 'Cold turkey, lobster salad, smoked trout, and a very good duck and truffles in aspic.'

'You bastard,' she whispered softly. She loves good food, and she had noticed my play with the envelope. I don't allow her to talk to me like that, but then I can't stop her either.

Five feet from me she sniffed, 'And peppermint-flavoured malt whisky! Yummy!'

I blushed, I can't help it. It's like my stutter – and she burst out laughing and came to perch on the edge of my desk.

'Come on, Ben.' She eyed the envelope frankly. 'I've been bursting since it arrived. I would have steamed it open – but the electric kettle is broken.'

Dr Sally Benator has been my assistant for two years, which is coincidentally the exact period of time that I have been in love with her.

I moved aside, making room for her behind the desk and uncovered the photograph. 'All right,' I agreed, 'let's see what you make of it.'

She squeezed in beside me, her upper arm touching my shoulder – a contact that shivered electrically through my whole body. In two years she had become like the children, she didn't seem to notice the hump. She was easy and natural, and I had a time-table worked out – in another two years our relationship would have ripened. I had to go slowly, very slowly, so as not to alarm her, but in that time

I would have accustomed her to the thought of me as a lover and husband. If the last two years had been long – I hated to think about the next two.

She leaned over the desk peering into the magnifying lens, and she was still and silent for a long time. Reflected light was thrown up into her face, and when she at last looked up her expression was rapt, the green eyes sparkled.

'Ben,' she said. 'Oh Ben – I'm so glad for you!' Somehow her easy acceptance and presumption annoyed me.

'You are jumping the gun,' I snapped. 'There could be a dozen natural explanations.'

'No.' She shook her head, smiling still. 'Don't try and knock it. It's true, Ben, at last. You've worked so long and believed so long, don't be afraid now. Accept it.'

She slipped out from behind the desk and crossed quickly to the shelf of books under the label 'K'. There are twelve volumes there that bear the author's name 'Benjamin Kazin'. She selected one, and opened it at the fly-leaf.

'*Ophir*,' she read, 'by Dr Benjamin Kazin. *A personal investigation of the prehistoric gold-working civilization of Central Africa, with special reference to the city of Zimbabwe and to the legend of the ancients and the lost city of the Kalahari.*'

She came to me smiling. 'Have you read it?' she asked. 'It's quite entertaining.'

'There's a chance, Sal. I agree. Just a chance, but—'

'Where does it lie?' she cut in. 'In the mineralized series, as you predicted?'

I nodded. 'Yes, it's in the gold belt. But it could, it just could, produce so much more than Langebeli and Ruwane.'

She grinned triumphantly, and bent over the lens again. With her finger she touched the indian ink arrow in the corner of the photo that gave the northerly bearing.

'The whole city—'

'If it is a city,' I cut in.

'The whole city,' she repeated with emphasis, 'faces north. Into the sun. With the acropolis behind it – sun and

13

moon, the two gods. The phallic towers – there are four, five – six. Perhaps seven of them.'

'Sal, those aren't towers, they are just dark patches on a photograph taken from 36,000 feet.'

'Thirty-six thousand!' Sal's head jerked up. 'Then it's huge! You could fit Zimbabwe into the main enclosure half a dozen times.'

'Easy, girl. For God's sake.'

'And the lower city outside the walls. It stretches for miles. It's enormous, Ben – but I wonder why it's crescent-shaped like that?' She straightened up, and for the first time – the very first wonderful time – she spontaneously threw her arms around my neck and hugged me. 'Oh, I'm so excited, I could die. When do we leave?'

I didn't answer, I hardly heard the question, I just stood there and revelled in the feel of her big warm breasts pressing against me.

'When?' she asked again, pulling back to look into my face.

'What?' I asked. 'What did you say?' I was both blushing and stuttering – and she laughed.

'When do we leave, Ben? When are we going to find your lost city?'

'Well,' I considered how to phrase it delicately, 'Louren Sturvesant and I will go in first. We leave on Tuesday. Louren didn't mention an assistant – so I don't think you will be coming along on the recce.'

Sally stepped back and placing her clenched fists on her hips, she looked at me unkindly and asked with deceptive gentleness: 'Do you want to bet on that?'

I like reasonable odds when I do bet, so I told Sally to pack. A week was too long for the job, for she is a professional and travels light. Her personal effects filled a single small valise and a shoulder-strapped carry-all. Her sketch-books, and paints, were more bulky, but we pooled our books to avoid duplication. My photographic equip-

14

ment was another big item, and then the sample bags and boxes together with my one canvas case made a formidable pile in the corner of my office. We were ready in twenty-four hours, and for the next six days we killed time by arguing, agonizing, squabbling and poring over the photograph which was starting to lose a little of its gloss. When our tensions built up to explosion point, then Sally would lock herself in her own office and try to work on the translation of the rock-engraving from Drie Koppen or the painted symbols from the Witte Berg. Rock-paintings, engravings and the translation of the ancient writings are her speciality.

I would wander fretfully around the public rooms, trying to find dust on the exhibits, dreaming up some novel way of displaying the treasures that filled our warehouse and upstairs store-rooms, counting the names in the visitors' book, playing guide to parties of schoolchildren – doing anything but work. Finally I would go upstairs to tap on Sally's door. Sometimes it was, 'Come in, Ben.' And then again it might be, 'I'm busy. What do you want?' Then I would drift through to spend an hour in the African languages section with my dour giant, Timothy Mageba.

Timothy started at the Institute as a sweeper and cleaner; that was twelve years ago. It took me six months to discover that apart from his own southern Sotho he spoke sixteen other dialects. I taught him to speak English fluently in eighteen months, to write it in two years. He matriculated two years later, graduated Bachelor of Arts in another three, Master's degree in the required further two years – and he is working on his doctorate in African languages.

He now speaks nineteen languages including English, which is one more than I do, and he is the only man I know, apart from myself – spent nine months in the desert, living with the little yellow men – who speaks the dialects of both the northern and Kalahari bushmen.

For a linguist, he is a peculiarly silent man. When he does speak it is in *basso profundo* which matches well his enormous frame. He stands six foot five inches tall and he is muscled like a professional wrestler and yet he moves with the grace of a dancer.

He fascinates me, and frightens me a little. His head is completely hairless, the rounded pate shaven and oiled to gleam like a midnight-black cannon ball. The nose broad and flat with flaring nostrils, the lips a thick purple black and behind them gleam big strong white teeth. From behind this impassive mask a chained animal ferocity glowers through the eye slits, and once in a while flashes like distant summer lightning. There is a satanical presence about him, despite the white shirt and dark business suit he wears, and though for twelve years I have spent much of my time in his presence I have never fathomed the dark depths beneath those dark eyes and darker skin.

Under my loose surveillance he runs the African languages department of the Institute. Five younger Africans, four men and a girl, work under him and, so far, they have published authoritative dictionaries of the seven main African languages spoken in southern Africa. They have also accumulated written and taped material to keep them busy for the next seven years.

On his own initiative, with just a little of my help and encouragement, he has published two volumes of African history which have raised a storm of hysterical abuse from white historians, archaeologists and reviewers. As a child Timothy was apprenticed to his grandfather, the witchdoctor and historical custodian of the tribe. As part of his initiation into the mysteries his grandfather placed Timothy under hypnosis and taped the entire tribal history on his brain. Even now, thirty years later, Timothy is able to throw himself into a trance and establish total recall of this mass of legend, folklore, unwritten history and magical doctrine. Timothy's grandfather was tried by an unsympa-

16

thetic white judge and hanged for his part in a series of ritual murders the year before Timothy had completed his training and been entered into the priesthood. However, his legacy to Timothy is a formidable mountain of material – much of it palpably spurious, a great deal of it unpublishable as being either too obscene or too explosive, and the remainder fascinating, puzzling or downright scary.

I have drawn on much of Timothy's unpublished material for my own book *Ophir* – particularly those unscientific and 'popular' sections which deal with the legend of the ancients, a race of fair-skinned golden-haired warriors from across the sea, who mined the gold, enslaved the indigenous tribes, built walled cities and flourished for hundreds of years before vanishing almost without trace.

I am aware that Timothy edits the information he passes on to me – some of it is too secret, the taboos which surround it too powerful to disclose to other than an initiate of the mysteries. I am sure that much of this withheld information relates to the legend of the ancients. I, however, never abandon my attempts to milk him.

On the Monday morning of Louren's return from Switzerland, Sally was so overwrought by the possibility that Louren would veto her inclusion in the preliminary expedition that her company was unbearable. To escape her and to kill the last long waiting hours, I went down to Timothy.

He works in a tiny room – we are a little pressed for space at the Institute, which is congested with neatly stacked pamphlets, books, folders, and piles of loose paper that reach almost to the ceiling – and yet there is room for my chair. This is a long-legged affair like a bar-room stool. For although my legs and arms are regulation size, or better, my trunk is squashed and humped so that from the seat of an ordinary chair I have trouble seeing over the top of a desk.

'Machane! Blessed one!' Timothy rose with his usual

greeting as I entered. According to Bantu lore those of us with club feet, albino pigmentation, squint eyes, and humped backs are blessed by the spirits and endowed with psychic powers. I derive a sneaky sort of pleasure from this belief, and Timothy's greeting always gives me a lift.

I hopped up on my chair, and began a desultory conversation which flicked from subject to subject and changed from language to language. Timothy and I are proud of our talents – and I suppose we do show off a little. There is no other man living, of this I am convinced, who could follow one of our conversations from beginning to end.

'It will be strange,' I said at last in I forget what language, 'not to have you along on a journey. It will be the first time in ten years, Timothy.'

He was immediately silent and wary. He knew I was going to start again on the lost city. I had shown him the photograph five days before, and had been pumping him steadily ever since for some significant comment. I changed into English.

'Anyway, you are probably not missing anything. Another groping for shadows. God knows there have been many of those. If only I knew what to look for.'

I broke off and froze with expectancy. Timothy's eyes had glazed. It is a physical thing, an opaque blueish film seems to cover the eyeballs. His head sinks down on the thick corded column of the neck, his lips twitch – and the goose flesh runs up my arms and the hair on the back of my neck fans erect.

I waited. As often as I had seen it I could never shake off the supernatural thrill of watching Timothy going into trance. Sometimes it is involuntary – a word, a thought will trigger it, and the reflex is almost instantaneous. Then again it can be a deliberate act of auto-hypnosis, but this involves preparation and ritual.

This time it was spontaneous, and I waited eagerly

18

knowing that if the material was taboo it would be but a few seconds only before Timothy broke the spell with a deliberate effort of will.

'Evil – ' he spoke in the quavering, high-pitched voice of an old man. The voice of his grandfather. A little spittle wet the thick purple lips, ' – an evil to be cleaned from the earth and from the minds of men, for ever.'

His head jerked, the conscious mind intervening, his lips worked loosely. The brief internal struggle – and suddenly his eyes cleared. He looked at me and saw me.

'I'm sorry,' he murmured in English, turning his eyes away now. Embarrassed by the involuntary display, and the need to exclude me. 'Would you like some coffee, Doctor? They have repaired the kettle at last.'

I sighed. Timothy had switched off, there would be no more communication that day. He was closed up and defensive. To use his own expression, he had 'turned nigger' on me.

'No thanks, Timothy.' I looked at my watch and slipped off the stool. 'Still some last-minute things to do.'

'Go in peace, Machane, and the spirits guide your feet.' We shook hands.

'Stay in peace, Timothy, and if the spirits are kind I will send for you.'

S tanding on the rail of the coffee bar in the main hall of Jan Smuts Airport I had a good view of the entrance to the international terminal.

'Damn it,' I swore.

'What is it?' Sal asked anxiously.

'B. Y. M. – a whole platoon of them.'

'What are B. Y. M.?'

'Bright young men. Sturvesant executives. There, you see the four of them beside the bank counter.'

'How do you know they are Sturvesant men?' she asked.

'Haircuts, short back and sides. Uniforms, dark cashmere suits and plain ties. Expressions, tense and ulcer-ridden but poised to blossom as the big man appears.' And then I added in an unaccustomed fit of honesty, 'Besides, I recognize two of them. Accountants. Friends of mine – have to prise money out of them every time I want a roll of toilet paper for the Institute.'

'Is that him?' asked Sally, and pointed.

'Yes,' I said, 'that's him.'

Louren Sturvesant came out of the doors of the international terminal, the first of the Zürich flight through customs and immigration, the airport public relations officer trotting to keep pace with him. Two other B. Y. M. a pace behind him on either side. Probably a third taking care of his luggage. The four waiting men broke into smiles that seemed to light the hall and hurried forward in order of seniority for a brief handclasp and then fell into formation around Louren. Two of them running interference ahead of him, the others closing in at either hand. The public relations officer fell back bewildered to the tail of the field, and Anglo-Sturvesant drove across the crowded floor like an advancing Panzer division.

In their midst Louren stood out by a golden curly head, his sun-bronzed features grim in contrast to the artificial smiles around him.

'Come on!' I caught Sally's hand and dove into the crowd. I am good at this. I go in at the level of their legs – and the pressure from this unexpected level cleaves them open like the waters of the Red Sea. Sally ran through behind me like the Israelites.

We intercepted Anglo-Sturvesant at the glass exit doors, and I dropped Sally's hand to crack the inner circle. I broke through at the first attempt and Louren nearly tripped over me.

'Ben.' I saw immediately how tired he was. Pale beneath

20

the gold skin, purply smudges under the eyes – but a warm smile cleared the fatigue for a moment. 'I'm sorry. I should have warned you not to come. Something has come up. I am on my way to a meeting now.'

He saw the expression on my face, and clasped my shoulder quickly.

'No. Don't jump to conclusions. It's still on. Be at the airfield at five o'clock tomorrow morning. I'll meet you there. I must go now. I'm sorry.'

We shook hands quickly.

'All the way, partner?' he asked.

'All the way,' I agreed, grinning at the schoolboy inanity, and then they swept on by and disappeared through the glass doors.

We were half-way back to Johannesburg before Sally spoke.

'Did you ask him about me? Is it fixed?'

'There wasn't time, Sal. You saw that. He was so rushed.'

Neither of us spoke again until I turned into the grounds of the Institute and parked the Mercedes beside her little red Alfa in the empty car park.

'Would you like a cup of coffee?' I asked.

'It's late.'

'It isn't. You won't sleep anyway – not tonight. We could have a game of chess.'

'All right.'

I let us in at the front door and we went through the public rooms, crowded with glass cases and wax figures, to the private staircase that led to my office and flat.

Sal lit the fire and set out the chessmen while I made coffee. When I came back from the kitchen she was sitting cross-legged on a tooled leather pouffe, brooding over the ivory and ebony chessboard. I caught my breath at the fresh dimension of her loveliness that the light and setting presented to me. She wore a patchwork poncho, as brilliantly coloured as the Oriental carpets strewn on the floor about her – and the gentle sidelighting glowed on the soft sun-touched olive of her skin. Watching her, I thought my heart might burst.

She looked up with those big soft eyes. 'Come,' she said, 'let's play.'

If I can weather the storm of her first lightning, volatile attacks then I can smother and wear her down with pawn play and superior development. She calls it the creeping death.

At last she toppled her king with a little groan of exasperation and stood up to pace restlessly about the room, hugging her own shoulders under the vivid poncho. I sipped coffee and watched her with covert pleasure until suddenly she swirled and faced me with long legs astride and clenched fists on her hips, her elbows tenting the poncho around her.

'I hate the bastard,' she said in a tight, strangled voice. 'A big arrogant god-man. I knew the type as soon as I saw him. Why, in the name of all that's holy, does he have to come with us? If we make any significant discovery, you can guess who will hog all the glory.'

I knew immediately she was talking of Louren – and I was startled by the acid and gall in her tone. Later I would remember it, and know the reason. But now I was stunned and then angry.

'What on earth are you talking about?' I demanded.

'The face, the walk, the flock of idolaters, the condescending air with which he dispenses favours, the immense overpowering conceit of the man—'

'Sally!'

'The casual, unthinking cruelty of his presumption—'

'Stop it, Sally.' I was on my feet now.

'Did you see those poor little men of his – shaking with fright?'

'Sally, you'll not talk of him like that – not in front of me.'

'Did you see yourself? One of the gentlest, kindest, most decent men I have ever known. One of the finest brains I have ever been privileged to work with. Did you see yourself, scampering and tail-wagging – God, you were rolling on your back at his feet – offering your belly to be tickled—' She was almost hysterical now, crying, tears of anger running down her face, shaking, white-faced. 'I hated you – and him! I hated you both. He was demeaning you, making you cheap and, and—'

I could not answer her. I stood stricken and numb – and her temper changed. She lifted her hand and pressed it to her mouth. We stared at each other.

'I must be mad,' she whispered. 'Why did I say those things? Ben, oh Ben. I'm sorry. So very sorry.'

And she came and knelt before me, her arms went around my body and she hugged me to her. I stood like a statue. I was cold with fear, dread of what was to come. For although this was what I had long prayed for, yet it had come so suddenly, without a moment's warning, and now I had been thrust far beyond the point of no return, into unknown territory. Sally lifted her head, still clinging to me, and looked up into my face.

'Forgive me, please.'

I kissed her, and her mouth was warm and salty with tears. Her lips opened under mine, and my fear was gone.

'Make love to me, Ben – please.' She knew instinctively that I must be led. She took me to the couch.

'The lights,' I whispered harshly, 'please switch off the lights.'

'If that's what you want.'

'Please, Sally.'

'I will,' she said. 'I know, my darling.' And she switched off the lights.

Twice in the darkness she cried out: 'Oh, please Ben – you're so strong. You are killing me. Your arms are – your arms.'

Then not long after, she screamed, an incoherent cry without form or meaning, and my own hoarse cry blended with it. Then there was only the ragged sound of our breathing in the darkness.

I felt as though my mind had broken free from my body and floated in warmth and darkness. For the first time in my life I was completely at rest, contented and secure. There seemed to be so many first times with this woman. When at last Sally spoke, her voice came as a small shock.

'Will you sing for me, Ben?' And she switched on the lights on the table beside the couch. We blinked at each other, owl-eyed in the muted glow. Her face was flushed rosily, and her hair a dark unruly tumble.

'Yes,' I said, 'I want to sing.' I went through into my dressing-room and took the guitar from the cupboard, and as I closed the door there was my reflection in the full-length mirror.

I looked with full attention, for a stranger stood before me. The coarse black hair framed a square face, with dark eyes and girlishly long lashes, a heavy simian jaw and a long pale forehead. The stranger was smiling at me, half shy – half proud.

I glanced down the strange, telescoped body over which I had agonized since childhood. The legs and arms were over-developed, thick and knotted with slabs of muscle, the limbs of a giant. Instinctively I glanced at the body-builder's weights in the corner of the room – and then back to the mirror. I was perfect around the edges – but in the centre was this squat, humped, toad-like torso, covered in a shaggy pelt of curly black hair. I looked at that remarkable body, and for the first time in my life, I did not hate it.

I went back to where Sally still lay on the soft monkey-skin kaross that covered the couch. I hopped up, and squatted cross-legged beside her with the guitar in my lap.

'Sing sad – please, Ben,' she whispered.

'But I'm happy, Sal.'

'Sing a sad song – one of your own sad ones,' she insisted, and as I picked out the first notes she closed her eyes. I was grateful, for I had never had a woman's body to gloat over. I leaned forward and as I touched the singing strings, I caressed the long smooth length of her with my eyes, the pale planes and rounds and secret shadows. Flesh that had cradled mine – how I loved it! I sang:

> 'In the lonely desert of my soul,
> The nights are long,
> And no other traveller journeys there.
> O'er the lonely oceans of my mind
> The winds blow strong—'

And in a short while a tear squeezed out behind her closed lids for there is a magic in my voice which can call up tears or laughter. I sang until my throat was rough and my picking finger tender. Then I laid the guitar aside and went on looking at her. Without opening her eyes she turned her head slightly towards me.

'Tell me about you and Louren Sturvesant,' she said. 'I would like to understand about that.'

The question took me by surprise, and I was silent for a moment. She opened her eyes.

'I'm sorry, Ben. You don't have to—'

'No,' I answered quickly. 'I'd like to talk about it. You see, I think you were wrong about him. I don't think you can apply ordinary standards to them – the Sturvesants. Louren and his father, when he was alive, that is. My own father worked for them. He died of a broken heart a year after my mother. Mr Sturvesant had heard of my academic record, and of course my father had been a loyal employee. There are a few of us, the Sturvesant orphans. We have nothing but the best. I went to Michaelhouse, the same school as Louren. A Jew at a church school, and a cripple at that – you can imagine how it was. Small boys are such utterly merciless little monsters. Louren dragged me out of the urinal where four of them were trying to drown me. He beat the daylights out of them, and after that I was his charge. I have been ever since. He finances this Institute, every penny of it. At first it was something just for me, but little by little he has become more and more involved. It's his hobby and my life – you will be surprised how knowledgeable he is. He loves this land, just as you and I do. He is caught up in its history and future more than you or I will ever be—' I broke off, for she was staring at me in a way that seemed to pierce my soul.

'You love him, Ben, don't you?'

I blushed then, and dropped my eyes. 'How do you mean that—'

'Oh, for God's sake, Ben,' she interrupted impatiently. 'I don't mean queer. You just proved the opposite. But I mean love, in the biblical sense.'

'He has been father, protector, benefactor and friend to me. The only friend I've ever had. Yes, you could say I love him.'

She reached up and touched my cheek.

'I'll try to like him. For your sake.'

It was still dark when we drove in through the gates of Grand Central Airport. Sal was huddled into her coat, silent and withdrawn. I was light-headed and brittle-feeling from a night of love and talk without sleep. There were floodlights picking out the private Sturvesant hangar at the east end of the runway, and as we approached I saw Louren's Ferrari parked in his reserved bay, and beside it another half-dozen late model saloons gleaming in the floods.

'Oh God,' I groaned. 'He's got the whole team with him.'

I parked beside the Ferrari, and Sal and I began unloading our equipment from the boot. She picked up her easel and slung it over her shoulder, then with a huge folder of parchment in one hand and a box of paints in the other she ducked through the wicket gate into the hangar. I should have gone with her, of course, but I was so absorbed in checking my luggage that it was three or four minutes before I followed her. By then it was too late.

As I stepped through the low aperture into the brightly lit hangar, my stomach churned with alarm. The gleaming sharklike silhouette of the Lear jet formed a backdrop for a tension-charged tableau. Seven of Louren's bright young men clad in the regulation casual garb – smartly cut safari suits and fleece-lined car coats – stood in a discreet circle about the two protagonists.

Louren Sturvesant very rarely loses his temper, and when he does it is only after severe and prolonged provocation. However, in less than two minutes Sally Benator had managed to achieve what many experts before her had never accomplished. Louren was in a towering, shaking, tight-lipped rage, which had his seven B.Y.M. awed and slack-mouthed.

Sally had dropped her load of equipment on the concrete floor and was standing with clenched fists on her hips and bright explosions of colour burning in her cheeks, trading Louren glare for glare.

'Dr Kazin told me I could come.'

'I don't care if the goddam King of bloody England told you that you could come. I'm telling you that the plane is full – and that I have no intention of dragging a female with me on the first break I've had in six months.'

'I didn't realize it was a pleasure jaunt—'

'Will somebody throw this bitch out of here?' shouted

27

Louren, and the B.Y.M. roused themselves and made a tentative advance. Sally picked up the heavy wooden easel, and held it in both hands. The advance petered out. I scuttled into the void and grabbed Louren's arm.

'Please, Lo. Can we talk?' I almost dragged him into the flight office – although I thought I detected a twinge of relief from Louren as I rescued him.

'Look I'm terribly sorry about this, Lo. I didn't have a chance to explain—'

Five minutes later Louren strode out of the office, and without a glance at either Sal or the frozen group of B.Y.M., climbed into the jet and a moment later his head appeared beside that of the pilot in the window of the cockpit as he adjusted his earphones.

I went to the junior B.Y.M. and gave him the word of the law.

'Mr Sturvesant asked me to tell you to arrange a charter to Gaberones for yourself.' Then I turned to the others. 'I wonder if you could give us a hand with the luggage.'

While a gang of the most highly paid stevedores in Africa carried Sally's luggage, she preened with shameless triumph. I managed to whisper a harsh warning.

'Back seat,' I snapped. 'And try and make yourself invisible. You will never know how close that was. Not only did you nearly miss the trip, but you almost talked yourself out of a job.'

We had been airborne for ten minutes before the pilot came back along the aisle. He stopped beside us and looked at Sal with open admiration.

'Jesus, lady.' He shook his head. 'I would have given a month's salary not to miss that! You were great.'

Sally, who had been suitably subdued since my warning, immediately perked up.

'With boys that size I don't even spit out the bones,' she declared, and a couple of B.Y.M. who heard it swivelled in their seats with startled expressions.

The pilot laughed delightedly and turned to me. 'The man wants to speak to you, Doctor. I'll change places with you.'

Louren was chit-chatting with flight control over the radio, but he waved me into the co-pilot's seat and I squeezed behind the wheel and waited. Louren ended his transmission and turned to me.

'Breakfast?'

'I've eaten.'

He ignored it and passed me a leg of cold turkey, and a huge slice of chicken and egg pie from the hamper beside him.

'Coffee in the Thermos. Help yourself.'

'Did you get your £25 million loan?' I asked with a full mouth.

'Yes – despite a last-minute panic.'

'I didn't think you needed to borrow, Lo. Have you fallen on hard times?'

'Oil prospecting.' He laughed at my suggestion. 'Risk money. I prefer to gamble with other people's money, and play the certainties with my own.' He changed the subject smoothly. 'Sorry about the detour. I am dropping the boys off at Gaberones. They've got a series of meetings with the Botswana government. Routine stuff, just settling the details of the concession. Anyway, it's not too far off our course. Then we can press on alone.' He filled his mouth with turkey and spoke around it. 'Met. report is lousy, Ben. Thick cloud down on the deck over the whole northern area. Happens about once in three years that you get low overcast in the desert – but today's the day. Anyway we'll have a stab at picking up the hills and the ruins, no harm done if we can't though. We'll not learn anything more from the air.' He was relaxed and easy, not a trace of his early rage, he could switch it on or off as he wished, and we talked and laughed together. I knew his mood, it was holiday and release. He was truly looking forward to it.

Lost city or no lost city, it was an excuse to get out into the wild country that he loved.

'This is like the old days. God, Ben, how long is it since we got away together? Must be all of ten years. Remember the canoe trip down the Orange River – when was that? 1956 or '7? And the expedition to find the wild bushmen.'

'We must do it more often, Lo.'

'Yes,' he said, really meaning it; as though he had a choice. 'We must, but there is so little time. It's running out so quickly – I'll be forty years old next year.' And his voice was wistful. 'God. If only we could buy time with money!'

'We've got five days,' I said, heading the conversation away from the quicksands, and he picked it up eagerly. It was another half an hour before he mentioned Sally.

'That assistant of yours, the prize fighter. What's her name?' And I told him.

'Are you having it away with her?' he asked. It was said so naturally, so casually, that for an instant I did not realize what had been said. Then I felt my vision blur with red rage, felt the blood pound in my temples and heat my throat and face. I think I could have killed him then, but instead I lied in a thick, shaken voice.

'No,' I said.

'Just as well,' he grunted. 'She's a wild one. Well, as long as she doesn't mess up the trip.' If only I had told him then, but it was too private a thing – too precious and fragile to despoil with words, especially the words he had chosen. Then the moment was passed, and I was sitting trembling and shaky as he talked on lightly about the five days ahead.

As we flew the cloud solidified beneath us, congealing into a dirty greyish blanket that stretched away in all directions to the horizon. We crossed the border between South Africa and the independent African state of Botswana. At Gaberones the ceiling was down to a thousand

30

feet when we landed. Despite Louren's assurance that we would be speedily airborne once more, there was a deputation of senior government officials, and an invitation to drinks and food in a private dining-room of the airport. Hot, sticky weather with intent white faces talking softly and greedily to shiny intent black faces – all of them sweating in the heat and whisky fumes, and the thick swirls of cigar and cigarette smoke.

Three hours more before the Lear jet with just four of us aboard slashed up into the cloud cover, then burst through into the high bright sunshine.

'Wow!' said Louren. 'An expensive little party. That black bastard Ngelane has just raised the price of his honour by another 20,000. I'll have to square him, of course. He could squash the whole deal. It has to go through his ministry.'

Louren flew northwards with the map on his lap and a stopwatch in his hand. His eyes darted from compass to airspeed indicator and back to the watch.

'Okay, Ben. You'd better let Roger take over the controls. We'll go down into the porridge and take a look-see.'

With Louren and the pilot, Roger van Deventer, at the controls and Sal and I braced in the doorway of the cockpit behind them, the jet slanted down towards the floor of dirty cloud. A few wisps of the stuff flickered past and then suddenly the sun was gone and we were enfolded in the dark grey mist.

Roger was flying, his attention completely on the instrument panel, and as the needle of the altimeter slowly unwound I saw his hands tightening on the wheel. We dropped steadily lower through the grey filth. Now Roger pulled on the flaps and airbrakes and throttled back. The three of us staring forward and down for the first glimpse of the earth. Down we sank, and still down. The pilot's tension turned to active fear. I could smell it, the rank

31

greasy tang of it. It was infectious. If he, the hardened fly-bird, was afraid, then I was prepared to be terrified. I knew suddenly that rather than risk Louren's wrath he would fly us straight into the ground. I decided to intervene, and opened my mouth. It was unnecessary.

'Overflown,' grunted Louren, checking the stopwatch. 'Ease up, Rog.'

'Sorry, Mr Sturvesant, there is no bottom to this stuff.' Roger said it like a sigh, and lifted the Lear's nose. He opened the throttle and let off the airbrakes.

'No go!' I murmured with relief. 'Forget it, Lo. Let's go on to Maun.'

Louren turned to look back at me, and instead looked into Sally's face. She stood behind his shoulder. I could not see her expression, but I could guess what it was by the tone in which she asked softly, 'Chicken?'

Louren stared at her a moment longer, then he grinned. I could have turned Sally over my knee and beaten that luscious backside to a pulp. The warm active fear I had felt the minute before, turned now to cold numbing terror for I had seen Louren grin like that before.

'Okay, Roger,' he said, slipping the map and stopwatch into the pocket beside his seat. 'I've got her.' And the Lear stood on one wing as he pulled her around in a maximum-rate turn. It was so finely executed that Sally and I merely sagged a little at the knees as gravity caught us.

He levelled out and flew for three minutes on even keel, retracing our course. I stole a glance at Sally's face. It was bright-eyed, and flushed with excitement – she was staring ahead into the impenetrable murk.

Again Louren banked the aircraft steeply and came out of the turn flying the reciprocal of our previous course and eased the nose downwards. This was no cautious groping with flaps and half throttle. Louren flew us in boldly and fast. Sally's hand groped for mine and squeezed. I was afraid and angry with both of them, I was too old for these children's games, but I returned her grip. As much for my own comfort as hers.

'Christ, Lo,' I blurted. 'Take it easy, will you!' And no one took the least notice of me. Roger was frozen in his seat, hands gripping the armrests, staring ahead. Louren was deceptively relaxed behind the controls, as he hurtled us into mortal danger – and Sally, damn her, was grinning all over her face and hanging on to my icy hand like a child on a roller coaster.

Suddenly we were into rain, pearly strings and snakes of it writhing back over the rounded Perspex windscreen. I tried to protest again, but my voice stuck somewhere in my parched throat. There was wind outside now. It buffeted the sleek gleaming body of the Lear, and the wings rocked. I felt like crying. I didn't want to die now. Yesterday would have been fine, but not after last night.

Before my own reflexes had even registered, Louren had seen the ground and caught the headlong plunge of the jet. With a soft shudder that threw Sally and me gently together he pulled us up level with the earth.

This was even more terrifying than the blind fall through space. The dark hazy outlines of the low scrubby tree-tops flicked by our wingtips close enough to touch, while ahead of us through the rain-mist an occasional big baobab tree loomed and Louren eased the jet over its greedily clutching branches. Seconds that seemed like a lifetime passed, then abruptly the filthy curtains of rain and cloud were stripped aside and we burst into a freak hole in the weather.

There before us, full in our path and washed by watery sunlight, stood a rampart of red stone cliffs. It was only the merest fleeting glimpse of red rock rushing down on us, then Louren had dragged the jet up on its tail and the rock seemed almost to scrape our belly as we slid over the crest and arrowed upwards into the clouds with the force of gravity squashing me down on buckling knees.

No one spoke until we had plunged out into the sunlight high above. Sally softly disengaged her hand from mine as Louren turned in his seat to look at us. I noticed with grim satisfaction that both he and Sally were looking slightly greenish with reaction. They stared at each other for a moment. Then Louren snorted with laughter.

'Look at Ben's face!' he roared and Sally thought that was very funny. When they finished laughing, Sally asked eagerly:

'Did anyone see the ruins? I just got a glimpse of the hills, but did anyone see the ruins?'

'The only thing I saw,' muttered Roger, 'was my own hairy little ring.' And I knew how he felt.

The cloud was breaking up by the time we reached Maun. Roger took us in through a gap and put us down sedately, and Peter Larkin was waiting for us.

Peter is one of the very few left. An anachronism, complete with fat cartridges looped to the breast of his bush jacket and his trousers tucked into the tops of mosquito boots. He has a big red beefy face and huge hands, the right index finger scarred by the recoil of heavy rifles. His single level of communication is a gravelly, whisky-raddled shout. He has no feelings and very little intelligence, so consequently never experiences fear. He has lived in Africa all his life and never bothered to learn a native language. He uses the lingua franca of South Africa, the bastard Fanagalo, and emphasizes his points with boots or fist. His knowledge of the animals on which he preys is limited to how to find them and where to aim to bring them down. Yet there is something appealing about him in an elephantine oafish way.

While his gang of hunting boys loaded our gear into the trucks he shouted amiable inanities at Louren and me.

'Wish I was coming with you. Got this bunch of Yanks arriving tomorrow – with a big sack of green dollars. Short notice, you gave me, Mr Sturvesant. But I'm giving you my best boys. Good rains in the south, be plenty of game in the area. Should run into gemsbok this time of year. And jumbo, of course, shouldn't be surprised if you get a simba or two—'

The coy use of pet names for game animals sickens me, especially when the intention is to blast them with a high-velocity rifle. I went to where Sally was supervising the packing of our gear.

'It's after one o'clock already,' she protested. 'When do we get cracking?'

'We'll probably push through to the top end of the Makarikari Pan tonight. It's about 200 miles on a fair road. Tomorrow we'll bash off into the deep bush.'

'Is Ernest Hemingway coming with us?' she asked, eyeing Peter Larkin with distaste.

'No such luck,' I assured her. I was trying to form some idea of those who were accompanying us. Two drivers, their superior status evident in the white shirts, long grey slacks and shod feet, with paisley-patterned scarves knotted at the throat. One for each of the three-ton trucks. Then there was the cook, carrying a lot of weight from his sampling, skin glossy from good food. Two gnarled and grey-headed gunboys who had jealously taken out Louren's sporting rifles from the other luggage, had unpacked them from their travelling cases, and were now fondling and caressing them lovingly. These were the elite and took no part in the frenzied scurryings of the camp boys as they packed away our gear. Bamangwatos most of them, I listened briefly to their chattering. The gunboys were Matabele, as was to be expected, and the drivers were

Shangaans. Good, I would understand every word spoken on this expedition.

'By the way, Sal,' I told her quietly, 'don't let on that I speak the language.'

'Why?' She looked startled.

'I like to monitor the goings-on and if they know I understand they'll freeze.'

'Svengali!' She pulled a face at me. I don't think I'd have laughed if anyone else had called me that. It was a bit too close to the bone. We went to shake hands and say goodbye to Roger, the pilot.

'Don't frighten the lions,' Roger told Sally. Clearly she had made another conquest. He climbed into the jet and we stood in a group and watched him taxi out to the end of the runway and then take off and wing away southwards.

'What are we waiting for?' asked Louren.

'What indeed,' I agreed.

Louren took the wheel of the Land-Rover and I climbed in beside him. Sally was in the back seat with the gunbearers on the bench seats.

'With you two – I feel a damned sight safer on the ground,' I said.

The road ran through open scrubland and baobab country. Dry and sun-scorched. The Land-Rover lifted a pale bank of drifting dust, and the two trucks followed us at a distance to let it settle.

There were occasional steep, rock-strewn dry river-beds to cross, and at intervals we passed villages of mud and thatched huts where the naked pot-bellied piccaninnies lined the side of the road to wave and sing, as though we were royalty. Sally soon ran out of pennies, throwing them to watch the resulting scramble, and clapping her hands with delight. When she started tossing our lunch out of the window I pulled my guitar from its case to distract her.

'Sing happy, Ben,' Sally instructed.

'And bawdy,' added Louren, I think it was to needle her, or perhaps test her.

'Yes,' agreed Sally readily. 'Make it meaty and happy.'

And I started with the saga of the Wild, Wild Duck, with Sal and Louren shouting the chorus at the end of each verse.

We were children going on a picnic that first day out, and we made a good run of it to the pan. The sun was a big fat ball of fire amongst the tattered streamers of cloud on the horizon when we came out on the edge of the pan. Louren parked the Land-Rover and we climbed out to wait for the trucks and stared out with silent awe across that sombre, glistening salt plain that stretched away to the range of the eye.

When the trucks arrived they spilled their load of black servants before they had properly stopped, and I timed it at seventeen and a half minutes to when the tents were pitched, the camp-beds made up and the three of us sitting around the fire, drinking Glen Grant malt on the rocks of glistening ice that dewed the glasses. From the cooking fire drifted the tantalizing smell of the hunter's pot as our cook reheated it and tossed in a dash more garlic and origanum. They were a good, cheerful gang that Larkin had given us and after we had eaten they gathered around their own fire fifty yards away and sweetened the night with old hunting songs.

I sat and listened half to them, and half to the involved and heated argument between Sal and Louren. I could have warned her that he was playing the devil's advocate, needling her again, but I enjoyed the interplay of two good minds. Whenever the discussion threatened to degenerate into personal abuse and actual physical violence, I intervened reluctantly and herded them back to safety.

Sally was staunchly defending the premise of my book *Ophir* that postulated an invasion of southern central Africa by Phoenician or Carthaginian colonizers in about 200 B.C. and which flourished until about A.D. 450, before disappearing abruptly.

'They were not equipped for a major voyage of discovery as early as that,' Louren challenged. 'Let alone a colonizing . . .'

'You will find, Mr Sturvesant, that Herodotus records a circumnavigation of Africa in the reign of King Necho. It was led by six Phoenician navigators as early as 600 B.C. or thereabouts. They started at the apex of the Red Sea and in three years returned through the Pillars of Hercules.'

'A single voyage,' Louren pointed out.

'Not a single voyage, Mr Sturvesant. Hanno sailed from Gibraltar to a point south in the west coast of Africa in about 460 B.C. a voyage from which he returned with bartered ivory and gold sufficient to whet the appetites of all the merchant adventurers.'

Still Louren attacked her dates. 'How do you get a date of 200 B.C., when the very earliest carbon-datings from the foundations of Zimbabwe are mid-fifth century A.D. and most of them are later?'

'We aren't concerned with Zimbabwe, but with the culture that preceded it,' Sally came back at him. 'Zimbabwe could have been built towards the end of the ancients' reign, probably only occupied for a short time before they disappeared; that would fit neatly with your carbon-dating of around A.D. 450. Besides the carbon-dating from the ancient mines at Shala and Inswezwe show results at 250 and 300 B.C.' Then she ended it with fine feminine logic. 'Anyway, carbon-dating isn't *that* accurate. It could be out by hundreds of years.'

'The mines were worked by the Bantu,' declared Louren. 'And Caton-Thompson – and of course, more recently, Summers – said—'

Fiercely she attacked Louren. 'Did the Bantu, who only probably arrived in the area about A.D. 300, suddenly conceive of a brilliant prospecting talent which enabled them to locate the metal lodes where not a scrap of it showed in the ore as visible gold or copper? Did they at the same time develop engineering know-how that enabled them to remove 250,000,000 tons of ore from rock at depth – remember they had never demonstrated these talents before – and did they abruptly forget or cease to use them for another thousand years?'

'Well, the Arab traders – they may have—' Louren began but Sally rode over him without a check.

'Why did they mine it at such risk and expenditure of energy? Gold has no value to the Bantu – cattle are their standard of wealth. Where did they learn how to dress and use rock for building? The Bantu had never done it before. Suddenly the art was fully fledged and highly skilled, and then instead of becoming more refined, the art *deteriorated* rapidly and then died out.'

With assumed reluctance Louren retreated steadily before her onslaughts, but he made his final stand when my own theory of incursion from the west instead of the east came under discussion. Louren had read the views and arguments of all my many detractors and critics and he repeated them now.

The accepted theory was that the point of entry was from the Sofala coast, or the mouth of the Zambezi. I had put forward the theory, based on the evidence of early texts and extensive excavations of my own, that a Mediterranean people left that sea through the Pillars of Hercules, and voyaged steadily down the western coast of Africa, probably establishing trading stations on the Gold, Ivory and Nigerian coasts, until their southward explorations led them into an unpeopled vacuum. I guessed at a river mouth long since dried and silted or altered in its course and depth in the present day. A river that drained what then would have been the huge lakes of Makarikari, Ngami, and others long since disappeared, shrivelled by the progressive desiccation of southern Africa. They entered the river, possibly the Cunene or the Orange, journeyed up it to the source, and from there sent their metallurgists overland to discover the ancient mines of Manica – and who knows but they discovered the diamonds in the gravel of the lakes and rivers, and certainly they would have hunted the vast herds of elephant that roamed the land. Sufficient wealth to justify the establishment of a city, a great walled fortress and trading station. Where would they site this city? Clearly at the limit of water-borne travel. On the shores of the furthest lake. Makarikari, perhaps? Or the lake that overflowed the present boundaries of the great salt pan.

Sally and Louren argued with increasing acrimony and bitterness. Sally called him 'an impossible man', and he countered with 'madam know-it-all'. Then suddenly Louren capitulated and the next minute all three of us were joyously anticipating the discovery of the lost city of Makarikari.

'The lake would have spread at least fifty miles beyond the boundaries of the present pan,' Louren pointed out. 'Only a hundred years ago Burchell describes Lake Ngami as an inland sea, and nowadays it's a puddle you can jump across without straining yourself. It's altogether probable that the ancient lake extended to the foot of the hills on which our ruins are placed. We have plenty of evidence of the gradual desiccation and drying up of southern Africa, read Cornwallis Harris' description of the forests and rivers which no longer exist.'

'Ben.' Sally grabbed my arm with excitement. 'The crescent-shape of the city, do you remember me puzzling on it? It could be the shape of the ancient harbour with the town following the shoreline!'

'God,' Louren whispered. 'I can hardly wait for tomorrow.'

It was after midnight, and the whisky bottles had taken a terrible beating before Louren and Sally went off to their tents. I knew I could not sleep so I left the camp, passing the fire around which lay the blanket-cocooned bodies of our servants, and I walked out onto the surface of the pan. The stars lit the salt a ghastly grey, and it crunched crisply with each pace I took. I walked for a long time, stopping once to listen to the distant roaring of a lion, from the edge of the bush. When I returned to the camp a lantern still burned in Sally's tent, and her silhouette was magnified against the pale canvas, a huge, dark portrait of my love. She was reading, sitting cross-legged upon her camp-bed, but as I watched she reached across and extinguished the lantern.

I waited a while, gathering my courage, then I went to her tent, and my heart threatened to hammer its way out of its malformed rib-cage.

'Sal?'

'Ben?' she answered my whisper softly.

'May I come in?' She hesitated before she replied.

'All right – just for a minute.'

I went into the tent, and in the gloom her nightdress was a pale blur. I groped for her face, and touched her cheek.

'I came to tell you that I love you,' I said softly, and I heard her little catch of breath in the dark. When she answered her voice was gentle.

'Ben,' she whispered. 'Dear, sweet Ben.'

'I would like to be with you tonight.'

And it seemed to me there was regret in her voice as she replied, 'No, Ben. Everyone would know about it. I don't want that.'

The morning started off as the previous day had ended. Everybody was in high spirits, laughing at the breakfast table. The servants sky-larked as they broke camp and repacked the trucks – and by seven o'clock we had left the road and were following the edge of the pan. The Land-Rover leading and the trucks following our tracks through scrub and rank grass, and across the dry ravines which meandered down to the pan.

We had been going for an hour when I saw a flash of pale movement among the trees ahead of us, and three stately gemsbok broke out onto the open pan and trotted in single file away from us. They moved heavily, like fat ponies, the pale mulberry of their coats and the elaborate black and white face masks standing out clearly against the grey of the pan surface.

Louren slammed the brakes on the Land-Rover, and with the smoothly executed timing of the professional the old Matabele gunbearer put the big .375 Magnum Holland Holland into Louren's hand and he was gone, running doubled-up behind the fringe of grass that lined the edge of the pan.

'Is he going to kill them?' asked Sally in her little girl voice. I nodded and she went on, 'Why – but why?'

'It's one of the things he likes doing.'

'But they are so beautiful,' she protested.

'Yes,' I agreed. Out on the pan, about six hundred yards from the Land-Rover, the gemsbok had stopped. They were standing broadside to us. Staring at us intently with heads held high, and long slender horns erect.

'What's he doing?' Sal pointed at Louren who was still running along the edge of the pan.

'He's playing by the rules,' I explained. 'It's an offence to fire within 500 yards of a vehicle.'

'Jolly sporting,' she muttered, biting her lip and glancing from Louren to the distant gemsbok. Then suddenly she had jumped from the Land-Rover and clambered up onto the engine bonnet. She cupped her hands around her mouth and yelled.

'Run you fools. Run, damn you!'

She snatched her hat and waved it over her head, jumping up and down on the bonnet and howling like a banshee. Out on the pan the gemsbok erupted into startled flight, galloping diagonally away from us in a bunch. I glanced at Louren's small figure, and saw him drop into a sitting position with elbows braced on his knees, head cocked over the telescopic sight. The rifle jerked, and smoke spurted from the muzzle – but it was a second or two before the flat report of the shot reached us. Out on the pan the leading gemsbok slid over his nose and rolled in a drift of white dust. Louren fired again, and the second animal tumbled with legs kicking to the sky. The last gemsbok ran on alone.

Behind me the old gunbearer spoke to the other in Sindebele. 'Hou! This is much man.'

Sally climbed down off the bonnet, and sat silently while I drove to where Louren waited. He handed the rifle to the gunbearer, and as I relinquished the wheel to him the bitter tang of burnt cordite filled the cab of the Land-Rover. He glanced at Sally. 'Thanks,' he said, 'I prefer a running shot.'

'Why didn't you kill all three of them?' Her tone was neutral, without rancour.

'You are only allowed two on a licence.'

'Christ,' said Sally in a voice that now reeked of anger and outrage, 'how bloody touching. It's not often you meet a true gentleman.'

And Louren drove us out to where the dead animals lay. While the servants skinned and butchered the carcasses, Sally remained in the back seat with her face averted, her hat pulled down low over her forehead, and her eyes glued to a book.

I stood beside Louren in the bright sunlight that was

intensified by the glare of the white salt surface, and watched the gunboys cut the incisions in the skin and flay the gemsbok with the skill of a pair of Harley Street surgeons.

'You might have warned me we had one of *them* on this trip,' Louren told me bitterly. 'Am I ever regretting having given in to you and letting her come along!'

I didn't reply and he went on, 'I've a bloody good mind to send her back to Maun on one of the trucks.' The suggestion was so unworkable that it didn't give me even a twinge, and Louren went on immediately, 'She's your assistant – try and keep her under control, will you!'

I moved away, giving him time to recover his temper, and took the map-case from the seat beside Sally. She didn't look up from her book. I walked around the vehicle and spread the aeronautical large-scale map on the bonnet of the Land-Rover, and within two minutes Louren was with me. Navigation is one of his big things, and he fancies himself no end.

'We'll leave the pan here,' he pointed to where a dry river-bed joined the eastern extremity of the pan, 'and strike in on a compass-bearing.'

'What kind of going will we meet, I wonder.'

'Sand veld, like as not. I've never been in there before.'

'Let's ask the drivers,' I suggested.

'Good idea.' Louren called the two of them across and the gunboys, who had by now finished the skilled work and were leaving the rest to the camp boys, joined us as was their right.

'This is where we want to go to.' Louren pointed it out on the map. 'These hills here. They haven't got a name marked, but they run in line with the edge of the pan, like this.'

It took a moment or two for the drivers to figure out their bearings on the chart, and then a remarkable change came over both of them. Their features dissolved into blank masks of incomprehension.

'What kind of country is it between the pan and the hills?' Louren asked. He had not sensed the change in them. The drivers exchanged furtive glances.

'Well?' asked Louren.

'I do not know that country. I have never heard of these hills,' Joseph, the elder driver, muttered, and then went on to give himself the lie. 'Besides there is much sand, and there are river-beds which one cannot cross.'

'There is no water,' agreed David, the second driver. 'I have never been there. I have never heard of these hills either.'

'What do the white men seek?' asked the old gunboy in Sindebele. It was obvious that maps meant nothing to him.

'They want to go to Katuba Ngazi,' the driver explained quickly. They were all convinced by now that neither Louren nor I had mastery of the language, and that they could speak freely in front of us. This then was the first time I heard the name spoken. Katuba Ngazi – the Hills of Blood.

'What have you told them?' demanded the gunbearer.

'That we do not know the place.'

'Good,' the gunbearer agreed. 'Tell them that there are no elephant there, that the wild animals are south of the pan.' The driver dutifully relayed this intelligence, and was disappointed in our obvious lack of dismay.

'Well,' Louren told them pleasantly, 'you will learn something today. For the first time you will see these hills.' He rolled up the map. 'Now get the meat loaded and let us go on.'

In five minutes the whole tone of the expedition had changed. Sally and the entire staff were all in the deepest depression. The smiles and horse-play were gone, there were sulky faces and meetings in muttering groups. The tempo of work dropped to almost zero, and it took almost half an hour to load the butchered gemsbok. While this was happening I led Louren away from the cluster of vehicles out of earshot and quickly told him of the exchange between the African servants.

'Hills of Blood! Wonderful!' Louren enthused. 'It means that almost certainly they know about the ruins – there is probably a taboo on them.'

'Yes,' I agreed. 'But now we are going to have to watch for attempts to sabotage the trip. Look at them.' We turned to watch the slow-motion, almost somnambulistic movements of our staff. 'My guess is that it's going to take longer to reach the Hills of Blood than we allowed for.'

We got off the pan once more, for the going is suspect with soft places beneath the crust that will bog a vehicle, and we followed the firm but sandy ground along the edge. We crossed another of the steep ravines, after having scouted for a place where the banks were flattened, and drove on for twenty minutes before we realized that neither of the trucks was following us. After waiting ten minutes, with both Louren and I fuming impatiently, we turned back and retraced our course to the dry river-bed.

One truck was hanging half over the edge of the ravine, one front wheel and one rear wheel not touching earth, but its belly heavily grounded. The other truck was parked nearby, and fourteen grown men were sitting or standing around in various attitudes of relaxation without making the least attempt to free the stranded truck.

'Joseph,' Louren called the driver. 'How did this happen?'

Joseph shrugged his shoulders disinterestedly, but he was having difficulty hiding his satisfaction.

'All right, gentlemen, let's get it out,' Louren suggested with heavy irony. Half an hour later, despite the ladylike efforts of all fourteen of them, and despite Joseph's hearty clashing of gears and desperate engine racing and stalling, the truck still hung over the edge of the ravine. Finally they all climbed out of the ravine and looked at Louren and me with interest.

'Okay, Ben?' Louren turned to me as he began to strip his bush jacket.

'All right, Lo,' I agreed. I was delighted to see how well Louren had taken care of himself. His body looked rock-hard, and denuded of fatty tissue. At six foot two, he carried a mass of muscle whose outlines beneath the skin were unblurred.

I kept my shirt on. My body, although it has the same utility as Louren's, is not so good to look at.

'Front end first,' Louren suggested.

The truck had been unloaded, petrol tank about half filled, I estimated the front end weight at a little over two thousand pounds. I windmilled my arms as I looked at the problem, loosening up cold muscles. The servants looked puzzled, and one of them giggled. Even Sally put aside her book and climbed out of the Land-Rover to watch.

Louren and I went to the front of the truck and stooped to it, placing our hands carefully, bending at the knee, spreading our legs a little.

'All the way, partner?'

'All the way, Lo.' I grinned back at him, and we began the lift. I started slow, just taking up the slack in my muscles, bringing on the strain evenly and letting it build up in shoulders, thighs and belly. It was a dead unmoving mass and I started to burn the reserves, feeling the tension turn to pain and my breathing start to scald my throat.

'Now,' grunted Louren beside me, and I let it all come, rearing back against it with my vision starting to star and pinwheel. It came away smoothly in our hands, and I heard the gasps and startled explanations from the watchers.

We lifted the front of the truck clear of the ravine, went around to the back and did the same there. Then we

47

started to laugh, a little shakily at first, but building up to a full gale. Louren put his arm around my shoulder and led me back to face our retinue of retainers who were looking discomfited and uneasy.

'You are – ' Louren told them, still laughing, ' – a bunch of frail old women and giggling virgins. Translate that for them, Joseph.'

I noticed that Joseph gave them a correct rendition of this pleasantry.

'And as for you, Joseph, you are a fool.' Louren stepped away from me towards Joseph, one quick dancing step, and hit him with an open hand across the side of the head. The sound of it was shockingly loud, and the force of it spun Joseph fully around in a tight circle before throwing him to the ground. He sat up groggily, with a thin trickle of blood running out of the corner of his mouth where teeth had cut into the thick under lip.

'You see that I am still laughing,' Louren pointed out to his startled audience. 'I am not even angry yet. Think a while on what may happen to anyone who makes me really angry.'

The truck was reloaded with alacrity and we went on.

'Well,' said Sally, 'we can be sure of full co-operation for the rest of this trip. Why didn't the big white bwana use a sjambok, rather than soiling his hands?'

'Tell her, Ben.' Louren did not look around at either of us, while I told Sally quickly about the campaign of deliberate obstruction that we had run into.

'I'm sure Louren didn't enjoy hitting the man, Sal. But he ditched the truck deliberately. We've got three and a half days left to get to these Hills of Blood, and we can't afford any more tricks.'

Sally immediately forgot her concern for Joseph. 'Hills of Blood,' she gloated. 'My God, it conjures up visions of human sacrifice and—'

'More likely it's merely the red colour of the cliffs,' I suggested.

'And this taboo thing.' She ignored me. 'It must be because of the ruins! Oh God, I can feel it in my blood – temples stuffed with treasures, relics and written records of a whole civilization, tombs, weapons—'

'You will notice my assistant's unbiased, unromantic and thoroughly scientific approach,' I pointed out to Louren, and he grinned.

'It irks me like hell, but for once I feel the way she does,' Louren admitted.

'For once that makes you smart, dearie,' Sally told him tartly.

I t was two in the afternoon before we reached the point on the eastern extremity of the pan where we were to cut off on compass for the hills, and almost immediately it became apparent that we would not reach them that day. The going was heavy, sand-veld clutched at the wheels of the vehicles and reduced our rate of progress to a low-gear slog. Half a dozen times the trucks bogged in the thick sand, and had to be dragged out by the four-wheel transmission of the Land-Rover. Each time this happened there was a profuse offering of apologies from the driver and crew concerned.

The sand had absorbed all traces of the recent rains, but they showed in the new growth of green that decked the thorn and acacia trees – and more dramatically in the display of wild flowers that were spread everywhere in carpets and thick banks.

Their seeds and bulbs had lain dormant for three long years of drought, waiting for this time of plenty – and now the bright crimson of King Chaka's fire burned brilliantly among the fields of Namaqua daisies. Star lilies, Ericas, golden Gazanias and twenty other varieties made a royal show, and helped to lessen the frustrations of our snail's progress.

At every enforced halt, I left the cursing and hustling to Louren, and wandered away from the vehicles with my camera.

Sunset found us still fifteen miles from the hills, and when I climbed into the top branches of the flat-topped acacia under which we camped, I could see their low outlines on the eastern horizon. The cliffs caught the last slanted rays of the sun, and glowed orange-red. I sat in the fork of the main trunk and watched them until the sun was gone and the hills melted into the dark sky.

A strange mood gripped me as I watched the far hills. A mystic sense of pre-destiny filled me with a languid melancholy – a sense of unease and disquiet.

When I climbed down into the camp, Louren sat alone by the fire, staring into the flames and drinking whisky.

'Where's Sally?' I asked.

'Gone to bed. In a sulk. We got into a discussion about blood sports and beating up blacks.' Louren glanced at her tent which glowed with internal lantern light. There was no singing from the servants' fire as Louren and I ate grilled gemsbok liver and bacon, washed down with warm red Cape wine. We sat in silence for a while after we had eaten, and finished the wine.

'I'm bushed,' Louren said at last, and stood up. 'I'll just call Larkin. I promised to check in every second night. See you in the morning, Ben.'

I watched him cross to the Land-Rover and switch on the two-way radio set. I heard Larkin's boozy voice through the buzz and crackle of static. I listened for a few minutes, while Louren made his report. Then I stood up also and moved away from the campfire.

Restless, and still under the spell of my mood of disquiet,

I wandered into the dark again. The gemsbok carcasses had attracted a pack of hyena to the camp, and they giggled and screeched out among the thorn trees. So I kept close to camp, passing Sally's tent and pausing for a while to draw comfort from her nearness, then walked on towards the servants' fire. My feet made no sound in the soft sand, and one of the old gunbearers was speaking as I approached. He had the attention of all the others who squatted in a circle about the low fire. His words came to me clearly, and stirred my memory. I felt the tingle of them run along my spine, and the ghost fingers stroked my arms and neck bringing the hair erect.

'This evil to be cleaned from the earth and from the minds of men, for ever.'

The words were exactly those that Timothy Mageba had spoken – the same words, but in a different language. I stared fascinated at the lined and time-quarried features of the old Matabele. It was as though he sensed my scrutiny for he looked up and saw me standing in the shadows.

He spoke again, warning them. 'Be careful, the spider is here,' he said. They had named me for my small body and long limbs. His words released them from the spell that held them, they shuffled their feet and coughed, glancing at me. I turned and moved away, but the old Matabele's words stayed with me. They troubled me, increasing my restless mood.

Sally's tent was dark now, and Louren's also. I went to my own bed and lay awake far into the night, listening to the hyenas and pondering what tomorrow would bring. One thing was certain, by noon we would know if the patterns on the photograph were natural or man-made, and with that thought I at last fell asleep.

51

W e could see the hills from the front seat of the Land-Rover by ten the following morning. They showed orange-red beyond the tops of the taller acacias, stretching across our front, higher at the centre of our horizon then dwindling in size as they strung out on either hand.

I took over the driving from Louren while he pored over map and photograph, directing me in towards the highest point of the cliffs. There was a distinctive clump of giant candelabra euphorbia trees on the skyline of the cliff – and these showed up clearly in the photograph. Louren was using them to orientate our approach.

The cliffs were between two and three hundred feet high, their exposed fronts furrowed and weather-worn, rising almost sheer to the crests. Later I was to find that they were a form of hardened sandstone heavily pigmented with mineral oxides. Below the cliffs grew a small grove of big trees, and it was clear that there was underground water trapped there to nourish these giants. Their exposed roots twisted and writhed up the face of the cliff like frenzied pythons, and their dense, dark green foliage was a welcome relief from the drab greenish grey of the thorn and acacia. In a strip about half a mile wide, the ground before the cliffs was open and sparsely covered with a low growth of scrub and pale grass.

I threaded the Land-Rover through the scrub towards the cliffs in a silence which momentarily grew more strained. Closer we crawled towards the towering red cliffs, until we had to crane our necks to look up at them.

Sally broke the silence at last, voicing our disappointment and chagrin. 'Well, we should be within the great walls of the main enclosure now – if there was one.'

We parked at the foot of the cliff and climbed out stiffly to look around us, subdued and reluctant to meet each other's eyes. There was no trace of a city, not a single dressed block of stone, not a raised mound of earth nor the faintest outline of wall or keep. This was virgin African bush and kopje, untouched and unmarked by man.

'You're sure this is the right place?' Sally asked miserably, and we did not answer her. The trucks came up and parked. The servants climbed down in small groups, peering up at the cliffs and talking in hushed tones.

'All right,' said Louren. 'While they set up the camp we will scout the area. I will go along the cliff that way. You two go the other way – and, Ben, take my shotgun with you.'

We picked our way along the base of the cliff, through the grove of silent trees. Once we startled a small troop of vervet monkeys in the high branches and they fled through the tree-tops in shrieking consternation. Their antics couldn't raise a smile from either Sally or me. We paused to examine the cliff at intervals, but there was little enthusiasm or hope in our efforts. Three or four miles from camp we stopped to rest, sitting on a block of sandstone that had fallen out from the cliff face.

'I could cry,' said Sal. 'I really could.'

'I know. I feel the same way.'

'But the photograph. Damn it, there was definitely *something* showing. You don't think it's his idea of a joke, do you?'

'No.' I shook my head. 'Lo wouldn't do that. He was just as keen as we were.'

'Then what about the photograph?'

'I don't know. It was clearly some sort of optical illusion. The shadow from the cliff, and cloud perhaps.'

'But those patterns!' she protested. 'They are geometrical and symmetrical.'

'Light can play funny tricks, Sal,' I said. 'Remember that photograph was taken at six o'clock in the evening – almost sunset. Low sun throwing shadows, you could get almost any effect.'

'I think this is the most disappointing thing that has

ever happened to me.' She really did look as though she might burst into tears, and I went to her shyly and put one long arm around her.

'I'm sorry,' I said, and she pulled a face and offered her lips to be kissed.

'Wow!' she said at last. 'Dr Kazin, you do carry on!'

'You ain't seen nothing yet.'

'I've seen too much.' She broke away gently. 'Come on, Ben. Let's circle back to camp, away from the cliff. There may be something out there.'

We tramped slowly through the heat. The flowers were out here also, and I noticed the bees crawling busily into the blossoms, their back legs thick with yellow pollen. We found where the recent rains had scoured a shallow ravine, although there was no remaining trace of moisture. I climbed down into the ravine and examined the exposed layers of stone and earth. Three feet from the surface the pebbles were rounded and water-worn.

'Good guess, Sal,' I told her as I picked out a few pebbles and found the shell of a bivalve encrusted in the half-formed sandstone. 'That proves at least a little of our theory. At one time this was the bed of a lake – look.'

Eagerly Sal clambered down beside me. 'What is it?'

'A type of *unionidae*, fresh-water African mussel.'

'I wish,' said Sally, 'that it were something a little more exciting.' She dropped the ancient shell in the sand.

'Yes,' I agreed, and climbed out of the ravine.

My only excuse is that my reasoning was clouded by intense disappointment and my recent physical excitement with Sally. I do not usually behave in such a cavalier fashion with scientific clues. Nor do I usually miss as many as four hints in the space of an hour. We walked away without a backward glance.

The camp was fully set up and functioning smoothly when Sal and I trailed in, sweaty and dusty, and sat down to lunch of tinned ham and Windhoek beer.

'Anything?' asked Louren, and we shook our heads in unison and lifted our beer glasses.

'Warm!' Sally spoke with disgust at her first taste of the beer.

'Cook has got the refrigerator going. It'll be cold by tonight.'

We ate in silence until Louren spoke. 'I raised Larkin on the radio while you were away. He will send in a helicopter tomorrow. We'll have a last search from the air. That will settle it once and for all. If there's nothing doing, I will fly out. Some things are brewing back in Johannesburg, and there is only one passenger seat, I'm afraid. You two will have to bus out the hard way.'

It was at that moment that a deputation arrived, headed by Joseph, to tell us that some unknown and foolish person had left the taps open on four of the water tanks. We had thirty-five gallons of water between seventeen people to last the rest of the trip.

'Therefore,' added Joseph, with evident relish, 'we will have to leave this place tomorrow, and return to the nearest water on the Maun road.'

There were a few expressions of disgust at this latest, clearly deliberate setback, but none of us could work up any real anger.

'All right, Joseph,' Louren agreed with resignation. 'Break camp tomorrow morning. We will leave before lunch.' There was an immediate improvement in employer-employee relations. I even noticed a few smiles, and heard a little laughter from the cooking fire.

'I don't know what you two intend doing this afternoon,' Louren lit a cigar as he spoke, 'but I noticed elephant spoor when I did my little recce this morning. I'm taking the Land-Rover and the gunbearers. Don't worry if I don't arrive back tonight, we may get hung up on the spoor.'

Sally looked up quickly; for a moment I thought she was going to start her anti-blood sport campaign again, but instead she merely frowned and went back to her ham. I watched the Land-Rover drive off along the base of the cliff before I suggested to Sally:

'I'm going to try and find a path up to the top – do you want to come along?'

'Deal me out, Ben,' she answered. 'I think I'll do some sketching this afternoon.'

Hiding my disappointment as best I could, I set off along the base of the cliff, and within half a mile I had found a game trail leading into one of the bush-choked gullies that furrowed the face of red rock.

It was a steep climb and I toiled up with the sun burning onto my back and bouncing off the rock into my face. From cracks and crannies in the cliff-face an army of furry little rock rabbits watched my endeavours with avid interest. It was forty minutes before I came out on the top, my arms scratched by the thorny undergrowth of the gully and sweat soaking my shirt.

I found a good vantage point on the front edge of the cliff under the spreading shade of a giant euphorbia, and my first concern was to sweep with the binoculars for any trace of ruins. The thorn bush at the base of the cliff below me was fairly open and scantily grassed, and immediately it was obvious that there was no trace of any human habitation or cultivation. I shouldn't really have hoped for more, but disappointment gave a sickening little lurch in my guts. Then I dismissed it, and turned the glasses towards the camp far below. A Bantu was cutting firewood, and for a while I amused myself by watching the axe-stroke, then listening for the sound of the blow seconds later. I searched further from the camp and picked up Sally's rose-coloured blouse at the edge of the grove. She had obviously given up all hope of a major discovery and, sensible girl, was deriving what other enjoyment she could from the expedition. I watched her for a long time, trying to decide how exactly to proceed with my campaign to make her my own. I had spent one night with her, but I was not so naïve as to believe that this proved a breathless and undying passion on behalf of a sophisticated highly intelligent and extravagantly educated modern Miss. Angel that she was, yet I was pretty damned certain that my Sally had played the game with other men before Dr Ben stumbled starry-eyed into her bed. The odds were extremely high she had been motivated by respect for my mind rather than my body, pity, and possibly a little perverse curiosity. However, I was almost certain she had not found the experience too repulsive, and I had only to keep working on her to change respect and pity into something a little deeper and more permanent.

A good quiet sense of peace came over me as I sat there in the high kranz; slowly I realized that this whole journey had been worthwhile and I found myself wishing that I could stay longer at these haunting Hills of Blood, with their mystery and silent beauty. Sally and I together here in the wilderness where I could teach her to love me.

A flicker of movement in the corner of my eye made me turn my head slowly, and within six feet of where I sat a marico sunbird was sucking the nectar from the blossoms of a wild aloe, its metallic green head shimmering as it dipped the long curved bill into the fiery red blossoms. I watched it with an intense pleasure, and when it was gone on quick darting wings I felt as though I had missed something. The feeling became stronger, making me rest-less; there was a message somewhere that was trying to come through to me but it was being blocked. I let my brain relax, and had the feeling that it was just there at the very fringe of my conscious mind. Another second and I would have it.

Dull on the hot breathless hush of afternoon the double boom-boom of distant heavy gunfire jerked my attention away. I sat up and listened for another thirty seconds – then it came again, boom, and again. Louren had found his elephant.

I picked Sally up in the field of the binoculars. She had heard it also, and was standing away from her easel staring out into the bush. I stood up also, my sudden restlessness still persisting, and started down the cliff path again. I could not shake off the mood, and it grew stronger. There is *something* here, I thought, something strange and inexplicable.

'You and I are lucky, my friend,' Timothy Mageba had told me once. 'We are marked by the spirits and we have the eye within that can see beyond, and the ear that can catch the sounds of silence.'

It was cool now in the heavily shaded gully and my shirt was still damp with sweat. I felt the goose pimples rising on my skin but not entirely from the chill. I began to hurry, I wanted to get back to the camp and Sally.

For dinner that night we ate grilled elephant heart sliced thin and covered with a biting pepper sauce, served with potatoes roasted in their jackets. The beer was icy cold as Louren had promised, and he was in an expansive mood. It had been a good day's hunt, fully compensating him for the other disappointments. Lying in the lantern light beyond the fire were four long, curved yellow tusks of ivory.

When Louren sets out to be charming, he is irresistible. Although Sally tried to maintain a disapproving attitude at first, she soon succumbed to his charisma and she laughed with us when Louren gave us the toast, 'To the city that never was, and the treasure we didn't find.'

I went to bed a little drunk, and I dreamed strange dreams – but I woke in the morning clear-headed and with an unformed sense of excitement buoying me, as though today something good was going to happen.

The helicopter came out of the south an hour before noon, drawn to us by the smudge fires of oil-soaked rag; it sank noisily down towards the camp on its glistening silver rotor, and raised a whirlwind of dust and debris.

There was a brief conference with the dark-haired young pilot, then Louren climbed into the seat beside him and the ungainly craft lifted into the air once more and began a series of sweeps along the cliffs, rising higher with each pass until it was a dark insect speck in the aching blue of that hot high sky. Its manoeuvres were so clearly indicative of failure that Sally and I soon lost interest and went to sit in the shade of the dining tent.

'Well,' she said, 'that is that, I guess.'

I didn't answer her, but went to the refrigerator and brought us each a can of Windhoek. For the first time in days the fabled Kazin brain began running on all cylinders. Thirty gallons of water shared between two persons meant a gallon a day for two weeks. Water? There was something else about water in the back of my mind. Sally and water.

The helicopter landed once more on the outskirts of the camp, and Louren and the pilot came to the tent. Louren shook his head.

'No go. Nothing. We'll have a bite of lunch and be on our way. Leave you to make the best of it home.'

I nodded agreement, not telling him my plans to forestall any argument.

'Well, Ben, I'm sorry about this. I just can't understand it.' Louren began building himself a sandwich of bread and cold slices of roast gemsbok fillet, smearing it with mustard. 'Anyway, it won't be the last disappointment we will ever have in our lives.'

Twenty minutes later Louren's essential luggage was packed in the helicopter and while the pilot started the motor we said our farewells.

'See you back in jolly Jo'burg. Look after those tusks for me.'

'Good trip, Lo.'

'All the way, partner?'

'All the way, Lo.'

Then he was ducking under the spinning rotor and climbing into the passenger's seat of the helicopter. It rose in the air like a fat bumble-bee and clattered away over the tree-tops. Bumblebee? Bee! Bee! My God, that was what had been niggling me.

Bees, birds and monkeys!

I grabbed Sally's arm, my excitement startling her.

'Sally, we're staying.'

'What?' She gaped at me.

'There are things here we've overlooked.'

'Like what?'

'The birds and the bees,' I told her.

'Why, you randy old thing,' she said.

We split the water fifteen to twenty gallons. That would give the servants a little over half a gallon a day each for two days, sufficient to get them out safely. Sally and I would have a full gallon a day for ten days. I kept the Land-Rover, making sure the petrol tanks were full, and there were twenty-five gallons in the emergency cans. I kept also the radio, one tent, bedding; a selection of tools including spade, axe and pick, rope, gas lanterns and spare cylinders, torches and spare batteries, tinned food, Louren's shotgun and half a dozen packets of shells, together with all of Sally's and my personal gear. All the rest of the equipment was loaded onto the two trucks and when the servants were all on board I took the old Matabele gunbearer aside.

'My old and respected father,' I spoke in Sindebele, 'I

have heard you speak of a great mystery that lives in this place. I ask you now as a son, and a friend, to speak to me of these things.'

It took him a few seconds to get over his astonishment. Then I went on to speak a sentence that Timothy Mageba had given me. It is a secret code, a recognition signal used at a high level among the initiates to the mysteries. The old man gasped. He could not question me now, nor ignore my appeal.

'My son,' he spoke softly. 'If you know those words then you should know of the legend. At a time when the rocks were soft and the air was misty,' an expression of the uttermost antiquity, 'there was an abomination and an evil in this place which was put down by our ancestors. They placed a death curse upon these hills and commanded that this evil be cleaned from the earth and from the minds of men, for ever.'

Again those fateful words, repeated exactly.

'That is the whole legend?' I asked. 'There is nothing else?'

'There is nothing else,' the old man told me, and I knew it was the truth. We went back to the waiting lorries and I spoke to Joseph first in Shangaan.

'Go in peace, my friend. Drive carefully and care well for those who ride with you – for they are precious to me.' Joseph gaped at me, his wits scattered. I turned to the camp boys and changed to Sechuana.

'The Spider gives you greetings and wishes you peace.' There was consternation amongst them as I used my nickname, but when they drove away they had recovered from the shock and were laughing delightedly at the joke. The trucks disappeared amongst the thorn trees, and the sound of their motors dwindled into the eternal silence of the deep bush.

'You know,' Sally murmured reflectively, 'I think I've been took! Here I am stranded 200 miles from anywhere with a man whose morals are definitely suspect.' Then she giggled. 'And isn't it lovely?' she asked.

I had found the spot on the top of the cliff where I could lean out over the drop, supported by a hefty young baboon apple tree, and obtain a good view of the rock screen on either side, as well as over the open plain below. Sally was down beyond the silent grove, and I could see her clearly.

The sun seemed at the right angle for her, although it was shining directly into my eyes. It was only ten or fifteen degrees above the horizon now and the golden rays brought out new soft colours from rock and foliage.

'Yoo hoo!' Sally's shout carried faintly up to me, and she held both hands straight up towards the sky. It was the signal we had evolved to mean, 'Come back towards me.'

'Good,' I grunted. She must have picked them up. I had explained to her carefully how to shade her eyes against the slant of the sun's rays and to watch for the arrow-straight flight of the tiny golden motes of light. It was an old trick used by bee hunters to find the hive, a bushman had taught it to me.

I pulled back from the cliff, and began working my way through the thorns and thick bush that clogged the crest. I had guessed where to begin the search, for the chances were enormously in favour of the hive being located in this tall wall of red rock with its many gullies and crevices, and now with Sally calling the range for me from below, it was only a matter of fifteen minutes before she windmilled her arms and I heard her call.

'That's it! Right under you.' Again I leaned out over the edge, and now I picked up the swift sunlit flight of the returning bees as they homed in on the cliff below me.

Leaning far out I could make out the entrance to the

hive; a long diagonal crack the edges of which were discoloured by old wax. It must have been an enormous hive, judging by the number of workers coming in, and by the extent of the waxing around the entrance. In such an inaccessible position it had probably remained undisturbed by man or beast for hundreds of years. A rarity in this land where honey is so highly prized.

I tied my white handkerchief to an overhanging branch to mark the spot and in the swiftly falling dark I went down to Sally on the plain. She was very excited by our small success, and we discussed the implications of it over our dinner.

'You are really quite clever, Doc Ben.'

'On the contrary, I was as slow as doomsday. I had to beat my head against all the signs for two whole days before I tumbled to it,' I told her smugly. 'The place is thick with birds, animals and bees, all of which must have a good permanent supply of surface water. There is supposed to be no permanent water for two hundred miles – well, that's wrong for sure.'

'Where will we find it, I wonder?' She was all big-eyed and enthusiastic again.

'I can't even guess, but when we do I promise you something interesting.'

That night when I came into the tent in my pyjamas, having modestly changed outside, she was already in her bed with the sheets up under her chin. I hesitated in the space between the two camp-beds, until with a mischievous grin she took pity on me and lifted the blankets beside her in invitation.

'Come to Mama,' she said.

In the chilly darkness before dawn I huddled in my leather jacket on the cliff above the hive, and waited for the sun. I was a very happy man again, some of my doubt dispelled during the night.

Down on the dark plain there was a flash of light. Sally

at her place beyond the grove again, probably lonely and a little scared in the African darkness with its night rustlings and animal cries. I flashed my torch down at her to reassure her, and the dawn started coming on quickly.

Dawn was a thing of soft pinks and roses, misty mauves and mulberry – then the sun burst up above the horizon and the bees began to fly. For twenty minutes I watched them to decide the pattern and purpose of their flight. There was a fan of workers winging wide out over the plain. These were the pollen-gatherers. I established this by leaning out and watching their return, through the binoculars, checking the bunches of yellow pollen on their hind legs as they alighted on the protruding bulge of the crack.

In so doing I discovered another pattern of flight that I might have missed. A steady stream of workers was dropping almost vertically down towards the dark foliage of the silent grove below me – and on their return there was no pollen on their legs. Water-carriers then! I signalled Sally in towards the base of the cliff; this morning our roles were reversed by the slant and angle of the sun's rays. After a while she waved to let me know she had spotted them, and I began the laborious climb down to the plain.

She had to point out to me the indistinct flight of bees down the cliff towards the grove, but even then the shadow cast by the cliff caused them to vanish before we could establish their exact destination within the grove. We watched them for thirty minutes, then gave it up and went into the trees to search at random.

By noon I could swear that there was no sign of surface water within the environs of the grove. Sally and I flopped down side by side with our backs to the sturdy trunk of one of the mhoba-hoba trees, the wild loquat tree that legend states the ancients brought with them from their homeland, and we looked at each other in despair.

'Another blank!' She was perspiring in a light dew across her forehead and temples and a dark curl was plastered to the skin. With one finger I pushed it gently back and tucked it behind her ear.

'It's here, somewhere. We'll find it,' I told her with the confidence I did not feel. 'It's got to be here. It just has to be.'

She was about to answer me, when I pressed my fingers to her lips to silence her. I had seen movement beyond the last trees of the grove. We watched the troop of vervet monkeys crossing the open plain at a gallop with their tails in the air. As they reached the grove they shot up the trunk of the nearest tree with comical relief. Their little black faces peered down anxiously from the massed green foliage, but they did not notice us sitting quietly at the base of the mhoba-hoba.

Confidently now they moved across the tree-tops towards the cliff, the big males leading with the mothers, with infants slung beneath their bodies, and the rabble of half-grown youngsters followed them.

They reached the top branches of a gargantuan wild fig tree, one of those whose roots and trunk were embedded in the vertical cliff wall of red rock, and whose branches spread wide and green fifty feet above the earth – and they began to disappear.

It was an astonishing phenomenon, sixty monkeys went into the tree and dwindled swiftly until the branches were deserted. Not a single monkey was left.

'What happened to them?' whispered Sally. 'Did they go up the cliff?'

'No, I don't think so.' I turned to her grinning happily. 'I think we've found it, Sal. I think this is it, but let's just wait for the monkeys to come back.'

Twenty minutes later the monkeys suddenly began reappearing in the branches of the wild fig again. The troop moved off in a leisurely fashion along the cliff, and we waited until they were all out of sight before we went forward.

The convoluted and massed roots of the wild fig formed a flight of irregular steps up towards the point where the trunk emerged from the cliff. We climbed up and began examining the trunk, working our way around it, peering up into the branches high overhead. The trunk was gigantic, fully thirty feet around, deformed and flattened by its contact with the uneven wall of red rock. Even then we might have missed it, had there not been a smoothly polished footpath leading into the living rock – a path worn by the passage of feet and paws and hooves over the course of thousands of years. The path squeezed between the gross yellow trunk of the wild fig, and the wall of rock. In the same manner as there is often a cave behind a waterfall hidden by the falling water so our wild fig screened the entrance.

Sally and I peered into the darkened recess behind the trunk, and then we looked at each other. Her eyes were sparkling bright and her cheeks flushed a dull rose.

'Yes!' she whispered, and I nodded, unable to speak.

'Come on!' She took my hand and we went in.

The opening was a long vertical crack in the cliff and good light came in from high above. Looking up I saw how the rock was polished by the paws of the monkeys who came in that way.

We moved on down the passage, the wall rising twenty feet on each side of us to a narrow vee of a roof. Immediately it was clear that we were not the first human beings that had entered here. The smooth red walls were covered with a profusion of magnificent bushman rock paintings. The most beautiful and well preserved that I had ever seen.

'Ben! Oh Ben! Just look at them!' One of Sally's specialities is bushman art. 'It's a treasure house. Oh, you wonderful clever man!' Her eyes shone in the gloom like lamps.

'Come on!' I tugged at her hand. 'There will be plenty of time for that later.'

We moved slowly along the narrow passage as it slanted steadily downwards for another hundred feet. The roof above us climbed progressively higher, until it was lost in the gloom above. We heard the squeak of bats from the dark recesses of the passage.

'There is light ahead,' I said, and we went on into an open chamber, rounded, perhaps 300 feet across with sheer walls which rose 200 feet upwards. Like the interior walls of a cone, they narrowed into a small aperture high above which gave a view of cloudless blue sky beyond.

I saw immediately that this was an intrusion of limestone into the red sandstone, and that it was a typical sink-hole formation, very similar to the Sleeping Pool at Sinoia in Rhodesia.

Here also the floor of the cavern was a basin which led down to a pool of water. The water was crystal clear, obviously very deep as the pale greenish colour showed, perhaps 150 feet across, the surface mirror-smooth and still.

Sally and I stood and stared at it. The beauty of this great cavern had paralysed us. Through the tiny aperture 200 feet above us the sun's rays poured in like the beam of a searchlight, striking the walls of shimmering limestone and lighting the entire cavern with an eerie reflected glow. From the arched roof and walls hung great butterfly wings and stalactites of sparkling white.

The walls of the main chamber were also decorated to a height of fifteen feet or more with the lovely bushman art. In places water seeping from the rock had destroyed the graceful figures and designs, but mostly it was well preserved. I guessed there was two years' work for Sally and me in this wondrous place.

Slowly she disengaged her hand from mine and walked

down to the edge of the emerald pool. I stayed where I was in the mouth of the tunnel, watching her with rapt attention as she stood at the edge of the pool and leaned forward to peer down into the still water.

Then she straightened and slowly, with deliberate movements, began to strip off her clothing. She stood naked at the edge of the pool and her skin was as pale and translucent as the limestone cliffs. Her body, for all its size and strength, had a delicacy of line and texture to it that reminded me of the Chinese carvings in old ivory.

Like a priestess of some old pagan religion, she stood beside the pool and lifted her arms. With a strange atavistic thrill this gesture brought to my mind an ancient forgotten ritual. There was something deep in me that I wanted to cry out, a blessing perhaps, or an invocation.

Then she dived, a long graceful curve of white body and flowing dark hair. She struck the water and went on down, deep. The sweet clean shape of her showed clearly through the crystal water, then she came up slowly from the depths and broke the surface. Her long dark hair was slicked down over her neck and shoulders, she lifted one slender arm and waved at me.

I felt like crying out aloud with relief. I realized then that I had not expected her to come up again from those mysterious green depths. I went down to the edge of the pool to help her out of the water.

Presently we moved slowly around the walls of the cavern and passage, awed by the profusion of paintings and engravings, Sally with her damp hair hanging to her shoulders and her face shining with wonder.

'There is work here spread over 2,000 years, Ben. This must have been a very holy place to the little yellow men.' The light failed before we had completed half the tour of the cavern, and it was chilly and scary in the passage as we groped our way out. It was only then that I realized we had not eaten that day.

While Sally warmed up a hash of bully beef and onions, I raised Peter Larkin on the radio and was relieved to hear that the two trucks had returned safely to Maun. I ended the transmission by asking Larkin to get a message through to Louren. 'Tell him we have found some very interesting rock paintings and will be staying on here indefinitely.'

'How are you for water?' bellowed Larkin, his voice distorted by static and Scotch whisky.

'Fine. We managed to find an adequate supply here.'

'You found water?' roared Larkin. 'There isn't any water there!'

'A small catchment in a rock basin from the last rain.'

'Oh, I see. Okay then. Keep in touch. Over and out.'

'Thanks, Peter. Over and out.'

'You are a fibber.' Sally grinned at me as I switched off the set.

'All in a good cause,' I agreed, and we began to prepare lanterns, and cameras, and sketching equipment for the following day.

The old bull elephant was mortally wounded. Blood, slick and shiny, poured from the wounds in throat and shoulder and the shafts of fifty arrows pin-cushioned his massive frame. He stood at bay, with his back humped in agony, while around him swarmed the brave little yellow hunters with drawn bows, and pelting arrows. A dozen of their number were strewn back along the path of the hunt, their frail bodies crushed and broken beneath the great round pads and cruel ivory shafts – but the others were closing in for the kill.

The ancient artist had filled his canvas of red rock with such movement and drama that I felt myself a witness to the actual hunt. However, the light was tricky and the best reading I could get was F.11. at 1/10th of a second.

Reluctantly I decided to use flash. I try to avoid it where possible for it tends to distort colour and throw in false highlights. I began setting up tripod and camera when Sally called.

'Ben! Come here, please!'

The echo effect and distortion caused by the lofty cavern could not disguise the urgency and excitement in her voice, and I went quickly.

She was in the main cavern beyond the emerald pool, where the rear wall cut back steeply to form a low recess. It was gloomy in there and Sally's torch beam jumped quickly over the smooth rock surface.

'What is it, Sal?' I asked as I came up beside her.

'Look.' She moved the torch beam down and I stared at the representation of a massive human figure before me.

'Good God!' I gasped. 'The White Lady of the Brandberg!* It's the same!'

Sally played the beam of the torch down across the figure until it spotlighted the vaunting erection that thrust from its thighs.

'That *lady* is beautifully hung,' she murmured, 'if you get the point.'

The figure was six feet tall, dressed in yellow breastplate and ornate helmet with a high arched crest. On his left shoulder he carried a rounded shield on which yellow ornamental rosettes were set in a circle about the central

---

* The White Lady of the Brandberg is one of the most celebrated and controversial rock paintings yet discovered in Africa. Its date is agreed at about A.D. 0–200, but its interpretation is the subject of much dispute. One source claims it is a Xhosa circumcision candidate daubed with white clay (one thousand miles from the territory of the Xhosa). The famous Abbé Breuil named it a lady, and Credo Mutwa in his recent book *Idaba My Children* gives an intriguing interpretation in which he concludes ' – It is not a Lady, but a strikingly handsome young white man, one of the great emperors who ruled the African Empire of the Ma-iti (Phoenicians) for nearly two centuries.'

boss. In his other hand he carried a bow and sheaf of arrows, and from his waist hung sword and battle-axe. His shins were protected by greaves of the same yellow metal and on his feet were light open sandals.

The figure's skin was depicted as deathly white, but a fiery bush of red hair hung onto his chest. The display of his sexual parts was clearly a stylized indication of his dominant and lofty status. The effect was in no way obscene but gave to the figure a masculine pride and arrogance.

'A white man,' I whispered. 'Armour and rounded shield, bow and battle-axe. Could it be—'

'A Phoenician king,' Sally finished for me.

'But the Phoenician type is more likely to have been dark-haired, hook-nosed. This man would have been an unusual figure among the ancients, to say the least. A throw-back, perhaps, to some north Mediterranean ancestor. How old is it, Sal?'

'I can't be sure yet, but I'd say 2,000 years. This wall of paintings is the most ancient in the whole cavern.'

'Look, Sal.' I pointed eagerly.

Beyond the central figure was an army of stick figures that followed the king. They were not executed in such detail, but the swords and helmets were unmistakable.

'And look there.' Sally directed the beam of the torch onto a row of white-robed figures that stood at the king's feet. Tiny figures, perhaps nine inches tall.

'Priests, perhaps – and, oh Ben! Look! Look!'

She played the beam across the stone canvas, and for a moment I did not recognize it – then my heart jumped. Like a huge frieze, that was obliterated in places by moisture, moss and lichens, or that was obscured by the myriad figures of men and animals drawn over it, and that yet managed to maintain its imposing majesty and power, swept the drawing of a stone fortress wall. It was built in blocks with the joints clearly shown, and along its summit was the decorative pattern of chevrons, identical to the one that graces the main temple wall at the ruins of Zimbabwe. Beyond the wall rose outlines of the phallic towers we had expected to find.

'It's our city, Ben. Our lost city.'

'And our lost king, Sally, and his priests, and warriors and – oh, my God! Sally, look at that!'

'Elephants!' she squealed. 'War elephants with archers on their backs, just like Hannibal used against the Romans. Carthaginian – Phoenician!'

There was so much of it, a curved wall 100 feet long and ten to fifteen feet high and every square inch of it thick with bushman paintings. The figures and forms were interwoven, some of the earlier pictures overlaid and smothered; others, like our white king, standing proudly untouched and unspoiled. It would be a major undertaking to unravel those portraits which related to our lost civilization, from the great mass of traditional cave art. This was Sally's special skill, my camera could only capture the whole confused scene, while she would patiently and painstakingly pick out a figure or group of particular interest that was almost entirely obliterated and recreate and restore it on her rolls of wax paper.

However, there was no suggestion of such work beginning now. Sally and I spent what was left of the day climbing and crawling along the back wall, peering and probing and exclaiming with wonder and delight.

When we got into camp that night we were physically and emotionally exhausted. Peter Larkin had a message for us from Louren:

'He says to wish you good luck, and that one of the oil helicopters will be in your area within the next few days. Is there anything you need, and if so give me a list. They will drop it to you.'

The next ten days were the happiest of my entire life. The helicopter came as Louren had promised with the name 'Sturvesant Oil' blazoned across its fuselage. It carried a full load of necessities and luxuries for us, another tent, folding chairs, a surveyor's theodolite, gas for the lamps, food, extra clothing for both of us, more paper and paints for Sally, film for me, and even a few bottles of Glen Grant malt whisky, that sovereign specific for all the ills of man. A note from Louren enjoined me to carry on with what I was doing as long as it looked promising. He would give me his full support, but I was not to keep him in the dark too long as he was 'dying of curiosity'.

I sent him my thanks, a roll of film showing the paintings which had no ancients in them, and a batch of polythene bags containing samples of pigments from the cavern for carbon-14 dating. Then the helicopter flew away and left us to our idyll.

We worked from early each morning until dark each evening, mapping the cavern in plan and elevation, and photographing an overlapping run of the walls and relating this to our map. Sally alternated between assisting me and continuing with her own task of isolating our ancient figures. We worked in complete harmony and understanding, breaking off now and then to eat our lunch beside the emerald pool, or to swim naked together in its cool limpid water, or at times just to lie idly on the rocks and talk.

At first our occupation of the cavern seriously affected the ecology of the local fauna, but as we hoped would happen, they soon adapted. Within days the birds were dropping down through the hole in the cavern roof to drink and bathe at the edge of the pool. Soon they ignored us as they went about their noisy and vigorous ablutions, shrieking and chattering and spraying water, while we paused in our labours to watch them.

Even the monkeys, driven by thirst, at last crept in through the rock passage to snatch a mouthful of water before darting away again. Rapidly these timid forays became bolder, until at last they were a positive nuisance, stealing our lunch, or any loose equipment that was left unguarded. We forgave them, for their antics were always appealing and entertaining.

They were wonderful days of satisfying work, good loving companionship, and the deep peace of that beautiful place. There was only one day on which anything happened to ruffle the surface of my happiness. As Sally and I were sitting below the portrait of our wonderful white king, I said: 'They won't be able to deny this, Sal. The bastards are going to have to change their narrow little minds now!'

She knew I was talking about the debunkers, the special pleaders, the politico-archaeologists, who could twist any evidence to fill the needs of their own beliefs, the ones who had castigated me and my books.

'Don't be so certain of that, Ben,' Sally warned. 'They will not accept this. I can hear their carping little voices now. It's second-hand observation by bushmen, open to different interpretations – don't you remember, Ben, how they accused the Abbé Breuil of retouching the paintings in the Brandberg?'

'Yes. That's the great pity of it – it *is* second-hand. When we show them the paintings of the fortified walls, they will say, "Yes, but where are the walls themselves?"'

'And our king, our beautiful virile warrior king,' she looked up at him, 'they'll emasculate him. He will become another "White Lady". His war shield will become a bouquet of flowers, his milky white skin will change to ceremonial clay, his fiery red beard will suddenly turn into a scarf or a necklace, and when they reproduce his portrait it will be subtly altered in all those ways. The *Encyclopaedia Britannica* will still read,' she changed her voice, mimicking a pedantic and pompous lecturer, '"modern scientific opinion is that the ruins are the work of some Bantu group, possibly the Shona or Makalang."'

'I wish – oh, how I wish we had found some definite proof,' I said miserably. I was facing for the first time the

74

prospect of delivering our discovery to my learned brothers in science, and the idea was as appealing as climbing into a pit full of black mambas. I stood up. 'Let's have a swim, Sal.'

We swam side by side, an easy breaststroke, back and forth across the pool. When we climbed out to sit in the spot of bright sunlight that fell from the roof above, I tried to alleviate my unhappiness by changing the subject. I touched Sally's arm and with all the finesse of a wounded rhinoceros, I blurted out, 'Will you marry me, Sally?'

She turned a startled face to me, her cheeks and eyelashes still bejewelled with water droplets, and she stared at me for fully ten seconds before she began to laugh.

'Oh, Ben, you funny old-fashioned thing! This is the twentieth century. Just because you done me wrong – doesn't mean you have to marry me!' And before I could protest or explain she had stood up and dived once again into the emerald pool.

For the rest of that day she was completely occupied with her paints and brushes, and she had no time to even look in my direction, let alone talk to me. The message was received my end loud and clear – there were some areas of discussion that Sally had put the death curse on. Matrimony was one of them.

It was a very bad day, but I learned the lesson well, and decided to clutch at what happiness I now had without pressing for more.

That evening Larkin had another message from Louren:

'Your samples 1–16 give C.14 average result of 1620 years ± 100. Congratulations. Looks good. When do I get in on the secret? Louren.'

I perked up at this news. Assuming our old bushman artist had been an eye-witness of the subjects he had drawn, then somewhere between A.D. 200 and A.D. 400 an armed Phoenician warrior had led his armies and war-elephants across this beloved land of mine. I felt guilty about

75

excluding Louren from the secrets of our cavern, but it was still too soon. I wanted to have it to myself a little longer – to gloat upon it, to have its peace and beauty to myself, unsullied by other eyes. More than that, it had become the temple of my love for Sally. Like the old bushmen, it had become a very holy place to me.

On the following day, it was as though Sally was determined to make up for the unhappiness she had caused me. She was teasing, and loving, and mischievous all at once. At noon with the beam of sunlight burning down on us, we made love on the rocks beside the pool, Sally skilfully and gently taking the initiative once again. It was a shattering and mystic experience that scoured the sadness from the cup of my soul and filled it to the brim with happiness and peace.

We lay together softly entwined, murmuring sleepily, when suddenly I was aware of another presence in the cavern. Alarm flared through me, and I struggled up on one elbow and looked to the entrance tunnel.

A golden-brown human figure stood in the gloomy mouth of the tunnel. He was dressed in a short leather loin-cloth, a quiver and short bow stood up behind his shoulder, and around his neck hung a necklace of ostrich egg-shell beads and black monkey beans. The figure was tiny, the size of a ten-year-old child, but the face was that of a mature man. Slanted eyes, and high flat cheekbones gave it an Asiatic appearance, but the nose was flattened and the lips were full and voluptuously chiselled. The small domed skull was covered by a pelt of tight black curls.

For an instant we looked into each other's eyes and then, like the flash of a bird's wing, the little manikin was gone, vanished into the dark passage in the rock.

'What is it?' Sally stirred against me.

'Bushman,' I said. 'Here in the cavern. Watching us.'

She sat up quickly, and peered fearfully about her.

'Where?'

'He's gone now. Get dressed – quickly!'

'Is he dangerous, Ben?' Her voice was husky.

'Yes. Very!' I was pulling on my clothes quickly, trying to decide on our best course of action, running over in my mind the words I would speak. Although it was a little rusty I found the language was still on my tongue, thanks to sessions of practice with Timothy Mageba. They would be northern bushmen here, not Kalahari; the languages were similar but distinctly different.

'They wouldn't attack us, would they, Ben?' Sally was dressed.

'If we do the wrong thing now, they will. We don't know how holy this place is to them. We mustn't frighten them, they have been persecuted and hunted for 2,000 years.'

'Oh, Ben.' She moved closer to me, and even in my own alarm I enjoyed her reliance upon me.

'They wouldn't – kill us, would they?'

'They are wild bushmen, Sally. If you threaten or molest a wild thing it will attack you. I've got to get an opportunity to talk to them.' I looked around for something to use as a shield, something strong enough to turn a reed arrow with a poisoned tip. Poison that would inflict a lingering but certain death of the most unspeakable agony.

I selected the leather theodolite case, and tore it open along the seams with my hands, flattening it out to give it maximum area.

'Follow me down the passage, Sal. Keep close.'

Her hand was on my shoulder as I led her slowly along the rock passage, using the four-cell torch to search every dark corner and recess before moving on. The light alarmed the bats and they fluttered and squeaked about our heads. The grip of Sally's hand on my shoulder became painfully tight, but we reached the tree-trunk that guarded the entrance to the cavern.

We crouched by the narrow slit between rock and tree-trunk, and the bright sunlight beyond was painful to my eyes. Minutely I examined each tree-trunk in the grove, each tuft of grass, each hollow or irregularity of earth – and there was nothing. But they were there, I knew, hidden waiting with the patience and concentration of the earth's most skilful hunters.

We were prey, there was no escaping this fact. The accepted laws of behaviour did not apply out here on the fringe of the Kalahari. I remembered the fate of the crew of a South African Air Force Dakota that force-landed in the desert ten years before. They hunted down the family of bushmen that did it, and I flew to Gaberones to interpret at the trial. In the dock they wore the parachute silk as clothing, and their faces were childlike, trusting, without guilt or guile as they answered my question.

'Yes. We killed them,' they said. Locked in a modern goal, like caged wild birds, they were dead within twelve months – all of them. The memory was chilling now and I thrust it aside.

'Now listen to me carefully, Sally. You must stay here. No matter what happens. I will go out to them. Talk to them. If,' I choked on the words, and cleared my throat, 'if they hit me with an arrow I'll have half an hour or so before – ' I rephrased the sentence, ' – I'll have plenty of time to get the Land-Rover and come back for you. You can drive. You'll have no trouble following the tracks we made back to the Makarikari Pan.'

'Ben – don't go. Oh God, Ben – please.'

'They'll wait, Sal – until dark. I have to go now, in the daylight.'

'Ben—'

'Wait here. Whatever happens, wait here.' I shrugged off her hands and stepped to the opening.

'Peace,' I called to them in their own tongue. 'There is no fight between us.'

I took a step out into the sunlight.

'I am a friend.'

Another slow step, down over the twisted roots of the wild fig, holding the flattened leather case low against my hip.

'Friend!' I called again. 'I am of your people. I am of your clan.'

I went slowly down into the silent hostile grove. There was no response to my words, no sound or movement. Ahead of me lay a fallen tree. I began sidling towards it, my guts a hard tight ball of tension and fear.

'I carry no weapon,' I called, and the grove was quiet and sinister in the hush of afternoon.

I had almost reached the fallen tree, when I heard the twang of the bow string and I dived for the shelter of the dead trunk. Close beside my head the arrow fluted, humming in the silence, and I went down. My face was pressed into the dry earth, my heart frozen with fear at the close passage of such hideous death.

I heard footsteps, running from behind me and I rolled over on my side ready to defend myself.

Sally was running down the wild fig roots towards me, ignoring my instructions, her face a pale mask of deathly terror, her mouth open in a silent scream. She had seen me fall and lie still, and the thought of me dead had triggered her panic. Now as I moved she realized her mistake and she faltered in her run, suddenly aware of her own vulnerability.

'Get back, Sal,' I yelled. 'Get back!' Her uncertainty turned to dismay and she stopped, stranded half-way between the cavern entrance and my dead tree-trunk, undecided on which way to move.

In the edge of my vision I saw the little yellow bushman rise from a patch of pale grass. There was an arrow notched to his bow and the feathered flights were drawn back to his cheek as he aimed. He was fifty paces from where Sally hovered, and he held his aim for a second.

I dived forward across the space that separated Sally from me at the instant the bushman released the arrow. The arrow and I flew on an interception course, two sides of a triangle with Sally at the apex.

I saw the humming blur of the arrow flash in belly-high at Sally and I knew I could not reach her before it struck. I threw the flattened leather case with a despairing under-hand flick of my wrist as I dived towards her. It cart-wheeled lazily, spinning in the air – and the arrow slapped into it. The deadly iron tip, with the poison-smeared barbs, bit into the tough leather of the case. Arrow and case fell harmlessly at Sally's feet, and I picked her up in my arms and spinning on my heels, doubled up under her weight, I raced back towards the cover of the dead tree-trunk.

The bushman was still on his knees in the grass ahead of me. He reached over his shoulder and pulled another arrow from his quiver; in one smoothly practised movement he had notched and drawn.

This time there was no hope of dodging, and I ran on grimly. The bow-string sang, the arrow flew, and instantly I felt a violent jerk at my neck. I knew I was hit, and with Sally still in my arms we fell behind the dead tree-trunk.

'I think I'm hit, Sal.' I could feel the arrow dangling against my chest as I rolled away from her. 'Break off the shaft – don't try and pull it out against the barbs.'

We lay facing each other, our eyes only a few inches apart. Strangely, now that I was a dead man I felt no fear. The thing was done, even if I was hit a dozen more times, my fate would be unaltered. It remained only to get Sally safely away before the poison did its work.

She reached out with shaking hands and took the frail reed arrow, lifting it gingerly – and then her face cleared.

'Your collar, Ben, it's lodged in the collar of your jacket. It hasn't touched you.'

Relief washed through me as I ran my hands up the shaft of the arrow, and found that I was not dead. Carefully lying on my side while Sally held the tip of the arrow from my flesh, I shrugged off my light khaki jacket. For a moment I stared in revulsion at the hand-forged iron arrow-head with the sticky toffee-coloured material clogging the wicked barbs, then I threw jacket and arrow aside.

'God, that was close,' I whispered. 'Listen, Sal, I think there is only one of them here. He's a young man, panicky, probably as afraid as we are. I will try to talk to him again.'

I wriggled forward against the reassuring solidity of the dead tree, and raised my voice in the most persuasive tones that would pass my parched throat.

'I am your friend. Though you fly your arrows at me, I will not war with you. I have lived with your people, I am one with you. How else do I speak your language?'

A deathly, impenetrable silence.

'How else do I speak the tongue of the people?' I asked again, and strained my ears for a sound.

Then the bushman spoke, his voice a high-pitched fluting, broken up with soft clucking and clicking sounds.

'The devils of the forest speak in many tongues. I close my ears to your deceits.'

'I am no devil. I have lived as one of yours. Did you never hear of the one named the Sunbird,' I used my bushman name, 'who stayed with the people of Xhai and became their brother?'

Another long silence followed, but now I sensed that the little bushman was undecided, puzzled, no longer afraid and deadly.

'Do you know of the old man named Xhai?'

'I know of him,' admitted the bushman, and I breathed a little easier.

'Did you hear of the one they called the Sunbird?'

Another long pause, then reluctantly, 'I have heard men speak of it.'

'I am that one.'

Now the silence went on for ten minutes or more. I

knew the bushman was considering my claim from every possible angle. At last he spoke again.

'Xhai and I hunt together this season. Even now he comes, before darkness he will be here. We will wait for him.'

'We will wait for him,' I agreed.

'But if you move I will kill you,' warned the bushman, and I took him at his word.

Xhai the old bushman came to my shoulder, and heaven knows I am no giant. He had the characteristically flattened features, with high cheekbones and oriental eyes, but his skin was dry and wrinkled, like an old yellow raisin. The wrinkling extended over his entire body as though he were covered with brittle parchment. The little peppercorns of hair on his scalp were smoky-grey with age, but his teeth were startling white and perfect, and his eyes were black and sparkling. I had often thought that they were pixie eyes, alive with mischief and intelligent curiosity.

When I told him how his friend had tried to kill us, he thought it an excellent joke and went off into little grunting explosions of laughter, at the same time shyly covering his mouth with one hand. The younger bushman's name was Ghal, and he was married to one of Xhai's daughters, so Xhai felt free to josh him mercilessly.

'Sunbird is a white ghost!' he wheezed. 'Shoot him, Ghal, quickly! Before he flies away.' Overwhelmed by his own humour, Xhai staggered in mirth-racked circles, giving an imitation of how he thought a ghost would look as it flew away. Ghal was very embarrassed and looked down at his feet as he shuffled them in the dust. I chuckled weakly, the sound of flighted arrows very fresh in my memory.

Xhai stopped laughing abruptly, and demanded anxiously, 'Sunbird, have you got tobacco?'

'Oh, my God!' I said in English.

'What is it?' Sally was alarmed by my tone, expecting that something else horrifying had happened.

'Tobacco,' I said. 'We haven't any.' Neither Sally nor I used the stuff, but it is very precious to a bushman.

'Louren left a box of cigars in the Land-Rover,' Sally reminded me. 'Is that any use?'

Both Ghal and Xhai were intrigued with the aluminium cylinders in which the Romeo and Julieta cigars were packed. After I showed them how to open them and remove the tobacco, they cooed and chattered with delight. Then Xhai sniffed the cigar like the true connoisseur he was, nodded approvingly and took a big bite. He chewed a while and then tucked the wad of sodden cigar up under his top lip. He passed the stub to Ghal who bit into it and followed Xhai's example. The two of them squatted on their haunches, positively glowing with contentment, and my heart went out to them. It took so little to make them happy.

They stayed with us that night, cooking on our fire a meal of bush-rats threaded on a stick like kebabs, and grilled over the open coals without gutting or removal of the skin. The hair frizzled off in the fire and stank like burning rags.

'I think I'm going to throw up,' murmured Sally palely as she watched the relish with which our two friends ate, but she didn't.

'Why do they call you Sunbird?' she asked later, and I repeated her question to Xhai.

He jumped up and did his celebrated imitation of a sunbird, darting his head and fluttering his hands. It was convincingly done, for bushmen are wonderful observers of nature.

'They say that's how I act when I get excited,' I explained.

'Yes!' Sally exclaimed, clapping her hands with delight as she recognized me, and then they were all laughing.

In the morning we went to the cave together, all four of us, and in that setting the little men were completely at home. I photographed them, and Sally sketched them as they sat on the rocks by the pool. She was fascinated by their delicate little hands and feet, and their enlarged buttocks, a recognized anatomical peculiarity named steatopygia, which enabled them to store food, like a camel stores water, against the contingencies of the wilderness. Ghal remarked to Xhai on the activity in which Sally and I had been engaged beside the pool when he discovered us the previous day, and this led to much earthy comment and laughter. Sally wanted to know the source of it, and when I told her she blushed like a sunset, which was a pleasant change, for I am usually the blusher.

The bushmen were enthusiastic over Sally's sketches, and this enabled me to lead them naturally to the rock paintings.

'They are the paintings of our people,' Xhai boasted. 'This has been our place from the beginning.'

I pointed out the portrait of the white king and Xhai explained frankly, without any of the reserve or secrecy I had expected.

'He is the king of the white ghosts.'

'Where did he live?'

'He lives with his army of ghosts on the moon,' Xhai explained – and my critics accuse *me* of being a romantic!

We discussed this at some length, and I learned how the ghosts fly between moon and earth, how they are well disposed towards the bushmen, but care should be taken as the common forest devils will sometimes masquerade as white ghosts. Ghal had mistaken me for one of these.

'Have the white ghosts ever been men?' I asked.

'No, certainly not.' Xhai was a little put out by the question. 'They were always ghosts, and they have always lived on the moon and these hills.'

'Have you ever seen them, Xhai?'

'My grandfather saw the ghost king.' Xhai avoided the question with dignity.

'And this, Xhai,' I pointed out the drawing of the stone wall with its chevrons and towers, 'what is this?'

'That is the Moon City,' Xhai answered readily.

'Where is it – on the moon?'

'No. It is here.'

'Here?' I demanded, my blood starting to race. 'You mean on these hills?'

'Yes.' Xhai nodded, and took another bite of his five-dollar cigar.

'Where, Xhai? Where? Can you show it to me?'

'No.' Xhai shook his head regretfully.

'Why not, Xhai? I am your brother. I am of your clan,' I pleaded. 'Your secrets are my secrets.'

'You are my brother,' Xhai agreed, 'but I cannot show you the City of the Moon. It is a ghost city. Only when the moon is full and the white ghosts come down, then the city stands upon the plain below the hills – but in the morning it is gone.'

My blood no longer raced, and my excitement cooled.

'Have you seen the Moon City, Xhai?'

'My grandfather saw it, once long ago.'

'Grandpa was a big mover,' I remarked bitterly in English.

'What is it?' Sally wanted to know.

'I'll explain later, Sal,' I said, and turned back to the old bushman. 'Xhai, in all your life have you ever seen such a city as this? A place of tall stone walls, of round stone towers? I don't mean here at these hills, but anywhere. In the north, by the great river, in the desert of the west – anywhere?'

'No,' said Xhai, 'I have never seen such a place.' And I knew that there was no lost city north of the great Pan or south of the Zambezi, for if there were, Xhai would have come across it in seventy years of ceaseless wandering.

'It was probably some old bushman who wandered 270 miles east of here and saw the temple at Zimbabwe,' I suggested to Sally that night as we sat around the fire and discussed the old bushman's story. 'He was so impressed that on his return he painted it.'

'Then how do you explain your white king?'

'I don't know, Sal,' I told her honestly. 'Perhaps it *is* a white lady with a bouquet of flowers.'

It seems that whenever I receive a serious disappointment – Sally's rejection of my proposal, and the story of the Moon City were both serious – my brain ceases to function for a period. I missed the clue completely, and the link-up was so obvious. I mean, for God's sake, I have a tested I.Q. of 156 – I'm a god-damned genius!

In the morning the two bushmen went, back to the families they had left by the Pan. They took with them the treasures we lavished upon them. A hatchet, Sally's make-up mirror, two knives and half a box of Romeo and Julieta cigars. They trotted away into the vastness of the Kalahari, without a backward glance, and left us poorer for their going.

T he helicopter came the following week, bringing in a full load of supplies and the special equipment I had asked Louren to send us.

Sally and I carried the rubber dinghy up to the cavern and inflated it beside the pool, taking it in turns to blow until we felt dizzy.

Sally launched it and paddled happily around the pool while I assembled the rest of the equipment. There was a short glass-fibre fishing-rod, a heavy one, twenty-five ounces, and in the case which held a 12/0 Penn Senator fishing-reel was a note from Louren: 'What are you after, for crying out aloud? Sand fish, or desert trout? "L"'

I fitted the reel to rod, threaded the line through the runners, and attached the five-pound lead weight to the end of it. Sally paddled us out into the centre of the pool. I dropped the lead weight over the side, disengaged the clutch on the reel, and let the line start running out.

As I had requested, the plaited Dacron line was marked at intervals of fifty feet, and as each marker of coloured cotton disappeared into the luminous green water, we counted aloud.

'Five, six, seven – my God, Ben. It's bottomless.'

'These limestone sink-holes can go down to tremendous depths.'

'Eleven, twelve, thirteen.'

'I hope we've got enough line.' Sally eyed what remained on the spool dubiously.

'We have got 800 yards here,' I told her. 'It will be more than enough.'

'Sixteen, seventeen.' Even I was impressed, I had guessed at a depth of around 400 feet, the same as the Sleeping Pool at Sinoia, but still the line unwound steadily from the big-game fishing-reel.

At last I felt the weight bump on the bottom, and the line went slack. We looked at each other with awe.

'A little over 850 feet,' I said.

'It makes me feel scary, hanging over a hole in the earth that deep.'

'Well,' I said with finality, 'I had plans to explore the bottom with a Scuba, but that's out now. Whatever is down there will stay there for ever. Nobody can dive that deep.'

Sally looked down into the green depths, and the dappled, moving, reflected light illuminated her face weirdly. There were shadows in her eyes, and her expression was dazed. Suddenly she shook herself violently, a shudder that went through her whole body, and she tore her eyes away from the green surface.

'Oh! I felt funny then. A really creepy sensation, as though something walked over my grave.'

I began to wind in the fishing-line, and Sally lay back flat on the floor of the dinghy staring up at the rock roof high above. It was a laborious task to recover all that line, but I worked away steadily.

'Ben.' Sally spoke suddenly. 'Look up there.' I stopped winding and looked up. We had never looked up at the opening in the roof from this angle. The shape of the opening was different.

'There, Ben. On the side,' Sally pointed. 'That piece of rock sticking out. It's square, too regular to be natural, surely?'

I studied it for a while.

'Perhaps.' I was dubious.

'You know we have never tried to find where the cavern opens out onto the top of the hills, Ben.' Sally sat up excitedly. 'Can't we do that? Let's go up and look at that piece of square stone. Can we, Ben?'

'Of course,' I agreed readily.

'Today. Now! Can we go now?'

'Hell, Sal. It's after two o'clock already. We will be out after dark.'

'Oh, come on! We can take torches with us.'

The growth of vegetation at the crest of the hills was dense and spiny. I was glad of the machete I had with me, and I hacked a path for us through it. We had marked the approximate position of the hole from the plain below, but even then we blundered about in the undergrowth for two hours before I nearly walked into it.

Suddenly the earth opened at my feet in that frightening black shaft, and I threw myself backwards, nearly knocking Sally down.

'That was a near one.' I was shaken, and I kept a respectful distance from the edge as we worked our way around to where a slab of stone jutted squarely out into the void.

I knelt on the lip to examine the stone. Far below, the surface of the emerald pool glowed in the gloomy depths. I do not like exposed heights, and I felt distinctly queasy as I leaned out to touch the flat surface of the stone.

'It is certainly regular, Sal.' I ran my hands over it. 'But I can't feel any chisel marks. It's been badly weathered though, perhaps—'

I looked up and froze with horror. Sally had walked out onto the stone platform as though it were a diving-board. She stood now with her toes over the edge, and as I watched in horror she lifted her hands above her head. She pointed them straight at the sky with all her fingers and both thumbs extended stiffly in that same gesture she had used when first she saw the emerald pool.

'Sally!' I screamed, and her head jerked. She swayed slightly. I scrambled to my knees.

'Don't, Sally, don't!' I screamed again, for I knew she was about to plunge into the hungry stone mouth. Slowly she leaned out over the gap. I ran out onto the stone platform and as she went forward beyond the point of balance my hand closed on her upper arm. For brief unholy seconds we teetered and struggled together on the lip of stone, then I dragged her back, and pulled her to safety.

Suddenly she was shaking and weeping hysterically, and I clung to her, for I also was badly scared. Something had happened that was beyond my understanding, something mystical and deeply disturbing.

When Sally's sobs had abated, I asked her gently, 'What happened, Sal? Why did you do it?'

'I don't know. I just felt dizzy, and there was a black roaring in my head, and – oh, I don't know, Ben. I just don't know.'

It was another twenty minutes before Sally seemed sufficiently recovered to begin the journey back to camp, and by then the sun was setting. Before we reached the path down the cliff face it was completely dark.

'The moon will be up in a few minutes, Sal. I don't fancy going down the cliff in the dark. Let's wait for it.'

We sat on the edge of the cliff huddled together, not for warmth, for the air was still hot and the rocks were sunbaked, but because both of us were still a little shaken from the experience we had just come through. The moon was a big silver glow beneath the horizon, then it pushed up fat and yellow and round above the trees, and washed the land with a soft pale light.

I looked at Sally. Her face was silver-grey in the moonlight with dark bruised eyes, and her expression was remote and infinitely sad.

'Shall we go, Sal?' I hugged her lightly.

'In a minute. It's so beautiful.' I turned to stare out over the moon-silver plain. Africa has many moods, many faces, and I love them all. Here, before us, she put on one of her more enchanting displays. We were silent and engrossed for a long time.

Suddenly I felt Sally stir against me, half rising.

'Ready?' I asked her, rising with her.

'Ben!' Her hand closed on my wrist with surprising strength, she was shaking my arm.

'Ben! Ben!'

'What is it, Sal?' I was seized with dread that her earlier mood had returned.

'Look, Ben. Look!' Her voice was choked with emotion.

'What is it, Sal? Are you all right?'

With one hand she was shaking my arm, with the other she was pointing down at the plain below us.

'Look, Ben, there it is!'

'Sally!' I put both arms around her to restrain her. 'Easy, my dear. Just sit down quietly.'

'Don't be a fool, Ben. I'm perfectly all right. Just look down there.'

Still holding her securely, I did as she asked. I stared and saw nothing.

'Do you see it, Ben?'

'No.' And then, like the face in the picture-puzzle, it was there. It was there, as it should have been from the beginning.

'Can you see it?' Sally was trembling. 'Tell me you can see it too, Ben. Tell me I'm not imagining it.'

'Yes,' I mumbled, still not certain, 'yes, I think—'

'It's the City of the Moon, Ben. The ghost city of the bushmen – it's our lost city, Ben. It is – it must be!'

It was vague, hazy. I shut my eyes tightly and opened them again. It was still there.

The double enclosure around the silent grove, vast symmetrical tracings on the silver plain, dark shadowy lines. There were the dark circles that marked the spots on which the phallic towers had stood, some of them obscured by the trees of the grove. Beyond the walls were the honeycomb cells of the lower city, crescent-shaped and spread around the shores of the ancient, vanished lake.

'The moon,' I whispered. 'Low angle. Picking up the

outline of the foundations. They must be so flattened that we have walked over them, lived on top of them for a month! The light of the full moon is just the right strength to cast shadows where the remains stand slightly proud.'

'The photograph!'

'Yes. From 36,000 feet, the light low enough and soft enough to give the same effect,' I agreed.

'We probably wouldn't have seen it from such a low altitude, the helicopter didn't go high enough,' Sally suggested.

'And it was noon,' I agreed. 'High-angle sun, no shadows. That is why Louren didn't see it from the helicopter.' It was so simple, and I had missed it. Some bloody genius – they must have botched the tests.

'But there are no walls, Ben, no towers, nothing. Only the foundations. What happened to it? What happened to our city?'

'We will find it, Sal,' I promised. 'But now let's mark it, before it disappears again.'

I handed her the one torch from the knapsack, 'One flash means "come towards me"; two flashes, "move away from me"; three, "move left"; four, "move right"; and a windmill means "you're on it".' Quickly we agreed a simple code. 'I'll go down onto the plain and you signal me. Put me on top of the large tower first, then guide me around the perimeter of the outer walls. We had better work fast – we don't know how long the effect will last. Give me a flat cut-out sign when it goes.'

It lasted a little over an hour with me scampering about on the plain in obedience to Sally's signals, and then the city faded, and slowly vanished as the moon rose towards its zenith. I went up to fetch Sally down from the cliff. I was bare to the waist, having ripped my shirt to shreds and tied strips of it onto clumps of grass and shrubs as markers.

Back in camp we built a huge fire and I got out the Glen Grant to celebrate. We were so elated, and there was so much to discuss and marvel over, that sleep was long delayed.

We went over the lighting phenomenon again in greater detail, agreeing how it worked and ruefully remembering how close we had come to the truth when we discussed the low sun effect on our very first day, the day we discovered the fresh-water mussel shells. We discussed the shells and their new significance.

'I swear here and now, with all the gods as my witness, that I will never again toss a piece of vital scientific evidence over my shoulder.' I made oath and testament.

'Let's drink to that,' suggested Sal.

'What a wonderful idea,' I agreed, and refilled the glasses.

Then we went on to the old bushman's story.

'It just goes to show you that every piece of legend, every piece of folklore is based on some fact, however garbled.' Sally becomes all philosophical after one shot of Glen Grant.

'And let's face facts, my blood brother Xhai is a champion garbler of facts from way back – the City of the Moon, forsooth.'

'It's a lovely name. Let's keep it,' Sally suggested. 'And what do you think about Xhai's grandfather actually meeting one of the white ghosts?'

'He probably saw one of the old hunters or prospectors, remember, we nearly had ghost status awarded us.'

'Literally and figuratively,' Sally reminded me.

The talk went on and on while the moon made its splendid transit of the sky above us. Every now and then serious discussion degenerated into effusive outbursts of, 'Oh, Ben. Isn't it wonderful. We've got a whole Phoenician city to excavate. All to ourselves.' Or, 'My God, Sal. All my life I've dreamed of something like this happening to me.'

It was long past midnight before we got our feet back on

the earth, and Sally brought up the subject of practical procedure.

'What do we do, Ben? Do we tell Louren Sturvesant now?'

I poured another drink slowly, while I considered this.

'Don't you think, Sal, we should sink a pothole, a small one, of course, on the foundations. Just to be certain we're not making fools of ourselves?'

'Ben, you know that's the first rule. Don't go scratching around haphazardly. You might destroy something valuable. We should wait until we go in on an orderly, organized basis.'

'I know, Sal. But I just can't help myself. Just one tiny little hole?'

'Okay,' she grinned. 'Just one tiny little hole.'

'I suppose we'd better try and get some sleep now, it's past two o'clock.'

Just before we finally drifted off, Sally murmured against my chest, 'I still wonder what happened to our city. If the bushman picture was correct then huge walls and towers of masonry have vanished into thin air.'

'Yes. It's going to be exciting to find out.'

W ith that strength of character which I am able occasionally to conjure up, I firmly thrust aside the temptation to open a trench within the temple enclosure, and instead I chose a spot upon the foundations of the outer wall where I hoped I would do minimum damage.

With Sally watching avidly, and volunteering more than her share of advice, I marked out with tapes torn from my sheets the outline of the intended excavation. A narrow trench three foot wide and twenty foot long, set at a right-angle to the run of the foundations so as to open a cross-section of the horizon.

We numbered the tapes at intervals of one foot, and Sally cross-referenced her notebook to the markings on the tapes. I fetched the cameras, tools and tarpaulin from the Land-Rover. Our trench was only thirty yards from the tents. We had camped almost on top of the ancient wall.

I spread the tarpaulin ready to receive the earth removed from the trench, and then I pulled off my shirt and threw it aside. I was no longer ashamed to expose my body in front of Sally. I spat on the palms of my hands, straddled the tapes, hefted the pick, and glanced at Sally, sitting attentively on the tarpaulin with a big floppy-brimmed hat on her head.

'Okay?' I grinned at her.

'All the way, partner!' she said, and I was startled. The words jarred, they were Louren's and mine. We didn't say them to other people. Then suddenly I thought, what the hell! I love her also.

'All the way, girl!' I agreed and swung the pick. It was good to feel the pick feather-light in my hands, and the head clunking deep into the sandy earth. I worked steadily, swinging pick and shovel easily, but soon the sweat was running in rivulets down my body and soaking my breeches. As I shovelled the earth from the trench and piled it on the tarpaulin, Sally began sifting it carefully. She chattered away happily as she worked, but my only reply was the grunt at each swing of pick.

By noon I had opened the trench along its full length to a depth of three feet. The sandy soil gave way at a depth of eighteen inches to a dark reddish loam which still held the damp of the recent rains. We rested and I ate a mess of canned food and drank a bottle of Windhoek to replace some of my lost moisture.

'You know,' Sally looked me over thoughtfully, 'once

you get used to it, your body has a strange sort of beauty,'
she said, and I blushed until my eyes watered.

I worked for another hour, and then suddenly the bite
of the pick turned up black. I swung again – still black. I
dropped the pick, and knelt in the trench.

'What is it?' Sally was there immediately.

'Ash!' I said. 'Charcoal!'

'An ancient hearth,' she guessed.

'Perhaps.' I didn't commit myself, luckily, so that later I
could chide her for her presumption. 'Let's take some
samples for dating.'

I worked more carefully now, trying to expose the layer
of ash without disturbing it. We sampled it and found that
it varied between a quarter of an inch and two inches deep
across the full horizon of the trench. Sally noted the depth
from the surface, and the position of each of the carbon
samples we took, while I photographed the trench and
tapes.

Then we straightened up and looked at each other.

'Too big for a hearth,' she said, and I nodded. 'We
shouldn't go deeper, Ben. Not like this, crashing in with
pick and shovel.'

'I know,' I said. 'We will stop on half the trench, leave
the layer of ash undisturbed – I'll make that concession to
the rules – but I am sure as hell going down on the rest of
it, to bedrock, if I can!'

'I'm glad you said that,' Sally applauded my decision.
'It's exactly what I feel as well.'

'You begin at the far end, I'll start here and we will work
towards each other,' I instructed, and we began lifting the
layer of ash from half the trench. I found that immediately
below it was a floor of hard clay and, though I didn't say
so, I guessed it was a building filler. A transported layer,
not occurring naturally.

'Go carefully,' I cautioned Sally.

'Quoth the pick-and-shovel man,' she muttered sarcastically without looking up, and almost immediately she made the first discovery from the ruins of the City of the Moon.

As I write I have her notebook in front of me, with her grubby, earthy fingerprints upon the pages and her big school-girlish handwriting filling it.

Trench 1.   Reference AC. 6.II.4. Depth 4′2½″.
Item: One glass bead. Oval. Blue. Circum.
             2½ mm.
             Pierced. Slightly heat-distorted.
Remarks: Found in layer of ash at Level I.
Index No.   CM. I.

This laconic notation can give no idea of our jubilation, the way we hugged each other and laughed in the sun. It was a typical blue Phoenician trade bead, and I cupped the tiny pellet of glass in my one hand.

'I'm going to take it and stick it up their backsides,' I threatened, referring of course to my critics.

'If that end is as narrow as their minds, Ben dear, then it will be a pretty tight fit.'

I started using a small pick and fifteen minutes later I made the next discovery. A charred fragment of bone.

'Human?' Sally asked.

'Possibly,' I said. 'Head of a human femur – the shaft has been burned away.'

'Cannibalism? Cremation?' Sally hazarded.

'You do run on,' I said.

'What do you think then?' she challenged. I was silent for a long time, then I made up my mind, and came out with it.

'I think at this level the City of the Moon was sacked and burned, its inhabitants were slaughtered, the walls thrown down and its buildings obliterated.'

Sally whistled softly, staring at me in mock amazement.

'On the evidence of one bead, and a piece of bone – that has to be the greatest flyer of all time!'

That evening, in reply to Larkin's bellowed queries, I replied, 'Thanks, Peter. We are fine. No, we don't need anything. Yes. Good. Please tell Mr Sturvesant there is no change here, nothing to report.'

I switched off the set, and avoided Sally's eyes.

'Yes,' she told me sternly. 'After a stinking one like that, you should look guilty!'

'Well, you said yourself it's only one bead and a piece of bone.'

But by the evening two days later, I had no such excuse, for I had sunk my trench seven feet five inches and there I uncovered the first of four courses of dry packed masonry. The stones were skilfully dressed, and squared. The joints between each block were so tight that a knife-blade would not go between them. The stones were bigger than those of Zimbabwe, clearly intended to support the weight of a substantial edifice; the average size was approximately four feet, by two, by two. They were cut from red sandstone similar to that of the cliffs and as I examined the workmanship I knew beyond any doubt that they were the work of artisans from a powerful and wealthy civilization.

That night I spoke to Larkin again.

'How soon can you get a message through to Mr Sturvesant, Peter?'

'He should have got back from New York today. I can put a phone call through this evening.'

'Please ask him to come right away.'

'You mean you want him to drop everything and come running – that's a laugh.'

'Just do it, please.'

The helicopter arrived at three o'clock the following afternoon, and I ran to meet it, pulling on my shirt.

'What have you got for me, Ben?' Louren demanded as he climbed, big and blond, out of the cabin.

'I think you are going to like it,' I told him, as we shook hands.

Five hours later we sat around the fire and Louren smiled over the rim of his glass at me.

'You were right, lad. I do like it!' This was the first opinion he had expressed since his arrival. He had followed Sal and me from excavation to cavern to cliff-top, listening attentively to our explanations, shaking his head with a rueful grin when I explained our theory of low-angle light on the ruins, firing a question occasionally in the same tone I had heard him use in a directors' meeting. Each time the question was relevant, incisive and searching, as though he were evaluating a business deal.

When Sally spoke he stood close to her, looking frankly into her face, those marvellous classical features of his rapt and still. Once she touched his arm to enforce a point and they smiled at each other. I was happy to see them so friendly at last, for they were the two people in the world I loved.

He knelt with me in the bottom of the trench and caressed the worked stone with his hands, he held the charred bone and melted glass bead in his palm and frowned at them as though trying to draw their secrets from them by sheer force of concentration.

Just before sunset, at Louren's insistence, we returned to the cavern and went to the rear wall. I lit one of the glass lanterns and placed it so that its light fell full on the painting of the white king. Then the three of us sat around it in a semi-circle and studied it in every detail. The king's head was in profile and Sally pointed out the features, the long straight nose and high forehead.

'A face like that never came out of Africa,' she said, and as a contrast she picked out the painting of another figure further down the wall. 'Look at that. It's a Bantu and no mistaking it. The artist was skilled enough to differentiate between the features of each type.'

However, Louren's attention never wavered from his scrutiny of the king. Again he seemed to be trying to wrest its secrets from it, but the king was regally aloof and at last Louren sighed and stood up. He was about to turn away when his glance dropped to the white-robed priest figures below the king.

'What are those?' he asked.

'We have named them the priests,' I told him, 'but Sally feels they could be Arab traders or—'

'The figure in the centre—' he pointed out the central priest figure, and his voice was sharp, almost alarmed, 'what is he doing?'

'Bowing to the king,' Sally suggested.

'Even though he is bowing, he stands taller than the others?' Louren protested.

'Size was the bushman artist's way of showing import-ance. See the relative size of the king – although they are pygmies they always show themselves as giants – the size of the central priest would signify that he was the High Priest, or the leader of the Arabs, if Sally is right.'

'If he is bowing, it's with the top third of his body only and he is the only one doing it. The others are erect.' Louren was still not convinced. 'It's almost as though—' his voice trailed away, and he shook his head. Then suddenly he shivered briefly, and I saw the goose-flesh appear on the smooth tanned skin of his upper arms.

'It's become cold in here,' he said, folding his arms across his chest. I had not noticed any drop in temperature, but I stood up also.

'Let's get back to camp,' Louren said, and it was only

after I had built up the fire to a cheerfully crackling, spark-flying blaze that he spoke again.

'You are right, lad. I do like it!' And he took a swallow of the malt whisky. 'Now let's start talking prices,' he suggested.

'Set it out for us, Lo,' I agreed.

'I will negotiate with the Botswana Government. I can put a little leverage on them. We'll have to have a formal agreement drawn up, probably split any finds fifty-fifty, they'll have to guarantee us access and exclusive rights. That sort of thing.'

'Good. That's certainly your bag of tricks, Lo.'

'Knowing you, Benjamin, you have a list of your requirements, the men you want, equipment – am I right?'

I laughed and unbuttoned my top pocket. 'As a matter of fact—' I admitted as I handed him three foolscap sheets. He glanced over them quickly.

'Very Spartan, Ben,' he congratulated me. 'But I think we can go in a bit bigger than this. I'll want at least a rough landing-strip here to start with, something to handle a Dakota. The hot weather is coming. You'll die living out under canvas. We'll need solid accommodation, also office and storage space with air-conditioning. That means a generator for lighting and to pump water down from the pool.'

'No one can ever accuse you of being half-arsed, Lo,' I told him, and we all laughed. Sally refilled my glass. I was jubilant and mightily pleased with myself that evening. I had much to be proud of, ferreting out a secret so well hidden for millennia, and Louren was going to back me all the way, partner. The whisky went down my throat like water.

I used to drink a lot of whisky. It was a way of forgetting certain things and making others easier to accept. Then about six years ago I found I hadn't worked on a book for a year, that my memory and intellect were blurry and unreliable, and my hands shook in the morning. I still drink a tot or two of an evening, and occasionally I take on a full blast of the stuff. But now I drink because I am happy not because I am sad.

'Come on, Ben. Tonight we've got something to celebrate.' Sally laughed and poured me another heavy portion.

'Wow! Gently, Doctor,' I protested weakly, but that night I got drunk, pleasantly, contentedly, floating drunk. With dignity I refused Louren's offer of assistance and made my own way to the tent wherein Sally had discreetly segregated me since Louren's arrival. I fell on top of my bed fully clothed and went to sleep. I half awoke when Louren came in and climbed into his bed across the tent. I remember opening one eye and seeing the glow of the waning moon through the fly of the tent – or was it the first glow of dawn? It didn't seem important then.

T he personnel for the project was the most important consideration, and here I was lucky. Peter Willcox was due for his sabbatical leave from Cape Town University. I flew down to see him, and in six hours convinced him that he wouldn't enjoy the fleshpots of Europe at all. Heather, his wife, was a little harder to sway, until I showed her the photographs of the white king. Like Sally, rock art is one of her big things.

They were good people to have on a dig. We had been together on the excavation of the Slangkop caves. They were both in their thirties; he a little paunchy and balding with steel-rimmed spectacles and trousers always on the point of falling down. He had to keep tugging at the waistband. She was thin and angular, with a wide laughing mouth and a snub, heavily freckled nose. They were childless, cheerful, knowledgeable and hard-working. Peter plays a very jazzy accordion and Heather has a voice that harmonizes well with mine.

Peter introduced me to two of his post-graduate students whom he recommended without reservation. I was startled at my first meeting with them. Ral Davidson was a young man of twenty-one – although the fact that he was a man was not immediately obvious. However, Peter assured me that beneath all the untidy hair lurked a promising young archaeologist. His fiancée was an intense bespectacled young woman, who had graduated at the head of her year. Although she was depressingly plain and I prefer my women beautiful, Leslie Johns endeared herself to me immediately by whispering breathlessly, 'Dr Kazin, I think your book, *Ancient Africa*, is the most exciting thing I've ever read.'

This display of good taste secured the job for them.

Peter Larkin found me forty-six African labourers from the southern territories of Botswana, who had never heard of the Hills of Blood nor of any curse upon them.

My only disappointment was with Timothy Mageba. I spent five days at the Institute in Johannesburg on my way back from Cape Town, mostly trying to convince Timothy that I needed him at the Hills of Blood.

'Machane,' he said, 'there is work here that no one else can do.' I was to remember those words later. 'Where you are going there is work that many men are capable of. You have these men and women already, specialists all of them. You do not need me.'

'Please, Timothy. It would be for six months or so. Your work here can wait.'

He shook his head vehemently, but I hurried on.

'I really want you, and need you. There are things that you alone can explain. Timothy, there are over fifteen thousand square feet of paintings on the rocks. Much of it is symbol, stylized emblems which only you—'

'Dr Kazin, you could send me copies of them. I can still give you my interpretation.' Timothy switched to English, which with him was always a discouraging sign. 'I hope you don't insist that I leave the Institute now. My assistants cannot work without my direction.'

We stared at each other for a few seconds. It was a deadlock. I could order him to come, but an unwilling helper is worse than none at all. There was a rebellious, independent spirit smouldering in Timothy's dark eyes and I knew that there was some deeper reason why he refused to accompany me.

'Is it—' I hesitated. I was about to ask him if the ancient curse was the reason for his refusal. It was always disquieting to find superstition influencing an intelligent and well-educated man. I was reluctant to come straight out with it, for even with an African like Timothy the direct question is considered gauche and discourteous.

'There are always reasons within reasons, Doctor. Please believe me when I tell you it would be better if I did not accompany you this time.'

'All right, Timothy,' I agreed with resignation, and stood up. Again we locked glances, and it seemed to me that he was different. The flickering fires burned brighter, and again I felt the stirring of unease, of fear even, deep within me.

'I promise you, Doctor, that my work here is at a critical stage.'

'I will be very interested to see it when you are ready, Timothy.'

My four new assistants arrived on the commercial flight from Cape Town the following morning and we drove directly to the Sturvesant hangar where the Dakota transport was waiting for us.

The flight in was noisy and gay. Peter had his accordion along, and I never travel without my old guitar. We hit a couple of easy ones like 'Abdul Abulbul Emir', and 'Green grow the rushes, oh!', and I discovered with delight that

Ral Davidson whistled with a clarity and purity that was truly beautiful, and that Leslie had a sweet little soprano.

'When we've finished this dig, I'm going to take you lot on tour,' I told them, and began teaching them some of my own compositions.

It was three weeks since I had left the Hills of Blood, and as we circled it I could see that changes had taken place in my absence. The landing-strip, complete with wind-sock, had been gouged out of the dusty plain. Near it stood a cluster of prefabricated buildings. One long central bungalow with the residential quarters grouped around it. A skeletal metal tower supported a 2,000-gallon galvanized iron water-tank, and beyond that was the encampment which housed the African labour force.

Sally was waiting for us at the landing-strip, and we piled our luggage into the Land-Rover and went to look at our new home. I expected Louren to be there but Sally told me he had gone the previous day after a stay of a few days.

Proudly Sally showed us over the camp. The central air-conditioned bungalow was divided into a small common room and lounge at the one end, in the centre was a large office and beyond that a storage warehouse. There were four residential huts, air-conditioned, but sparsely furnished. Sally had allotted one to the Willcoxes, one for Leslie and herself, one for Ral and me, and the fourth for Louren or other visitors, pilots, and overnight guests.

'I could think of a few improvements in the sleeping arrangements,' I muttered bitterly.

'Poor Ben.' Sally smiled cruelly. 'Civilization has caught up with you. By the way, I hope you remembered to bring your bathing costume, no skinny dips in the pool any more.'

And perversely I regretted all that Louren had done for me. The Hills of Blood were no longer a lonely, mysterious place in the wilderness, but a bustling little community, with aircraft landing regularly, Land-Rovers kicking up the dust and even the clatter of an electric water-pump shattering the dreaming silence of the cavern and disturbing the still green waters of the emerald pool.

Quickly my group settled into their allotted tasks. Sally worked on at the cavern, with a single young African assistant. Each of the other four was placed in charge of a team of ten labourers and assigned an area in which to work.

Peter and Heather shrewdly elected to work outside the main walls, in the ruins of the lower city. It was here that the ancients would have disposed of their rubbish, broken pottery, old weapons, discarded beads and the fascinating debris of a vanished civilization.

Ral and Leslie with dreams of gold and treasure jumped at the chance of excavating within the enclosure, an area which the ancients would have kept swept and scrupulously clean, and therefore much less likely to yield finds of interest. That is the difference between experience and inexperience, between the impetuosity of youth and the cool calculations of an older head.

I kept myself free, in a supervisory and advisory capacity. Spending my time at those places where it could do the most good. Anxiously I watched Ral and Leslie to assure myself that their approach and technique were satisfactory, then I relaxed as Peter Willcox's recommendation proved correct. They were clever, enthusiastic youngsters and, more important, they knew their way around an archaeological dig.

The four teams shook themselves out as the dullards amongst the African labourers were sorted from the bright ones. In a shorter time than I had hoped for, the firm of Kazin and Company was breaking ground and doing good business.

It was slow, painstaking and thoroughly satisfying work. Each evening, before the nightly singsong in the common room, the day's work was discussed and any discoveries evaluated and related to their place in the general picture of the site.

The first conclusive discovery we made was that the ash layer at Level I persisted throughout the site, even in the lower city. It was by no means evenly distributed, but showed up in patches of varying thickness. Carbon-dating, however, gave a fairly constant result, and we settled at a date of A.D.450. This date seemed to be concurrent or to slightly pre-date the oldest bushman paintings in the cavern.

We were agreed that bushman occupation of the cavern would have followed immediately after the departure or disappearance of the ancients from the city. Scrupulously we referred to the first occupations as 'ancients', considering the term 'Phoenician' as yet unproven. A condition which it was my most dearly-held hope would soon be altered.

Associated with the ash layer were haunting scraps of human remains. Ral uncovered an incisor in the ash against the base of the main tower, Peter a complete humerus together with many other unidentifiable bone fragments. These unburied human remains went a long way to ensuring a general acceptance of my theory of a violent end to the City of the Moon.

This was reinforced by the baffling disappearance of walls and towers, which we could reasonably accept once stood on these bases of clay, with their vestigial stone foundations which occurred spasmodically along the outline of the temple enclosure.

Ral hesitantly suggested an enemy so crazed with hatred, that he had set out to obliterate all trace of the ancients from the earth. We could all accept this.

'Fair enough. But what happened to thousands of tons of massive masonry?' Sally spoke for all of us.

'They scattered it out across the plain,' Ral hazarded.

'A Herculean task, besides the plain was a lake in those days. To get rid of it they would have scattered it along the area between cliff and lake. There is no sign of it.'

Apologetically Peter Willcox reminded us of the account in Credo Mutwa's book *Indaba My Children* of how an ancient city was carried by its people, block by block, out of the west, and how the city was rebuilt at Zimbabwe.

'This is red sandstone,' Sally cut in brusquely. 'Zimbabwe is granite, quarried from the rock on which it stands. Zimbabwe is 275 miles east of here. The labour involved is unthinkable. I will accept that the building skills and techniques were transported, but not the material itself.'

There were no more ideas forthcoming and we could turn from theories to facts. At the end of six weeks Louren Sturvesant visited us for the first time. All digging and other work was suspended as for two days we held a seminar, with myself as Chairman, in which we presented Louren with all our accomplishments and conclusions to date.

These were very impressive. To begin with, the list of artefacts, pottery sherds, and other relics filled 127 type-written foolscap pages. Peter and Heather were responsible for most of these and they opened the seminar.

'So far all excavation without the enclosure has been confined to the area north of it, and lying within 1,000 feet of the outer perimeter. In the main it seems to have been a complex of small rooms and buildings built from adobe clay and roofed with poles and thatch—'

Peter described the area in detail, giving the average size of the rooms and the exact position of each object discovered. Louren started thrashing around in his chair, and fiddling with his cigar. Peter is meticulous, almost old-maidish, in his approach to his work. Finally he reached his conclusions. 'It seems, therefore, that this area was an extensive bazaar and market.' And he led us through into the warehouse to examine the finds from this area. There were fragments of badly rusted iron, a bronze comb, the handle of a knife fashioned in the shape of a woman's body, fourteen rosettes of bronze that we guessed had embossed a leather shield, twenty-five pounds' weight of bronze discs, and stars and sun objects which were clearly ornaments, sixteen shaped and beaten bronze plates that we hoped might comprise part of a suit of body armour, a magnificent bronze dish twenty-four inches in diameter chased with a sun image and set around with an intricate border pattern, and another forty pounds' weight of bronze scraps and fragments so badly battered and damaged as to be unidentifiable.

'These are all the bronze objects so far discovered,' Peter told Louren. 'The workmanship is crude, but not recognizably Bantu in conception and execution. It would relate more closely to what we know of Phoenician craftsmanship. Unlike the Romans and Greeks, they placed little value on the arts. Their artefacts, like their buildings, were massive and roughly executed. One other fact that emerges is the veneration of the sun. It was clearly a generally polytheistic community but one in which sun-worship predominated. In this settlement, it appears that Baal, the Phoenician male deity, was personified by the sun.'

I thought Peter was verging on the mistake of special pleading but I let him continue without interruption. After discussing each item separately, Peter led us to the next row of tables that carried all the glass and pottery.

'One hundred and twenty-five pounds' weight of glass beads – the colours are predominantly blue and red. Phoenician colours, with greens and whites and yellows recovered only in Levels I and II. In other words, later than A.D. 50 which coincides approximately with the final phase of absorption of Phoenician civilization by the Romans in the Mediterranean area, and its gradual disappearance.'

I interrupted. 'The Romans were so thorough in their absorption of Phoenicia and all her works, that we know very little of them . . . .'

My attention wandered to Sally. She was in a sparkling mood, a complete change from the previous six weeks when she had been moody and withdrawn. She had washed her hair and it was shiny and springing with soft lights. Her skin also shone with golden hues where the sun had touched it, and she had coloured her lips and dramatized her eyes. Her beauty squeezed my heart. I forced my mind back to the row of tables.

'. . . A case in point is this recovery of pottery,' Peter was saying. He indicated the huge display of fragments, portions, and a very few complete pieces. 'On all of this, with one exception, there is not a single inscription. This is the exception.' He picked up a sherd which was set out in a place of honour, and passed it to Louren. Although we had all gloated over it before, we crowded around Louren as he examined it. There was a symbol cut into the baked clay.

'A chip from the lip of a cup, or vase. The symbol could conceivably be a Punic T.'

Louren burst in impulsively, turning to me and laying a hand on my shoulder, 'Conclusive, Ben. They must accept that, surely?'

'By no means, Lo.' I shook my head regretfully. 'They will cry, "Imported." The old trick of discrediting anything you can't explain, or which doesn't support your theories, by saying that it was brought in during the course of trade.'

'Looks as though you can't win, Ben,' Louren sympathized, and I grinned.

'At least we haven't uncovered any fourteenth-century Nanking pottery – or a chamber pot with Queen Victoria's portrait on it!'

Laughing we moved on to the next display of copper

and copperware. There were bangles and brooches, green-encrusted and eaten away. Bales of copper wire and, significantly, ingots cast into the shape of a St Andrew's Cross each weighing twelve pounds.

'Those aren't something new,' Louren remarked.

'No,' I agreed. 'They turn up all over central and southern Africa. And yet the shape is exactly that of the ingots taken from the tin mines of Cornwall by the Phoenicians – or the copper ingots from the ancient mines on Cyprus.'

'Still not conclusive?' Louren looked at me and I shook my head, leading him on to see the iron work we had recovered. All of it was so badly rusted and damaged that the original shape was a matter of conjecture and guess-work. There were hundreds of arrow-heads, mostly associated with Levels I and II, spear-heads and sword-blades, axe-heads and knives.

'Judging by the quantities of weapons, or what we take to be weapons, the ancients were a warlike people. Alternatively they were a people fearful of attack and well armed against it,' I suggested, and there was a general murmur of agreement. From the iron section we went on to a display of my photographs, showing each stage of the excavations, views of the lower city, the temple, the acropolis and the cavern.

'Pretty good, Ben,' Louren admitted. 'Is that all you have for me?'

'The best comes last.' I couldn't help a little showmanship in my presentation, and I had screened off the end of the warehouse. I led him beyond the first screen with all my team hovering anxiously to judge his reaction. It was gratifying.

'Good God!' Louren stopped short and stared at the phallic columns with their ornamental tops. 'Zimbabwe birds!'

There were three of them. Although incomplete, they

stood about five foot high, and were thirty inches in circumference. Only one of them was relatively undamaged, the other two had been mutilated so as to be hardly recognizable. The carving on top of each pillar had obviously originally depicted a vulturine bird shape with heavy beak, hunched shoulders, and predatory claws. They were similar in design and execution to those recovered from Zimbabwe by Hall, MacIver, and others.

'Not Zimbabwe birds,' I corrected Louren.

'No,' Sally affirmed. 'These are the ones from which the Zimbabwe birds were copied.'

'Where did you find them?' Louren asked as he moved in for a closer scrutiny of the green soapstone figures.

'In the temple,' I smiled at Ral and Leslie, who looked suitably modest, 'within the inner enclosure. They are probably religious objects – you see the sun symbols around the collar of the column – clearly they are associated with the worship of Baal as the sun god.'

'We have named them the sunbirds,' Sally explained, 'as Ben felt a name like the birds of Ophir was a bit too pretentious.'

'Why have they been damaged like this?' Louren indicated where deliberate blows had shattered the brittle green stone.

'That's anybody's guess.' I shrugged away the question. 'But we know that they had been toppled and were lying without design or direction in the layer of ash at Level I.'

'That's very interesting, Ben.' Louren's eyes were drawn to the final screen at the end of the warehouse. 'Now come on, you secretive old bastard, what have you got behind there?'

'What the whole city and colonization was based on – ' I opened the screen, ' – gold!'

There is something about that beautiful buttery metal that holds the imagination captive. A hush came over the party as we stared at it. The objects had been carefully cleaned, and the surfaces shone with the special soft radiance which is unmistakably gold.

To coldly itemize the collection detracts in some way from its excitement and mystery. The gross weight of the pieces was 683 fine ounces. There were fifteen rods of native gold as thick and as long as a man's finger. There were forty-eight pieces of crudely wrought jewellery, pins, brooches and combs. There was a statuette of a female figure four and a half inches tall –

'Astarte – Tanith,' Sally whispered as she stroked it, 'Goddess of the moon and the earth.'

In addition there were a handful of gold beads with the string long ago disintegrated, dozens of sun discs and many chips, tacks and flakes and buttons of no definite shape or discernible purpose.

'And then,' I said, 'there is this,' picking up the heavy chalice of solid gold. It had been crushed and flattened, but the base was undamaged. 'Look,' I said, pointing to the design worked into it with uncommon delicacy of line.

'Ankh? The Egyptian sign of eternal life?' Louren looked to me for confirmation, and I nodded.

'For the Christians and heathens amongst you. We know that the Pharaohs on occasions used the Phoenicians to supply treasure for their empire. Was this,' and I turned the chalice in my hands, 'a gift from a Pharaoh to the King of Ophir?'

'And do you remember the cup in the right hand of the White Lady of the Brandberg?' Sally asked.

It was enough to keep us arguing and locked in discussion into the early hours, and the next day Sally, helped by Heather Willcox, presented her drawings and paintings from the cavern. When she showed the tracing of the white king, that frown of concentration again creased Louren's brow, and he stood up and went to examine it more closely. We waited for a long time in silence, before he looked up at Sally.

'I would like you to make a copy of this, for my own personal collection. Would you mind?'

'With the greatest of pleasure.' Sally smiled happily at him. The mood of sparkle and smile was still strong upon her and she was enjoying the sensation that the display of her work was causing. Sally, like most beautiful women, is not completely averse to standing in the limelight. She knew her work was damned good, and she liked the plaudits.

'Now I haven't been able to decide what these are.' Sally smiled as she hung a new sheet on the common-room board. 'There are seventeen symbols similar to this which I have so far isolated. Heather calls them the walking cucumbers, or the double walking cucumbers. Have you any ideas?'

'Tadpoles?' Ral tried.

'Centipedes?' Leslie was a bit more feasible.

That was the end of our imagination, and we were silent.

'No more offers?' Sally asked. 'I thought that with the formidable collection of academic qualification and worldly wisdom we have assembled here we could do better—'

'A bireme!' Louren said softly. 'And a trireme.'

'By Jove.' I saw it immediately. 'You're right!'

' "Quinquereme of Nineveh, from distant Ophir," ' Peter quoted joyously.

'The shape of a ship's hull, and the banks of oars,' I enlarged upon it. 'Of course – if we are right then vessels like that must have plied regularly across the lakes.'

We could accept it, but others certainly would not.

After lunch we went for a tour of the excavations, and Louren again distinguished himself with an inspired guess. A series of large regular cell-like rooms had been uncovered by Peter's team in the angle formed by the cliff and the enclosure wall. They were joined by a long corridor, and there was evidence of paved floors and a system of drainage.

Each room was approximately twenty-five feet square, and it seemed that these were the only buildings outside the enclosure which had been made of stone blocks and not adobe clay.

The closest we could come to a purpose for these cells was to call them 'the prison'.

'Do I have to do all the work around here?' Louren sighed. 'When you've just shown me pictures of the war elephants?'

'Elephant stables?' I asked.

'Very quick, lad!' Louren clapped me on the shoulder and I blushed. 'But I believe they are called elephant lines in India.'

After dinner I worked for an hour in my dark room, developing three rolls of film, and when I was finished I went to look for Louren. He was leaving again early the following morning and there was much for us to discuss.

He wasn't in the guest room, nor in the lounge, and when I asked for him, Ral told me, 'I think he has gone up to the cavern, Doctor. He borrowed a torch from me.'

Leslie looked at him in a way which was clearly meant to be highly significant, a frown and a quick little shake of the head, but it meant as much to him as it did to me. I went to fetch my own torch, and set off through the silent grove, picking my way carefully around the open excavations. No light showed from the entrance of the tunnel beyond the great wild fig tree.

'Louren!' I called. 'Are you there?' And my voice bounced hollowly from cliff and rock. There was silence once the echoes died, and I went forward into the tunnel. Flashing my torch into the darkness ahead, ducking my head under the zooming flight of the bats, and hearing my own footsteps magnified in the silence.

I could see no light, and I stopped and called again.

'Louren!' My voice boomed around the cavern. There was no reply, and I went on down the passage.

As I stepped out from the mouth of the tunnel, suddenly the beam of a powerful torch flashed from across the cavern shining full in my eyes.

'Louren?' I asked. 'Is that you?'

'What do you want, Ben?' he demanded from the darkness behind the torch. He sounded irritable, angry even.

'I want to talk to you about the plans for the next step.' I shielded my eyes from the beam.

'It can wait until tomorrow.'

'You are leaving early – let's talk now.'

I started to cross the cavern towards him, averting my eyes from the dazzling beam.

'Point that light somewhere else, won't you,' I protested mildly.

'Are you deaf!' Louren's voice rasped, the voice of a man used to being obeyed. 'I said tomorrow, damn you.'

I stopped dead, stunned, confused. He had never spoken to me like that in my life before.

'Lo, are you all right?' I asked anxiously. There was something wrong here in the cavern. I could sense it.

'Ben,' his voice crackled, 'just turn around and walk out of here, will you. I'll see you tomorrow morning.'

I hesitated a moment longer. Then I turned and walked back down the passage. I hadn't even had a glimpse of Louren in the darkness beyond the torch.

In the morning Louren was as charming as only he can be. He apologized handsomely for the previous evening. 'I just wanted to be alone, Ben. I'm sorry. I get like that sometimes.'

'I know, Lo. I am the same.'

In ten minutes we had agreed that although the circumstantial evidence of a Phoenician occupation of the city was most encouraging, it was not conclusive. We would not make any public announcement yet, but in the mean-

116

time Louren gave me complete *carte blanche* to proceed with a full-scale excavation and investigation.

He flew out with the dawn, and I knew he would be in London for breakfast the following morning.

The weeks that followed Louren's departure were dissatisfying for me. Although the work on the ruins went forward steadily, and my assistants never faltered in their enthusiasm and industry – yet the results were uniformly disappointing.

There were other finds, many of them, but they were repetitive. Pottery, beads, even the occasional gold fragment or ornament no longer thrilled me as it had before. There was nothing that added a scrap of knowledge to the store we had accumulated already. I roved the site restlessly, anxiously hovering over a new trench or exposed level, praying that the next spadeful of earth turned would expose an inscribed pallet or the headstone to a burial vault. Somewhere here was the key to the ancient mystery but it was well hidden.

Apart from the lack of progress on the excavation, my relationship with Sally had deteriorated in some subtle fashion which I was at a loss to explain. Naturally there had been no opportunity for any physical intimacy since the arrival of the others at the City of the Moon. Sally was adamant in her determination not to allow our affair to become common knowledge. My amateurish manoeuvrings to get her alone were deftly countered. The nearest I came to success was when I visited her at the cavern during the day. Even here she had her assistant with her, and often Heather Willcox as well.

She seemed withdrawn, taciturn, even surly. She worked over her easel with a fierce concentration during the day, and she usually slipped away to her hut immediately after dinner. Once I followed her, knocking softly on the door of her hut, then hesitantly pushing the door open when there was no reply. She was not there. I waited in the shadows, feeling like a peeping Tom, and it was after midnight before she returned, slipping out of the silent grove like a ghost and going directly to her room where Leslie had long ago switched out the light.

It was distressing for me to see my laughing Sally so withdrawn, and finally I visited her at the cavern.

'I want to talk to you, Sal.'

'What about?' She looked at me with mild surprise, as though it were the first time in days that she had noticed me. I sent the young African assistant away and prevailed on Sally to join me on the rocks beside the emerald pool, hoping that its beauty and associations would soften her mood.

'Is something wrong, Sal?'

'Good Lord, should there be?' It was an awkward unsatisfying conversation. Sally seemed to feel I was prying into affairs that did not concern me. I felt my anger rising, and I wanted to shout at her:

'I am your lover, damn you, and everything you do concerns me!'

But good sense prevailed, for I am sure presumption of that magnitude from me would have severed the last tenuous threads of our relationship. Instead I took her hand and, hating myself for the blush that burned my cheeks, I told her softly, 'I love you, Sally. Just remember that – if there is ever anything I can do—'

I think it was probably the best thing I could have said, for immediately her hand tightened on mine and her face softened, her eyes went slightly misty.

'Ben, you are a sweet dear person. Don't take any notice of me for a while. I've just got the blues, there is nothing

118

anybody can do about it. They will go on their own, if you don't fuss.'

For a moment she was my old girl again, a smile quivering precariously on the corners of her mouth, and in those great green eyes.

'Let me know when it's over, won't you?' I stood up.

'That I will, Doctor. You'll be the first to know.'

T he following week I flew back to Johannesburg. There was the Annual General Meeting of the trustees of the Institute which I could not avoid, and I was committed to a series of lectures for the Faculty of Archaeology at the University of Witwatersrand.

I was scheduled to be away from the site for eleven days. I left it all in Peter Willcox's safe hands, after extracting from him a promise that he would cable me immediately if any new development broke.

The three girls fussed around me, packing my case, making a picnic lunch for me to eat on the plane, and lining up to kiss me goodbye at the airstrip. I must admit that I rather enjoyed all the attention.

I have often found that living too close to any problem narrows one's view of the whole. Three hours after leaving the City of the Moon, I made a minor breakthrough. If there had been walls and towers standing on the ruined foundations, then the rock must have been brought from nearby. The obvious place was from the cliffs themselves. Somewhere in those cliffs, close to the city, there was a quarry.

I would find it, and from its extent I would calculate the actual size of the city.

For the first time in weeks I felt good, and the days that followed were gratifying and solidly enjoyable. The meeting

119

of the trustees was the type of festive affair which can be expected when funds are unlimited and prospects are favourable. From the Chair Louren was most complimentary when he renewed my contract as Director of the Institute for a further twelve months. To celebrate the thirty per cent rise in my remuneration, he invited me to a dinner at his home where forty people sat down at the yellow wood table in the huge dining-room, and I was the guest of honour.

Hilary Sturvesant, in a gown of yellow brocade silk and wearing the fabled Sturvesant diamonds, gave me her almost undivided attention during the meal. I have a weakness for beautiful things, particularly if they are women. There were twenty of them there that night, and in the drawing-room afterwards I held court like royalty. The wine had loosened my tongue, and washed away my confounded shyness. No matter that Hilary and Louren had probably primed the other guests to make a fuss of me, for when at two o'clock in the morning I went down to the Mercedes with Hilary and Louren escorting me I swaggered along seven feet tall.

This new-found confidence carried me through the series of four lectures at the University of the Witwatersrand. The first of which was attended by twenty-five students and faculty members, the latter outnumbering the former two to one. The word got out, however, and my final venue was changed to one of the main lecture theatres to handle the audience of 600 that turned up. I was an unqualified success. I was prevailed upon to return at an early date – and there was an unsubtle hint from the Vice-Chancellor of the University that the Archaeology Chair would be vacant the following year.

For the last three days of my visit I spent every minute at the Institute. With relief I found that not much had suffered in my absence, and my multitudinous staff had kept things running smoothly.

The bushman exhibition in the Kalahari Room was completed, and open to the public. It was magnificently executed, and the central figure of the main group reminded me sharply of my little friend Xhai. The model was depicted in the act of painting on the stone wall of a cave abode. With his stoppered buck-horn paint pots, and reed pipes and brushes, I imagined that this was how the artist who had painted my white king had worked. It gave me an odd sensation, as though two millennia had rolled away, as though I could send my mind back along the years. I spoke of it to Timothy Mageba.

'Yes, Machane. I have told you before that you and I are marked. We have the sign of the spirits on us, and we have the sight.'

I smiled and shook my head. 'I don't know about you, Timothy, but I've never been able to pick a winner—'

'I am serious, Doctor,' Timothy rebuked me. 'You have the gift. It is merely that you have not been taught to develop it.'

I will accept hypnotism, but talk of clairvoyance, necromancy, mantology and the like leaves me feeling embarrassed. To divert the conversation from me and my gifts, I asked, 'You have told me before that you are also marked by the spirits . . .'

Timothy looked at me steadily from out of those disturbing black eyes. At first I thought I had insulted him by my thinly disguised question, but suddenly he nodded that cannon-ball head. He stood up, closed and locked the door of his office before returning to his seat. Quickly he stripped shoe and sock from his right foot, and showed it to me.

The deformity was shocking, although I had seen photographs of it before. It was of fairly common occurrence among the Batonga tribe of the Zambezi Valley. There had been a paper on it published in the *British Medical Journal* during 1969. The condition was known as 'ostrich-footed', and consisted of a massive division between the metatarsus of the big toe and the second toe. The effect was to make the foot resemble the claw of an ostrich or predatory bird. Timothy was obviously very sensitive about this deformity, and almost immediately replaced his sock and shoe. I realized later that he had shown it to me in a deliberate attempt to enlist my sympathy, to create a bond between us.

'Both feet?' I asked, and he nodded. 'There are many people in the Zambezi Valley with feet like that,' I told him.

'My mother was a Batonga woman,' he answered. 'It was this mark that qualified me for training in the mysteries.'

'Does it hinder you at all?' I asked.

'No,' he answered brusquely, and then went on almost defiantly in Batonga. 'We men of the cloven feet outrun the fleetest antelope.'

It was a beneficial mutation then, and I would have enjoyed discussing it further but I was warned by Timothy's expression. I realized the effort it had taken him to show me.

'Will you have some tea, Doctor?' He reverted to English, closing the subject. When one of his young African assistants had poured cups of strong black tea for us, Timothy asked, 'Please tell me how the work at the City of the Moon is progressing, Doctor.'

We chatted for another half hour, then I left him.

'You must excuse me now, Timothy. I am flying back tomorrow morning early and there is still much to do.'

I was awakened by a soft but insistent knocking on the door of my suite in the Institute. I switched on the bedside light and saw that the time was three o'clock in the morning.

'Who is there?' I called and the knocking stopped. I slipped out of bed, shrugged into a dressing-gown and slippers, and started for the front door, when I realized the risk I was taking. I went back to my bedroom and took the big ugly automatic .45 from the drawer. Feeling a little melodramatic, I pumped a round into the chamber and went back to the front door.

'Who is it?' I repeated.

'It's me, Doctor, Timothy!'

I hesitated a moment longer – anybody could call themselves Timothy.

'Are you alone?' I asked in Kalahari bushman.

'I am alone, Sunbird,' he answered in the same language, and I slipped the pistol into my pocket and opened the door.

Timothy was dressed in dark blue slacks and a white shirt with a windcheater thrown over his shoulders and I noticed immediately that there were spots of fresh blood on the shirt and that there was a rather grubby cloth wrapped around his left forearm. He was clearly much agitated, his eyes wide and staring in the light, and his movements jerky and nervous.

'Good God, Timothy, are you all right?'

'I've had a terrible night, Doctor. I had to see you right away.'

'What have you done to your arm?'

'I cut it on the window pane of my front door, I fell in the dark,' he explained.

'You'd better let me have a look at it.' I went towards him.

'No, Doctor. It's only a scratch. What I have come to tell you is more important.'

'Sit down at least,' I told him. 'Can I get you a drink?'

'A drink, thank you, Machane, as you can see I am upset and nervous. That is how I came to injure my arm.'

I poured both of us whisky, and he took his glass in his right hand and continued moving nervously around my sitting-room while I sat in one of the big leather armchairs.

'What is it, Timothy?' I prompted him.

'It is difficult to begin, Machane, for you are not a believer. But I must convince you.'

He broke off and drank whisky, before turning to face me.

'Yesterday evening we spoke at length about the City of the Moon, Doctor, you told me how there are mysteries there that still baffle you.'

'Yes.' I nodded encouragement.

'The burial grounds of the ancients,' Timothy went on. 'You cannot find them.'

'That is true, Timothy.'

'Since then I have thought heavily on this matter.' He changed into Venda, a language better suited for the discussion of the occult. 'I went back in my memory over all the legends of our people.' I imagined vividly how he must have thrown himself into hypnotic trance to search. 'And there was something there, like a shadow beyond the firelight, a dark memory that eluded me.' He shook his head and turned away, pacing restlessly, sipping at his drink, muttering softly to himself as though he still searched in the dark archives of his mind.

'It was no use, Doctor. I knew it was there, but I could not grasp it. I despaired of it, and at last I slept. But it was a sleep greatly troubled by the dream demons – until at last . . .' he hesitated, '. . . my grandfather came to me.'

I stirred uneasily in my chair. Timothy's grandfather had lain twenty-five years in a murderer's grave.

'All right, Doctor.' Timothy saw my small movement of disbelief, and changed smoothly to English. 'I know you do not believe such things can happen. Let me explain it in terms you can accept. My imagination, heated by my search for a long-forgotten fragment of knowledge, threw up a dream image of my grandfather. The one from whom the knowledge was learned in the first place.'

I smiled to cover my spooky feelings; at this time of night with this half-demented black man talking of dark things, I felt myself falling under his spell.

'Go on, Timothy.' I tried to say it lightly, but my voice croaked a little.

'My grandfather came to me, and he touched my shoulder and he said, "Go with the blessed one, to the Hills of Blood and there I will make the mysteries known to you and open up the secret places." '

I felt my skin prickle. Timothy had said 'The Hills of Blood', and nobody had told him that name.

'The Hills of Blood,' I repeated.

'That is the name he used,' Timothy agreed. 'I can only believe he meant your City of the Moon.'

I was silent; reasonable man at war with primitive superstitious man within me.

'You want to come with me tomorrow, Timothy?' I asked.

'I will go with you,' Timothy agreed. 'And perhaps I will be able to show you something for which you search – then again I may not be able to.'

There was certainly nothing to lose. Timothy was obviously sincere, he was still tense and nervously aware.

'I have already invited you to join me, Timothy, and I was very disappointed when you refused. Of course you may come with me – we can certainly see if the sight of the ruins stirs something in your memory.'

'Thank you, Doctor. What time will you leave?'

I glanced at my watch.

'Good Lord, it's four o'clock already. We will leave at six.'

'Then I must hurry home and pack.' Timothy replaced his glass on my cabinet, then he turned to me. 'There is a small snag, Doctor. My travel papers have expired and we will have to cross an international border into Botswana.'

'Oh, damn it,' I muttered, deeply disappointed. 'You will have to get them renewed and come up with me on the next trip.'

'As you wish, Doctor,' he agreed readily. 'Of course, it will take two or three weeks – and by then the whole thing might have faded from my memory.'

'Yes.' I nodded, but I felt a prick of temptation. I am usually a law-abiding person, but now as I thought about it I saw that no harm could come from what I intended. The chance that Timothy might lead me to the burial grounds of the ancients was worth any risk.

'Would you like to take a chance, Timothy?' I asked. Formalities concerned with the coming and going of Sturvesant aircraft had been reduced to a minimum. There were daily arrivals and departures, and a phone call to the airport authorities was all that was necessary before departure. The Sturvesant name carried such weight that there was never a head count on arrival or departure. At the City of the Moon Louren had arranged special status with the Botswana Government, and we were virtually free from bothersome red tape.

I could have Timothy in and out within three days with nobody the wiser and no damage done. Roger van Deventer would accept my word that Louren had sanctioned the flight. I could see no problems.

'Very well, Doctor, if you think it's safe.' Timothy agreed to my proposal.

'Be at the Sturvesant hangar before six.' I sat down to scribble a note. 'If you are questioned at the airport gate, which I doubt, show them this. It's a note authorizing you to deliver goods to the Sturvesant hangar. Park your car behind the flight office, and wait for me in the office.'

Quickly we made our arrangements, and when I stood at the window of my bedroom and watched Timothy's old blue Chevy pull out of the Institute car park I felt a mixture of elation and apprehension. Idly I wondered what the penalty was for aiding illegal exit and entry, then dismissed the thought and went to make myself some coffee.

T imothy's Chevy was in one of the parking bays when Roger van Deventer and I drove up in the Mercedes. We went through into the hangar. The big sliding doors were open and the ground crew was readying the Dakota for the flight, and through the glass doors of the flight office I saw Timothy sitting hunched at the desk. He looked up and smiled at me.

'I'll get the clearance, Roger,' I suggested smoothly. 'You go and start the engines.'

'Okay, Doctor.' He handed me the flight dossier. We had done this before, and I had banked on the same procedure. Roger climbed up through the door of the fuselage, while I went quickly into the office.

'Hello, Timothy.' I looked at him and felt a twinge of concern. He was huddled into his blue windcheater, and there were lines of pain cut into his forehead and the corners of his nostrils. His skin was grey and his lips pale purplish blue. 'Are you all right?'

'My arm is a little painful, Doctor.' He opened the front of his jacket. The arm was in a sling, freshly bandaged. 'But it will be all right. I've had it attended to.'

'Do you feel up to this trip?'

'I'll be all right, Doctor.'

'Are you sure?'

'Yes, I'm sure.'

'All right, then.' I sat down at the desk and picked up the phone. It was answered at the first ring.

'Airport police!'

'This is Dr Kazin – from Sturvesant, Africa.'

'Oh, good morning, Doctor. How are you this morning?'

'Fine, thank you. I want to clear a flight to Botswana on ZA-CEE.'

'Hold on, Doctor. Let me get the particulars. Who are the passengers?'

'One passenger, myself – and the pilot is Roger van Deventer as usual.'

I dictated while the constable on the other end took it down in laborious shorthand. Until finally he said: 'That's okay, Doctor. Have a good flight. I'll give your clearance to control.'

I hung up and smiled at Timothy.

'All clear.' I stood up. 'Let's go.' And I led the way out of the office. The engines of the Dakota were ticking over. The three black ground crew inexplicably left their positions beside the landing gear and began walking rapidly towards me.

'Doctor!' Timothy's voice behind me, and I turned back towards him. It took me four or five seconds to realize that he had a short-barrelled Chinese model machine-pistol in his uninjured hand and the muzzle was pointing into my belly. I gaped at him.

'I am sorry, Doctor,' he said softly, 'but it is necessary.'

The ground crew closed in on each side of me, they gripped my arms.

'Please believe me, Doctor, when I tell you that I will not hesitate to kill you if you do not co-operate.' He raised his voice without taking his eyes off me. 'Come,' he called in Venda.

Five others came through the outer door of the hangar. I immediately recognized two of the young Bantu assistants from the Institute, and one of the girls. All of them carried those stubby, lethal-looking machine-pistols and between them they supported a badly wounded stranger. His feet

128

dangled loosely, and blood-soaked bandages covered his chest and neck.

'Get him into the plane,' Timothy ordered crisply.

All this time I had stood dumbly, paralysed with shock, but now the party carrying the wounded man squeezed past between my captors and the side wall. They were blanketing each others' line of fire, the whole group was off balance and at that moment I regained my wits. I braced my legs, leaned forward slightly and heaved. The men on my arms shot forward like thrown darts, crashing headlong into Timothy and knocking him down in a floundering heap.

'Roger!' I shouted. 'Radio! Get help!' Hoping my voice would carry over the sound of the aircraft engines. The third ground crew leaped on my back, one arm locking around my throat. I reached up, took him at wrist and elbow and wrenched against the joint. His elbow went with a rubbery popping sound and he screamed like a girl, his arm loose and flabby in my grip.

'Don't shoot,' shouted Timothy. 'No noise.'

'Help!' I screamed, the engines drowning my cry. They dropped the wounded man and came at me. I ducked and went in low. I kicked for the groin of the leader, and felt my boot sock into him, fleshy and soft. He doubled over and I swung my other knee up into his face. It crunched as the gristle of his nose collapsed.

Timothy and the ground crew were scrambling to their feet.

'No shooting.' Timothy's voice was desperate. 'No noise.' I went for him. Leopard-mad with rage, hating him for this betrayal with the full strength of my being, wanting to see his blood splash and feel his bones break in my hands.

One of the girls hit me with the steel butt of the machine-pistol, as I brushed past her. I felt the sharp edge of it cut into the flesh of my scalp, it threw me off balance. One of the ground crew grappled with me, and I took him to my chest and hugged him. He screamed, and I felt his ribs buckling in my grip.

They hit me again, steel biting into the bone of my skull. Blood poured warmly down my face, blinding me. My arms went soft, I dropped the man I was crushing and turned to charge into the others. Blinded with my own blood, my maniacal roars deafening me, they hit me again, crowding around me as I flailed and groped for them. The blows rained on my head and my shoulders. My knees collapsed, and I went down. I was still conscious, hot waves of anger buoying me. The boots started then, crashing into my chest and belly. I doubled up, blind, rolled into a ball on the cold oily concrete, trying to ride that storm of booted feet.

'Enough, leave him.' Timothy's voice. 'Get him to the aircraft.'

'My arm. I'll kill him.' The voice pig-squealing with agony.

'Stop that.' Timothy again, and the sound of a palm slapping against a face. 'We need hostages. Get him into the plane.'

They dragged me across the floor, many hands. I was lifted and thrown heavily onto the metal floor of the fuselage. The door slammed closed, muting the engine noise.

'Tell the pilot to take off,' Timothy ordered. 'Get the Doctor into the radio compartment.'

I was hustled down the length of the aisle. Blinking the blood out of my eyes, I saw the white ground engineer and his black ground crew lying bound and gagged against the wall of the fuselage. They were stripped of their overalls, which the gang had used to impersonate them.

Rough hands forced me into the steel chair in the radio compartment, and they tied me so tightly that the ropes bit painfully into my flesh. My face felt swollen and numb, and the taste of my own blood was thick and metallic in my mouth.

I turned my head, looking into the cockpit. Roger van Deventer was at the controls. There was a livid red swelling under his eye, and his grey hair was rumpled, his face pale and terrified. One of them stood over him with the muzzle of a machine-pistol pressed firmly against the back of his head.

'Take off,' instructed Timothy. 'Observe all routine procedures. Do you understand?'

Roger nodded jerkily. I felt sorry for him, I had guessed he was not cast in the heroic mould.

'Sorry, Doctor,' he tried to explain. 'They jumped me the moment I stepped aboard.' His full attention was on the job of taxiing the big aircraft out onto the still dark airfield. He did not look at me. 'I didn't have a chance.'

'That's all right, Roger. I didn't do so good either,' I replied thickly. 'I only got in two good licks.'

'That is enough talking for now, please, Doctor. Mr van Deventer must attend to the business of take-off,' Timothy admonished me, and I turned to give him the most expressive glare of hatred that I could force from my numbed features.

Roger asked for and received control clearance, and the take-off was routine and uneventful. The tense, anxious black faces relaxed and there were a few nervous laughs.

'You will fly on course for Botswana,' Timothy instructed Roger. 'Once you are over the border I will give you a new course.'

Roger nodded stiffly, the machine-pistol still held at his head. I was assessing the strength of the gang, I had already formed a working idea of their motives. Apart from Timothy and the eight who had overwhelmed me, there were five others. These were the ones who had captured and guarded Roger and the ground crew. The wounded man and the two I had damaged were laid out on the floor of the cargo hold. The two girls were working over them, both girls from the Institute, they were fitting a splint and changing bloody bandages.

As I watched, the gang members began changing from civilian clothing into camouflage paratrooper battle-dress. I saw the red star shoulder flashes, and my last doubts were dispelled. I turned my head and found Timothy was watching me.

'Yes, Doctor.' He nodded. 'Soldiers of freedom.'

'Or the bringers of darkness, depending how you look at it.'

Timothy frowned at my retort. 'I had always believed you to be a man of humanity, Doctor. You, I would have expected, could understand and sympathize with our aspirations.'

'I find it hard to sympathize with gangsters carrying guns in their hands.'

We stared at each other for a few moments. Then abruptly he stood up and came to the radio equipment beside my chair. He switched on the set, glanced at his watch, and began sweeping the bands. The station came on loudly, and immediately all movement in the aircraft arrested, all attention fixed on the announcer's voice:

'This is the South African Broadcasting Corporation. The time is seven o'clock and here is the news. A spokesman for the South African Police states that at 2.15 a.m. this morning a detachment of the Security Police, acting on information received, raided a farm house on the outskirts of Randburg, a suburb of Johannesburg. A pitched battle between police and a large gang of unidentified persons armed with automatic weapons ensued. Elements of the gang escaped in four motor-cars, and after a chase by the police, two vehicles managed to evade pursuit. Initial reports are that eight of the gang were shot dead, and four were captured wounded or unhurt. It is anticipated that many of those escaping were also wounded. A full-scale police hunt is now in progress, and all roads out of the Witwatersrand area are under surveillance, together with all airports. It is with deep regret that we announce the death of three members of the South African Police Force, and the critical wounding of two—'

A ragged cheer rang out through the aircraft, and one or two of the gang clenched their fists over their heads in the Communist salute.

'Congratulations,' I murmured sarcastically to Timothy and he looked down at me.

'Death is ugly, slavery is worse,' he said evenly. 'Doctor, there is a bond between us.'

'My head is sore, my face is too painful to listen to your Communistic cant,' I told him, 'don't give me fancy words, you bastard. You want to burn my land and soak it in blood. You want to tear down everything I hold dear and sacred. It is my country and with all its faults I love it. You are my enemy. There is no bond between us – except that of the knife.'

Again we held each other's eyes for a long moment, then he nodded. 'To the knife then,' he agreed and turned away. The Dakota bore on steadily into the north, and my injuries began to ache. I closed my eyes, and rode the long dizzy swells of pain that rose up out of my guts and exploded in my head.

The Mirage jet came up out of the east and flashed silvery sleek across our nose, and as it passed with incredible speed I saw the Air Force roundels and the goggled face of the pilot staring at us. Then it was gone, but immediately the Tannoy crackled into life.

'ZA-CEE. This is Air Force Red Striker Two. Do you read me?' I stared out of the window beside my head, and saw the Mirage turn sparkling in the sunlight high above us. Timothy came running forward to the set beside me and stared at it for a moment. The atmosphere was hushed and tense. Timothy could not reply, his Bantu accent was too thick for deception.

Again the jet howled across our front. The gunman crouched low behind Roger's seat hidden from view.

'ZA-CEE.' Again the call was repeated. Timothy was sweating lightly, his face blue-grey with strain and the pain of the arm-wound. He turned from the set and motioned to two of his men.

'Bring him,' he pointed to the white ground engineer. They dragged him into the radio compartment and held him in front of me. His face was pale and shiny with sweat, his terrified eyes held mine in pitiful appeal, the gag cut into his mouth. One of them stood behind him and pulled his head back, exposing his throat and stretching the pale skin so that the arteries showed blue and pulsing. He reached around in front of the man, and laid the glistening blade of a trench knife against his throat.

'I am serious, Doctor,' Timothy assured me as he freed the rope from my arms and put the microphone of the radio transmitter into my hand. 'Reassure them. Tell them there are only two aboard, and that you are bound for the City of the Moon on a routine flight.' He placed his finger on the transmit switch of the set ready to cut if off.

The terrified engineer moaned into his gag, the knife pressed to the softly throbbing skin of his throat. They pushed him towards me, closer so that I could see his face clearly.

'Air Force Striker Two this is ZA-CEE standing by.' I croaked into the mike, staring fascinated into the engineer's terrified face.

'Report your complement and destination.'

'This is Dr Kazin of Sturvesant, Africa on a routine flight from—' As I spoke I saw them relax, the tension

134

eased and Timothy's hand moved from the transmit switch of the set. The engineer's eyes held mine and I wanted to tell him that I was sorry, that I wished I could save him. I wanted to explain that I was trading his life for those of fourteen of my country's most dangerous enemies, that the sacrifice was worthwhile, and that I would willingly add my own life to the price. Instead I shouted into the handset:

'Hi-jacked by terrorists! Fire into us! Disregard our safety.' Timothy's hand darted to the transmit switch, and at the same moment he turned towards the hostage. I think he was going to intervene, to try and stop it. He was too late.

The knife slashed across the tensed throat, slitting it deeply beneath the line of the jaw. The blood burst forth like a ruptured garden hose, it sprayed out in a red fountain that drenched both Timothy and me. It pumped in great liquid jets that splashed against the roof of the cabin, then dribbled in thick cords and strings to the floor. The engineer was keening a high wailing sound like steam from a kettle, and the air from his lungs burst from the severed windpipe in a pink froth that spattered the radio set.

The Tannoy was squawking, 'Reverse your course! Conform to me! Conform to me immediately, or I will fire into you.'

Timothy was cursing as he wrestled the microphone out of my hand: I was screaming and fighting against the ropes.

'You animals! You filthy murdering bloody animals.'

One of the gang lifted his machine-pistol to hit me in the face, but Timothy knocked his arm away.

'Get him out of here!' He jerked his head towards the still twitching, kicking corpse of the engineer – and they dragged him out into the cargo hold.

'Mirage is attacking!' shouted Roger, from the cockpit, and we saw it coming from ahead of us, a silvery flash as it bore in on a head-on interception course.

Timothy snatched the microphone to his mouth. I saw

that his face was speckled with the engineer's blood. 'Hold your fire!' he shouted. 'We have hostages aboard.'

'Attack!' I screamed, tearing and jerking at my bonds. 'They'll murder us anyway! Open fire!'

The Mirage jet pulled up steeply ahead of us, without opening fire, and howled a few feet over our heads. The Dakota rocked violently in the slipstream. I was still screaming and struggling to tear myself loose. I wanted to get at them. The steel chair was rocking from side to side. I got to my feet against the side of the fuselage and heaved with all my strength. The seat buckled a little, and again the guard lifted his machine-pistol.

'No,' shouted Timothy. 'We need him alive. Tell Mary to bring the morphine.'

The Mirage sheered off, then circled in to take up station a hundred feet off our starboard wingtip, I could see the pilot staring helplessly across the gap at us.

'You have spoken to Dr Kazin,' Timothy warned the pilot of the jet. 'And we have four other hostages. We have already executed one white hostage and we will not hesitate to execute another if you take any further hostile action.'

'They're going to kill us anyway,' I shouted, but Timothy broke the contact.

It took five of them to hold me still for the hypodermic, but at last they got it into my arm, and though I tried to resist the drug, I felt myself going muzzy and misty. I tried to maintain my struggles, but my movements became lethargic and uncoordinated and slowly I drifted off into unconsciousness. My last waking memory was hearing Timothy giving Roger a new course to fly.

Pain and thirst woke me. My mouth was thick and scummy and my head was a mass of solid blinding agony. I tried to sit up and cried out aloud.

'Are you all right, Doctor? Take it easy.' Roger van Deventer's voice, and I focused my eyes on him.

'Water?' I asked.

'Sorry, Doc.' He shook his head, and I looked around the bare white-washed room. Four wooden bunks and a lavatory bucket were all the furnishings, and the door was barred and grilled. The three Bantu ground crew sat on one of the bunks across the room, looking lost and unhappy.

'Where are we?' I whispered.

'Zambia. Some sort of military camp. We landed an hour ago.'

'What happened to the Air Force jet?'

'It turned back when we crossed the Zambezi. Nothing they could do.'

And there was nothing we could do, either. For five days we sat in the airless, oven-like room with its stinking bucket, until on the fifth day our guards came to fetch me. With much shouting and many unnecessary shoves and blows I was marched down a corridor and into a sparsely furnished office whose main furnishing was a portrait of Chairman Mao. Timothy Mageba rose from behind the desk and motioned my guards to leave.

'Sit down, Doctor, please.' He wore paratrooper camouflage, and the bars and stars of a Colonel in the Chinese People's Army.

I sat on the wooden bench, and my eyes fastened on the half-dozen bottles of Tusker beer that stood on a tray. The bottles were bedewed with cold, and I felt my throat contracting.

'I know how fond you are of a bottle of cold beer, Doctor.' Timothy opened one of the bottles, and offered it to me. I shook my head.

'No, thank you. I don't drink with murderers.'

'I see.' He nodded, and I saw the little shadows of regret in those dark brooding eyes. He lifted the bottle to his own lips and drank a mouthful. I watched him thirstily.

'The engineer,' he said, 'the execution, it was not intended. I did not mean it to happen. Please understand that, Doctor.'

'Yes. I understand. And when the smoke of our burning land blackens the skies, and the stink of our dead sickens even your dark spirits, will you cry out, *I did not mean it to happen?*'

Timothy turned away and went to stand at the window, looking out over a parade ground where squads of uniformed Bantu drilled under a dazzling sun.

'I have been able to arrange for your release, Doctor. You will be allowed to return in the Dakota.' He came back to stand before me, and then he changed from English into Venda. 'My heart cries out to see you go, Machane, for you are a man of gentleness, and strength, and great courage. Once I hoped that you might join us.'

In Venda I answered, 'My heart weeps also, for a man who was a friend, one I trusted, one who I believed was a man of goodwill, but he is gone now into the half-world of the criminals and the destroyers. He is dead to me, and my heart weeps.'

It was true, I realized. It was not just an attempt to shame him. Beneath my hatred and anger, there was a sense of sorrow, of loss. I had believed in him. I had seen in a man such as he was, a hope for the future of this poor tormented continent of ours. We looked at each other wistfully, regretfully across a space of four feet that was as wide as the span of the heavens and as deep as the chasms of Hell.

'Goodbye, Doctor,' he said softly. 'Go in peace, Machane.'

They took us in the covered back of a three-ton truck to the airstrip, bare-footed and stripped to our underclothes.

They formed a double line from the truck to the Dakota. There were perhaps 200 of them in paratrooper uniform, and we were forced to walk down the narrow aisle with jeering black faces on each side of us. There were Chinese instructors with them, their lank black hair flopping out from under the cloth uniform caps, grinning hugely as we passed. I was bitterly aware of the mocking eyes and jibes aimed at my crooked exposed back, and I hurried towards the refuge of the Dakota. Suddenly one of them stepped out of the ranks in front of me. Deliberately he spat at me, and a storm of laughter went up from them. With a thick gob of yellow phlegm plastered in my hair, I scrambled up into the cabin of the aircraft.

The Air Force Mirages picked us up an hour after we crossed the Zambezi river and they escorted us to the military airfield at Voortrekker Hoogte. However, my almost hysterical relief at our safe home-coming was shortlived. Once a doctor had cleaned and dressed the clotted and suppurating gashes in my head, I was hustled away in a closed car to a meeting with four unsmiling, grimly polite, officers of the police and military intelligence.

'Dr Kazin, is this your signature?'

It was my recommendation for the issue of Timothy Mageba's passport.

'Dr Kazin, do you remember this man?'

A Chinaman I had met when I visited Timothy at London University.

'Are you aware that he is an agent of the Communist Chinese government, Doctor?'

There was a photograph of the three of us drinking beer on the tow-path beside the Thames.

'Can you tell us what you spoke about, please, Doctor?'

Timothy had told me that the Chinaman was an anthropology major, and we had discussed Leakey's discoveries at Olduvai Gorge.

'Did you recommend Mageba for the Sturvesant travel scholarship, Doctor?'

'Did you know that he went to China and received training as a guerrilla leader?'

'Did you sign these order forms for twenty-seven drums of fuller's earth from Hong Kong, Doctor – and these customs declarations?'

They were standard Institute forms, I could recognize my signature on the customs form across the desk. I did not remember the shipment.

'Were you aware that this shipment contained 150 lb. of plastique explosives, Doctor?'

'Do you recognize these, Doctor?'

Pamphlets in a dozen African languages. I read the first line of one of them. Terrorist propaganda. Exhortations to kill, burn and destroy.

'Were you aware that these were printed on your press at the Institute, Doctor?'

The questions went on endlessly, I was tired, confused, and began contradicting myself. I pointed out the wounds on my head, the rope burns at my wrists and ankles, and the questions went on. My head throbbed, my brain felt like a battered jelly.

'Do you recognize these, Doctor?'

Machine-pistols, ammunition.

'Yes!' I shouted at them. 'I had pistols like that against my head, in my belly!'

'Did you know that these were imported in cases of books addressed to your Institute?'

'When you obtained police clearance for the Dakota flight, Doctor, you stated—'

'They jumped me after the phone call. I've explained that a dozen times, damn you!'

'You've known Mageba for twelve years. He was a protégé of yours, Doctor.'

'Do you mean to tell us that you were never approached by Mageba? Never discussed politics with him?'

'I'm not one of them! I swear it—' I remembered the blood spraying against the cabin roof, the crunch of steel biting into the bone of my skull, the spittle clinging in my hair. 'You've got to believe me, please! Oh God, please!' And I think I must have fainted, it went all dark and warm in my head and I slumped sideways off the chair onto the floor.

I woke in a hospital room, between clean crisp sheets – and Louren Sturvesant sat beside the bed.

'Lo, oh thank God.' I felt all choked up with relief. Louren was here, and it would be all right now.

He leaned forward, unsmiling, that marvellous face cold and hard as though it had been cast in bronze. 'They think you were one of the gang. That you set it up, that you were using the Institute as the headquarters for a terrorist organization.'

I stared at him, and he went on remorselessly, 'If you have betrayed me and your country, if you have gone over to our enemies, then you can expect no mercy from me.'

'Not you also, Lo. I don't think I can stand that.'

'Is it true?' he demanded.

'No!' I shook my head. 'No! No!' And suddenly there were tears streaming down my face and I was shaking and blubbering like a baby. Louren leaned forward and gripped my shoulder hard.

'Okay, Ben.' He spoke with infinite gentleness and pity. 'It's okay, partner. I'll fix it. It's all over now, Ben.'

Louren would not let me go back to my bachelor quarters at the Institute, and I was installed in a guest suite at Kleine Schuur, the Sturvesant residence.

The first night Louren woke me from a screaming nightmare of blood and mocking black faces. He was in a dressing-gown, with his golden curls disordered from sleep. He sat on the side of my bed, and we talked of the good, sane things we had done together and the things we would do together in the future, until at last I slipped off into untroubled sleep.

For ten lazy, idyllic days I stayed at Kleine Schuur, spoiled by Hilary and fussed by the children, protected from the news-hungry Press, and sheltered from the realities and alarums of the outside world. The bruises faded, the scabs dried and fell away, and I found it more and more difficult to respond to the children's cry of 'Story' with something new. They shouted the punch-lines in chorus, and corrected me on the details. It was time to go back into the stream.

In one unpleasant day-long session I told the story of the hi-jacking at the public inquiry, and afterwards faced the Press of the world. Then Louren flew me north in the Lear jet, back to the City of the Moon.

On the way I told him how I intended to find the stone quarries – and then the tombs of the ancients.

When he grinned and told me, 'That's the tiger – get in there, boy, and tear the bottom out of it!' I realized that I had been enthusing and emoting a little. I remembered Old Xhai's imitation of the Sunbird, and put my fluttering hand firmly back in my lap.

A hero's welcome was waiting for me at the City of the Moon, they had followed my adventures on the radio. But now they opened a case of Windhoek beer and sat round me in a circle while I told the whole story again.

'That Timothy, he always gave me a funny feeling.'

Solemnly Sally demonstrated her amazing gift of hind-sight. 'I could have told you there was something fishy about him.' Then she stood up and came to kiss me on the forehead in front of them all, while I blushed crimson. 'Anyway, we are glad you're safe, Ben. We were so worried about you.'

The next morning, after I had driven Louren to the airstrip and watched him take off, I went looking for Ral Davidson. I found him in the bottom of a trench measuring a slab of sandstone. He was covered by a skimpy pair of shorts and a mass of hair that almost completely obscured his features, but he was burned a deep mahogany brown by the sun and was lean and fit. I had become very fond of him. We sat on the edge of the trench dangling our feet over the side, and I explained to him about the quarry.

'Gee, Doc! Why didn't we think of that before?' he enthused. That evening we drew up an elaborate search pattern, with a schedule to enlarge the area of search in expanding spirals each day. Ral's gang was temporarily withdrawn from the excavations within the temple, and armed with machetes for the assault on the thick, spiny vegetation on top of the cliffs.

The whole search was planned like a military operation. I had been dying to find an opportunity to use the walkie-talkie radio sets with which Louren had, unbidden, supplied us. This was it. Ral and I checked the radios, shouting things like, 'Over to you' and 'Roger!' and 'Read you five five!' at each other.

Peter Willcox muttered something about 'boy scouts', but I think he was a little jealous that he hadn't been invited to join the search. Leslie and Sally, however, were infected by our enthusiasm and they victualled the expedition with sufficient food and drink to keep an army bloated and drunk for a week. They turned out in a pink dawn, still in their pyjamas and dressing-gowns, Leslie with her hair in curlers, to wave us off and wish us luck. At the head of my gang of stalwarts, laden with food and equipment, feeling a little like Scott or bold Cortez, I led them towards the gap in the cliffs which had become our regular route to the top – and ten hours later, sweaty, bedraggled, scratched by thorns, stung by hippo fly and other insects, broiled by the sun and in a filthy temper, I led them down again.

We repeated this routine daily for the next ten days, and on the tenth evening when we paused half-way down the gap in the cliff to rest, Ral suddenly looked at the steep sides of the gap and said in a voice of wonder:

'Gee, Doc! This is it!'

For ten days we had been using the steps cut by the ancients into their quarry. Thick growth had covered the neat terraces from which they had sawn the red stone. We found some of the half-formed blocks of masonry still *in situ*, only a little undercut and almost unweathered in this protected gully. The marks of the saws were fresh upon them as though the workmen had laid down their tools the day before, instead of 2,000 years ago. Then there were blocks, cut in the rough, and abandoned half-way through the process of dressing. Others were completed, ready for transporting – yet others were in transit, discarded haphazard along the floor of the gully.

We cleared the undergrowth from around them and were then able to follow each fascinating step of the process of manufacture. The whole team came up to assist. They were jubilant with this new success, for we had all been a little put down with the recent total lack of progress. We sketched and mapped, measured and photographed, argued and theorized, and there was an evident renaissance of enthusiasm in all of us. The feeling that we had reached a dead end in the investigations was dispelled. I have a photograph, taken by one of the Bantu foremen who thought us all mad. We are clowning it up, posing on one of the bigger blocks of masonry. Peter strikes a Napoleonic attitude, hand in the breast of his jacket. Ral's hairy visage is adorned with a ferocious squint, and he poises a pick-axe murderously above Peter's head. Leslie is coyly showing a little cheesecake, and that is almost as bad as Ral's squint, with those legs she could kick elephants to death. I am sitting on Heather's lap, sucking my thumb. Sally has Peter's glasses on her nose and my hat pulled down over her ears; she is trying to look hideous, but failing resoundingly. This photograph illustrates the mood of those days.

After their assistance was no longer needed, the others went back to their separate tasks with renewed energy. Ral and I stayed on in the quarry. I brought up my theodolite and we set about calculating its extent and the amount of masonry removed from it. It was impossible to measure accurately the irregular excavation, but we decided that approximately a million and a half cubic yards of rock had been removed.

Then by a study of the method of quarrying and using the volume of abandoned blocks as a very rough guide, we guessed that the ratio of dressed finished blocks to waste material would be about 40:60. Finally we arrived at a figure of 600,000 cubic yards.

Up to this point we had been working with fairly factual figures, but now we pushed off into an ocean of conjecture.

'At least it's not as bad as drawing a dinosaur from its footprints,' Ral defended us, as we used the map of the foundations of the temple together with our calculation of rock volumes to reconstruct a complete elevation of the vanished City of the Moon.

'Here, let me do that!' Irritably Sally took the paintbrush out of my hand on the first evening, after she had watched my efforts for ten minutes.

'I think the batter of the main walls is a little excessive,' Peter murmured critically, watching her, 'if you compare the walls of the elliptical building at Zimbabwe—'

'Yes, but take the temple of Tarxien at Malta,' Heather

interceded. 'Or the main walls of Knossos.' And before Ral and I could do a thing to prevent it, the project had become a group effort that replaced the nightly song-fest in the common room.

With everybody contributing from their own particular area of the dig, and from their own specialized talents and interests, we built up a series of pictures of our city.

Massive red walls, ornamented with the chevron patterns of the waves that made Phoenicia great. Red walls that caught the rays of the setting sun, the evening blessing of the great sun god Baal. The tall towers, symbols of fertility and prosperity, rising from the dark green foliage of the silent grove. Beyond it, the vertical gash in the cliffs that led through a secret passage into the mysterious cavern. Again a symbol of the organs of reproduction. Surely this must have been sacred to Astarte – more commonly worshipped by the Carthaginians as Tanith – goddess of earth and moon, and so ranks of white-clad priests wound in procession through the grove, past the towers and into the secret cavern.

We knew that the Phoenicians made human sacrifice to their gods and goddesses. The Old Testament described the infants delivered to the flaming belly of Baal, and we wondered what dreadful ritual our peaceful emerald pool had seen, depicting the victim dressed in gold and finery and poised on the edge of the pool with the high priest lifting the sacrificial knife.

'If only it weren't so deep!' Sally exclaimed. 'Ben wanted to get divers to go down, but he says they couldn't work so deep.'

In the area between the inner and outer walls of the temple, where the layer of ash lay thick and where the majority of golden beads and richer ornaments had been discovered, we drew in the quarters of the priests and priestesses. This would be a maze of mud walls with thatched roofs. We reconstructed the streets and courts of the priests and nobles.

'What about the king and his court?' Peter demanded. 'Wouldn't they live within the main walls also?'

So we divided the area between the quarters of the priests and the court of the king, drawing on what little we knew of Knossos, Carthage and Tyre and Sidon to give our paintings life. Ral had found the gate through the outer wall, it was the only opening and it looked towards the west.

'From it a road would have led directly down to the harbour.' Sally drew it in.

'Yes, but there would have been a market, a place of trade beside the harbour,' Ral suggested, and pointed to the map. 'This would be it. The area Peter has been puzzling over.'

'Can you imagine the piles of ivory and copper and gold,' Leslie sighed.

'And slaves standing on the blocks to be sold,' Heather agreed.

'Hold it! Hold it! This is supposed to be a scientific investigation.' I tried to restrain them.

'And the ships lying on the beach.' Sally started to paint them in. 'Huge biremes with their prows shaped like rams' heads, covered with gilt and enamel.'

The walls and towers rose again, the lake refilled with bright waters, and the harbours and taverns were peopled with hosts dead for two thousand years. Warriors strutted, and slaves whined, noble ladies rode in their litters, caravans poured in from the land to the east laden with gold and treasure, and a white king strode out through the great stone gates with a rosetted shield on his shoulder and his armour asparkle in the sun.

The project was fun, and it served also to prod our imagination. By the time Sally had put the last touches to our painting, four weeks had passed, and as a direct result of it Peter had discovered the shipyards suggested by Sally's biremes beached below the city.

There was the keel of a ship laid on the slip, with the main frames in place. The unfinished vessel had been burned, and its charred parts scattered. Only imagination and faith could recognize it as a ship. I knew my scientific opponents would challenge it, but carbon-14 on the charred wood gave us an approximate date of A.D. 300, the date which we had defined as that of the 'great fire'.

The project gave me an excuse to spend more of my time with Sally. I began taking my lunch and bathing costume up to the cavern. At first there was an awkwardness between us, but I worked hard at setting Sally at ease and soon we were back in that friendly bantering relationship that made us such a good working team. Only once I referred back to our more intimate association.

'Have you still got the blues, Sal?' I asked, and she gave me a long frank gaze before replying.

'Please give me time, Ben. There is something I have to work out with myself.'

'Okay.' I smiled as cheerfully as I could, and resigned myself to a long, long wait.

Sometimes the others joined our lunch-time sessions at the pool, for even when the heat was a hissing 115° outside, it was cool in the cavern. We splashed and shouted, and the echoes boomed back at us. One of my indelible memories is that of Leslie clad in a frilly little pink bikini romping skittishly around the pool like a lady hippopotamus in the mating season, pursued by the indefatigable Ral.

Five weeks after my return I went up to the cavern with good news.

'I just received a radio message from Larkin, Sal. Louren is arriving tomorrow.'

I was disappointed in her negative reaction, because I

was sure she had overcome her initial dislike of Louren for my sake – and that she had begun to like him.

I went to meet Louren at the airstrip, and I was shocked. He had lost 20lb in weight, and his skin which usually glowed with golden health was now chalky grey. Beneath his eyes were smears of dark plum that looked like bruises.

'Ben!' He put an affectionate arm around my shoulder and squeezed. 'It's good to see you, you old bastard.' But his voice was weary and I noticed the threads of silver at his temples which were newly acquired.

'My God, Lo, you look terrible.'

'Thanks.' He grinned wryly, and slung his bags into the back of the Land-Rover.

'Seriously, Lo. Are you sick or something?' I was distressed to see him looking so ill and haggard.

'I've been on a rough one, Ben,' he confided as he climbed into the Land-Rover beside me. 'Four weeks at the bargaining table, I had to do it all myself – could not trust anyone else to handle it. The other side sent in teams, changing them when they were worn out.'

'You're going to kill yourself,' I scolded him, sounding a little like a nagging wife. And he leaned across, punched my arm lightly, and laughed.

'You're a shot in the arm, partner.'

'Was it worth it? What was it about?'

'It's big, Ben! E – bloody – normous! Copper and iron, South West Africa, near the Cunene River, massive ore bodies lying in association, low-grade copper and high-grade iron – together they are a treasure chest.' The weary tone was gone from his voice. 'I put those little Jap bastards over the table and I roasted their arses. They will put in the finance for a deep-water harbour and a railway line to get the stuff out. That will cost them 150 million.' He was exultant, colour coming back into the pale cheeks. 'One of my companies will do the construction work, of course.'

He touched a finger to his lips in a conspiratory gesture and I giggled delightedly. I enjoyed him in this mood. 'I'll put up for the pelletization plant and . . .' He went on to outline the scheme, laughing and punching my arm when he recounted each bargaining point on which he had scored.

'What will it make for you?' I asked at last, and he looked at me, slightly put down.

'You mean in terms of money?' he asked.

'Sure! What else?'

'Hell, Ben. I've explained it before. That's not the important thing. It's not the money, it's exports and employment, and opening up new resources, and building for the future, realizing the potential of our country and – and—'

'And getting one hell of a kick out of it,' I suggested.

He laughed again. 'You are too shrewd, Ben. I suppose that's a lot of it. The game not the score.'

'Have you seen last week's *Time* magazine?' I asked. I knew it would needle him.

'Oh, for God's sake, Ben,' he protested.

'Your name is on the list of the world's thirty richest men.'

'Those bastards,' he muttered darkly. 'Now everybody doubles their prices. Why don't they mind their own business and let me get on with mine.'

'And in the process you are killing yourself.'

'You're right, Ben. I do feel a little spent, so I'm taking a week. A whole week's holiday.'

'Big deal,' I sneered, 'a holiday with your B.Y.M. arriving every half-hour for conferences, and the rest of the time with you hanging over the radio set.'

'Forget it,' he smiled. 'I'm getting away, and you're coming with me.'

'What do you mean, Lo?' I asked.

'Tell you later.' He avoided the question for we were

approaching the branch in the dirt track, and I automatically slowed to turn down to the huts.

'Straight on, Ben,' Louren instructed. 'I want to go up to the cavern. I've been thinking of that place for weeks.' His voice went soft and reflective. 'When things got really tough there at the table, I'd think about the peace and tranquillity of that place. It seemed to . . .' He stopped, and coughed with embarrassment. Louren doesn't often talk that way.

Sally was working at the rear wall of the cavern. She wore a green silk blouse and tailored khaki slacks, with her hair loose and shiny. As she looked up to greet Louren, I saw with mild surprise that she wore lipstick for the first time in weeks.

She noticed his haggard features immediately, and I saw the concern in her eyes although she said nothing about it. Her greeting was subdued, almost offhand, and she turned back to her easel. Louren went immediately to the portrait of the white king. I drifted across to join him and we sat in a friendly relaxed silence examining the strange figure. Louren spoke first.

'Do you get the feeling he's trying to tell you something, Ben?'

It was a fanciful question for Louren, but I treated it with respect for he was clearly in deadly earnest.

'No, Lo, I can't say that I do.'

'There is something here, Ben,' he said with certainty. 'Something you – we have overlooked. The key to this place, the whole secret of it is in this cavern.'

'Well, Lo, we could . . .' I began but he wasn't listening. Sally left her easel and came to join us, she sat beside Louren and watched his face with complete attention.

'This feeling has never let me down, Ben. Do you remember the Desolation Valley mine? My geologist gave it a thumbs down, but I had this feeling. Do you remember?'

I nodded. Desolation Valley was now yielding twenty thousand carats of gem diamonds a month.

'There is something here. I am sure of it, but where?' He turned to stare at me, as though I had hidden whatever he was searching for. 'Where is it, Ben? The floor, the walls, the roof?'

'And the pool,' I said.

'All right, let's start with the pool,' he agreed.

'It's too deep, Lo. No diver—'

'What do you know about diving?' he demanded.

'Well, I've dived a couple of times.'

'Oh, for God's sake, Ben!' he interrupted brusquely. 'When I need a heart operation I go to Chris Barnard, not the local vet. Who is the best diver in the world?'

'Cousteau, I suppose.'

'Fine. I'll get my people onto him. That takes care of the pool. Now the floor.'

Dealing with Louren is like being caught in a hurricane. At the end of an hour, he had outlined a scheme for a thorough investigation of the cavern, and at last he suggested casually, 'Okay, Ben. Why don't you go on back to camp? I'd like an hour or so alone here.' I was reluctant to miss a minute of his company but I stood up immediately.

'Are you coming, Sal?' I asked. Louren wanted to be alone.

'Oh, Ben. I'm in the middle of—'

'That's okay, Ben,' Louren told me, 'she won't disturb me.' And I left the cavern.

The guest hut was long ago prepared, but I went with one of the servants to supervise the unpacking of Louren's bags. I noticed that someone had cut a spray of wild cave-lilies that grew under the cliffs, and placed them in a beer tankard beside the bed. I meant to compliment the Matabele who acted as our cook, butler and house-keeper for this thoughtful little touch. It relieved the bleakness of the hut.

After checking Louren's accommodation I went down to the big bungalow and made sure there was ice in the refrigerator and plenty of cold water. Then I cracked the seal on a fresh bottle of Glen Grant – Louren and I have a common fondness for this nectar. While I was busy with the whisky bottle, Ral and Leslie came in off the dig and I heard them clump into the office next door. I did not intend eavesdropping, but the partition walls were paper-thin.

Ral growled like an enraged beast, and Leslie squealed.

'Oh, you are naughty!' she cried breathlessly, and it was clear that she had been physically molested. 'Someone will catch you doing that.'

'As long as they don't catch me doing what I'm going to do tonight,' Ral declared.

'Shh!' Leslie enjoined silence, but to no avail.

'Five weeks. I thought he'd never come. I was going mad.'

'Oh, Rally Dally darling,' wheezed Leslie in high passion.

'Toodles, my little Toodles,' Ral replied, and I blushed for them. Silently I set down the bottle and stole from the room. I was slightly puzzled as to how Louren's arrival, for that was obviously what Ral was referring to, could make such a dramatic improvement in their physical relationship, and I envied them for I had no such expectation.

We were all of us sick to the stomach with a diet of canned and preserved food. Louren had brought with him a full load of fresh fruit, vegetables and meat. That night we had a sucking pig, golden brown in its suit of crackling, with roast potatoes, green peas and a gigantic bowl of fresh salad. There was very little conversation at the dinner-table.

Once the dishes were cleared, Louren lit a cigar. I

153

refilled the glasses and we all settled down in a circle about Louren. First I reported to Louren the discovery of the quarry, and the deductions we had made from it. This led on to an exhibition of Sally's reconstruction of the city.

I had not expected Louren to react the way he did. I had thought he might be mildly amused, as we were, not that he would accept our fantasy as proven fact. He worked himself into a fever of excitement, jumping up from his chair to examine each illustration, firing his abrupt searching questions at us, or simply sitting hunched forward in his seat staring at the painting with glitter-eyed concentration. His face was still pale and ravaged, which gave an almost demented intensity to his expression.

Sally, with a touch of canny showmanship, had kept the painting of the white king for the last. As she lifted it onto the board I saw Louren stiffen in his seat. The white king was in full battle armour, helmet and breastplate in glistening bronze, shield slung, and a short sword girt around his waist. His red-gold beard was curled and clubbed, and his bearing regal. His attendants followed him through the gates of the high outer wall, one carried his battle-axe, another his bow and a quiver of arrows, a third bore the golden chalice of eternal life.

Sally had lavished patient skill upon this particular illustration, and it was the most impressive of the whole series. We all stared at it in silence until suddenly I uncrossed my legs and leaned forward quickly, spilling a little of my whisky in surprise. I had not noticed it before, the gold beard had masked it, but now I realized suddenly whom Sally had used as her model for the white king. I turned to stare at Louren, and there was the same deep forehead, the noble brow above wide-set piercing pale blue eyes, the same straight nose with delicately chiselled nostrils, and the proud curve of mouth with the slightly sensual pout of the lower lip.

'Ben!' His voice was husky, he did not take his eyes off

the portrait. 'This is remarkable – I hadn't realized until this evening what this meant. Up to now it was just intriguing blocks of stone, and a few beads and scraps of gold. I never really thought about the people. That's the important thing, Ben! These men that voyaged to the ends of the world; that built something magnificent in the wilderness—' He broke off, and shook his head slowly, considering the magnitude, the grandeur of it. Then he turned to me.

'Ben. We have got to find out what happened to them, and their city. I don't care how long it takes, how much it costs. I have got to know.'

Now he stubbed out his cigar and jumped up from his chair, began pacing with a barely controlled violence.

'It's about time we announced this, Ben. I will set up a press conference. I'll want you all there to explain it. The world must know about these men.'

My stomach dropped steeply with alarm, and I stuttered a protest.

'But, Lo, we can't do that. Not now, not yet – please!'

'Why not?' He wheeled on me belligerently.

'We haven't got enough proof yet.' I went chill with horror, as I thought how my critics would hang, draw and quarter me if I went out on stage with such a sorry script. 'They'll scalp us, Lo. They'll tear us to pieces.'

'We'll show them these.' He pointed at the paintings.

'God!' I shuddered at the thought. 'Those are just conjecture, fantasy, in that picture the only single detail we could substantiate would be the chalice.'

Louren stared at me, but I saw the madness fading in his eyes. Suddenly he laughed guiltily, and struck his forehead with the heel of his hand.

'Wow!' he laughed. 'I must be tired! For a moment there those paintings were real, from life!' He went to stand before the painting again and examined it wistfully. 'I've got to know, Ben,' he said again, 'I've just got to know.'

155

The following day, while we ate lunch beside the emerald pool, Louren told me how he and I were to get away together. He used Sally's charcoal stick to draw on the flat surface of a rock.

'Here we are, and here sixty-five miles to the north-east are the ruins at Domboshaba. If your theories are correct then there was an ancient caravan route between the two cities. You and I are going to take the Land-Rover, and go cross-country, trying to pick up the old trail.'

'It's pretty rough country,' I pointed out, without enthusiasm. 'Completely unexplored, no roads, no water.'

'And no B.Y.M.,' Louren smiled.

'That makes it irresistible.' I returned his smile, remembering that this was therapeutic not scientific. 'When do we leave?'

'Tomorrow morning at first light.'

It was still dark when I awoke, and my bedside clock showed four-thirty. It was too late to go back to sleep and too early to get up. I was pondering the problem when the door of the hut opened stealthily and, as I prepared to repel burglars, Ral's hairy head silhouetted by the moonlight appeared around the jamb.

He had given me a fright so I shouted at him, 'What are you doing?'

If I had been frightened, it was nothing to Ral's reaction to my question. Letting out a howl of terror he leapt about three feet in the air with his arms flapping, rather like a crested crane doing its mating dance. It took him a minute or two to recover himself sufficiently to shamble across to his bed and reply in a shaky voice, 'I've been to the toilet.' Which was just as well, I thought, otherwise my challenge could have had disastrous consequences. I got up, dressed and went out to check the Land-Rover. I suppose I guessed that Ral had been with Leslie, but I did not realize the implications of this.

It took Louren and me most of the first day to find a way

over the Hills of Blood that the Land-Rover could negotiate. We followed the line of cliffs northward until they dwindled away and broke up into low kopjes and we could climb one of the gullies between them. It was a rugged ascent that taxed even that sturdy vehicle, but once on top the going was through open savannah and scattered acacia forest and we made good progress, swinging away southward again to pick up the caravan route that Louren had hopefully drawn in on his large-scale map.

That night we camped astride it, or at least where we hoped it might have been. With the amount of gasoline and water aboard, there was scant room for the luxuries of camp life. Besides it was meant to be a rough trip to dispel the smogs and grimes of civilization, a nostalgic return to the expeditions we had made together in our youth.

We grilled a brace of sand-grouse over the coals, and drank Glen Grant and sun-warmed water from enamel mugs. Then with hollows scraped from the hard earth for hip and shoulder we rolled into our sleeping bags beside the Land-Rover and chatted drowsily and contentedly for an hour before falling asleep.

In the dawn Louren massaged his back and gingerly worked the stiffness out of his muscles.

'I've just remembered I'm not twenty any longer,' he groaned, but by the third day he was looking it. The sun coloured him again, the bruises under his eyes were gone and he laughed freely.

Our progress was slow. Often it was necessary to retrace our spoor out of broken ground whose kopjes and ridges denied us passage. Then we would leave the Land-Rover and go in on foot to try and pioneer a way through. There was no hurry, however, so we could fully enjoy each mile as we groped our way north and east through country that changed its character and mood with the bewitching rapidity that is Africa's alone.

Each hour of eastward travel rewarded us with more

157

evidence of bird and animal life. The dry-land birds gave way for guinea fowl, francolin, and the gigantic korrie bustard. While amongst the mopani and masasa trees there was the occasional silver-grey flash of a running kudu, with his long corkscrew horns laid flat along his back.

'Water not far away,' Louren commented as we stopped the Land-Rover at the edge of one of those open glades of yellow grass and watched a herd of sable antelope move away into the trees on the far side. The most stately antelope in Africa, proud heads holding the curved scimitar horns high and the dazzling contrast of snowy breast against the black body.

'Another endangered species,' I remarked sadly. 'Making way for the greed and excesses of man.'

'Yes,' Louren agreed. 'And you know something, there's not one single specimen of *homo sapiens* that's half as beautiful, and that,' he said, 'includes Raquel Welch.'

That night we camped in a grove of masasa trees, clad in their outlandish spring foliage which has the colours of no other tree on earth – pinks, soft shiny beige, and flaming reds. Louren had shot a young impala ram during the day and he wrapped the fillets in bacon and roasted them in a heavy iron pot while I made a sauce of onions and tomato and plenty of garlic. We ate it with thick slices of brown bread and yellow tinned butter and it tasted like no other food I had ever known.

'If you ever need a job, Lo, you can come cook for me,' I told him around a mouthful. He grinned and went to the Land-Rover to switch on the radio.

'What was the deal?' I asked.

'Just the news.' He had the grace to look guilty. 'Can't lose touch entirely.'

We listened to the strivings and strugglings of a world gone mad. Somehow, in this remote and tranquil place the affairs of man seemed unimportant, petty and transient.

'Switch it off, Lo,' I said. 'Who needs it?'

He reached for the control knob of the set, but checked his hand as the voice of the announcer spoke a familiar name.

'Lusaka Radio reports that the leader of the terrorist gang which yesterday ambushed a detachment of police in the Wankie district of Rhodesia, killing four and wounding two others, is the self-styled "Colonel" Timothy Mageba who two months ago made world headlines in his dramatic hi-jacking bid. A spokesman for the Rhodesian police said that Mageba is probably one of the most dangerous terrorists in Africa. A reward of 10,000 Rhodesian dollars has been offered for information leading to his death or capture.'

With a savage gesture Louren switched off the set and came back to the fire. He sipped his whisky before speaking.

'He's operating only a hundred miles or so north of here. I'd give anything to get a chance at that one.'

News of Timothy disturbed me deeply, and that night I lay long awake with my hands behind my head staring up at the starry splendour of the night sky. Venus had dropped below the horizon before I fell into a sleep troubled with ugly dreams.

The morning sun lit the crests of the kopjes a fresh gold and inflamed the sky with virulent reds and purples, driving away dark thoughts, and we talked and laughed together as we picked our way slowly towards the east.

In the middle of the morning we saw the vultures circling off towards the north, a vast wheel of specks turning slowly beneath the hard blue sky. Following the flight of these grotesque scavengers is one of the most intriguing invitations that Africa has to offer. For every time they will lead you to the scene of some desperate incident in the never-ending drama of the wilderness.

'A couple of miles off,' Louren commented, peering eagerly ahead through the windscreen. I shared his curiosity. The hell with ruined cities and lost civilizations, this was the stark, raw rule of tooth and claw we were going to witness.

A quarter of a mile ahead of us we saw the hunch-backed bird shapes squatting obscenely in the tree-tops, thick as some devil's fruit in the orchards of hell.

'They are off the kill.' Louren was jubilant. 'Something's keeping them up in the trees and sky.'

He stopped the Land-Rover, and switched off the ignition. We climbed out, and Louren checked the load of his big .375 magnum, changing the solid bullets for soft-nosed ones that would deliver a heavier knock-down blow.

'We'll walk up,' he said. 'I'd love a chance at a big black-maned lion.' He snapped the bolt of the rifle closed. 'Take the shotgun, Ben, load with buckshot.'

This is my sort of thinking. If a lion is far enough away to warrant the use of a rifle then he and I have no quarrel; closer than that I like a weapon that I can't miss with.

Louren set off through the waist-high grass, I followed him, keeping out on his flank to open my line of fire, the shotgun loaded for lion and my pockets bulging with spare shells. We moved in slowly, trying to find the focal point of this gathering of vultures for they were scattered in the trees over an area of half a square mile.

Every step heightened our tension with the expectation of walking on top of a pride of lions lying in the grass. Louren signalled each change of direction to me, as we quartered carefully back and forth over the ground. From the trees around us the birds launched into flight, changing miraculously from ungainly repose into something graceful and beautiful as they entered their true element.

My throat was dry with excitement, and a pleasurable fear. I could see Louren was sweating through the back of his shirt, not entirely from the heat. His every movement was charged with restrained energy, ready to explode at the first sign of the quarry. I loved this part of the hunt, for there is the atavistic urge of hunter still hidden in most of us, it was only the killing that repulsed me.

Louren froze, rifle at high port. He was staring ahead, and I braced myself for the heavy detonation of the shot that I knew must follow; but the seconds passed slowly as dripping oil and still Louren stood with only the slightest movements of his head as he searched.

Quietly I moved up beside him. Ahead of us was an area of flattened and trampled grass. In the centre of it lay the body of a dead buffalo, his belly bloated with gas, and big shiny green flies swarming over his dead eyes and into his open mouth. I could see no marks of claws in the thick hide, with its coarse black hair blotched with patches of shiny baldness and rough scab.

I looked down at the ground, not wishing to tread on a twig as I moved again, and I saw the small childlike human footprint in a patch of ant-turned earth.

I felt the hair at the back of my neck prickle, we had walked into something a damned sight more dangerous than a pride of lions. Quickly I looked back to the dead buffalo, and for the first time noticed two inches of a frail reed stalk protruding from the folded skin of the neck. The flesh around it was swollen tight and hard.

'Lo!' I croaked huskily. 'Let's get the hell out of here – this is a bushman kill.'

Louren's head jerked around and he stared at me. I saw the rim of his nostrils fade to china white.

'How do you know?' he demanded hoarsely.

'Footprints at your feet.' He glanced down. 'Arrow in the buffalo's neck.'

He was convinced. 'This is your shauri, Ben. What do we do?' Now he was sweating as heavily as I was.

I said, 'Slowly, slowly! Don't turn your back and don't move suddenly. They are watching us, Lo. Probably right here.'

We began backing off, clutching our weapons with sweat-greasy hands, eyes darting restlessly from side to side.

'Talk to them, for God's sake, Ben!' Louren whispered. I found time to examine the discovery that the threat of poison could turn even a man like Louren into a coward.

'Can't take the chance. Anything could trigger them.'

'They may be behind us.' His voice shook, and I felt my skin between the shoulder-blades cringe as I listened for the flute of the arrow. With each pace backwards I felt my fear shrinking, and fifty yards from the kill I risked hailing them.

'Peace,' I called. 'We mean you no harm.'

The reply came immediately, birdlike and disembodied, seeming to emanate from the heated air itself.

'Tell the big white-head to lay down his weapon, for we do not know him.'

'Xhai,' I cried out my relief and delight. 'My brother!'

> 'His eye was bright as the yellow moon,
> His hoof struck fire from the iron hills.'

We sang the buffalo song together, the men squatting around the leaping fire, clapping out the complicated rhythm with our hands. The women danced in an outer circle around us, swaying and shuffling, miming the buffalo and his gallant hunter. The firelight shone on their golden-yellow skins, their tiny childlike bodies with the startling bulge of buttocks and the fat little yellow breasts joggling to the dance rhythm.

> 'The arrow-bird flew from my hand
> Swift as a bee, or a stooping hawk.'

The branches of the trees around us were heavy with festoons of raw meat, hung out to dry, and beyond the firelight the jackal and hyena howled their frustrations to the star-bright heavens, as they snuffed the tantalizing odours.

'The blood when it flowed was bright as a flower
And sweet as wild honey was the flesh of his body.'

The dance ended at last, and the women giggled and trilled as they flocked to the fire to cram more meat into their little round bellies. Bushmen and women are awed by physical size, and to them Louren was a huge golden giant. They discussed him in a frank and intimate manner, starting at his golden head and working downwards until I laughed out aloud.

'What's so funny?' Louren demanded, and I told him.

'My God, they didn't say that!' Louren was shocked, staring at the women in horror, and they covered their mouths with their hands as they giggled.

I sat between Xhai and Louren, one of them smoking and the other eating a Romeo and Julieta cigar, and I translated for them. They spoke of the animals and the birds for they had a common love of the chase.

'My grandfather told me that when he was a young man the buffalo in this land below the great river were as locusts, black upon the earth – but then the red sickness came.'

'Rinderpest,' I explained to Louren.

'And they died so that they fell one upon the other, so thick that the vultures could not fly with the load of their bellies, and their bones lay in the sun like the fields of white Namaqua daisies in the spring time.'

They talked on after the women and children had curled up and fallen asleep like little yellow puppies in the dust. They spoke of noble animals and great hunts, and they became friends beside the fire so that at last Xhai told me shyly, 'I should like to share the hunt with such a one. I could show him an elephant, like those that my grandfather knew, with teeth as thick as my waist and as long as the shaft of a throwing spear.'

And there goes any further pretence of looking for ruins and caravan routes, I thought, as I watched Louren's face light up at the suggestion.

'But,' I added, 'he says you must leave the Land-Rover here. They heard us coming for half an hour before we arrived today and he says this elephant is old and cunning. Which means we will have to get some sleep now. We've got a hell of a day ahead of us tomorrow.'

By the time the sun came up we had been on the march for three hours, dew had soaked our trousers to the knees but we had walked the night's chill out of our joints and were extending ourselves, stepping out with full stride to keep the two tiny brown figures in view. Xhai and Ghal were into that loose-limbed trot that would eat away the miles all day without flagging, their little brown forms danced ahead of us through the thickening thorns and jessie bush.

'How you doing, Ben?'

I grunted and changed the shotgun to my other shoulder.

'The little bastards can certainly foot it.'

'Brother, you have only just started,' I warned him. They led us into bad, broken country where harsh black ridges of ironstone thrust from the earth and the thorn was grey and spiny and matted, where deep ravines rent the walls of steep tableland outcrops and the heat was a fierce dazzling thing that sucked the moisture from our bodies and dried it in rings of white salt on our shirts. It was the type of country that a canny old elephant bull, pursued by men all his life, might choose as a retreat.

We rested for half an hour at noon, seeking shade in the lee of a boulder whose black surface was scalding to the touch and drinking a few mouthfuls of lukewarm water, then we went on and almost immediately cut the spoor.

'There and there.' With the point of a poison arrow, Xhai traced the outline of a padmark on the iron-hard earth. 'Do you not see it?' he asked with exasperation, and though we circled the area, tilting our heads learnedly, neither of us could make it out.

'If that's an elephant spoor,' muttered Louren, 'I'm a Chinese tinker.' But Xhai set off confidently on a new bearing through the thorns, and we climbed one of the rocky tablelands, following a trail that Louren and I could not even see. Near the crest of the hill lay a pile of elephant dung, still moist despite the furnace-dry heat, and a cloud of yellow and orange butterflies hovered over it attracted by the wetness. The dung looked like the contents of a coir mattress.

'Velly solly,' I whispered to Louren, 'pleese fixee pottee – chop chop.'

'The man's a bloody magician.' Louren shook his head in amazement, as he unslung the heavy rifle from his shoulder and tucked it under his arm.

We went on again, but slowly now, pausing frequently while Xhai and Ghal searched the impenetrable thickets of thorn ahead of us. It was a gut-aching business in this close bush, each step planned and made only at a signal from Xhai's dainty pink-palmed hand, moving forward when the hand beckoned and freezing when it froze.

'Come,' said the hand and we went on again, then abruptly –

'Stop!' A quick cut-out sign, with the hand like a blade, then balling into a fist and pointing ahead, bad luck to point with a finger at the quarry.

We stood still as death, sweat-shiny faces staring ahead into the wall of thorn – and then suddenly the elephant loomed ghostly grey amongst the grey thorn, moving from us in a leisurely sway-backed shamble, grey skin wrinkled and old, hanging in bags and pouches at the belly and in the crotch of his back legs, the tail bare of tuft hair, the knuckles of the spine showing clearly through the ridged skin on his back. Old elephant. Big elephant.

'Stay here!' Xhai's hand pointed at Ghal and me, and I nodded in acknowledgement.

'Come with me!' Xhai's forefinger crooked at Louren, and they went on together, circling out on the elephant's flank through the thorn. The bushman doll-like beside Louren's bulk, leading him around for a clean shot at the head or shoulder.

The elephant paused, and began feeding from one of the thickets, delicately plucking the pale green shoots with the tip of his trunk, stuffing them into his mouth, completely unaware of danger – while out on his flank Louren reached a firing stance and braced himself, legs spread, leaning forward to meet the recoil of the heavy rifle.

The shot was stunningly loud, shocking in the heat-drugged silence. I heard the bullet slap into flesh, and the elephant spun away from the impact, turning to face Louren, with its long yellow ivories lifted high, the huge grey ears cocked back, and it squealed as it saw the man. It squealed in anger, and a long smouldering hatred now burst into flame.

It crabbed sideways as it began the charge, blanketing Louren's line of fire with a thicket of thorns. I saw Louren turn and run out to the side, trying to open his front for a clear shot. His foot hit an ant-bear hole and he fell in full run, going down heavily, the rifle flying from his hand, lying stunned full in the path of the charge.

'Louren!' I screamed, and then I was running also, armed with only a shotgun, racing to head off the charge of a wounded bull elephant.

'Here!' I screamed at it as I ran. 'Here!' Trying to lead it off him, in the corner of my vision I saw Louren on hands and knees crawling painfully towards his rifle.

'Yah! Yay!' I screamed with all the strength of my lungs, and the bull checked his charge, his head swinging towards me, piggy eyes seeking me, trunk questing for my scent.

I threw up the shotgun, and at thirty yards' range I aimed for his little eyes, hoping to blind him.

Blam! Blam! I fired left and right into his face, and he came at me. I felt a vast sense of relief as his charge exploded towards me, I had taken him off Louren – that was all that counted. With clumsy fingers I groped for fresh cartridges, knowing that before I could reload he would be upon me.

'Run, Ben, run!' Louren's voice, high above the ground-thudding charge of the bull. But I found my legs would not function, and I stood in the path of the charge, groping stupidly for cartridges which were useless as thrown pepper-corns against this grey mountain of flesh.

The blast of Louren's rifle beat against my numbed brain, once – twice, it crashed out and like an avalanche the grey mountain fell towards me, dead already, the brain shattered like an overripe fruit at the passage of the heavy bullet.

My feet were rooted to the earth, I could not move, could not dodge, and the outflung trunk hit me with savage force. I felt myself thrown through the air, and then the cruel impact of earth and my brain burst into bright colours and stabbing lights as I went out.

'You silly bastard! Oh, you silly brave little bastard.' I heard Louren's voice speaking to me down a long dark tunnel, and the sound of it echoed strangely in my head. Cool wetness splashed over my face, blessed wetness on my lips and I opened my eyes. Louren was sitting on the ground, my head cradled in his lap and he was splashing water from the bottle into my face.

'Who are you calling a bastard?' I croaked up at him, and the expression of relief that flooded over his worried features was one of the most satisfying things I have ever seen.

I was stiff and sore, bruised of shoulder and across the small of my back, and there was a lump above my temple that was too painful to touch.

'Can you walk?' Louren fussed over me.

'I can try.' It wasn't too painful, and I even found the inclination to photograph the huge dead beast as it knelt in a prayerful attitude with the head supported on the curved yellow tusks. Louren and the bushman sat on its head.

'We will camp tonight at the Water-In-The-Rocks,' Xhai told me, 'and tomorrow we will return and take the teeth.'

'How far is it?' I asked dubiously.

'Close!' Xhai assured me. 'Very close.' And I scowled at him uncertainly. I had heard him use the same words to describe a march of fifty miles.

'It had bloody well better be,' I said in English, and to my surprise it was much closer than I had expected – and a lot of other things I had not expected either.

We crossed one ridge with me hobbling along on Louren's arm and then came out on a wide granite sheet, a great curved dome of rock almost four acres in extent. I took one look at it, at the lines of shallow rounded holes that dimpled the entire surface, and I let out a whoop of joy. Suddenly I no longer needed Louren's support, and both of us ran down onto the stone floor, chortling with glee, as we examined the regular lines of worn depressions.

'It must have been a big one, Ben,' Louren exulted, he made a guess at the number of holes. 'A thousand?'

'More!' I said. 'More like two thousand.'

I paused then, imagining the long regular lines of naked slaves kneeling on the rock floor, each beside one of the smooth depressions, each of them linked to his neighbours by the iron slave chains, each of them with a heavy iron pestle in his hands, pounding away at the gold-bearing ore in the stone mortar between his knees.

168

I saw in my imagination the slave masters walking along the lines, the leather whips in their hands as they checked that the rock was crushed to a fine powder. I saw the endless columns of slaves with ore baskets balanced on their heads coming up from the workings. All this had happened here nearly 2,000 years before.

'I wonder where the mine is.' Louren was paralleling my thoughts.

'And the water?' I added. 'They'd need water to wash the gold out.'

'The hell with water,' Louren shouted. 'It's the mine I want, those old boys only worked values of three ounces and over and they stopped at water level – there's a bloody treasure house around here somewhere.'

This was how all the ancient mines had been destroyed. It was a credit to the skill of the ancient metallurgists that the site of nearly every modern mine in central Africa had been discovered by them 2,000 years before. The modern miners ripped out all trace of the ancient workings in their haste to expose the abandoned reef. I made a vow that at the least I would be first into this one, before the vandals with their drills and dynamite.

The water was at the bottom of a fifty-foot well, cut cleanly through the living rock, its walls lined with masonry. It was the finest example of an ancient well I had ever seen; clearly it had been kept in good repair by the bushmen, and I gloated over it while Xhai fetched a raw-hide rope and leather bucket from a hiding place among the rocks. He brought the bucket up brimming with clear water in which floated a few dead frogs and a drowned bush rat. I made a resolution to boil every drop before it passed my lips.

Louren spent a full thirty seconds in admiring the well, before he set off into the narrow valley between the two ridges of granite. I watched him disappear amongst the trees searching diligently, and twenty minutes later his faint shouts drifted up to me.

'Ben! Come here! Quickly!' I dragged myself off the coping of the well and limped down into the valley.

'Here it is, Ben.' Louren was wild with excitement and I was struck again by the power that gold has to quicken the most sluggish pulse, and to put the glitter of avarice in even the most world-weary eyes. I am not a materialistic person, but the lure and magic of it quickened my own breathing as I stood beside Louren and we looked upon the mine of the ancients.

It was not an impressive sight in itself, a shallow depression, a trench sunk about three feet below the level of the surrounding earth, its banks gently rounded, it meandered away amongst the trees like a footpath that had been worn into the earth.

'Open stope,' Louren told me. 'They followed the strike of the reef.'

'And back-filled.' I commented on the peculiar habit that the ancients had of filling in all their workings before abandoning them. This shallow trench was caused by the subsidence of the loose soil with which they had filled it.

'Come on,' said Louren. 'Let's follow it.'

For a mile and a half we followed the old stope through the forest before it petered out.

'If only we could find one of their dumps,' Louren muttered as we searched the rank vegetation for a pile of loose rock. 'Or at least a piece of the ore that they overlooked.'

My back was hurting so I sat on a fallen log to rest, and left Louren to continue the search. He moved away through the trees leaving me alone, and I could enjoy the sense of history which enveloped me when I was alone in a place such as this.

The water level in the well was fifty feet, so I guessed that this was the depth to which the ancients had worked their stope. They did not have the pumps or equipment to evacuate the workings, and as soon as water started pouring in they refilled it and left to find another reef.

This mine had been an open trench, one and a half miles long and fifty feet deep by six feet wide, hacked from the earth with adzes of iron and iron wedges pounded into the grain of the rock with stone hammers. When the rock was hard enough to resist this method, then they built fires upon it and poured water mixed with sour wine on the heated surface to shatter it. This was the same method that Hannibal used to break up the boulders that blocked the passage of his elephants across the Alps – a Carthaginian trick, you might call it. From the sheet of reef they prised lumps of gold quartz and packed it into baskets to be haulted to the surface on raw-hide ropes.

Using these methods they removed an estimated 700 tons of fine gold from workings spread over 300,000 square miles of central and southern Africa, together with vast quantities of iron and copper and tin.

'That's 22 million ounces of gold at $40 an ounce, 880 million dollars.' I worked it out aloud, then added, 'And that's a big loaf of bread.'

'Ben, where are you?' Louren was coming back through the trees. 'I found a piece of the reef.' He had a lump of rock in his hand and he handed it to me.

'What do you make of that?'

'Blue sugar quartz,' I said. And I licked at it to wet the surface, then held it to catch the sunlight. 'Wow!' I exclaimed as the native gold sparkled wetly back at me, filling the cracks and tiny fissures in the quartz like butter in a sandwich.

'Wow, indeed!' Louren agreed. 'This is good stuff. I'll send a couple of my boys in to peg the whole area.'

'Lo, don't forget about me,' I said, and he frowned quickly.

'You'll be cut in on it, Ben. Have I ever tried—'

'Don't be a clot, Lo. I didn't mean that. I just don't want your rock hounds tearing up the countryside before I've had a chance to go over it.'

'Okay, Ben. I promise,' he laughed. 'You can be here when we reopen the workings.' He juggled the lump of quartz in his hand. 'Let's get back, I want to pan this and get some idea of its value.'

Using one of the stone mortars in the granite cap and a lump of ironstone as a pestle, Louren pounded a piece of the quartz to a fine white powder. This he collected in our cooking pot, and with well-water washed off the powdered stone. Swirling the contents of the pot with an easy circular motion, letting a little spill over the rim of the pot with each turn. It took him fifteen minutes to separate the 'tail' of gold. It lay curled around the bottom of the pot, greasy shiny yellow.

'Pretty,' I said.

'They don't come prettier!' Louren grinned. 'This stuff will go five ounces to the ton.'

'You are an avaricious bastard, aren't you,' I teased him.

'Put it this way, Ben,' he was still grinning, 'the profits from this will probably keep your Institute running for another twenty years. Don't kick it, partner, money isn't the root of all evil if you use it right.'

'I won't kick it,' I promised him.

We camped that night beside the well, feasting on boiled elephant tongue and potatoes and keeping a bonfire going to compensate for our lack of blankets. We spent the following morning cutting out the tusks. These we buried beneath a huge pile of rocks to keep off the hyenas, and it was after noon before we started back for the Land-Rover.

Night caught us out again, but we reached the Land-Rover in the middle of the following morning. I had blisters on my heels the size of grapes and my lumps and bruises ached abominably. I collapsed thankfully into the passenger seat of the Land-Rover.

'Up to this moment I have never truly appreciated the invention of the internal combustion engine,' I announced gravely. 'You can take me home now, James.'

We left Xhai and his small tribe to their eternal wanderings in the wilderness and we arrived back at the City of the Moon eight days after we left it. We were blackened by the sun and an accumulation of dirt, we had sprouted beards, and our hair was stiff with dust and grime. Louren's beard came out a burnished red-gold that glistened in the sunlight.

He had been AWOL for three days, and the pack was clamorous. A tall pile of messages waited for him in the radio shack, and before he could shave or bath he had to spend an hour on the radio taking care of the most urgent matters that had arisen in his absence.

'I should get on back to the salt mines right away,' he told me as he came out of the shack. 'It's four-thirty. I could make it.' He hesitated a moment, then his resolve hardened. 'No, damn it! I'm going to steal one more night. Get out the Glen Grant while I take a bath.'

'Now you're talking sense.' I laughed.

'All the way, partner.' He punched my shoulder.

'All the way, Lo,' I assured him.

We talked a lot, and sang a little, and drank whisky until after midnight.

'Bed!' said Louren then, and rose to go, but suddenly he paused. 'Ben, you promised to let me have some photographs of the "white king" painting to take back with me.'

'Sure, Lo.' I stood up a little unsteadily and went through into the office. I took a sheaf of nine-by-six-inch glossy prints from my files and went back with them to Louren. Standing under the light he shuffled through them.

'What's wrong with this one, Ben?' he asked suddenly, and handed it to me.

'What? I can't see anything.'

'The face, Ben. There is a mark.'

173

I saw it then; a faint shadowy cross which marred the death-white face of the king. I studied it a moment. It puzzled me. I hadn't noticed it before – like a dark grey hot cross bun.

'It's probably a flaw in the printing, Lo,' I guessed. 'Is it on the others?' He glanced through the other prints quickly.

'No. Just that one.'

I handed it back to him. 'Just a faulty print,' I said.

'Okay.' Louren accepted my explanation. 'Good night.'

I poured myself a nightcap while Sally and the others trooped off after Louren, and I drank it slowly, sitting alone, running over in my mind the plans that Louren and I had formulated for the thorough investigation of the cavern.

I will admit that I never gave the mark on the white king's face another thought. My excuse is that I was more than a little drunk.

The next two months passed swiftly. Ral and I devoted ourselves to a thorough excavation of the floor of the cavern.

The results were surprising only in their paucity. The cavern had never been used for human habitation, there was no midden or hearth level. We found an accumulation of animal detritus that extended down to bed-rock. On the bed-rock itself we found a single square block of dressed stone, and that was the total bag.

Our excavations had given the cavern a forlorn and gutted appearance, and the bed-rock was uneven limestone, so I had the dig refilled and neatly levelled. Then we used the ancient blocks to lay a pavement around the emerald pool. I saw this as a concession to the convenience of the thousands of future visitors who would come to view this wonderful gallery of bushman art once its existence was known to the world.

As he had promised, Louren radioed me when his company was ready to begin re-opening the ancient mine we had discovered on the hunt for the elephant. A helicopter fetched me and I spent three weeks with the engineers who were doing the work.

The reef was there below the water-table as we had hoped, and although its values varied widely from place to place along its length, yet the average was exceptionally high. Secretly I was glad of my ten per cent interest in the mine, despite my non-materialist values. We recovered many hundreds of artefacts, mostly mining tools. There were badly rusted adzes and wedges, stone hammers, scraps of chain, a few well-preserved fibre baskets and the usual beads and pottery.

Of these I was most pleased with the fibre baskets which enabled us to obtain a carbon-14 date from the laboratories. This was slightly prior to, if not concurrent with, the date of the great fire, and served to link the elephant mine with the City of the Moon.

However, the most interesting find at the elephant mine was that of fifteen human skeletons lying like a string of beads along the stope at its deepest point. The arrangement of the bodies was so regular as to preclude the idea that they might have been killed in a rockfall. Although the skeletons had been flattened by the weight of earth from above, I was able to determine that five of them were female and ten were males. All of them were elderly, and one of them showed traces of arthritis, another had lost an arm between elbow and wrist but the bone had encysted, proving that it had not been a recent injury. Most of them had lost teeth. On all of them I found traces of iron chains, and the picture I had was that of fifteen elderly and infirm slaves laid deliberately along the bottom of the stope before it was filled.

After supervising the cataloguing, packing and despatch to the Institute of all these finds, I returned to the City of the Moon, and I went immediately to the cavern. As I hoped, Sally was hard at work there. I do not think her pleasure was affected as she came to meet me and kissed me.

'Oh, Ben. I've missed you.' Then she launched immediately into a technical discussion, and while I made the right answers my thoughts were far from bushman paintings.

I watched the way she crinkled her nose as she spoke, and the way she kept pushing her hair back from her cheek with the back of her hand, and my whole being throbbed with love of her. Down in my stomach I felt a squirming dread. Our work at the City of the Moon was almost finished, soon we would be returning to Johannesburg and the hushed halls of the Institute. I wondered how this would affect Sally and me.

'We'll be leaving soon, Sal.' I gave expression to my thoughts.

'Yes,' she agreed, immediately sobered. 'The thought saddens me. I've been so happy here, I'm going to miss it.'

We sat in silence for a while, then Sally stood up and went to stand before the portrait of the white king. She stared at it moodily, her arms folded tightly across her breast.

'We've learned so much here,' she paused for a moment, and then went on, 'and yet there was so much that was denied us. It was like chasing clouds, often I felt we were so close to having it in our hands.' She shook her head, angrily. 'There are so many secrets still locked away from us, Ben. Things we will never know.'

She turned and came back to where I sat; she knelt in front of me with her hands on her knees, staring into my face.

'Do you know that we haven't got proof, Ben! Do you

realize there is nothing we have found here that can't be discredited by the old arguments.' She leaned closer towards me. 'We have a symbol on a scrap of pottery. Imported in the course of trade, they will say. We have the golden chalice, the work of native goldsmiths using the Ankh motif by chance, they will say. We have the paintings – hearsay is not evidence, they will say.'

She sat back on her haunches and stared at me.

'Do you know what we've got, Ben, after it's all been sifted and sorted? We've got a big fat *nothing*.'

'I know,' I said miserably.

'We haven't even a single fact to knock them off their smug little perch. Our City of the Moon – our beautiful city – will be simply another culture of obscure Bantu origin, and there isn't a damn thing we can do about it. We will never know what happened to the great walls and towers, and we will never know where our white king lies buried.'

I planned to shut down the dig on the 1st of August, and we spent the last weeks of July tidying it all, leaving the foundations exposed for others who might follow us, packing our treasures with loving care, making the last entries in the piles of notebooks, typing the long lists of catalogues and attending to the hundreds of other finicky details.

The field investigation was over, but ahead of me lay months of work, filing and correlating everything we had discovered, fitting each fact into its niche and comparing it with evidence gathered by others at other sites, and finally there would be the summation and the book. Months before, I had hoped I might be able to entitle my book *The Phoenicians in Southern Africa*. Now I would have to find another title.

The Dakota arrived to take away the first load of crates, and with it went Peter and Heather Willcox. They would still have two or three months of their European holiday, but we were sorry to see them go, for we had been a happy group.

That evening Louren spoke to me over the radio.

'We have got hold of Cousteau at last, Ben. He's been cruising in the Pacific but my office in San Francisco spoke with him. He thinks he may be able to help, but there is no chance that he will be able to come before next year. He has a full schedule for the next eight months.'

That was my last excuse for staying on at the City of the Moon, and I began packing my own private papers. Sally offered to help me. We worked late, sorting through the thousands of photographs. Now and then we would pause to examine a print of particular interest, or laugh over one that had been taken in fun, remembering the good times we had spent together over the months.

Finally we came to the file of prints of the white king.

'My beautiful mysterious king,' Sally sighed. 'Isn't there anything more you can tell us? Where did you come from? Who did you love? Into what battles did you carry your war shield, and who wept over your wounds when they carried you home from the field?'

We went slowly through the thick pile of prints. They were taken from every angle, with every type of variation in lighting, exposure and printing technique.

A detail of one of the prints caught my eye. I suppose that subconsciously I was alerted to pick it up. I stared at it, with eyes that began to see for the first time. I felt something fluttering inside of me like a trapped bird, felt the electric tickle run up my arms.

'Sal,' I said and then stopped.

'What is it, Ben?' She picked up the quaver of suppressed excitement in my voice.

'The light!' I said. 'Do you remember how we found the city in the moonlight? The angle and intensity of the light?'

'Yes,' she nodded eagerly.

'Do you see it, Sal?' I touched the white king's face. 'Do you remember the print I gave to Lo? Do you remember the mark on it?'

She stared at the photograph. It was fainter than on Louren's print, but it was there, the same shadowy cross shape superimposed upon the death-white face.

'What is it?' Sally puzzled, turning the photograph in her hands to catch the light.

'I don't know,' I said as I hurried across the room to the equipment cupboard, and began scratching around in it, 'but I'm damned well going to find out.'

I came out of the cupboard and handed her one of the four-cell torches. 'Take this and follow me, Watson.'

'We always seem to do our best work at night,' Sally began, and then realized what she had said. 'I didn't mean it that way!' She forestalled any ribald comment.

The cavern was as still as an ancient tomb, and our footsteps echoed loudly off the paving as we skirted the pool and went to the portrait of the white king. The beams of our torches danced upon him and he stared down at us, regal and aloof.

'There's no mark on his face,' Sally said, and I could hear the disappointment in her voice.

'Wait.' I took my handkerchief from my pocket. Folding it in half, and in half again, I masked the glass of my torch. The bright beam was reduced to a steady glow through the cloth. I climbed up on to the timber framework that had been left in position.

'Switch yours off,' I ordered Sally, and in the semi-darkness I stepped up to the portrait and began examining the face with the dimmer light.

The cheek was white, flawless. Slowly I moved the light, lifting higher, lowering it, moving it in a wide circle around the king's head.

'There!' we cried together, as suddenly the hazy mark of the cross appeared over the pale features. I steadied the light in its correct position and examined the mark.

'It's a shadow, Sal,' I said. 'I think there must be an irregularity beneath the paint. A sort of groove, or rather two grooves intersecting each other at right angles to form a cross.'

'Cracks in the rock?' Sally asked.

'Perhaps,' I said. 'But they seem to be too straight, the angles too precise to be natural.'

I unmasked my torch, and turned to her.

'Sal, have you an article of silk with you?'

'Silk?' She looked stunned, but recovered quickly. 'My scarf.' Her fingers went to her throat.

'Lend it to me, please.'

'What are you going to do with it?' she demanded, holding her hand protectively over the scrap of pretty cloth that showed in the neck of her blouse. 'It's genuine Cardin. Cost me a ruddy king's ransom.'

'I won't spoil it,' I promised.

'You'll buy me a new one if you do,' she warned me, as she unknotted the scarf and passed it up to me.

'Give a light,' I requested and she directed her torch onto the king. I spread the scarf over the king's head, holding it in position with the fingers of my left hand.

'What on earth are you doing?' she demanded.

'If you are ever buying a second-hand car, and you want to be sure it has never been in a smash, then this is the way you feel for blemishes that the eye can't see.'

With the finger-tips of my right hand I began feeling the surface of the painting through the silk. The cloth allowed my finger-tips to slip easily over the rock, and seemed to magnify the feel of the texture. I found a faint

180

groove, followed it to a crossroads, moved down the south axis to another cross-roads, moved east, north, and back to my starting point. My finger-tips had traced a regular oblong shape, measuring about nine by six inches.

'Do you feel anything?' Sally could not contain her impatience. I did not answer her for my heart was in my mouth, and my fingers were busy, running all over the rock beneath the silk, moving well away from the portrait, down almost to floor level, and up as high as I could reach.

'Oh, Ben. Do tell me! What is it?'

'Wait!' My heart was drumming like the flight of a startled pheasant, and the track of my finger-tips trembled with excitement.

'I will not wait, damn you,' she shouted. 'Tell me!'

I jumped down off the framework and grabbed her hand. 'Come on.'

'Where are we going?' she demanded as I dragged her across the cavern.

'To get the camera.'

'What on earth for?'

'We are going to take some photographs.'

I had two rolls of Kodak Ektachrome Aero-film type 8443 in the small refrigerated cabinet which housed my stock of films. I had ordered this infra-red film to experiment with photographing the unexcavated foundations of the city from the top of the cliffs, but the results had not been encouraging. There were too many rock strata and too much vegetation confusing the prints.

I filled my Rolleiflex with a roll of the infra-red film, and I fitted a Kodak No. 12 Wratten filter over the lens. Sally pestered me while I worked, but I replied to all her queries with, 'Wait and see!'

I took up two arc-lights, and we arrived back at the cavern a little after midnight.

I used a direct frontal lighting, plugging the arc-lights into the switch-board of the electric water-pump beside the pool. I set the Rolleiflex on a tripod and made twenty exposures at varying speeds and aperture-settings. By this time Sally was on the point of expiring with curiosity, and I took mercy on her.

'This is the technique they use for photographing canvases and picking out the signatures and details overlaid by layers of other paints, for aerial photography through cloud, for photographing the currents of the sea, things which are invisible to the human eye.'

'It sounds like magic.'

'It is,' I said, clicking away busily. 'The filter takes out everything but the infra-red rays, and the film is sensitive to it. It will reflect any temperature or texture differences in the subject and show them in differing colours.'

There was an hour's work in the dark room before I could project the images onto our viewing screen. All colours were altered, becoming weird and hellish. The king's face was a virulent green and his beard purple. There were strange dapplings, speckles, and spots which we had never noticed before. There were irregularities in the surface, extraneous materials in the paint pigments, colonies of lichens and other imperfections. They glowed like outlandish jewels.

I hardly noticed these. What held all my attention, and set my pulses pounding, was the grid of regular oblong shapes that underlaid the entire image. An irregular chequer-board effect; they showed in lines of pale blue.

'We've got to get Louren here immediately,' I blurted.

'What is it? I still don't understand. What does it mean?' Sally pleaded, and I turned to her with surprise. It was so clear to me that I had expected her to understand readily.

'It means, Sal, that beyond our white king is an opening in the rock wall which has been closed off by a master mason with perfectly laid blocks of sandstone. The white king has been painted over it.'

Louren Sturvesant stood before the rock wall in the cavern and stared angrily at the white king. His hands were clasped behind his back. He was balanced on the balls of his feet, with his jaw thrust out aggressively. We stood around him in a semi-circle, Ral, Sally, Leslie and I, and we watched his face anxiously.

Suddenly Louren tore the cigar out of his own mouth and hurled it onto the paved floor. Savagely he ground the stub to powder, then he swung away and went to the edge of the emerald pool and stared down into its shadowy depths. We waited in silence.

He came back, drawn to the painting like a moth to the candle.

'That thing,' he said, 'is one of the world's great works of art. It's two thousand years old. It's irreplaceable. Invaluable.'

'Yes,' I said.

'It doesn't belong to us. It's part of our heritage. It belongs to our children, to generations not yet born.'

'I know,' I said, but I knew more than that. I had watched Louren over the months as his feelings towards the portrait grew. It had developed some deep significance for him, which I could only guess at.

'Now you want me to destroy it,' he said.

We were all silent. Louren swung away and began pacing, back and forth, in front of the portrait. All our heads swung to watch him, like spectators at a tennis match. He stopped abruptly, in front of me.

'You and your fancy bloody photographs,' he said, and began pacing again.

'Couldn't we—' Leslie began timidly, but her voice faded out as Louren spun around and glared at her.

'Yes?' he demanded.

'Well, could you sort of go round behind it, I mean, well—' Her voice faded and then grew stronger again. 'Drill a passage in the wall off to one side, and then turn back behind the king?'

For the first time in my life I felt like throwing my arms around her neck and kissing her.

Louren flew up one of his mine captains with a crack team of five Mashona rock-breakers from the Little Sister gold mine near Welcome. They brought with them an air-compressor, pneumatic drills, jumper bars, and all the other paraphernalia of their trade. The mine captain was a big, ginger-haired man, with cheerful cornflower-blue eyes, and a freckled baby face. His name was Tinus van Vuuren, and he threw himself wholeheartedly into the project.

'Reckon we will be able to cut her fairly easy, Doctor. This sandstone is like cheese, after the serpentine and quartz that I am used to.'

'I want the smallest opening you can work in,' Sally told him sternly. 'I want as little damage as possible done to the paintings.'

'Man,' Tinus turned to her earnestly, 'I'll cut you one no bigger than a mouse's—' he cut the word off, and substituted another, 'ear-hole.'

Sally and I taped the outline of the mouth of the shaft on the wall of the cavern. We positioned it carefully to avoid the most beautiful and significant paintings. Though we took Tinus at his word and made the opening a mere two feet wide by four high – yet we would destroy part of a lovely group of giraffe, and a dainty little gazelle with big listening ears.

We kept thirty feet away from the white king, to avoid undue vibrations from the drills which might have loosened flakes of stone or paint pigments. Tinus would go in for thirty feet, then turn his shaft at right angles to the face and cut in behind the king. Tinus was set to begin first thing the following morning, but that night we entertained him in the common room. The atmosphere was similar to that of a fighter squadron mess on the eve of a dangerous sortie. We were all voluble and tense, and all of us were drinking a little too much.

To begin with, Tinus was very reserved, clearly over-awed by the company of the legendary Louren Sturvesant, but the brandy loosened him up and he joined in the conversation.

'What do you want the respirators for, Doc?' he asked. 'You expecting gas or a fire?'

'Respirators?' Louren broke off a private conversation with Sally. 'Who ordered respirators?'

'They specially told me six respirators.' Tinus looked dismayed at Louren's direct questioning. 'They told me that, sir.'

'That's right, Lo.' I rescued the poor man. 'I asked for them.'

'Why?'

'Well, Lo. What we are all hoping to find is a passage, a – ' I was about to say tomb, but I did not want to tempt the gods, ' – cave of some sort.'

He nodded. They were all watching me – and with a receptive audience I can seldom resist a touch of the theatrical.

'That cave will have been sealed, airtight, for two thousand years or so, which means there could be a danger of—'

'The Curse of the Pharaohs!' Sally interjected. 'Of course, do you remember what happened to the men who first entered Tutankhamen's tomb?' She drew a finger across her own throat and rolled her eyes horribly. She was onto her second Glen Grant.

'Sally, you ought to know better,' I cut in severely. 'The Curse of the Pharaohs is of course a myth. But there is a danger of a peculiarly unpleasant lung disease.'

'Well, I must say, I don't believe in curses and all that sort of bulldust,' Tinus laughed, a little too loudly. His inhibitions were way down around his ankles.

'That makes two of us,' agreed Ral Davidson.

'It's not a supernatural thing,' Leslie told them primly. 'It's a fungus disease.'

I seemed to have lost control of the situation completely, so I raised my voice.

'If you are all finished, I'll go on,' which got their attention back to me. 'The conditions would have been ideal for the development of *cryptococcus neuromyces*, a fungoid saphrophitic growth whose air-borne spores are the cause of a fatal disease.'

'What does it do?' Tinus asked.

'The spores are breathed into the lungs, and in the warm moist conditions they germinate almost immediately and develop into dense granulitic colonies.'

'Sies!' said Tinus, which is an expression of the deepest disgust. 'You mean it starts growing on your lungs like that green stuff on mouldy bread?'

'What are the consequences?' Louren asked.

I had it word-perfect. 'Primarily they are extensive lesions of the lung tissue, with haemorrhage, high temperature and rapidly painful breathing, but then the fungoid colonies begin generating wastes which are readily absorbed into the blood and carried to the brain and central nervous system.'

'My God!' Tinus was blanched and horrified, his blue eyes stared out of the white freckled face. 'Then what happens?'

'Well, the wastes act as a virulent neurotoxin and induce hallucination. There is inflammation of the meninges, and severe brain malfunction, similar to the effects of lysergic acid or mescalin.'

'Groovy!' said Ral, and Leslie kicked his shin.

'You mean it drives you crazy?' Tinus demanded.

'Clean out of your little skull,' Sally assured him.

'Fatal?' asked Louren.

'Seventy-five per cent, depending on individual immunity and the rate of antibody formation.'

'In the event of survival, is there permanent damage?'

'Scarring of the lungs similar to healed tuberculosis.'

'Brain damage?'

'No.' I shook my head.

'Hell, man,' said Tinus carefully, setting his glass down. 'I don't know that I am so keen on this deal. Rock falls, methane gas, pressure bursts – those don't worry me. But this fungus thing,' he shuddered, 'it is creepy, man. Just plain bloody creepy.'

'What precautions are you going to take, Ben?' Louren asked.

'The first party in will be protected by respirators,' I explained. 'I will take air and dust samples for microscopic examination.'

Louren nodded, and smiled at Tinus.

'Satisfied?'

'What will you do if you don't find it – but it's sort of lurking there? Like, ready to pounce, you know. Like in those science fiction books,' Tinus hedged.

'If it's there, it will be thick. Every dust sample will be full of it. You can't miss it under the microscope. A black, three-ball structure like a pawnbroker's sign.'

'Are you sure, Doc?'

'I'm sure, Tinus.'

He took a deep breath, hesitated a moment longer, then nodded. 'Okay, Doc. I'll trust you,' he said.

The buffeting, fluttering roar of the rock drills chased my agonized brain into a corner of my skull and started kicking it to a jelly. The party had ended in the early hours.

'How are you feeling, Doc?' Tinus van Vuuren came across to where I stood watching the work and shouted above the din. My nerves vibrated like guitar strings. Tinus looked as fresh and baby-faced as though his nightcap had been hot milk and honey and he had slept twelve hours. I knew the type – Louren was one of them.

'I feel bloody awful, thanks,' I shouted back.

'There won't be anything to see here for a couple of days,' Tinus told me. 'Why don't you go lie down for a bit, Doc?'

'I'll stick around,' I said, which seemed to be the general sentiment. Louren piloted the course of the Sturvesant empire from the radio shack, unable to tear himself away from the City of the Moon. Sally made a few desultory attempts at cataloguing and filing, but these never lasted more than an hour or two and then she was back at the cavern. Ral and Leslie made no pretence, and spent all day in the cavern, except for brief simultaneous absences which Louren and I guessed were exercise periods.

Tinus was a top man in his trade, and his team cut the tunnel swiftly and skilfully. The walls were shaped smoothly and precisely. They were shored with heavy timber baulks, and electric lights were strung along the roof. Thirty feet in, Tinus constructed a large chamber from which a new drive was made, aimed at the area behind the painting of the white king.

Tinus and I had made careful measurements and calculations, and we had decided exactly where we could expect to strike whatever the wall of masonry concealed.

The Bantu drill-men were warned of the need for respirators, and Tinus and I crouched behind them in the cramped rock tunnel as they began the assault on the last few feet of rock. Their backs were naked glistening bunches of black muscles as they worked the heavy drills. The noise in the confined space was thunderous, and despite the ventilation fans circulating air, the heat was appalling. The sweat poured down inside the face-mask of my respirator, and the eye goggles were fogged and blurry.

The tension was becoming almost painful as the long steel bit of the drill hammered itself into the rock, sinking in inch by inch, the muddy lubricating water running back from the drill hole. I glanced sideways at Tinus. He appeared monstrous in the black rubber mask, but the blue eyes twinkled out of the eye glasses and he winked and held up a thumb in a gesture of assurance.

Suddenly the drill-man was thrown off balance, as the drill ran away with him. It slid, unresisted, into its hole, and he staggered wildly as he tried to control the enormous weight of steel. Tinus slapped his shoulder, and he slammed the valve of the drill closed. The silence was almost painful, and our laboured breathing was the only sound.

Through, I thought, *we've holed through into God knows what.*

I saw my own excitement reflected in Tinus's blue eyes. I nodded at him, and he turned and tapped the drill-men's shoulders and jerked his thumb in a gesture of dismissal. They shuffled back, bowed in the low tunnel, and disappeared around the bend.

The two of us went forward and crouched at the face. Gingerly we withdrew the drill steel from its hole, and a wisp of fine dust followed it out, smoking in the harsh glare of the electric lights. Tinus and I exchanged glances. Then I jerked my head at Tinus. He nodded, and followed his gang back along the tunnel. I worked on alone at the face.

I used the long plastic rod, with a piece of sterile white cloth attached to the end of it, to probe the drill hole to its limit. It ran fourteen feet into the rock before meeting resistance, and when I withdrew it the cloth was thick with grey floury dust. I dropped it into the sample bottle, and attached another cloth to the rod. In all I collected six separate samples, before I followed Tinus back along the passage. There was a bench and an angle-poise lamp set up ready for me in the rock chamber. The microscope was under the light, with its mirror adjusted and it was the work of only a few minutes to smear my dust samples onto the slides and spread the red dye over them.

It was difficult to get a view into the eyepiece of the microscope through my befogged goggles. One quick scrutiny was sufficient, but I doggedly inspected all six samples before I ripped off my respirator and sucked big relieved breaths. Then I scampered down the passage and out into the cavern.

They were all waiting for me, crowding around me eagerly.

'We've drilled into a cavity,' I shouted, 'and it's clean!'

Then they were on me, pounding my back and shaking my hand, laughing and chattering excitedly.

Louren would let no one else work with me at the face, though Ral and Sally were clearly breaking their hearts to do so.

The two of us worked carefully, slowly chipping away at the drill hole with chisel and four-pound hammer, enlarging it gradually until we had exposed a slab of dressed masonry. It was a massive slab of red sandstone which blocked off the end of our tunnel from floor to roof, and from wall to wall. It was obviously the lining of the cavity into which the drill had bored.

The drill hole cut through the centre of it like a single black eye-socket. All our efforts to peer through it were rewarded with a vista of impenetrable blackness and we had to content ourselves with the slower painstaking approach.

For three days we worked shoulder to shoulder, stripped to the waist, chipping steadily at the living rock until, despite our gloves, our hands were mushy with blisters and smeared skin. Slowly we exposed the massive slab over its full width and height to find that it butted on either side against identical slabs and that it appeared to carry across its summit the cross-pieces of an equally massive stone lintel.

We used two fifty-ton hydraulic jacks to take the strain of the lintel off the slab. Then we drilled and attached ring bolts to the slab itself and hooked steel chains to them. We jammed a brace of steel H-sections across the tunnel to anchor the chains and with two heavy ratchet winches we began to haul the slab bodily out of its seating.

We knelt side by side, each of us straining against one of the winches, taking up the pull one pawl at a time. With each click of the ratchet the strain on the chains increased until they were as rigid as solid steel bars. Now the handles of the winches were almost immovable.

'Okay, Ben. Let's both get onto one of them,' Louren panted. His golden curls were dark and heavy with sweat and dirt, plastered against his skull, and the sweat highlighted his great shoulder muscles and the straining, swollen biceps as we heaved together at the winch.

'Clank!' went the ratchet and the chain moved a sixteenth of an inch.

'Clank!' Again she moved. Our breathing hissed and whistled in the silence.

'All the way, partner,' Louren gasped beside me.

'All the way, Lo.' And my body arched like a drawn bow, I felt the muscles in my back begin to tear, my eyes strained from their sockets.

Then with a soft grating sound the great slab of sandstone swung slowly out of the face, and then fell with a heavy thump to the floor of the tunnel, and beyond it we saw the square black opening.

We lay together side by side, fighting for breath, sweat trickling down our faces and bodies, our muscles still quivering and twitching from our exertions, and we stared into that sinister hole.

191

There was a smell; a stale, long-dead, dry smell as the air that had been trapped in there for 2,000 years gushed out.

'Come!' Louren was the first to move, he scrambled to his feet and snatched up one of the electric bulbs in its little wire cage, the extension cable slithered after him like a snake as he went forward. I followed him quickly, and we crawled through the opening.

It was a jump of four feet down to the floor of the chamber beyond. We stood side by side, Louren holding the light above his head, and we peered around us into the moving mysterious shadows.

We were in a long commodious passage that ran straight and undeviatingly 155 feet from the cavern end to terminate against a blank wall of stone. The passage was eight foot six inches high, and ten foot wide.

The roof was lined with lintels of sandstone laid horizontally from wall to wall, and the walls themselves were tiled with blocks similar to the one we had removed from its seating. The floor was paved with square flags of sandstone.

Let into the walls on each side of the passage were stone-lined cupboards. These were seven feet wide and five feet deep and reached from floor to roof height. Each of these recesses was fitted with shelves of stone slab, rank upon rank of them, three feet apart, and upon the shelves stood hundreds upon hundreds of pottery jars.

'It's some sort of store room,' Louren said, holding the light high and moving slowly down the passage.

'Yes, probably wine or corn in the jars.' I have never learned not to guess aloud. My heart was hammering with excitement and my head swivelled from side to side, as I tried to take in every detail.

There were twenty of these recesses, ten on each side of the passage, and I guessed again.

'Must be two or three thousand pots,' I said.

'Let's open one.' Louren was consumed by a layman's impatience.

'No, Lo, we can't do that until we are ready to work properly.'

There was a thick soft shroud of pale dust over everything, it softened the outlines and edges of all shapes. It rose lazily around our legs like a sea mist as our movements stirred it.

'We will have to clean up before we can do anything else,' I said, and sneezed as the dust found its way into my nostrils.

'Move slowly,' Louren told me. 'Don't stir it up.' He took a further pace and then stopped.

'What's this?' Scattered along the passage floor were dozens of large shapeless objects, their identity concealed by the blanketing dust. They were lying singly, or in heaps, strange fluid shapes that teased my memory. Compared with the orderly ranks of jars on their shelves, the objects were strewn with a careless abandon.

'Hold the lamp,' I told Louren, and crouched over one of them. I touched it gently, running my fingers through the velvety dust, brushing it softly aside until I recognized what it was and I drew back with an involuntary exclamation of surprise.

Through the soft mist of dust and ages a face stared up at me. A long-dead, mummified face over which was stretched dry tobacco-brown skin. The eyes were empty dark holes, and the lips had dried and shrunken to expose the grinning yellow teeth.

'Dead men,' Louren said. 'Dozens of them.'

'Sacrifices?' I pondered. 'No, this is something else.'

'It looks like a battle. As though they have been killed in a fight.'

Now that we knew what they were, it was possible to make out the way the bodies were piled upon each other like the debris of a hurricane, or were thrown loosely about the stone floor. A corpse in a mantle of grey dust sat with his back to the wall, his head sagged forward on his chest, and one outflung arm had knocked four of the jars from their shelf – they lay on the floor beside him like fat rolls of French bread.

'It must have been a hell of a fight,' I said with awe.

'It was,' said Louren softly, and I turned to him with surprise. His eyes glowed with some intense inner excitement, and his lips were parted, a reckless half-smile on his lips.

'What do you mean?' I demanded. 'How do you know that?'

Louren looked at me. For a second or two he did not see me, then his eyes focused.

'Hey?' he said, puzzled.

'Why did you say that, as though you knew?'

'Did I?' he asked. 'I don't know. I meant – it must have been.'

He moved on slowly down the passage, stepping over the wind-rows of dead men, peering in each recess as he passed, and I followed him slowly. My mind was thrashing around like a corralled bull, charging madly at each fleeting idea that crossed its path, spinning back on its track and charging again. I knew there was no chance of it being capable of calm, logical thought until this first surging excitement waned.

Of one thing, and one thing only, I was certain. This was big. This was something to rank with Leakey's discoveries at Olduvai Gorge, something to startle and dazzle the world of archaeology. Something that I had prayed for and dreamed about for twenty years.

We had reached the end of the passage. The end wall was another panel of sandstone, but this was decorated. A swirling, stylized engraving of the sun image. Three feet in diameter, it looked like a Catherine wheel with the rays radiating from its circumference. The image evoked in me a strange sense of reverential awe, a hushed feeling of the spirit such as I experience sometimes in a synagogue or the cloisters of a Christian cathedral. Louren and I stood and stared at the image for a long time, then suddenly he turned and looked back to the bricked-in wall 155 feet away.

'Is that all?' he asked, and there was an irritable tone to his voice. 'Just this passage and pots and old bones? There must be something more!'

It came as a shock to me to realize that he was actually disappointed. For me the universe could hold no richer prize, this was the culminating moment of my life – and Louren was disappointed. I felt anger start to hiss and bubble within me.

'What the hell do you want?' I demanded. 'Gold and diamonds and ivory sarcophagi and—'

'Something like that.'

'You don't even know what we've got here yet, and already it's not enough.'

'Ben, I didn't say that.'

'You know what's wrong with you, Louren Sturvesant? You're bloody well spoiled. You've got everything, so nothing is good enough for you.'

'Now, listen here!' I saw my own anger reflected in his eyes, but I rushed on regardlessly.

'I've planned and saved and worked for this all my life. And now I achieve it, and what do you do?'

'Hey, Ben!' I saw comprehension in his eyes suddenly. 'I didn't mean it that way. I'm not knocking your achievement. I really think it's the most incredible discovery ever made in Africa, I was just—'

It took him a few minutes of hard talking to mollify me, but at last I grinned reluctantly.

'Okay,' I relented, 'just don't go saying things like that, Lo. All my life the bastards have been putting down my discoveries and theories, so don't you start!'

'One thing they'll never be able to say about you is that you're frightened to speak your mind!' He punched my shoulder lightly. 'Come on, Ben, let's see what we've got in these pots.'

'We shouldn't disturb them, Lo.' I was ashamed of my outburst now, and eager to make it up to him. 'Not until we have mapped and charted—'

'A couple of them are lying on the floor, knocked off the shelves,' Louren pointed. 'There are thousands of the bloody things. We will just snaffle one of them. Hell, Ben, it won't do that much harm!'

He was not asking permission, not Louren Sturvesant, he was merely giving an order in the pleasantest possible fashion. Already he was making his way back to where the jars were lying beside the dusty bowed corpse, and I hurried after him.

'Okay,' I agreed unnecessarily, in an attempt to keep nominal control of my find. 'We will remove one of them only.' I felt a sneaking sense of relief that the wrong decision had been made for me. I was also in a fever of impatience to find out what was in the jars.

The jar stood in the centre of the work-shop bench in our prefabricated warehouse. Night had fallen outside, but the overhead lights were all on. We stood around the bench, Sally, Ral, Leslie and I. Tinus van Vuuren was still up at the cavern, his status having changed from mine captain to night watchman. Louren had decided to place a twenty-four-hour armed guard over the entrance to the tunnel, and Tinus was it – until we could get others. Through the thin partition walls of the hut I could hear

Louren's voice as he shouted into the microphone of the radio.

'A vacuum cleaner. *Vacuum cleaner*. VACUUM CLEANER! V for Venereal, A for Alcoholic – that's *right*. Vacuum cleaner. You know the heavy-duty model for cleaning factories. Two of them. Have you got that? Good! Now I want you to get on to Robeson, Head of Security at Sturvesant Diamond Mines. He is to send me his two best men, with half a dozen Bantu guards. Yes, that's right. Yes, I want them armed.'

None of us paid attention to Louren's voice, we were all staring in mesmerized fascination at the earthenware jar.

'Well, it's not filled with gold.' Ral was certain. 'Not heavy enough.'

'Nor is it liquid – not wine or oil,' Leslie agreed. And we relapsed into silence. The pot was about eighteen inches high, and thick around as a pickle jar. It was of unglazed red pottery, without inscription or ornamentation, and the lid was like that of a teapot with a small knob for a handle. It was sealed with a layer of black substance, probably gum or wax.

'Get that lot on the Dakota first thing tomorrow morning, do you hear?' Louren was still busy next door.

'I wish he'd hurry up!' Sally stirred impatiently. 'I'm dying to find out what it is.'

Suddenly I was afraid. I didn't want to know – I didn't want to find the jar filled with African millet or some other indigenous grain. I could hear my critics howling like wolves out there in the wilderness. Suddenly I was doubting my own premonition of some momentous discovery and I sat on the edge of my stool, miserably rubbing my grimy hands together and staring at the jar. Perhaps Louren was right, perhaps we would echo his cry, 'Is that all?'

From the radio shack we heard Louren's voice end the transmission, and he came through into the warehouse. He was still filthy from the work in the tunnel, and his golden hair was stiff with dust and dried sweat. Yet the grime and unruly curls gave him an air of romance, the jaunty look of an old-time pirate. He stood in the doorway with his thumbs hooked into his belt, and all our attention was on him. He grinned at me.

'Okay, Ben. What have you got for us?' he asked and sauntered across the room to stand behind my shoulder. Instinctively the others drew closer, crowding into a circle around me and I picked up the surgical scalpel and touched the point of it to the joint of the lid.

The first touch told me that my guess had been correct.

'Beeswax, I think.'

Carefully I scraped it away, then laid the scalpel aside and gently tried the lid. It came away with surprising ease.

All heads craned forward, but the first view of the contents was disappointing. An amorphous mass of substance that was stained dirty yellow-brown by time.

'What is it?' Louren demanded of his experts, but none of us could answer him. I was not sure whether to be disappointed or relieved. It certainly wasn't corn.

'It smells,' said Sally. There was a faintly unpleasant, but familiar odour.

'I know that smell,' I said.

'Yes,' agreed Leslie.

We stared at the pot trying to place it. Then suddenly I remembered.

'It smells like a tannery works.'

'That's it!' agreed Sally.

'Leather?' asked Louren.

'Let's see,' I said, and carefully tipped the jar onto its side with the mouth facing me. Gently I began easing the contents out of the jar. It became immediately clear that it held something cylindrical in shape and of a hard, brittle texture.

It seemed to have stuck to the inside of the jar, but I twisted carefully and with a faint rending sound it was loose. I inched it out of the jar, and as it emerged, there was a running commentary from the watchers.

'It's a long round thing.'

'Looks like a polony sausage.'

'It's wrapped in cloth.'

'Linen, I hope!'

'It's woven anyway. That will take some explaining away as Bantu culture!'

'The cloth is rotten, it's falling away in patches.'

I laid it on the table, and as I stared at it I knew all my dreams had become reality. *I knew what it was.* A treasure beyond all the gold and diamonds Louren had hoped for. I looked up quickly at Sally to see if she had guessed, her expression was eager but puzzled. Then her eyes met mine and my jubilation must have been obvious.

'Ben!' She guessed then. 'It isn't? Oh, Ben, it couldn't be! Open it, man! For God's sake, open it!'

I took up a pair of tweezers, but my hands were too unsteady to work. I clenched my fists, and drew a couple of deep breaths to try and calm the racing of my blood and the pounding of it in my ears.

'Here, let me do it,' said Ral, and reached to take the tweezers from my grip.

'No!' I snatched my hand away. I think I would have struck him if he had persisted. I saw the shock on Ral's face, he had never before seen the violence that lurks in my depths.

They all waited until I had got control of my hands again. Then carefully I began to peel the wrappings of brittle yellow cloth from the cylinder. I saw it appear from under the wrappings, and there were no more doubts. I heard Sally's little gasp from across the bench, but I did not look up until it was done.

'Ben!' she whispered. 'I'm so happy for you.' And I saw that she was crying, big fat tears sliding slowly down her cheeks. This was what triggered me, I am certain that if she hadn't started it I would have been all right, but suddenly my own eyes were burning and my vision blurred with moisture.

'Thanks, Sal,' I said, and my voice was soggy and nasal. When I felt the droplets start to spill onto my cheeks I struck them away with an angry hand, and groped for my handkerchief. I blew my nose like a bugler sounding the charge, and my heart sang as loudly.

It was a tightly rolled cylindrical scroll of leather. The outer edges of the scroll were tattered and eaten by decomposure. The rest of it, however, was miraculously preserved. There were lines of writing running like columns of little black insects along the length of the scroll. I recognized the symbols immediately, identifying the individual letters of the Punic alphabet. It was written in a flowing Punic script, of which the first thirty lines were exposed on the roll of ancient leather. The language was not one I understood, but I looked up at Sally again. This was her speciality, she had worked with Hamilton at Oxford.

'Sal, can you read it? What is it?'

'It's Carthaginian,' she spoke with complete certainty. 'Punic!'

'Are you sure?' I demanded.

In reply she read aloud in a voice that was still choked up and muffled with tears, '*Into Opet this day a caravan from the* . . .' she hesitated, 'that piece is obscure but it goes on, *In fingers of fine gold one hundred and twenty-seven pieces, of which a tenth part unto—*'

'What the hell is going on?' Louren demanded. 'What does all this mean?'

I turned to him. 'It means we have found the archives of our city – completely intact and decipherable. We have the whole written history of our city, of our dead civilization, written by the people themselves in their own language. Their own words.'

Louren was staring at me. It was clear that the significance of our discovery had not yet occurred to him.

'This, Lo, is what every archaeologist prays for. This is proof in its most absolute form, in its most detailed and elaborate form.'

He still didn't seem to understand.

'In one line of writing we have proved conclusively the existence of a people who spoke and wrote the ancient Punic of Carthage, who traded gold, who called their city Opet, who—'

'And that's only in one line of writing,' Sally interrupted. 'There are thousands of jars, each with its scroll of writings. We will know the names and deeds of their kings, their religion, their ceremonial—'

'Their battles and strivings, where they came from and when.' I took the verbal ball from Sally, but just as adroitly she snatched it back.

'And where they went to and why!'

'My God!' Louren understood at last. 'This is everything we've been looking for, Ben. It's the whole bloody shebang and shooting-match rolled into one!'

'The works!' I agreed. 'The whole ruddy lot!'

Within an hour of my triumph, right at the zenith of my career when nothing but the prospect of fame and brilliant success lay ahead of me, Dr Sally Benator managed to bring it all crashing down around me.

We were sitting in the same tight circle around the scroll, still talking eagerly, one of those talk sessions which could only end in the early morning, for already the Glen Grant bottle was out and all our throats were oiled, the words pouring out smoothly.

Sally had translated all the writing visible on the scroll. It was an accounting of trade into the city, a cataloguing of goods and values that in itself held intriguing references to places and peoples.

'*Twenty large amphora of the red wines of Zeng, taken by Habbakuk Lal of which a tenth part to the Gry-Lion.*'

'What's a gry-lion?' Louren's hunter's instincts were roused.

'Gry is a superlative,' Sally explained. 'So a gry-lion is a great lion. Probably a title of the king or governor of the city.'

'*From the grass seas of the south one hundred and ninety-two large tusks of ivory in all two-hundred and twenty-one talents in weight of which a tenth part to the Gry-Lion and the balance outwards on the bireme of Al-Muab Adbm.*'

'How much is a talent?' Louren asked.

'About 56 pounds avoirdupois.'

'My God, that's over 10,000 lb. of ivory, in one load,' Louren whistled. 'They must have been great little hunters.'

We had discussed in detail every line of exposed writing, and again Louren's impatience came to the surface.

'Let's unroll a little more,' he suggested.

'That's a job for an expert, Lo.' I shook my head regretfully. 'That leather has been rolled up for nearly 2,000 years. It's so dry and brittle it will fall to pieces if it isn't done correctly.'

'Yes,' Sally agreed with me. 'It will take me weeks to do each one.'

Her presumption left me flabbergasted. Her practical knowledge of palaeography and ancient writings was limited to three years as a third assistant to Hamilton, I doubted if she had actually done much work on preservation and preparation of leather or papyrus scrolls. She could read Punic with about the same aplomb as the average ten-year-old can read Shakespeare, and she was taking it for granted that she would be placed in sole control of one of the greatest hoards of ancient writings ever discovered.

She must have read my expression, for her own alarm showed clearly.

'I *am* to do the work, aren't I, Ben?'

I tried to make it easier for her, I do not like hurting anyone, let alone the girl I love.

'It's an enormous and difficult job, Sal. I really think we should try and get someone like Hamilton himself, or Levy from Tel Aviv, even Rogers from Chicago.' I saw her face starting to fall to pieces, the lips drooping and trembling, the eyes clouding, and I went on hurriedly. 'But I'm sure we can arrange for you to become first assistant to whoever does the work.'

There was a deadly silence for five seconds, and during that time Sally's despair changed swiftly to a blind all-consuming rage. I saw it coming like a build-up of storm clouds but I was powerless to divert it.

'Benjamin Kazin,' she began with deceptive softness of voice, 'I think you are the most unmitigated bastard it has ever been my misfortune to meet. For three long difficult years I have given you my complete and unswerving loyalty—'

Then she lost control and it was a splendid spectacle. Even while her words lashed my soul raw and bleeding I could still admire the flashing eyes, the flushing cheeks and the masterly choice of invective.

'You are a *little* man, in mind as well as body.' She used the adjective deliberately, and I gasped. No one should ever call me that, it is a word that eats away the fabric of my soul and she knew it. 'I hate you. I hate you, you *little* man.'

I felt the blood rush to my face, and I stuttered, trying to find the words to defend myself, but before I could do so Sally had turned on Louren. Her rage still blazed, her tone was not moderated in the least as she shouted at him.

'Make him give it to me. Tell him to do it!'

Even in my own distress I felt alarm for poor Sally. This wasn't a crippled, soft-hearted little doctor of archaeology she was talking to now. This was like prodding a black mamba with a short stick, or throwing stones at a man-eating lion. I could not believe that Sally would be so stupid, would presume so upon the mildly friendly attitude which Louren had shown to her. I could not believe that she would dare that tone with Louren, as though she had some special right to his consideration, as though there was some involvement of emotions or of loyalties which she could call upon in such imperious terms. Even I who had such rights would never misuse them in such a fashion. I knew no one else who would.

Louren's eyes flashed cold blue light, like the glinting of spearheads. His lips drew into grim lines, and the rims of his nostrils flared and turned pale as bone china.

'Woman!' His voice crackled like breaking ice. 'Hold your tongue.'

If it were possible then my despair plunged even deeper as Louren responded precisely as I had expected. Now the two persons I loved were on collision course, and I knew each of them so well, knew their pride and pig-headedness, that neither would deviate. Disaster was certain, inevitable.

I wanted to cry out to Sally, 'Don't, please don't. I'll do what you ask. Anything to prevent this happening.'

And Sally's bravado collapsed. All the fight and anger went out of her. She seemed to cringe beneath the lash of Louren's voice.

'Go to your room and stay there until you learn how to behave.' Louren gave the order in the same coldly furious tone.

Sally stood up and with eyes downcast she left the room.

I could not believe it had happened. I gaped at the door through which she had gone – my saucy, rebellious Sally – as meekly as a chastened child. Ral and Leslie were writhing in a sea of agonized embarrassment.

'Bedtime, I think,' Ral muttered. 'Please excuse us. Come, Les. Good night, all.' And they were gone, leaving Louren and me alone.

Louren broke the long silence. He stood up as he spoke in an easy natural voice. His hand dropped on my shoulder in a casually affectionate gesture.

'Sorry about that, Ben. Don't let it worry you. See you in the morning.' And he strolled out into the night.

I sat alone with my suddenly worthless roll of old leather, and my breaking heart.

'I hate you, you *little* man!' Her voice echoed through the lonely wastes of my soul, and I reached for the Glen Grant bottle.

It took me a long time to get completely drunk, to the stage where the words had lost some of their sting, and when I staggered down the steps into the bright silver moonlight, I knew what I was going to do. I was going to apologize to Sally, and let her do the work. Nothing was important enough to warrant her displeasure.

I went to the hut where Sally now slept alone. Leslie had moved into Peter and Heather's old room. I scratched softly on the door, and there was no reply from within. I knocked louder, and called her name.

'Sally! Please, I must talk to you.'

At last I tried the door, and it opened into the darkened room. I almost went on in, but then my courage deserted me. I closed the door softly, and staggered to my own hut. I fell face down across the bed, and still dirty and fully dressed I found oblivion.

'Ben! Ben! Wake up.' Sally's voice and her hand shaking me gently but insistently. I turned my head and opened my burning eyes. It was bright morning. Sally sat on the edge of my bed, leaning over me. She was fully dressed, although her skin glowed from the bath and her hair was freshly brushed and gay with a scarlet ribbon, yet her eyes were puffy and swollen as though she had slept badly, or had been crying.

'I've come to apologize for last night, Ben. For the stupid, hateful things I said, and my disgusting behaviour—'

As she talked the shattered pieces of my life fell back into place, and the pain in my head and heart abated.

'Even though you've probably changed your mind, and I don't deserve it anyway, I'd be honoured to act as first assistant to Hamilton or whoever does the work.'

'You've got the job.' I grinned at her. 'That's a promise.'

Our first task at the archives was to clean away the thick accumulation of grey dust that blanketed everything. I was puzzled as to the source of this dust in a sealed and airless space like the passage, but I soon found that the joints of the roof lintels were not as tight as those of the walls, and during the centuries a fine sprinkling of dust had filtered down through these cracks.

When the equipment which Louren had ordered arrived on the Dakota, along with a detachment of Louren's security police, we could begin the work.

The security police set up a hut at the entrance to the tunnel, where there was a permanent guard posted. Only the five of us were allowed to enter.

The vacuum equipment simplified the removal of dust from the archives. Ral and I worked from the outer end of the passage like a pair of busy housewives, and the suffocating clouds of grey dust made it necessary to wear respirators until the job was finished.

We were then able to assess our discovery more accurately. There were 1,142 sealed jars of pottery in the stone recesses. Of these 148 had been knocked from their niches and 127 were broken or cracked, with their scrolls exposed to the air and obviously much the worse for it. These we sprayed with paraffin wax to prevent them crumbling, before lifting, labelling and packing them.

We then turned our full attention to the evidence of

the deadly battle that had raged through the archives, and wrought the damage to the shelves of jars.

There were thirty-eight corpses strewn down the passage between the shelves in all the abandoned attitudes of sudden and violent death, and their state of preservation was quite remarkable. A few of them had crawled away into the recesses to die, groaning out their last breaths, and clutching the terrible wounds that still gaped in their mummified bodies. Their dying agonies were clearly stamped into their contorted features. Others had died swiftly, and most of these had received hideous wounds that had severed limbs, or split their skulls down to the shoulders, or, in a few cases, had struck the head clean from the trunk and sent it rolling yards away.

There was evidence here of a diabolical fury, the unleashing of an almost superhuman destructive strength.

All the victims were clearly negroid in type, and wore loin-cloths or aprons of tanned leather, with beadwork or bone decorations. On their feet were light leather sandals, and on their heads caps or head-dresses of leather, feathers or plaited fibre also decorated with beads, shells or bones.

Around them were strewn their weapons; crudely forged iron spearheads bound on shafts of polished hardwood. Many of these shafts were broken, or severed by the blows of some razor-sharp weapon. With them lay hundreds of reed arrows, fledged with the feathers of wild duck and tipped with wickedly barbed heads of hand-forged iron. The arrows had nicked and chipped the soft sandstone walls, and it was easy to determine that they had been fired from outside the mouth of the passage before it had been sealed off. Not one of them had found a mark in a human body, and so we reasoned that a barrage of arrows had preceded the attack by these men who lay scattered in death down the length of the passage.

Fifteen feet from the sealed mouth of the passage there

was evidence of a large bonfire which had blackened the walls, roof and floor around it. A pile of charred logs still lay where the lack of air had stifled the fire when the mouth of the tunnel was sealed. This fire puzzled us until Louren reconstructed the battle for us. He paced restlessly back and forth along the passage, his footsteps ringing on the stone slabs, his shadow falling grotesque and monstrous on the stone walls.

'They drove them into this place, the last of our men of Opet, a small party of the strongest and the bravest.' His voice rang with the truth of it, like a troubadour singing the legends of the old heroes. 'They sent in their champions to finish the slaughter but the men of Opet cut them down and the others fled. Then they drew up their archers at the mouth of the passage, and fired volleys of arrows into it. Again they went in, but the men of Opet were there waiting for them and again they died in their dozens.'

He turned and came down the passage to stand beside me under the swaying electric bulb, and we were silent for a moment imagining it.

'My God, Ben. Think of it. What a fight to end with. What glory these men won on that last day.'

Even I, a man of peace, was stirred by it. I felt my heartbeat quicken and I turned to him like a child at story-time. 'What happened then?' I asked.

'They were dying already, weak with a dozen wounds each. There was no strength left in them to continue and they stood shoulder to shoulder, companions in life, and now in death also, leaning wearily on their weapons, but the enemy would not come again. Instead, they built a fire in the mouth of the passage to smoke them out, and when that did not do it, they abandoned the attack and bricked up the entrance, turning it into a tomb for the dead and the living alike.'

We were all silent then, thinking about Louren's story. It made sense, it fitted the evidence in all but one respect.

I did not want to say it, did not want to spoil such a stirring tale, but Sally had no such compunction.

'If that's true, then what happened to your band of heroes – did they change into moonbeams and flit away?' Her tone was slightly derisive, but of course she was right. I wished she was not.

Louren laughed, a little embarrassed chuckle. 'So *you* think of something better,' he challenged her.

Of the heroes of this ancient drama there was no trace, except that which lay at the foot of the passage below the graven sun image of Baal. It was blanketed by the thick grey dust and it was the final discovery on the archives floor. It was a battle-axe. A weapon of striking beauty and utility. When first I took it up from the paving where it had lain for almost 2,000 years, my hand closed snugly around the haft, the grooves in the handle fitted my fingers as though they had been moulded from them. A broken wrist-strap of leather dangled from the end of the handle.

The haft was forty-seven inches long, and fashioned from lengths of rhinoceros horn that had been laminated into a solid rod of steely resilience and strength. The handle was of ivory and the whole had been bound with electrum wire to reinforce its already surpassing strength and to protect the shaft from the cuts of enemy blades. The blade was shaped like a double crescent moon, each side exposing seven and a half inches of razor edge. From its extreme end protruded an unbarbed spike twelve inches long, thus the weapon could be used on the cut as well as the thrust.

The head was exquisitely worked and engraved, with the shapes of four vultures with wings spread, one on each side of the double blade. The birds were rendered in such detail that every feather was shown, and beyond the figures a sun rose in a burst of rays like a flower. The engravings were inlaid with electrum, an alloy of gold and silver, and from the silvery sheen of the blades it was clear that they had been tempered. The weapon was caked and dulled with what must have been dried blood, it was obviously the author of those horrible wounds that bloomed upon so many of the corpses scattered along the passage.

Holding that beautiful weapon in my hand I was infected by a sudden madness. I was not truly aware of my own intention until the axe was flying in a wide glittering circle around my head. The balance and weight of the great axe was so pure and sweet that no effort was involved as I swung it high, and then into a long overhand killing stroke. The blade whickered eagerly at the kiss of moving air across its bright edge. The flexing of the handle seemed to bring it alive in my hand, alive again after nearly 2,000 long years of sleep.

From some deep atavistic depths of my soul I felt a cry rising, an exultant yell which seemed the natural accompaniment to the deadly song of the axe. With an effort I checked the flight of the axe and the cry before it reached my lips, and looked around at the faces of the others.

They were staring at me as though I had begun raving and frothing at the mouth. Quickly I lowered the axe. I stood there feeling utterly foolish, appalled at my treatment of such a rare treasure. The horn handle could easily have become brittle, and snapped at such harsh usage.

'I was just testing it,' I said lamely. 'I'm sorry.'

T hat night we pondered and puzzled the riddle of the archives until well after midnight. We found no answer and afterwards Louren walked with me to my hut.

'The Lear is coming to pick me up tomorrow morning, Ben. I've been here two weeks already, and I just cannot stay another day. God, when I think of how I've neglected my responsibilities since we started on this dig!'

We stopped at the door of my hut and Louren lit a cigar.

'What is it about this place that makes us all act so strangely, Ben? Do you feel it also? This strange sense of,' he hesitated, 'of destiny.'

I nodded, and Louren was encouraged.

'That axe. It did something to you, Ben. You weren't yourself for a few minutes there today.'

'I know.'

'I am desperate to discover the contents of the scrolls, Ben. We must start on that as soon as possible.'

'There is ten years' work there, Lo. You will have to be patient.'

'Patience is not one of my virtues, Ben. I was reading of the discovery of Tutankhamen's tomb last night. Lord Carnarvon made the discovery possible, and yet he died before he could look on the sarcophagus of the dead Pharaoh.'

'Don't be morbid, Lo.'

'All right,' Louren agreed. 'But don't waste time, Ben.'

'You get Hamilton for me,' I said. 'We can't do a thing without him.'

'I'll be in London on Friday,' Louren told me. 'I'll see him myself.'

'He is a difficult old codger,' I warned him.

Louren grinned. 'Leave him to me. Now, listen to me, Benjamin my boy, if you find anything else here, you let me know immediately, you understand? I want to be here when it happens.'

'When what happens?'

'I don't know – something. There is something else here, Ben. I know it.'

'I hope you are right, Lo.' And he clapped my shoulder and walked away into the night towards his own hut.

While we worked on in the archives, lifting the human remains and the piles of weapons, a construction crew arrived on the site by Dakota to erect a repository for the scrolls. This was another large prefabricated warehouse, fitted with airtight doors and a powerful air-conditioning unit to maintain the scrolls in an atmosphere of optimum temperature and humidity. A high barbed-wire fence was erected around the building for security reasons, and every precaution for the safety of the scrolls was taken.

At the same time the construction crew erected another half-dozen living quarters for the expanded team, and the first inhabitants of these were four high officials of the Botswana Government. It was the Government who had forbidden the removal of the scrolls from the territory and made the erection of the new buildings necessary. The Government deputation stayed for two days, and left satisfied that their interests in the discovery would be adequately protected, but not before I had exacted a solemn promise of secrecy. The announcement of the site would be at my signal only.

We began labelling and removing the pottery jars from their shelves. Taking the greatest pains to record, both photographically and by written notes, the exact position of each. It seemed likely that they had been stacked in chronological order, and this would assist the work of interpretation.

On the Monday I received a crippling blow to my plans in the form of a laconic message from Louren.

'Hamilton unavailable. Please suggest alternative.'

I was disappointed, hurt and angry. Disappointed because Hamilton was the best in the world, and his presence would have immediately given weight and authenticity to my site. I was hurt because Hamilton obviously believed my claims were spurious, my reputation had been damaged by the vicious attacks of my critics and scientific opponents, Hamilton had clearly been influenced by this.

He did not want to be party to some mistaken or blatantly fraudulent discovery of mine. Finally, I was angry because Hamilton's refusal to undertake the work was a direct insult. He had put the mark of the pariah on me and it would discourage others from giving the assistance I desperately needed. I might find myself discredited before I had even started.

'He didn't even give me a chance,' I protested to Sally. 'He didn't even want to listen to me. Christ, I didn't realize I was such a professional leper. Even talking to me can ruin a reputation!'

'He's a skinny, bald-headed old goat!' Sally agreed. 'He's a lecherous old feeler of bottoms, and—'

'And the greatest living authority on ancient writings in the world,' I told her bitterly. There was no reply to that, and we sat in forlorn silence for a while.

Then Sally perked up. 'Let's go and fetch him!' she suggested.

'He might refuse to see us,' I gloomed.

'He won't refuse to see me,' Sally assured me, and behind the words was an untold story that set my jealousy coursing corrosively through my veins. Sally had worked for him three years, and I could only console myself that her standards were high enough to exclude Eldridge Hamilton.

Seventy-two hours later I sat in the front lounge of the Bell at Hurley with a pint of good English bitter in front of me, and watched the car park anxiously. It was only a fifteen-minute drive from Oxford and Sally should have been here long ago.

I felt tired, irritable and depressed from that soul-destroying overnight flight from Johannesburg to Heathrow. Sally had phoned Hamilton from the airport.

'Professor Hamilton, I do hope you don't mind me phoning you,' she had cooed. 'Sally Benator, do you remember I worked under you in 1966. That's right, Sally Green-Eyes.' And she giggled coyly.

'Well, I am on my way through England. Just here for a day or two. I felt so lonely and nostalgic – those were wonderful times.' Her tones had a hundred intimate shades of invitation and promise.

'Lunch? That's wonderful, Professor. Why don't I pick you up. I have a hire car.' She gave me a triumphant thumbs-up sign.

'The Bell at Hurley? Yes, of course, I remember. How could I forget.' She made a sick face at me. 'I so look forward to it.'

The silver Jaguar slid into the car park, and I saw Sally at the wheel. With a scarf in her hair and laughter on her lips, she didn't look like a girl who had sat fourteen hours in the cramped seat of an intercontinental jet.

She slid out of the car, giving me a flash of those wonderful sun-browned thighs, and then she was coming towards me. Hanging on the arm of Eldridge Hamilton, and laughing gaily.

Hamilton was a tall stoop-shouldered man in his fifties, a baggy Harris tweed suit with leather patches on the elbows hung like a sack on his gaunt frame. His nose was beaky, and his bald pate shone in the pale sunlight as though it had been buffed up with a good wax polish. All in all he was not formidable competition, but his little eyes sparkled behind the heavy horn-rimmed glasses and his lips were slack with desire, exposing a mouthful of bad teeth, as he looked at Sally. I found it a hard price to pay for his services.

Sally led him to my table, and he was six feet from me before he recognized me. He stopped dead, and I saw him blink once. He knew instantly that he had been taken, and for a moment the whole project hung in the balance. He could so easily have turned on his heel and walked out.

'Eldridge!' I leapt to my feet, crooning seductively. 'How wonderful to see you.' And while he still hesitated, I had him by the elbow in a grip like a velvet-lined vice. 'I've ordered you a large Gilbey's gin and tonic – that's your poison, isn't it?'

It was five years since last we had met, and my memory of his personal tastes mollified him slightly. He allowed Sally and I to ease him into a seat and place the gin convenient to his right hand. While Sally and I bombarded him with all our considerable combined charm he maintained a suspicious silence, until the first gin had gone down. I ordered another and he began to thaw; half-way through the third he became skittish and voluble.

'Did you read Wilfred Snell's reply to your book *Ophir* in the *Journal?*' he asked. Wilfred Snell was the most vociferous and merciless of all my scientific adversaries. 'Jolly amusing, what?' And Eldridge neighed like a randy stallion, and clutched at one of Sally's beautiful thighs.

I am a man of peace, but at that moment I was having difficulty remembering it. My expression must have been a sickly grin, my fingernails were driven like claws into the flesh of my palms as I fought down the temptation to drag Eldridge around the room by his heels.

Sally wriggled out from his exploring hand, and I suggested in a strangled voice, 'Let's go through to lunch, shall we?'

There was a quick game of musical chairs at the dining-room table, as Eldridge tried to get a seat within clutching distance of Sally and I tried to prevent it.

We out-foxed him on a cunning double play, allowing him to settle down triumphantly beaming over the top of his menu at Sally who was backed into a corner beside him, before I cried, 'Sally, you are in a draught there.' And smoothly as a pair of ballet dancers we changed seats.

Then I could relax and give the pheasant the attention it deserved, although the burgundy that Eldridge suggested was nothing if not gauche.

With characteristic tact Eldridge brought up the subject we had all been flirting with.

'Met a friend of yours the other day, big flashy chap like a cross between a male model and a professional wrestler. Accent like an Australian with the 'flu. Had some cock-and-bull story about scrolls you'd found in a cave outside Cape Town.' And Eldridge neighed again at a volume that momentarily stopped all other conversation in the room. 'Damned man had the cheek to offer me money. I know the type, not a bean to bless himself with, and talks like he's made of the stuff. He had "shyster" written all over him in letters two feet high.'

Sally and I gaped at him, struck dumb by his astute grasp of the facts and his masterly summation of Louren Sturvesant's character.

'Sent him packing of course,' said Eldridge with relish, and stuffed his mouth with breast of pheasant.

'You probably did the right thing,' I murmured. 'Incidentally the site is in northern Botswana – 1,500 miles from Cape Town.'

'Oh, yes?' Eldridge asked, expressing disinterest as politely as one can with a mouthful of pheasant and rotten teeth.

'And Louren Sturvesant was on *Time* Magazine's list of the thirty richest men in the world,' murmured Sally. Eldridge stopped chewing with his mouth ajar, and afforded us a fine view of a semi-masticated pheasant-breast.

'Yes,' I affirmed. 'He is bank-rolling my dig. He has put in 200,000 dollars already, and he has set no limit.'

Eldridge turned a stricken face towards me. That sort of patron of scientific research was almost as rare as the unicorn, and Eldridge realized suddenly that he had been within range of one and let him escape. All the bumptious-ness was gone out of Professor Hamilton.

I signalled the waitress to clear my plate, and I swear that I felt true compassion in my heart for Eldridge as I unlocked my briefcase and took from it a cylindrical bundle wrapped in its protective canvas jacket.

'I have an appointment with Ruben Levy in Tel Aviv tomorrow, Eldridge.' I opened the canvas wrapping.

'We have 1,142 of these leather scrolls. So Ruby will be pretty busy for the next few years. Of course, Louren Sturvesant will make a donation of 100,000 dollars to the Tel Aviv University Faculty of Archaeology for their co-operation, and I shouldn't be surprised if the faculty doesn't have some of the scrolls given to them as well.'

Eldridge swallowed his mouthful of pheasant as though it were broken glass. He wiped his fingers and mouth with his napkin, before leaning forward to examine the scroll.

'*From out of the southern plains of grass,*' he whispered as he read, and I noticed the difference from Sally's translation, '*received 192 large ivory tusks, weighing 221 talents—*' His voice died but his lips moved as he read on. Then he began speaking again, and his voice quavered with excitement.

'Punic in the style of the second century B.C., do you see the use of ligatures to join the median "m", still using the hang of the characters from the line, that's definitely pre-first century B.C. Here, Sally, do you see the archaic crossing of the "A"?'

'We have over a thousand of these scrolls, preserved in chronological order – Levy is very excited,' I interrupted this flow of technicalities with a gentle untruth. Levy didn't know they existed.

'Levy,' Eldridge snorted, and his spectacles flashed with outrage. 'Levy! Take him outside Hebrew and Egyptian and he's a babe in the bloody woods!' He had hold of my wrist now.

'Ben. I insist, I absolutely insist on doing this work!'

'What about Wilfred Snell's criticism of my theories? You seemed to find it amusing.' I had him by the ackers now, and I could afford to be a little cocky. 'How do you feel about working with somebody whose views are so suspect?'

'Wilfred Snell,' said Eldridge earnestly, 'is a monumental jackass. Where did he ever find a thousand Punic scrolls?'

'Waiter,' I called, 'please bring us two large Cordon Argent brandies.'

'Make that three,' said Sally.

As the brandy diffused a gentle warmth through my body, I listened to Eldridge Hamilton effusing about the scrolls and demanding of Sally information as to exactly where, when and how we had discovered them. I found myself beginning to like the man. It was true that he had teeth like the stumps of a pine forest devastated by fire, but then I am not a perfect physical specimen myself. It was also true that he had a weakness for Gilbey's gin and pretty girls – but then he differed from me only in his choice of liquor, and who am I to hold that Glen Grant is in any way superior?

No, I decided, despite my prejudices, I would be able to work with him, just as long as he kept his bony little claws off Sally.

Eldridge followed us out a week after our return to the City of the Moon, and we met him at the airstrip. I was concerned that he might find that the transition from a northern winter to our 110°F summer impaired his abilities. I need not have worried. He was one of those Englishmen who, solar topee cocked, go out in the midday sun without raising a sweat. His luggage consisted of a single small valise which contained his personal effects and a dozen large packing-cases filled with chemicals and equipment.

I gave him the Grade 'A' tour of the site, trying without

success to fan his interest in the city and the cavern. Eldridge was a single-minded specialist.

'Yes,' he said. 'Jolly interesting – now where are the scrolls?' I think even then he had doubts, but I took him into the archives and he purred like an angular old tom cat as he moved down the burdened stone shelves.

'Ben,' he said, 'there's just one thing still to settle. I write the paper on the actual scrolls, agreed?' We are a strange breed, we work not for the gold but for the glory. Eldridge was making certain of his share.

'Agreed.' We shook hands.

'Well then, there is nothing to stop me beginning right away,' he said.

'No,' I said, 'there isn't, is there.'

The treatment of the scrolls was an art form more than an exact science. For each of them the treatment varied, depending on their state of preservation, the quality of the leather, the composition of the ink and other interrelated factors. Sally admitted to me in a weak moment that she would not have been able to handle the task, it required a fund of acquired experience which she did not have at her command.

Eldridge worked like a medieval alchemist, steaming and soaking and spraying and painting. His domain stank of chemicals and other weird smells, and his and Sally's fingers were stained. Sally reported that his absorption with the task had reduced his animal instincts to the level where he made only spasmodic and half-hearted clutches at the protruding parts of her anatomy.

As each scroll was unrolled, its contents were evaluated and the detailed translation begun. One after the other they proved to be either books of account on the city's trade, or proclamations made by the Gry-Lion and the council of the nine families. The authors were nameless clerks, and their style was brisk and economical with little time for poetic flights or unnecessary descriptive passages. This starkly utilitarian outlook echoed the lifestyle which we had so far reconstructed from our finds on the site. We discussed it at the nightly talk sessions.

'It's typically Punic,' Eldridge agreed. 'They had little taste in the visual arts, their pottery was coarse and mass-produced. In my opinion their sculpture, what little there was, was downright hideous.'

'It requires wealth and leisure and security to produce art,' I suggested.

'That's true – Rome and Greece are examples of that. Carthage and, earlier, Phoenicia were often threatened, on occasion struggling for survival – they were the bustlers and hustlers. Traders and warriors, more concerned with wealth and the acquisition of power than the niceties of living.'

'You don't have to go back that far, modern art comes from the great wealthy and secure nations.'

'And we white Africans are like the old Carthaginians,' Sally said, 'when there's gold in them thar hills who gives a hoot about painting pictures.'

The scrolls reinforced the theory. Gold from Zimbao and Punt, ivory from the southern plains of grass or from the forests along the great river, hides and dried meat, salted fish from the lakes, wine and oil from the terraced gardens of Zeng, copper from the hills of Tuya, and salt from pans along the west shores of the lakes, tin from the juncture of the two rivers, corn from the middle kingdom in baskets of woven cane, sun stones from the southern river of the crocodile, iron bars from the mines of Sala – and slaves, thousands upon thousands of human beings treated as domestic animals.

The chronicle was dated from some undisclosed point

in time, we suspected this as the date of the founding of the city, and each entry was prefaced by such dating as, 'In year 169 the month of the elephant.' From these we deduced a ten-month year based on a calendar of 365 days.

Once the nature of the scrolls had been established, I suggested to Eldridge that rather than work systematically through the collection from beginning to end, we sample them and try to establish the overall history of our city.

He fell in with my wishes, and there evolved a picture of a widespread colonization of central and southern Africa by a warlike and energetic people, based on the city of Opet, and ruled by a hereditary king, the 'Gry-Lion', and an oligarchy of nine noble families. The decrees of this Council covered a range as wide as the measures adopted for dredging the channels of the lake and preventing the encroachment of water weed, to the choice of messengers to be sent to the gods Baal and Astarte. Here Astarte seemed to have taken precedence over the more usual Carthaginian form, Tanith. 'Messengers', we suspected, were human sacrifices.

We discovered carefully recorded family trees, based like the Jewish system on a matrilinear system. Each noble man or woman could trace his or her line back to the founding of the city. It was also clear from the chronicle that their religion was part of their scheme of living, and we could reasonably guess that it was a conventional form of polytheism, with leading male and female godheads, Baal and Astarte.

As we moved forward in time so we found new factors intruding, new contingencies occupying the attention of the ruling king. The rapid shrinking of the waters of the lake of Opet began to threaten the city's life line, and in the year 296 the Gry-Lion sent 7,000 slaves to assist with the work of keeping the channels open to the sea. He also despatched a column of 1,000 of his own guards under the war-captain Ramose with orders to 'venture eastwards towards the rising sun stopping not, nor failing in determination' until he had reached the eastern sea and had discovered the route to the lands of the north whose existence was postulated by the sea captain and navigator, Habbakuk Lal.

A year later Ramose returns, with only seventy men, the others having perished in a land of pestilential swamps and putrid fevers. He had, however, reached the eastern sea and there found a city of traders and seafarers 'dark men, and bearded, dressed in fine linens, and binding their brows with the same material'. They come from a land beyond the eastern sea, and Ramose is rewarded with twenty fingers of gold and twenty slaves. Our men of Opet have made their first contact with the Arabs, known to them as 'the Dravs', who are colonizing the Sofala coast.

We learned how the Gry-Lion's search for a new source of slave-labour becomes desperate. Orders are despatched to the mine overseers to take all measures to prolong the working lives of their slaves. Rations of meat and corn are increased, inflating the cost of production but increasing the life expectancy of the slaves. Owners are enjoined to breed all female slaves regularly, and the practice of infibulation is discontinued. The slaving expeditions are sent further and further afield, as the Yuye are hunted down. From the description of these yellow-skinned Yuye we guessed they were the ancestors of Hottentot people.

Then suddenly the Gry-Lion is delighted by the return of a northerly expedition with 500 'savage Nubians, both tall and strong' and the leader of the expedition is rewarded with ten fingers of gold. This delight fades slowly over the following hundred years as a solid mass of black humanity builds up north of the great river. The vast Bantu migrations have begun and now the concern of the Gry-Lion is to dam the flood southwards and his legions march constant patrol upon the northern border.

Our samplings gave us these fleeting glimpses into the

past, but they were recorded as bland impersonal statements of fact. How we longed to find the writings of a Pliny or Livy to give flesh and breath to these meticulous records of acquired wealth.

Each fact seemed to present us with a hundred unanswered questions. Of these the most pressing was: where did they come from these men of Opet, and when? Where did they go to and why? We hoped the answers to the major questions were here somewhere in this maze of writings, and in the meantime we occupied ourselves with finding the lesser answers.

It was easy enough to locate the places mentioned in the chronicles, Zimbao and Punt were the southern and northern territories of modern Rhodesia, the great river was the Zambezi, the lakes had disappeared, the gardens of Zeng were clearly the hundreds of thousands of acres of terraced hillsides in the Inyanga area of eastern Rhodesia, the hills of Tuya must be the copper-rich country above Sinoia; step by step we established the presence of our men of Opet at nearly all of the ancient sites, and at the same time we had a picture of the building-up of an immense treasure. For although the bulk of this wealth was sent 'outwards' yet there re-occurred the words 'a tenth part to the Gry-Lion'.

Where had this treasure been stored, and what had become of it? Had it perished with the city, or was it still here in some secret storehouse carved from the red rock cliffs of the Hills of Blood?

As a mental exercise I made an estimate of the extent of this treasure. Assuming that a 'finger' of gold was one of the finger-like rods of the precious metal we had discovered among the foundations of the city, I listed the total inflow of gold recorded in twenty-odd sample years beginning in the year 345 and ending in the year 501. I found that previous estimates had been hopelessly inadequate. Instead of 750 tons of gold, I found that the total recovery from

223

the ancient mines could not have been less than 4,000 tons – of which a tenth part to the Gry-Lion.

Assuming half of this 400 tons had been spent on the maintenance of his army, the building of the temple and other public works, this still left the staggering figure of 200 tons of gold that might be hidden in or near the city – 200 tons represents a fortune of almost £80,000,000.

When I showed my calculations to Louren on his next visit to the site, I saw the gold-greed glitter in the pale blue eyes. He took away the sheet of paper with my workings on it, and the following morning as he was about to board the Lear for Johannesburg, he remarked casually, 'You know, Ben, I really think that you and Ral should spend more time exploring the area along the cliffs, rather than living in those archives.'

'What should we look for, Lo?' As if I didn't know.

'Well, those old boys were dab hands at hiding things away. They must have been the most secretive people in history, and we still haven't found their burial grounds.'

'So you want me to go grave-hunting.' I grinned at him, and he laughed.

'Of course, Ben, if you happened to stumble on their treasury I wouldn't hate you for it. After all eighty Big M's are a nice piece of petty cash.'

We had transferred 261 jars from the archives to the repository and Eldridge and Sally had sufficient material to keep them busy for the next two or three months, so I decided to follow Louren's suggestion and suspend work in the archives and undertake another detailed search of the area. My timing was impeccable, Ral was within five feet of where the small jars with the sunbird seals on their lids were standing in the darkest corner of the last recess. They were tucked away behind the front rank of jars twice their size and so effectively hidden by them that we had not included them in our original count. Ral was working his way steadily towards them, another three days would have been enough, but I took him away to search the cliffs.

This was November which we call the 'suicide month' in Africa. The sun was a hammer, and the earth an anvil but we worked the cliffs despite it. We rested only for two hours in the middle of the day, when the heat was murderous and the cool green waters of the emerald pool were irresistible.

We were alert now to the tricks and subterfuges of the ancient men of Opet. Having learned from bitter experience how skilfully they could cover their tracks and how cunningly their masons could conceal the joints in their masonry, I went back over ground I had already covered. I used my own tricks to try and out-think them. Ral and I re-photographed every inch of the cavern walls, but this time with infra-red film. We found no more concealed passages.

From there we worked outwards. Each day I marked off a 300-foot section and we combed this minutely. Not content merely to eyeball the rocks, we searched by sense of touch also. Groping our way over them like blind men.

Each day brought its small adventures. I was chased by a black mamba, eight feet of irritability and sudden death, with eyes like glass beads and a flicking black tongue, that resented my prodding around in the crack which was its home and castle. Ral was very impressed with my turn of speed over broken ground, and suggested I took it up professionally.

A week later I could return his sallies in kind by remarking on the improvement that twenty wild bee stings made to his appearance. His face looked like a hairy pumpkin, and his eyes were slits in the swollen flesh. For five days poor Ral was of no use to me at all.

November passed and in mid-December we had a quarter of an inch of rain, which is about par for the course in this part of Africa. It laid the dust for an hour or so, and that was the end of the rainy season. I guessed that the ancient lake of Opet would have ensured a higher and more regular rainfall for the area. Open water encourages rain, both by its evaporation and by cooling the air to aid precipitation.

Ral and I worked on without results, but also without any diminution of our determination or enthusiasm. Despite our days of wearing labour under the killer sun, we spent most of our evenings poring over the map of the foundations of the city. By a process of guess, deduction and elimination, we tried to work out where the ancients would have sited their tombs. I had by now become extremely fond of Ral Davidson, and I saw in this big gangling indefatigable youth the makings of one of the giants of our profession. There would be a permanent post for him at the Institute once this dig was finished, I would see to that.

In contrast to our results, Eldridge Hamilton, assisted by Sally, and Leslie, continued to reap the rich and enchanting harvest of the scrolls. Each evening I would spend an hour in the air-conditioned repository with them, reviewing the day's work. Steadily the sheets of typed translation piled up, the margins thick with notes and references in Eldridge's spidery and untidy hand.

Christmas came and we sat out under a moon as big as a silver gong, exchanging gifts and companionship. I gave them 'White Christmas' in the style of Bing Crosby, even though the night temperature was in the high eighties. Then Eldridge and I did 'Jingle Bells' as a duet. Eldridge had forgotten the words, all except the jingling part. He was a great little jingler was our Eldridge, especially after ten large gins. He was still jingling away merrily when Ral and I carried him off to bed.

Early in the new year we had what amounted to a royal

visit. Hilary Sturvesant had at last prevailed on Louren to bring her to see the site. We had a week to prepare for the family. Hilary was bringing the elder children with her and I was beside myself with excitement at the prospect of having all my favourite women at the City of the Moon. I left the search of the cliffs to Ral, while I rushed about re-arranging the accommodation and checking our stores for such essentials as Coca-Cola and chocolates. Commodities which make life bearable for Bobby Sturvesant.

They arrived in time for the lunch of cold meats and salads which I had personally prepared, and immediately the visit began souring. Sally Benator was not at the meal, she sent a message that she had a headache and was going to lie down. However, I saw her sneaking off with towel and bathing costume towards the emerald pool.

Eldridge Hamilton and Louren Sturvesant took one look at each other, and remembered their last meeting. They were as hostile as a pair of rutting stags. I recalled Eldridge's boast that he had sent Louren packing. They began making elaborately offensive remarks at each other, and I was fully extended in trying to prevent active physical violence breaking out, and when Eldridge spoke about people with 'more money than either breeding or sense', I thought I had lost my expert on ancient writings.

As if this was not sufficient, it was also obvious that Hilary and Louren were engaged in a domestic dispute which made it impossible for them to address each other directly. All communication was conducted through the agency of Bobby Sturvesant and was preceded by remarks of the order, 'Please ask your step-mother if . . .' or 'If your father wants . . .'

Hilary wore dark glasses at the lunch-table, and I could guess her eyes bore the traces of recent weeping. She was silent and reserved, as were both Ral and Leslie. The two youngsters were overcome with shyness in the presence of

the Sturvesants, and when Louren and Eldridge also subsided into a smouldering truce, there were only two of us
left articulate, Bobby Sturvesant and me.

Bobby took full advantage of the temporary breakdown
in parental control to become an utterly impossible little
bitch. She spent the entire meal either showing off shame-
lessly or being insolent to her step-mother. I would dearly
have loved to turn her over my knee and paddle her stern.

Immediately after the meal dragged to its tortured
conclusion, Eldridge retreated to his repository, Ral and
Leslie muttered excuses and fled. Louren asked me for the
keys of the Land-Rover and I saw him take his shotgun and
drive away towards the north, leaving Hilary and the
children to me. I took Hilary through the site museum and
she soon forgot her unhappiness in the fascination of our
exhibits.

I had carefully cleaned and polished the great battle-
axe. It glittered silver, gold and ivory, and we examined
the craftsmanship of its manufacture together before going
across to the repository of the scrolls. Sally was too busy to
talk to us. She hardly lifted her head when we entered, but
Hilary turned her gentle charisma on to Eldridge Hamilton
and he was not proof against it. When we left an hour later
Hilary had another devoted admirer.

We went up to the cavern, and sat together above the
emerald pool while the children splashed and shrieked in
the cool green water. We talked together like the old and
dear friends we were, but even then it was some time before
Hilary could bring herself to mention that which was
troubling her.

'Ben, have you noticed anything different about him?'
The old question of an unhappy woman, and I made the
old excuse for him.

'He works so hard, Hil.' And she snatched at it.

'Yes, he's been tied up in this hotel business for months.
He's building a chain of luxury vacation hotels across the

228

islands of the Indian Ocean. Comores, Seychelles, Madagascar, ten of them. He is exhausting himself.'

Then as we walked down towards the huts in the dusk, she said suddenly, 'Do you think he has found another woman, Ben?'

I was startled. 'Good Lord, Hil. What on earth makes you think that?'

'I don't know. Nothing I suppose. It's just that—' She stopped and sighed.

'Where would he find more than he has now?' I asked softly, and she took my hand and squeezed it.

'My dear Ben. What would we do without you?'

When I went to tuck Bobby up and kiss her good night, I told her what I thought of her behaviour at lunch and she snuffled a bit and said she was sorry. Then we kissed and hugged and agreed that we still loved each other. She was asleep before I had switched out the light, and with dread in my heart I went across to the common room for a repeat of the midday performance.

At the threshold I blinked with surprise. Louren, Eldridge and Sally were in a friendly and animated huddle over the typed pile of translation sheets, while Ral and Leslie were eagerly discussing their marriage plans with Hilary. The transformation was miraculous. I made my way with relief towards the Glen Grant bottle, and poured a medium-sized one.

'One for me also.' Sally came across to me. I could see no evidence of headache. Her mouth was a hectic slash of bright lipstick, and the silk dress she wore was draped to expose her strong brown back and shoulders. She had piled her hair up on her head, and I thought I had seldom seen her look so lovely.

I poured her a drink, and we went to join the discussion of the scrolls. In contrast to his earlier mood, Louren was at his most charming, and even Eldridge could not resist him.

'Professor Hamilton has done a most remarkable job here, Ben,' he greeted me. 'I can only congratulate you on your choice of a colleague.' Eldridge preened modestly.

'There is something we cannot put off much longer, Ben,' Louren went on. 'We are going to have to make an announcement soon. We can't keep this a secret much longer.'

'I know,' I agreed.

'Have you had any thoughts on it, yet?'

'Well, as a matter of fact—' I hesitated. I hate having to ask Louren to spend money. 'I was thinking of something on a rather grand scale.'

'Yes?' Louren encouraged me.

'Well, I thought if we could have the Royal Geographical Society convene a special symposium on African prehistory. Eldridge is a member of the Council, I'm sure he could arrange it.'

We looked at him, and he nodded.

'Then perhaps Sturvesant International could play host to the delegates, fly them to London and pay their expenses to make sure they all attend, or at least some of them.'

Louren threw his head back and laughed delightedly. 'You are a scheming son-of-a-gun, Ben. I see your plan exactly. You are going to get all your critics and enemies together in one bunch within the hallowed precincts of the R.G.S., and you are going to play the Al Capone of archaeology in a scientific St Valentine's day massacre. In the jargon, you are going to murder da bums. That's right, isn't it?'

I blushed at having my plans so readily exposed.

'Well,' and then I grinned sheepishly and nodded, 'I guess that's about it, Lo.'

'I love it.' Sally clapped her hands with delight. 'We will draw up a guest list.'

'We will do this in style,' Louren promised. 'We'll fly

230

them in first class and we'll put them up at the Dorchester. We'll give a champagne lunch to lull them and then we'll turn Ben and Eldridge loose amongst them like a pack of ravening wolves.' He had entered fully into the spirit of the thing and he turned to Eldridge.

'How long would it take to arrange?'

'Well, it would have to go before the Council for approval. We would have to give them some idea of the agenda, but of course your offer to pay the expenses would make it a lot easier. I will lobby a couple of the other Council members.' Eldridge was enjoying it also. There is a rather perverse thrill to be had out of planning and executing the professional assassination of one's enemies. 'I think we could arrange it for April.'

'April the first,' I suggested.

'Lovely,' laughed Louren.

'We must have Wilfred Snell,' Sally pleaded.

'He's top of the list,' I assured her.

'And that slimy little Rogers.'

'And De Vallos.'

We were still gloating and scheming when we sat down to eat the fiery curry of wild pheasant that I hoped would make the sultry night air seem cool by comparison. There were pitchers of cold draught beer to go with it, and the meal developed into a festive occasion. We were still gloating on the discomfort of our scientific enemies and planning the confrontation in detail, when Sally turned suddenly to Hilary who had been sitting quietly beside me.

'You must forgive us, Mrs Sturvesant. This must be terribly boring for you. I don't suppose a word of it makes sense to you.' Sally's tone was honeyed and solicitous. I was as surprised as Hilary, for I understand enough of the secret language of women to recognize this as an open declaration of war. I hoped that I was mistaken, but five minutes later Sally attacked again.

231

'You must find the heat and primitive conditions here most trying, Mrs Sturvesant. Not the sort of weather for your tennis parties, is it?'

The way she said it made tennis seem the pastime of a spoiled and ineffectual social butterfly. But this time Hilary was ready for her, and with a face like an angel and tones every bit as sugary as Sally's, she ripped back in a devastating counter-attack.

'I'm sure it can be most unhealthy, especially after any length of time, Dr Benator. The sun can play havoc with one's skin, can it not? And you are still looking peaky from your headache. We were very worried about you. I do hope you are feeling better now.'

Sally found that despite her gentle nunlike air, Hilary was an opponent worthy of her steel. She changed her attack. She turned all her attention onto Louren, laughing gaily at his every word and not taking her eyes from his face. Hilary was helpless in the face of these tactics. I seemed to be the only one in the party aware of this duel in progress, and I sat silently trying to puzzle out the meaning of it all – until Hilary played her trump.

'Louren, darling, it has been such a busy, exciting day. Won't you take me to bed now, please.'

She swept off the field on Louren's arm, and reluctantly I had to admit that my Sally had received the treatment she deserved.

I woke to the awareness of somebody else in my bedroom with me, and I tensed myself for sudden violent action as I rolled my head stealthily and looked towards the door. It was open. The moonlight outside was bright and clear. Sally stood in the opening.

She wore a flimsy nightdress, which did not conceal the lovely outline of her nude body against the silver moonlight. The long legs, the swelling womanly hips, the nip-in of waist and flare of breast, the long gazelle neck with tilt of dainty head.

'Ben?' she asked softly.

'Yes.' I sat up, and she came quickly to me. 'What is it, Sal?'

In reply she kissed me with open mouth and probing tongue. I was taken completely by surprise, frozen in her arms and she laid her cheek against mine. In a small gusty voice she whispered, 'Make love to me, Ben.'

There was something wrong here, desperately wrong. I felt no awakening of desire, only a warm rise of compassion for her.

'Why, Sal?' I asked. 'Why now?'

'Because I need it, Ben.'

'No, Sally. I don't think you do. I think that is the very last thing in the world you need now.'

And suddenly she was crying, big broken silent sobs. She cried for a long time, and I held her. When she was quiet I laid her on the pillow and covered her with the blankets.

'I am a bitch, aren't I, Ben?' she whispered, and went to sleep. I stayed awake all that night, watching over her. I think I knew then what was happening, but I did not want to admit it to myself.

At breakfast Louren abruptly announced that the family would return immediately to Johannesburg, rather than stay the extra day as had been originally planned. I found it hard to hide my disappointment, and when I asked Louren for a reason as soon as we were alone, he merely looked towards the heavens and shrugged with exasperation.

'You are plain lucky you never married, Ben. My God – women!'

Life at the City of the Moon returned to its normal satisfying routine for a week, during which Ral and I pursued our search for the tombs and the others worked steadily at the scrolls. Then while Ral and I sat in a sizzling midday sun under the meagre shade of a camel thorn, a little puckish figure rose from the grass seemingly at my feet.

'Sunbird,' said Xhai softly, 'I have travelled many days to seek the sunshine of your presence.' He turns the prettiest compliment, and my heart went out to him.

'Ral,' I said, 'let me have your tobacco pouch, please.'

We sat together all that afternoon under the camel thorn and we talked. The conversations of primitive Africa are an art form, with elaborate rituals of question and answer, and it was late before Xhai reached the subject which he had come to discuss.

'Does Sunbird remember the water-in-the-rock at the place where we slew the elephant?'

Sunbird remembered it well.

'Does Sunbird remember the little holes that the white ghosts made in the rock?'

Sunbird would never forget them.

'These holes gave Sunbird and the big golden one much pleasure, did they not?'

They did indeed.

'Since that day I have looked with fresh eyes upon the rocks as I hunted. Would Sunbird wish to visit another place where there are many such holes?'

Would I!

'I will lead you there,' Xhai promised.

'And I will give you as much tobacco as you can carry away,' I promised him in return, and we beamed at each other.

'How far is this place?' I asked, and he began to explain. It was beyond the 'big wire' he told me. This was the 300-mile-long game fence along the Rhodesia border which was erected to control movements of the wild animals as a precaution against foot and mouth disease. We would need

234

clearance from the Rhodesians, and when Xhai went on to describe an area which seemed fairly close to the Zambezi river border with Zambia, I knew I would have to ask Louren to arrange an expedition. It was obviously squarely within the zone of terrorist activity.

Xhai refused to accompany me back to a camp which was filled with his traditional enemies, the Bantu. Instead we arranged to meet under the camel thorn three days later, once Xhai had completed the rounds of his trap line.

I was fortunate enough that evening to find Louren had returned an hour before from Madagascar.

'What's the trouble, Ben?' His voice boomed above the radio static.

'No trouble, Lo. Your little bushman friend has found another ancient gold working site. He's happy to take me to it.'

'That's great, Ben. The elephant mine is in production already, and looking very good indeed.'

'There is only one problem, Lo. It's in Rhodesia, in the closed area.'

'No problem, Ben. I'll fix it.' And the following evening we spoke again.

'It's set up for Monday week. There will be a Rhodesian police escort to meet us at the Panda Matenga border gate.'

'Us?' I asked.

'I'm stealing a couple of days off, Ben. Just couldn't resist it. You take the bushman with you, go by Land-Rover through to Panda Matenga. I will come in from Bulawayo by helicopter. See you there. Monday week, morning, okay?'

The commander of the police escort was one of those beefy, boyish young Rhodesians with impeccable manners, and an air of quiet competence which I found most reassuring. He was an assistant inspector with an askari sergeant and five constables under him. His rank and the composition of the escort gave me some indication of the level to which Louren had applied for cooperation.

We had two Land-Rovers, both with mounted medium machine-guns on the bonnet, and the armament of the rest of the party was impressive, as was to be expected on the borders of a country subjected to unceasing harassment by terrorist infiltrators from the north.

'Dr Kazin.' The inspector saluted and we shook hands. 'My name's MacDonald. Alaistair MacDonald. May I introduce my men?'

They were Matabeles, all of them. The big moon-faced descendants of Chaka's fighting impis, led here 150 years ago by the renegade general, Mzilikazi. They were dressed in camouflage fatigues with soft jungle hats, and they stood to rigid attention as MacDonald led me down the single rank.

'This is Sergeant Ndabuka.' And when I acknowledged the introduction in fluent Sindebele, the stern military expressions dissolved into huge flashing smiles.

Xhai was obviously very ill at ease in this company. He followed on my heels like a puppy.

'Did you know, Doctor, that there is still a field order issued to the British South Africa Police that hasn't been rescinded,' MacDonald told me, as he looked Xhai over with interest. 'It is an instruction to shoot all bushmen on sight. This is the first one I've ever seen. Poor little blighters.'

'Yes.' I had heard of that order which was maintained as a curiosity, but too faithfully reflected the attitude of the last century. The time of the great bushmen hunts, when a hundred mounted men would band together into a commando to hunt and kill these little yellow pixies as though they were dangerous animals.

White and black had hunted them mercilessly. The atrocities committed against them were legion. Shot and speared – and worse. In 1869 King Khama had enticed a whole tribe of them to a feast of reconciliation, and while they sat at his board, with their weapons laid aside, his warriors seized them. The king had supervised the subsequent torture personally. The last bushman died on the fourth day. With this history to remember it was no wonder that Xhai stayed within arm's length of me, and watched these colossal strangers with frightened Chinese eyes.

I explained to MacDonald our approximate destination, pointing out the general area on his map as accurately as I could reckon it from Xhai's description, and the inspector looked grave. He picked a shred of sun-burned skin from the tip of his nose before replying.

'That's not a very good area, Doctor.' And he went off to talk to his men.

It was midday before the helicopter came clattering over the tree-tops from the south-east. Louren jumped from the cabin lugging his own bag.

'Sorry I'm late, Ben. I had to wait for a phone call from New York.'

MacDonald came forward and touched his cap-brim.

'Afternoon, sir.' His attitude was deferential. 'The prime minister asked me to give you his respects, Mr Sturvesant, and I am to place myself at your disposal.'

We left the track before we reached the ranching country near Tete, and we swung away northwards towards the Zambezi. MacDonald was in the leading Land-Rover with a driver and a trooper on the machine-gun. We followed in the central spot, Louren driving and another trooper riding shotgun in the passenger seat, Xhai and I together in the back. The second police Land-Rover took the rearguard with Sergeant Ndabuka in command.

The slow miles ground past, as the column wound through forests of mopane, and climbed the low ranges of granite. At any hesitation in our advance, Xhai's arm would signal the direction and we would move forward, jolting and pitching over the rough places or humming swiftly through open glades of brown grass. I realized that Xhai was guiding us along the elephant trail, the migratory road that the huge beasts had beaten out from the river to the sanctuary of the Wankie game reserve in the south. Skilled trail blazers, they had picked a route that required the minimum effort to negotiate. Always it was the easy gradient, the low pass through the hills, and the river drifts with gentle sloping banks that they chose.

We camped beside one of these drifts. The river-bed was dry, choked with polished black boulders that glittered like reptiles in the sunset. There were banks of sugar-white sand, patches of tall reeds and a pool of slimy green water overhung with the branches of fever trees.

Beyond the river the ground rose steeply in another of those rocky ridges dotted with marula trees and patches of scrub. However, on this side the bush was open, offering a clear field of fire around our camp. MacDonald drew the three vehicles into a defensive triangle, and while he placed his sentries, Louren and I, followed by Xhai, went down the bank to the pool.

We sat on the rocks and watched a colony of yellow weaver birds chattering and fluttering around their nests of woven grass that hung from the fever trees over the green water.

Louren gave Xhai a cigar, and while we talked the little bushman's eyes never left our faces, like those of a faithful dog. The talk was fitful, changing from one subject to

238

another without design. Louren told me about the hotel project on the islands. He was very certain of its success.

'It's one of my really good ones, Ben.' And when I thought about his other good ones – the cattle ranches, the diamond mines, gold, chrome and copper – I knew how big it must be.

I touched lightly on his difficulties with Hilary.

'My God, Ben. If only they understood that they don't buy you with the marriage certificate!' There were three others who had found that out the hard way, I hoped that Hilary would not be the fourth.

It was almost dark when MacDonald came down the bank.

'Excuse me, Mr Sturvesant. Could I ask you to come into the perimeter now. I don't like taking unnecessary chances.' And with good grace Louren flicked the stub of his cigar into the pool, and stood up.

'This used to be a country where a man could range to the full extent of his fancy. Times are changing, Ben.'

When we entered the camp there was coffee brewing on a low screened fire, and while we sipped from the steaming mugs I saw the precautions MacDonald had taken for our safety and I realized that his competent looks were not deceiving. He finished his sentry rounds and came to sit with us.

'I should have asked you sooner, but do you gentlemen know how to use the FN rifle and the 60-calibre machine-gun?' Louren and I both told him we did.

'Good.' MacDonald looked out towards the north. 'The closer we get to the border the more chance there is of a clash. There has been a big step-up in the terrorist activity recently. Something brewing up there.'

He poured a mug of coffee and sipped before he asked:

'Well, gentlemen, what are your plans for tomorrow? How far are we from our destination?'

I looked at Xhai. 'How far is it to the holes in the rock, my brother?'

'We will be there before the sun stands so,' indicating noon with one delicate little hand, 'my people are camped at the waterhole near the holes in the rock. We will go there to find them first, for they have long awaited my coming.'

I stared at him, realizing for the first time the extent of Xhai's friendship. Then I turned to Louren. 'Do you realize, Lo, that this little devil had made a trek of 150 miles on foot merely to tell us something that might give us pleasure.'

'What do you mean?'

'As soon as he discovered the old workings he left his tribe and set off to find me.'

That night Xhai slept between Louren and me. He still didn't trust the big Matabele troopers one little bit.

It was eleven o'clock the following morning when we saw the vultures in the northern sky. MacDonald halted the column, and came back to our vehicle.

'Something up ahead. Probably only a lion kill, but we had better not take any chances.'

Xhai slipped off the seat and clambered up onto the roof of the Land-Rover. For a minute he watched the distant birds, then he came down to me.

'My people have killed a large animal. Perhaps even a buffalo, for the birds are above my camp. There is nothing to fear. Let us go forward.'

I translated for MacDonald, and he nodded.

'Okay, Doctor. But we'll keep our eyes peeled all the same.'

The bushmen had erected five rude shelters beside a hole of mud and filthy water. They had merely bent a number of saplings inwards to form the framework, and then thatched it roughly with leaves and grass. There was no smoke and no sign of the little yellow people as we

240

drove towards the encampment. Xhai was looking puzzled, darting little birdlike glances into the thick bush, and whistling softly through his teeth. The vultures sat in the tree-tops all around the camp, and as we approached there was a sudden commotion from amongst the huts and twenty or thirty of the big ugly birds flapped into the air.

Xhai let out a soft wailing cry. I did not understand what had happened, it merely seemed odd that the vultures were on the ground amongst the huts, but Xhai had guessed it. He began rocking slowly on the seat, hugging his chest and emitting that low-pitched wail.

MacDonald stopped his Land-Rover and climbed out. He stooped over something on the ground, then he straightened up and shouted an order. His troopers jumped from the vehicle and spread out with their weapons held ready. Louren parked our Land-Rover and we went to where MacDonald was standing amongst the huts. Xhai remained in the back seat, still rocking and wailing.

For the Bantu the bushman girls are an object of peculiar lust. I do not know why this should be so, perhaps it is their golden yellow colour, or it may be their tiny doll-like bodies. They had raped Xhai's women, all of them, even the little immature girls. Then they had bayoneted them and left them lying in that pathetically vulnerable attitude of love. Ghal and the other two males they had shot. Bursts of automatic fire had smashed their bodies so that slivers and chips of bone protruded from the mangled flesh. The blood had dried in black splashes and puddles. There were flies everywhere, big green metallic flies that buzzed like hiving bees and came to settle on my lips and eyes. I struck them away angrily. The birds had been at the bodies; that was the truly horrible part of it, the birds.

'God,' said Louren. 'Oh God. Why? Why did they do it?'

'It's their style,' MacDonald answered. 'Frelimo, Mau Mau, all of them hit their own people hardest.'

241

'But why?' repeated Louren.

'They've got guns. They want to use them. This is easier than going for white ranchers or police posts.' Two of the police troopers carried a tarpaulin from one of the Land-Rovers. They began wrapping the bodies. I walked back to our vehicle and leaned against the door. Suddenly I was sick, an acid bitter flood gushing up my throat, and I retched painfully.

When I was finished I wiped my mouth on my sleeve and looked up to find Xhai watching me. He was a man deprived of everything except the breath of life. There was such agony in those dark eyes, such sorrow twisted that mouth that I felt my own heart breaking for him.

'Let us find who has done this thing, Sunbird,' he whispered, and he led me into the short grass around the camp. He worked quickly, like a gundog.

There were spills of the bright brass cartridge cases scattered on the sandy earth. Shoddily manufactured, and stamped with Chinese characters, hundreds of them. The gunners had fired with childish gusto, pouring a torrent of bullets into the camp. Their boots had left the character-istic chevron-patterned imprints. There seemed to be hundreds of them, for the earth was churned and the grass flattened.

'They came in the night,' Xhai explained softly. 'See! Here is where they waited.' He pointed to the scuffed places amongst the bushes. 'There were many of them.' And he showed both his hands with fingers spread, three times. Thirty of them. A big party. 'They struck in the dawn. Yesterday at dawn.' Thirty-two hours ago. They would be miles away now, I realized. When we returned to the encampment the nine bodies were wrapped in canvas and laid out in a neat line, like parcels ready for posting. Four of the troopers were digging a shallow communal grave.

Xhai went to squat beside the line of dead. He was silent

242

now, and the silence was more distressing than his despairing wail. Once he leaned forward and timidly touched one of the green canvas-wrapped bundles. How many of these little men had squatted like this in the sun to mourn the massacre of their tribe, I wondered. It is at times such as this that I hate the savage ferocity of this land of ours. I could not watch Xhai's grief and I turned away and went to where Louren and MacDonald stood together talking quietly.

'It's a big party, Ben,' Louren greeted me as I came up.

'Xhai says there are thirty of them,' I told him, and he nodded.

'Very likely. The inspector feels we should turn back, and I reckon I agree with him.'

MacDonald explained, 'Should we run into them, they outnumber us heavily, Doctor. These swine are well trained and armed with the most modern weapons. It's not like a few years ago when they sent in a half-baked rabble. They are really dangerous now, and we aren't an offensive patrol. I think we must get out as quickly as possible, and call in the helicopters. Once they locate them the Hunter jets will give them a whiff of napalm.'

'Yes,' I agreed. The ancient workings were no longer important in the face of this horror. I looked across to where the troopers were lifting the bundles down into the grave. Xhai stood watching them. When the grave was filled with loose earth I went across to Xhai and placed an arm around his shoulder.

'Come, little brother,' I said and led him to the Land-Rover. The column turned and in the same order made its way back into the south.

The journey slowly developed into a nightmare of tension and straining nerves. The revving and gear-changing that was necessary to negotiate the rough and broken ground broadcast our progress far ahead of us. Every mile there was a location ideal for an ambush, with thick cover pressing in closely on either hand. Our trail was laid clearly, and we must follow it on our return. They would know this and wait for us there. It was possible they carried landmines and we watched anxiously for disturbed earth in the trail ahead. The strain was on all of us. Louren drove in grim silence, with an unlit stub of cigar rolling restlessly in the corner of his mouth.

The trooper behind him rode with the butt of the machine-gun pulled into his shoulder, and occasionally he traversed the heavy weapon experimentally. All our heads moved constantly, swinging slowly from side to side, searching, searching.

'Have you noticed there is no sign of game, Ben?' Louren asked suddenly. He was correct. Since leaving the bushman encampment we had seen none of the wildlife which had enlivened our outward journey, not even a herd of the dainty brown impala.

'I don't like it, Lo.'

'Join the club,' Louren grunted.

'In thirty-two hours the bastards could have moved miles. They could be anywhere.' I fiddled restlessly with the rate of fire selector on the rifle in my lap. MacDonald had insisted on us taking the spare weapons from two of the troopers on the heavy machine-guns. I was glad of it now. There was much comfort to be drawn from that hunk of wood and steel.

Suddenly the Land-Rover ahead of us skidded to a halt, and Louren slammed on his own brakes and snatched the automatic rifle from the bracket behind him. We sat with our weapons poised, peering into the wilderness of rock and scrub around us. Waiting for the sudden shuddering roar of machine-guns. The slow seconds passed and my own pulse drummed in my ears deafening me.

'Sorry,' MacDonald called from up front. 'False alarm!'

The engines revved, hideously loud in the vast silence of Africa, and we went on.

244

'For Christ's sake stop fiddling with that bloody thing!' Louren snapped at me with unnecessary violence. I had not realized that I had been clicking the selector of the rifle.

'Sorry,' I muttered guiltily. The tension was infectious. Louren's outburst was a symptom of it, but almost immediately he glanced over his shoulder and grinned apologetically.

'This is bloody murder.'

It seemed hours later that we crossed a ridge and went twisting down amongst the trees to the pool in the dry water-course where we had camped the previous night. MacDonald signalled the column to a halt on the far bank, and he came back to us.

'We will top up the fuel tanks here, Mr Sturvesant. I'll see to that. Will you take a party down to the pool and refill the water containers.'

Louren went down the bank with two of the troopers lugging the five-gallon jerry cans while I watched Mac-Donald begin refuelling. The gasoline fumes swirled like a mirage in the heat, and the smell was biting in my throat. One of the troopers splashed the liquid in a spurt down the side of the lead vehicle and MacDonald reprimanded him sharply.

'Stay here,' I told Xhai. 'Do not move.' And he nodded at me from the back seat of the Land-Rover.

I left him and followed Louren down to the edge of the pool. It was a tranquil scene, so typical in Africa. Tall reeds languidly drooping their fluffy heads, black mud, pocked with the hooves of a thousand beasts, water green and thick with slime bubbling sulkily with marsh gas, the weaver birds hanging upside down below their swinging basket nests. The two troopers were talking quietly as they filled the jerry cans, Louren standing over them with the automatic rifle.

'Another hour's travel will see us in the clear,' he

remarked as I joined him. He took a cigar from his top pocket and began unwrapping it without interrupting his search of the surrounding trees and brush.

There was a fleck of white on the rocks at the water's edge. It caught my eye and I glanced at it, and was about to dismiss it as a splash of bird droppings. Then I noticed something else, and I felt the first cool draught of apprehension blow down my spine. Casually I strolled along the edge of the pool averting my eyes from the white object until it was at my feet. Then I glanced down, and my breath jammed in my throat. My first impulse was to scream a warning to Louren and run for the Land-Rover, but I controlled the urge and forced myself to look away casually. Despite the racing of my heart and the difficulty I had in breathing I managed to stoop and pick up a pebble from the water's edge and toss it out into the pool where it fell with a plop in a widening ring of ripples. Quickly I glanced down again.

The white fleck was a piece of domestic soap, with a wet lacework of bubbles still frothing around it. There were damp marks on the rocks, that the sizzling sun had not yet dried, and in the mud at the water's edge, amongst all the thousands of hoof marks was a print. A strange half-human print, like that of a giant bird. The big toes deeply divided from the rest of the foot, split half-way back to the heel, and I knew that Timothy Mageba was watching me over the sights of an automatic weapon.

My skin prickled as from the stings of the myriad insects of fear. They crawled over my body and along the strings of my nerves. Slowly I walked back to Louren. The cigar was in his mouth and he struck a match as I approached. It flared in a puff of blue nitrous smoke in his cupped hands, and he bowed over it.

'Lo,' I said softly. 'Don't do anything suddenly. Behave as naturally as you can. They are here. Right here, watching us.'

He puffed four times then waved the match to extinguish it, and he looked around naturally.

'Where?' he asked.

'I don't know, but they are very close. We must show ourselves here until Mac is ready.'

'Tell the troopers,' Lo said.

The troopers were recapping the jerry cans, and as they moved back past us I stopped them.

'Go very gently. Do not run. Do not look behind you. The evil ones are here. Go to the inspector. Tell him to start the engines, when we hear them we will come running.'

They nodded, expressionlessly, understanding immediately, and I knew then why these were famed as the finest native troops in Africa. They went calmly up the bank, leaning away from the weight of the jerry cans.

'I feel like one of those little mechanical ducks in a shooting gallery,' I said, and tried to smile. It hung all crookedly on my face. 'What are they waiting for?' I asked.

'They probably didn't have time to set it up properly.' Louren laughed, a very good effort. It rang convincingly. 'They'll be moving into position now. Then they wait until we are all together in a bunch, not spread out like this.'

'God, I wish I knew where they are, where to expect it to come from.'

'What tipped you?' Louren asked, anything to keep this conversation flowing naturally.

'Piece of soap, and wet footprints on the rocks. They were bathing when they heard us coming.'

Louren tapped ash from his cigar, and glanced at the rocks, seeing the soap. Then his eyes flicked back to me. Above the bank we heard the starters whirring loudly in the silence, and then the engines running steadily. One, two, and the third one.

Louren ground the fresh cigar into the mud at the edge

247

of the pool, then turned to me. He let his hand fall onto my shoulder.

'All the way, partner?' he asked.

'All the way, Lo.' And we whirled together and went for the path up the bank, unslinging the rifles as we ran. I felt a lift of relief, the waiting was over. It had begun.

I had the strange sensation of not moving, of marking time, rather than running. The climb up the bank seemed endless, my feet dragged leadenly and a hot hushed silence persisted in which the engines of the Land-Rovers seemed muted, but our footsteps pounded like stampeding hooves.

We came out on top of the bank.

Sergeant Ndabuka was at the wheel of our vehicle swinging in towards us, slowing for the pick up.

The other two Land-Rovers were backing up, ready to cover us, turning for the path with the gunners traversing the heavy machine-guns.

'Jump!' shouted MacDonald. 'Let's hit out!'

I leapt for the side of the Land-Rover and Louren piled in beside me.

'Go!' he snapped urgently at the sergeant. The engine roared and we surged forward. From the moment when we started to run to the moment we boarded the speeding vehicle perhaps six seconds had elapsed. It had all gone very quickly, and I scrambled onto my knees, pushing the automatic rifle forward to cover one flank. In that instant they opened on us. The air around me was torn by the sound of a thousand bull whips, while the gunfire sounded like a stick dragged swiftly across a corrugated-iron fence.

MacDonald's vehicle was leading us out, back along our tracks. It was drawing fire also. I saw the gunner hit. His head snapping backwards as though from a heavy punch and his hat flying from his head. He collapsed over the seat, his untended weapon spiralling idly on its mounting.

They were below the river bank, lining it, hidden in the

reeds and scrub there. I saw the muzzle flashes, glinting like swords. I let off a burst, swinging on them, but with the Land-Rover bucking I was low. Dust flew in a line below the bank as though churned up by a whiplash. I corrected my aim and fired, the weapon shuddering in my hands. Seeing the reeds shake and tremble as my bullets raked them. Someone screamed, a thin passionless sound, and my weapon clicked empty.

I snatched for a fresh magazine, looking ahead, to estimate how much longer we must receive fire. MacDonald was just entering the forest, there were big trees on either side of the path indicating the passage. I saw the loose earth in the path ahead of MacDonald swept neatly, and I knew then why they had held their fire until it served to drive us into the trap.

I opened my mouth to scream a warning, but it was lost in the continuous clamour of gunfire and engine roar.

MacDonald hit the landmines they had laid for us across our old tracks and the detonation was a burst of bright white light that seared the retina of the eye. The concussion slammed painfully into my eardrums, and Mac-Donald's Land-Rover reared like a wounded lion. Its front end was smashed in, one of the wheels spinning lazily through the air. It toppled backwards, crushing the occupants beneath it. The second Land-Rover drove into it at thirty miles an hour. There was a rending screeching sound of metal as the two came together.

'Look out!' shouted Louren and the sergeant swung the wheel violently to avoid colliding with the mass of wrecked vehicles. Our Land-Rover hung over on two wheels, then flopped over on its side. We were thrown out on to the rocky earth.

There was a silence that lasted for three or four seconds. A stunned silence, even the enemy frozen by the sudden-ness of the havoc they had created. We were perhaps fifty yards from the river-bed where Timothy's men lay. The intervening ground was sparsely studded with fever trees. These and the bodies of the vehicles gave us a little cover.

I had lost my rifle and as I groped for it I found Xhai huddled next to me. I had one glimpse at his terrified face, as I crawled towards Louren.

'Are you all right?'

For answer he pointed. 'Look!' Twenty feet away Alaistair MacDonald lay on his back with the full weight of the Land-Rover lying across his pelvis. He was pushing the mass of metal with weak fluttering hands. He moaned then softly.

I stood up to go to him, and at that moment the guns opened again. Flailing us, rattling and clanging against the Land-Rovers, lashing billows of dust and storms of stone fragments, ricocheting with the sound of tearing silk – and Louren dragged me down.

I was aware of movement beside me and as I turned towards it little Xhai wailed softly like a restless baby. I put out my hand to calm him, but my touch galvanized him. He jumped to his feet, his dark amber eyes ablaze with terror, and he ran.

'Wait, little brother,' I shouted, and I scrambled up to follow him. Louren grabbed and held me and I watched as Xhai ran out into that hell storm.

He drew all their fire immediately. They hunted him, hosing bullets at him. He ran like a rabbit caught in a car's headlights, making no attempt to hide. I struggled in Louren's grip.

'No!' I shouted. 'Leave him! No! No!' And they hit him, knocking him down so he rolled across the stony earth like a small brown ball. He came up on his feet again, still running but his left arm was shot away above the elbow, holding only by a tatter of wet flesh, and it bounced loosely against his flank. They hit him again, squarely this time, between the shoulder-blades and he went down hard and skidded on his face. He lay very still and small in the harsh white sunlight. I was quiet in Louren's grip, while around me the surviving troopers crawled into position to return the enemy fire. Louren rolled away from me, lying prone and fired a burst around the tailboard of the overturned Land-Rover.

The storm of bullets returned to sweep over us, and MacDonald was still moaning. Nobody could reach him across that bullet-swept space. I knelt on the hard earth staring at Xhai's frail little body, and I felt the hot winds of my rage blow through my soul. They came from deep and far, crescendoed and overwhelmed my reason.

I jumped up and ran to the mined Land-Rover, I tore the pin from the mounting and hefted the heavy machine-gun out of its seating. Then I threw four loops of the cartridge-belt over my shoulders, draping myself with death as though it were an Hawaiian lei. Then, with my gun on my hip, I went after them, running towards the river-bed, straight at the centre of their line.

I heard myself screaming, and the violent disruption of the air around me as shot passed close, buffeted my ears and fanned my face with a hot dry wind. I ran screaming and the gun shook my body as though it were a giant fist. The spent cartridge cases spewed from the breech in a glittering stream, ringing like silver bells as they bounced off the stony earth. I saw the lip of the bank dissolve in spurting, swirling clouds of dust as I traversed it, saw one of them hit and flung backwards.

Their fire was shrivelling, I saw movement in the reeds as they ran. One of them leapt to his feet and fired a burst. Beside me slabs of white bark exploded from the trunk of a fever tree, and I swivelled the gun onto him. He was in camouflage battledress, a pudding-basin helmet of steel on his head, and he crouched over his weapon, the muzzle winked its hot red eye at me and I wondered that it could miss me at such close range.

251

One of my bullets caught him in the mouth, spinning his helmet away and the contents of his skull blew out of the back of his head in a pink cloud. He dropped below the bank.

'Follow him! Cover him!' I heard Louren yelling somewhere behind me, but I did not care. I reached the bank of the river and looked down into the dry bed. They were running, panicky, for the far bank and I turned the gun on them. Watching as they fell, with the white sand dancing in sudden soft fountains amongst them. I was still screaming.

The last loop of cartridges flipped off my shoulder and fed into the hungry breech of my weapon. The gun went dead and useless in my hands, and I hurled it after them. Rage and sorrow had driven me far beyond the boundaries of reason and fear. I stood unarmed and unafraid and from the far bank Timothy Mageba turned back towards me. He had a pistol in his right fist, and he aimed at me. I felt the passage of the bullet close beside my head.

'Murderer!' I screamed, and he fired again, twice. It was as though the angels of death had draped their wings around me, shielding me, for I did not even hear the bullets. I saw him glaring at me, those terrible smoky eyes, the great cannon-ball head like that of some wounded beast at bay.

Then suddenly Louren was beside me, he threw up his rifle and snapped a shot at Timothy. I think Louren may have nicked him, for I saw him wince and stagger slightly, but then he was gone into the thick scrub that covered the high ground on the far bank. The police troopers went past us, moving forward in line of skirmishers down the bank and across the river-bed where the dead men lay. They fired a few rounds into the bush, then Louren called them back.

Louren turned to stare at me with a look of disbelief. 'They didn't touch you,' he said with wonder. 'Not a single bullet – my God, Ben, my God!' He shook his head. 'You frightened me, you crazy bastard. You frightened the hell out of me.' He put his arm around my shoulder and led me back to the vehicles.

MacDonald was still moaning softly. We lifted the side of the Land-Rover, Louren and I between us. MacDonald screamed as the troopers drew him out from under the vehicle. His legs were twisted at an odd angle and his face was very pale, his tan a dirty brown over it and little beads of sweat dewed his upper lip.

I left Louren to administer morphine and try to splint the badly shattered bone, and I went across to where Xhai still lay.

The entry hole was a blue-black pucker in the centre of his back, there was no bleeding from it. Yet he lay in a puddle of thick gelatinous blood, and I knew what hideous damage the exit of the bullet from his chest must have caused. I did not turn him over. I could not bring myself to do it, but his head was twisted sideways and I squatted beside him. With my finger-tips I closed the lids over those staring Chinese eyes.

'Go in peace, little brother,' I whispered.

'Come on, Ben. They'll be back. We must hurry,' Louren called.

Two of our troopers were dead, and the sergeant rolled them in their blankets.

'The bushman also,' I told him. He hesitated, but then he saw my expression and went quickly.

We rolled the third vehicle back onto its wheels and while the troopers lifted our dead and wounded aboard, Louren and I checked it out. Two of the tyres were shot through, the petrol tank was riddled, the steering box was severed by a bullet and another had shattered the engine sump cover. Oil poured from it, stinking in the heat.

Quickly Louren placed the sergeant and the three remaining troopers in a defensive perimeter amongst the fever trees and we pushed the crippled Land-Rover into the lee of the wrecked vehicles, giving ourselves some cover to work behind.

There was a tool box in MacDonald's Land-Rover. We changed the wheels as quickly as a pair of Grand Prix mechanics, cannibalizing from the wrecks. As we tightened the last wheel bolts the sniping began. It was long range, from the far ridge a quarter of a mile away. They had learned their lesson well, and kept a respectful distance now. Our troopers answered, blazing away with the two heavy machine-guns to discourage them further.

In the middle of a fire fight Louren and I worked, greasy to the elbows. Smearing skin from knuckles on sharp steel in our haste, burning blisters into our skin on the red-hot manifold and exhaust system.

We pulled the sump cover off the capsized Land-Rover, and lay on our backs with hot oil dripping into our faces as we bolted it back onto our vehicle. The gasket was worn, it would leak, but it would hold oil long enough to get us clear.

Louren changed the steering-box, while I found a cake of soap in my pack and plugged the bullet holes in the fuel tank. As we worked, I blessed the Chinese artisans who had manufactured those shoddy weapons on the far ridge, with their limited range and accuracy.

We refuelled and replaced the engine oil, standing by necessity fully exposed to the marksmen on the hill, forcing ourselves to work methodically and trying to shut from our ears the terrifying sound of passing shot.

Louren jumped into the driver's seat, and pressed the starter; it whirled dismally, on and on, and I closed my eyes tight and prayed. Louren released the starter button and in the silence I heard him swearing with bitter vehemence. He tried again, the battery was weakening now, the whirring of the engine slowed and faltered.

A stray bullet smashed the windscreen, spraying us with

glittering glass fragments. Louren was still swearing. In despair I glanced at the setting sun, only half an hour or so of daylight left. In the darkness the hyenas would come down from the ridge. As though they had read my thoughts the fire from up there intensified. I heard a bullet whine away off the metal of the Land-Rover. Louren jumped out of the driver's seat and opened the bonnet again. As he worked I shouted across to Ndabuka.

'Why aren't you firing, Sergeant? You are letting them have target practice. Keep their heads down, dammit!'

'The ammunition is almost finished, sir,' he called back, and a coldness closed about my guts. No ammunition, and darkness coming on fast.

Louren slammed the bonnet closed, and ducked back into the driver's seat. He looked at me through the shattered windscreen.

'Say another prayer, Ben. The last one was no damned good.' And he pressed the starter. It wheezed wearily but the engine would not turn.

'We've had it, Ben,' Louren told me. 'Both the other batteries are *kaput*.'

'Sergeant – all of you. Shove,' I shouted. 'Come on, help me.'

They ran to me at the rear of the Land-Rover.

'Try her in second,' I shouted at Louren, and a burst of bullets kicked around my legs, stinging them with fragments of stone.

We threw our combined weight on the Land-Rover and it bumped over rough ground, back towards the river.

'Now,' I shouted at Louren. The Land-Rover juddered and slowed and we hurled ourselves against it, keeping it moving against compression.

It fired once. 'Keep going!' I gasped. And abruptly the engine roared into life and we howled with triumph.

'Climb on,' Louren yelled and swung the Land-Rover back towards the trail, but I ran beside him.

'Matches!' I panted.

'What?'

'Give me your matches, damn you.' I snatched them from his hand and ran to the tangled wreckage. Gasoline was dribbling from one of the ruptured tanks and I flicked a match at it. The sucking, roaring torrent of flame licked across my face, singeing my eyelashes away, and I turned and ran after the Land-Rover, scrambling in over the tailboard, falling face forward onto the pile of dead and wounded men in the back.

Louren smashed a new route through a belt of scrub thorn, avoiding the mined trail, and then angled back to pick it up further out.

The firing from the ridge died away as the forest blanketed us. I watched the column of black sooty smoke climbing up into the flushed evening sky, pleased that I had denied them the spoils of victory, and suddenly I found myself shaking like a man in high fever. Icy waves of shock and reaction engulfed me.

'Are you all right, Ben?' Louren called to me.

'Yes, I'm fine,' I answered and looked down at the pathetic blanket-wrapped bundles at my feet.

All that night we crawled southwards, jolting and bumping over the rough ground, often losing the track and having to search for it, shivering in the cold of an African night when the wind blew through the shattered windscreen.

In a dawn that was grape-purple and smoky blue I asked Louren to stop the Land-Rover. The troopers helped me to dig a shallow grave in the sandy bottom land between two kopjes. I lifted Xhai out of the Land-Rover still wrapped in the dark grey police blanket and he was as light as a sleeping child in my arms. I laid him in the earth and we stood around in a circle and looked down at him. Blood had soaked through the blanket and dried in a black stain.

I nodded to the troopers. 'All right. Cover him.' They did it quickly and went back to the Land-Rover. It was still cold, and I shivered in my thin cotton shirt. Up on the kopjes an old bull baboon barked, his cry boomed across the valley.

I followed the troopers back to the Land-Rover and climbed up beside them. As we drove on I looked back, and saw a herd of buffalo moving down out of the bush. They were grazing, heads down and tails swinging towards Xhai's grave. This was where my brother belonged, with the animals in the wilderness he loved.

'I'm very much afraid that they have slipped back across the river,' the assistant commissioner of police told me. 'There is nothing we would have liked more than to get our hands on this fellow Mageba.'

We had flown out with MacDonald in the police helicopter to Bulawayo two days before. Louren had left me to help the Rhodesian police as best I could while he sent for the Lear and went on direct to Johannesburg. Now I was having a final debriefing at police headquarters, while a charter flight stood by to take me back to the City of the Moon.

The assistant commissioner was a tall man with a military set to his shoulders, and a brush of closely cropped grey hair. His face was seamed and furrowed and burned darkly by a thousand suns. There were ribbons on his chest that I recognized, the emblems of courage and honour.

'He is top of our list of the chaps we'd like to meet, actually. A nasty piece of work, but then you'd know that as well as anybody.' And he turned those steely grey eyes onto me, giving me the feeling that I was being interrogated.

'I know him,' I agreed. My part in the hi-jacking incident was common knowledge.

'What do you make of the man?'

'He is an intelligent man, and he has a presence. There is something about him.' I tried to find the words to describe him. 'He's the type of man who sets out to get what he wants, and the type that other men will follow.'

'Yes,' the assistant commissioner nodded. 'That's a fair summation of our own intelligence. Since he joined them there has been an escalation of hostile activity from our friends across the river.' He sighed, and massaged his iron-grey temples. 'I thought we might have got him this time. They left their dead unburied, and made a run for the river. We could only have missed them by minutes.'

He walked down with me to where a police car waited under the jacaranda trees with their clouds of purple blossoms.

'What news have you of MacDonald?' I asked as we stood beside the police car.

'He will be all right. They saved both legs.'

'I am glad.'

'Yes,' agreed the assistant commissioner. 'He is a good type. Wish we had more of them. By the way, Doctor, we would rather you kept mum about this business. We don't like to make too much fuss about these incidents. Rather playing into their hands, you know. Gives them the publicity they want.'

We shook hands and he turned and strode back into the building. As we drove through the busy streets and I saw the smiles on the faces around me I wondered why anybody should want to destroy this society – and if they succeeded, with what would they replace it?

It seemed natural to think then of the City of the Moon.

A great civilization, a nation which held dominion over an area the size of Europe, a people who built great cities of stone and sent their ships in trade to the limits of the known world. All that remained of them were the few poor relics which we had so laboriously gleaned. No other continent was so fickle in the succour it gave to men, to raise them up so swiftly and then to pluck them down and devour them so that they were denied even a place in her memory. A cruel land, a savage and merciless land. It was a wonder that so many of us loved her so deeply.

My return to the City of the Moon was disappointing. After the events of the last few days it was an anticlimax. It seemed that the others had hardly noticed my absence.

'Did you enjoy yourself?' Sally asked over the typewriter and a pile of translation sheets.

'Well, it was interesting.'

'That's good. What happened to your eyelashes?' she asked and without waiting for an answer began pounding the keyboard with two fingers, biting her tongue with concentration, pausing only to push her hair off her cheek with the back of one hand.

'Glad you are back, Ben,' said Eldridge Hamilton. 'I've been wanting to talk to you about this.' And he led me to a table on which a portion of one of the scrolls was spread. I didn't seem to be able to concentrate. Suddenly, for the first time in my life I felt that it was ancient and unimportant compared with the blood that I so recently had seen spurt fresh and red.

Ral and Leslie had obviously used my absence to scheme out an approach. Ral spoke for both of them, with Leslie prompting him when he faltered. 'So you see, Doctor, we don't feel it's right to marry until at least one of us has a steady job. So, well, we thought we'd sort of ask your advice. I mean we love it here, both of us. We'd like to stay on, but we'd also like to get married. It's just that, well, we've got such a high opinion of you, Doctor. We wouldn't like to miss the rest of the investigation, but—'

I spoke to Louren that evening and then called them from the supper table.

'The job is worth three and a half thousand, and Leslie will get two. Of course, there is a free flat at the Institute and I'll help you with the furnishing, as a wedding present.'

Leslie kissed Ral, and then me. A novel way in which to accept the offer of employment, I felt.

Ral threw himself into the search of the cliffs with renewed energy, but I spent little time with him. Instead, I began to prepare my address to the Royal Geographical Society. This should have been a labour of love and excitement, but I found myself floundering. There was so much detail in the scrolls, but all of it seemed irrelevant to those unanswerable questions: where did they come from and when, where did they go to, and why?

Each time, my efforts became so long-winded and convoluted that they bored even me. Then I would rip the sheets from my typewriter, ball them and hurl them at the wall. There is no more lonely place in the world than a blank sheet of paper, and it frightened me that my unruly emotions should intrude and prevent me marshalling my thoughts and facts in orderly ranks. I told myself that it was reaction from the horrors of our journey to the north, that Sally's enigmatic behaviour was worrying me deeply, that it was merely the fear of the imminent confrontation with my enemies.

I tried all the tricks, forcing myself to sit at the typewriter until I had completed 10,000 words or rising at midnight to try and shake loose a flow of words from my stalled brain.

The address remained unwritten, and I found myself mooning about my office polishing the great battle-axe until it gleamed and glittered, painful to the eye, or strumming fitfully on my guitar and composing new songs which all seemed sad and mournful. At other times I would sit for hours before the painting of the white king, dreaming and withdrawn, or I would wander all day along the cliffs, oblivious of the sun and the heat, and it seemed that often a little birdlike presence was near me, moving like a mischievous brown sprite just beyond the fringe of my vision. Or again, I would sit alone in the dim depths of the archives, deep in a trance of despair as I remembered the hatred in Timothy's smoky eyes as he glared at me across the water-course where the dead men lay. Neither Timothy nor I were all of what we seemed to be, there were dark and ugly depths in both of us. I remembered the savagely mauled bodies of the tiny bushmen left lying for the birds, and my own screaming madness as I cut down the running men on the white sand of the river-bed. I do not know how long my despondency might have lasted except for the discovery which uncovered the answer to so many of the mysteries that still shrouded our city.

Eldridge's team had been countering my apathy by an accelerated advance through the scrolls. Practice had sharpened Sally's grasp of the language, until she was as quick and as fluent as Eldridge himself. Even Leslie was now able to make an appreciable contribution to the work, while Eldridge had arrived by a process of trial and error at the most suitable method of unrolling and preserving our scrolls and he was now saving a great deal of time in this procedure.

At breakfast, which seemed to be the only time we spent together these days, Eldridge asked me to resume the work of removing the pottery jars from the archives. To be truthful I welcomed the excuse not to have to face the blank accusing stare of the sheet of paper in my typewriter, and Ral seemed as pleased to have a change from his fruitless search of the cliffs.

In the cool, peaceful gloom of the archives we worked in our established routine, photographing and marking the position of each jar after we had labelled it and entered it in the master notebook. The work was unexacting, and Ral did most of the talking for my mood of lethargy still persisted. Ral lifted down another of the jars from its slab, and then he peered curiously into the space beyond where the wall opened into a squared stone cupboard.

'Hello,' Ral exclaimed. 'What's this?' And I felt my lethargy fall away like a discarded article of clothing. I hurried across to him and I had a feeling of pre-knowledge as I stared at the row of smaller, squatter jars of the same pottery which had been hidden away in this carefully prepared recess. I knew that we had made another major advance, a significant step forward in our search for the ancient secrets. This idea came into my mind fully formed, it was as though I had simply mislaid these small jars and now I had rediscovered them.

Ral moved the arc-light to obtain a better lighting of the recess, and immediately we noticed another unusual feature. Each of the jars that we could see were sealed – a loop of plaited gold wire linked lid and body of the jar, and a clay seal bore the imprinted figure of a bird. I leaned forward and gently blew away the dust that obscured the impression on the seal. It was of the crouching vulture, the classical soapstone bird of Zimbabwe culture with its base of sun discs and rays. It came as a distinct shock to find this emblem of modern Rhodesia upon a seal of indisputably Punic origin 2,000 years old, as it would be to find the lion and unicorn of the British coat of arms in an Egyptian tomb of the twentieth dynasty.

We worked as quickly as was reconcilable with accuracy;

labelling and photographing the large jars which obscured the recess, and when we lifted them down we discovered that there were five of the smaller jars concealed behind them. All this time my excitement had been increasing, my hope of a major discovery becoming more certain. The concealment of the jars, and the seals indicated their importance. It was as though I had been marking time, waiting for these jars, and my spirits surged. When finally we were ready to remove them from the recess, I reserved this honour for myself despite Ral's protests of, 'But I found them!'

Balancing on the top rungs of the step-ladder, I reached in and attempted to lift the first of them.

'It's stuck,' I said, as the jar sat immovably on its slab of stone. 'They must have bolted it down.' And I leaned further into the recess and carefully groped behind the jar for the fixings which held it in place. I was surprised to find that there were none.

'Try one of the others,' Ral suggested, breathing heavily on the back of my neck from his lofty perch atop those lanky legs. 'Can I give you a hand?'

'Look, Ral, if you don't give me a bit of room you're going to suffocate me.'

'Sorry, Doc,' he muttered, moving back a full quarter of an inch.

I tried the next jar and found that it was also solidly anchored to the shelf, as were the next three.

'That's very odd,' Ral understated the position, and I returned to the first jar, and bracing my elbows on the edge of the shelf I began to twist it in an anti-clockwise direction. It required my full strength, and the muscles bulged and knotted in my forearms before the jar moved. It slid towards me an inch, and immediately I realized that the jar was held down on the slab not by bolts but by its own immense weight. It was fifty times heavier than the jars twice its size.

'Ral,' I said. 'You are going to have to give me a hand, after all.'

Between us we moved the jar to the front edge of the shelf, and then I cradled it in my arms like a new-born infant and lifted it down. Later we found that it weighed 122 pounds avoirdupois, and was not much bigger than a magnum of champagne.

Gently Ral helped me to settle it into the fibre-glass cradle we had designed for transporting the jars. We each took a handle and carried it down the archives, out through the access tunnel and past the guard post at the entrance. I was surprised to find it was already dark, and the stars were pricks of light in the high opening above the emerald pool.

Our disparity of heights made it awkward carrying the cradle, but we hurried down the rock passage and down towards the camp. I was relieved to see that lights still burned in the respository. When Ral and I carried in our precious burden the others hardly glanced up from their work.

I winked at Ral, and we carried the jar to the main workbench. Concealing it with our bodies, we lifted it out of the cradle and stood it in the centre of the bench. Then I turned back to the three bent heads across the room.

'Eldridge, would you mind having a look at this one.'

'One moment.' Eldridge went on poring over an unrolled scroll with his magnifying glass, and Ral and I waited patiently until at last he laid the glass aside and looked up. Like I had, he reacted immediately. I saw the glitter of his spectacles, the rosy glow suffuse his bald pate like sunset on the dome of the Taj Mahal. He came quickly to the bench.

'Where did you find it? How many are there? It's sealed!' His hand was actually trembling as he touched the clay tablet. His tone alerted the girls and they almost ran to join us. We stood about the jar in a reverent circle.

'Open it.' Sally broke the short silence.

'It's almost dinner-time.' I glanced at my watch. 'We had better leave it until tomorrow,' I suggested mildly, and both girls turned on me furiously.

'We can't,' Sally began, then she saw my expression, and relief flooded her face. 'You shouldn't joke about things like that,' she told me sternly.

'Well, Professor Hamilton, what are we waiting for?' I asked.

'What indeed?' he demanded, and the two of us went to work on the seal. We used a pair of side-cutters to nip the gold wire, and then carefully worked the seal loose. The lid lifted easily, and there was the usual linen-wrapped cylinder. However, there was not a suggestion of the unpleasant leathery odour. Eldridge, whose arms are like a pair of thin white candles, was unable to lift the jar. I tilted it carefully onto its side, and while he steadied it I withdrew the weighty roll. The wrapping was well preserved and folded off in one piece.

Nobody spoke as we stared at the exposed cylinder. I had guessed what it would contain. There is only one material which is that heavy, but it was still a delicious thrill to have my expectations realized.

It was another writing scroll, but it was not of leather. This scroll was a continuous rolled sheet of pure gold. It was one-sixteenth of an inch thick, eighteen inches wide and a fraction over twenty-eight feet long. It weighed 1,954 fine ounces with an intrinsic value of over \$85,000. There were five of them – \$425,000, but this was a fraction of the value of the contents.

The beautifully mellow metal unrolled readily as though eager to impart its ancient secrets to us. The characters had been cut with a craftsman's skill into the metal with a sharp engraver's tool, but the reflected light from its surface dazzled the reader.

We all watched with complete fascination as Eldridge spread lamp-black across the blinding surface and then carefully wiped off the excess. Each character stood out now, etched in black against the golden background. He adjusted his spectacles, and pored deliberately over the cramped lines of Punic. He started making non-committal grunts and murmurs, while we crowded closer, like children at story-time.

I think I spoke for all of us when at last I blurted out, 'For God's sake, read the bloody thing!'

Eldridge looked up, and grinned wickedly at me. 'This is very interesting.' He kept us all in aching suspense for a few seconds longer while he lit a cigarette. Then he began to read. It was immediately clear that we had chosen the first scroll in a series, and that Eldridge was reading the author's note.

'Go thou unto my store and take from thence five hundred fingers of the finest gold of Opet. Fashion therefrom a scroll that will not corrupt, that these songs may live for ever. That the glory of our nation may live for ever in the words of our beloved Huy, son of Amon, High Priest of Baal and favourite of Astarte, bearer of the cup of life and Axeman of all the Gods. Let men read his words and rejoice as I have rejoiced, let men hear his songs and weep as I have wept, let his laughter echo down all the years and his wisdom live for ever.

'Thus spoke Lannon Hycanus, forty-seventh Gry-Lion of Opet, King of Punt and the four kingdoms, ruler of the southern seas and keeper of the waterways, lord of the plains of grass and the mountains beyond.'

Eldridge stopped reading, and looked about the circle of our intent faces. We were all silent. This was something far removed from the dry accounts, the list of trade and the Council orders. This scroll was imbued with the very breath, the essence of a people and a land.

'Wow!' Ral whispered. 'They had a pretty good press agent.' And I felt irritation scratch across my nerves at this irreverence.

'Go on,' I said, and Eldridge nodded. He crushed out the stub of his cigarette in the ashtray at his elbow and began to read again. Pausing only to unroll and lamp-black each new turn of the scroll, he read on steadily while we listened, completely entranced. The hours fled on nimble feet, as we heard the poems of Huy Ben-Amon sung again after 2,000 years.

Opet had produced her first philosopher and historian. As I listened to the words of this long-dead poet, I felt a curious kinship of the spirit with him. I understood his pride and petty conceits, I admired his bold vision, forgave his wilder flights of fancy and his more obvious exaggerations, and was held captive by the story-web he wove about me.

His story began with Carthage surrounded by the wolves of Rome, besieged and bleeding, as the legions of Scipio Aemilianus pressed forward on her walls to the chant of 'Carthage must die'.

He told us how Hasdrubal sent a swift ship flying along the shore of the Mediterranean to where Hamilcar, the last scion of the Barcas, a family long since fallen from power and politics, lay with a war fleet of fifty-seven great ships off Hippo on the north African coast.

How the besieged leader called for succour and of the storm and adverse winds that denied it to him. Scipio broke through into the city, and Hasdrubal died with a reeking sword in his hand hacked into pieces by the Roman legionaries below the great altar in the temple of Ashmun upon the hill.

As Eldridge paused, I spoke for the first time in half an hour.

'That gives us our first date. The third Punic war and the final destruction of Carthage, 146 B.C.'

'I think you'll find that is also about the date point of the Opet calendar,' Eldridge agreed.

'Go on,' said Sally. 'Please go on.'

Two biremes escaped the carnage, the sack and rape of Carthage. They fled with the great winds to where Hamilcar lay fretting and storm-bound at Hippo and they told him how Hasdrubal had died and how Scipio had dedicated the city to the infernal gods, had burned it and thrown down the walls, how he had sold the 50,000 survivors into slavery and had sowed the fields with salt and forbidden under pain of death any man to live amongst the ruins.

'So great a hatred, so cruel a deed, could only spring from the heart of a Roman,' cried the poet, and Barca Hamilcar mourned Carthage for twenty days and twenty nights before he sent for his sea captains.

They came to him all nine of them, and Huy the poet named them, Zadal, Hanis, Philo, Habbakuk Lal and the others. Some would fight but most would fly, for how could this pitiful remnant of Carthaginian power stand against the legions of Rome and her terrible fleet of galleys?

There seemed to be no sanctuary for a Carthaginian, Rome ground all the world beneath her armoured heels. Then Habbakuk Lal, the old sea lion and master navigator, reminded them of the voyage that Hanno had made 300 years before beyond the gates of Hercules to a land where the seasons were inverted, gold grew like flowers upon the rocks, and elephants lived in great herds upon the plains. They had all of them read the account that Hanno had written of his voyage inscribed on tablets in the great temple of Baal Hammon at Carthage, now destroyed by Rome. They recalled how he spoke of a river and a mighty lake, where a gentle yellow people had welcomed him and traded gold and ivory for beads and cloth, and how he had lingered there to repair his ships and plant a harvest of corn.

'It is a good land,' he had written. 'And rich.'

Thus in the first year of the exodus Barca Hamilcar had led a fleet of fifty-nine great ships, each with 150 oarsmen and officers aboard, westward beneath the towering gates of Hercules and then southward into an unknown sea. With him went 9,000 men, women and children. The voyage lasted two years, as they made slow progress down the western coast of Africa. There were a thousand hardships and dangers to meet and overcome. Savage tribes of black men, animals and disease when they landed, and shoals and currents, winds and calms upon the sea.

Two years after setting out they sailed into the mouth of a wide, placid river and journeyed up it for sixteen days, dragging their ships bodily through the shallows, until finally they reached the mighty lake of which Hanno had written. They landed upon the furthest shore under a tall red cliff of stone, and Barca Hamilcar died of the shaking fever which he had carried with him from the pestilential lands of the north. His infant son Lannon Hamilcar was chosen as the new king and the nine admirals were his counsellors. They named their new land Opet, after the legendary land of gold, and they began to build their first city at a place where a deep pool of water sprang from the cliffs. The pool and the city were dedicated to the goddess Astarte.

'My God, it's four o'clock.' Ral Davidson broke the spell which had held us all for most of the night, and I realized how tired I was, emotionally and physically exhausted, but well content. I had found my Pliny, now I could go to London in triumph. I had it all.

How swiftly the days passed now. I was at work each morning before sunrise. My typewriter clattered steadily and the filled sheets piled up beside it. I worked until noon each day, and spent the afternoons and evenings in the repository. Listening to the songs from the golden books of the poet Huy. There was no question that the translation could be completed before April the first. Indeed we would be lucky to have the two first scrolls out of the five completed by then. There was equally no possibility that we could postpone the symposium that had been approved by the Council of the Royal Geographical Society for that date. The public relations office of the London branch of Anglo-Sturvesant had completed the arrangements, invitations had been issued and accepted, accommodation, transport and a hundred other details had been arranged and confirmed.

It was a race to marshal and present as much of this incredible plethora of facts and legend as I could in the time left to me. Always I must guard against the temptation to romanticize my subject. The words of Huy were inflammatory to my emotions, I wanted to copy his ebullient style, to laud his heroes and castigate the villains as he did. All of us at the City of the Moon were becoming deeply involved in the story, even Eldridge Hamilton, who was the only one of us not of Africa, was caught up in the grandeur of it. While to the rest of us for whom Africa was, academically and emotionally, the well of our existence, these songs were a compulsive living cavalcade.

How often I found our recent history but an echo of the endeavours and adventures of these men of Opet. How closely they seemed linked to us despite the passage of nearly 2,000 years.

For the first five years the settlement on the shores of the lake prospered. The buildings were of log and mud, the men of Opet came to terms with their new land. They fell into a trading relationship with the Yuye. These were the yellow people that Hanno had described 300 years before, tall graceful men with slanted eyes and delicate features. Clearly they were the ancestors of the Hottentots. They were a pastoral people, with herds of goats and small scrub cattle. They were also hunters and trappers, and gatherers of the flakes of alluvial gold from the gravel beds of the rivers. In the name of the infant king, Habbakuk Lal concluded a treaty with Yuye, King of the Yuye. A treaty that granted all the land between the great river and the hills of Tuya to the men of Opet in return for five bolts of linen and twenty swords of iron.

Well satisfied, Habbakuk Lal, to whom the set and scent of the sea were as the coursing of blood through his own veins, returned with five of his swiftest ships laden with the gold and ivory of Opet to the middle sea. He completed the return journey in nine months, setting up staging posts along the western shores of Africa, and returned with a cargo of beads and linen and the luxuries of civilization. He had pioneered the trade route along which the treasures of southern Africa would pour to the known world, but ever wary of Rome's vengeful eye he covered his tracks like the crafty old sea-fox he was.

He brought with him also new recruits for the colony at Opet. Metallurgists, masons, shipbuilders and gentlemen adventurers. However, the trickle of Yuye gold and ivory shrivelled as the accumulated stores of ages were exhausted. Habbakuk Lal led a company of 100 men to the city of Yuye. He sought the right to prospect and hunt throughout the kingdom of the Yuye, and the king agreed readily, placing his mark at the foot of a leather scroll covered with characters he did not understand. Then he called a feast to entertain his honoured guests. The beer was brought in great gourds, the oxen roasted whole over the pits of glowing coals, and the lithe Yuye maids danced naked, their yellow bodies glistening with oil in the sunlight.

At the height of the revelry Yuye, the king, stood, and pointed his fist at the men whose demands became ever more excessive.

'Kill the white devils,' he cried, and his warriors who had lain in readiness without the mud walls of the city fell upon them.

Habbakuk Lal cut himself a road to safety, his battle-axe swinging in a furious arc about him. Three of his men followed him out, but the rest of them were dragged down and their skulls crushed beneath the war clubs of the Yuye.

271

Habbakuk Lal and his gallant three outran the warriors that pursued them, and reached the bank of the great river where their ship was moored. Flying on white sails they carried the warning to Opet. When the Yuye regiments, 40,000 strong, swarmed down through the pass of the red cliffs, they found 5,000 men of Opet standing to meet them.

All that day the yellow horde broke like the waves of the sea on the ranks of the Opet archers, and all that day the arrows flew like clouds of locusts. Then at the moment when the Yuye drew back exhausted, their resolve broken, Habbakuk Lal opened his ranks and let his axemen run. Greyhounds on the rabbit, wolves on the sheep herds, they pursued until darkness halted the slaughter. Yuye died in the flames of his burning city, and his people were taken into slavery. This is the law of Africa, a land that favours the strong, where the lion alone walks proud.

Now suddenly the colony which had been quietly establishing itself, putting down its roots and making sure of its base, exploded into growth and bloom.

Her metallurgists sought out the mother lodes of metal, her hunters ranged widely, her ranchers bred the scrub cattle of the Yuye to the blood bulls that Habbakuk Lal's ships brought from the north. Her farmers sowed the corn, and watered it from the lake. To protect her citizens and her gods a start was made on the walls of Opet. The land and its treasures were divided amongst the nine noble families, the sea captains of the exodus, who were now the members of the king's council.

Habbakuk Lal, with his huge frame twisted and tortured by arthritis, and with the flaming red beacon of his hair and beard long ago changed to grey ash, died at last. But his eldest son, already admiral of the fleet of Opet, took his father's name. Another Habbakuk Lal directed the growing fleet of Opet in trade and exploration. His ships still beat the well-worn sea-lanes to the north, but also they voyaged southwards to where the land turned back upon itself and a great flat-topped mountain guarded the southern Cape. Here a sudden gale out of the north-west smashed half the Opet fleet upon the rocks below the mountain. The priests read this as an omen from the gods, and never again would a ship of Opet venture this far southwards.

The centuries pass. Kings take the throne and then pass from it. New customs arise, the ways of the gods and their worship are altered to suit this land, a new breed of man arises from the mixed blood of Opet and Yuye. He is a citizen, but only the noble families may govern. He may enjoy all the privileges and carry all the responsibilities of citizenship, except that of directing the affairs of state. This is reserved for those of the old blood, pure and untainted. As an offshoot of this nobility a clan of warrior priests arises. These are the sons of Amon, and it amused me to learn that the clan has its origin in a man from the old kingdom, that is, the kingdom of Tyre and Sidon, on the borders of Canaan. These priests probably spring from Jewish stock. You cannot keep us out of a good proposition, can you?

New heroes spring up and fight along the borders, or crush a rising of slaves, or slay the wild beasts. The old art of elephant-training is revived, and the king's elephants spearhead his army and lighten the heavy labours of building and mining.

From the golden books we had an occasional exciting flash of physical contact with the past. Huy describes the lay-out of the walls, and the towers of Baal. They tally exactly with the foundations we had exposed. Huy gives the dimensions of walls thirty-five feet high and fifteen thick, and again we wonder how they had disappeared.

At another place he describes a gift of treasure from the Egyptian agents at Cadiz to the Gry-Lion, as the king is now called; amongst the items is a gold cup marvellously worked with the signs of eternal life. It is our chalice found among the ruins of the temple, and that night I went to examine it again. Seeing its battered beauty with new eyes.

Always running through the songs of Huy was the puzzle game of guessing the modern names of the animals and places he mentions. Towns and garrisons had long since gone, or had been reduced to those mysterious piles of old stone which dot the landscape of central Africa. However, we were enthralled to hear how the men of Opet began a search for land where the vine and olive will grow. The oils and wines from the north were more precious than their weight in gold by the time they had completed the journey in the ships of the fifth Habbakuk Lal.

The Gry-Lion's horticulturists and viticulturists discover a range of high mountains far to the east. Mountains of mist and cool pure air. The terracing and developing of the benign slopes begins, with tens of thousands of slaves employed in the project. Living plants in pottery jars are sped southwards in the swiftest ships, then carried on the backs of elephants to the mountains of Zeng, and from them come the sweet red wines of Zeng which the poet Huy so loudly and lovingly extols. Here then is a description of the building of those terraced gardens which cover the Inyanga mountains to this day.

From the descriptions of the animals and wild birds of Punt and the four kingdoms we could recognize most of them. The sacred sunbird, who carried offerings of meat to Baal, flying upwards into a cloudless sky until it disappeared beyond the range of the human eye was obviously the vulture. Then we realized the significance of the carved vulture birds and the seal on the golden scrolls. The vulture had been taken as the emblem of the warrior priests, the sons of Amon, Ben-Amon. Huy had placed his personal seal on the jars which contained the scrolls.

There were other animals described by the poet which could only be extinct species, types which had vanished in the intervening 2,000 years. Chief of these was the Gry-

Lion. For we learned that the king took his title from a real beast. This was a large predatory cat which lived along the southern shores of the lake amongst the reed beds that grew there. As early as the year of Opet 216, laws were passed to protect this animal, already threatened by extinction. This protection was afforded it because of the role it played in the ritual of coronation of a new king; a ceremony which Huy referred to as 'taking the Gry-Lion'. He described it as reddish roan-brown in colour with a face masked in lines of black and white, and standing five feet high at the shoulder. Its eye-teeth protruded from its jaw in a set of great curved fangs ten inches long. Despite the doubts of the others as to Huy's veracity, I thought I recognized a description of the giant sabre-toothed lynx. A skeleton of this animal had been discovered amongst the upper level of bones at Sterkfontein caves.

Huy describes how the trade in live animals begins. Their ancient enemy, Rome, is denuding north Africa of lion and rhinoceros and elephant, for use in her circuses. Hanis, the hunter of the southern plains of grass, develops a method of capturing these animals alive and drugging them with a distillation of the seeds of the wild hemp. In a comatose state they are placed aboard the ships of Habbakuk Lal, and sped swiftly northwards from staging-post to post along the coast. Huy reports an unexpectedly high survival rate of fifty per cent, and these fetch astronomical prices for the entertainment of the sensation-hungry populace of Rome.

In the Opet year of 450, the nation is at the zenith of her wealth and power, but she has outgrown herself. Her boundaries are extended, her slave population hardly sufficient to support her multifarious enterprises. In desperation the Gry-Lion sends a slaving expedition for ten days' march to the north of the great river. Hasmon Ben-Amon returns with 500 superb black Nubian captives, and claims his reward from the Gry-Lion.

275

We had reached the end of Huy Ben-Amon's second golden book, and the Lear was waiting for us. Reluctantly we had to interrupt our readings and go.

Leaving Ral and Leslie to supervise the site, Eldridge, Sally and I flew out to meet the international flight from Luanda. We had to pay the excess on 200 lb. of overweight luggage, and the fare of the Botswana Police Inspector sent by his Government to guard their interests in the ancient relics we carried with us.

I n London we had one free day, one precious day to ourselves and as usual I tried to do it all. The crocuses were out on the lawns of Lincoln's Inn Fields, the bitter at the Barley Mow in Duke Street tasted better than I remembered, and the new crop of girls in the King's Road were prettier than the last. When the National Gallery closed at six o'clock Sally and I took a cab directly to San Lorenzo in Beauchamp Place and ate Lorenzo's wonderful ossobucco washed down with red Chianti. We were only just in time for the curtain at the Queen's Theatre. It was all so different from our life at the City of the Moon.

By the time we returned to the Dorchester it was after midnight, but Sally was still wrought-up with the first impact of that fabulous city.

'I'm too excited to sleep yet, Ben. What shall we do?'

'Well, I've got a bottle of champagne in my suite,' I hinted, and she looked at me with an amused twinkle in her eyes.

'Ben Kazin, my favourite boy scout. Always prepared. Okay, let's go drink it.'

It was Krug, very pale and dry. When the bottle was half finished we made love for the first time in six months. If it were possible this was for me a more cataclysmic experience than our first time. Afterwards I lay exhausted physically and spiritually, and it was Sally who took the empty glasses and carried them through into the lounge. She came back with the brimming pale wine and stood over me naked, and lovely.

'I don't know why I did that,' she said, and gave me a tulip-shaped glass.

'Are you sorry?' I asked.

'No, Ben. I have never regretted anything between us. I only wish – ' But she stopped and instead she sipped at her glass and sat down beside me on the bed.

'You know that I love you,' I said.

'Yes.' She looked at me with an expression I could not fathom.

'I will always love you,' I said.

'No matter what?' she asked.

'No matter what,' I told her.

'I believe you, Ben,' she nodded, her eyes dark brooding green. 'Thank you.'

'Sally—' I began again, but she placed one long tapered finger on my lips, and shook her head so the soft dark wings of her hair swung against her cheeks.

'Be patient, Ben. Please be patient.' But I lifted her finger from my mouth.

'Sally—' She leaned forward and silenced my lips with hers. Still holding the kiss she placed her glass on the floor beside my bed, she took mine from my unresisting fingers and placed it beside hers. Then she made love to me with such devastating skill and subtlety that there were no questions nor protest left in me. At nine o'clock the next morning I got Sally into a taxi headed for Elizabeth Arden in Bond Street, a little apprehensive as to what would happen to that dark silky head of hers. What some of those faggots do to a pretty girl they should be hanged for. Then I climbed into another taxi and headed for the M4 and

Heathrow to become snarled in one of those traffic jams which make British motoring such a leisurely and soothing experience.

Louren's flight had landed by the time I paid off my taxi and ran through into the International Terminal, that seething cauldron of humanity.

I heard someone in the crowd exclaim, 'It must be Dicky and Liz!' and I was immediately alerted to the whereabouts of the Sturvesant party. With the limited horizon that I have from my altitude above ground, I am forced to rely on these gratuitous sighting reports.

I fought my way through to the entourage which had been mistaken for that of the Burtons, and realized that the error was excusable. This was Louren Sturvesant travelling heavy, in the grand manner, with his foreriders running interference and clearing a path for the doors. There was a light screen of the gentlemen of the Press skirmishing along the flanks of the advance, but unable to break through the ranks of B.Y.M. Their methods were too conventional. I got into a head-on position and went in low and dirty, and there were a few yelps and cries of, 'Watch that one,' and, 'Get him,' which changed quickly to, 'Sorry, Doctor.'

And I was through into the soft centre. Bobby Sturvesant let out a shriek and landed around my neck, and the entire advance broke down for the minute it took for us to accomplish the greeting ceremony. Hilary was in a soft wrap of honey mink which was made to look shabby by the lustre of her hair, and over her towered Louren, his mane of hair sun-bleached to white gold and his face burned dark nut-brown.

'Ben, you old bastard.' He grabbed me around the shoulder. 'Thank God you made it. Will you look after Hil and the kids for me. I've got a few things to clear up, then I'll see you back at the Dorchester.'

There were two long shiny black limousines waiting

under the portico and the party split neatly, but not before Louren had doubled back to tell me proudly, 'I got a black marlin in the Seychelles – 900 pounder, Ben. A real beauty.'

'That's the tiger,' I congratulated him.

'Get out the Glen Grant, sport. I won't be long.'

I sat in the jump seat opposite Hilary, having beaten one of the B.Y.M. to it, and I was delighted to see how radiant she looked. It was that bright shiny look of happiness which you cannot fake with cosmetics and eyeliner.

'We had ten days on the islands, Ben. It was wonderful.' She went all misty and soft at the memory. 'Our anniversary. Look!' And she held up her left hand which was overburdened with a ring of red gold and a solitaire diamond. I was accustomed to Louren's style of living, but even I blinked. The diamond was bluey-white in colour and looked good, it was certainly not a shade less than twenty-five carats.

'It's beautiful, Hilary.' And for no good reason I thought, 'The deeper the guilt, the bigger the gift.'

When we reached the Dorchester Hilary gasped and covered her mouth with surprise at the baroque super-abundance of the Oliver Messel suite.

'It's not true, Ben,' she laughed. 'It just can't be!'

'Don't laugh,' I warned her. 'We must be costing Louren over £100 per day.'

'Wow!' She flopped into one of the enormous armchairs. 'You can get a drink, Ben, my love. I need it.'

While I poured I asked unnecessarily, 'Your problems were of a temporary nature then, Hil?'

'I have forgotten I ever had any, Ben. He's better than he ever was.'

When Louren arrived I saw what she meant. He was in high humour, laughing and restless with energy, sleek and hard and tanned. He disposed of the last two B.Y.M. while

I poured him a Glen Grant, then he threw his coat and tie over a chair, rolled his sleeves up over brown bulging muscle and settled with the drink.

'Okay, Ben. Show it to me.' And we plunged into an examination and discussion of the scrolls and their translation.

Louren picked on the first line of the first page.

'Go thou unto my store and take from thence five hundred fingers of the finest gold—' He repeated the line, then looked up at me. 'That's right from the old boy's mouth, Ben. My *store*! That's his treasury. That clot Hamilton mistranslated it. It should read "treasury".'

'Suddenly your Punic is pretty hot,' I commended him.

'Well, for cat's sake, Ben, when did you ever send down to a store for your gold?' He tasted the Glen Grant. 'If your theories are correct—'

'Don't give me that *if* bit, Lo. Your name is not Wilfred Snell.'

'All right, let's accept that there was a violent and sudden death to our city. Fire and dead men, the archives which they obviously held so dear are untouched, then there is a better than ever chance the treasury was untouched also. We've just got to find it.'

'Great!' I nodded, and grinned sarcastically. 'This is a major breakthrough. I've been breaking my heart searching for it these last six months.'

'It's there, Ben.' He did not answer my grin.

'Where, Lo? Where?'

'Close. Somewhere within the main walls, probably within the cavern area.'

'Hell, Lo. I've been over every inch of it fifty times.' I spoke with mild but rising irritation.

'And when you've been over it for the hundredth time, you'll realize how blind you've been.'

'Damn it, Lo!' I started. 'I don't think—'

'Get yourself a drink, partner, before you blow up.'

I did as he advised, and Louren went on. 'I'm not knocking what you've done, Ben. But let me just remind you that in 1909 Theodore Davis ended his book by saying, "I fear that the valley of the kings is now exhausted."'

'Yes, I know, Lo, but—'

Ignoring me Louren went on, 'And it was thirteen years later that Howard Carter discovered the tomb of Tutankhamen, the greatest treasure that the valley had ever yielded.'

'Nobody is talking about giving up the search, Lo. I'll go on just as long as you keep paying.'

'And I'll bet that my cheque book is more tenacious than your resolve.'

'That's a bad bet,' I warned him, and we were laughing again.

We parted in the middle of the afternoon, Louren being borne away in a flood of B.Y.M., across the lobby to where a black Rolls waited in front of the hotel, and I slipping out of the side entrance to hail my own taxi in Park Lane.

Eldridge Hamilton was waiting for me on the pavement outside the Royal Geographical Society, having motored up from Oxford in his bright red mini. He was dressed as always in his tweed with the elbow patches, but was feverish with anticipation of the morrow.

'I can hardly wait for it, Ben,' he chortled with malicious glee. 'Have they arrived at the hotel yet?'

'No, but Snell is due in this evening.'

Eldridge did a little hop and skip of excitement and said. 'Like a hippopotamus lumbering into the dead fall.' Cruel but apt, I thought, and we went up through the double oaken doors into the panelled hall which is a high temple of our profession. There is a hushed dignity about the building which I find reassuring and permanent in this insane and transitory modern world.

Side by side we climbed the sweeping staircase, past the portraits of great men and the lists of former medallists honoured by the Society.

'You'll have to give some thought as to who should paint you, Ben.' Eldridge indicated the portraits. 'They do say this foreign Johnny – what's his name, Annigoni? – is not too bad.'

'Don't talk tripe,' I snapped, and he let out one of those startling neighs of laughter that rang like a bugle call through the hallowed precincts. I was irritated by Eldridge's assault on one of my most private and treasured fantasies. I am a modest and almost painfully retiring person, but the very first time I had entered here, and looked up at the portraits, I had imagined my own dark visage peering down from the wall of honour. I had even selected the pose – seated to avoid undue emphasis on my body, with my head turned half away. I have a good right-hand profile. There would be a flecking of dignified grey at the temples, a gay little ribbon of some foreign decoration in my lapel, Legion of Honour, perhaps. The expression pensive, the brow furrowed. . .

'Come on,' said Eldridge, and we went to where the President and a handful of Council Members waited for us with sherry and biscuits, and not a decent whisky in sight. Nevertheless, I was aware that these gentlemen had it in their power to make into reality my imaginings of a few minutes previously. I set out to be as affable and charming as is possible, and it seemed to have the desired effect.

We discussed the opening of the symposium, which was set for two-thirty the following afternoon.

'His Grace will make the opening address,' one of them explained. 'We've asked him to keep it down to forty-five minutes, and if possible to avoid reference to orchid-growing or steeple-chasing.'

I would then read my paper. It would rank as a follow-on to the one I had read six years earlier. 'The Mediterranean Influence on Central and Southern Africa of the Pre-Christian Era', the paper which had afforded Wilfred Snell and his pack so much sport. They had set aside four hours for me.

Eldridge would read his paper the following morning, 'Certain ancient writings and symbols of south-western African origin.' The title Eldridge had chosen was purposely vague, so as not to telegraph my punch.

Eldridge and I reassured ourselves that the exhibits we had brought with us from Africa were safe in the strongroom of the Society, then Eldridge gave me a bad attack of the shakes by driving me back to the Dorchester through London's rush-hour traffic in his satanical red mini. We were carried around Hyde Park Corner four times, with Eldridge cursing fluently and his bald head shining like a warning beacon while I hung terrified to the door handle ready to bale out, before Eldridge managed to break out of the traffic stream into Park Lane.

I led him, both of us still palpitating, into the cocktail bar and shot a pair of double Gilbeys into him, and then left him. I had plans for the evening and it was already past six.

Sally came out of the lifts as I approached them. I mentally apologized to her hairdresser. He had let it lie, still loose and cloudy. They had wrought some sort of magic with her face also. It was all eyes and soft pink mouth. She had on a full-length dress of a floating green material that picked up the green of those eyes.

'Ben,' she came to me quickly. 'I'm so glad I found you. I left a note for you under your door. About this evening, I'm terribly afraid that I won't be able to make it, Ben. I'm sorry.'

'That's all right, Sal. It wasn't definite anyway,' I told her, hiding my disappointment behind a grin as my plans collapsed like soggy pastry.

'I have to see them. They are old friends, Ben. They've come all the way from Brighton.'

I went up to Louren's suite, and hung around waiting for him to return, chatting to Hilary and the children. At seven-thirty he phoned, and Hilary put me on after she had spoken to him.

'I was hoping we could have had dinner, Ben, but I'm screwed up here for heaven knows how long. They have made a complete hash of the tax clause in the contract. We are trying to redraft it. Why don't you take Hilary for dinner, instead?'

But she pleaded exhaustion, and announced her intentions of making it an early night. I ate alone at Isow's, a real kosher meal begun with chopped liver and onions. Afterwards I crossed the alley to Raymond's, and for five pounds watched the loveliest girls in London taking off their clothes. It was a distressing experience. It made me feel even more lonely and despondent, and afterwards, though I am not a lecher, I teetered on the edge of temptation when the girls beckoned from the dark doorways in Wardour Street.

I rang Sally's room when I got in a few minutes before midnight, and again an hour later when I had given up my efforts at sleep. Neither call was answered, and the telephone buzzed dismally like an insect sending out an unanswered mating call. It was almost morning before I found sleep.

Louren woke me, boorishly healthy and hearty at eight, bellowing into the phone, 'It's the big day, Ben. Come and have breakfast up here. I'll order it now, what do you want?'

'Coffee,' I mumbled, and when I arrived in his suite he had a huge platter of steak and bacon, kidneys and eggs, with smoked kippers and porridge to start and toast, marmalade and coffee to end it. An average sort of breakfast for Louren.

'You are going to need your strength, partner. Get in there and eat, boy.'

With my spirits bolstered by this solid bulwark, I was carried through the morning on a cresting wave of expectation and I felt like a lion when we went down to meet our guests at noon. When I say lion, I mean a man-eating lion. I had anointed my smoothly shaven cheeks with a double handful of Dior aftershave, I wore my dark cashmere suit with a white shirt and maroon tie, and Hilary had found a carnation for my button-hole. I smelt like a rose garden, and there was an eager snap to my step and the hunter's warm thrill in my belly.

Louren and I entered the private lounge together, and the buzz of conversation dwindled. I don't pretend that my entrance to a room can command silence, but Louren's certainly can. Only one voice continued raised; in a convincing imitation of the British upper class, it brayed across the lounge. Wilfred Snell stood in a circle of his sycophants, towering above them much bigger than life size, almost like a badly executed monument to himself. His legs were set apart and his body braced in the stance of a heavily pregnant woman to counter-balance his monstrous gut. It was as though he carried a half-filled winesack under his vest. The expanse of pearl-grey suiting material necessary to cover this bulge was as vast as a theatre curtain. His face hung down on his chest in a series of chins like the ripples on a pond. It was white and soft-looking as though a plastic skin had been filled with dirty milk. His mouth was a deep purple gash in the whiteness, loose, perpetually open, even when he was not talking, which was seldom. His hair was a wild curling bush from which a gentle white rain of dandruff sifted down onto his shoulders and lapels, and he was hung with things – a pair of reading glasses around his neck like a tank commander's binoculars, a golden cigar-cutter from his money pocket, from his lapel a monocle on a black ribbon, a watch chain and key ring.

I approached him obliquely, stopping to greet friends, to chat with colleagues, but moving in on him steadily. Someone put a glass in my hand and I looked around.

'Scotch courage,' Sally smiled at me.

'I don't need it, luv.'

'Let's go talk to him,' she suggested.

'I was sort of making the pleasure last.'

We looked at him openly, this self-appointed drummer of archaeology, whose half-dozen books had sold 500,000 copies, books that aimed at and struck squarely in the centre of popular tastes. Books in which he flirted dangerously with the laws of plagiarism and criminal libel; books in which cant masqueraded as erudition, and facts were squeezed, ignored or subtly altered to suit the argument.

I am not a bitter man, not one who bears grudges, but when I looked at this great bloated executioner, this torturer, this – well, when I looked at him I felt the blood bubble and fizz behind my eyes. I started towards him directly.

He saw me coming, but ignored it. The entire room was aware of what was happening, had probably been anticipating this confrontation since the day they received their invitations. The circle about the master opened, giving me space to approach the presence.

'There is no doubt—' Wilfred brayed, his gaze passing several feet over my head. He usually precedes each of his statements with an advertising plug.

'As I have always said—' his voice carried to the furthest corners, and I waited patiently. I have a carefully rehearsed smile which I use at times like this. It is shy, self-effacing.

'It is generally agreed—' Such a recommendation from Wilfred usually means that the theory in question is the subject of a raging controversy.

'To tell the truth—' And he went on to tell a blatant lie.

At last he glanced down, stopped in mid-sentence,

screwed his monocle into his eye, and to his delight and surprise, discovered his old friend and colleague Dr Benjamin Kazin.

'Benjamin, my dear little fellow,' he cried, and the diminutive stung like a dart in the hump of the bull. 'How very good to see you!'

Then Wilfred Snell did a very rash thing. He dangled his great soft white hairy paw languidly in my direction. For an instant I could not believe my good fortune; at the same instant Wilfred remembered the last time we had shaken hands six years before and tried to snatch it back. His reactions are no match for mine, and I had him.

'Wilfred,' I cooed, 'my dear, dear chap.' His hand felt like a glove full of warm jelly, it was only when my fingers had cut in for an inch or two that you could actually feel the bones.

'We were absolutely delighted that you could come,' I told him, and he made a little mooing sound. A few loose drops of spittle spattered from the slack purple lips.

'Did you have a good trip?' I asked, still smiling shyly. Wilfred had begun to do a little jig, skipping from foot to foot. My fingers had almost disappeared in the soft white flesh, I could now feel every knuckle very clearly. It was rather like playing a jelly fish on a trout rod.

'We must make time for a little private chat before the end of the symposium,' I said, and the air started to leak out of Wilfred. He was making a soft hissing sound, and he seemed to shrink like a punctured balloon. Suddenly I was disgusted with my brutality, my weakness in giving in to it. I let him go, and the return of blood to the abused hand must have been more painful than my treatment of it. He held it tenderly to his chest, his big pansy eyes were filled with tears and his lips trembled like those of a petulant child.

'Come,' I told him gently. 'Let me get you another drink.' And I led him away unprotesting like an elephant and its mahout. However, Wilfred Snell is nothing if not resilient, and he came back strongly. Throughout the luncheon snatches of his monologue carried across to our table. He was 'making no bones about it' and 'letting them in on a little secret' in his best form. From what I could hear he was repeating his conviction as to the medieval age and Bantu origin of the central African ruin system, and was lightly and amusingly debunking my own writings. At one stage I glanced across to see that he had *Ophir* open beside his plate and was reading from it to the general merriment of his table companions.

However, I had another crisis threatening which took all my skill to avert. Sally was my lunch partner and we sat opposite the Sturvesants. Within five seconds of seating ourselves, Sally noticed Hilary's new diamond. She could hardly overlook it, it was throwing slivers of light about the room, bright as arrows. Sally was silent for half the meal, but her eyes were drawn to that flaming jewel every few seconds. The rest of us were vying for an opportunity to speak, and there was much laughter and excited banter. Louren seemed to be especially attentive to Hilary, but suddenly there was a momentary silence.

Sally leaned forward, and in her sweetest voice, told Hilary, 'What a pretty ring. You are so lucky to be able to wear costume jewellery, my dear. My bones are too small. It doesn't suit me, I'm afraid.' And she turned back to me and started chattering brightly. She had ruined the mood with one expert thrust. I saw Louren frown, and flush angrily. Hilary pursed her lips, and I saw a hundred retorts pass in review behind her eyes but she withheld them. I plunged gamely into the void, but even my charm and social grace could not restore the mood. I was relieved when at last Louren glanced at his watch, then looked across at the B. Y. M. who was in charge of the arrangements and nodded. Immediately this gentleman was on his feet, shepherding the unwieldy party out to where the cavalcade of cars waited. As we passed through the lobby, Wilfred Snell cleaved a path to my side with a swarm of his admirers following him in grinning anticipation.

'I was glancing through your book again during lunch. I had forgotten how amusing it was, my dear chap.'

'Thank you, Wilfred,' I replied gratefully. 'That's jolly decent of you to say so.'

'You must sign it for me.'

'I will. I will.'

'Looking forward to your paper this afternoon, my dear little chap.' And again I shuddered with the effort of suppressing my feelings and keeping my voice mild.

'I hope you'll find it as amusing.'

'I am sure I will, Benjamin.' He let go a fruity chuckle and moved off like a crowd. I heard him saying to De Vallos as they climbed into their limousine, 'Mediterranean influence! My God, why not Eskimo while he is about it.'

We went through the park like the mourners at a state funeral, a convoy of black limousines, and turned out of the second gate into Kensington Gore.

We were set down at the door of the Society, and moved into the lecture hall. The speakers and Council Members were on the platform, and the body of the hall filled solidly. Wilfred was in his place, front centre, where I could watch every expression on his face. He was surrounded by his hatchet men.

They led in His Grace, smelling of cigars and good port. They pointed him at the audience like a howitzer, and let him go. In forty-five minutes he had covered orchids, and the steeple-chase season. The President began tugging discreetly at his coat-tails, but it was another twenty minutes before I had my chance.

'Six years ago I had the honour of addressing this Society. My subject was "The Mediterranean Influence on Central and Southern Africa of the Pre-Christian Era". I come before you now with the identical subject, but armed with further evidence that has come to light in the intervening period.'

Every few minutes Wilfred would heave himself around in his seat to address a remark to either Rogers or De Vallos in the row behind him. He used a stage whisper, covering his mouth with his programme. I ignored the distraction and ploughed through my introduction. It was a resumé of all the previously known evidence, and the various theories that had been applied to them. I made it purposely dull, pedestrian, letting Wilfred and his party believe that I had nothing further to support my views.

'Then in March of last year a photograph was shown to me by Mr Louren Sturvesant.' Now I changed my delivery, let a little electricity come into my tone. I saw a flare of interest in faces which had taken on glazed expressions. I fanned it steadily. Suddenly, I was telling them a detective story. There were longer intervals between Wilfred's pompous asides. The snickers from his admirers died away. I had the audience by the throat now, they were there with Sally and me in the moonlight looking down on the ghostly outlines of a long-dead city. They shared our thrill as we exposed the first blocks of dressed stone.

At the moment when I needed it, the lights were turned down into darkness and the first image was flashed upon the screen behind me.

It was the white king, proud and aloof, regal in his rampant maleness and golden armour. Out of the darkness the images flashed upon the screen. The audience sat in rapt silence, their fascinated faces lit by the reflected glow of the screen, the only movement was the frantic scribbling of the Pressmen in the front row as my voice went on weaving spells about them.

I carried the story to the point where we had investigated the plain and cavern, but had not yet discovered the walled-up tunnel beyond the portrait of the white king.

At my signal the lights went up, and the audience

stirred back to the present, all except His Grace who had succumbed to the port and was sleeping like a dead man. He was the only one of two hundred who I had not captivated by my tale. Even Wilfred looked groggy and shaken, like a badly beaten prize fighter trying to rouse himself to meet the gong. I had to accord him a grudging admiration, the man was game to the core. He heaved himself around towards De Vallos and in a penetrating whisper told him:

'Typical Bantu stonework of the thirteenth century A.D., of course. But very interesting. Reinforces my theories about the dating of the immigrations.'

I waited silently, clenched fists on the lectern, my head bowed over it. Sometimes I believe I could have been a truly great motion picture actor. I lifted my head slowly and stared at Wilfred, my expression was desolate. He took heart from it.

'The painting means nothing, of course. To tell you the truth it's probably a Bantu initiation candidate, similar to the White Lady of the Brandberg.'

I maintained my silence, letting him take out line as though he were a marlin. I wanted him to swallow it down deep, before I set the hook.

'There is no new evidence here, I'm afraid.'

He looked around him with a satisfied smirk, and his followers' heads started nodding and grinning like puppets.

I addressed him directly then.

'As Professor Wilfred Snell has just remarked, fascinating as all of this was, it presented no new evidence.' They all nodded more vigorously. 'And so, I determined to look deeper.'

And I was away again into a description of the discovery of the blocked tunnel, the decision to preserve the white king and cut through living rock, the hole through into the tunnel, and again I paused, and looked at Wilfred Snell. Suddenly I felt sorry for him; where before he had been my implacable enemy, an open running canker in my professional life, now he was just a fat and rather ridiculous figure.

Like the poet Huy, Axeman of all the Gods, I hacked into him then. Cutting him to pieces with my account of the scrolls, the vulture axe, and the five golden books.

As I spoke, one of the attendants wheeled in a barrow covered with a green velvet cloth. It pulled all their eyes, and at my signal he drew aside the cloth and there lay the great gleaming battle-axe and one of the scrolls.

Wilfred Snell slumped in his seat with his gut in his lap and his purple mouth hanging open slackly while I read the opening words of the first golden book of Huy.

'"Let men read his words and rejoice as I have rejoiced, let men hear his songs and weep as I have wept."'

I ended and looked around at them. They were gripped by the heart strings, every one of them. Even Louren, Hilary and Sally who knew it all were leaning forward in their seats, shiny-eyed and intent.

It was after seven-thirty, I noticed with surprise. I had overrun my time by an hour and there had been no rebuke from the President beside me.

'Our time is finished, but not the story. Tomorrow morning Professor Eldridge Hamilton will read his paper on the scrolls and their contents. I hope you will be able to attend. Your Grace, President, ladies and gentlemen, I thank you.'

The silence was complete, nobody moved nor spoke for a full ten seconds, then suddenly they were on their feet applauding wildly. It was the first time since the formation of the Society in 1830 that a paper had been applauded as though it were a stage performance. They came out of their seats, crowding around me to shake my hand and ask their questions which I could not hope to answer. From my vantage-point on the dais I saw Wilfred Snell rise from his seat and lumber ponderously towards the door. He walked alone, his band of followers had left him to join the crowd around me. I wanted to call out to him, to tell him that I felt sorry for him, that I wished I could have spared him, but there was nothing to say. He had said it all a hundred times before.

Every single national paper had it the following morning, and even *The Times* had allowed itself a touch of the dramatic. 'Discovery of Carthaginian Treasure,' it stated, 'one of archaeology's most significant finds since the tomb of Tutankhamen.'

Louren had sent out for them all, and we sat in a sea of newsprint as we ate another of those gargantuan breakfasts. I was touched by Louren's pride in my achievements. He read each article aloud, interspersing his own comments:

'You rocked them, partner.'

'Ben, you murdered the bums.'

'The way you told it, you even had me wetting my pants, and, hell! I was there!'

He picked one of the left-wing tabloids from the pile and opened it. His expression changed immediately. Suddenly he was scowling furiously, a look of such concentrated venom that I asked quickly, 'What is it, Lo?'

'Here.' He almost flung the sheet at me. 'Read it yourself, while I finish changing.' He went through into the bedroom and slammed the door.

I found it almost immediately. A full page of photographs under a big banner 'The forces of freedom'. Black men with guns, with tanks. Black men marching, rank upon endless rank. Eggshell helmets like evil toadstools of hatred, modern automatic weapons slung on camouflaged shoulders, booted feet swinging. It was not these that held me. In the centre of the page was a picture of a tall man with shoulders wide as the crosstree of a gallows, and a bald cannon-ball head that shone in the bright African sunshine. He walked unsmiling between two grinning Chinamen in those shabby rumpled uniforms that look like pyjamas.

The caption was in bold lettering: 'The Black Crusader. Major-General Timothy Mageba, the newly appointed commander of the People's Liberation Army with two of his military advisors.'

I felt a sinking sensation of dread as I looked at the brooding hatred in that face, the power and terrible purpose in those set shoulders and thrusting gait.

In some inexplicable fashion it seemed to detract from my own personal triumph. What had happened 2,000 years ago seemed of lessened importance when I looked at the picture of this man, and I thought of the dark forces in movement through the length of my land.

Yet it came to me then that this man was not unique, Africa had bred many like him. The dark destroyers who had strewn her plains with the white bones of men, Chaka, Mzilikazi, Mamatee, Mutesa, and hundreds of others that history had forgotten. Timothy Mageba was only the latest in a long line of warriors which stretched back beyond the shadowy, impenetrable veils of time.

Louren came out of the bedroom, and with him was Hilary. She came to kiss me and congratulate me again, and I dropped the sheet of newspaper from my hand, but not my mind.

'I'm sorry I can't be with you to hear your friend Eldridge this morning, Ben. I can't get out of this meeting. Please look after Hil for me. Give her a good lunch, will you?' Louren told me as the three of us went down in the lift.

Eldridge, in his tweeds and elbow patches, massacred his subject. For three and a half hours he mumbled about 'hangs' and 'abridgements', occasionally letting fly with that laugh of his, a sound which woke the sleepers. I was grateful to him as I looked around the slowly emptying hall, and the doodling yawning members of the Press. He certainly wasn't stealing my glory from me.

An hour before lunch Sally slipped me a note from her seat behind me. 'I can't take any more. Going out to do some shopping. See you. S.'

And I smiled as I watched her slide gracefully out of the side exit. Hilary turned and winked at me, and we both smiled.

Eldridge ground to a slow, inconclusive halt and beamed around at his depleted audience.

'Well,' he said. 'I think that covers just about everything.' And there followed a relieved scramble for the doors.

In the lobby of the Society I was once more surrounded by an enthusiastic mob, and we made slow progress towards the door and our lunch.

When at last we reached the taxi, with Eldridge and myself flanking Hilary on the seat, I was just about to give the driver the address of the Trattoria Terrazza when Hilary looked down at her hands in her lap and gave a little stricken cry.

'My ring!' And for the first time we noticed that the great jewel was no longer flamed upon her hand. I stared aghast at the naked finger, a fortune beyond my dreams was missing. That diamond must certainly be worth £30,000.

'When did you last have it?' I demanded of her, and after a second's thought a look of relief replaced her worried frown.

'Oh, I remember now. At the hotel, I was painting my nails. I put it in the alabaster cigarette box beside my chair.'

'Which room? Which chair?'

'The lounge, the tapestry chair beside the television set.'

'Eldridge, will you take Mrs Sturvesant on to the

restaurant, please. I'd better take another cab and dash back to the hotel before one of the cleaning staff discovers it. Have you your key with you, Hil?'

She dug into her handbag and came out with the key.

'Ben, you are an old sweetheart. I'm so sorry about this.' And she handed it to me.

'Damsels in distress are my speciality.' I stepped out onto the pavement. They pulled away and for five minutes I behaved like a berserk semaphorist towards the passing stream of taxis. I can never tell if those little yellow lights on top are burning or not, so I flag them all.

I let myself into the Oliver Messel suite with Hilary's key and hurried down that long passage past the bedrooms. With a little grunt of relief I found the ring amongst the cigarettes in the alabaster box. With it in my hand I moved across the light from the window to admire it for a moment. It was a thing of such brilliant beauty that my stomach turned within me. I felt a fleeting envy, a twinge of unhappiness that I should never own an object of such pure enchantment. Then I pushed the feeling aside and quickly tied the ring into the corner of my handkerchief, and I started back down the passage.

As I came level with the bedroom door I noticed that it was slightly ajar, and I paused with my hand going out towards the handle to draw it closed.

From the room beyond came a woman's voice, a voice husky with emotion, a voice broken by the panting of breath aroused and tremulous.

'Yes, oh God, yes. Do it! Do it!' And a man's voice blended with it, a voice rising in a hoarse cry like a wounded animal.

'Darling! My darling!' The voices washed, and swirled and broke together, the high surf of passion driven by the storm winds of love. With it was another sound, rhythmic, urgent, pounding out the pulse of creation, a sound as old as man, as unchanging as the courses of the stars. As I stood frozen, my hand still out-stretched towards the door handle, the thudding heartbeat of love was arrested and then there was only the sound of ragged breathing and the small sighs and moans of emotions spent and exhausted.

I turned away like a sleep walker. Silently I went to the front door and silently I closed it behind me.

I sat quietly through a lunch I do not remember eating, through conversations I do not remember hearing, for the voices I had heard beyond that door were those of Sally Benator and Louren Sturvesant.

I do not remember the return to the Royal Society, and only vague snatches of the concluding papers and ceremonial remain with me.

I sat in my seat in the front row, hunched down in my chair and stared at a crack in the polished wooden floor. My mind cast back, working over the past like a gun-dog hunting a hidden bird.

I remembered a night at the City of the Moon when I had gone drunk to bed, drunk on whisky poured for me by Sally's own hand. I remembered waking when Louren came into the tent, and seeing the pale flush of dawn in the sky beyond the tent-flap.

I remembered my visit to the cavern in the night, when Louren had dazzled me with the torch beam and sent me away.

I remembered that conversation overheard between Ral and Leslie. I remembered Sally's friends from Brighton, her violent unreasonable attacks on Hilary, her moods and silences, her sudden gaiety and even more sudden depressions, the half-statements, the hovering upon the verge of revelation, the midnight visit to my bedside, and a hundred other clues and hints – and I marvelled at my own blindness. How could I not have seen it, nor sensed it?

My name had been spoken, and I struggled to rouse myself, to try and listen to what was said. It was Graham Hobson, the President of the Society, speaking and looking down at me, smiling. Around me heads were craning, smiling also, friendly kind faces.

'Awarded the Society's Patron's and Founder's Medal,' said Hobson. 'In addition, my Council has instructed me to announce that a sum has been set aside from the fund provided, and that a commission will be awarded to a leading artist to paint a portrait of Dr Kazin. At an appropriate ceremony the portrait will be hung—'

I shook my head to clear it. I felt fuzzy and stupid. Hobson's voice kept fading and I tried to concentrate. Then gentle but insistent hands were pulling me to my feet, pushing me towards the stage.

'Speech!' they called, laughing, applauding.

I stood before them. I felt dizzy, the room turned and steadied again, blurred and refocused.

'Your Grace,' I began and choked, my throat felt flannelly, the words came out thickly. 'I am honoured.' I stopped and groped for words, they were silent, expectant. I looked desperately about the hall, seeking deliverance or inspiration.

Sally Benator was standing beside the side entrance. I did not know how long she had been there. She was smiling, white teeth in her sun-brown and lovely face, dark hair hanging in shining wings to her shoulders, her cheeks aflame and eyes sparkling, a girl freshly arisen from the bed of her lover.

I stared at her. 'I am thankful,' I mumbled, and she nodded and smiled encouragement at me – and my heart broke; it was a physical thing, a sharp pain, tissue tearing in my chest, so intense that I caught my breath. I had lost her, my love, my only love, and all these honours, all this acclaim was meaningless.

I stared across at her, desolate and bereft of purpose. I

felt the tears flood and burn my eyes. I did not want them all to see it, and I stumbled from the stage towards the door. The applause swelled again, and I heard voices in the tumult.

'Poor fellow, he's completely overcome.'

'How touching.'

'He's overwhelmed.'

And I ran out into the street. It was raining a soft drizzle and I ran wildly. Like a wounded animal I wanted to be alone to recover from this hurt. The cold rain soothed my burning eyes.

I craved solitude and surcease from pain, and both I found at the City of the Moon. Eldridge had a month's lecturing commitments to meet in England, and Sally had disappeared. I had not spoken to her since that night, but Louren told me casually that she had taken two weeks of her accumulated vacation time and had joined a tour to Italy and the Greek Islands. At the City of the Moon an airmail letter from Sally reached me, postmarked Padua, confirming this and regretting that her efforts to see me before I left London had failed. This was not surprising, for I had not returned to the Dorchester, but had my luggage sent to Blue Bird House and flown out on the early morning flight for Africa. Sally sent her congratulations, and ended by saying she would return to Johannesburg at the end of the month and take advantage of the first flight to the City of the Moon.

Reading her letter gave me a feeling of unreality, like receiving a message from beyond the grave. For she was dead to me, gone beyond my reach for ever. I burned the letter.

Louren visited the site for one day. I found that I had nothing to say to him. It was as though we were strangers;

his features, once so well remembered and beloved, were unfamiliar to me now.

He sensed the gap that separated us, and tried to reach across it. I could not respond, and he cut short his visit and left. I knew his puzzlement, and vaguely I regretted it. I could not find it in myself to blame or hate him.

Ral and Leslie were shadowy figures on the borders of my solitude. They did not intrude in the private world in which I now lived.

This was the world of Huy Ben-Amon, a place beyond pain and sorrow. During the time that Eldridge worked upon the scrolls, I had followed daily each detail of his translation. Language is my greatest talent, it comes to me without effort. Lawrence of Arabia learned to speak Arabic in four days – in ten I had taught myself Punic, and in so doing had gained the key to the fairyland of the golden books of Huy.

The third book was a continuation of the history of Opet up to the lifetime of the poet. This was as fascinating a document as the two that preceded it, but the true magic for me was in the remaining two golden books.

These were the poems and songs of Huy, poems and songs in the modern sense of the words. This was Huy the warrior, the Axeman of all the Gods, writing an ode to the shiny wing of the bird of the sun, his battle-axe.

He described the ore brought from the mines of the south, and its smelting in the womb-shaped furnace, the smell of the glowing charcoal and the trickle of the molten metal.

How it was purged, and alloyed, forged and shaped, its edging and engraving, and when he described the figures of the four vultures and the four suns I looked up at the great axe that hung above my working desk with wonder.

With Huy I heard the gleaming blade moan in flight, heard the snick of the edge into bone, the sucking withdrawal from living flesh. I read with awe the list of the enemies who had died beneath it, and wondered at their crimes and transgressions.

Then Huy's mood changed and he was a roistering fellow, tipping back the jug of red Zeng wine, roaring with laughter in the firelight with his companions in arms.

Now he was the dandy dressed in white linen, perfumed with sweet oils, his beard twisted and plaited into ropes.

Now the priest, walking with his gods. Sure of them, tending to their mysteries, and rendering unto them their portion of the sacrifice. Huy kneeling alone in silent prayer, Huy in the dawn lifting his arms in greeting to Baal, the sun-god. Huy in a frenzy of religious revelation.

Then again Huy is the friend, the true companion, describing his joy in the company of another man. The interlock of personalities, the spice of shared pleasures, dangers faced together and overcome. There is a strong hint in this poem that Huy is a hero-worshipper, blind to the faults of his friend, describing his physical beauty with an almost womanly insight. He details the breadth of shoulder, the regal curve of flaming red beard down onto a chest where the muscle bulges smooth and hard as the boulders upon the hills of Zimbao, the legs like strong saplings, the smile like the warm blessing of the sun-god Baal, and he ends with the line, 'Lannon Hycanus you are more than King of Opet, you are my friend.' Reading it, I felt that to have the friendship of Huy was to have something of value.

The mood of the poet changes again and he is the observer of nature, the hunter, describing his quarry with loving care, missing no detail, from the curve in the ivory tusk to the creamy softness of a lioness's underbelly.

Then he is a lover, bemused by the beauty of his sweetheart.

Tanith whose wide brow is shining white and full as the

moon, whose hair blows soft and light as the smoke from the great papyrus fires in the swamps, whose eyes shine green as the deep pool in the temple of the goddess Astarte.

Then suddenly Tanith is dead, and the poet cries his grief, seeing her death as the flight of a bird, her ivory arms gleaming like spread wings, her last cry echoing across the vault of heaven to touch the hearts of the gods themselves. Huy's lament was mine, his voice was mine, his terrors and triumphs became my own, and it seemed that Huy was me, and I was Huy.

I rose early and retired late, I ate little and my face grew gaunt and pale, a haunted face that stared back at me from my mirror with wild eyes.

Then suddenly reality caught up with me, shattering the fragile crystal walls of my fairyland. On the same aircraft Louren and Sally arrived together at the City of the Moon. The torment which I had for so long avoided had now begun again.

Again I tried to hide. I chose the archives as my sanctuary, and spent each day there trying to avoid all contact with either Sally or Louren. Still there was that dreaded hour of the evening meal, trying to smile my way through it and join in the banter and discussion, trying not to notice the private intimate exchange of glances and smiles between Louren and Sally until I could reasonably leave.

Twice Louren came to me.

'There is something wrong, Ben.'

'No, Louren. No. I swear to you. You are mistaken.' And I escaped to the stillness of the archives.

There was Ral's quiet company and the physical labour of cataloguing, photographing and packing the jars, and besides these I found another distraction. This cavern sealed for almost 2,000 years had been sterile, devoid of any life form when first we opened it. Now it was establishing its own ecology, first the tiny midge flies, then sand fleas, ants, spiders, moths, and finally the little brown gecko lizards. I had started making a film record of this colonization of the archives.

I spent many hours a day sitting quietly with my camera poised, waiting to obtain some difficult close-up shot of fly or insect and it was thus that I made the last major discovery at the City of the Moon.

I was working alone at the furthest end of the archives, close by the wall on which was graven the image of the sun. One of the gecko lizards ran down the wall, and across the stone floor. At the spot where the great battle-axe had lain when we discovered it, the lizard stopped. It stood poised, the soft skin of its throat pulsing and its little black beady eyes shiny with expectation. I noticed then the insect it was stalking. A white moth that sat quietly with spread wings on the sun image.

Quickly I reached for my camera, and set the flash bulb and exposure. I was anxious to record one of the lizards in the moment of its kill. Slowly I moved into a position from which I could focus on the moth, and I waited while the lizard approached in a series of swift dashes. Twelve inches from the moth it stopped again, and seemed to gather itself for the final assault. I waited breathlessly, my finger on the trigger button. The lizard shot forward and I exploded the bulb.

The lizard froze with the body of the moth crammed in its mouth. Then it turned and darted head-down towards the floor; when it reached the corner formed by wall and floor it disappeared and I laughed at its ludicrous fright.

I wound the film, replaced the flash bulb, returned the camera to its case, and was about to resume my work when a thought occurred to me. I went back to the end wall of the cavern, to the point where the lizard had disappeared and stooped to examine the juncture of floor and wall. It seemed solid, and I could see no hole or crack for the lizard to use as a refuge. Intrigued now by the lizard's

303

disappearance, I went to fetch one of the electric arc-lights on its cable and I set it so that the beam fully illuminated the wall.

Then on hands and knees I crawled along the wall. I felt my heart start to pound like a war drum, and the hum of blood in my ears, the warmth of it in my cheeks. My hand as I reached for my pen-knife was unsteady, and I nearly broke my thumbnail as I tried to open the blade.

Then I was probing the faint crack line, plugged with dust, that separated wall and floor. The blade of my knife slipped into the crack to its full length.

I rocked back on my heels and stared at the wall, seeing the image of the sun throwing weird shadows in the arc-light.

'Perhaps,' I whispered aloud, 'it's just possible . . .' And then I was grovelling again beneath the image of Baal, almost as though I were one of his worshippers. Frantically I probed the crack, following it along the floor, until abruptly it turned ninety degrees, and climbed the wall. Here the crack was secret-jointed, riveted and turned back onto itself, making it all but invisible. The cunning skill with which this joint had been concealed convinced me that it hid something vital. The workmanship of this piece of the wall was a far cry from the rough joints on the roof slabs through which the dust had filtered down.

Now I jumped up and paced restlessly back and forth before the blank wall. I was alive again for the first time since my return to the City of the Moon. My skin tingled, my step was full of spring, my fists clenched and unclenched and my brain was racing with excitement.

'Louren,' I thought suddenly. 'He should be here.' I almost ran back down the archives, and out through the tunnel. In the wooden guard hut which enclosed the entrance to the tunnel one of the security guards was sprawled in a chair with his boots on the desk. The collar of his blue uniform was unbuttoned, his cap pushed back on his head. On the wall behind him his gunbelt hung from a hook, with the black butt of the revolver sticking out of the holster. He looked up from his paperback Western, a thick beaky-nosed face with cold eagle eyes.

'Hi, Doc. You in a hurry?'

'Bols, can you get hold of Mr Sturvesant for me? Ask him to come up here right away.'

I was on my knees below the sun image when Louren arrived.

'Lo, come over here. I want to show you something.'

'Hey, Ben!' Louren laughed, and it seemed to me that his expression was one of relieved pleasure. 'That's the first time I've seen you really smile in two weeks. God, I was worried about you.' He slapped my shoulder, still laughing. 'This is more like the old Ben again.'

'Lo, look at this.' And he knelt beside me.

Ten minutes later he was no longer smiling, his face was cold and intent. He was staring at the wall with those pale blue eyes as though he were seeing through the solid rock.

'Lo,' I began, but he waved me to silence with a peremptory gesture. He never took his eyes from the wall and now it seemed to me that he was listening to a voice I could not hear. I watched that cold god-like face with a sudden feeling of almost superstitious awe. I had a premonition of something unnatural about to happen.

Slowly, step by step, Louren approached the sun image. His hand went out and lay against the centre of the great disc. His fingers were spread, seeming to echo the shape of the image. He began to press against the wall, I saw the tips of his fingers flatten against the rock, changing shape beneath the pressure of his hand.

For a few long seconds nothing happened, then suddenly the wall began to move. There was no sound, no grating or squeal of protesting hinge, but the whole wall began to revolve upon a concealed axis. A ponderous, deliberate movement that revealed the square dark opening to a further passageway concealed beyond the image of Baal.

Staring into that dark prehistoric opening I whispered without glancing at Louren, 'How did you do that, Lo? How did you guess?'

His tone as he replied was puzzled. 'I knew – I just knew, that's all.' We were both silent again, staring into the opening. I was seized by a sudden unaccountable dread of what we would find in there.

'Get the light, Ben,' Louren ordered without taking his eyes from the doorway. I fetched the portable arc-light, and Louren took it from my hand. I followed him as he walked through the doorway.

Before us a passageway slanted down into the earth at an angle of forty-five degrees. The passage was seven foot six inches high, and nine feet wide. There was a flight of stone steps cut into the floor. Each step was worn, with edges smoothed and rounded. The walls and roof of the tunnel were of unadorned stone, and the depths of the tunnel were hidden from us by shadow and darkness.

'What's this?' Louren pointed at two large circular objects which lay at the head of the staircase. I saw the gleam of bronze rosettes upon them.

'Shields,' I told him. 'War shields.'

'Someone dropped them in a hurry.'

We stepped over them carefully and started down the staircase. There were 106 steps, each six inches high.

'No dust in here,' Louren remarked.

'No,' I agreed. 'The seal of the door was tight.'

His words should have acted as a warning, but I was lost in the wonder and excitement of this new discovery. The surface of the stairs was as clean as though freshly swept.

At the bottom of the staircase we reached a T-junction. On our right the passage led to a gate of barred ironwork which was closed and bolted. On the left it descended another twisting staircase that disappeared into the living rock.

'Which way?' Louren asked.

'Let's see what's behind the gate,' I suggested in a voice choking with excitement, and we went to it.

The heavy bolts were not locked but a thread of gold wire was twisted around the jamb of the gate, and a heavy clay seal closed the entrance.

The figure on the seal was of a crudely wrought animal, and the words, 'Lannon Hycanus, Gry-Lion of Opet, King of Punt and the four kingdoms.'

'Give me your knife,' Louren said.

'Lo, we can't,' I began.

'Give it to me, damn you.' His voice was shaking, thick with a peculiar lust and passion. 'You know what this is? It's the treasury, the gold vaults of Opet!'

'Wait, let's do it properly, Lo,' I pleaded, but he took the seal in his bare hands and ripped it from the gate.

'Don't do it, Lo,' I protested, but he pulled the bolts open, and flung his weight against the gate. It was rusted closed, but he attacked it with all his weight. It gave, swinging back far enough for Louren to squeeze through. He ran forward, and I ran after him. The tunnel turned again at right angles and led directly into a large chamber.

'God!' shouted Louren. 'Oh God! Look at it, Ben. Just look at it.'

The treasury of Opet lay before us with all its fabulous wealth untouched. Later we could count and weigh and measure it, but now we stood and stared.

The chamber was 186 feet long and 21 wide. The ivory was stacked along most of one wall. There were 1,016 large elephant tusks. The ivory was rotten and crumbly as chalk, but in itself must have been a vast treasure 2,000 years ago.

There were over 900 large amphorae, sealed with wax.

The contents of precious oils had long since evaporated into a congealed black mass. There were bolts of imported linen and silk, rotted now so that they crumbled to dust at the touch.

The metals were stacked along the opposite wall of the vault – 190 tons of native copper cast into ingots shaped like the cross of St Andrew; 3 tons of tin, cast into the same shape; 16 tons of silver; 96 of lead; 2 of antimony.

We walked down the aisle along the centre of the vault, staring about us at this incredible display of wealth.

'The gold,' Louren muttered. 'Where is the gold?'

There was a stack of wooden chests, carved from ebony, the lids decorated with ivory and mother-of-pearl inlay. These were the only objects of an artistic nature in the vault, and even they were crudely executed battle scenes or hunting scenes.

'No, don't do it, Lo,' I cried another protest as Louren began ripping open the lids.

They were filled with semi-precious stones, amethyst, beryl, tigers' eyes, jade and malachite. Some of these were crudely cut and incorporated in gold jewellery, thick clumsy pieces, collars, brooches, necklaces and rings.

Louren hurried on down the aisle, and then stopped abruptly. In another recess that led off the main chamber, behind another iron gate, the gold was stacked in neat piles. Cast in the usual 'finger' moulds. The piles of previous metal were insignificant in bulk, but when, months later, it was all weighed the total was over sixty tons.

Its value was in excess of £60,000,000 sterling. In the same recess as the gold were two small wooden chests. These yielded 26,000 carats of uncut and rough-cut diamonds of every conceivable colour and shape. Not one of these was smaller than one and a half carats, and the largest was a big sulky yellow monster of thirty-eight carats, and this added a further £2,000,000 to the intrinsic value of the treasure.

Here was the wealth of forty-seven kings of Opet, accumulated painstakingly over the course of 400 years. No other treasure of antiquity could compare with this profusion.

'We'll have to be bloody careful, Ben. No word of this must leak out. You understand what might happen if it did?' He stood with a finger of solid gold in each hand, looking down on the piles of treasure. 'This is enough to kill for, to start a war!'

'What do you want me to do, Lo? I must have help in here. Ral or Sally even.'

'No!' He turned on me ferociously. 'No one else will be allowed in here. I will leave orders with the guards, no one but you and I.'

'I need help, Lo. I can't do it myself, there is too much here.'

'I'll help you,' Louren said.

'It will take weeks.'

'I'll help you,' he repeated. 'No one else. Not a word to anyone else.'

Until six o'clock that evening Louren and I explored the treasure vault.

'Let's find out where the other branch of the tunnel leads to,' I suggested.

'No,' Louren stopped me. 'I want to keep normal hours here. I don't want the others to guess that we are up to something. We will go down to the camp now. Tomorrow we will have a look at the other fork of the tunnel. It can't be anything like this anyway.'

We closed the stone door behind us, sealing off the secret passage, and at the guard post Louren made his orders clear, repeating them and writing them on the guard's instruction sheet. Ral's and Sally's names were removed from the list of those allowed into the tunnel. And later he mentioned it to them at dinner. He explained it away as an experiment that he and I were attempting. It was a difficult evening for me. I was over-wrought by the day's excitement, and now that I had shaken off my mood of apathy I was over-reacting to the normal stimuli of living. I found myself laughing too loudly, drinking too much, and the agony of my jealousy returned more intensely than ever.

When Louren and Sally looked at each other like that, I wanted to shout at them, 'I know. I know about it, and damn you, I hate you for it.'

But then I knew it was not true. I did not hate them. I loved them both and this made it all the harder to bear.

There was no chance of sleep for me, that night. When I get myself into a certain state of nervous tension, then I can go for two or three nights without being able to still the racing of my overheated brain. I did not mean to spy on her. It was a mere coincidence that I was standing at the window of my hut staring out from my darkened room at the moonlit night when Sally left her own hut.

She wore a long pale-coloured dressing-gown and her hair was let down in a dark cloud around her shoulders. She paused in the doorway of her own hut and looked around carefully, making sure that the camp was asleep. Then guiltily, quickly, she hurried across the open moonlit yard to the hut in which Louren was living. She opened the door and went in without hesitating and for me a long harrowing vigil had begun.

I stood by my window for two hours, watching the moon shadows change shape, watching the patterns of the stars swing and turn across the heavens, stars as fat and bright as they are only in the sweet clean air of the wilderness. The beauty of it was wasted on me this night. I was watching Louren's hut, imagining each whispered word, each touch, each movement, and hating myself and them. I thought of Hilary and the children, wondering what madness it is that makes a man gamble his all on a few hours of transient pleasure. In that darkened hut how many confidences were those two betraying, how many people's happiness were they risking.

Then suddenly I realized that I was assuming that this affair was merely play on Louren's part, and I faced the possibility that he was serious. That he would desert Hilary and go to Sally. I found this thought intolerable. I could no longer watch and wait, I must have some distraction and I dressed quickly and hurried across to the repository.

The night-watchman greeted me sleepily, and I unlocked the door and went to the vault in which the golden books were kept. I took out the fourth book of Huy. I carried it across to my own office, and before I settled down to read I went to fetch a bottle of Glen Grant. My two opiates, words and whisky.

I opened the scroll at random and re-read Huy's ode to his battle-axe, the gleaming wing of the bird of the sun. When I had finished I was taken by an impulse and I lifted the great axe down from its place of honour. I caressed the shimmering length of it, studying it with new attention. I was convinced that this was the weapon of the poem. Could there be another answering the description so accurately? I held it in my lap, wishing that I could draw from it the story of the last days of Opet. I was sure it was involved intimately in the final tragedy. Why had it been left abandoned, a thing so well beloved and yet thrown carelessly aside to lie uncared for and discarded for nearly 2,000 years? What had happened to the Axeman Huy, and his king and his city?

I read and dreamed, disturbed less frequently by thoughts of Sally and Louren. However, at every pause in my readings they came to me with a sick little slide of jealousy and despair in my guts. I was torn between the present and the distant past.

I read on, sampling those portions of the scroll which were still unknown territory while the level in the whisky bottle sank slowly and the long night passed.

Then when midnight had flown and the new day was being born, I came upon a small piece of writing which touched a new depth of response in me. Huy makes a sudden heart-felt cry from the depths of his being. It is as though some long-suppressed emotion will no longer be contained and must come out in this appeal to have his physical form discounted when his value is assessed. From base earth flowers the purest gold, Huy cries, in his own poor distorted clay there were treasures concealed.

I re-read the passage half a dozen times, making sure of my translation before I could accept that Huy Ben-Amon was like me. A *cripple*.

Dawn's first promise was tracing the silhouette of the cliff tops with a pale rose colour when I laid the golden book away in its vault and walked slowly back towards my hut.

Sally stepped out of Louren's doorway and came towards me in the darkness. Her gown was ghostly pale and she seemed to float above the ground. I stood still, hoping she would not see me. There was a chance for I stood in the deeper shadow of her hut and I turned my face away, standing quietly.

I heard the rustle of her skirts, the whisper of her feet in the dust very close in the dark, then her startled gasp as she saw me. I looked at her then. She had seen but not recognized me. Her face was a pale moon of fear and her hands were at her mouth.

'All right, Sally,' I said. 'It's only me.'

I could smell her now. On the clean night air of the desert it was a perfumed smell like crushed rose petals, and mingled with it the warm smell of perspiration and love. My heart slid in my chest.

'Ben?' she said, and we were both silent staring at each other.

'How long have you been here?'

'Long enough,' I answered, and again the silence.

'You know, then?' It was said in a small voice, shy and sad.

'I didn't mean to spy,' I said, and another silence.

'I believe you.' She began to move away. Then she turned back. 'Ben, I want to explain.'

'You don't have to do that,' I said.

'Yes, I do. I want to.'

'It doesn't matter, Sal.'

'It does matter.' And we faced each other. 'It does matter,' she repeated. 'I don't want you to think that I, well, that I am so terrible.'

'Forget it, Sally,' I said.

'I tried not to, Ben. I swear to you.'

'It's all right, Sally.'

'I couldn't help it, truly. I tried so hard to fight it. I didn't want it to happen.' She was crying now, silently, her shoulders shaking as she sobbed.

'It doesn't matter,' I said, and went to her. I took her gently to her room and put her on the bed. In the light I saw how her lips were swollen and kiss-inflamed.

'Oh, Ben, I would have given anything for it to be different.'

'I know, Sally.'

'I tried so hard, but it was too much for me. He had me in some kind of spell, from the very first moment I saw him.'

'That evening at the airport?' I could not help but ask the question, remembering how she had watched Louren that first time she met him and how later she had ranted against him.

'That's why – later, with me – that's why we—' I did

313

not want to hear her answer, and yet I must know if she had first come to me inflamed with thoughts of another man.

'No, Ben.' She tried to deny it, but she saw my eyes, and turned her face away. 'Oh, Ben, I'm sorry. I didn't want to hurt you.'

'Yes,' I nodded.

'I truly didn't want to hurt you. You are so good, so gentle, so different from him.' There were dark shadows of sleeplessness beneath her eyes, and the peach-coloured velvet of her cheek was rubbed pink by Louren's unshaven skin.

'Yes,' I said with my heart breaking.

'Oh, Ben, what shall I do?' she cried in distress. 'I am caught in this thing. I cannot escape.'

'Does Lo – has he said what he is going to do? Has he told you he, well, that he will leave Hilary, and marry you?'

'No.' She shook her head.

'Has he given you reason—'

'No! No!' She caught my hand. 'Oh, Ben. It's just fun for him. It's just a little adventure.'

I said nothing, watching her lovely tortured face, glad at least that she knew about Louren. Realized that he was a hunter and she the quarry. There had been many Sallys in Louren's life, and there would be many more. The lion must kill regularly.

'Is there anything I can do, Sally?' I asked at last.

'No, Ben. I don't think so.'

'If there is, tell me,' I said and moved towards the door.

'Ben,' she stopped me, and sat up. 'Ben, do you still love me?'

I nodded without hesitation. 'Yes, I still love you.'

'Thank you, Ben,' she sighed softly. 'I don't think I could have taken it if you had turned away from me.'

'I'll never do that, Sally,' I said, and walked out into the lemon and rose glow of dawn.

L ouren and I descended the staircase beyond the sun image. We went first to the treasure vault. While Louren gloated over the stacks of golden fingers, I watched his face. I was light-headed from lack of sleep, and I could taste the spirits I had drunk in the back of my throat. Watching Louren, I tried to find hatred for him in my heart, I searched diligently without success. When he looked up and smiled at me, I could not but answer him with a smile.

'This will keep, Ben,' he said. 'Let's go and have a look at the rest of it.'

I had guessed what we would find beyond the junction of the tunnels, and once we had descended the last spiralling stairs and come into another short level passage I had my last doubts dispelled.

The passage ended against another solid stone wall. Here, however, there was no attempt at concealment, for carved into the stone was an inscription. We stood before it, and Louren held the arc-lamp full upon it.

'What does it say?' he asked.

I read it through slowly. Even with all my practice I read slowly, for in Punic there are no symbols for the vowels and each must be guessed from the context of the word.

'Come on,' Louren muttered impatiently.

'"You who come here to interrupt the sleep of the kings of Opet, and to despoil their tomb, do so at your peril, and may the curse of Astarte and great Baal hound you to your own graves."'

'Read it again,' Louren commanded, and I did. He nodded.

'Yes,' he said, and stepped to the stone door. He began to seek the pivot point which we knew would trigger the mechanism. Here we were not so fortunate as we had been at the threshold of the sun door. After two hours, our way was still barred by that solid slab of uncompromising stone.

'I'm going to blow the bloody thing open,' Louren warned, but I knew he would not commit such an atrocity in this sacred place. We rested and discussed the problem, before returning to the door. It had to be another simple leverage system, but the trick was to find the pressure point and the angle of movement.

When we found it at last, I cursed my own stupidity. It should have been my first attempt. The symbol for the name of the sun-god Baal was once more the pressure point.

The door swung open, ponderous and slow, and we went through into the tomb of the kings of Opet.

There is only one other place I have known with the same atmosphere. That is Westminster Abbey which contains the tombs of so many of the kings of England. There was the same hushed cathedral sense of time past and history reborn.

Neither of us spoke as we went to the centre of the long narrow vaulted tomb. The silence was an oppressive weight upon my eardrums. Utter silence, so complete as to be sinister and threatening. Here again the air was long disused, but with an even heavier musty quality to it. I thought I detected the faint, stale smell of dust and mushrooms.

Along each wall, parallel to it, stood the sarcophagi of the kings of Opet. They were carved of massive granite. Solid, squat and grey. The lids were held in place by their own immense weight, and the upper surface had been polished and engraved with the name and style of the body that lay within. The mighty names that had echoed through the golden books of Huy. I recognized them, Hamilcar, Hannibal, Hycanus. Forty-seven great coffins, but the last was empty, its lid propped against the wall beside it. Its interior cut out into a man's shape, ready to swallow the last king of Opet.

At the foot of the great stone coffin a man lay stretched

upon his back on the floor of the tomb. His helmet was missing and his red-gold hair and beard formed a soft frame for the wizened, mummified features. His breast-plate had been removed exposing the dried parchment skin stretched over the gaunt skeletal rib-cage. The broken shaft of an arrow protruded from a long-dead chest. He wore a kilt of leather, studded with bronze rosettes and on his shins were greaves of bronze, on his feet light sandals.

His arms lay at his sides, his heels were together. The dead body had been laid out with care and obvious love.

Over him stooped another figure, kneeling like a man in prayer. A figure in full armour, with only the war helmet and breast-plate discarded on the floor beneath the empty sarcophagus. Long black hair hung forward to conceal his bowed face. Both hands clutched at his chest at the level of the diaphragm. From his chest a blade of steel protruded, a reversed sword, with its hilt securely anchored against the stone slabs of the floor, the point driven up under the ribs and lodged in his vitals.

Here was a man in the attitude of final escape from the shame of defeat, a man who in despair had fallen upon his own sword. The weapon had supported his weight these many centuries, propping him up in that kneeling position.

Neither Louren nor I could speak, as we drew closer to this tableau of ancient tragedy. For me there was no doubt as to the identity of these dried-out human husks.

Lannon Hycanus, the last King of Opet, lay stretched on the cold stone floor. Above him knelt his friend and high priest Huy Ben-Amon.

I felt choked with a sense of destiny, with a cold aching dread – for Huy Ben-Amon, the Axeman of the Gods, was a *hunchback*.

I had to see his face. I had to see it! I ran forward, and knelt beside him.

I touched his gaunt bony shoulder, covered by a tunic of brittle yellow linen. It was the lightest touch, a breath almost, but it was enough to shatter that delicately poised mummy.

The corpse of Huy Ben-Amon slid forward and crashed down on the body of the king. Steel and bronze rang on the stone floor, and echoed about the vaulted tomb of Opet.

The two figures burst into dust at the impact, a soft yellow explosion of mustard-yellow dust, swirling like smoke in the arc-light. There was nothing left of them but the metal of armour and sword, and two hanks of gold and sable hair in the puddle of talcum-soft dust.

I stood up, choking with the yellow dust. My eyes were swimming with tears of wonder and burning with the dust. The dust smelled of mushrooms.

Louren Sturvesant and I stared at each other without speaking. We had witnessed a miracle.

I awoke from a screaming nightmare of blood and flame and smoke, a horror of shining black faces and sweat-polished bodies lit by crackling roaring flames and the scream of the dying and the animal roar of blood-crazed voices. I woke panting and choking from the memory, and the terror and horror of it stayed with me long after I had found myself alone in my quiet hut in the silent night.

I switched on the bedside light and looked at my watch. It was still early, a little before eleven. I threw back my sheets and stood up, surprised to find my legs shaky and my breathing ragged. There was a twinge of pain at each breath I drew, and a dull tight sensation behind my eyes. My body felt hot, fever hot. I went to the wash-stand across the hut, and shook three aspirin from the bottle. I swallowed them with a mouthful of water, and then the tickling sensation in my lungs grew stronger. I coughed as though I was on sixty cigarettes a day, and the effort left me sweaty and trembling. My skin seemed to be aflame.

Without really knowing why, I took my dressing-gown off the hook behind the door, pulled it on and went out into the yard. There was half a moon in the sky, horned and yellow. The shadows under the trees and around the buildings were very dark and ugly. I felt the lingering dread and horror of my nightmare still upon me as I hurried across towards my office, and I glanced about me nervously. I could smell the tinge of smoke on the night air, and it troubled me also. I sniffed at it, feeling the faint sting deep in my lungs.

I reached the door of my office, and there was something waiting for me in the deep shadow beside the building. I saw it rush at me from the corner of my vision, a big dark thing, rounded and shapeless and deadly silent. I spun to face it, falling against the wall of the hut, weak with terror. A scream bubbled and died in my throat for there was nothing there. It was gone, I had imagined it, but now the pain in my head beat like hammer blows on the anvil.

I pulled the door open, and fell into my office, slammed the door behind me, locked it, gasping with unnamed and baseless fear. Something scratched against the door from the outside, a terrifying clawing animal sound that ripped my quivering nerves.

I backed away from the door towards my desk, crouching there, trembling, shaking and weak.

The sound came again, but from the wall beside me, I spun to face it, and I heard myself whimper.

I needed a weapon, I looked around desperately and the great battle-axe of Huy hung on the wall above my desk. I snatched it down and backed into a corner, holding it ready, at the present position across my chest. I coughed.

There was a thick sheaf of white paper on my desk. It moved and I felt the gooseflesh crawl all over my hot body.

The white square of paper quivered and wavered, it changed shape, crawled across my desk, and spread white bats' wings. Then suddenly it launched into flight, wings whispering, and it flew at my face. I saw the wide open mouth ringed with needle vampire teeth, heard the shrill squeaks as it attacked. I shouted with horror, and struck with the axe. The white thing fluttered and squeaked against my throat and face, and I fought and shouted, striking it down onto the floor where it crawled and slithered loathsomely. I struck with the edge of the axe, and inky black blood spurted from the thing and puddled the wooden floor of the hut.

I backed away from the thing, and lay back against the wall. I felt weak, and terribly afraid. I began to cough. The cough took hold of my whole body and shook it, rocking me, doubling me against the wall. I coughed until my vision burst into bright lights, and there was a salty sweet taste in my mouth.

I sank to my knees against the wall, my mouth was filled with warm wetness and I spat a thick gob of bright blood onto the floor. I stared at it, not understanding what was happening to me. I lifted my hand to my mouth and wiped my lips. My hand came away smeared with blood.

I knew then what it was. Louren and I had passed beyond two sealed doorways into the depths of a tomb closed for 2,000 years – and we had breathed air loaded with the spores of *cryptococcus neuromyces*, the curse of the Pharaohs.

It was too late now for me to berate myself for overlooking the precautions. I had believed that because the archives were safe, the rest of it was also. In my eagerness and excitement I had not given another thought to the fungus danger, even when Louren and I had discussed the door seals and even when I had smelled the mushroom odour in the tomb of the kings.

Now my lungs were clogged with the horrible colonies

of living fungus, a growing living thing within me, feeding on the soft tissues of my body, and pouring out its poisons into my blood to be carried to my brain.

'Treatment,' I gasped, 'got to find the treatment.' And I staggered across to my bookshelves. I tried to read the letters on the spines of the books, but they changed to little black insects and crawled away. Suddenly a thick mottled snake uncoiled from the top shelf, and dangled down towards my face, a thick bloated puff-adder with a flicking black tongue. I backed away, then turned and fled out into the night.

The smoke was thick, swirling around me, choking me so that I coughed wildly. The flames around me lit all with a lurid satanic glow, a flickering glow. There were dark shapes and strange sounds. I saw Louren's hut, and ran towards it.

'Louren,' I screamed, bursting in through the door. 'Louren!' panting, coughing.

The light went on. Sally was alone in Louren's bed, she sat up, sleepy, soft-eyed, naked, and looked at me with unfocused vision.

'Where is he?' I shouted at her. She looked confused, not understanding.

'Ben, what is it? You're bleeding!'

'Where is Lo?' It was desperately urgent. I had to find him. He had been exposed to the fungus also. I had to find him.

Sally looked down at the bed beside her. There was the indentation on the pillow where Louren's head had lain.

'I don't know,' she said, big-eyed, puzzled. 'He was here. He must have gone out.'

I coughed, great choking sobs, and felt fresh blood in my mouth. Sally was fully awake now. She stared at me.

'Ben, what is it?'

'Neuromyces,' I told her, and she gasped seeing the blood streaming down my chin.

321

'Louren and I have opened a secret passage beyond the sun image in the archives. It's infected with the spores. We took no precautions. It has got us. I'm sure he's there now. I'm going to him.' I stopped to breathe. Sally was out of bed slipping into her gown, coming to me.

'Get Ral Davidson. Respirators. Take all precautions. Follow us. I will prop the doors open. Down steps. Turn left at bottom. Follow us. Louren will have it also, drives you mad. Crazy. Terrible things. Come quickly – do you understand?'

'Yes, Ben.'

'Get Ral,' I said and turned. I ran out into the smoke and flames and darkness, running for the cliffs and the cavern. The great walls of the temple towered above me, walls long gone. The great phallic towers of Baal pointed to the moon, lit by the flames of a burning city. Towers that stood again after so long. They were screaming, the women, burning alive with their children. Dead men lay strewn in my path, cut down like the harvest of the devil, their dead faces terrible in the moonlight.

'Louren,' I shouted and ran on through the temple. They were in my path, dark and savage, crowding forward to oppose me. Dark, shapeless, terrifying, and I flew at them with a strange battle cry yelled from a blood-glutted throat. The mighty axe spun its silver circles in the firelight, and I was through them, running.

I reached the cavern, saw it lit by the guttering torches, saw the pavement of stone bordering the circular green beauty of the emerald pool. The rows of stone benches, rising in tiers around it as they had 2,000 years before. With a last enormous effort of will, I forced my brain to discount this fantasy and to recognize reality.

The wooden guard hut stood across the cavern from me. I staggered towards it. The guard sat at his desk reading. He looked up, his expression changing to surprise and incredulity.

'Good God, are you all right, Doctor?'

'Mr Sturvesant, is he in the tunnel?'

'Yes.'

'When did he go in?'

'An hour ago.' The guard came towards me. 'Is something wrong? You are bleeding, Doctor!'

'Wait here,' I told him. 'The others are coming. They know what to do.'

I hurried on into the archives, smelling the smoke still and hearing the clamour of a dying city ring in my ears.

Before the image of the sun-god I let the great battle-axe slip from my hand and left it lying on the stone floor. I pushed the stone door open, and propped it with one of the war shields to prevent it swinging closed behind me.

I ran down the staircase. Half-way down I saw the glow of light from the tomb below.

The inscribed doorway with its graven curse of the gods stood open, jammed in the hinge by the cable of the arc-light. The light lay on its side in the centre of the tomb where Louren had dropped it. The bulb still burned, lighting the tomb vividly.

Louren lay on his back at the foot of the huge granite sarcophagus of Lannon Hycanus, the last king of Opet.

He was naked to the waist. His face was deathly pale, his eyes closed, and bright blood stained the corners of his mouth and ran back down his cheeks into his ears and hair.

With the last of my strength I staggered to where he lay and dropped onto my knees beside him. I stooped over him and tried to lift him, my arms around his shoulders.

His skin was moist and burning hot, and his head flopped helplessly backwards. A new bright gush of blood ran out of his mouth, wetting my hands.

'Louren,' I cried, holding him to my chest. 'Oh please, God, help me! Help me!'

There was still life in him, just the last flicker of it. He opened his eyes, those pale blue eyes with the first shadows of death darkening them.

'Ben,' he whispered, choking with his own blood. He coughed, spattering droplets of the bright lung blood.

'Ben,' he whispered so softly I could scarcely hear it. 'All the way?'

'All the way, Lo,' I whispered, holding him like a sleepy child. His head of golden curls cradled against my shoulder. He was quiet for a little while, then suddenly he stirred again, and when he spoke it was in a clear strong voice.

'Fly!' he said. 'Fly for me, Bird of the Sun.' And the life went out of him, he turned to nothing in my arms, the great wild spirit flown – gone.

I knelt over him, feeling my own senses reel. The world turned and swung beneath me. I slipped over the edge of it, down into the swirling darkness of time. Down into a kind of death, a kind of life, for in my dying I dreamed a dream. In my poisoned sleep of death which lasted a moment and a million years I dreamed of long-dead men in a time long passed . . .

PART II

Of the thirty days of the prophecy there were but two remaining when Lannon Hycanus and his train came at last to the Bay of the Little Fish on the furthest southerly shores of the great lake. It was already dark when ten ships of the fleet anchored in the shallow waters of the bay, and their torches and lamps smeared long ruddy paths of light across the black waters.

Lannon stood beside the wooden gunwale of his steering-deck, and looked out across the fields of papyrus and hidden waterways to the south where the open country began and spread away endlessly into the unknown. He knew that here lay his destiny and that of the nation. For twenty-eight days he had hunted and now he felt an unaccustomed chill of fear ran his arms and neck, fear not of the terrible animal he had come to find, but of the consequences of the animal continuing to evade him.

Behind him there were light footsteps on the wooden deck and Lannon turned quickly. His hand on the hilt of the dagger beneath his leather cloak relaxed as he saw the unmistakable shape of the man in the light of the torches.

'Huy,' he greeted him.

'Highness, you must eat now and sleep.'

'Have they come yet?'

'Not yet, but they will before morning,' replied the hunchback, moving closer to his prince. 'Come now. You will have need of a steady hand and clear eye on the morrow.'

'Sometimes it seems I have ten wives, not nine,' laughed Lannon, and regretted the jest when he saw the blood darken the face of the hunchback; quickly he went on.

'You pamper me, old friend, but I think that tonight I will hunt sleep with as little success as I have hunted the gry-lion these twenty-eight days since my father's funeral.' He turned back to the bridge rail and looked across at the other nine ships. The ships of the nine families, come to watch him make good his claim to the throne of Opet and the four kingdoms, come to watch him take his gry-lion.

'Look at them, Huy.' And his friend came to his side. 'How many of them have made sacrifices to the gods for my failure?'

'Three of them, certainly – you know which I mean. There are perhaps more of them.'

'And those who are loyal to house Barca, those we can count upon without question?'

'You know them also, my lord. Habbakuk Lal will stand with you until the seas turn to sand, house Amon, house Hasmon—'

'Yes,' Lannon interrupted. 'I know them, Huy, every one of them, for and against. I was but talking to have the comfort of your voice.' He touched the hunchback's shoulder in a gesture of affection, before turning away to gaze once more into the southern wilderness.

'When the prophecy was made did they ever foresee the day when the great gry-lion would pass from the land? When a prince might search for all thirty of the days allotted to the task without seeing even the marks of the beast's paws in the earth of Opet?' Lannon spoke with sudden anger. He flung his cloak back over his shoulder and folded his arms across his naked chest. His skin was freshly oiled and the muscles glowed in the torch light, he kneaded his own flesh with the long powerful fingers.

'My father killed on the twenty-fifth day, and that was forty-six years ago. They said even then that the gry-lion was finished. Since then how many have the scouts reported?'

'My lord, the gods will decide,' Huy tried to soothe him.

'We have hunted every covert where the gry-lion has been seen in the last 200 years. Five full legions have swept the swamps in the north, three more along the great river.' He broke off and began pacing the deck, pausing to look down into the hull where the tiers of naked slaves slept chained upon their benches, leaning on the mighty oars in the position in which they would die. The stench of the rowing decks came up to him as a solid thing in the humid night. He turned back to Huy.

'This reach of the swamps is the last place in the whole of my kingdoms which might hide a gry-lion. If it does not, then what will happen, Huy? Is there no other way in which I might prove my right? Is there no escape in the scrolls?'

'None, my lord.' Huy shook his head with regret.

'The kingship must fall?'

'Unless there is a gry-lion taken then Opet will have no king.'

'Who will rule without a king?'

'The Council of Nine, alone.'

'And the royal house? What will become of house Barca?'

'Let us not talk of it,' Huy suggested softly. 'Come, my lord. A slave is preparing a jug of hot spiced wine and a stew of fish. The wine will help you to sleep.'

'Will you make an oracle for tomorrow, my priest of Baal?' Lannon asked suddenly.

'If the oracle is unfavourable, will it help you sleep?' asked Huy, and Lannon stared at him a moment before barking with harsh laughter.

'You are right, as always. Come then, I am hungry.'

Lannon ate with vast appetite from the bowl of fish, sitting naked on his fur-covered bed. He had let his hair loose and it hung to his shoulders, curling and gleaming strangely golden in the light of the hanging lamp. He was a god-like figure among his dark-haired people.

The leather awnings were opened, and a light breeze came up from the south-east to cool the cabin and blow out the galley stench. The ship moved to the breeze and the light chop of the surface, her timber popped and creaked softly, a slave cried out in nightmare, and from the deck above came the steps of the night guard – all the familiar comforting sounds of the flagship at sea.

Lannon wiped out the bowl with a piece of millet bread, popped it into his mouth, and washed it down with the last of the wine. He sighed with content, and smiled at Huy.

'Sing for me, my bird of the sun.'

Huy Ben-Amon squatted on the deck at the foot of the prince's bed. He held his lute in his lap, and crouched over it. The curve of his back exaggerated the attitude, the long tar-black tresses of hair hung forward to hide his face, his massively developed arms seemed too powerful for the long delicate fingers that held the lute. He struck a note, and a listening hush fell upon the night. The footsteps overhead ceased, two slave girls ceased their work and came to kneel beside Lannon's bed, the arguing voices from the ship anchored alongside quieted, and Huy sang.

His voice rang sweetly across the dark waters, and the prince and the fleet listened. Dark shapes moved to the rails of the nearest ships and stood quietly there looking across at the flagship. On the cheeks of one of the pretty slave girls stood teardrops that glistened in the lamp light, when Huy sang of a lost love. Then she smiled through her tears when Huy changed the song to one of the bawdy marching tunes of the Sixth Legion.

'Enough.' Huy looked up from his lute at last. 'There will be work tomorrow, my lord.'

Lannon nodded and touched one of the slave girls on the cheek. Immediately she stood up and loosed the shoulder strap of her linen tunic, letting it fall from her body. She was young and lithe, her body almost boyishly slim in the lamp light. She stooped and gathered her robe, dropped it across the bench beside the door and stepped naked into Lannon's bed. The other girl went to snuff the lamp, and Huy rose from the deck with his lute slung on his shoulder.

A voice hailed from the darkness, a great bull bellow from the edge of the papyrus beds that carried across the water to the flagship.

'Open your lines for a friend!'

'Who calls himself friend?' One of the guards shouted a challenge, and the reply was bellowed hoarsely.

'Mursil, huntmaster of house Barca.' And Lannon was out of his bed in one bound.

'He has come!' he exclaimed, flinging his cloak over his shoulders and hurrying to the companion ladder with Huy scampering beside him.

A small canoe bumped alongside and Mursil came up through the entry-port as Lannon and Huy reached the deck, a huge figure, gross and apelike with his big beefy round face ruddy from sun and wine.

The ship was awake now. Her officers swarming up onto the deck, new torches flaring to light the scene as day, the bustle and hum of excitement affecting them all.

Mursil saw Lannon and hurried to him down the aisle which opened for him across the crowded deck. He was followed closely by a pygmy figure, a tiny brown naked manikin that looked about him from slanted eyes in obvious terror at these unfamiliar surroundings.

'My lord.' Mursil opened his cloak and dropped heavily to one knee in front of Lannon. 'I bring good news.'

'Then you are welcome.'

'This one,' Mursil reached behind him and dragged the little bushman forward, 'this one has found what we seek.'

'You have seen it?' Lannon demanded.

'The tracks of his paws only, but this one has seen the beast itself.'

'If it is true, you will be well rewarded, both of you,' promised Lannon Hycanus and turned to grin triumphantly at Huy.

'The gods have decided. House Barca will have its chance once more.'

The sky was only a shade lighter than the black brooding swampland; the dawn-flighting duck ghost-whistled unseen overhead and each minute the light strengthened.

Half a mile out on the open plain a herd of buffalo grazed in a dark bunch. Heads down, tails swinging lazily, they moved back steadily towards the tall dense banks of papyrus reed.

They moved faster as the light strengthened, hurrying to reach the sanctuary of the reedbeds, 200 huge bovine shapes with their armoured heads and bunched black shoulders. Dawn's first light showed the white tick birds which hovered above the dark herd in a cold pink sheen. The swampy earth smoked with mist and the endless banks of papyrus stood frozen in the hush of dawn, for once their fluffy white heads were not nodding and dancing – except where something moved amongst the reeds.

Following its track the papyrus heads stirred, an opening and closing movement that set them nodding briefly before settling into stillness once more. The movement was sedate and yet so weighty that it betrayed the size of the animal which stalked beneath it.

The big bull buffalo that led the herd stopped suddenly fifty yards from the edge of the papyrus bed. He lifted his nose high and spread his ears wide beneath the heavy boss of horn. With little suspicious piggy eyes he examined the bed of reeds ahead of him. Behind him the herd stopped also, alerted by his stillness.

The gry-lion came out of the reeds at full charge, a blur of soft roan-brown, an animal as tall and almost as heavy as the quarry it hunted. It crossed the open ground so swiftly that the bull had only begun to turn away before the gry-lion was on him.

It landed on his back, curved yellow claws hooked through thick black skin and flesh at shoulder and haunch. The long fangs sank into the back of the buffalo's neck, holding it steady while one paw reached forward and grasped the bull's nose. A single powerful wrench twisted the black neck back against the holding fangs, the spine snapped with a sharp report and the bull folded in full run.

Before he went down the gry-lion had left him, dropping lightly to the ground, seeming hardly to touch it before he was in the air again, a long arcing leap, flashing soft brown against the pink dawn sky to land easily across the back of an old black cow that ran beside the bull.

Lightly as a humming bird flashing from flower to flower, the gry-lion had killed again. Bone breaking sharply in the dawn, the victim carrying the great lion forward in the press of galloping buffalo, and as the cow died the gry-lion was gone, flitting to the next, killing again in one fleeting movement and flitting again.

Six times the gry-lion killed before the surging, plunging, panicking herd had run 300 paces. Then he let them run, the thunder of their hooves dwindled, a far bank of papyrus swallowed them and they were gone.

The gry-lion stood in the silky light of dawn. His long, black-tufted tail still slashed from side to side with the thrill of the hunt. Every muscle was tight and swollen and the great beast half crouched, the flat snakelike head lifted as though to counter the weight of those long white fangs that curved down almost to touch the fluffy fur of his chest.

The face mask was elaborately patterned in black and

startling white, an effect that enhanced the golden glowing savagery in the wide-set eyes, but the whiskers and eye-lashes were long white bristle, and seemed to soften the animal's expression. However, when it stood up from its crouch, with the short ruff of mulberry-brown mane along its back still fully erect, any illusion of softness vanished.

As tall as a man, and as heavy as a horse, armed with those legendary fangs and claws, this was the most danger-ous cat that all nature's twists and evolutions had ever produced.

The cat turned and paced back to where its last victim lay in the short grass of the plain. It stood over the dead buffalo, and it seemed impossible that such a large animal could move as swiftly as this one had at the height of the hunt.

The gry-lion lifted its head, the massive jaws parted, the long pink tongue curled out between those unbelievable fangs, and it roared.

It was a sound that seemed to shake the purple skies of dawn, that made the earth shudder and ruffled the quiet waters of the great lake.

In the dawn, upon the narrow muddy beach beside the reed banks, Huy Ben-Amon greeted his god. Huy wore light hunting armour of leather, a leather breast-plate and arm-guards over a short linen tunic and bronze-studded leather kilt, but his weapons were laid aside, for he was about to offer the sacrifice, to send a messenger to great Baal. A messenger to carry the request of Lannon Hycanus to his god. The prince and his nobles were gathered in a half-circle about the priest, all of them facing the eastern sky. Baal showed the tip of his fiery orb above the horizon, and they lifted their hands to him. Fingers spread in the sun-sign.

'Great Baal,' Huy called the greeting in sweet shimmering tones that seemed must carry to the sky. 'Your children greet you!' Huy's swarthy, beak-nosed features were lit by a mystic glow which gave him a strange beauty.

'We have come to this place to choose a king for your people and we ask your blessing on our endeavours.' Huy knew his gods intimately, and though he loved them yet he knew their all too human weaknesses. They were vain, inconsistent, touchy, greedy, and sometimes bone-lazy. They must be flattered and cajoled, bribed and jollied along, they needed special ceremony and display to capture their jaded interest and attention, sacrifice, which Huy personally found revolting, to assuage their lust for warm blood. It was not enough that sacrifice was made, it must be made in all the correct forms before the gods would accept it, and as one of his lesser priests led the white bull forward Huy wondered if he had done the right thing in persuading Lannon to offer an animal rather than a slave. The gods preferred human blood, but Huy had argued with Lannon that a bull now and the promise of a slave later might be more effective. Huy had no compunction in bargaining with the great immortals, especially if it delayed the moment when he must look into the terrified, pleading eyes of a doomed slave. In the five years that Huy had directed the religious life of Opet, not more than 100 human messengers had been sent to the gods. Whereas there had been times in the city's history when that number had been sent at a single ceremony.

'We send you a fine white bull to carry our message.' Huy turned and approached the animal. It was of the short stocky Opet type, white and grey dappled, with a fat hump on its shoulders and wide straight horns. It stood quietly as Huy took the vulture axe from one of his priests. The circle of nobles drew back a little, giving the axe space to swing and the blood to spurt.

'Great Baal, receive our messenger!' Huy shouted, and

the axe went up, reflecting the low rays of the sun from its flashing blade. It hissed angrily as it fell, and the bull's thick neck severed cleanly, the head seeming to leap from the trunk. Headless, the body fell to its knees and the blood pumped and gushed.

Huy leaned upon his weapon in the typical stance of the resting axeman.

'A sign, great Baal!' Huy shouted, making it more a demand than a request. 'Give your children a sign!' And his voice was tiny in the immensity of swamp and sky and water. The timeless silence of the swamps fell upon them, the silence of the ages in the smoky purple dawn.

A flight of spur-winged geese passed overhead, wings beating heavily, long necks out-stretched, silhouetted darkly against the rosy streamers of sun-touched mist. Huy watched them hopefully, tempted to claim them as god-forms.

'A sign, great Baal!' He thrust aside the temptation, but his irritation was increasing. The sacrifice had been meticulously performed right down to the single clean stroke of the axe – was this to be one of those occasions when the god's attention had wandered, or was he being obstinate, pig-headed? A hippopotamus splashed and snorted out in the bay, and Huy turned towards it expectantly, but the fat grey sea-cow merely fluttered its ears like bees' wings, then submerged with a swirl.

'A sign, great Baal!' The third and final request, and almost immediately it was answered.

A sound rose from beyond the papyrus beds that startled the water birds into flight, that shook the fluffy white heads of the reeds, that seemed to roll across the heavens like thunder. A sound such as none of them had ever heard before. The roaring of the gry-lion.

Huy's dark scowl vanished beneath a beatific smile, and he turned those long-lashed gazelle eyes on his prince.

'The gods have answered you, Lannon Hycanus.' He

was seeing the faces of the priests and nobles and warriors and huntsmen, the superstitious awe with which they gazed at him. He would sacrifice privately to Baal later, nothing ostentatious or expensive, a chicken perhaps, as a gesture of thanks for this magnificent co-operation. It would rank with one of his best performances ever. Huy was so delighted with his success that he could not resist a further histrionic gesture.

'Go out, Prince of Opet, and take your gry-lion,' said Huy.

The little bushman led them along one of the buffalo paths. It was a green tunnel of reeds, the papyrus closing overhead to hide the sky, the damp peaty swamp earth underfoot, the musty animal swamp smell in their nostrils. They came out at last into the open grassland. Short, bright green grass cropped down by the countless herds of buffalo that infested this reach of the shore.

The bushman turned and led them along the edge of the papyrus beds. They were an unwieldy procession, four or five hundred strong, for some of the noble nine would not come ashore to look for the gry-lion without a thick screen of archers and axemen around them. They trailed far behind Lannon's party which consisted of Mursil the huntmaster, smelling richly of fruity Zeng wine, the bushman, Huy, the prince and his two arms-bearers.

The gods were as good as their promise that morning. The bushman led them around the bank of papyrus that thrust out into the plain like an accuser's finger, and as they turned the point of it they came upon another bay of open grassland. It was a natural arena, fenced on three sides by the stands of dark reeds, a huge circular extent of lush grass about half a mile across.

Down the centre of this opening, lying at regular intervals, were six large dark objects, clearly visible on the open plain, but the range was too long for immediate identification.

Mursil, the huntmaster, spoke quickly to the pygmy scout in a formless dialect. Huy made a note to study this language, it was the only spoken word in all the four kingdoms in which he was not fluent.

'My lord, he says they are dead buffalo killed by the gry-lion,' Mursil translated on a warm wave of wine fumes.

'Where is the beast?' Lannon asked, and the bushman pointed.

'It is there, behind the second carcass. It has seen and heard us, and it is lying hidden,' Mursil explained.

'Can he see it?' Lannon demanded.

'Yes, my lord. He can see the tips of its ears and its eyes. It is watching us.'

'At that distance?' Lannon asked with disbelief, looking down at the bushman. 'I do not believe it.'

'It is true, my lord. He has the eyes of an eagle.'

'At your peril, if he is mistaken,' Lannon warned.

'At my peril,' Mursil agreed readily, and Lannon turned to Huy.

'Make ready, my Bird of the Sun.'

While they stripped Lannon of his armour, bound his loins in a cloth of linen, and set light hunting sandals on his feet, the rest of the party straggled up. Some of the older nobles were in litters. Asmun, looking frail and white-haired, stopped his bearers beside Lannon.

'A clean kill,' he wished the prince. 'Like the one your father made.' And they carried him to where he could have a view of the field. The party spread out along the edge of the reed bank, their arms and armour glinting in the sunlight, their robes purple and white and red, spots of gay colour against the dark reed beds. A silence fell upon them as Lannon stepped forward and turned to face them.

His body was naked but for the loin-cloth, and the skin was smooth and startlingly white except where the sun had gilded his face and limbs. It was a beautiful body, tall and gracefully proportioned, heavy in the shoulder and narrow at waist and belly. His curls were bound with a purple headband and his red-gold beard was clubbed and turned up against his throat.

He looked at the waiting ranks before him.

'I make claim to the city of Opet, and all the four kingdoms,' he said with simplicity, and his voice carried clearly to every one of them.

Huy took his weapons to him. The shield. Hide of the buffalo, shaped in a long oval, tall as a man and as wide as his shoulders. In its centre were the 'eyes', a pair of fierce owl eyes painted in white and yellow. When these were exposed to a beast they represented the natural aggressive stare which would usually trigger the charge of a predator.

'May this shield cover you well,' Huy told him softly.

'Thank you, old friend.'

Next Huy offered him the lion-spear. This was such a heavy cumbersome weapon that only a powerful man could handle it. The shaft was of carefully selected hard wood, fire-treated, and bound with green leather which had been allowed to dry and shrink upon it. It was as thick as Lannon's wrist, and twice as tall as he was.

The unbarbed blade was in proportion wide and heavy, bound into the shaft with leather strips, the round point honed to a razor edge. It was designed to allow the maximum penetration into flesh and, once buried, to open a massive wound that would induce heavy bleeding.

'May this blade find the heart,' Huy whispered, and then louder: 'Roar for me, Gry-Lion of Opet.'

Lannon reached out and touched the priest's shoulder. He squeezed it briefly.

'Fly for me, Bird of the Sun,' he said and turned away. With the shield on his back, careful not to show the 'eyes',

Lannon walked out towards the waiting beast. He walked tall and proud in the sunlight, a king in all but name, and Huy's heart went with him. Quietly Huy began to pray, hoping that the gods were still attentive.

Lannon strode through the soft grass that brushed his knees. As he went he remembered the advice of the oldest and best of his huntmasters, rehearsing each move, each word of it.

'Wait until he growls before you show him the eyes.'

'Make him come to you at an angle.'

'He charges with head held low. You must open his chest from the side.'

'The skull is like iron, the bones of the shoulder will turn the finest metal.'

'There is one place only. The base of the neck, between spine and shoulder.'

Then the words of the only man amongst them all who had ever faced the gry-lion, Hamilcar Barca, the forty-sixth Gry-Lion of Opet, 'Once the spear is in, hold it, my son, cling to it with your life. For the gry-lion is still alive and that shaft is all that will keep him from you until he dies.'

Lannon walked on steadily watching the black swollen-bellied carcass of the buffalo, seeing no sign of the beast he was hunting.

'They are mistaken,' he thought. 'There is nothing here.'

He could hear his own heart beating in the silence, his own footfalls, and the hiss and suck of his breath. He watched the dead buffalo and walked on, tucking the butt of the lion spear more firmly under his right armpit.

'There is nothing here. The gry-lion has gone,' he thought, then suddenly he saw movement ahead of him. Just the flick of two ears held erect for a moment then flattened again, but he knew that it was there waiting for him. He felt his steps begin to drag, feet heavy with fear, but he forced himself onwards.

'Fear is the destroyer,' he thought, and tried to force it down, but it was a cold heavy thing like oil in his guts. He walked on, and suddenly the gry-lion stood up beside the carcass of the buffalo. It stood facing him, with ears erect, its tail swinging lazily, head up, watching him, and Lannon gasped aloud. He had not expected it to be so large. He missed a step, hesitating. It was huge, unbelievable, like something from a nightmare.

He was 200 paces from it, and he walked on towards it, concealing the 'eyes', and watching the giant cat's tail swish faster with agitation as he approached.

A hundred paces from it, and now the tail began to slash angrily, like a whip against the gry-lion's flanks. The cat crouched a little, the ears flattening against the skull. Lannon could see the eyes now, hot yellow eyes in the patterned face-mask.

He walked on, and the gry-lion's ruff of mane came erect, swelling out the shape of its head, it sank a little lower into its crouch. Its tail slashed furiously, and Lannon walked on towards it.

Fifty paces separated them now, and the gry-lion growled. It was the muttering menace of distant thunder, the drumming of the earth in quake, a belly-jarring sound like the crash of surf on a storm-swept beach. Lannon stopped, he could not walk on with that sound in his ears. He stood frozen, staring at this terrible animal in its mounting rage.

Long seconds he hesitated, then with an abrupt movement born of fear he swept the shield from his back and showed the 'eyes'. The glaring roundels were all that was needed to precipitate the beast's anger. The black tufted tail froze rigid, lifted slightly above the level of its back, the head dropped low against its chest, and it charged.

At the same moment as the charge began Lannon went up on his toes, and jumped forward. The shackles of fear fell from his limbs, and he bounded towards the charging cat with long light strides. He was angling his run across the gry-lion's front, forcing it to keep turning towards him, bringing it in at an angle, exposing the neck and the side of the chest.

As Lannon ran the spear blade danced above the earth ahead of him, like a firefly of light in the sun.

The gry-lion came fast, and low, head down so that the incredible fangs almost touched its chest, curved and ivory pale. It seemed to snake against the grass as it closed for the kill, and its enormous bulk filled the whole of Lannon's vision.

At the last possible instant Lannon lifted the spear-tip slightly, centring it on the vital spot at the base of the neck, and the gry-lion came onto the spear with its whole weight driving it.

The blade plunged into the brown furry body, sucked into unresisting flesh, and the shock of the impact drove up the shaft and hurled Lannon backwards onto his knees – but he held onto the spear.

A storm raged about him, great waves of sound engulfed him, battering his eardrums, as the gry-lion roared out its death throes. The shaft of the lion-spear whipped and thrashed in his grip, smashing against his ribs, crushing and bruising his flesh, shaking him so his teeth clashed together in his skull, lacerating his tongue. He clung to the spear.

He was lifted from his feet, riding high on the shaft of the spear as the gry-lion reared, then he was smashed down onto the earth again as the great cat plunged. He felt muscle and sinew tear in his arm and shoulders, felt the gry-lion's claws raking the flimsy leather shield, felt weakness in his body and darkness in his head, but still the storm raged and shook him.

Once more the gry-lion roared and reared. Lannon felt himself hurled towards the heavens, the shaft of the lion-spear snapped like a brittle twig, and Lannon was thrown with the butt of it still in his hands. He flew for long seconds, bird free, then earth thumped the breath from his lungs. Painfully he dragged himself into a sitting position, and looked around him stunned, clutching the broken shaft of the spear to his chest.

Ten paces away the gry-lion was crawling towards him through the grass. The broken hilt of the spear protruded from the exact spot in the neck where Lannon had aimed. The gry-lion's throes had worked the blade mercilessly in its own flesh, opening a hideous wound from which the bright heart-blood pumped, but the gry-lion's yellow eyes were still upon him, and those great curved fangs gleamed for his flesh.

Slowly it crawled towards him, its breath drumming in the mighty throat, dragging its paralysed hindquarters, dying but still deadly.

'Die,' thought Lannon, watching it with facination, crushed by the conflict, unable to move. 'Die,' he thought. 'Please die.' And suddenly the final spasm caught the giant cat. Its back arched, the legs stiffened, claws ripping into the earth, the mouth opened wide and pink, and it groaned. One last long pitiful groan, and it died.

The half-circle of watchers shouted, a cheer that was lost in the great silence of the swamps, and they began moving forward slowly towards the tiny figure of the king out on the grassy plain. But Huy was running. On legs too long for his crumpled trunk he seemed to dance over the ground, his long black tresses flowing out behind him and the vulture axe on his shoulder.

He was half-way to where Lannon sat bowed in the grass when the second gry-lion stood up from where it had lain concealed behind the carcass of the nearest buffalo. Huy saw it and shouted as he ran.

'Lannon! Behind you! Beware!'

Lannon looked back and saw it. It was the female,

lighter in colour, daintier in build, but notoriously more savage than the male. It moved towards Lannon with the deadly concentration of a stalking cat.

'Baal speed me!' Huy prayed as he ran towards his prince, and saw him trying to struggle to his feet. The gry-lion was slinking low along the ground, moving forward in short dashes.

Huy ran with all his might, driven by horror and fear for his prince. Lannon was on his feet now, reeling weakly away from the stalking cat. The movement triggered the hunting reflex of the gry-lion; it closed remorselessly.

Huy shouted at it. 'Here!' he yelled. 'Come!' And the cat noticed him for the first time. It lifted its head and looked at him. The fangs glinting long and pale, the eyes yellow and splendid.

'Yes!' shouted Huy. 'Here I am!' He saw Lannon stagger and fall, dropping out of sight into the grass, but he watched the beast. Saw the tail stiffen and the head drop. It began to charge, and Huy checked his advance.

He stood to meet the gry-lion, braced on long powerful legs, with the axe on his shoulder, and he let the cat come straight.

As it closed he fastened his gaze on the black diamond pattern between the gry-lion's eyes, and he adjusted his grip on the axe, settling it carefully.

The axe went up and the gry-lion covered the last few paces in a soft roan-coloured blur of fluid movement, towering over the little hunchback.

'For Baal!' howled Huy and the axe moaned in flight. The blade cracked into skull, buried in the gry-lion's brain and was instantly torn from his grip as the full weight of the dead beast smashed into his chest.

Huy came back from deep down and far away along a tunnel of roaring darkness, and when he opened his eyes Lannon Hycanus, the forty-seventh Gry-Lion of Opet, knelt over him in the sunlight.

'The fool,' said the king, his own face bruised and swollen, caked with drying blood. 'Oh! The brave little fool.'

'Brave, yes,' whispered Huy painfully. 'But fool never, majesty.' And saw the relief dawn in Lannon's eyes.

They spread the wet skins of the two gry-lions on the main mast of the flagship, and Lannon Hycanus received the oaths of allegiance from the heads of the nine houses of Opet while reclining on a couch of soft fur beneath them. Huy Ben-Amon carried the cup of life, despite the protests of his king.

'You must rest, Huy. You are badly wounded, I believe the ribs of your chest are stove—'

'My lord, I am the cup-bearer. Would you deny me that honour?'

Asmun was the first of the nine to make oath. His sons helped him from the litter, but he shrugged away their hands as he approached Lannon.

'In respect of the snow upon your brow, and the scars of your body, you need not kneel, Asmun.'

'I will kneel, my king,' replied Asmun, and went down on the deck in the sunlight. Baal must witness the oath of this frail old man. When Huy held the cup of life to his lips he sipped it, and Huy carried the cup to the king. He drank and then offered it back to Huy.

'Drink also, my priest.'

'It is not the custom,' Huy demurred.

'The King of Opet and the four kingdoms makes the custom. Drink!'

Huy hesitated a moment longer, then lifted the cup and took a long draught. By the time Habbakuk Lal, the last of the nine, came forward the cup had been refilled five times with the heavy sweet wine of Zeng.

'Do your wounds still trouble you?' Lannon asked softly as Huy brought the cup to him for the last time.

'Majesty, I feel no pain,' Huy replied and then giggled suddenly and spilled a drop of wine down the king's chest.

'Fly high, Sunbird,' laughed Lannon.

'Roar loudly, Gry-Lion,' said Huy, and laughed with him. Lannon turned to the nobles who crowded the steering deck.

'There is food and drink.' The ceremony was over, Lannon Hycanus was king. 'Habbakuk Lal!' Lannon picked out the big ginger-bearded seaman with his freckled and sea-brined face.

'My lord.'

'Will you weigh, and set for Opet?'

'A night run?'

'Yes, I wish to reach the city before noon tomorrow, and I trust your seamanship.'

Habbakuk Lal inclined his head at the compliment and the heavy gold ear-rings dangled against his cheek. Then he turned on his heel, and stumped across the deck, bellowing orders at his officers.

The anchors came up over the stern, and the drummer on the forecastle of the flagship struck the hollow tree trunk with the wooden drumstick, beating out the rhythm for the racing start.

Three swift, two slow, three swift. The bank of oars dipped and swung and rose and swung forward and dipped to the beat. In perfect unison, an undulating movement, like the wet silver wing-beats of a great water bird. The long narrow hull slicing boldly through the sunset blush of lake water, the clean run of the wake streaming out behind her, the standard of house Barca hoisted at the crosstree of her masthead and her high castles fore and aft standing tall and proud above the papyrus banks on either hand.

As she swept past the other vessels of the fleet they

dipped their standards, and fell in behind the flagship. Each of them holding their station meticulously in line ahead, the steersmen leaning on the rudder oar and the drum-beats booming out across the lake.

His hobbling gait was all that betrayed Huy's discomfort as he moved from group to group upon the torch-lit deck; with each of them he pointed the bottom of the wine bowl to the starry bright night sky, and bounced the ivory dice across the deck.

'Damn your luck,' laughed Philo, but the laughter did not hide the anger in his brooding gypsy dark features. 'Am I mad to dice with a favourite of the gods?' But he stacked gold upon the board, covering Huy's pile, and Huy scooped the dice and threw the three black fish again. Philo pulled his robes closer about him and moved away with the laughter and the shouted gibes of the watchers following him.

The bright white star of Astarte had set when at last Lannon and Huy stood together beneath the spread skins of the gry-lions and looked about the deck. It was a battlefield when the battle is spent. The bodies lay strewn about in the torch light, lying where they had fallen, loose and senseless. A wine bowl rolled back and forth with the easy motion of the ship that still sped on into the darkness.

'Another victory,' Lannon spoke thickly, peering blear-ily around at the carnage.

'A notable victory, Majesty.'

'I think,' Lannon began, but did not finish. His legs buckled under him. He swayed and swung forward. Huy caught him neatly as he fell, and settled him across one shoulder. Ignoring the pain in his chest he lifted the king and carried him down to the main cabin below the deck. He dropped Lannon on the bed, and arranged his limbs and head more comfortably. A moment longer he stayed, hanging over the supine figure.

'Sweet sleep, my beautiful king,' he blurted and turned to stagger away to his own cabin. The slave girl rose at his entrance.

'I have set out your writing pallet,' she told him, and Huy peered at the scroll, ink bowl and stylus under the hanging lamp.

'Not tonight.' He started towards the bed, lost direction, crashed into the bulkhead and bounced backwards. The slave girl ran to help him, and steered him into port.

Huy lay on his back and looked up at her. She was one of Lannon's household. Huy wished he could afford one like her, but she would fetch ten fingers of gold at the least.

'Is there anything else, my lord?' she asked. She was a pretty little thing with dark soft hair and pale ivory-yellow skin. Huy closed one eye the better to focus on her.

'Perhaps,' he said shyly. 'If you will help a little.' But his aspirations were too ambitious, and in a few moments his snores shook the ship to its keel. The girl rose, pulled on her robe and for a moment smiled down at him before she slipped out of the cabin.

In the darkness before dawn Huy stood on the forecastle of the galley and worked the axe, keeping it in flight, humming and hissing in the gloom. He felt the sluggish old wine in his veins begin to course faster, the sweat broke out on his body that the cool lake could not quench. He changed hands smoothly on the cut, and the great axe sang. The dullness in his head lightened and the sweat poured now, streaming down his muscled legs and arms, over the bull-humped back, soaking the loin-cloth, running into his eyes, and Huy began to dance, lightly he spun and leapt and waved, and still the axe flew.

Dawn was pinking the sky when at last he stopped and leaned upon the axe. His breath steamed and gasped in the cold stream of air, but his blood raced through his body and he felt like a man again.

In the cabin one of Lannon's slave girls scraped the

sweat from his body with the gold strigil that was a gift from Lannon. Then she rubbed him down with perfumed oil, plaited and set his hair and beard, and held a loose unbelted robe of white linen for him.

He came up on the steering-deck just as the order to heave to was passed to the fleet, and they swung towards the east to await the coming of the sun with the slave oarsmen collapsing thankfully over their oars. As the sun showed over the horizon Huy led the praise chant to Baal. Then there was breakfast on the open deck with the company squatting on mats of plaited reeds. Huy looked at their faces, grey and crumpled, baggy-eyed and bad-tempered. Even Lannon was pale and his hands shook as he breakfasted on a bowl of warm milk and honey.

Huy started on millet cakes dripping with oil and honey, then he ate a large smoked and salted lake bream, and when he called for a broiled duck reeking with rank wild garlic and more millet cakes the company watched him with awe. Huy ripped the duck to pieces and forced an expression of relish as he ate, for he was jealous of his reputation.

Philo spoke for them all when he cried at last, 'Great Baal! You insult not only your own belly but mine as well.' And he jumped up and hurried below.

'He is right.' Lannon laughed for the first time that day. 'You look like a child who has drunk nothing more poisonous than his mother's milk.'

'He was weaned on red Zeng wine, and he cut his teeth on the blade of a battle-axe.'

'If the lake was wine he would lower the level so we could walk across.'

Huy twinkled at them like a mischievous gnome, and tore another leg from the carcass of the duck.

In the middle morning they reached the shallows and Habbakuk Lal went forward to pilot the ship through the narrow channel. Water hyacinth, papyrus and a dozen other varieties of vegetation threatened to clog the life-line of Opet. The channel boats pulled out of the lane as the ten great ships flew past on their silver-wet wings. The officers saluted the standard of Barca at the masthead with a clenched fist, but the slave gangs who were doomed for ever to fight the lake weed stood dumbly and watched with patient animal eyes.

Closer to Opet now they began passing the fishing fleet, the nets coming in over the side with fish shining silver in the mesh like captured stars, and the white clouds of gulls shrieking and fussing overhead.

Then the cliffs came up on the horizon, glowing dusky red in the sunlight, and the rail was crowded with those who were enjoying this moment of homecoming.

Mursil, the huntmaster, came to Lannon on the steering deck and knelt briefly.

'You sent for me, Majesty.'

'Yes – and the pygmy.'

'He is here, King.'

'I promised you a reward. Name it.'

'My lord, I have three wives. All of them avaricious.'

'Gold?'

'If it please you, my lord.'

'Huy, write an order on the treasury for five fingers of gold.'

'May Baal shine upon you always!'

'What of the pygmy?'

Mursil called the little yellow bushman to him, and Lannon examined him with interest.

'What is he named?'

'Xhai, my lord.'

'Does he not understand the language?'

'No, my lord, he speaks only his own primitive tongue.'

'Ask him what he desires – freedom, perhaps?'

'He does not understand the idea of freedom. He is like

a dog, Majesty. Deprive him of a master and you deprive him of the reason for life.'

'Ask him what he wants.'

Mursil and the bushman spoke for a long while in that birdlike chittering tongue, before the huntmaster turned back to the king.

'It is a strange request.'

'Name it.'

'He wishes to hunt with the slayer of the gry-lion.'

Lannon stared at the bushman, who grinned at him with the beguiling candour of a child.

'He thinks, my lord, and you will forgive the impertinence,' Mursil was sweating a little, ill at ease, 'he thinks you are a god, and he wants to belong to you.'

Lannon let out a bull roar of laughter and slapped his thigh.

'So be it then. He is elevated to a master of the royal hunt – with the pay and privileges. Take him, Huy. Teach him to speak the language, or failing that learn to speak his!'

'All the strays and cripples,' thought Huy ruefully. His household was filled with them, whenever he had accumulated sufficient gold for a luscious young slave maid it went on another who was too old or infirm to justify his keep and who was consigned by his master to the pool of Astarte. At least the pygmy would have his pay as a huntmaster to help with the costs.

Lannon dismissed the subject and turned back to the rail. The mother city came up over the horizon at last. The walls of the temple shone a ruddy rose in the sunlight, and the lower city was brilliant white, the walls of the houses painted with the ash of the lake shell-fish.

The war fleet of Opet streamed out from the harbour to meet them. The shields and helmets of the legionaries sparkled in the sun as each ship in turn wheeled across the flagship's bows with the gilt work on her arrow-sharp prow catching the sunlight. They saw the raw skins hanging below the standard of house Barca and a cheer roared out across the water.

The flagship led them into the harbour, still scudding to the drive of her banked oars. Habbakuk Lal aimed at the stone jetty below the city where the crowds thronged the shore. The entire population of the city was out in their best and most brilliant robes, shrieking and cheering their new king from 100,000 throats.

At the last possible moment Habbakuk Lal dropped his hand in a signal to the drummer and steersman. The ship spun on her heel, with every oar clawing at the water to drag her to a halt, her side lightly touching the stone jetty. Lannon Hycanus and his train stepped ashore.

Lannon's wives were the first to greet him. Nine of them, one from each of the noble houses, young matrons of the blood, proud and beautiful. Each one came forward to kneel before Lannon, and call him 'sire' for the first time.

Huy looked at them with a heart that ached. These were not the pliant, brainless slave girls whose company was all he had ever known. These were full women. He needed someone like that to share a life with, and he had tried so hard. He had carried his suit to every one of the great houses of Opet, and had it rejected. They could see no further than his back, and he could not blame them for it.

The dignity of the occasion was abruptly shattered by a loud chorus of 'Hoo! Hoo!' and the twins broke away from their nursemaids and raced each other across the jetty. Ignoring their father and the gathered nobles, they ran to Huy and danced about him, tugging at his robe and demanding his attention. When he picked them up they competed so fiercely for his kisses that it developed into a hair-pulling bout. The nursemaids flew to the rescue and dragged them away.

Imilce's hands still locked in Helanca's golden tresses, and from the scowl on Lannon's face Huy knew that there would be retribution and that those plump little bottoms would soon be glowing red. He wished there was some way he could prevent it.

Huy slipped away into the crowd. On the way to the temple he haggled for a chicken with one of the merchants and struck a good bargain. After he had sacrificed he went to his own house in the precinct of the priests between the outer and inner wall of the temple. His household were all there to meet him, doting and doddering, fussing about him with their grey heads and toothless gums. All agog for the news of his latest exploits, demanding the story of the hunt, while they bathed and fed him.

When at last he escaped to his sleeping quarters to rest, he had not lain for long when the four eldest princesses arrived. Aged from ten to six, they broke through the feeble defences of his slaves and invaded his room as if by right.

With a sigh Huy abandoned rest and sent one of them to fetch his lute, and as he began to sing the slaves, one at a time, crept into the room and sat quietly along the wall. Huy Ben-Amon was home again.

I n the year 533 from the founding of Opet, six months after he had taken the gry-lion and claimed the four kingdoms, Lannon Hycanus, the head of house Barca, left the city of Opet and went out to march around his borders, a custom that would bind his claim irrevocably. He was twenty-nine years old in that spring, a year older than his high priest.

He marched with four of his wives, the childless ones, hoping to change their status upon the two-year journey. He took with him two legions each of 6,000 hoplites, light infantry, axemen and archers. The legions were composed mostly of Yuye freedmen with officers from the noble families of Opet. These legions were organized along the Roman lines, in the manner that Hannibal had adopted during his campaign in Italia. There were ten cohorts to a legion and six centuries to a cohort. They were uniformed in leather body armour with conical iron helmets and circular leather shields studded with bronze rosettes. On their legs and feet they wore leather greaves and nailed sandals, and they sang as they marched.

The officers were more magnificently appointed as befitted their noble origins. Their armour was of bronze and their cloaks were of fine linen dyed purple and red, and they marched at the head of their divisions.

There was no cavalry. In 500 years no attempt to bring horses from the north had succeeded. Every one of the animals had succumbed to the sea voyage, or surviving that had died soon after arrival at Opet of a mysterious disease that made their coats stand on end and turned their eyeballs to bloody red jelly.

In place of cavalry were the elephants. Huge, ugly-tempered beasts, who struck terror into the hearts of the enemies of Opet when they charged with the archers in the castles upon their backs loosing a shower of arrows as they came on. In battle frenzy, however, they could wreak as much havoc amongst their own army as that of the enemy, and their handlers were equipped with a mallet and a spike to drive into the brains of the berserk animals. Lannon took twenty-five of these beasts upon his march.

With him went his high priest and a dozen lesser priests, engineers, physicians, armourers, cooks, slaves and a huge flock of camp followers: merchants, prospectors, gamblers, soothsayers, liquor-sellers and prostitutes. The bullock train carrying the tentage and supplies stretched for seven miles, while the whole unwieldy column spread out over fifteen miles. This was no problem in the huge unpeopled grass plains of the south with their plentiful supplies of water and forage, but when Huy Ben-Amon stood on a low hill with his king and saw the slow straggling mass coming down out of the north he thought of the time when they would turn north again in a great circle amongst the forests and broken country along the great river. Such a collection of wealth would be a sore temptation to the pagan war bands from the unknown land beyond the river. He told Lannon his misgivings and Lannon laughed, crinkling his pale blue eyes into the sun.

'You think more like a soldier than a priest.'

'I am both.'

'Of course.' Lannon dropped a hand on his shoulder. 'Not for nothing the command of the sixth legion – well, Huy, I have thought much of this march. In the past, it has always been a great time-waster and a sorry expense on the treasury of Opet. My march will be different. I intend to turn a profit.'

Huy smiled at that magic word, the one understood by all in Opet, noble or commoner, king or priest.

'I intend to make this a different type of march. In the south kingdom we will hunt – hunts such as you have never conceived, and the meat will be smoked and dried and sold to the houses and mines to feed their slaves. We will hunt also for elephant. I would like my army to have 200 of these animals to meet the threats from the north of which you have just reminded me.'

'I had wondered at the multitude of empty wagons that follow us.'

'They will be filled before we turn northwards again,' Lannon promised. 'And when we pass through the gardens of Zeng, I will change the garrisons there, leaving these men in their place. Troops who stay too long in one billet grow lazy and corrupt. At Zeng I will meet the emissaries of the Dravs from the east and renew our treaty with them.'

'But what of the north?' Huy came back to his original question.

'From Zeng we will march north in battle array. The women and the others will be sent home to Opet along the road through the middle kingdom. We will come to the river with two full legions to reinforce the two already there, and we will cross the river on a burning and slave-taking raid that will warn the tribes beyond that a new king reigns in Opet.'

Lannon turned and glared towards the north, and his mane of golden and red hair and beard shone in the sunlight.

'For a hundred years now they have plagued us, and we have been too soft with them. Each year they have grown more numerous, more daring. I will show them the iron of my hand, Sunbird. I will show them that the river is held by a barrier of bright steel, and they will press against it at their cost.'

'Where do they come from, I wonder, and how many of them are there?' Huy asked softly.

'They are the hosts of darkness, black because they are not of the sun-god Baal as we are. They were spawned in darkness in the forests of eternal night to the north, and when you can number the greedy locusts then you will count them also.'

'Are you afraid, Lannon?' Huy asked, and the king turned to him with a fiery anger darkening his face.

'You presume, priest,' he snarled.

'Call me friend, not priest – and I do presume to show you that unreasoning hatred is based on fear.'

Lannon's anger faded, and he fiddled with the hilt of his sword, glancing about to make sure that his aides were out of earshot.

'There is reason for fear,' he said at last.

'I know,' said Huy.

uy led the praise chant to Baal in the dawn, but they kept the volume of their voices low so as not to alarm the nearest herds, and afterwards Huy asked the gods to look with favour upon the hunt, promising that a part of the spoils would be left for the Sunbirds to carry on high. Then Huy and Lannon drank a bowl of wine and ate a dry millet cake together as they waited for the hunt to develop.

Mursil, the huntmaster of the south, had chosen the ground with cunning and care. From where they sat on the low line of the escarpment they could look down the vast funnel-shaped plain hemmed in by hills on either hand; along the summit of the hills the signal fires smoked in the early morning to show that the warriors were in position to turn any of the game that tried to cross out of the valley.

In the distance, beyond the range of the eye the two legions were spread out across the plain. Already they were moving forward, 10,000 men, sweeping the grassland like a wave across the beach. The dust of their advance rose palely against the eggshell blue of the morning sky, and below the pall an occasional flash of light came from helmet or spear.

'It has begun,' said Lannon with satisfaction.

Huy looked out on the tens of thousands of grazing animals scattered in herds about the plain. This was the tenth great hunt in fifty days, and the slaughter was beginning to sicken him a little.

He glanced down to where the plain narrowed and the river that bisected it ran down into the neck. At the base, squeezed into a wedge shape by the hills, was a gap of 500 paces which promised escape to the limitless expanse of grassland beyond. The whole plain was thinly scattered with tall flat-topped acacia trees.

Even from where they sat above the gap they could barely see the treble line of concealed pits across the gap

357

that joined the spurs of the two ranges of hills. A thousand of Lannon's archers lay in ambush there, each with a bundle of 300 arrows and a spare bow.

Beyond them still was a double line of netting, heavy woven mesh standing on flimsy poles that would collapse when a heavy body charged into it, smothering the animal in its folds until one of the hoplites could jump up from his hiding-place and run forward with a javelin to despatch the animal and reset the net. Here another 1,000 javelin throwers lay in waiting.

'We should go down now.' Lannon finished the last of the wine and brushed a few crumbs from his cloak.

'A little longer,' Huy suggested. 'I should like to watch this.'

A restlessness was running through the herds upon the plain, beginning with the animals nearest the lines of beaters. The long lines of gnu began running in aimless circles with their noses almost raking the ground, black bodies with long flowing manes kicking and frolicking. The herds of zebra grouped themselves in compact masses of some 200 or 300 animals and looked curiously towards the line of approaching beaters. Their close relatives, the quagga, short and sturdier, assembled in lesser herds, a darker bay colour than the grey zebra. Mixed with them were herds of brilliant yellow and red hartebeest, purple sassaby, and the great bovine eland, striped and maned and majestic. This vast multitude began a stirring and moving, a general slow retreat down the valley towards the gap – and the dust rose around them.

'Ah,' said Lannon. 'What a booty.'

'There could never have been a greater in the history of the hunt,' Huy agreed.

'How many, do you think?' Lannon asked.

'I do not know – fifty, a hundred thousand – it would not be possible to count them.'

Now the long-necked giraffe were infected by the

growing alarm, they left the shelter of the acacia trees and their calves followed them as they joined the mass movement down the valley. Amongst the host trotted an occasional rhinoceros, big and cumbersome, horned and snorting, lifting his massive hooves high as he ran.

Like a flux holding the entire mass together moved the smoky brown herds of dainty springbok. They came on down the valley, moving more urgently, like flood waters, and the dust rose thicker, swirling up in choking clouds. The hills squeezed the herds into a denser mass, and when the hartebeest and sassaby tried to cross the ridges on either hand there was a line of screaming, weapon-brandishing men to meet and turn them from the crest. They charged down the slopes again carrying and spreading the panic through the closely packed herds below.

They surged forward, and the sound of their hooves rose like the sound of storm, surf and wind. The ground began to shake. 'Come,' shouted Lannon and he jumped up and went bounding down the slope. For a moment longer Huy watched that unbelievable phalanx of living creatures thundering down on the gap, then he shouldered his axe and went racing down the slope after Lannon. His long black hair streamed out behind him, and he ran goat-footed, rabbit fast, so that he and Lannon came out on the plain together and Huy led the way into the centre of the gap where a pit had been dug for them and a dozen bundles of javelins lay ready.

Lannon jumped down beside him. 'There was no gold on that race,' he laughed.

'There should have been,' said Huy, and they went to the front lip of the pit and looked up the valley. It was a terrifying sight. The entire valley from side to side was clogged with a great tide of living things, and above them rose a high brown wall of dust through which the low sun glared balefully.

The heads and manes of the lead animals tossed and

heaved like the surface of a torrent, and above them rose the stick-like necks of the giraffe and ostrich. The whole bore down upon them, and the earth trembled beneath them and they stared in awe and wonder.

Lannon was judging his moment carefully, waiting for the first wave of game to cross his range-markers. The moment came and he snapped an order to his trumpeter. The single urgent note of the attack rang out, repeated stridently over and over again.

From the earth at the feet of the advancing wall of living things rose the line of archers. They loosed four times before the wall swept over them. Four thousand arrows in twenty seconds and those that followed fell over the wind-rows of dead animals, screaming with the agony of broken bone and arrow-impaled flesh.

Borne by the weight of their own forward momentum the masses of game pressed onwards while flight after flight of arrows decimated their ranks, and the corpses and wounded piled in ridges and huge mounds.

The smaller game were wiped out by the archers, but the larger thick-skinned animals came through with the arrows bristling in their flanks. Great grey rhinoceros, lumbering, wild-eyed towards the line of nets, tossing their long curved nose horns. Giraffe galloping long-legged and terror-driven. A squadron of black buffalo running in a mass, shoulder to shoulder like a team in span.

They came into the nets, and fell struggling and screaming. The javelins whipped into them as they rolled and roared, smothered in the folds of heavy netting. Desperately Lannon and his men worked to clear the dead from the netting and reset the poles, but it was effort wasted. There were too many of them now, and there was death out there in the open beyond the security of the pits. Arrow-maddened, the wounded game charged for any man who showed himself.

Huy saw a soldier tossed by an angry rhinoceros. He

cartwheeled in the air, and fell on the hard earth to be kicked and trampled to a muddy pulp in the dust by the hordes that followed.

From the pit now Lannon hurled his javelins with an uncanny accuracy and power, aiming each bolt for the soft ribs behind the shoulder of the passing game. He piled the bodies about the pit, shouting and laughing in the frenzied excitement of the hunt.

Huy also was infected by it. He danced and shouted and waved his axe, guarding Lannon's back and flank, hurling a javelin when some huge animal seemed about to crash into the pit on top of them.

Both he and Lannon were soaked with their own sweat and caked with the swirling dust; a stone flung by a dashing hoof had cut Huy's forehead open to the bone of the skull and he ripped the hem from his tunic and bound the wound quickly, hardly interrupting his dance of excitement.

In front of them the archers had been overwhelmed by the sheer weight of animal flesh. With their arrows exhausted they cowered in their pits and let the solid ranks pour over them.

Huy saw the fresh ranks driving down on them and he grabbed his blood-crazed king and dragged him struggling to the floor of the pit, and they lay with their heads covered by their arms while the edges of the pit crumbled in on top of them under the impact of hooves. Earth smothered them and they covered their faces with the hems of their tunics and gasped for breath.

A young zebra stallion fell into the pit on top of them, kicking and neighing in terror with its powerful yellow teeth snapping indiscriminately, it was a deadly danger.

Huy rolled away from its flying razor-sharp hooves. He paused a moment to aim and then shot his right arm upwards. The spiked head of the vulture axe lanced up under the terrified animal's jaw, entering the brain cleanly.

It collapsed warm and limp, shivering on top of them, and its corpse was a protection from the storm of hooves that raged about them.

The storm dwindled, passed over, and rumbled away into the distance. In the quiet that followed, Huy rolled towards Lannon.

'Are you safe?' And Lannon crawled with difficulty from under the dead zebra. They dragged themselves from the pit and looked about them with wonder.

Across a front of 500 paces, and to a depth of the same distance the ground was covered by a thick carpet of dead and dying game. From their pits amongst this terrible carnage the archers and javelin-throwers climbed and stood staring with the dazed air of drunken men.

The line of beaters seemed to wade towards them out of a swamp of hanging dust, even the sky was dulled with the dust, and the pitiful cries and the bleating of the dying and wounded animals shamed the silence.

The beaters came forward in lines through the fields of bleeding flesh and their swords rose and fell as they killed the wounded. Huy reached under his tunic and brought out a leather flask of Zeng wine.

'I can always trust you for comfort.' Lannon grinned, and drank greedily. The wine drops shone like blood in his dusty beard.

'Was there ever a hunt like that?' he asked as he handed the flask to Huy.

Huy drank and then looked about him at the field. 'I cannot believe there ever was,' he said softly.

'We will smoke and dry this kill – and then hunt again,' Lannon promised and strode away to order the butchery.

A high dome of orange light hung over the plain, light reflected from 10,000 fires. All afternoon and all that night the army worked to butcher the enormous bag. To cut the flesh into strips and hang it on the racks over the smoking fires. The smell of sweet raw flesh, the musty reek of split entrails, and the sizzle of the cooking meat drifted across the camp where Huy sat beneath the awning of his leather tent and worked by the fluttering light of an oil lamp.

Lannon came out of the darkness, still filthy with dust and dried blood.

'Wine! Sunbird, for the love of a friend.' He pretended to stagger with thirst, and Huy passed both amphora and bowl to him. Scorning the bowl Lannon drank directly from the neck of the jug and wiped his beard on his arm.

'I come with news,' he grinned. 'The bag was 1,700 head.'

'How many of them men?'

'Fifteen men died, and there are some wounded – but was it not worth it?'

Huy did not answer, and Lannon went on.

'There is more news. Another of my javelins has struck the mark. Annel has missed her moon.'

'The southern air must be beneficial. All four of them with child in two months.'

'It is not the air, Sunbird,' Lannon laughed and drank again.

'I am pleased,' said Huy. 'More of the old blood for Opet.'

'When did you ever care for blood, Huy Ben-Amon? You are pleased to have more of my brats to spoil – I know you.' Lannon came to stand behind Huy. 'You are writing,' he said, unnecessarily. 'What is it?'

'A poem,' said Huy modestly.

'What of?'

'The hunt – today's hunt.'

'Sing it to me,' commanded Lannon and dropped onto Huy's fur bed, with the amphora still grasped by the neck.

Huy fetched his lute, and squatted on the reed mat. He sang, and when he had finished Lannon lay quietly on the bed staring out through the opening of the tent into the night.

'I did not see it like that,' he said at last. 'To me it was just a taking, a harvest of flesh.'

He was silent again.

'I have displeased you?' Huy asked, and Lannon shook his head.

'Do you truly believe that what we did today has destroyed something that will never be replaced?' he asked.

'I do not know, perhaps not – but if we hunted like that every day, or even once every ten days, would we not soon turn this land into a desert?'

Lannon brooded quietly over the half-empty amphora for a long while, then he looked up at Huy and smiled.

'We have taken sufficient meat. We will not hunt again this year – only for ivory.'

'My lord, has the wine jug stuck to your hand?' Huy asked softly, and Lannon stared at him for a moment then laughed.

'A trade, Sunbird, another song and I will give you wine.'

'A fair trade,' Huy agreed.

When the amphora was empty, Huy sent one of his ancient slaves for another.

'Bring two,' suggested Lannon. 'It will save time later.'

At midnight Huy was soft from the wine, and desolated by the beauty of his own voice and the sadness of his own song. He wept, and Lannon seeing him weep, wept with him.

'I will not have such beauty recorded on the skin of beasts,' cried Lannon with tears cutting runnels through the dust on his cheeks and pouring into his beard. 'I will have a scroll made of the finest gold, and on it you will inscribe your songs, my Sunbird. Then they will live for ever to delight my children and my children's children.'

Huy stopped weeping. The artist in him aroused, his mind quickly assimilating the offer which he knew Lannon would not remember in the morning.

'I am truly honoured, my lord.' Huy went to kneel at the side of the bed. 'Will you sign the treasury order now?'

'Write it, Huy, write it now, this instant,' Lannon commanded. 'I will sign it.'

And Huy ran for his writing pallet.

The column moved on slowly in a great circle to the south and east through the southern plains of grass. It was a land of such limitless dimensions that the fifteen-mile column was as significant as a file of safari ants. There were rivers and ranges of hills, forests and plains teeming with game. The only men they met were the garrisons of the king's hunting camps. Their task was primarily to provide a steady supply of dried meat for the multitudes of slaves that were the foundation of the nation's prosperity.

They crossed the river of the south* six months after departure from the city of Opet and 100 miles beyond they reached the range of thickly forested blue mountains† which marked the border of the southern kingdom.

They went into camp at the mouth of a dark rocky gorge that tore its way through the heart of the mountains, and Lannon and Huy with a cohort of infantry and archers took the precipitous path through the gorge. It was an eerie place of tall black stone cliffs hanging high above the

* Limpopo River.
† Zoutspansberg.

roaring frothing torrent in the depths below. It was a cold dark place where the warmth of the sun seldom penetrated. Huy shivered, not from the cold, and clutched his axe firmly. He prayed almost continually during the three days that they marched through the mountains for it was most certainly a place frequented by demons.

They camped on the southern slopes of the mountains and built signal fires, sending the smoke aloft in tall columns that could be seen for fifty miles. To the southward stretched a land as vast as that to the north.

Looking out across its golden rolling grasslands and its dark green forests, Huy felt a sense of awe. 'I would like to go down into that land,' he told Lannon.

'You would be the first,' Lannon agreed. 'I wonder what it holds. What treasures, what mysteries?'

'We know there is a Cape to the far south with a flat-topped mountain where the fleet of Hycanus IX was destroyed, but that is all we know.'

'I have a mind to defy the prophecy and lead an expedition southwards beyond these mountains – what say you, Huy?'

'I would not counsel it, my lord,' Huy answered formally. 'No good ever comes of challenging the gods, they have damnably long memories.'

'I expect you are right,' Lannon conceded. 'Yet I am sorely tempted.'

Huy changed a subject which was making him uncomfortable, he should never have broached it.

'I wonder when they will come.' He looked up at the smoke from the signal fires streaming up into the calm blue of the midday sky.

'They will come when they are ready,' Lannon shrugged. 'But I wish they would make it soon. Whilst we wait, we will hunt the leopard.'

For ten days they hunted the big spotted cats which

abounded in the misty cliffs and woody gorges of the mountains. They hunted with specially trained hounds and lion-spears. They would run the quarry with the pack, until it was cornered or bayed and they would then surround it and close in until the charge was provoked.

Then the man selected by the leopard would take the snarling, slashing animal on the point of his spear. Two of the hunters were killed in those ten days – and one of them was a grandson of Asmun, the old nobleman. He was a fine brave lad and they all mourned, although it was a good and honourable death. They cremated his body, for he had died in the field, and Huy sacrificed for a safe passage of his soul to the sun.

On the eleventh day, in the dawn after Huy had greeted Baal, and they had breakfasted and were dressing and arming for the hunt, Huy noticed the agitation and restlessness of the little bushman huntmaster, Xhai.

'What is it that troubles you, Xhai?' he asked him in his own language, which he now spoke with authority.

'My people are here,' the bushman told him.

'How do you know that?' Huy demanded.

'I know it!' Xhai answered simply, and Huy hurried through the camp to Lannon's tent.

'They have come, my lord,' he told him.

'Good.' Lannon laid aside his lion-spear and began stripping his hunting armour. 'Call the stone-finders.' And the royal geologists and metallurgists came hurrying to the summons.

The meeting place was at the foot of the mountains where thick forest ended abruptly at the edge of a wide glade.

Lannon led his party down amongst the rocks and at the edge of the glade they halted, and threw out a protective screen of archers. In the centre of the glade, well out of arrowshot of the forest edge or the rocky slope, a pole had been driven into the soft earth and the tail of a reed buck dangled from it like a standard. It was the sign that the trade could begin.

Lannon nodded to his senior stone-finder, Aziru, and Rib-Addi, master of the royal treasury. The two of them walked out into the glade unarmed and with two slaves following them. The slaves each carried a leather bag.

At the foot of the pole was a dried gourd which contained a handful of bright pebbles and stones of various colours ranging from glassy to fiery red.

The two officials examined each stone, rejecting some by dropping them in a neat pile on the earth, selecting others by returning them to the gourd. Then from the leather bags they doled out glass beads into a pottery jar which they placed beside the gourd. They withdrew to the rocky slope where Lannon and his archers stood.

They waited until a dozen tiny figures left the edge of the forest and approached the pole. The troop of little bushmen squatted beside the gourd and jar and there was a long heated debate before they withdrew to the forest once more. The two officials went out into the glade and found gourd and jar untouched. The offer had been refused. They added a dozen iron arrow heads to the offering.

At the third attempt a bargain was struck when the bushmen accepted the beads and arrow heads and copper bangles, leaving the stones to be collected.

Then another batch of stones was set out beside the pole and haggled over. It was a tedious business which occupied four whole days, and while they waited Huy added considerably to his knowledge of geology.

'From where do these sun-stones come?' he asked Aziru, as he examined a yellow diamond the size of an acorn which had been traded for a pound's weight of glass beads.

'When sun and moon show together in the sky, then it may happen that their rays mingle and become hot and heavy. They fall to earth, and if they strike water then they are quenched and freeze into one of these sun-stones.' Huy found this explanation utterly convincing.

'A love-drop of Baal and Astarte,' he whispered with reverence. 'No wonder then that they are so beautiful.' He looked up at Aziru. 'Where do the pygmies find them?'

'It is said that they search in the gravel beds of the rivers, and also the edge of the lakes,' Aziru explained. 'But they are not adept at recognizing the true sun-stone and their offerings contain many common stones.'

When the bushmen had traded their entire gathering of diamonds, they offered for sale the unwanted children of the tribe. These little yellow mites were left bound and shivering with terror beside the trading pole. The slave masters, experts in appraising human flesh, went out to examine them and offer payment. The pygmies were much in demand as slaves, for they were tractable, loyal and hardy. They made excellent hunters, guides, entertainers, and, strangely, children's companions.

Xhai stood behind his tall yellow-haired king and watched the trade, exactly the bargaining which had been conducted over him as a child.

At the end of the fourth day the treasury of Opet had acquired five large pottery jars of fine diamonds. Trade in these stones was a jealously guarded monopoly of the ruling house of Barca. In addition there were eighty-six bushman children between the ages of five and fifteen years. They were wild slaves, and had to be bound until tamed.

Huy devoted himself almost entirely to their welfare during the return across the mountains. With the help of Xhai and the other tame bushmen he was able to save most of them. Only a dozen of the tiny creatures died of terror and heartbreak before they could be handed over to the slave women of the main camp.

Lannon broke the camp under the southern mountains and they turned north and east, recrossing the river and picking up the mountains of Bar-Zeng* on the horizon. They began passing through the populous kingdom of the east, where the Yuye peasants farmed the corn lands along the Lion River.†

At each settlement the freedmen turned out to welcome them, and make tribute to their new king. They were a cheerful throng, and the mud-walled villages were clean and prosperous-looking. Even the slaves in the fields were sleek and well cared for, only a fool would abuse a valuable possession. The slaves were mostly blacks, taken in the north, but amongst them were those of mixed blood, sired by their own masters, or by selected stud slaves. They were unbound, differing little in dress or ornament from their masters.

Along their way the legionaries who had completed their military service left their regiments and returned to their villages. Their places in the ranks were filled by the young recruits.

They camped each night at one of the walled and fortified garrisons that studded the road to the mountains of Zeng. They were passing now through the fringes of the wide gold belt that ran east and west across the middle kingdom. It was this belt on which the wealth of Opet was based, and the king's stone-finders had developed an almost supernatural ability to find the enriched reefs in which the gold was hidden. The results of their efforts were numerous mines where the ore was prised from the earth by platoons of black slaves working naked in the narrow stifling stopes. At the surface it was crushed and the powdered rock washed from the grains of native gold in specially designed copper basins.

Lannon paused in his march to inspect many of these works, and Huy was impressed by the ingenuity of the

* The Chimanimani Mountains.
† The Sabi River.

engineers who overcame the problems that the extraction of the ore presented at each separate site.

Where the gold-bearing reef was narrow, they kept the headroom in the stopes as low as possible by using only women and children in the workings.

They employed elephants for hauling the ore baskets to the surface, and for carrying water to the mines situated in the drier areas.

They had developed a method of undermining massive ore bodies and collapsing them under their own weight. It was a dangerous procedure, and at one of the mines practising this method Lannon and Huy were kept from sleep the entire night by the mourning wailing from the slave compound. During the day an ore body had collapsed prematurely and over a hundred slaves with a few slave-masters had been crushed beneath it. Huy wondered how much of that hideous sound was on account of the dead slave-masters.

Driven by his insatiable curiosity, Huy had himself lowered in one of the ore baskets to the lower levels of one of the workings. It was a hellish place of foul air, and heat and sweat, lit by the flickering oil lamps. The naked slaves toiled in cramped and dangerous chambers hacked from the living rock. Huy watched an intrusive outcrop of harder rock demolished by the means Hannibal had used hundreds of years before to clear his passage across the alps. A slow fire was lit and kept burning upon the rock until it had heated to a dull glow. It was quenched then with buckets of liquid, a mixture of water and sour wine, that exploded in a swirling cloud of steam, and split the rock into chunks which were hacked out and dragged away by the slaves. Huy went to the face where he saw the native gold shine in the mother lode, rich and yellow, and he mused at the price that must be paid for its extraction.

When Huy was again hoisted to the surface he was soaked with sweat, and filthy with dirt from the stopes.

Lannon shook his head. 'What did you want to do that for? Have the birds got your brain, that you must grovel around in the earth?'

At one of the mines the ore had been exhausted above the level of the subterranean water. It was impossible to go down below this level, for no method had yet been devised to clear the water from the workings. Bucket chains of slaves were seldom able to lower the level by more than a few inches. The mine must be returned to Astarte the mother of moon and earth. She had given of her bounty, and in return she must receive.

Lannon, as was his right, selected the messengers, conferring with his slave-masters to decide which fifteen slaves would be the least loss to the labour force. The gods were not particular about the quality of the sacrifice. To them a life was a life, and therefore acceptable.

Huy's heart went out to them as they were led down into the workings for the last time. They wore the symbolic chains of the sacrifice, and they shuffled along, stooped and maimed and coughing with the lung disease of the miners.

Huy delegated one of his priests to supervise the sending, and when his emissary emerged from the evil dark pit Huy led the praise chant to Astarte, and the work of refilling the mine began. It would continue for many weeks because of the amount of rock that must be carefully repacked into the caverns.

This refilling was necessary to placate the earth mother further and also to allow new gold to grow.

Aziru explained the need for this. 'This is benevolent ground, suitable for the growth of gold. We replace rock in the earth and the action of the sun upon it will, in time, engender a fresh growth of the precious metal.'

'All life is in Baal,' Huy intoned formally.

'Our children's children will one day thank us for this seeding of the earth,' Aziru predicted smugly, and Huy was impressed with this forethought – and he recorded every detail of it all in his neatly flowing script.

Three hundred days after leaving the city of Opet, the column climbed the foothills of the Zeng Mountains.* The air was cool and fresh after the heat of the lowlands, and at night the mist hung heavily along the slopes and woke the fever in men's bones so that they shivered and huddled in their cloaks about the campfires.

Those hills were the gardens of Opet, where tens of thousands of acres of land had been terraced and cultivated, and where tens of thousands of slaves tended the olive groves and vineyards. The centre and citadel of these gardens was a fortified hilltop town named after the twelfth Gry-Lion of Opet, Zeng-Hanno. Here there were temples to both Baal and Astarte, the religious strongholds of the eastern kingdom, and Huy spent twenty days in synod with his priests and priestesses. Huy also exercised and inspected his own personal legion, the sixth Ben-Amon, which was the only one of the eight legions of Opet composed entirely of warriors of the blood. Their standard was a golden vulture set on a shaft of polished ebony.

These religious activities were interrupted when Lannon summoned Huy to accompany him on a short journey to the east, from whence word had come that the Dravs awaited Lannon to renew the five-year treaty.

Three sheikhs of the Drav met them when they descended the mountains of Zeng towards the eastern sea. They were tall, brown-skinned men with fierce eagle features and dark glittering eyes. They wore head-dresses

* Inyanga Mountains.

of white over their long black hair, and they dressed in full-length robes belted with sashes of filigree and semi-precious stones. Each carried a magnificent broad curved dagger at his waist, and wore slippers with long pointed toes.

Their warriors dressed differently, wearing baggy panta-loons, on their heads onion-shaped helmets, body armour of silver breast-plates; and they were armed with round iron shields and long curved scimitars, spears and short oriental bows. Most of them were Negroes, but they had clearly adopted the Drav manner of speech and dress. Two hundred years of relentless warfare had preceded the treaty between the Drav and the kings of Opet.

The two armies bivouacked on each side of a wide valley, with a stream of clear water overhung with shady green trees separating the camps.

Under these trees the council tents were pitched, and here for five days the two delegations feasted and bargained and manoeuvred diplomatically.

Huy spoke the language of the Dravs and he translated for Lannon the negotiations towards a treaty of unrestricted trade and mutual military aid.

'My lord, Prince Hassan is concerned to know how many warriors Opet could put into the field in the event of a threat to the security of the two nations.'

They sat on piles of silken cushions and lovely woven woollen rugs of vivid design and colour, drinking sherbet, for the Drav would not touch even the finest wines, eating a dish of mutton and fish spiced with herbs, smiling at each other and not trusting each other further than the range of the eye.

'Prince Hassan,' replied Lannon, nodding and smiling at him, 'is concerned to know with what force we would oppose an attempt to seize the gardens of Zeng and the gold mines of the middle kingdom.'

'Of course,' Huy agreed. 'What shall I tell him?'

'Tell him I can field fourteen regular legions, as many auxiliaries, and 400 elephants.'

'He will not believe those figures, my lord.'

'Of course not, no more do I believe his. Tell him anyway.' And so the bargaining proceeded in an atmosphere of mutual trust.

They agreed to secure each other's flanks, combine to hold the line of the great river in the north against invasion by the migrant black tribes, and to come to each other's assistance if that border was violated.

'The prince would like to revise the unit of trade, my lord. He suggests that 500 mikthals should equal one Opet finger of gold.'

'Tell him politely to swing on his own testicles,' Lannon replied, smiling at the prince, and the prince nodded and smiled back at him, the gemstones sparkling and glittering on his fingers.

They set the rate of exchange at 590 mikthals per finger, and went on to negotiate the slaving agreement, and the cotton and silk clauses. On the fifth day they ate salt together and exchanged extravagant gifts, while the armies gave displays of archery and swordsmanship and drill. These were intended to impress the other side.

'Their archers are ineffectual,' Lannon appraised them.

'The bow is too short, and they draw to the waist not the chin,' Huy agreed. 'They limit their range and accuracy.'

Then later when the infantry drilled:

'Their infantry are lighter armed and armoured, my lord. They have no axemen, and I doubt those breastplates would turn an arrow.'

'And yet they move fast, and they have a fiery spirit – do not dismiss them lightly, my Sunbird.'

'No, my lord. I will not do that.'

The elephants charged across the open ground with the archers in their castles spraying a shower of arrows ahead of the line. The huge grey beasts tossed and trampled the lines of straw dummies and their squeals and trumpets rang against the crest of the hills.

'See their faces,' Lannon murmured. 'The prince seems to be looking on the eternal seas!' And it was true that the Dravs were silent and subdued for they had no elephants of their own, they had not mastered the art of training them.

They parted and when Lannon and Huy looked back into the valley they saw the Drav army winding away eastwards in column, with the sunlight sparkling on helmets and spearheads.

'Our eastern border is secure for five more years,' Lannon declared with satisfaction.

'Or until the princes change their minds,' Huy qualified.

'No, Sunbird. They must honour the treaty – it is in their own best interest. Trust me, old friend.'

'You, I trust,' said Huy.

O n the return to Zeng-Hanno the legions assembled and preparations began for the burning which Lannon planned to lead across the great river.

Huy's legion was one of those chosen, and he spent much time with his priest-officers. They dined with him in the splendid quarters set aside for him within the enclosure of the temple of Baal. Huy invited the reverend priestesses of Astarte, and provided magnificent fare for he had hunted the day before and there was game to add to the beef and chicken and fish seasoned with spices traded from the Drav, while the gardens of Zeng provided the best of their fruits and wines.

Lannon was the guest of honour, and they were all decked with wreaths of flowers and boisterous with wine.

'Reverend Mother,' one of Huy's priests, a handsome young rake named Bakmor, called across the board to the

High Priestess of Astarte. 'Is it true that you have discovered a new oracle among your novices to replace the Lady Imilce who died two years ago of the shivering sickness?'

The reverend mother turned wise old eyes on the young officer. She had pale, brittle-looking skin and her hair was fine and fluffy white. Her arms were thin and pale also and her hands skeletal and corded with blue veins. Up until now she had sat withdrawn from the revelry.

'It is true that one of the temple novices shows wisdom and wit beyond her years or training, it is true also that she has seen beyond the veil and made prophecy, but the sisterhood has not yet decided to send her to the High Priest for examination.'

'Is there doubt then, Reverend Mother?' Bakmor insisted.

'There is always doubt, my son,' the priestess answered, in a tone that clearly rebuked his presumption and the youngster sat back discomfited.

'I have not heard of this,' Huy remarked with interest and a trace of accusation in his tone. For two years the priesthood had been without the services of an oracle, and the search had been diligent. Fees for divination and prophecy formed a significant proportion of the temple income, and there were also political reasons why Huy was anxious to find a successor to Lady Imilce.

'Forgive me, Holy Father. I had determined to discuss this with you privately.' The High Priestess spoke confidentially, but Lannon leaned across Huy to join the discussion.

'Send for the wench,' he said, speaking thickly with wine. The priestess stiffened at his choice of words. 'Send for her, let her entertain us with her prophecies.'

'My lord,' Huy wished to remonstrate but Lannon brushed his protest aside, and raised his voice.

'Send for the oracle – let her speak on the outcome of the campaign to the north.'

Huy turned back to the priestess with an apology in his eyes.

'The king commands,' he said, and the priestess inclined her head then turned to whisper to her body slave. The slave hurried from the hall.

When she came the loud voices and laughter stilled, and they stared at her with curiosity. She was a tall girl with finely boned wrists and ankles. She wore the long green robes of the temple novice which left her arms bare, and her skin had a lustre and smoothness which made it glow in the lamp light. Her hair was dark and soft, so that it floated cloudlike to her shoulders. She wore the gold crescent moon emblem of Astarte on her deep bulging forehead, dangling from a fine chain of gold, and her ear-rings were two small sun-stones that shone like the stars of heaven.

Her eyes were green, a colour that reminded Huy of the pool of Astarte in the cavern of the temple of Opet. Her lips were full and quivered faintly, betraying her agitation at his unexpected summons, while there were spots of colour in her cheeks. However, her manner was calm and controlled, and she moved with dignity to where Huy sat. He saw then that she was very young.

'Pray for me, Holy Father,' she greeted him and bowed her head. Huy studied her avidly, taken with her direct manner and her dignity.

'Greet your king, my child,' he murmured and the girl turned to Lannon. While she made the formal greeting Huy continued to examine her.

'What is your name?' he asked, and the girl turned back to Huy and fixed him with those solemn green eyes.

'Tanith,' she answered. It was the ancient name of the goddess, from the days of the old city of Carthage.

'It is a pretty name,' Huy nodded. 'I have always loved it.' And the girl smiled at him. It was a smile that took him by surprise, for it was as warm and uplifting as the dawn of Baal.

'You are kind, Holy Father,' she said, smiling at him and Huy Ben-Amon fell in love. He felt the bottom fall out of his stomach, and his vitals sucked downwards in a long sliding sensation. He stared at Tanith, unable to speak, feeling his cheeks flush with hot blood, searching desperately for the right word but not finding it.

Lannon broke the spell by shouting at a slave, 'Bring a cushion.' And they seated Tanith before the king and priests.

'Make an oracle,' Lannon commanded, and leaned towards her, breathing heavily and with the wine flushing his face. Tanith looked at him calmly with the faintest trace of a smile on her lips.

'If it were within my power, I would speak an oracle for you, lord, but then there would be a matter of fee and question.'

'What is the fee?' Lannon demanded; he had flushed a little darker with the first stirring of anger. He was not accustomed to this treatment.

'Holy Father, would you set the fee?' Tanith asked of Huy – and the devil took Huy.

'One hundred fingers of fine gold,' he spoke before he realized what he had done. It was an enormous fee, and it constituted a challenge to Lannon, daring him to back down or pay. Tanith smiled again now, a provocative dimple appeared in her cheek and she held Lannon's scowl with a cool amused stare. Huy was suddenly aware that he had placed the girl in a position of peril. Lannon would not forgive this readily, and Huy hastened to give Lannon a graceful escape.

'For this fee the Gry-Lion may put as many questions as he has fingers on his sword hand.'

Lannon hesitated, Huy could see that he was still angry but slightly placated by Huy's amendment.

'I doubt that the wisdom of a child will be worth that much, but it amuses me to test this wench,' Lannon mumbled, looking anything but amused. He took up his wine bowl and drank deeply, then he wiped his beard and looked at Tanith.

'I go northwards on a mission. Speak to me of the outcome,' he ordered, and Tanith settled herself on the leather cushion, spreading her green robe about her. She lowered her head slightly, and her green eyes seemed to look inwards. There was an expectant hush on the guests now, and they watched her eagerly. Huy noticed that her cheeks paled, and her lips also rimmed with white.

'There will be a mighty harvest,' Tanith whispered hoarsely in a strange unnatural monotone, 'more than the Gry-Lion expects or realizes.'

The guests stirred, glancing at each other, whispering, pondering the answer. Lannon frowned over the girl's words.

'Do you speak of a harvest of death?' Lannon asked.

'You will take death with you, but death will return with you unknown and secretly,' Tanith replied. It was an unfavourable oracle, the young officers were restless, sobering rapidly. Huy wanted to intervene – he was regretting the whole business. He knew his king, knew he would not readily forget or forgive.

'What must I fear?' Lannon asked.

'Blackness,' Tanith answered readily.

'How will I find death?' Lannon was shaking with anger now, his voice guttural and his pale blue eyes deadly.

'At the hand of a friend.'

'Who will reign in Opet after me?'

'He who kills the gry-lion,' Tanith replied, and Lannon struck the wine bowl aside and it shattered on the earthen floor, the red wine splattering the feet of a waiting slave.

'The gry-lion is finished,' he shouted. 'I killed the last of them – do you dare prophesy the death of house Barca?'

'That is your sixth question, my lord.' Tanith looked up. 'I cannot see the answer to it.'

380

'Get her out of here,' Lannon roared. 'Take the witch away.'

And Huy signalled quickly for the High Priestess to take her, for a slave to replace Lannon's wine bowl, and for another to fetch his lute.

After Huy's third song Lannon laughed again.

O n the eve of the departure of the legions from Zeng-Hanno, Huy sent for the priestess and the novice Tanith. It was five days since her disastrous prophecies to Lannon Hycanus, and it had taken all Huy's strength of will not to send for her earlier.

When she came she was fresher and lovelier than he remembered. While the priestess sat in the shade, Huy walked with Tanith upon the walls of the city, looking down on the one hand upon the streets and courtyards with the bustle of the army preparing for its march, while on the other hand they looked across the wooded hills and terraces where the slaves tended the neatly laid out vineyards and orchards.

'I have instructed the reverend mother that you will join the convoy to Opet through the middle kingdom. You will travel with the wives of the king, and at Opet you will enter the sisterhood of Astarte – and await my return.'

'Yes, my lord.' Her humble tone was at odds with her saucy expression. Huy stopped and looked into her green eyes, she held his gaze easily, smiling a little.

'Do you truly possess the sight, Tanith?'

'I do not know, my lord.'

'The words you spoke to the king, what did they mean?'

'I do not know. They are words that came into my mind unbidden. I cannot explain them.'

Huy nodded, and paced on in silence. There was an appealing innocence about this girl, coupled with a bright mind and a sunny disposition it was impossible to resist. Huy stopped again, and she waited for him to speak.

'Do you love the gods, Tanith?'

'I do.'

'Do you believe that I am their appointed one?'

'I do, Holy Father,' she answered with such conviction, with such transparent honesty and respect, that Huy's reservations were set at rest. There was no doubt that she was an instrument which could be used, as long as it was used with skill.

'What is your destiny, Tanith?' he asked suddenly.

'I cannot see it,' she answered, but she hesitated then and for the first time Huy knew she was uncertain. 'But this I know, that this – this meeting between you and me is part of that destiny.'

Huy felt his heart swell, but his voice was gruff as he replied, 'Caution, child. You are a priestess, dedicated to the goddess. You know better than to speak like that to a man.'

Tanith dropped her eyes and colour stained her skin a dusky rose. The soft wing of dark hair swung forward against her cheek, and she pushed it away with her hand. Huy felt his soul shrivel with despair. Her presence was a physical agony, for no matter how great his need of her it could never be slaked. She belonged to the gods, forbidden, untouchable.

'You know that,' Huy warned her sternly. 'Do not trifle with the gods.'

She looked up at him demurely, but Huy could have sworn there were glints of laughter and teasing mockery in the green eyes.

'Holiness, you wrong me. I did not mean as man and maid.'

'How then?' demanded Huy, disappointed and with a hollow feeling in his guts at the denial.

'We will find the answer to that when we meet at Opet,

Holiness,' she murmured and Huy knew that the months until then would pass slowly.

Lannon stood over a clay box in which was modelled a relief map of the great river area. In the east rose the Clouds of Baal, a mighty waterfall where the river fell hundreds of feet into a dark gorge and the spray from the torrent rose high into the heavens, a perpetual cloud that stood upon the plains.* From here the river flowed into a deep valley, a hot unhealthy place where rough and rocky ramparts rose on each bank, heavily forested and rich with the ivory-bearing herds. Six hundred miles further east the river entered the territory of the Dravs, and ran through a wide alluvial plain which was inundated in the season of rain. Then at last the river joined the eastern sea through a dozen fan-shaped mouths.

Lannon pointed out the main features of this country on the model to his generals, occasionally turning for verification to his garrison commanders who had held the river during the past year. There were twenty men in the large leather tent, and the sides were lifted to allow a dry breeze to enter – and to show the view across the wide valley below the camp. The great river itself was obscured by the tall dark green growth of trees along its bank. There was an occasional flash of reflected sunlight from the water amongst the trees. Far to the north the opposite escarpment of the valley rose in smoky blue tiers of hills.

'Our spies have marked the main towns at which the tribes are gathered. They are mostly on the high ground, a day's march beyond the river, and it is important that each tribe be attacked on the same day.'

* Victoria Falls.

He went on to assign a target to each of his commanders, a crossing place over the river, and a return route.

'There will be no danger of attack on the return march, as long as you break their spirit on the first day. Each of the tribes is at war with the others, and they will not rally to the assistance of each other. The only way in which we can fail is if warning is carried to the barbarians and they scatter before our thrust.'

He explained the plan in detail, dwelling on the logistics of supply and routes of march, until at last Lannon set a date for the attack.

'Twelve days from now. That will give each of your legions time to march to the crossing places, and reach the towns of the barbarians.'

From the camp on the escarpment of the valley, Huy marched the Sixth Ben-Amon to the garrison fort on the banks of the great river at Sett, and here he put the legion into camp in a forest of mopane trees which would screen them from observers on the opposite bank. Fires were forbidden during the day and were carefully screened at night and the men were kept busy building the rafts for the crossing. Heavy rains in the west had swollen the river and the ford was impassable.

Mago Tellema, the garrison commander, was a tall balding disillusioned man with the yellowish skin and eyes of the shivering sickness which was endemic along the river. He seemed pathetically glad of Huy's company during the waiting days, and Huy found his information valuable, so they dined together every evening – Huy provided the wine out of the ample stocks he had brought from Zeng.

'I have kept my patrols on their usual routine, as you ordered.'

'Good.' Huy nodded over a bowl of baked river fish and wild rice. 'Have they noticed any increase in activity since my arrival?'

'No, Holiness. A war party of a few hundred crossed last night and attacked one of my outposts. We drove them off readily enough, killing fifty of them.'

'What do they gain by these raids?'

'Weapons, and an appraisal of our strength.'

'Is the whole border so active?'

'No, Holy Father. But here at Sett we oppose one of the more warlike tribes, the Vendi – they are exceptional. You recall how four years ago they crossed in strength, 20,000 of them overwhelmed the garrison here and left the valley—'

'Yes,' Huy interrupted. 'I was with the legions when we met them at Bhor.'

'Ah! Of course. I remember now that your legion's number was on the honour list.' The commander chuckled. 'Of that 20,000 not one returned across the river.'

'They fought well, though – for pagans,' Huy conceded.

'Indeed, Holiness, they are exceptional in that respect also and in the years since then they have become more formidable.'

'Have you seen their town?'

'No, Holiness, but I have many spies. It is set on the first slopes of the northern escarpment, where the tributary river Kal comes down from the plateau.'

'What is the population?'

'I believe them to number 50,000.'

'So large!' Huy looked up with a mouthful of fish and stared at the commander.

'They are a numerous tribe – not all of them live in the town. They tend large herds of cattle and are spread over a vast area.'

'Is the town fortified?'

'It is a large and sprawling huddle of huts, Holiness. Some of the huts are ringed with primitive palisades, but these are defence against wild animals only.'

A slave refilled Huy's wine bowl and took away his

empty dish. Huy cupped the bowl in his hands and stared moodily into the dark red liquid. His silence discomfited the commander who at last blurted, 'Is it true that the king will arrive here on the morrow?'

'Yes. Lannon Hycanus will march with my legion in the raid.'

'I have never been presented to him,' the man murmured, and Huy had a penetrating insight into the career of an elderly officer doomed to a minor outpost in the wilderness without patron or prospects.

'I will commend you to him,' Huy promised, and saw the pathetic gratitude in the man's eyes.

One of the biremes that patrolled the river landed a century of axemen and archers on the far bank in the night, and before dawn they had rigged the lines across the river.

The river was 300 paces wide at this point, a dirty green flow of water between steep banks which were thickly wooded and covered with reed and dense vegetation. The rafts were carried down to the river's edge and attached to the looped lines. The legion boarded in groups of fifty, and the elephants walked away with the lines drawing the rafts smoothly across the river.

The crossing went with well-drilled precision – it was not the first time a legion had crossed the great river. There were a few minor incidents – two hoplites fell from their rafts and sank swiftly beneath the weight of their armour, one of the rafts capsized a struggling mass of men and equipment into the shallow water beside the bank but all waded to safety, a legionary entangled his arm in one of the lines and had it neatly severed below the elbow – but the crossing was completed before mid-afternoon and Lannon turned to Huy:

'Bravely done, my Sunbird. Now explain to me your order of march.'

Huy left a cohort to hold the crossing, and to act as a base for his stores, a pile of dried meat and corn in leather bags. His legion would be tired, hungry, and perhaps hard pressed on its return and if all went as was planned, there would also be many thousands of extra mouths to feed.

Then behind a screen of light infantry and archers he began his march on the barbarian town of Kal. Here the weeks of training and hardening during the march from Zeng-Hanno showed. For although the ground was broken and heavily forested, the legion moved swiftly in compact columns, covering the ground at a pace that pushed a steady five miles behind them every hour. Ahead of them the scouts ensured that no one would carry a warning to the town. The few hundred herders and hunters and root gatherers that were met with by the scouts were despatched with a silent shower of arrows or a swift clean axe stroke. Their bodies lay where they had fallen beside the track, and the columns trudged on past them with hardly a sidelong glance. Huy saw that they were well-formed men and women, dressed in kilts of animal skins and with tribal scars on their cheeks and breasts. Like most of the tribes from the north their skins were a very dark blueish black. Some of them had mutilated their teeth by filing them to a sharp point like those of a shark, and the men were armed with throwing spears and light axes with half-moon-shaped blades.

The legion halted after dark, and ate cold cooked meat and corn cakes from their pouches while the wine-carriers moved amongst them filling the bowls.

'Look.' Huy touched Lannon's shoulder and pointed towards the northern hills. The sky glowed, as though the moon was rising from the wrong direction. It was the reflected light from thousands of cooking fires.

'A rich harvest,' Lannon nodded. 'Just as the witch prophesied.'

Huy stirred uncomfortably at the mention of Tanith, but remained silent.

'Her words have troubled me – I've spent many nights pondering them.' Lannon wiped his greasy fingers and lips, before he reached for the wine bowl. 'She preaches death and darkness and betrayal by a friend.' He rinsed his mouth with wine and spat it on the ground before drinking.

Huy murmured, 'She did not preach, Majesty – she replied to a question.'

But Lannon said, 'I believe she is evil.'

'Sire!' Huy protested quickly.

'Do not be misled by a pretty face, Huy.'

'She is young, innocent,' he began but saw Lannon leaning towards him and peering into his face, and he stopped.

'What is this witch to you, my Sunbird?'

'As a maid, she means nothing. How could she, she belongs to the goddess.' Huy denied his love, and Lannon leaned back and grunted sceptically.

'It is as well – you are wise in all things but women, my friend. You must let me guide you.'

'You are always kind,' Huy muttered.

'Keep away from that one, Huy. Be warned by one who loves you, she will bring you nothing but sorrow.'

'We have rested long enough.' Huy stood up and settled the strap of his axe about his wrist. 'It is time to march.'

After midnight they crested the low line of hills that formed the first slope of the escarpment, and before them spread a wide-open basin of land through which the dark river Kal meandered. The basin was moon-washed silver and blue, and the smoke from 10,000 cooking fires spread like a pale sea mist across the river, lying in layers in the still night air.

The fires had died to pin-points of dull red that speckled the town, and the huts were dark and shapeless, scattered thickly without plan or pattern, a vast agglomeration of primitive dwellings.

'He estimated 50,000 – and he's not far wrong.' Huy looked out across the basin, and beside him Lannon asked:

'How will you proceed?' And Huy smiled in the moonlight.

'You taught me how to hunt game, my king.'

His cohort commanders came for their orders, cloaked and helmeted and grim. Huy ordered out a thin screen of light infantry and covering bowmen to the east. During the day the scouts had captured 4,000 of the rangy little scrub cattle belonging to the Vendi.

'Take the cattle with you. You remember Hannibal's ruse in Italia, it will serve us as well upon the great river.'

Lannon laughed delightedly and clapped Huy's shoulder when he had explained it. 'Fly for me, Sunbird.'

'Roar for me, Gry-Lion,' Huy grinned back at him as he settled and buckled his helmet.

Silently Huy led 4,500 of his heavy infantry and axemen around to the west and laid them in a crescent shape at the edge of the forest beyond the town. Huy slept for an hour and when one of his centurions shook him awake he was stiff and cold with the night dew.

'Stand to!' he ordered quietly, and the word was passed from mouth to mouth. There was a stirring and a dark movement along the edge of the forest as the legionaries slung their axes and swords and bows, and took up instead the slavers' wooden clubs.

Huy and Lannon hurried to the command position at the centre of the line, shrugging off their cloaks and flexing cold muscles.

Huy looked out across the sleeping town and the smell of it was wood smoke and cooking food and human excrement, a great sour smell of humanity that wrinkled his nostrils. The town was silent except for the lonely barking of a cur, and the petulant wail of a sleepless baby.

Huy said softly, 'The time is now.' And Lannon nodded. Huy turned and gave the order to one of his centurions and the man stooped over a clay fire pot and blew flame to life on the bunch of pitch-dipped rags that tipped the signal arrow. When the flame had caught and blossomed he notched the arrow and loosed it in a high arching parabola against the dark sky. From along the line the signal was repeated, orange flame soaring briefly in the darkness, but the silence was unbroken and the town slept on.

'They have set no guards, no picket, nothing,' Lannon remarked scornfully.

'They are barbarians,' Huy pointed out mildly.

'They deserve slavery,' Lannon said.

'They will fare better as slaves than free men,' Huy pointed out mildly. 'We will dress them and feed them and show them the true gods.'

Lannon nodded. 'We have come to lead them out of the darkness and into the sun.' And he shifted the heavy slaving club into his right hand.

From the east, appearing suddenly out of the edge of the forest, stampeded a mass of bellowing, maddened cattle. On their horns burned torches of pitch and grass, behind them they dragged flaming dry branches and they were driven by their own terror and by a line of yelling whooping warriors. The whole scene was hellish with dust and smoke and flame. The line of cattle crashed into the town, knocking down the flimsy grass huts, leaving fire to bloom and spread in their wake, trampling the sleep-drugged naked Vendi that stumbled into their path. Behind them ran the warriors, clubbing down the survivors and leaving them lying in the hoof-churned dust.

Huy heard a steady climbing wail from the town, the

sound of thousands of terrified voices. He heard the drumming of running hooves and saw the explosions of yellow flame and sparks mount into the night sky as the tinder-dry huts burned.

'Hold your line,' he called to the men in the darkness around him. 'Leave no gaps in the net for the fish to slip through.'

The night was filled with movement and sound and flame. The flames spread quickly, lighting the scene with a great flickering orange light, and the Vendi darted and milled and screamed as the grim line of marauders moved down upon them. The clubs rose and fell and the sound of the blows against bone was that of woodsmen working in a forest. They fell black and naked, and lay in the glaring firelight, or crawled and wriggled and wailed.

One woman with her infant clutched to her breast saw the relentless line bearing down on her, and she whirled like a doe startled from cover and ran into the tall bellowing flames of burning thatch. She burned like a torch, her hair exploding, and she screamed once and then fell scorched and unrecognizable into the flames. Huy saw it, and his blood madness cooled, congealing into revulsion and disgust.

'Hold!' he shouted. 'Lighten your blows!' And slowly out of this terrible confusion order emerged. The slave-masters were there ordering the captives into squatting lines, the infantry swept the town clear, and the flames burned themselves out, leaving only black mounds of smoking ash.

The dawn came up, a red and angry dawn – across which drifted banks of dark smoke. When Huy led the praise chant to Baal, the cries and wailing of the captives rose with the voice of the legion.

Huy hurried through the devastation ordering and organizing the retreat. Already two cohorts under the young Bakmor had started back towards the great river driving an uncounted herd of captured cattle before them. Huy guessed there might be as many as 20,000 head of the scrubby little beasts. Bakmor had Huy's orders to swim the cattle across the river and return immediately to cover the retreat.

Now his concern was to get the slow unwieldy columns of slaves moving. The approach march that his legion had made in half a day and night would surely take two or three days on the return. The newly captured slaves must be chained, and unaccustomed to their bonds they would move but slowly, retarding the march. Every hour's delay was dangerous, and would make the heavily encumbered legion more vulnerable to attack or reprisal.

One of his centurions accosted him, his tunic blackened with smoke and his beard singed. 'My lord!'

'What is it?'

'The slaves. There are few young men amongst them.'

Huy turned to examine one of the masses of squatting black humanity. They were festooned with the light marching chains, shackled at the neck like hunting dogs in leash.

'Yes.' He saw it now, they were mostly women and immature youths. The slave-masters had weeded out the old and infirm, but there were very few men of warrior age and status. Huy picked a bright-looking youngster from the squatting ranks and spoke to him in the vernacular.

'Where are the warriors?' The youth looked startled at being addressed in his own language, but he dropped his eyes sullenly and would not answer. The centurion half drew his sword, and at the scrape of steel in the scabbard the boy glanced up fearfully.

'A drop more blood will mean nothing,' Huy warned him, and the boy hesitated before replying.

'They have gone to the north to hunt the buffalo.'

'When will they return?' Huy demanded.

'I do not know,' the slave shrugged expressively, and Huy now had a more telling reason for haste. The fighting regiments of the Vendi were intact, and this towering beacon of smoke would draw them as meat draws the vultures.

'Get them up, and moving,' he ordered the centurion and hurried away. Lannon came out of the smoke followed by his armour-bearers and men-at-arms. One glance at his face was enough to warn Huy, for it was flushed and scowling.

'Did you order the slave-masters to spare those they reject?'

'Yes, sire.' Suddenly Huy was impatient with the king's rages and tantrums, there were more important matters to occupy him now.

'By what authority?' Lannon demanded.

'By the authority of a commander of a Royal Legion in the field,' Huy answered him.

'I commanded a burning.'

'But not a massacre of the aged and infirm.'

'I want the tribes to know that Lannon Hycanus passed this way.'

'I leave witnesses to it,' Huy told him shortly. 'If these old ones would burden us, will they not also be a burden upon their tribe?' Lannon drew himself up, Huy saw his rage boil over – and he took Lannon's arm in unexpectedly conspiratorial grip.

'Majesty, there is something of importance I must tell you.' And before Lannon could give vent to his rage Huy had led him aside. 'The regiments of Vendi have escaped us, they are in the field and out in battle array.'

Lannon's rage was forgotten. 'How close are they?'

'I do not know – except that the longer we talk the closer they come.'

It was past noon before the long files of shuffling slaves were all tallied and moving. The slave-masters reported in to Huy's command post, and the final count was almost 22,000 human beings.

Despite Huy's orders to keep the column bunched and under control, the files of chained Vendi stretched over four miles and their pace was that of the slowest. At a laboured crawl like a crippled centipede, they wound through the hills and down into the bad broken ground of the valley bottom.

The first attack hit them a little after midnight on the first night. It came as a shock to Huy, for although he had taken every precaution for a night camp in enemy territory, he had not expected anything like this from the tribes. A few sentries with slit throats, a flight of arrows from ambush, even a swift rush and withdrawal at some weak spot along the line, but not a full-scale night attack which showed every evidence of planning and control, and which was pressed home with murderous intent.

Only training and discipline held his legion together before that howling torrent that hurled itself upon them from the darkness. For two hours they closed up and fought, with the trumpets blowing the standfast and the rallying cries of the centurions ringing out in the darkness.

'On me, the Sixth.'

'Steady, the Sixth.'

'Hold hard, the Sixth.'

When the moon came out and lit the field, the attackers melted away into the forests and Huy could stride among his cohorts and assess his position.

The dead tribesmen were piled chest deep about the square where the cohorts had stood. In the torch light the skirmishers were finishing the enemy wounded with quick sword thrusts, while others were tending their own wounded and laying out their dead for cremation. Huy was relieved to see how small a toll the enemy had exacted from the defence, and how grievous a price they had paid themselves.

In the confusion of the battle many of the files of slaves had responded to the calls of the attackers and, with a concerted rush, had broken out of the square and escaped into the night still linked together. But there were still more than 16,000 of them howling with terror and hunger and thirst.

The legion lit its cremation fires in the dark and sang the praise chant to Baal on the march. Before the sun had been up an hour, it was clear what tactics the Vendi had decided upon for that day. Each feature along the route was contested by groups of archers and spearmen. They had to be laboriously dislodged, always falling back before the charges of Huy's axemen, but at the same time the flanks of the column and the rear were harried and tested by repeated attacks in considerable strength.

'I have never heard of this happening before,' protested Lannon during a lull while he unbuckled his helmet to air his sweat-sodden curls, and wash his mouth out with wine. 'They behave like drilled and trained troops.'

'It is something new,' Huy agreed as he accepted a cloth one of his armour-bearers had wetted for him. Huy's arms and face were speckled with droplets of thrown blood, and blood had dried black and crusty on the blade and shaft of the vulture axe.

'They have direction and purpose – I have never known tribesmen regroup after a charge has broken them. I have never known them come back after a mauling.'

Lannon spat red wine upon the ground. 'We may have better sport than we bargained for before the day is out,' he laughed with anticipation and passed the wine bowl to Huy.

There was a place where the track crossed a narrow stream and then passed between two symmetrical rounded maiden's breast hills. There was a ford at the stream and on the approaches to it sixteen spears had been set in the earth and spiked upon them were the severed heads of legionaries who had been with Bakmor's cohorts that had gone ahead with the cattle.

'Bakmor has not got through unscathed either,' Huy remarked, as he watched the heads taken down and hurriedly wrapped in leather cloaks.

'Sixteen from twelve hundred is hardly a disaster to rank with Lake Trasimene,' Lannon remarked easily. 'And with their grisly display they have warned us of their intention to hold the ford – weak tactics, Sunbird.'

'Perhaps, my lord,' Huy conceded, but he had noticed the faces of his men who had seen the ragged red throats and the dull staring eyes of the trophy heads. Their stomachs had cooled a little.

The ford was held as Lannon had predicted. It was held by a force that Huy guessed was not less than twice his own, and while they attempted to hack their way through the attacks upon the flanks and rear never let up. Twice Huy pulled his axemen and infantry out of the reddened mud of the ford to rest and re-form. By now the day was baking hot and the legionaries were tiring.

Lannon had received a spear-thrust in the face which had opened his cheek to the bone, a wound that looked uglier than it really was, and his beard was thick with blood and dust. A physician was stitching the wet lips of the wound closed when Huy joined the group around the king, and Lannon dismissed his anxious enquiry with a chuckle.

'It will leave an interesting scar.' Then without moving his head he told Huy, 'I have discovered the solution to the mystery, Huy, and there it is!' He pointed across the stream to the closest of the two hills. The crest was just out of random arrow range, perhaps 500 paces away. Although the slopes of the hill were forested the crest was a dome of rounded bare granite, and upon the dome stood a small group of men. They were gathered about a central figure.

Huy would always remember him as he was that fateful noon on the hilltop beside the ford. The distance did not dwarf him as it did the men about him. In some strange fashion it made his physical presence more imposing. He was a huge man, fully a head and shoulder taller than his companions. The sun shone on the oiled black muscles of his chest and arms, and a tall head-dress of blue heron feathers stood wind-tossed and proud upon his head. He wore a short kilt of leopard tails around his waist, but Huy did not need that to know he was a king.

'Ah!' he said softly, and he felt something stir in him, a cold sliding thing like an uncoiling snake. On the hilltop the Vendi king made a sweeping gesture, and then stabbed towards the ford with his heavy war spear. It was clearly the delivery of a command, and from the group around him a messenger broke away and raced down the slope of the hill carrying the order.

'At last the tribes have found a leader,' said Huy. 'I should have guessed it earlier.'

'Take him for me,' Lannon commanded. 'I want him. Nothing else is important. Take that man for me.' And Huy heard a new tone in Lannon's voice. It puzzled him and he glanced at his king. He saw it then. It was not the pain of his crudely stitched cheek that made dark shadows play in the pale blue eyes. For the first time in all the years Huy knew that Lannon was afraid.

Huy timed it carefully for the last hour before dark, for the last of the day when the shadows were long and the light uncertain. During the afternoon he skirmished at the ford in half-cohort strength, but in the thick forest on the banks of the stream he held his main strength in reserve. He let them rest during the heat of the afternoon, let them eat and drink and sharpen their blades while he made his preparations. He chose fifty of his finest, selecting them by name from the ranks, and he took them well back where they would be screened from prying eyes on the heights beyond the stream.

From the bottoms of the cooking-pots they scraped the thick black soot and mixed it into a thick paste with cooking oil. There was not enough to darken the skins of fifty men so for their arms and legs they used the black mud from the river. They were all of them stripped stark naked when the slave chains were shackled about their throats, but instead of the iron pins a thin dry twig was used to close the links on every collar. They could not take shields with them, and they smeared their weapons with a thick coating of black mud to hide the twinkle and flash of naked metal, then they strapped them to their backs so they could run empty-handed.

'You are slaves, not legionaries,' Huy told them. 'Run like a slave, scamper like a beaten dog.'

When they broke from the trees and ran for the river with half a century of legionaries in pursuit, they howled with terror and the carefully aimed arrows patterned around them. They reached the bank 500 paces upstream from the ford. As they blundered across, still linked together by the slave chain, the Vendi king from his vantage point saw their escape and sent two large parties of archers and spearmen to screen their crossing.

A fierce bloody little battle flared up on the river bank, and under cover of the tumult Huy got his group over the river and into the shelter of the forest on the far bank. There was a thin detachment of tribesmen in set positions amongst the trees, but by the time they realized the deception Huy's band had dropped their chains and cut into them in a silent murderous rush.

Then they were through with nothing opposing them to the foot of the command hill. Bunched up, and hidden by the forest, Huy led them at a run around the back of the hill. They had moved fast, and he rested them here for a few minutes. The mud had washed from legs and arms during the crossing of the river and the soot and oil was streaky with sweat giving them a wild and desperate appearance.

The clamour of the fighting at the river had died away and the forest was silent and still as Huy led his band up the back slope of the hill. There were sentries posted here, but they were inattentive and did not see the weird blackened figures amongst the forest shades until it was too late.

Below the bare dome of granite Huy waited again, listening for the diversion which Lannon had promised. The distant yells and tiny scraping sounds of metal from the ford were almost blanketed by the distance and the intervening bulk of the hill.

Huy said softly, 'Now. All together.' And they burst from the forest edge and went racing away up the granite dome. Huy led them easily, bounding ahead with the loping long-armed gait of an old bull baboon.

When he was twenty paces from the crest, the Vendi king sensed his presence and turned to face Huy. He shouted a warning to his staff, and Huy went at him like a terrier at the throat of a lion. Two of the king's bodyguard leapt to intervene, but Huy flicked a casual axe stroke at them, rolling his wrist slightly in midstroke so the blade whimpered as it changed direction, killing the one guard cleanly and taking the spear arm of the other away above the elbow with a single cut. They fell aside and Huy went on to take the king.

He was a big man, perhaps the biggest Huy had ever met, and his skin was a shiny purplish black. The muscles of shoulders and arms were bunched and knotted. The sinews of his neck stood out starkly, corded into the heavy bone of his jaw. His head was round as a river-washed boulder, and without head-dress the scalp was bald and polished black.

He moved to meet Huy, sliding in on thick black legs with his leopard-skin kilts swirling, crouching slightly with the stabbing spear held underhand, the blade glistening hungrily for the softness of Huy's belly. He moved with leopard speed, reacting instantly to Huy's attack, and there was a sense of savage power and energy about him that checked Huy's charge and made him whirl instinctively to the side, just as the blade of the stabbing spear slashed upwards through nothingness where Huy's belly should have been.

The huge black man grunted as his stroke died in air, and his tawny yellow eyes fastened on Huy. He struck again and Huy hopped aside as the point hissed past him, and Huy reached out as he sprang and ran the stabbing point of the axe across the giant's exposed ribs. The purple black skin opened and for an instant white bone showed in the depths of the wound before the rush of dark blood obscured it. The king bellowed at the sting of it, and he struck and slashed and cut at the dancing gadfly before him. Each stroke wilder, each charge more reckless as Huy goaded him, watching for his moment. It came and suddenly Huy was through the circle of the spear. With the point of the axe he probed for the femoral artery in the giant's groin, running the engraved steel into the tight flesh half an inch too far to the right, missing the artery but dropping the king to one knee. Huy twisted out of close contact. The axe flew high and Huy went into the kill stroke aiming at the round black skull of the kneeling king, a stroke which would split him to the chest.

'For Baal!' he shouted, sending the axe down from on high. Then in full stroke he changed. He never knew what impulse it was that made him check, made him twist the weapon, presenting the flat of the blade and not the edge, holding the stroke half back so that the side of the axe cracked against the king's skull with enough force to topple him forward senseless onto his face but not enough to stove in the bone of the great round head.

Huy jumped back and with one quick glance made certain that the Vendi king's train were all lying lifeless on the dome of granite, and his legionaries were grouped around him resting on their bloody swords. The surprise had been complete and overwhelming.

Huy turned and ran to the highest point of the hill. Naked and filthy with soot and mud he brandished his axe above his head, and his band cheered and waved their weapons also. From the ford a trumpet began to blare the advance, and immediately the call was taken up and shrilled from cohort to cohort.

Huy watched Lannon lead the first wave across the ford. The legion crashed into the leaderless tribesmen who opposed them, and drove through them with scarcely a check, splitting them and driving them back against the hills in a disorganized rabble. They had seen their king cut down and there was no spirit left in any of them.

From the hilltop Huy watched Lannon commit his last two reserve cohorts at exactly the right moment. The tribesmen broke and made a rout of it. Throwing aside their weapons they streamed back in a wailing panic-stricken mob into the bottleneck between the hills.

At that moment the handsome young Bakmor, with the two cohorts which had driven the captured cattle to the great river, marched out of the forest. He deployed the cohorts neatly across the only line of retreat open to the tribes. His return was timely indeed, and Huy watched him with grudging professional approval as he made his dispositions. As the sun touched the horizon in a splendour of red and purple the trumpets sounded the advance once again, and the slaughter and the slave-taking lasted until after midnight.

Huy crossed his legion and the host of wild slaves, using the elephant-drawn rafts at Sett. After the battle at the ford the return march had been unopposed. The regiments of the Vendi had been shattered, all their war chiefs killed or captured and Lannon was jubilant.

He told Huy, 'My Sunbird! It was more than I asked of you. Even I did not guess that such a dangerous enemy had grown up upon my borders. If we had left him another year, only the gods know how deadly he might have become.'

'Baal smiled upon me,' Huy disclaimed modestly.

'And so does Lannon Hycanus,' Lannon assured him. 'What was the harvest, Sunbird? Has old Rib-Addi made the accounting yet?'

'I hope so, my lord.'

'Send for him,' Lannon commanded, and Rib-Addi came with his scrolls and his ink-stained fingers and his untrusting little book-keeper's eyes. He read out the lists of cattle and slaves of each grade, every one of them carefully categorized by the slave-masters.

'The prices will be much depressed, sire,' Rib-Addi pointed out pessimistically. 'For the other legions have taken a great tribute from all the tribes across the river. It will be two or three years before the markets of Opet have absorbed this mass of wealth.'

'Nevertheless, the prize money taken by the Sixth Ben-Amon must be considerable, Rib-Addi.'

'As my lord says.'

'How much?' Lannon demanded.

Rib-Addi looked alarmed. 'I could only hazard a guess, Majesty.'

'Guess, then,' Lannon invited him.

'It could be as much as 25,000 fingers – and as low as—'

'You would smell dung in an alabaster jar of perfume,' Lannon chided the old man. 'Do not give me your low figure.'

'As my lord pleases.' Rib-Addi bowed, and Lannon turned to Huy and clasped his shoulder.

'Your share is one part in a hundred, Sunbird. Two hundred and fifty fingers – you are a rich man at last! How does it feel?'

'It does not sicken me,' Huy grinned at him, and Lannon laughed delightedly as he turned back to Rib-Addi.

'Write in your book, old man. Write that Lannon Hycanus sets aside half of his share of the prize. He makes it over as an award to the legion commander, Huy Ben-Amon, for his conduct of the campaign.'

'My lord, that is one part in twenty,' Rib-Addi protested vehemently. 'It is an award of over 1,000 fingers!'

'I have learned my figures also,' Lannon assured him, and the book-keeper might have protested further, but he saw Lannon's expression.

'It shall be written,' he mumbled, and Huy came to kneel before his king in gratitude.

'Up!' Lannon ordered him, smiling. 'Do not grovel for me, old friend.' And Huy went to stand beside Lannon's stool, as the king called each of the officers who had acted with distinction and made the awards.

Huy was lost in a trance of avarice, hardly able to credit his fortune. He was rich – rich! He must sacrifice to the gods this very day. A white bull, at the least. As Rib-Addi had pointed out, the market was flooded and Huy would be able to get one cheaply. Then he remembered that he no longer had to stint.

He could afford any luxury he had ever coveted, and still have enough over for an estate on the terraces of Zeng, a share in one of Habbakuk-Lal's trading galleys. A seat on one of the gold-mining syndicates, a secure income for life. No more patches in his tunics, no more bullying his household to cut down on the consumption of meat, no more of the cheap sour wines from the harbour taverns. And then his mind jumped, no more reliance on Lannon's hospitality and on the goodwill of his young slave girls. He would have one of his own – no damn it, two – three! Young and pretty and pliant. He felt his body stir. He could afford a wife now, even the daughters of the noble houses might turn a blind eye to his back when dazzled by such a pile of the golden metal.

Then suddenly he remembered Tanith, and the phantom slave girls and wives faded back into the mists of his imagining. His spirits plunged sickeningly. The priestesses of Astarte were dedicated to the goddess, they could never marry. Suddenly Huy did not feel as rich as he had a moment before.

'Do you not hear your king when he speaks?' Lannon demanded, and Huy started guiltily.

'My lord, I was dreaming. Forgive me.'

'It is no longer necessary to dream,' Lannon told him.

'What was it the Gry-Lion asked?'

'I said we should send for the barbarian – we can deal with him before the legion assembles.'

Huy looked around at his cohorts drawn up in an open square before the leather awning under which Lannon sat. The legions' standards glittered in the sunlight, and the officers stood at ease before their men. They waited expectantly, and Huy sighed quietly.

'As the Gry-Lion wishes.'

'Order it so,' Lannon commanded.

They had chained him at wrists and ankles, as well as at the throat. The slave-masters could pick a dangerous one at a glance, and two of them held him in leash by the chains from his throat collar.

He was as big as Huy remembered, and his skin even darker, but he was a young man. This came as a shock to Huy, he had thought of him as being in his prime years but this was an illusion. The man's physical bulk and his commanding presence made him older than his years.

Huy saw how he had fought against his bonds, tearing

his own flesh, smearing the skin on the unyielding iron shackles, and the wound in his groin had been crudely dressed with leaves and bark. There were the first watery yellow discharges of putrefaction soiling the dressing, and the flesh around it looked hard and swollen. Although he limped, although the chains jangled mockingly at every pace, and although the slave-masters braced against him as though he were a captured animal, there was no mistaking that he was a king. He stood before Lannon and lowered his head slightly on the thick sinewed neck. His eyes were ferocious, even the whites were smoking yellow and covered with a fine lacework of blood vessels, and he stared at his captors with a hatred that was a palpable thing.

'You captured this – this great black beast, Huy?' Lannon returned the giant's stare. 'Without help, you took him?' Lannon shook his head with wonder and turned to Huy, but Huy was watching the Vendi king.

'What is your name?' Huy asked softly, and the big round head swivelled towards him, the fierce eyes held his.

'How do you have the tongue of Vendi?'

'I have many tongues,' Huy assured him. 'Who are you?'

'Manatassi, King of the Vendi.' And Huy translated for Lannon.

'Tell him he is king no longer,' Lannon snapped, and Manatassi shrugged and smiled. His smile was a frightening thing for although the thick purple lips drew back to expose strong white teeth, yet his eyes still smoked with hatred.

'Fifty thousand warriors of Vendi call me king still,' he answered.

'A slave king of a slave people,' Lannon laughed, and then to Huy, 'What of him, Huy? Is he not a dangerous enemy? Can we afford to let him live?'

Huy tore his gaze from the slave king and considered the question, trying to think logically but finding it difficult. Huy had conceived a sudden but powerful proprietary interest in Manatassi. He was impressed with the man's power and presence, with the military skills he had displayed, with the cunning and cleverness and the strange smouldering depths of him. Huy had taken him, he could claim him, even from Lannon, and he was strongly tempted to do so now, for he sensed that here was some extraordinary opportunity. To take this man and educate him, civilize him – what might be made of him! He felt an excitement as a new idea tried to struggle to the surface of his mind.

'I think not,' Lannon answered himself. 'From the first moment I saw him, on the hill above the ford, I knew he was dangerous. Deadly dangerous. I do not think we can let him live, Huy. He would make a fine messenger to the gods. We will dedicate him to Baal and send him as a messenger to express our gratitude for the outcome of the campaign.'

'My lord,' Huy dropped his voice for Lannon alone, 'I have a feeling about this man. I feel I could enlighten him, teach him the true gods. He is young, my lord, I could work upon him, and when we are ready we could return him to his people.'

'Have the birds picked out your brain?' Lannon looked at Huy in astonishment. 'Why should we return him to his people, when we have spent so much effort on capturing him?'

'We could use him as an ally then.' Huy was trying desperately to get his idea over. 'Through him we could make a treaty with the tribes. We could win him over and use him to secure our northern borders.'

'Treaties with barbarians!' Lannon was angry now. 'What nonsense is this? Secure our northern borders, you say? One thing, and one thing only will secure our northern borders, and that is a sharp sword in a strong hand.'

'My lord, please hear me out.'

'No, Huy. I will have no more of it. He must die – and

quickly.' Lannon stood up. 'Tonight at sunset. Prepare to send him.' And Lannon strode away.

'Dismiss the legion,' Huy ordered his commanders, and nodded to the slave-master to lead the captive away. But Manatassi stepped forward, dragging the slave-masters with him on the chains.

'High born!' Manatassi called Huy, who turned back to him with surprise. He had not expected a title of respect.

'What is it?' Huy looked at him.

'Is it death?' Manatassi asked, and Huy nodded.

'It is death,' he admitted.

'But you argued for me?' Manatassi insisted, and again Huy nodded.

'Why?' demanded the slave king, and Huy could not answer. He spread his hands, a gesture of weariness and incomprehension.

'Twice already,' the slave king said. 'First you turned the blade which should have killed, and now you speak for me. Why?'

'I do not know. I cannot explain.'

'You feel the bond – the bond between us,' Manatassi declared, and his voice sank low, rumbling and soft. 'The bond of the spirits. You felt it.'

'No.' Huy shook his head, and hurried away to his tent. He worked on his scrolls for most of the afternoon, recording the campaign, describing the burning and the battle at the ford, listing the battle honours and the slaves taken, the booty and the glory – but he could not bring himself to describe Manatassi. The man would soon be dead, let his memory die with him, let it not linger on to haunt the living. A phrase that Lannon had used stuck in his mind, 'the black beast', and he used it as the only reference to the doomed slave king.

He ate the noon meal with Bakmor and a few others of his young officers, but his mood infected them all and the meal was awkward, the conversation trivial and stilted. Afterwards Huy spent an hour with his adjutant and quartermaster ordering the legion's affairs, then he worked with the axe until his sweat ran down his body in streams. He scraped and oiled and changed into fresh robes for the sacrifice, and went to Lannon's tent. Lannon was in conference, a group of his advisers and officials sitting in a half-circle around him on the skins and cushions. Lannon looked up and smiled and called Huy to him.

'Sit by me, my Sunbird. There is something here on which I would value your thoughts.' And Huy sat and listened to Lannon directing the affairs of the four kingdoms with a quick and confident logic. He made decisions which would have tormented Huy for days, and he made them easily, without doubts or hesitations. Then he dismissed his court, and turned to Huy.

'A bowl of wine with me, Huy. It will be many days before we have the chance again, for in the morning I leave you.'

'Whither, my lord?'

'I return to Opet, but at speed. I will leave you and your slaves and herds to make the best of it.'

They drank together, exchanging the seemingly easy desultory talk of old friends, but Huy was manoeuvring for an opening to speak of Manatassi, and Lannon was deftly denying it to him. At last Huy in desperation approached the subject directly.

'The Vendi king, my lord.' And he got no further, for Lannon slammed the wine bowl down so that it cracked and a ruby gush of the lees spurted onto the furs on which they sat.

'You presume on friendship. I have ordered his death. Except for the axe-stroke the matter is settled.'

'I believe it is a mistake.'

'To let him live will be a greater mistake.'

'My lord—'

'Enough, Huy! Enough, I say! Go out now and send him.'

In the sunset they brought the Vendi king to a clear place on the river bank below the garrison walls of Sett. He was dressed in a cloak of leather, worked with the symbols of Baal, and he wore the symbolical chains of the sacrifice. Huy stood with the priests and nobles, and when they led the doomed king forward his eyes fastened on Huy's. Those terrible yellow eyes seemed almost to hook into his flesh, seemed to draw Huy's soul out through his eye sockets.

Huy began the ritual, chanting the offertory, making the obeisance to the flaming god image in the western sky and all the while he could feel those eyes eating into the core of his existence.

Huy's assistant offered him the vulture axe, polished and glinting red and gold in the last rays of the sunset. Huy went to where Manatassi stood, and looked up at him.

The slave-masters stepped forward and lifted the cloak from the shoulders of the sacrifice. Except for the golden chains he was naked and magnificent. They had removed the raw-hide sandals from his feet. The slave-masters waited with the chains in their hands, at Huy's signal they would jerk the sacrifice off his feet and stretch him out upon the ground. His neck drawn out for the axe blade.

Huy hesitated, unable to force himself to give the order, held fascinated by those fierce yellow eyes. With an effort he tore his gaze free and looked downwards. He had started to give the signal, but his hand froze. He was staring at Manatassi's bare feet.

Around him the watchers stirred restlessly, glancing towards the horizon where the sun was rapidly sliding below the trees. Soon it would be too late.

Still Huy stared at Manatassi's feet.

'The sun goes, priest. Strike!' Lannon called abruptly, angrily in the silence and the sound of his voice seemed to arouse Huy. He turned to Lannon.

'My lord, there is something you must see.'

'The sun is going,' Lannon called impatiently.

'You must see it,' Huy insisted, and Lannon strode forward to stand beside him.

'Look!' Huy pointed at the Vendi king's feet, and Lannon frowned on a quick intake of breath.

Manatassi's feet were monstrously deformed, deeply divided between the toes so that they resembled the claws of some preternatural bird. Involuntarily Lannon stepped backwards, making the full-handed sun sign to avert evil.

'He is bird-footed,' Huy said, 'he has the feet of the sacred sunbird of Baal.' And there was a rustle and murmur from the watchers. They craned forward with a ghoulish, superstitious curiosity.

Huy raised his voice. 'I declare this man god-marked. He is favoured by the gods – and cannot be sent as a messenger.'

As he spoke the sun dropped below the rim of the world and there was a chill and a dankness in the air.

Lannon was in a towering, shaking rage that paled his lips and face so that the black clotted scab of his wound stood out clearly on his cheek.

'You defied me!' He said it softly, but in a voice that trembled with his rage.

'He is god-marked!' Huy protested.

'Do not try to hide behind your gods, Priest. You and I both know that many of Baal's decisions are made by Huy Ben-Amon, for Huy Ben-Amon.'

'Majesty,' Huy gasped at the accusation, at the dreadful blasphemy of it.

'You defied me,' Lannon repeated. 'You think to place this barbarian beyond my reach, you aspire to play the game of power and politics with me.'

'It is not true, my lord. I would not dare.'

'You *would* dare, Priest. You would dare to steal the teeth from the mouth of the living Gry-Lion, if the fancy came upon you.'

'My lord, I am your true, your most loyal—'

'Tread lightly, Priest. I warn you. You fly high in the four kingdoms, but remember always that you do so by my favour alone.'

'I know this well.'

'I who exalted you, have it in my power to throw you down as readily.'

'I know this also, my lord,' said Huy humbly.

'Then give me this barbarian,' Lannon demanded, and Huy looked up at him with an expression of deep regret.

'He is not mine to give, my lord. He belongs to the gods.'

Lannon let out a bellow of frustrated rage, and snatched up a heavy amphora of wine. He hurled it at Huy's head, and Huy ducked nimbly. The amphora slapped into the leather side of the tent, cushioning the impact and it dropped to the ground without breaking, wine gurgled from the mouth and soaked into the dry earth.

Lannon was on his feet now, towering over Huy, holding out towards him fists bunched into bony clubs, the muscles in his forearms knotted and ridged with exasperation. He held those fists under Huy's nose, and his eyes were pale glittering blue and deadly, the thick red-golden ringlets danced on his shoulders as he shook with the tempests of his rage.

'Go!' he said in a strangled voice. 'Go quickly – before – before I—'

Huy did not wait to hear the rest of it.

Lannon Hycanus marched from Sett with a body-guard of 200 men, and Huy watched him go from the walls of the garrison. He felt a chill of apprehension, vulnerable now and lonely without the king's favour.

Huy watched the small travelling party march out between the ranks of the legion, and saw that Lannon wore only a light tunic and that he was bare-headed in the early morning sunlight, his hair shining like a beacon fire. His armour-bearers followed him with helmet and breastplate, bow and sword and javelins. At Lannon's heels followed the little pygmy huntmaster, Xhai the bushman; he was attentive as a shadow to the king.

The legion cheered Lannon away, their voices ringing from the escarpment of the valley, and Lannon moved through the gates. He stood taller than those that surrounded him, smiling and proud and beautiful.

He looked up and saw Huy on the wall, and the smile changed to a quick fierce scowl; ignoring Huy's hesitant salute he marched out through the gates and took the road that ran southwards into the pass, and over the hills to the middle kingdom.

Huy watched until the forest hid him from sight, and then he turned away, feeling very alone. He went down to where the slave king lay dying on a bed of dry straw in a corner of Huy's own tent.

In the rising heat of the morning the smell of the wound was the rank, fetid odour of fever swamps and things long dead.

One of the old slave women was bathing his body, trying to lower the fever. She looked up as Huy entered and answered his query with a shake of her head. Huy squatted beside the pallet, and touched the slave king's skin. It was burning hot and dry, and Manatassi moaned in delirium.

'Send for a slave-master,' Huy ordered irritably. 'Have him strike away these chains.'

It was amazing to watch the fever eat away the flesh from that huge black frame, to see the bone appear beneath the skin, to watch the face collapse, and the skin change colour from shiny purple black to dry dusty grey.

The wound in his groin swelled up hot and hard, with a crusty evil-smelling scab from which a watery greenish-yellow fluid wept slowly. Each hour the slave king's hold on life seemed to slacken, his body grew hotter, the wound swelled to the size of a man's bunched fist.

In the noon of the second day Huy left the camp alone and climbed to a high place upon the escarpment where he could be alone with his god. Here in the valley of the great river the sun-god's presence seemed all-pervading and his usually warm benevolent countenance was oppressive. It seemed to fill the entire sky, and to beat down upon the earth like the hammer of a smith upon the anvil.

Huy sang the prayer of approach, but he did so in a perfunctory fashion, gabbling out the last lines, for Huy was very angry with his gods, and he wanted them to be aware of his displeasure.

'Great Baal,' he omitted the more flowery titles, and came swiftly to the main body of his protest, 'following your evident wishes, I have saved this one who bears your marks. Although I do not wish to complain, nor to question your motives, yet you should know that this has been no easy task. I have made serious sacrifices. I have weakened the position of the High Priest of Baal in the king's favour – I think not of myself, naturally, but only of my influence as your agent and servant. What weakens me, weakens the worship of the gods.' Huy said this with relish, that must surely catch their attention, and Huy was delighted with it. He felt it was entirely justified, it was high time that certain things were said and that the reciprocal duties of loyalty were stated.

'You know of old that no command of yours is too difficult of execution, no burden you place upon me but I shoulder it cheerfully, for always I have been secure in the certainty of your wisdom and purpose.'

Huy paused for breath, and thought. He was angry, but he must not let anger run away with his tongue. He had offended the king, best not offend the gods also. Quickly he moderated his closing address.

'However, in the matter of this marked barbarian I have no such certainty. I have saved him at great cost – to what purpose? Is it your intention that he must now die?' Huy paused again, letting his point sink in.

'I ask you now, most humbly,' Huy spread a drop of honey, 'most humbly, to make your intentions plain to your always attentive and obedient servant.'

Huy paused once more, should he dare the use of stronger terms? He decided against it, and instead spread both hands in the sun sign and sang the praise of Baal, with all the skill and beauty at his command. The sound of his voice shimmering and aching sweet in the breathless heat-rush of the wilderness was enough to make the gods weep, and when the last pure note had died upon the heated air Huy went down to the camp and with a bronze razor he lanced the grotesque swelling in the slave king's loin. Manatassi screamed with pain even in his delirium, and the poison gushed out thick and yellow and stinking. Huy poulticed the open wound with boiled corn wrapped in a linen cloth, scalding hot to drain the poisons.

By evening the fever had passed, and Manatassi lay in exhausted, but natural sleep. Huy stood over him smiling and nodding happily. He felt that he had won this wasted giant, wrested him from death's dark jaws with prayer and endeavour. He experienced a proud warmth of ownership and when the old slave crone brought him a brimming bowl of good Zeng wine, Huy lifted it in a salute to the sleeping giant.

'The gods have given you to me. You are mine. You live

414

under my protection now, and I pledge it to you.' And he drained the bowl.

T he weakness of his body smothered him, pressing him down on the hard mattress of straw. It was an effort to lift head or hand, and he hated his body that had failed him now. He rolled his head slowly and opened his eyes.

Across the tent, on a mat of woven reeds sat the strange little man. Manatassi watched him with a quick flaring of interest. He was stooped over a roll of the strange glowing metal that had been beaten out into a thin pliable length, and with a pointed knife he was scratching and cutting marks into the soft surface. He spent many hours of each day at this unusual activity. Manatassi watched him, noticing the quick nervous birdlike movements of head and hands that set the golden ear-rings jangling and the thick black plaits of hair dangling down his back.

The head seemed too large for the oddly hunched body, and the legs and arms were long and thick and brutal-looking, dark hair grew on the forearms and the back of the long tapered hands – and Manatassi remembered the speed and strength of that body in battle. He lifted his head slightly and glanced down at the linen bandages which swathed his lower body.

At the movement Huy was on his feet in one swift movement, and he came to the pallet and stooped over him, smiling.

Huy said, 'You sleep like a breast-fed baby.' And Manatassi looked up at him, wondering that a man could speak such a deadly insult to the paramount king of Vendi – and smile as he said it.

'Aia, bring food,' Huy shouted for the old slave woman,

and settled down on a cushion beside Manatassi's couch. While Manatassi ate with huge appetite he listened with only a small part of his attention to a ridiculous description of the moon as a white-faced woman. He wondered that such a skilled warrior could be so naïve. It was only necessary to look at the moon to see that it was a cake of ground corn, and as the Mitasi-Mitasi the one great god devoured it, so the shape of his bite could clearly be seen cut from the round cake.

'Do you understand this?' Huy asked with deep concern, and Manatassi answered readily:

'I understand, high-born.'

'You believe it?' Huy insisted.

'I believe it.' Manatassi gave the answer which he knew would please, and Huy nodded happily. His efforts to teach the slave king were most rewarding. He had explained the theory of symbolic representation very carefully, showing Manatassi that the moon was not Astarte but her symbol, her coin, her sign and promise. He had explained the waning and waxing as the symbolic subjugation of the female to the male, repeated in the human female by the periodic moon-sickness.

'Now, the great god Baal,' Huy said, and Manatassi sighed inwardly. He knew what was coming. This strange person would now talk about the hole in the sky through which Mitasi-Mitasi made his entrances and exits. He would try to make Manatassi believe that this was a man with a flowing red beard. What a contradictory people they were, these pale ghost-like beings. On the one hand they had weapons and clothes and wonderful possessions and almost magical skills in civil and military matters. He had seen them fight and work, and it had amazed him. Yet these same people could not recognize truths that even the unweaned infants of his tribe understood completely.

Manatassi's first conscious thoughts when he had emerged from the hot mists of fever had been of escape.

But now, forced by his weakness into the role of observer, he had time to reconstruct his plans. He was safe here, this hunchbacked manikin wielded some strange power, and he was under its protection. He knew this now. No one would touch him as long as his new master held his shield over him.

The other thing he knew was that there was much to learn here. If he could acquire the skills and knowledge of this people, he would be armed a thousand times. He would be the greatest war chief the tribes had ever known. They had used these skills to defeat him, he would defeat them with the same skills that he learned from them.

'Do you understand?' Huy asked earnestly. 'Do you understand that Baal is the master of the whole of heaven and earth?'

'I understand,' said Manatassi.

'Do you accept Astarte and great Baal as gods?'

'I accept them,' Manatassi agreed, and Huy looked very pleased.

'They have placed their mark upon you. It is right that you should be dedicated to their service. When we reach the city I will perform the ceremony in the temple of great Baal. I have chosen a god-name for you – you will no longer use the old style.'

'As you wish, high-born.'

'From henceforth you will be called Timon.'

'Timon,' the slave king tested the sound of it.

'He was the priest-warrior in the reign of the fifth Gry-Lion. A great man.'

Timon nodded, not understanding but content to watch and wait and learn.

'High-born,' he asked softly, 'the marks you scratch upon the yellow metal – what are they?'

Huy jumped up and fetched the golden scroll to the couch.

'This is how we store words and stories and ideas.' He

plunged into an explanation of the writing process, and was rewarded by Timon's quick grasp of the principle of the phonetic alphabet.

On a scrap of leather he wrote Timon's name in sooty black ink, and in unison they spelled it out aloud, Timon laughing delightedly at his first achievement.

'Yes,' he thought, 'there is much to learn here – and so little time.'

A cross the clay box Caius Terentius Varro, Consul of Rome, fought once more, pressing his legions into Hannibal's soft centre. The centre gave, with the sucky reluctance of dough, the Spaniards and Gauls there withdrew at Hannibal's design.

'Do you see it, Timon? The beauty of it, the sheer genius of it!' Huy called excitedly, speaking in Punic now, manipulating the counters.

'And where was Marhabal now?' Timon demanded as excitedly in the same language. After two years his Punic was fluent, with only the dragging vowels marring its perfection.

'He was here,' Huy touched the cavalry counters, 'holding his horse on a short rein.' Timon understood a horse to be a swift animal like a zebra on whose back armed men rode.

'Varro is entangled now?' Timon asked.

'Yes! Yes! Hannibal has crumpled his front and enveloped him – then what does he do, Timon?'

'The reserves?' Timon guessed.

'Yes! You have it! The Numidians and African reserves.' Huy was hopping up and down in his agitation. 'With the timing of the great master, he unleashes them. Taking Varro in the flanks, squeezing him in a vice, packing his ranks so they cannot manoeuvre nor wield their weapons. Then what, Timon, what then?'

'The cavalry?'

'Ah! The cavalry – Marhabal! The faithful brother. The master of horse, who has waited all that long day. Go! cries Hannibal.' Huy threw his arm in a wide gesture. 'Go! My brother, ride with your wild Iberians! They crash into them, Timon. It is the moment, the exact moment. Five minutes earlier is too soon – five minutes later and it is too late. Timing! Timing! The talent of the great military commander, timing! Of the statesman, the lover, the businessman, the merchant. The right action, at the right time.'

'And the result, high-born, what was the result?' Timon pleaded, in an agony of suspense. 'Was it victory?'

'Victory?' Huy asked. 'Yes, Timon. It was victory. Victory and massacre. Eight legions of vaunting Rome wiped out to the man, two entire consular armies.'

'Eight legions, high-born.' Timon marvelled. 'Forty-eight thousand men in a single battle?'

'More than that, Timon. The auxiliaries were lost also. Sixty thousand men!' Huy swept his hand across the board, exterminating the Roman legions. 'We won the battles, Timon, but they won the wars. Three of them. Three bloody wars, that crushed us—' Huy broke off, his voice choking. He turned away quickly and went to the water jug. Timon hurried across and held the basin for him while Huy washed his hands and combed his beard. 'That brings us to the end of our study of Hannibal's campaigns, Timon. I kept the battle of Cannae for the last.'

'Who will we study next, high-born?'

'The one who Hannibal himself rated the most skilful General of all history.'

'Who was that?'

'Alexander III,' Huy said, 'King of Macedonia, who

smashed the Persian Empire – whom the oracle at Delphi proclaimed invincible, and men called the Great.'

Timon held Huy's cloak for him, and Huy fastened the clasp as he left the precincts of the temple college through the small gate in the inner wall. Timon followed a pace behind him, wearing the short blue tunic of Huy's household with a light gold chain, dagger and purse belting his waist, the mark of high trust as a body slave. He walked a pace behind Huy's left shoulder, so as not to mask his master's sword arm, and he kept his hand on the dagger.

'High-born, the manner in which Hannibal invested Varro?'

'Yes?' Huy encouraged him.

'Could he not have advanced his flanks, and held his centre firm?'

'It is the difference between defence and offence,' Huy explained, and they plunged into discussion of battle tactics and strategy until they left the main gate in the outer wall of the temple area. From here any conversation was impossible, for the crowds spotted this strange couple. Giant black slave and diminutive gnome-like master. They cheered Huy, crowding around him to touch his arm in greeting, to listen to his banter and perhaps receive an alms coin from the purse on Timon's belt.

Huy loved his popularity. He smiled and joked and pushed his way gently through the press. A successful General – there had been two other campaigns since the great slave-taking – a well-beloved priest, a noted wit and song-writer, and a rich philanthropist (Huy's investments had prospered exceedingly in the last two years), he was the object of popular adulation throughout the city.

They crossed the market-place with its fascinating smells and sights and sounds of hides and humanity, of spices and open sewers. On one of the slave blocks was a light-skinned girl of mixed Yuye blood, and the auctioneer spotted Huy in the crowd and called out to him.

'My lord, a work of art for you. A statue in yellow ivory,' opening the girl's cloak to display her body.

Huy laughed and waved a hand in refusal. They moved along the stone jetty at the lakeside where the ships lay with stern almost touching stern, their hatches open and a boiling of stevedores running over them, loading and unloading the merchandise. From the taverns and wine-shops flanking the jetty came the sour stench of cheap wine and gusts of drunken laughter. The street girls beckoned from the narrow lanes between the shops. The uncertain light of dusk softened their raddled features and hectic painted cheeks and lips – Huy wondered what solace a man would find with the likes of them.

Beyond the bustle of the harbour area lay the town houses of the noble families and rich merchants, each protected by the high mud outer wall and a heavy carved wooden gate. Huy's new residence was one of the least pretentious of these, with the entrance off a narrow walled lane, and a view from the flat roof over the lake.

Once through the gate Huy shed his sword and cloak and handed them to Timon with a sigh of pleasure at the moment of homecoming, and he went through into the paved central courtyard.

The princes and princesses were waiting for him, four-teen of them, headed by the twins, Helanca and Imilce. The two of them had grown in the past years, and they were stranded now in that awkward period between girl-hood and womanhood. Too young to giggle, yet too old to greet Huy with a kiss.

There were no such inhibitions upon the younger members of house Barca, and they swarmed forward to engulf Huy. The religious instruction of the children of the royal house was a duty Huy had imposed upon him-self, and despite the estrangement between king and priest, Lannon had not interfered with this arrangement. He had not sanctioned it, but he had not forbidden it. Huy led his students through into the airy living-room of the house.

In the courtyard one of the royal nursemaids waited until her charges had followed the priest before she turned and her eyes sought those of Timon. She was a tall girl with strong shoulders, long-waisted and with fruitful hips. Her legs also were straight and strong, but her hands were narrow and pink-palmed and delicately shaped. She wore her hair oiled and dressed in the manner of the Vendi, for she was of Timon's tribe. Taken in the great raid, she was not slave born, not of the humble dependent breed that had known nothing but captivity. There was a fierce spirit in her to match Timon's. Her skin was a shade lighter than his, her face was round, moon-shaped, her nose flat and broad, her lips full and pouting, but her teeth were small and even, and very white when she smiled at Timon.

Timon inclined his head sharply in a command, and Sellene the slave girl nodded in acknowledgement. When Timon left the courtyard and went through the kitchens into the slave quarters she followed him.

He was waiting for her in his own tiny room with its single pallet of reed mat and furs. She went to him without hesitation, and lay against the great hard muscles of his chest and belly and thighs. Her round breasts jutting through the purple tunic of house Barca pressed against Timon.

They held their faces together, sniffing softly but eagerly at each other's eyes and mouths and nostrils, clinging to each other in their need and wanting.

'When I hold you, then once again I am King of Vendi, and no slave dog,' Timon whispered, and the girl groaned against him with her love.

With gentle hands that could crush the life from a man Timon loosened her tunic and carried her to the pallet. He laid her upon the bed, and as he came over her he said,

'You shall be the first of my wives. You shall be my queen and the mother of my sons.'

'When shall it be?' she asked him and her voice shook with the emotions locked within her.

'Soon,' he promised. 'Very soon now. I have what I came for, and I will take you back beyond the river. I shall be the greatest king the tribes have ever known, and you shall be my queen.'

'I believe you,' whispered Sellene.

'My royal lords and fair ladies.' The children squealed with glee, it was one of their jokes when Huy addressed them that way. 'Today I have a special treat for you!' Again pandemonium broke out. Huy's treats were usually something special indeed.

'What is it?' Imilce demanded breathlessly.

'This evening you will meet the oracle of Opet,' Huy announced, and the uproar subsided swiftly. The small ones not understanding but none the less infected by the solemnity of their elders. The bigger children had heard of the oracle, their nurses often frightened them into obedience with the name. Now that they were about to meet this mythical creature the atmosphere was charged with tension. They were all of them suffering from an onset of the creeps and ghostlies.

Anna spoke for all of them when she asked in a very subdued voice, 'She won't eat us, will she?'

When Tanith came she seated herself amongst them, and threw the hood of her cloak back from her face. She smiled at the children, and said softly, 'I am going to tell you a story.' The smile and the promise were enough to ease the tension and they edged in closer to her. 'It's the story of the marriage of the great god Baal to the goddess Astarte.'

Tanith began the tale from religious mythology which was the basis of the Festival of the Fruitful Earth, a festival celebrated every five years. This year of Opet 538 was the 106th ceremony since the founding of the city, and the following day would begin the festivities that would last for ten days.

Tanith held her young audience enthralled, speaking in the compelling voice which Huy had trained so carefully, using the mannerisms and gestures he had taught her. Huy watched her with an unusual mixture of professional appraisal and the adulation of a besotted lover.

In two years she had lost the last traces of gawkiness and uncertainty, and although she was not yet twenty years of age, there was an inner calm, a serenity of mind and expression, that befitted her role of seeress and occult adviser to a nation. No matter that her pronouncements were carefully coached and rehearsed by Huy Ben-Amon, it was she that made the delivery, and made it convincingly. Much of Huy's material success in the last two years stemmed from the questions and requests for guidance addressed to Tanith by the rich merchants and trading syndicates of Opet – and Tanith's replies. The supplicants were usually well satisfied with Tanith's advice, though it was always couched in terms of ambiguity to ensure against recriminations. Did it matter that Huy Ben-Amon was also well satisfied?

In the same way Huy, despite his loss of the king's ear, kept a guiding hand on the rudder of the ship of state. Huy was certain that Lannon Hycanus was fully aware of the ultimate source of the advice and guidance which he received from Tanith. In any event, Lannon visited the oracle regularly in her shrine in the grotto beside the silent green pool of Astarte.

On the morrow Lannon's visit to the oracle would be his first official act that would signal the commencement

424

of the Festival of the Fruitful Earth. This was the true reason why Huy had summoned Tanith to his residence. He must brief her carefully on the replies she would make to the king's queries. Huy knew with a high degree of accuracy what these would be, for his informers were close to the king and again Huy guessed that Lannon intentionally leaked his questions in advance, certain that they would reach Huy and that the replies would come through the oracle.

Thinking of Lannon always brought on a mood of deep melancholy. Two years Huy had been without solace of Lannon's smile and handclasp and companionship, and during that time the sharp edge of his loss had not blunted but grown keener. He would wait for hours for a passing glimpse of his old friend, he would pester others for accounts of the banquets at the palace to which he was not invited. On each anniversary of the king's birth, and also on his throne day Huy had composed a sonnet and sent it with a handsome gift to the palace. The gift had been unacknowledged and the sonnet unsung – as far as he knew.

Huy tore himself out of this sad mood, and looked instead at his love. The children had crowded her now, silent and big-eyed and intent. Four-year-old Hannibal, named after his illustrious ancestor, had crawled into Tanith's lap and was sucking his thumb as he stared up into her face.

Tanith's mask of solemnity had slipped a little, with these children she was childlike, her expression animated and her voice excited. Seeing her thus seemed to add a new dimension to Huy's feelings for her, and his heart swelled in his chest until it seemed his chest must burst. How much longer must he wait, he wondered, and for what? If it had taken two long carefully planned years to win her confidence, how much longer to win her heart, and having won it what could he hope for – for she was dedicated to the goddess and could never belong to mortal man.

Tanith's story ended, and the children exclaimed and clamoured for more, besieging her with demands and entreaties and bribery kisses – but Huy feigned outrage, and scolded them while they laughed and clapped their hands with delight. He shouted for the nursemaids and they came – among them that tall brooding fiery woman who always made Huy feel disquiet when she looked at him from those unfathomably dark eyes.

He said to her. 'Sellene, darkness falls, tell Timon to carry a lamp for you to the palace gate.' And she acknowledged him with an inclination of the head, showing no gratitude at the order nor resentment either.

After the children had gone they ate the evening meal, the three of them, Tanith, Huy and Aina the ancient priestess who was Tanith's chaperone. Huy had selected her for two good reasons. She was half blind and completely deaf. Huy had tested her by making obscene gestures at her from a range of twenty paces. Aina had shown no reaction, nor had she when Huy crept up behind her and shouted a rude name in her ear. She was just the type of chaperone that Huy wanted.

They ate with the lamps trimmed low and the food served by one of the ancient slaves, and when they were finished Huy led Tanith up the outside staircase to the roof and they sat together below the parapet on reed mats and leather cushions. The night wind off the lake was cool and the stars very yellow and bright. Huy crouched over his lute, and strummed softly the rippling tune which he had trained Tanith's unconscious mind to accept as the signal for hypnotic concentration. Before he had finished the last bars of the tune she was breathing slowly and evenly, her body still and her eyes dark green and unseeing.

While his fingers ran over the strings of the instrument,

repeating the tune again and again, Huy began to speak. He kept his voice at a monotonous sing-song tone, speaking softly but insidiously and Tanith sat in the starlight and listened with an inner ear.

On the first day of the 106th Festival of the Fruitful Earth, Lannon Hycanus the forty-seventh Gry-Lion of Opet went in procession to the temple of Astarte to take the oracle.

He passed through the enclosure of the temple of Baal where the sacred towers pointed to the sun, guarded by the carved sunbird monoliths, and where the silent populace of the city waited, but when he reached the cleft in the red cliffs that guarded the entrance to the sacred grotto he unbuckled his sword and handed it to his little pygmy huntmaster, his shield and helmet he gave to his armour-bearers, and bareheaded and unarmed he entered the opening in the cliff.

He passed through the paved tunnel and into the silent beauty of the grotto. The surrounds of the pool were paved with slabs of sandstone and the pool itself was edged with a rounded coping of the same material. Tiers of stone benches rose against the sheer walls of the grotto, and against the far wall the shrine of Astarte was built half into the living rock. Its portals were columned in the Hellenic style, and it contained the cells of the priestesses and the chamber of the oracle.

Beyond the stone throne of the oracle was concealed the entrance to the city archives cut into the rock, and beyond that again, guarded by a massive stone door and the curse of the gods, was the treasury and the tomb of the kings.

Lannon paused beside the pool, and the priestesses came forward to meet him and escort him to the edge of the pool. Here they helped him to shed his armour and under-garments.

He stood tall and naked, golden-headed and beautifully formed, at the head of the steps leading down into the green water. His body was finely muscled as that of a trained athlete, although there was heavy bunched muscle in the shoulders and neck, the mark of the swordsman. His belly and flanks, however, were lean with the shape of muscle beneath the skin but lightly stated. A gilding of red-gold hair ran down from his navel across the flat stomach to explode in a sunny burst of curls in the angle of his legs. The legs were shapely, long and moulded, and balanced his regal bulk easily.

The High Priestess blessed him, and called down the goddess's favour upon him. Then Lannon went down the steps and immersed himself in the sacred, life-giving water.

While two young novices dried his body and dressed the king in robes of fresh linen, Huy Ben-Amon sang the praise chant to the goddess and when it ended all eyes looked up to the opening in the roof of the cavern high above the green pool.

Lannon called out in a loud voice. 'Astarte, mother of moon and earth, receive the messenger we send you – and hear our plea with favour.'

The throng about the pool lifted their hands high in the sign of the sun, and at the signal the body of the sacrifice plunged from the slab that jutted into the opening in the grotto roof. The wail of the doomed soul echoed briefly about the cavern, until he struck the water and was dragged down swiftly into the green depths by the weight of the chains he wore.

Lannon turned from the pool, and passed between the ranks of the priestesses into the entrance of the shrine. The audience chamber of the oracle was only a little larger than the living-room of a rich man's house. The lamps burned with a steady light. The flames were tinted an unnatural greenish hue, and the incense of burning herbs was heavy and oppressive. There were draperies beyond the oracle's throne hanging from roof to flagged floor.

The oracle sat upon the throne, a small figure completely swathed in white robes, the face hidden in the shadows of her hood.

Lannon halted in the centre of the chamber and before he spoke he admired for a moment the arrangements that put the interviewer at such a disadvantage. Bare-footed, damp from the pool, stripped of weapons and finery, dressed in strange robes and forced to look up at the figure on the throne while he inhaled the subtly drugged air – he must be off balance. Lannon felt his anger stir, and his voice was harsh as he made the formal greeting and asked the first question.

Huy watched from his place of concealment behind the draperies. He revelled in the closeness of his friend's physical presence, remembering his mannerisms and voice tones, watching the familiar and well-loved face, smiling at an expected change of expression, the quick smoulder of anger in the pale blue eyes, the quickening of interest at a warning, the glimmer of a smile as he recognized good advice.

Tanith spoke in the same sing-song cadence as Huy had used, picking the answers from the wide selection with which Huy had armed her.

When Lannon was finished and would have left the chamber, Tanith's voice stopped him.

'There is more.'

Lannon turned back with surprise, for he was not accustomed to unsolicited – and unpaid for – counsel from the oracle. But Tanith spoke, 'The lion had a faithful jackal to warn him of the hunter's approach, but drove the jackal away.

'The sun had a bird to carry the sacrifices on high, but turned his countenance away from the bird.

'The hand had an axe to defend it, but cast the axe aside.

'Oh, proud lion! Oh, faithless sun! Oh, careless hand!'

Behind the drapery Huy held his breath. It had sounded very clever when he had composed it, but now spoken out in the bare stone chamber it shocked even him.

Lannon's pale eyes seemed to glaze over as he puzzled the riddle, but it was not that subtle and as the import struck him his eyes cleared to the chill sparkle of sapphire and the blood engorged his face and neck.

'Damn you, witch,' he shouted. 'Must I have it from you also? That cursed priest plagues me at every turn. I cannot walk the streets of my city but I hear the crowds sing his piddling songs. I cannot dine in my own banquet-room but my guests will repeat his empty mouthings. I cannot fight, nor drink a bowl of wine, nor toss a dice but his shadow stands at my shoulder.' Lannon was panting with anger, as he stamped across the audience chamber and shook his fist in the oracle's startled face. 'My children even, he bewitches them also.'

Behind the drapes Huy felt his spirits soar on bright wings, this was not an enemy speaking.

'He struts and lords it in the streets of my city, his name echoes through my kingdoms.'

Lannon's anger was changing to righteous indignation.

'They cheer him when he passes, I have heard it, and, by great Baal, they cheer him louder than they do their own king.'

Lannon swung away from the throne, unable to control his agitation. His eyes swept over the draperies and for an instant seemed to stare into Huy's soul. Huy drew back with a quick intake of breath, but Lannon paced quickly about the chamber before approaching the oracle again.

'He does all this, mark you, *without my favour*. He should be an outcast, a—' He broke off and paced again, and his voice changed, the cutting edge of it dulled, and he said almost inaudibly, 'How I miss that terrible little man.'

Huy doubted for a moment that the words had been spoken, but almost immediately Lannon's voice rose in a bellow.

'But he defied me. He took from me what was mine, and that I cannot overlook!'

Lannon whirled and stormed from the shrine. His gentleman-at-arms and his huntmaster saw the expression on his face and they signalled the warnings ahead of the king's furious progress back to the palace.

O n the final day of the festival Lannon Hycanus prayed in the temple of great Baal, alone in the sacred grove among the towers and the sunbird monoliths. Then he emerged to receive the renewed pledges of loyalty from his subjects. Each of the nine noble families would be represented, as well as the order of priesthood, the guilds of craftsmen and the powerful trading syndicates of the kingdom. They would restate their oaths of allegiance to the throne, and present gifts to the Gry-Lion.

Huy Ben-Amon was absent from the ceremony. Bakmor made the oath for the priesthood and presented the gift. Lannon growled softly at the young warrior priest as he made obeisance before him.

'Where is the Holy Father of Ben-Amon?'

'My lord, I speak for him and all the priests of great Baal.' Bakmor avoided the question as Huy had coached him, and Lannon could protest no further in the presence of his assembled nobles.

The ceremony ended the festival and Opet plunged into an orgy of food and wine and frolic and licence. While

Lannon feasted with his nobles in the palace, the commoners thronged the narrow streets singing and dancing. The wine vendors passed freely amongst them, but during the daylight hours the restraints of custom and law checked the behaviour of the crowds. Darkness would bring on the lewd and wanton revels which characterized the festival. In the night the noble matrons and their pretty daughters would slip out, cloaked and hooded, into the streets to join the debauchery – or at the very least to watch it with shining eyes and breathless laughter. For a day and night the rules of society were suspended, and no husband nor wife could demand explanation or accounting from their spouses. It happened but once every five years, and when the festival ended there were wine-sore heads, pale faces and shaking hands, as well as smug and secret smiles.

By the middle of the afternoon Lannon was drunk, expansively and happily drunk, as were most of his guests. The banquet-room of the palace was sweltering. The sun beat down fiercely upon the flat mud roof, while the body heat of 500 excited nobles, and the heat from the steaming dishes of rich food turned it into an oven.

The roar of voices drowned the valiant efforts of the musicians, and the artistry of the naked girl dancers was impaired by a barrage of ripe grapes aimed by a group of young and noble knights. Hits upon various parts of the girls' anatomy scored for the marksmen in a contest upon which large amounts of gold were wagered.

Deep in wine and talk, Lannon was not aware of the change in the feast until almost complete silence had descended upon the hall. He looked up, frowning quickly, and saw that the musicians' hands had frozen upon their instruments, the dancers stood paralysed, and the guests gawked.

Lannon's frown deepened to a scowl as he saw Huy Ben-Amon approaching him down the hall. Huy was dressed in a blue tunic with a border of woven gold wire. He wore a gold belt, and a jewelled dagger. His hair and beard were carefully oiled and curled, and golden ear-rings dangled to his shoulders.

His expression was solemn as he knelt quickly before Lannon, and his voice rang golden and sweet to every corner of the hall.

'My king, I come to renew my allegiance to you. Let all men know that I honour you above all things, and my loyalty is unto death and beyond.'

Lannon was caught off balance, as Huy had intended. His brain was fuddled with surprise and wine. He fumbled for words, but before he found them, Huy had risen swiftly.

'As a mark of my faith, I offer a gift.' He signalled with one hand behind his back, and all heads in the hall swung to the main doors.

The towering figure of Timon stalked into the hall, passed down its length and stopped beside Huy. He stared into Lannon's face with those ferocious smoky eyes.

Huy whispered. 'Down!' And nudged the giant slave, and slowly Timon lowered himself to one knee and bowed his head.

'But he belongs to the gods,' Lannon challenged harshly. 'You declared him god-marked, Priest.'

And Huy gathered his resolve, steeling himself to tell the lie, to commit this sacrilege. Despite the fact that he had already explained it to the gods and to Timon, he was uneasy. It was necessary to regain the king's favour, Huy had explained, there was but one way of doing so. Lannon was bound by his pride. He could not move to break the deadlock. Huy must make the offer. He asked great Baal for permission to deny the bird-footed marking of the slave. He asked aloud, while pacing the roof of his house in the noon day. A distant muttering of summer thunder had been all the answer Huy needed. The gods had answered, but Huy felt nervous, the answer had been in a very minor key, and not without ambiguity. It was also very difficult for Huy to admit that he was wrong – it jarred the very foundations of his soul.

'My lord,' said Huy. 'I was mistaken. The gods have shown me that the markings are not sacred.'

Lannon stared at Huy. He shook his head slightly, as though he doubted the evidence of his own ears.

'You mean – you give him to me without reservation? I can have him despatched immediately, if I wish to?' He leaned forward staring at Huy. 'Do you give him to me without conditions?'

'I have declared my love for the king,' said Huy, and with his foot he nudged Timon.

In a great rumbling bass, Timon spoke his lines in near perfect Punic. 'I come to you as a living proof of that love.'

Lannon rocked back on his cushions. He thought about it, and the scowl reappeared, as he saw it.

'You seek to chain me! There are still conditions – only better concealed,' he growled.

'Nay, my lord. Not chains, but the silken threads of friendship,' Huy told him softly. They held each other's eyes. Lannon beginning to flush with anger, Huy steady and calm.

Then suddenly Huy's face cracked, and the dark eyes sparkled. The ringlets on his cheeks began to dance with suppressed laughter. Lannon opened his mouth to bellow at him, to reject the gift and the offer of friendship. Instead, laughter rattled up his throat and burst from his open lips. He laughed, until the tears poured down his cheeks and between gusts of laughter he moaned with the pain of his aching belly muscles.

'Fly for me, bird of the sun,' he sobbed, and Huy flopped down beside him on the cushions and shook and quivered with laughter.

'Roar for me, Lion of Opet,' he cried and a slave girl filled a wine bowl and brought it to him. Huy quaffed half of it, then passed the bowl to Lannon. He drained it. A

434

little wine ran from the corners of his mouth into his golden beard. He smashed the bowl on the stone floor, then clasped Huy about the shoulders.

'We have wasted much time, my Sunbird. Let us make up for it. What shall we do first?'

'Drink,' said Huy.

'Ah!' cried Lannon. 'And then what?'

'Hunt,' suggested Huy, choosing those activities dearest to the king.

'Hunt!' Lannon echoed. 'Send for my huntmasters – we march tomorrow to hunt the elephant!'

'Astarte, mother of earth, your beauty is multiplied until it floods my soul,' muttered Huy, swaying gracefully, as he looked up at the night sky. He reeled backwards, but fell against a wall. It steadied him, and he went on studying the astronomical phenomena in the heavens. Four silver moons hung above the night-revelling city. Huy closed one eye, and three of the moons vanished – he opened it and they reappeared.

'Astarte, guide your servant's footsteps,' Huy entreated, pushed himself away from the wall and went on down the narrow lane towards the harbour. He stumbled over a body lying in the shadows, and stooped unsteadily to check for signs of life.

The body snored and grunted as he rolled it onto its back, and a warm fruity gust of winey breath came up to Huy. It reminded him of the recumbent figures he had left strewn about the banquet hall at the palace. Lannon chief among them, smiling as he slept.

'Tonight you are in good company, citizen of Opet,' Huy chuckled, and went tottering onwards down the lane. In an angle of the wall a dark shape moved. Huy peered at it curiously, saw one body, two heads, heard broken gusty breathing, soft incoherent cries. The movements were small, but unmistakable. Huy smiled, tripped and nearly fell. He saw a startled girl's face turn towards him from the gloom. 'Let all things be fruitful,' he told her solemnly and went on, and as he went another figure slipped silently from the dark lane and followed Huy. The figure was cloaked and hooded in rough woven brown cloth, and its movements were stealthy and deliberate.

The quayside of the harbour was crowded with revellers, and there were bonfires burning here. The reflections of the flames smeared ruddy and bright upon the still black waters of the lake. Around them, arms linked in a circle, danced the crowds. Some of the women were past all restraint, stripped naked to the waist, spilled wine snaking down their white bodies like blood.

Huy stopped to watch them a while, and the following figure hung back, mingling with the throng of merry-makers.

When Huy started forward, the cloaked figure hurried forward also. The lane that led up to Huy's house was in deep darkness, but a lamp burned dimly in a niche above the gate, left there to welcome the master home.

As Huy groped his way towards the light, the following figure closed with him silently and swiftly. The blundering sounds of his own progress blanketed the rustle of cloth and the light footfalls behind him.

Huy reached the gate, and he stood in the dim lamp-light. His dagger was under his cloak, and his sword hand reached out for the latch of the gate. In that instant while he was unready and off balance, the dark figure flew at him from out of the darkness. A hand closed on his wrist, and he was thrown back against the wall beside the gate. Wine had slowed his reflexes, he twisted his face upwards in surprise and alarm. He saw the dark figure, with its face hidden in the recesses of the hood, come at him – and before he could shout soft lips were pressed against his, and a little muffled chuckle broke through these lips into his startled mouth – and he felt warm breasts and thighs moving against him.

The shock of it paralysed Huy. For long seconds he stood utterly still while lips and cunning hands teased and goaded him. Then with a hoarse cry he reached for the taut warm woman shape, and immediately it was gone, slipping away beyond his reach.

He lunged for it wildly, his hands groping air, and the shape danced away, swirled through the gateway into Huy's house and slammed the gate closed.

Cursing desperately, Huy struggled with the gate, wrenched it open at last and ran into the entrance court.

There was a flash of dark movement across the court, disappearing into the house, and Huy raced after it, tripped over a cushion and fell full length, knocked over a stool on which a house slave had left an amphora and wine bowl. They shattered loudly, splashing wine across the mud floor. A mocking whisper of laughter, from the dim recess of the house, sent Huy scrambling to his feet and charging onwards. He saw the cloaked figure silhouetted against the lamplit doorway of his sleeping quarters.

'Wait!' he shouted. 'Who are you?' And his house slaves roused by the uproar came running, still half asleep, panicky and hastily armed.

'Be gone!' Huy shouted at them furiously. 'All of you – the first one I catch out of his room before morning, I will have flogged.' And they retreated to their quarters, not seriously alarmed by the threat. Huy maintained his dignity until the last of them had disappeared, then he turned and charged towards the doorway of his sleeping quarters.

There was a night lamp burning here also, on a low stool beside his bed. The wick was trimmed low, a soft orange puddle of light which left the furthest reaches of the room in darkness. Beside the lamp stood the cloaked woman. She stood motionless and the face within the hood was completely hidden although Huy thought he caught the sheen of reflected light off watching eyes.

The force of Huy's charge carried him half across the room, but in the wrong direction. He swung towards her, and at that moment she stooped and snuffed the lamp flame. The room was plunged into darkness, and Huy's charge ended against the wall. He gathered himself quickly, he was sobering fast now, and he crouched beside the wall listening.

He heard the rustle of cloth, and he pounced. His fingers closed on a hem of the cloak. There was a muted shriek of surprise, and the fold of material was plucked from his fingers. He swore bitterly, and with arms wide-spread groped like a blind man about the room.

He sensed movements near him, the lightest breathing, the softest stirring in the darkness. He reached out quickly, and his fingers brushed against smooth skin. He recognized the shape of a nude back, and the plump warm bulge of a buttock. A soft chuckle and it was gone again. Huy froze with his heart hammering at his ribs, and his physical arousal making him momentarily dizzy.

Whoever she was, she had discarded the cloak. He was alone with a woman who was elusive as a darting lake pike, and as naked as a new-born babe. Like a stalking leopard he went after her, stripping his own tunic and breech clout as he went, dropping them carelessly on the floor, until, except for the gold rings in his ears, he was bare as his own passion.

She was panicky in the darkness now, unable to control the gasps and nervous giggles. And Huy hunted her by ear, closing in on her, driving her into the corner beside the bed.

She nearly escaped him again, ducking under his searching hands but one of his long arms whipped around her waist and he lifted her easily. She squealed now, kicking like a captive animal, her fists beating against his face and chest.

He carried her to the thick pile of furs that made up his bed.

H uy woke with a sense of peace, a feeling of deep happiness.

His body seemed softened and enervated, but his mind was clear and sharply focused. The soft pinks of dawn suffused his chamber and the cry of the winging lake birds carried clearly to him.

He raised himself on one elbow and looked down at the girl who slept beside him in the storm-tossed bed. She had cast aside her covering in the warm spring night. Her hair was moist at the temples, and a fine sheen of moisture shone on her softly pouting upper lip. Her eyes were closed, and she slept so lightly that her breathing barely stirred the mass of soft dark hair which lay upon her cheeks.

One arm was thrown over her head, pulling the surprisingly large breasts out of shape. Her breasts were big and full and round for the long slim length of her body, and the tips were still flushed dark red from the loving of the night. Her skin was smooth and pale creamy olive, with violent puffs of black silky hair in her armpits and at the base of her belly.

Huy saw all of this in the first startled glance, before his eyes fastened on her calm and sleeping face.

Incredulously Huy stared at her, all sound locked away in his throat. He felt horror, and awe, and superstitious terror.

The girl opened her eyes, and saw him and smiled.

'Baal's blessings on you, Holy Father,' she said softly.

'Tanith!' gasped Huy.

'Yes, my lord.' She was still smiling.

'This is sacrilege,' Huy whispered. 'This is an offence against the goddess.'

'To deny my love for you would have been an offence against all nature.' Tanith sat up on the bed, and kissed him without remorse, without the least sign of guilt.

'Love?' Huy asked, his misgivings temporarily forgotten.

'Yes, my lord,' Tanith nodded, and kissed him again.

'But—' Huy stuttered, and his cheeks turned bright as bush fires. 'You cannot – how can you love me?'

'How can I not, my lord?'

'But my body – my back.'

'Your back I love because it is part of you, part of your goodness and kindness and wisdom.'

He stared at her for many seconds, then clumsily he took her in his arms and buried his face in the fragrant dark cloud of her hair.

'Oh, Tanith,' he whispered. 'What are we going to do?'

Huy stood on the hilltop in the dawn and waited for his god. Below him the camp stirred. The cooking fires paled in the growing light of day. Small sounds carried up to him, the sounds of 6,000 men preparing for the hunt. The 6,000 warriors of Huy's legion, and the king's train. Small wonder that the camp filled the entire valley on both sides of the small river that flowed down the escarpment of the hills. Thirty miles away to the north lay the sluggish green ribbon of the great river, sweltering in its hot and unhospitable valley. One of Lannon's legions was camped there already, and for days now they had been harassing the elephant herds that were feeding along the river. They had attacked them with archers, and javelin-throwers and war elephants.

Under this harassment the herds would leave the valley,

taking to their ancient roads out over the escarpment. Lannon was encamped now astride these well-blazed trails, and scouts from the valley had reported the previous evening that the herds were already on the move. They were massing and moving in towards the escarpment wall, and in the next few days they would come pouring up out of the valley in long majestic files, as the old bulls led them to sanctuary from the persistent hunters who plagued them.

Huy Ben-Amon pondered this as he stood in the dawn. He wore light hunting armour and running sandals, and he leaned comfortably on the shaft of the vulture axe. The splendid blade was covered with a soft leather sheath to protect the finely honed edge and the delicate engravings. It seemed to Huy that the gods had so arranged circumstances as to provide him with this opportunity.

For two weeks, ever since that last night of the Festival of the Fruitful Earth, Huy had spent most of his waking moments pondering his dilemma. He had spent hours poring over the sacred books, examining the roles of priest and priestess, their duties and relationship to the gods, and to each other. He thought that from all this research he had built up a case for his behaviour. He could not bring himself to call it sacrilege. He had come now to plead his case, and to receive judgement.

The sun shot its first golden lance against the crest of the hill, and Huy sang the praise chant with all the beauty at his command. Then he made his plea. It was complicated dialectic, based on the concept of earthly representation, and amounting to a line of reasoning which supposed that what was good behaviour between Baal and his mate Astarte would be equally justifiable between their earthly representatives – although, of course, not between a priestess and any other person than the High Priest of Baal. Huy glossed over the more evidently weak spots in his case.

He ended, 'It may be, however, great Baal and heavenly Astarte, that I am mistaken in my reasoning. It may well be that I have sinned. If this is the case then I deserve your full wrath and despite my life of service and faithful duty, I deserve the most dire punishment!'

Huy paused for effect. 'I go now to hunt the elephant. I swear on my life that wherever the chase is hottest, there I shall be. Wherever the danger is deadliest, there I shall be.

'If I have sinned – then let the tusked beasts strike me down. If I have not sinned then let me live and return to the bosom of your priestess. If you grant me life and love – I swear my duty and service will last to the end of my days, and no man nor woman will ever know of the dispensation you have granted me.' He was quiet a while longer then he spoke again, 'You who have loved, take pity on one who loves also.'

Huy came down the hill well satisfied with his bargain. He would give the gods full measure. He would not hang back in distaste from the slaughter today, the gods would have every opportunity to demonstrate their outrage. In any event, Huy was well aware that only death could keep him out of Tanith's arms. The taste of that fruit had been too sweet for him ever to deny it.

'Huy,' Lannon shouted as Huy entered the camp. 'Where have you been?' He was armed and striding impatiently back and forth outside his tent. He came towards Huy quickly. 'The day wastes away,' he cried. 'Already from the hills our look-outs have seen the approach of the herds.'

The war elephants were ready, drivers sitting on their necks and the tall castles on their backs. Lannon's hunting party was assembled about the tent. Among them Huy noticed some of the king's most renowned huntmasters: Mursil, with his purple boozy face, the lean and saturnine Zadal, Huya the celebrated bowman, and the diminutive yellow Xhai whose fame as a tracker had grown apace in the last few years. Beyond them amongst the horde of body slaves towered the colossal black bulk of Timon. Huy smiled at him, and then he hurried beside Lannon to the elephant lines.

Lannon told him, 'You will ride with me, Sunbird.' And Huy replied, 'I am honoured, my lord.'

Mursil handed Huy one of the elephant bows. Few men could draw these massive weapons. Carved from solid baulks of wild ebony, they were as thick at the centre as a man's wrist and strung with twisted strands of lion gut. It required immense strength in the arms and chest to draw one of the five-foot arrows, that were armed with a heavy steel head and flighted with wild duck feathers. However, once drawn to the limit and loosed, they could fly 100 paces and bury the arrow up to its feathers in the living flesh of an elephant. They could reach the mighty heart in its castle of ribs, they could cut deep into the massive pink lungs, or loosed with skill they could cut through the ear-hole in the great bony skull and find the brain.

'I know you prefer the bow to the spear, Holy Father,' Mursil murmured respectfully. 'As for me, my old arm can no longer draw.'

'Thank you, huntmaster.'

'The quivers are full. I have tested and selected each of the arrows,' Mursil assured him, and Huy followed Lannon to where his war elephant knelt. It was a rangy old cow, more steady than the bull in the heat of battle, more reliable and even-tempered than the bull in the hunt.

Huy followed Lannon up into the castle. There was room for three men in the wooden box. The arrow quivers were fitted to the outside, but with the arrow-heads standing up ready to the hand. The javelins were racked on the front of the castle and Lannon selected one and tested it thoughtfully.

'A nice balance,' he judged it, and then looked down to where his huntmasters waited anxiously. Each of them eager for the honour of riding with the Gry-Lion. Lannon glanced over them, but his eye stopped on Xhai. He nodded, and with pathetic gratitude the pygmy scrambled up the elephant's side.

With a heavy lurch that threw Huy against the edge of the castle, the elephant came up on its feet. They looked down from the majestic height of nearly eighteen feet, and the driver goaded the old cow into a stately swaying walk. They took the trail down towards the escarpment of the valley.

'I have selected a good place for it,' Lannon told Huy. 'Where the steep path comes out suddenly into a small flat bowl. We will wait for them there.'

Huy looked back and saw the other war elephants following them. Twenty of them in single file, ears flapping, trunks swinging, they trundled sedately along. The huntsmen in the castles were checking and testing their weapons, and chattering excitedly.

'For what do we hunt, my lord?' Huy asked. 'Calves or ivory?'

'Calves first. The elephant trainers have asked for two dozen youngsters between five and ten years old. We will capture those this morning, for it will be the breeding herds that come up out of the valley first. Then later we will hunt for ivory. The scouts report many fine bulls scattered along the great river.'

The saucer which Lannon had selected was hemmed in with steep broken ground. It was circular in shape, perhaps 500 paces across. The elephant road came into it through a narrow rocky pass, crossed the saucer and climbed out of it up a steep pitch to the high ground above. The saucer was thickly wooded, and Lannon placed his war elephants in ambush, concealing them about the perimeter of the bowl in the good cover. The war elephants were forced to kneel for better concealment, and while they waited Huy and Lannon breakfasted on cold corn cakes, cheese and roast salt beef washed down with red wine. It was a hunter's meal, taken in cover with the mounting excitement of the chase sharpening their appetites, and as they ate they kept glancing up at the look-outs on the high ground above the saucer whose task it was to watch for and to signal the approach of the herds.

The dew was still on the grass when a figure waved frantically from the skyline above them, and Lannon grunted with satisfaction and wiped the grease from his fingers and lips.

'Come, my Sunbird,' he said, and they mounted the kneeling elephant once more.

It was a long wait that stretched and tightened their nerves, then suddenly little Xhai stirred expectantly beside Huy and his dark amber eyes snapped.

'They are here,' he whispered, and almost immediately a single wild elephant came out through the rocky portals of the pass and paused on the lip of the saucer. It was an old cow, grey and lean and tuskless. Suspiciously she looked about the saucer, lifting her trunk to sample the air and then blowing the sample into her mouth against the olfactory glands in her upper lip. The breeze was behind her, a soft dry movement of air that carried the smell of waiting men away from her, and she lowered her trunk and moved forward.

From the pass behind her poured an avalanche of great grey bodies.

'Breeding herd,' murmured Lannon, and Huy saw the calves at heel. They ranged in size from almost full grown to not much bigger than a large pig. The smaller they were the more noisy and mischievous, squealing and frolicking and chasing between the legs of their mothers. Huy smiled at the attempts of one to suckle from his moving mother, groping for the teats between her front legs with his miniature trunk until in exasperation the mother picked up a fallen branch and swatted him mercilessly across the rump. The calf squealed and fell in at her heels again, demure and chastened.

The saucer was full of wild elephants now, their grey humped backs showing above the thick bush as they streamed along the ancient road to safety.

Lannon leaned forward and touched the driver on the shoulder, and the war elephant rose beneath them, lifting them high so that they could look down from their castle upon the quarry. All around the saucer, the war elephants rose from cover with the armed men upon their backs. They closed in on the herd quietly, the squealing and uproar from the calves blanketing their approach until they were right in amongst the herd.

Lannon selected a young cow with a half-grown calf and leaning out from the castle he hurled his javelin into her neck, aiming for the great arteries there. The cow squealed in pain and alarm, and bright red arterial blood blew in a cloud from the tip of her trunk. She reeled backwards, mortally wounded, and from the other castles a torrent of missiles flew into the herd. Hundreds of huge bodies burst into flight and the forest shook and rang with their trumpeting and their frantic efforts at escape.

Despite his promise to the gods, Huy did not raise his bow, but watched in awful fascination the slaughter of the terrified beasts. He saw an old cow, bristling with arrows and javelins, charge one of the war elephants and knock it down on its knees; the men were hurled from the castle to fall beneath stampeding hoofs, and the old cow tottered away to fall and die, still in her battle rage. He saw a calf, hit in error, trying to tear the arrow from its own flank and squealing pitifully as the barbs clung stubbornly in the flesh. He saw another calf attempting vainly to rouse its dead mother, tugging at her with its little trunk.

Lannon was shouting with excitement, hurling his javelins into the neck and spine with that deadly accuracy that dropped the great grey bodies in profusion about them.

One of the herd mothers charged them from the side; a bad-tempered old queen as big and as strong as their mount, she bore down on them. Lannon swung to face her, braced himself and threw, but the old queen lifted her trunk and the javelin struck it squarely, biting deep into that pulpy sensitive member just below the level of her eyes. She squealed in agony but never faltered in her run, and regretfully Huy lifted his bow. He knew she would charge home, and that only death would stop her.

The old queen lifted her head and trunk high, bracing herself for the impact of her charge. Her mouth was wide open, with the pointed lower lip dangling, and Huy drew, and loosed his shaft into the back of her throat. All five feet of the arrow disappeared into her gaping mouth, and he knew the point had found the brain for she reeled back onto her haunches, shuddering and quivering, a strangled gurgling cry bubbling from her throat. The lids of her eyes twitched violently and she fell forward and was still.

They killed forty-one cows, thirty of them with calf. However, nine of the calves were adjudged by the trainers too young for survival as orphans and they were put down with a single merciful arrow. The others were cut out and rounded up by specially trained nursing cows and led away from the mountainous bleeding carcasses of their mothers. By noon the work was done, and the slaves could busy themselves in butchering the carcasses and carrying the meat away to the smoking racks. The saucer was a reeking charnel-house, and the vultures turned overhead in a dark cloud that almost obscured the sun.

Lannon ate the midday meal with his nobles and huntmasters. Fresh grilled elephant tripe seasoned with hot pepper sauce, broiled elephant heart stuffed with wild rice and olives, platters of golden corn cakes and the inevitable earthen amphorae of Zeng wine made it a meal fit for a hunter's appetite.

Lannon was in a high good humour, striding amongst his men, laughing and jesting with them, picking out one or another for a special commendation. He was still wrought up by the excitement of the chase, and when he paused beside Huy he meant to chaff him when he said:

'My poor Sunbird, you loosed but one arrow during the whole hunt.' And Huy was about to answer lightly that one arrow for one elephant was as good a score as any, when suddenly Zadal the huntmaster from the middle kingdom laughed.

'Was the bow too strong for you, Holiness, or the game too fierce?'

There was sudden and deathly silence on the entire group, and all their faces turned towards the lean dark man with the thin sneering mouth and bright acquisitive eyes.

It took a few seconds of the silence for Zadal to realize what he had said, then he glanced quickly about the circle of watching faces. With a small chill he saw they were looking at him with the same detached curious expression that men looked upon those doomed to sacrifice. Beside him a noble said softly but matter-of-factly, 'You are a dead man.'

Swiftly, with real alarm, Zadal looked back at Huy Ben-Amon. Too late he recalled the reputation of this priest. It was said that no man still lived who had sneered at his back or his height or his courage. With relief he saw that the priest was smiling slightly, and delicately wiping his fingers on the hem of his tunic.

'Thank you, great Baal,' Huy prayed silently, smiling a little. 'It was right that you remind me of my promise. I held back from the hunt. Forgive me, great Baal. I will give you your chance now.'

Zadal's relief was short-lived for when Huy looked directly at him he saw the smile was on the priest's lips only. His eyes were bright and black and cold.

'Zadal,' Huy said softly, and the crowd pressed closer to hear his words. 'Will you fly with me on the wings of the storm?'

They stirred at the challenge, a quick buzz of comment

and they watched Zadal's face. It had paled to a dirty yellow, and his lips compressed into a thin white line.

'I forbid it,' said Lannon loudly. 'I will not let you do this, Huy. You are too valuable to me to waste your life in—'

Huy interrupted him quietly, 'Majesty, it is a matter of honour. This one called me coward.'

'But no man has hunted in that manner for fifty years,' Lannon protested.

'Fifty years is too long,' Huy smiled, 'is it not, Zadal? You and I will revive the custom.'

Zadal stared at him, hating his own unruly tongue.

Huy still smiled at him. 'Or is it that the game is too fierce for you?' he asked softly. For long moments it seemed that Zadal might refuse, then he nodded curtly, his lips still white.

'As you wish, Holiness.' And he knew they were right, he was a dead man.

In two large baskets, slaves had collected from one of the elephant carcasses the contents of the lower intestines. As Huy and Zadal, stripped naked, smeared their bodies with the yellow dung he overheard young Bakmor discussing the hunt with Mursil.

'I do not believe it is possible to kill a full-grown bull elephant with a battle-axe. It sounds to me like an unpleasant form of suicide.'

'That's why they call it flying on the wings of the storm.'

The elephant dung had a rank odour, strong enough to mask the man smell. It was the one protection the hunters would have. Their one chance of getting into close contact with the great beasts without being discovered. The sharp sense of smell of the elephant is its main defence, for its vision is weak and near-sighted.

Timon came over from the king's entourage and assisted Huy, spreading the dung across his back. Quickly Timon had understood the method that they would use.

'High-born, I fear for you,' he said softly.

'I fear for myself,' Huy admitted. 'Spread the dung thickly, Timon. I would prefer to stink, rather than die.'

Huy looked down the steep slope which stretched down into the valley from the saucer. The elephant road zig-zagged up through the sparse forest. They would intercept the next herd here, before it was alarmed by the smell of blood in the saucer.

Huy glanced around him and saw that the huntsmen had spread out along the ridge, selecting vantage points from which to view the sport. His eyes met those of Zadal. The huntmaster was daubed with the yellow filth from his head to his feet, and he gripped the handle of his axe too hard. There was fear in those dark eyes, and fear in the taut manner in which he held himself. Huy smiled at him, enjoying his discomfort, and Zadal looked away. His lips quivered.

'Are you ready, huntmaster?' Huy asked, and Zadal nodded. He could not trust his voice.

'Come,' said Huy, and started down the slope, but Lannon stepped into his path. There was a foreboding in his eyes, and his smile was unconvincing.

'That fool Zadal spoke in haste and without meaning it. No man here doubts your courage, Huy, except you yourself. Do not seek to prove it too convincingly. Life will hold little for me without my Sunbird.'

'My lord,' Huy's voice was hoarse. He was touched to the heart by Lannon's concern.

'The first cut is the dangerous one, Huy. Be careful that when he drops, he does not fall upon you.'

'I will remember.'

'Remember also to bathe before you dine with me this evening.' Lannon smiled and stepped aside.

Twice during the afternoon small herds of elephant passed them, moving swiftly up the slope amongst the trees. Each time Huy shook his head at Zadal and let them pass for they were cows and calves and immature bulls.

The day drew towards its close, and Huy felt an uneasy sense of relief. Perhaps the gods had decided in his favour and would not seek to put him to the test.

There was an hour of light left now. Huy and Zadal sat quietly beside the path, hidden by a screen of monkey apple vines that hung from one of the trees.

The dung had dried upon their bodies, making Huy's skin feel stiff and uncomfortable. He sat with the vulture axe across his lap and watched the path, hoping that nothing would come up it before darkness and he could abandon this mad adventure to which he was committed by honour and hasty choice. It was strange how inactivity dulled even the brightest passion, Huy thought, and grinned wryly as he fondled the handle of the axe.

He saw movement far down the slope, a grey drifting movement like smoke amongst the trees and he felt his skin prickle. Zadal had seen it also, he stopped his restless fidgeting and sat woodenly beside Huy.

They waited, and suddenly two elephants came out of the trees. Two big old bulls, with heavy ivory, stepping lightly up the slope. They were a hundred paces apart, spaced out on the path and there was an alertness and a sense of purpose in their tread that warned Huy they had been freshly disturbed, possibly wounded, by the huntsmen down in the valley.

'We will take these two,' Huy whispered. 'Choose one.'

Zadal was silent a moment, watching the two bulls with an experienced eye. The leading bull was older, and his one tusk was broken off at the lip. He was leaner and rangier-looking than his companion, and his leading position showed he was the more experienced, the more alert, and the broken tusk would make him meaner and his temper more uncertain.

'The second one,' Zadal whispered, and Huy nodded. He had expected it.

'I will move back now. We must try to attack at the same moment.' He left the cover of the hanging vines, and slipped back along the path opening a gap between him and Zadal approximately equal to that between the bulls.

Huy dropped into a patch of coarse grass beside the trail, and looked back. The elephants were striding steadily up towards them. The leading bull passed Zadal's hiding-place, and came on. Huy saw that the gap between the two bulls had closed. Zadal's elephant would reach him before Huy's came level with the clump of grass where he lay.

If one of the hunters launched his attack prematurely the other bull would be alerted, and the danger multiplied many times. Huy knew he could not rely on consideration from Zadal. The man would think only of his own best interests.

As the thought came to him he saw Zadal leave the shelter of the vines, and run silently out into the path behind the second bull. Huy's elephant was still fifty paces from where he lay, and it was facing him.

Zadal was following his elephant, running close upon its heels. Huy felt a moment's admiration for him. Perhaps he had misjudged him. Perhaps Zadal would follow the second bull and wait for Huy to get into position.

Then Huy saw the huntmaster's axe go up and glint at the top of its swing; as it flashed down, Huy transferred all his attention to the leading bull.

There was a squeal of pain and alarm as Zadal's axe struck, and Huy's bull burst into a full run. Sweeping down on him until it seemed to fill the whole field of Huy's vision, an animal as large as the very earth it sprang from.

As Huy rose from his hide he knew he had a few fleeting seconds in which to strike. Then the bull would be gone.

He went bounding along beside the bull, keeping uphill of him for when he fell he would roll down the slope. The pace stretched Huy's long legs to the full, and he was losing ground swiftly, falling back to the bull's hindquarters.

With every pace, as the huge weight of the grey body fell on the hind legs, so the hamstring tendons running down the back of the leg from knee to heel tightened under the coarse eroded skin. The tendon was a thick cord that flexed and bulged, thick as a girl's wrist; it carried the whole weight of the bull at each stride.

Huy swerved in his run, crossing behind the bull and as the tendon in the nearest leg tightened he slashed the blade of the vulture axe across it, severing it cleanly so that the sound of it was a sharp snapping, like the sheet of a sail parting in a gale.

The bull lunged off balance as the leg collapsed under him, he teetered wildly on the edge of the path, his weight held only on the good leg.

'For Baal!' Huy shouted with excitement and the axe went high as he swung. The second tendon parted as sharply, and the huge grey beast dropped heavily. The sound of its fall carried clearly to the watchers on the ridge, and a cloud of dust boiled up from the dry earth. Huy had danced back from under the rolling body and that terrible flailing trunk.

He steeled himself for the final act, as he danced about the rearing floundering animal, knowing he had only seconds to exploit his surprise, seconds before the maimed animal braced itself and saw him, and he searched for his opening desperately.

The bull reared up on its front legs, dragging its crippled hind legs behind it. In its unreasoning rage it was tearing at the trees, and slashing its terrible trunk in wild circles, gouging the earth with its single tusk.

But its back was turned to Huy, it had not recognized its attacker yet. Lightly Huy ran in, ducking under the flailing trunk. He vaulted up on the bull's wide back, landing on his knees with the axe high above his head.

The knotted spine stood out clearly through the wrinkled dry skin, great knuckles of bone braced for the blade. Huy struck, the killing stroke that crashed through the bone, and severed the soft yellow core of the spinal tissue. The bull shrieked, and collapsed, kicking and shaking spasmodically in its death throes.

Huy jumped down from its pulsating body and danced back out of danger from the legs and trunk of the dying beast. He felt a soaring sense of triumph and relief. It was done, he had flown upon the wings of the storm – and lived through it.

He heard the wild shrill trumpeting of the other bull, and he spun around. One glance showed him that the task was not yet completed, the gods were not finished with him.

Zadal had blundered. His second cut had missed the tendon and the bull was on three legs, but moving with agility and speed as it hunted the man. Zadal had thrown his axe aside, and was running, dodging up the slope with the bull close upon him. The bull was shrieking with rage, its trunk out-stretched, gaining swiftly on the fleeing man.

As Huy started forward it caught him. It wrapped its trunk around Zadal's body and flung him high in the air, above the tops of the tallest trees, and his body spun loosely in the air.

He fell face down on the rocky earth, and the bull placed one foot in the small of his back while with its trunk it plucked his head from his body, the way a farmer kills a chicken, and it tossed the head aside. It bounced and rolled down the slope like a child's ball.

Huy ran towards the bull, scrambling up the slope. The bull knelt on the mangled corpse and drove one tusk through Zadal's chest. It was so preoccupied with the mutilation of Zadal's body that Huy came up easily behind it.

He saw the deep gash in the back of the bull's knee

where Zadal's stroke had failed to find the tendon, and the vulture axe moaned softly in flight. This time there was no mistake.

'I give you a new title.' Lannon lifted his wine bowl, and silence fell expectantly on the nobles and knights who sat about his board. 'I give a battle honour for the man who has flown on the wings of the storm.'

Huy dropped his eyes modestly, blushing a little in the torch light under the leather awning of Lannon's campaign tent.

'Huy Ben-Amon – Axeman of the Gods!' Lannon shouted the title, and the nobles echoed it, saluting Huy with clenched fists.

'Drink, Huy! Drink, my Sunbird!' Lannon offered Huy his own wine bowl. Huy sipped the wine, smiling around at the company. Tonight he would not look too deeply in the wine bowl. He did not want to cloud or befuddle this sense of joy. The gods had answered him, and he sat quietly smiling in the midst of noisy revelry, hardly hearing the laughter and the banter, listening instead to the voice deep inside him which sang, 'Tanith! Tanith!'

When he rose to leave, Lannon was outraged, dragging him down into his seat by the hem of his tunic.

'You'll not leave here on your feet, Axeman. You deserve to be carried to your couch this night! Come, I challenge you to a bout with the wine cups.'

Huy shrugged aside the challenge, laughing and shaking his head.

'One challenge a day, my lord, I beg of you.'

Outside the night was still, and the sky was brilliant with the stars. The heat of the day was cooling, and the feel of the night wind in his face was like the caress of Tanith's silky tresses against his cheek.

'Astarte!' The goddess rose out of the valley, the golden disc of her countenance lighting the land with a soft radiance. 'Mother of earth. I thank you,' Huy whispered, and felt the tears of happiness flood his eyes.

He moved on through the camp towards his own tent, hugging the warmth of his love secretly to him.

'Tanith,' he whispered, 'Tanith.'

He moved on through the shadows until movement caught his attention, and he stopped. Beside one of the cooking fires crouched a figure, a slave woman working on the grinding stone, crushing corn for cakes.

The firelight caught her handsome features, and shone on the dark skin of her strong arms. It was the nurse Sellene.

Huy was about to move on, when the slave girl looked up expectantly. A man came towards her out of the darkness, and the girl's face lit with such a look of adoration, such unashamed love, that Huy felt his heart go out to her.

The man stepped into the firelight, and it needed only one glance at the powerful body and rounded bald head for Huy to recognize Timon.

Sellene stood up and went quickly to meet Timon, and they embraced. They sniffed at each other's faces in the strange love greeting of the pagans, holding each other closely. Huy smiled tenderly, feeling the warm sympathy of the lover for all other lovers.

Timon drew back from the girl, holding her at arm's length and he spoke softly. Huy could not catch the words. He heard only the soft rumble of Timon's voice, and the girl nodded quickly.

Timon left her and disappeared amongst the tents. Sellene went to the grinding stone and filled a leather bag with ground corn, then she glanced about furtively and followed Timon into the darkness. Huy watched her go, and smiled.

'I must talk to Lannon,' he thought. 'I could arrange a pairing between those two.'

In his own tent Huy took the golden scroll and spread it upon his writing pallet. He adjusted the lamp wicks, picked up his engraving tool, and began to write the poem to Tanith.

'Her hair is dark and soft as the smoke from the papyrus fires upon the great lake,' he wrote, and the incident between Timon and Sellene was forgotten.

Exhaustion overcame him a little after midnight, and he fell forward across his writing pallet and he slept with one cheek pressed to the love poem to Tanith on the golden scroll. The lamp flames smoked and faded and died.

Rough hands shook him awake in the dawn, and he looked up groggily. It was Mursil, the huntmaster.

'The Gry-Lion sends for you, Holiness. The hounds are in leash, and the slave-masters assembled. Two of the king's slaves have run, and the king bids you join the chase.'

Even in his half-wakening state, Huy knew who the running slaves were, and he felt the sick sliding of his guts.

'The fools,' he whispered. 'Oh, the stupid fools.' Then he looked at Mursil. 'No,' he said. 'I cannot – I will not go with them. I am sick, tell him I am sick.'

Sellene stood in the shadows and listened to the drunken bellowing and laughter from the king's tent. Beneath the short cloak was concealed the leather grain-bag, a bundle of smoked meat dried into hard black sticks, and a small earthen cooking pot. There was food for two of them for four days, and by then they would be across the great river. She was fearful, and elated at the same time. They had planned this moment for two years, and many emotions played behind her round impassive face as she waited.

Timon came at last; quietly he appeared beside her with such suddenness that she gasped with fright. He took her hand, and led her away towards the perimeter of the camp. She saw that he wore a cloak also, and that a bow and quiver stood behind his shoulder and a short iron sword was belted at his waist. These were weapons forbidden to a slave, and death was the penalty for carrying them.

There were two guards at the gate of the stockade, and while Sellene spoke with them, offering favours, Timon came from the darkness behind them. He broke their necks with his bare hands. Taking one in each hand and shaking them the way a dog will shake a rat. There was no outcry, and Timon laid the bodies gently beside the stockade gate and they went through.

They passed through the saucer where the elephant had been butchered, and the night was hideous with the snarling and yammering of the scavengers. Hyena and jackal fought over the bloody scraps and bone chips. With the sword bared in one hand Timon led Sellene through, and though the slinking hump-shouldered hyena followed them, moaning and sniggering, they reached the pass and started down the elephant road into the valley. The moon gave them good light, and they moved fast. They stopped only once at the ford of the stream to rest and drink a little water, then they hurried on towards the north.

Once they came upon a lion in the path. A big male whose body was ghostly grey in the moonlight, with a dark ruff of mane. They stared at each other for long seconds before the lion grunted softly and leapt into the under-growth beside the path. He had fed recently, and the two human shapes did not interest him.

The moon, four days past full, wheeled across the star-furry sky and sank towards the dark horizon. When it set, there was only the indistinct glow of the stars to light their way, and at a steep and broken place in the path Sellene fell heavily.

Timon heard her cry out and he turned back quickly. She was lying on her side, making a soft moaning sound.

'Are you hurt?' he asked as he dropped to his knees beside her.

'My ankle,' she whispered, agony making her voice husky and Timon groped down her leg. Already the ankle was hot to the touch, and as he held it he could feel it swelling, blowing up into a hard hot ball.

With the sword Timon cut strips from his cloak, and he bound the ankle tightly as Huy had taught him. He worked with frantic haste, and the worms of dread were already gnawing his guts.

When he lifted Sellene to her feet, she cried out as her weight came on the injured foot.

'Can you walk on it?' Timon asked, and she tried a few painful hobbling steps. She was panting with pain and her breathing whistled in her throat. She clung to Timon and shook her head hopelessly.

'I cannot go on. Leave me here.' Timon lowered her to the ground, and then straightened up as he discarded his weapons and her provisions. He kept only the short sword. He folded and knotted the two leather cloaks into a sling seat for Sellene, and placed it about her body. Then he looped the end over his neck and shoulder and lifted her. She was in his arms, with her own clasped about his shoulders. Half of her weight was taken by the sling, hanging about Timon's neck. He started forward, striding out down the steep path towards the valley floor.

By mid-morning the sling had rubbed the skin from his neck, a weeping pink graze through the dark skin. The heat was strong now, that heavy oppressive heat of the valley floor sucking away the last of his energy. The spring had long gone from Timon's step, and he reeled forward with spirit outlasting his physical strength.

On the edge of one of the glades of open grass, Timon stopped and leaned against the trunk of a mhoba-hoba tree. He was afraid to lower the girl's body to the ground lest he could not find the strength to lift it again. His lips were white and rimmed with dried spittle, and his eyes were laced with red veins. His chest heaved and shook with his breathing.

'Leave me, Timon,' Sellene whispered. 'This way both of us will die.'

Timon did not answer, but gestured her to silence with an impatient inclination of his head. He held his breath and listened. She heard it also then, the faint and distant baying of the hound pack.

He said, 'It is too late for that.' And he looked about quickly for a place to stand. They could not hope to outrun the dogs.

'You can still escape,' she urged him. 'The river is not far.'

'Without you there is no escape,' he said, and she clung to him as he carried her across the glade to a place where the mother rock outcropped. A jumble of fragmented granite like the ruins of an ancient castle.

He laid her gently amongst the rocks, with her back against one of the slabs. He folded her cloak and placed it as a pillow for her head, then he squatted beside her and caressed her face and neck with a surprisingly gentle touch for so big a man.

'They will kill us,' Sellene said. 'They always kill those who run.'

Timon did not answer, but his fingers stroked her cheek lightly.

'They kill in the worst way,' Sellene said, turning her head to look at him. 'Would it not be better if we died now, before the dogs come?' But he did not answer, and after a while she went on.

'You have a sword, Timon. Will you not use it?'

'If the little priest is with them, then we have a chance. He has power over the king – and there is a thing between him and me. There is a bond. He will save us.'

The dogs were closer now and it seemed that their baying had become more urgent as the scent ran hotter. Timon stood up and unsheathed the sword. He went out amongst the rocks and looked back towards the escarpment. Half a mile back the pack streamed from the forest into the glade. There were thirty of the tall sinewy hounds, long-legged and with rough ginger-brown coats and the heads and fangs of wolves. They were bred to chase and drag down the quarry.

Timon felt his skin tighten and prickle as he watched them string out across the glade towards him. Behind them, running on the heels of the pack were the handlers, with their distinctive green tunics and the dog-whips over their shoulders.

Beyond them again came the war elephants, five of them with the knights and slave-masters in their castles. The elephants followed the pack easily, in that ambling gait which could cover fifty miles a day.

Timon shaded his eyes and tried to pick out the distinctive figure of the priest amongst the men in the castles. They were too far off still, but the hounds were closing swiftly.

He wrapped his cloak carefully about his left forearm, and settled his grip on the sword. Swinging the weapon in a short arc to stretch his muscles.

The leading hounds saw him amongst the rocks, and immediately the deep regular baying changed to an excited yammering. Their ears flattened as they ran, and long pink tongues flopped over white fangs in the wolf jaws, and they fanned out across his front.

Timon stepped back into the opening where Sellene lay, guarding her from the vicious clamouring rush of brown bodies.

The first hound rushed in at him, with its jaws snapping, and it leapt at his face.

Timon took him on the point, in the base of his throat, killing the dog instantly, but before he could clear his blade another had sprung at him. He thrust his cloaked arm into its jaws, and hacked at a third hound.

They swarmed over him as he stabbed and hacked and thrust. He swung the hound that hung on his arm against the rock beside him, crushing in its ribs, but another had locked its fangs in his calf and was tugging him cruelly off balance. He drove the point into its shaggy back and the hound shrieked and released him.

Another went for his face and he struck at its head with the sword hilt. A great furry body smashed into his chest, a fang ripped his shoulder muscles.

There were too many of them, overwhelming him, ripping and tearing at him, smothering him with their weight and strength. He went down on his knees, holding a frothing slavering animal away from his throat and face with one hand, strangling it – but he felt other teeth slashing at his back and belly and thighs.

Then abruptly the dog-handlers were there, whipping the pack away from him, shouting to the animals by name, dragging them back and leashing them in the strangling collars.

Slowly Timon pulled himself up on to his feet. He had lost his sword, and blood streamed down his shining black body from the deep cuts and lacerations that covered him.

He looked up at the war elephant which towered over him. His last hope faded as he saw that Huy Ben-Amon was not amongst the hunters – and that Lannon Hycanus, the Gry-Lion of Opet was laughing.

'A good run, slave,' Lannon laughed. 'I thought that you might reach the river.' He looked beyond Timon to where Sellene lay. 'My huntmasters were correct then. They judged by the sign that the woman had damaged her leg and that you were carrying her. A noble gesture, slave, most unusual for a pagan. All the same it will cost you dear.' Lannon looked away to one of his slave-masters. 'There seems little to be gained by returning with them. Execute them here.'

Timon looked up at the king and spoke in a strong clear voice.

'I am the living symbol of that love,' he said, and Lannon's head jerked around as he remembered the words. With the laughter gone from his lips he stared at the bleeding slave king, meeting those smoky yellow eyes. For long seconds, Timon's life teetered on the verge of extinction, then suddenly Lannon's eyes dropped away from those of Timon.

'Very well,' he nodded. 'You remind me of my duty to a friend. I will honour it, but I swear you will live to curse the moment you spoke those words. You will live – but in life you will long for the sweetness of death.' Lannon's face was a mask of cold anger, as he turned back to his slave-masters. 'This man will not be executed, but he is declared "incorrigible" and he will be chained with a weight of two talents.' Almost a hundred pounds' weight of chains to be carried night and day, waking and sleeping. 'Send him to the mines at Hulya, tell the overseer there that he is to be used at the deep levels.'

Lannon watched Timon's face as he went on. 'The woman cannot claim my protection, but we will take her back with us, none the less. Let her be chained to the castle of one of the war elephants and marched.'

For the first time Timon showed emotion. He stepped forward and in appeal lifted one badly savaged arm from which the dark tattered flesh hung.

'My lord, the woman is hurt. She cannot walk.'

'She will walk,' said Lannon. 'Or she will be dragged. You will ride upon the elephant and encourage her. You will have time to decide if the swift death I offered you would not have been preferable to the life you have chosen.'

They chained Sellene at the wrists with a light marching chain twenty paces long. The other end of the chain was shackled to the rear wall of the elephant castle.

Timon, wearing his massive chains at neck and ankles, was seated in the castle. He was made to face backwards to where Sellene stood swaying slightly on one leg, favouring her grotesquely swollen ankle. Her face was greyish with pain, but she tried to smile up at Timon.

The first jerk of the chain as the elephant started forward pulled her face downwards on the hard earth, with its sharp shales and harsh clumps of razor grass. She was dragged fifty paces before she managed to roll onto her feet again and hop and stumble after the striding elephant. Her knees and elbows were raw, and there were scratches across her belly and breasts.

She fell and regained her feet a dozen times, each time her body was more battered and torn. She went down for the last time a little before sunset.

As Timon sat in the castle, draped in his chains, he swore an oath. In his anger and grief and pain he swore an oath of vengeance, watching Sellene's lifeless body bounce and slide over the rough places, leaving a damp brown smear across the dry red African earth. Then Timon wept, for the last time in his life he succumbed to tears. They ran down his face and dripped from his chin to mingle with the blood and dust that caked his body.

Huy filled a wine bowl from one of his choice amphorae, one that he had set aside for a rare occasion. He was humming softly to himself, and there was a small smile which came and went upon his lips and made his dark eyes sparkle.

He had returned to Opet in the middle of the night, slept five hours and now, bathed and dressed in his best linen, he had sent a slave to summon the oracle of Opet to meet with him. All the blood and passion of these last weeks upon the escarpment of the great river were forgotten now in his anticipation of his reunion with Tanith. Forgotten were the memories of Sellene's mutilated corpse dragged into camp behind the war elephant, the tall figure of Timon bowed beneath his chains and grief, led away by the slave-masters, those terrible accusing eyes turned towards Huy, the manacled wrists lifted in a gesture of menace or of appeal – Huy could not guess which. Then the slave-master's whip hissing and snapping across the purple black shoulders, lifting a welt as thick as a finger without cutting the skin. For the first time since it had happened Huy was free of it, his whole being taken up with the joy of his love.

Pursing his lips thoughtfully he let four drops of the clear liquid drip from the blue glass vial into the wine. He stoppered the bottle and stirred the wine with his forefinger, sucking his finger thoughtfully and wrinkling his nose at the faint musty taste of the opiate. He added a little wild honey to mask it, tasted again and at last satisfied he set the bowl on one of the wooden stools beside the pile of cushions. There was a dish of cakes and sweetmeats there already. Huy covered the wine bowl with a silken cloth, then surveyed his preparations with pleasure. He picked up his lute and climbed the staircase to the parapet of the roof and seated himself. He tuned the instrument and strummed upon it, loosening his voice and fingers, watching the narrow lane that led up to the front gate.

In the bright morning sunlight the lake waters were a cheery blue, only slightly darker than the sky. The breeze had flecked the surface with little floppy waves, and one of Habbakuk Lal's galleys had shipped her oars and was running in towards the harbour under a big lateen sail. The sea birds followed her, planing and soaring across her stern.

High above the lake the midday clouds were building tall, frothy thunder-heads. There would be rain before sunset, Huy thought, feeling the thunder in the air, in the touch of his garments upon his skin and the curl of his beard.

His breath caught, and the music died under his fingers as two figures turned into the lane and came up towards the gate. They wore the coarse brown-hooded robes that the priestesses of Astarte affected while travelling abroad. However, the bulky garment could not disguise the quick step and youthful carriage of the taller figure that hurried ahead, nor the age and aggravation of the bent figure that hobbled after her. The ancient voice, breathless and high, called with exasperation:

'My lady, slower! I pray you.' And Huy grinned. A slave opened the gate, and as they crossed the courtyard Huy struck a single authoritative note on the lute, and Tanith stopped dead. The old chaperone, unhearing, moved on into the house mumbling and muttering while Tanith looked up at Huy upon the parapet of the roof.

He began to sing, and the girl below him lifted the hood from her face and let it fall back on her shoulders. She shook her hair loose, watching his face with large green eyes and her expression was rapt and solemn. He sang the song he had written in the wilderness, the song to Tanith inscribed in the golden book, and as he let the last sweet note fall on the bright morning, Tanith's cheeks were flushed and her lips trembled.

Huy went down the staircase and stood close to her, without touching her.

'You are my soul,' he said gently, and she swayed towards him as if drawn by a force beyond her control.

'My lord, I cannot trust myself to be with you where other eyes may see us. I fear I shall betray my love to the blindest of them. Be strong for me.'

Huy touched her elbow, guiding her towards the house. As they passed through into the main room, Tanith stumbled slightly, for a moment pressed against him.

'Oh! I cannot bear it,' she said, and Huy's voice shook as he answered.

'In a while, my love. In a very short while.'

The old priestess was seated on the cushions already, mouthing a cake with bald gums, dropping crumbs and spittle down her robe and mumbling bitterly about her pains and aches.

Huy moved around behind her, and picked up the prepared wine bowl in both hands. Secure in the old priestess's deafness he asked Tanith, 'Is she strong?'

'As strong as most men,' Tanith smiled. 'Though she'll not admit it.'

'She does not complain of chest pains or shortness of breath?'

'Never.' Tanith was intrigued. 'Why do you ask?'

'I have placed star-drops in her wine,' Huy explained. 'But I do not want her sleep to be eternal.'

Tanith's smile flamed, lighting the green depths of her eyes and sparkling on her teeth. 'Oh, Holy Father, how clever of you.' She clapped her hands, a childlike gesture that never failed to touch Huy to the core of his being.

'How many drops?' Tanith demanded.

'Four,' Huy admitted.

'Perhaps a few more would not hurt her,' Tanith said. 'I have not seen you in many weeks, Holiness. There is much to discuss.'

During this exchange the old priestess had been nodding

and grimacing intelligently, quite as though she had under-stood every word. Huy studied her a moment, then firmly thrust aside the temptation.

'No,' he said. 'Four is sufficient.' And he came around in front of the priestess. The wrinkled monkey-like face split into a huge toothless grin and she reached for the bowl with a pair of bony claws, on which the old-age blotches and blue veins stood out clearly.

'You have a kind heart, Holiness,' she keened.

They seated themselves in front of her, and while they talked they watched her anxiously. The crone was drawing out her pleasure, sipping the wine and rolling it noisily around her mouth before swallowing and smacking her gums.

'Since we have been apart, I have thought much upon what has happened between us,' Huy admitted, without looking at Tanith.

'I have thought of nothing else.'

'As a man whose life is devoted to the service of the gods, I was greatly troubled that we had sinned against them,' Huy told her.

'There can be no sin in something which gives so much pleasure and happiness.'

'I asked the gods to set a test for me, a trial of my sins.' Huy had still not looked at her, but Tanith glanced at him sharply and her voice snapped.

'You did not indulge in foolish risk, did you?'

'The trial was a fair one – the gods were not cheated.' Huy wanted her to understand, and she understood too well.

'I forbid you to do these stupid male things. I shiver to think of what madness you committed out there in the wilderness.' She was angry now.

'It was necessary. They must have the opportunity to express their wrath.'

'They could as readily express their wrath with a

lightning bolt or a falling tree! I will not have you provoking them to destroy you.'

'Tanith, please let me—'

'I can see, my lord, that you will require stricter supervision in the future. I want a lover not a hero.'

'But, Tanith, the gods' answer was favourable. Don't you see, now we need feel no guilt.'

'I never felt guilt, then or now. But, Holiness, I will feel wrath beside which that of the gods will pale if again you risk your life needlessly.'

Huy turned to her, and shook his head with mock sorrow.

'Oh Tanith, what would I ever do without you?' And her stern expression softened.

'My lord, that question will never arise.' And at that moment the empty wine bowl slipped from the old priestess's fingers and spun on one end across the mud floor. Its circles narrowed, until it settled into silence and the priestess let out a long contented snore and bowed forward. Huy caught her and eased her backwards onto the cushions. He laid her out comfortably, and arranged her robe modestly about her. She was smiling and burbling and whistling in her sleep.

Huy straightened up and Tanith stood close beside him. They turned to each other and embraced, coming together slowly and carefully. Her lips had a glossy feeling, cool and firm. Her soft hair brushed his cheeks, and her body pressed boldly against his.

'Tanith,' he whispered. 'Oh Tanith, there is so much I want to tell you.'

'My lord, your voice is the most beautiful I have ever heard. Your wisdom and wit are celebrated throughout the four kingdoms – but please do not talk now.'

Tanith pulled gently out of his embrace, took his hand and led him softly from the room.

Over the months that followed, Tanith's chaperone developed a peculiar taste for Huy's wine. At the temple feasts she was wont to disparage the quality of the wine served by the Reverend Mother, comparing it most unfavourably against the other, and she would always end with a word of praise for the Holy Father himself.

'A dear, dear man,' she would tell her audience. 'None of the nonsense you find with some of the others. Did I ever tell you about Rastafa Ben-Amon, the Holy Father in the reign of the forty-fourth Gry-Lion when I was a novice. Now there was a one!' Her old eyes went a little misty, and she drooled a thread of saliva.

'Drink!' she said with outraged virtue. 'Fight! And other things.' Then she nodded sagely. 'A terrible, terrible man!' And she grinned fondly at her ancient memories.

From the leather pipe, with its pitch-sealed joints, feeble gusts of air puffed like the dying breaths of a dinosaur. Driven by the great bellows at the surface, the circulation of fresh air had lost most of its force here, seventy feet below.

Timon leaned against the sweating rock surface, pressing his face to the hose outlet, gasping at that scanty trickle of air in the hellish heat and sulphurous atmosphere of the underground workings. He was lean, every rib showed clearly through the black skin, each sinewy muscle was outlined. His head was skull-like, with gaunt cheek-bones and deep eye-sockets in which the smouldering fires of his indomitable spirit still burned.

All fat and spare flesh had been burned off him by the ceaseless toil and the heat. Even now a sheen of moisture squeezed from the pores of his skin, highlighting the scars which criss-crossed his back and curled around his rib-cage – scars that patterned his arms and legs, scars long healed into thick ridges and shiny grooves, scars fresh and pink, scars still thick-scabbed and oozing. The chain shackles hung loosely at his neck and wrists and ankles. They had rubbed coarse calloused circles around his neck and limbs, slave marks that he would carry to his grave.

He sucked in the air, his chest pumping, swelling and subsiding, the ribs beneath the skin fanning open and closing. Around him the smoke swirled, dimming the lamp flames. The heat was a violent shimmering thing, and the rock at the face glowed still, although the fires had burned to thick beds of ash.

For five days now they had been attempting to break up this intrusion of hard green serpentine rock which was obscuring the gold reef. Sixteen men had died in the attempt, suffocated by the steam and smoke, struck down by flying shards of exploding rock or merely overcome by the heat to fall swooning onto the glowing floor and to sizzle while their flesh stuck to the hot rock and came away in stinking slabs from the bone.

From the shaft above him, dangling on a plaited reed rope, one of the water bladders was lowered to him. Made from the whole skin of an ox, carefully stitched and with the joints waterproofed with pitch the bladder contained forty gallons of liquid, a mixture of sour wine and water.

Timon doused his leather cloak in the filthy warm water of the wooden trough beside him, then one at a time he lifted his feet and dipped them into the trough, soaking his leather leggings and the sandals. The soles of the sandals were reinforced with five thicknesses of leather to withstand the heat of the rock floor. Timon threw the cloak across his shoulders, bound the linen cloth over his mouth and nose, took one last breath from the air pipe and held it. Then he ducked under the dangling water bladder and took the weight on his shoulders. Reaching up, he jerked loose the tail of the knot that held it, and, bowed under the weight of the liquid, he staggered up the tunnel.

As he approached the face, the wet soles of his sandals began spluttering and stinking. He could feel the heat through the thick leather. Heat from the rock walls hammered at him, a physical force against which he had to fight his way forward.

There was little time in which to work. Already his abused lungs were pumping painfully, but he dared not draw a breath of this poisonous smoke-laden air. The heat was scalding the exposed skin on his arms and face, his feet were agony as the rock burned away the protective soles.

Against the face of the drive, he eased the bladder from his shoulder. He moaned with the pain as his careless elbow touched the rock, searing away an inch of skin and leaving the pink raw flesh exposed.

He lowered the bladder to the floor, whirled and ran back through swirling fumes and heat down the tunnel with his chains jangling loosely under the cloak. This was the moment when men died, when the hot rock ate through the water bladder too swiftly, before the bearer was out of the danger area.

Behind Timon the bladder popped, forty gallons of liquid drenched the hot rock, the sudden contraction of the strata shattered the surface, the rock burst explosively and a sharp sliver of it hit Timon in the back of the head, a glancing razor touch that sliced down to the bone of his skull. He staggered, knowing that to fall on this burning floor was to die horribly. He kept his feet while with his senses reeling he reached the water trough and plunged his head quickly into the filthy scummy water. Then with dirty water and fresh blood streaming down his back, he clutched the air pipe with both hands and panted into it. He was coughing and retching and his eyes were blinded with the tears of pain.

It took him minutes to recover a little of his strength, and he staggered to the ladder that led to the level above. As he climbed, the next water bladder was being lowered, and he squeezed himself against the side of the narrow shaft to allow it past. He climbed fifty feet in darkness and then crawled over the edge into a dimly lit low-roofed cavern.

The slave-master saw him grovelling on the lip of the shaft.

'Why have you left your station?' And the long lash of the hippo-hide kiboko curled wickedly around Timon's ribs. He writhed at the sting of it.

'My head,' he gasped. 'I'm hurt.' And the slave-master stepped closer to him, stooping to examine the clotted cut in the back of Timon's scalp from which dark blood still welled. He grunted impatiently.

'Rest, then.' And turned to a row of ten squatting slaves. They were all incorrigibles, wearing the same heavy chains as Timon, and their bodies were also scarred and abused. The slave-master selected one of them, prodding him with the sharpened point of the whip.

'You next. Quickly now.' The slave stood, and shuffled to the mouth of the shaft, moving stiffly for the damp of the workings was in all their bones. At the edge of the shaft the slave paused and peered fearfully into that dreadful fuming pit.

'Move!' grunted the slave-master and the kiboko whistled and clapped against his flesh. He went down the ladder.

Timon dragged himself to the low bench against the wall. He sat with his elbows on his knees and his face in his hands. His lungs ached with the smoke and the cut in his scalp burned and stung. None of the other slaves looked at him. Each man was sunk in his own private hell, uncaring and silent. Beside Timon a man began to cough, a monotonous hacking sound, and a little bloody saliva wet his lips and glistened in the lamp light. He was dying of the lung sickness of the miners. The dust of powdered rock had filled his lungs, solidifying like concrete and turning his lungs to stone. None of them moved, none of them spoke.

The younger slave-master paced restlessly back and forth before them. He was a swarthy bearded man, part Yuye, a freed-man as like as not. He wore a linen tunic with light body armour, enough to turn a dagger's point, and an iron helmet to protect his skull from the rough roof of the tunnel. At his waist were belted a short iron sword and a slave club studded with iron nails. He was tall and hard-looking, with flat sinewy muscle in his arms and legs. A cruel man, selected to work with the incorrigibles because of his brutality. There were always two of them. The other slave-master was an older man with a frosting of grey in his beard and a pale sickly-looking face. But he was big in the shoulder, and dangerous, as cruel as the younger man and more experienced. From above, five bladders of liquid were lowered into the shaft, and five times a thick rush of steam swirled from the dark mouth as they were used to quench the heated rock.

'Enough!' the younger slave-master bellowed down, and the slave crawled up out of the pit and lay on the edge coughing and retching. He was filthy with ash and sweat and mud, and he vomited a little yellow bile into the mud.

'Take him away,' ordered the slave-master and two of them shambled forward and dragged him away to the bench.

The younger slave-master's eyes travelled along the row, and they stiffened into awareness, each trying to will the choice away from himself.

'You.' The sharp point of the whip dug spitefully into Timon's ribs. 'You did not finish your shift.'

There was no right of appeal, protest was folly, Timon had learned long ago. He stood up, and shuffled to the shaft. He steeled himself to the descent, but the delay was too long, and the hippo-hide whip seared its white flash of agony across the tenderness beneath his armpit.

It began as a reflex of pain, Timon lifted his arms to protect himself and the chains swung. In a sudden orgasm of anger and pain, Timon whirled the heavy links just as the slave-master swung the next whip stroke. The chain wrapped about the slave-master's forearm and the bone snapped with a sharp brittle sound.

He backed away with a startled cry, and his broken arm dangled loosely at his side. Behind him the older man drew his sword. It came out of the scabbard with a harsh rasp. He was fifty paces away down the tunnel.

Two of them now, for the younger man was groping left-handed for his sword. Somewhere beneath the slave dullness, the blankness of the slave animal mind, a spark burned. Huy Ben-Amon's training came back to Timon: of two enemies – separate them and attack the weaker first.

Flailing the chain Timon leapt at the younger slave-master, and the man went down in the mud.

Timon leapt over him, and caught the second man's sword stroke on the iron shackle at his wrist. The blow jarred him to the shoulder, and numbed his arm, but he ran in under the next stroke and threw a twist of the chain about the man's throat. He drew tight and held it.

The older man dropped his sword and clutched desperately at Timon's hands, at the links of iron that were strangling him.

Timon found that he was growling like a dog as he jerked and twisted the chain tighter. Suddenly the slave-master's hands dropped away, his tongue fell out between slack and swollen lips and there was the sharp acrid odour of faeces as his sphincter muscle relaxed. Timon let him down onto the floor, and picked up his sword from the mud.

He turned to the younger slave-master who had crawled

to his knees, still stunned. He had lost his helmet, and he was cradling his broken arm against his chest.

Timon stood over him and with the short sword chopped his skull open. The slave-master fell face downwards into the mud.

Timon stood back and looked about the drive quickly. From the first blow to the last only ten seconds had passed, and there had been no outcry.

Timon looked down at the sword in his hand, the blade was dulled with mud and blood, but he felt the despondency of abject slavery fall away. He felt the spark burst into flame, felt himself become a man again.

He looked at the other slaves sitting on the bench. Not one of them had moved. Their eyes were dull, incurious. They were not men. Timon felt a chill as he looked at them. He needed men. He must have men.

There was one of them. His name was Zama. A young man of Timon's age. A wild slave, taken beyond the river. He had not worn his chains for a year yet. Timon stared at him, and saw his eyes come into focus, saw his chin lift and the muscles in his jaw clench.

'Hammer!' Timon commanded. 'Bring a hammer!' Zama stirred. It was an effort of will for him to break the pattern of slavery.

'Hurry,' said Timon. 'There is little time.' Zama picked up one of the short-handled iron-headed mining adzes, and stood up from the bench.

Timon felt his heart soar within him. He had found a man. He held out his wrists, with the bloody sword in his hand.

'Strike off these chains,' he said.

Lannon Hycanus was pleased, but trying not to make it obvious. He stood by the window, and looked down towards the harbour where five galleys lay against the stone jetty. Lannon twisted a curl of his beard about one finger, and smiled secretly.

In the room behind him Rib-Addi was reading in his prim and precise voice, combing his fingers through his scraggily grey beard.

'Into Opet this day from the southern plains of grass, fifty-eight large tusks of ivory, in all sixty-nine talents.'

Lannon turned quickly, a scowl masking his pleasure.

'You attended the weighing?' he demanded.

'As always, my lord,' Rib-Addi assured him, and his clerks looked up from their writings, saw the Gry-Lion's expression soften and they grinned and bobbed their heads ingratiatingly.

'Ah!' Lannon grunted, and turned back to the window, while Rib-Addi resumed his reading. The voice was monotonous, and Lannon found his attention wandering although his subconscious was alert for a false note in the book-keeper's voice. Rib-Addi had the habit of raising his voice slightly whenever he reached a portion of the accounting which might cause the Gry-Lion's displeasure – a lower return, an estimate unfulfilled – and immediately Lannon pounced on him. This convinced Rib-Addi that the Gry-Lion was a financial genius, and that he could hide nothing from him.

Lannon's mind drifted away, picking idly at stray thoughts, turning over mental stones to see what scurried out from under. He thought of Huy, and felt a cold breeze ruffle the surface of his contentment. There was a flaw in their friendship. Huy had changed towards Lannon, and he searched for the reason. He discarded the thought that it might be the aftermath of their long estrangement. It was something else. Huy was withdrawn, secretive. Seldom would he spend his nights in the palace, sharing the dice and wine and laughter with Lannon. Often when Lannon sent for him in the night, instead of Huy arriving with his lute slung on his shoulder and a new ballad to sing, the slave would return with a message that Huy was sick or sleeping or writing.

Lannon frowned now, and at that moment he heard the tell-tale rise in Rib-Addi's voice and he swung around and glared at them.

'What?' he bellowed, and their faces were yellow-white with fright. The clerks ducked their heads over their scrolls.

'My lord, there was a heavy fall of rock in the southern end of the mine,' Rib-Addi stuttered. It never ceased to amaze him that from a mass of figures Lannon would instantly pounce on a ten per cent decrease of output from one of the dozens of tiny mines of the middle kingdom.

'Who is the overseer?' Lannon demanded, and ordered the man replaced.

'It is carelessness, and I will not have it so,' Lannon told him. 'The yield is affected, valuable slaves wasted. I would rather spend more on shoring timber, it is cheaper so in the end.'

Rib-Addi dictated the order to one of the clerks, and Lannon turned back to the window and his thoughts of Huy. He remembered how it had been before, how Huy's presence had provided the zest that made each triumph more valuable, and each disappointment or disaster easier to surmount. All the good things happened when Huy was there.

In a rare moment of self-honesty Lannon realized that Huy Ben-Amon was the only human being that he could look upon as a friend.

His position had isolated him from all others. He could not approach them for the warmth and comfort that even a king needs. His wives, his children feared him. They were uneasy in his presence, and left it with obvious relief.

In all his kingdom there was only one person with the blend of courage, honesty, and disregard of consequence which allowed him to live in the king's presence without shrivelling.

'I need him,' Lannon thought. 'I need him much more than he needs me. Everybody loves him, but he is the only one who truly loves me.' And he grimaced as he remembered how Huy had defied him, and it was he, Lannon Hycanus the forty-seventh Gry-Lion of Opet, who had suffered most during the estrangement.

'I will not let him go again,' he vowed. 'I will not let him draw away from me like this.' And his self-honesty persisted. He saw that he was jealous of his priest. 'I will destroy anything which comes between us. I need him.'

He thought of this latest journey of Huy Ben-Amon's. Was it truly a matter of such urgency that the High Priest must travel 400 miles, taking with him two cohorts of his legion and the priestess and oracle of Opet, to consecrate some minor shrine to the goddess at a desolate garrison outpost in the northern kingdom? Lannon thought it more likely that Huy was leaving Opet for some devious reason of his own, and the result was that Lannon was bored, lonely and irritable. Huy knew that Lannon had planned a feast for his name-day.

The clash of urgent armoured feet interrupted Lannon's thoughts. He turned from the window as three of his high officers burst into the room. With them was a centurion in dusty cloak and unburnished armour. There was dust in his beard and dust coated his sandals and greaves. He had travelled fast.

'My lord. News of the worst possible kind.'

'What is it?'

'A slave rising.'

'Where?'

'At Hulya.'

479

'How many?'

'A great many. We are not sure. This man,' indicating the centurion, 'has seen it.'

Lannon turned to the weary officer. 'Speak!' he ordered.

'I was on patrol, Majesty. Fifty men on a sweep to the north. We saw the smoke, but by the time we returned to the mine it was finished. They had opened the compounds, slaughtered the garrison.' He paused, remembering the dead men with their bowels ripped open and the bloody mush of castration between their legs. 'They had gone, all except the sick and the lame. Those they left.'

'How many?'

'About 200.'

'What did you do with them?'

'We put them to the sword.'

'Good!' Lannon nodded. 'Continue.'

'We followed after the main party of slaves. There were more than 5,000 when they left Hulya, and they moved northwards.'

'Northwards,' Lannon growled. 'The river, of course.'

'They are moving slowly, very slowly. And they plunder and burn as they go. We could follow them by the smoke and the vultures. The population ahead of them flees, leaving all to them. They devour the land like locusts.'

'How many? How many?' Lannon demanded. 'We must know!'

'They have opened the compounds at Hulya, and Tuye and a dozen other mines – all the field slaves have flocked to join them,' the centurion answered.

One of the officers hazarded, 'There must be 30,000 of them, then?'

'At least, Majesty,' the centurion agreed.

'Thirty thousand, in Baal's holy name,' whispered Lannon. 'Such a multitude!' Then his anger came and he spoke harshly. 'What force have we to oppose their march? How many legions are mobilized?'

'There are two legions at Zeng,' an officer volunteered.

'We could not move them in time,' Lannon answered.

'One legion here at Opet.'

'Too far, too far,' Lannon growled.

'And two more along the south bank of the great river.'

'And they are scattered in garrisons spread over a distance of 500 miles. All the others are disbanded?' Lannon asked. 'How long to call them up?'

'Ten days.'

'Too long,' Lannon snapped. 'We must put down this rising with the uttermost ruthlessness. Rebellion is a plague, it spreads like fire in dry papyrus beds. We must isolate it, and quench it. Every spark of it. What other force have we?'

'There is His Holiness,' one of the officers murmured diffidently, and Lannon stared at him. He had forgotten Huy. 'He is at Sinal, directly in the slaves' lines of march to the north.'

'Huy!' said Lannon softly, and then was silent while his officers plunged into an animated discussion.

'He has only two cohorts with him – 1,200 men – he would not engage an army of 30,000.'

'No army, but a slave rabble.'

'Thirty thousand, none the less.'

'We cannot reinforce him in time.'

'It would be folly to try odds like that – and, my lord, Ben-Amon is no fool.'

'The nearest reserves are at Sett on the river.'

'Ben-Amon will not fight,' one of them declared, and they looked to Lannon for his opinion.

Lannon smiled. 'Content yourselves. Ben-Amen will fight. At a time and a place of his own choosing His Holiness will fight.' Then the smile was gone. 'I will march in four hours with all available troops to support Ben-Amon. Issue mobilization orders to all the disbanded legions, send runners to Zeng.'

'Will there be a battle?' Tanith asked. Her eyes sparkled green with anticipation, and her lips were parted expectantly. 'I mean, a real battle like the ones you sing about?'

Huy grunted without looking up from his writing pallet where he was formulating his orders to the garrison commander at Sett.

'Gather to you all troops within your sector and hold them within your walls. Account to me for your store of javelins, arrows and other weapons. What force of elephant do you command? Command the galleys of the river patrol to anchor beneath your walls and await my orders. Inform me of the level of the river. What fords are passable?

'I will join you within six days to assume command. It is my intention to dispute the enemies' passage of the river at—'

Tanith slipped off the couch and crossed the tent. She came up behind Huy and put a finger in his ear.

'My lord.'

'Please, Tanith. I am busy on affairs of moment. This is urgent.'

'No more urgent than a reply to my question – will there be a battle?'

'Yes,' Huy replied testily. 'Yes, there will.'

'Oh, good!' Tanith clapped her hands. 'I have never watched a real battle.'

'Nor will you now!' replied Huy grimly as he resumed his writing. 'You will leave tomorrow morning on a war elephant with an escort of fifty men. You are going home to Opet until this trouble is over.'

Tanith returned to the couch and plumped herself down upon it with the skirts of her tunic drawn up wantonly about her smooth thighs. She glared at the back of Huy's head, and her lips compressed into a stubborn line.

'That, Holy Father,' she whispered inaudibly, 'may be *your* plan!'

Tanith lay unsleeping and listened to the voices of Huy and his officers as they planned the campaign. Her tent was placed conveniently close to that of the High Priest, and the unlit space between them could be crossed without observation by the sentries. This journey to Sinal had been planned by Huy as a love tryst, an escape for them from the restraints of Opet.

Across the tent from her, Aina, the ancient priestess, burbled and muttered in her sleep. Tanith picked up one of her sandals from beside the couch and threw it at her. Aina hiccupped and subsided into silence.

Tanith was too excited by the momentous events in which she had been caught up for her to even contemplate sleep. A savage slave army was trundling down upon them, tens of thousands of wild men, leaving behind them a wide swathe of rape and slaughter and fire-blackened earth.

All that day the refugees had poured into the camp, each of them bringing fresh tales of horror and death. To oppose these savages was Huy Ben-Amon and his small band of heroes, outnumbered twenty to one. It was the stuff of legend, and Tanith would not miss a moment of it. In her mind the outcome was assured, in the ballads the hero always triumphed. He was the favourite of the gods, and therefore invincible. It was a pity merely that the favourite of the gods in the usual masculine fashion was being tiresome, but Tanith had laid her plans.

It was long after midnight before Tanith heard the officers taking loud leave of Huy, and clumping away to their own tents. She sat up, and started to induce tears to flood her eyes. She could usually achieve this by remembering a puppy she had owned as a child. A leopard had taken it. Tonight the trick would not work and she had to resort to rubbing her eyes with her knuckles.

Huy lay on his couch, with the lamp wick trimmed low so the corners of the tent were in darkness. He came up quickly on one elbow when Tanith slipped in through the tent flap, and before he could speak she had thrown herself on the couch beside him and wrapped her arms about his neck. She was shivering violently.

'What is it, my heart?' Huy was alarmed.

'Oh my lord, a dream. A dream of ill omen.' And Huy felt icy little prickles of dread upon the back of his neck. In two years he had learned that Tanith was truly possessed of the gift of prescience. She was capable of vivid glimpses of the future, from small incidents to matters of the gravest moment. If Huy primed her on the course her prophecies should take, it was only on the more mundane consultations. He had, however, developed a hearty respect for her abilities. Tanith knew this as she whispered, 'I walked upon a night field lit only by the funeral fires.' And Huy held her closer, feeling the chill spreading through his body – night, funeral fires, ill-omens indeed.

'I was weeping, my lord. I do not know why, but there was a great sense of loss. There had been a battle. The field was littered with weapons, and broken shields. I came upon the standard of the sixth legion, the sunbird, broken and discarded in the dirt.' Huy shuddered with awe, the sunbird thrown down! It was not only the symbol of his legion, but his own personal totem.

'Then our Lady Astarte was with me. She also was weeping. Silver tears that ran down across her white face. She was very beautiful and very sad. She spoke to me, chiding me sorrowfully. '"You should have stayed with him, Tanith. This would never have happened if you had stayed with him."'

Huy felt the quick stab of doubt through his superstitious awe. He placed his hands on Tanith's shoulders and held her away to study her face. Her eyes were reddened, and tears had washed her cheeks, but still he was suspicious. It seemed a little too neat, and he had learned that when Tanith set her heart on something she was not easily put off.

484

'Tanith,' he said severely. 'You know how grave a matter it is to misrepresent the words of the gods.'

Tanith nodded fervently. 'Oh yes, my lord.'

'As a seeress you have a sacred duty,' Huy insisted, and Tanith wiped her cheeks and remembered how Huy had used that sacred duty to steer the political and economic life of the nation, not to mention his personal profit. She could not deny herself a wicked pleasure in paying him in his own coin.

'I know it well, Holy Father.' Huy stared at her but could find no evidence of guile. Unable to withstand the scrutiny of those dark eyes a moment longer, Tanith buried her face in his neck once more and waited silently. The silence lasted a long time, before Huy finally admitted defeat.

'Very well,' he gruffed. 'I will keep you with me, if that is what the goddess wants.' And Tanith hugged him closer and smiled triumphantly into Huy Ben-Amon's curly beard.

For five days Huy probed and tested that moving mass of humanity as it flowed on towards the great river like a vast black jelly-fish. Always he moved back, retreating ahead of it, keeping his tiny force compact and well under his hand, using it with economy and purpose.

On the fifth day he linked up with the garrison at Sett. Mago, the elderly commander, placed himself under Huy with 1,800 archers and light infantry, 12 war elephants, 2 patrol galleys of 100 oars each, and the garrison's considerable arsenal.

Huy greeted him in the heated noonday on a small hill a dozen miles south of the river, and he led Mago aside out of earshot of the staff.

'I am honoured to serve under you, Holy Father. They say there is glory for those that follow the standard of the Sunbird.'

'There will be enough glory for all here, I warrant you,'

Huy told him grimly, and pointed across the open forest land. 'There they are.'

The slave army moved like a thick column of foraging ants, and a pale mist of dust rose above the trees.

'What thought comes first to your mind, Captain?' Huy asked quietly, and Mago studied the distant army.

'From here, my lord, they look like any other army on the march,' he muttered doubtfully.

'And does that not strike you as odd? This is not an army, Mago, it is a rabble of escaped slaves. Yet it moves like an army.'

Mago nodded quickly, understanding. 'Yes! Yes! They are in hand, you can see it. It is true, you would not expect such control.'

'There is more to it than that,' Huy told him. 'You will see it demonstrated in a moment, for I have arranged a little entertainment. I believe in giving these slaves plenty of pepper in their diet. We will raid their baggage in a moment, and then you will see what I mean.'

They were silent for a moment, watching the enemy move slowly down towards them.

Then Huy asked, 'What is the state of the river, Mago?'

'My lord, it is very low.'

'The ford is passable?' Huy insisted. 'How deep is it?'

'It can be crossed on foot. The water at the deepest is neck-deep, but flowing fast. I have had the guide ropes cut.'

Huy nodded. 'They are moving towards the ford at Sett. I have been sure of that from the moment when they chose the Lulule pass of the escarpment.' Huy was silent a moment longer. 'That is where I will destroy them,' he went on firmly, and Mago glanced sideways at him. 'Destroy' seemed a strange word for a General of 3,000 men to use in connection with an army of 30,000.

'My lord!' one of Huy's officers shouted. 'The attack begins!' And Huy hurried across to join the group.

'Ah!' he said with satisfaction. 'Bakmor has chosen his moment well.'

From their carefully prepared ambush, Bakmor's 500 heavy infantry men charged into the flank of the column. Huy's favourite had picked a weak spot in the protective screen of black spearmen. His axemen hacked their way through to the baggage train, and the drivers of the bullock wagons jumped from their seats and ran, the women bearers dropped the baskets of grain from their heads and followed them in a shrieking panic.

Swiftly the attackers slaughtered the oxen in their traces, and piled the grain baskets in heaps. Fire from the earthenware pots was fanned to life and within minutes the plundered food stores of the slave army were ablaze.

'Look!' Huy pointed out to Mago the response of the slaves to this sudden onslaught. From head and tail of the column formations of spearmen were doubling back and forward in the classical manoeuvre of envelopment. The movement was not executed with any of the precision of a trained legion. It was slow and unwieldy, a mere parody of the correct formations, but it was recognizable.

'Remarkable!' Mago exclaimed. 'A soldier commands them, one at least who has read the military statutes. Your officer must be careful now.'

'Bakmor knows what to do,' Huy assured him, and as he spoke the distant axemen formed up quickly into the testudo formation, an armoured tortoise of shields, and they trotted out between the enclosing arms of spearmen, beating the encircling movement with minutes to spare. Behind them the baggage train burned, smearing black smoke across the tree-tops.

'Good! Good!' Huy grinned his pleasure and relief, slapping his thigh with pleasure. 'Sweetly done! Now, let the slave commander show if he is as great a quartermaster as he is a tactician! There will be growling bellies in the enemy camp tonight.' Huy took Mago's arm and led him away. 'A bowl of wine,' he suggested. 'Watching and waiting is almost as thirsty work as swinging the axe.'

Mago smiled. 'Speaking of wine, Holiness. I have a few amphorae of wine that I am sure will give no offence even to a palate as knowledgeable as yours. Will you dine with me this night?'

'I look forward to it with the keenest anticipation,' Huy assured him.

The wine was drinkable, and after the meal Huy and Tanith sang together for the guests. It was a fanciful piece of pornography of Huy's composition, a love duet between Baal and Astarte. Tanith sang the part of the goddess in a sweet and true voice, rendering the more suggestive and ambiguous lines with modestly downcast eyes, that had the guests shouting with laughter and pounding the board with their wine bowls. Huy ignored the pleas for an encore, and setting his lute aside, he became serious. He spoke of the impending battle, warning Mago and his officers not to judge the enemy too lightly.

'I nearly paid dearly for that mistake,' he told them. 'I was tempted to probe their centre in strength, and I found it as soft as freshly kneaded dough. I sensed a quick rout, a chance of victory at a single stroke. With their centre collapsing I would drive through them and split them.' Huy paused, and made the sun sign. 'Praise unto Baal, but a moment before I gave the order to commit and change the probe to a full frontal attack I was warned by an impulse from the gods.' The company assumed expressions of suitable religious solemnity, and a few of them made the sun sign as Huy went on. 'I looked to the enemy's flanks which, naturally, overlapped mine, and I saw how firmly they stood. It seemed to me that the enemy's steadiest and best troops were posted there, and suddenly I remembered Cannae. I remembered how Hannibal had enmeshed the Roman Consul.' Huy broke off suddenly, and an expression of revelation dawned upon his face.

'Cannae! Hannibal!' Clearly he remembered the clay box with the battle counters of Cannae set out upon it. He remembered his own voice lecturing, and a black face intent and listening. 'Timon!' he whispered. 'It's Timon! It must be!'

A round him lay his army, a vast agglomeration of black humanity, hungry and afraid and restless in the night. The fires blossomed like a flower garden upon the southern bank of the great river, and the night sky glowed orange. The fires were for warmth alone, there was no food. There had been no food for two days now, not since they had burned his baggage.

Timon moved silently amongst them, and saw how they huddled about the fires. Hunger had made them cold, and they whispered and moaned, so the sound of his camp was murmurous, a sibilance like the hive sound of wild bees.

He hated them. They were slaves, weaklings. One in fifty of them was a man, one in a hundred was a warrior. When he had longed for a war spear in his hands, they had been a rotten twig. They were slow and clumsy in response to the lightning sallies of the enemy. Fifty of them were no match for one of the splendid warriors that opposed him. He longed for the men of his own tribe, longed to teach them what he had learned, to imbue them with his own sense of purpose, his own dreams of destiny and retribution.

On the bank of the river he stood and looked across the slick black flow of water. The reflection of the stars danced upon the surface, at the shallow place of the ford there were whorls and eddies, a disturbance, as though some monster swam deep.

Three hundred paces out, half-way across the river, was a small islet. The flood waters would cover it, and it was thick with driftwood and mats of stranded papyrus. This was the first stage of the ford. It was here that he would anchor his lines of twisted bark that his men were plaiting now. He would rig the lines at dawn, and attempt to make the crossing in a single day. He knew how heavy his losses must be. They were weak with hunger and wounds and exhaustion, the bark ropes were unreliable, the current was swift and treacherous, and the enemy was as swift and unrelenting.

Timon moved away downstream, passing amongst his sentries, talking quietly with them, stopping to examine the huge coils of bark rope that were laid ready upon the bank, and at last he came to the perimeter of his camp.

Downstream was the garrison of Sett, 1,000 paces away, a Roman mile as Timon now thought of it. There were torches burning upon the walls and Timon could see the sentries moving vigilantly in the light.

Out on the river, anchored in a deep placid pool were the galleys of the river patrol. With oars shipped and sails furled they were saurian in shape, and Timon watched them uneasily. He had never seen warships in action and he did not know what to expect of them. When Huy Ben-Amon had spoken of the great sea battles of the Romans and Greeks and Carthaginians, he had paid scant attention. He regretted it now. He wished he could form some estimate of the threat that these strange craft afforded his crossing.

The sound of voices came faintly to him across the water, and though he could not recognize the words, yet the familiar modulation of the Punic language fanned his hatred. He listened to them and he felt it come up out of the pit of his belly. He wanted to destroy every trace, every memory of this grotesque light-skinned people with their skills and strength and strange gods and monstrous cruelties.

Standing in the darkness and staring at the distant fortress, hearing their voices in the night, he remembered the body of his woman sliding and bouncing over the rough ground, he remembered the slaves wailing in the compounds of Hulya, he remembered the slave smell, the sound and kiss of the lash, the jangling weight of the chains, the searing heat of the rock, the voices of the slave-masters, the thousand other memories burned and branded into his brain. He massaged the thickened chain callouses at his wrist, and stared at his enemies, and from the core of his soul his hatred bubbled and boiled, threatening to flood his reason like the red-hot lava of an active volcano.

He wanted to swing his army about and fall upon them. He wanted to destroy them, destroy every last trace of them.

He found with surprise that he was shaking, his whole body shuddering with the force of his hatred, and with an immense effort of his will, he controlled himself. Sweat poured down his face and chest in the night cool, the rank-smelling sweat of hatred.

'My time is not now,' he thought. 'But it will come.'

There was a presence beside him in the darkness and he turned to it.

'Zama?' he asked, and his lieutenant answered softly.

'The dawn is coming.'

'Yes,' Timon nodded. 'It is time to begin.'

With loving attention Tanith braided his beard, and then twisted it up under his chin and clubbed it out of the way where it would not catch in Huy's breastplate nor afford a grip for a desperate enemy.

She whispered endearments as she worked, the endearments of a childless woman, speaking to him as though he were her infant. Huy sat quietly on his couch, delighting in the deft and gentle touch of her hands, the soft words and the loving tone of her voice; all this contrasted so violently with what the day would bring, and when Tanith rose from the couch and went to fetch his heavy breastplate, he felt a sharp sense of loss.

She helped him to arm, kneeling to buckle the straps of his greaves, fussing with the folds of his cloak, and although she smiled, he could hear the fear in her voice.

He kissed her awkwardly, and the iron crushed her breast as he held her. She made a small movement of protest, half pulling away, then she surrendered to his embrace and, ignoring the pain, pressed herself to him.

'Oh Huy,' she whispered, 'my lord, my love.'

The old priestess pulled aside the hanging reed mat and stepped into the chamber. She saw the two of them clinging to each other, oblivious of all else. Aina stared at them through rheumy old eyes, then her mouth sagged open into a toothless grin and she drew back silently and let the reed mat fall into place.

Tanith drew away at last. She went to the wall against which the vulture axe leaned beside Huy's couch, and she took it up and untied the soft leather sheath from the blade. She came to Huy, standing before him, and she lifted the blade to her lips and kissed it.

'Fail him not!' she whispered to the axe and handed it to Huy.

In the pre-dawn darkness there was an eager group of officers on the ramparts of the fort staring upstream to where the slave army was camped. They were all armed and were eating the morning meal as they stood. They greeted Huy and Tanith with boisterous high spirits, and Tanith watched and listened as they discussed the day. She found it difficult to understand how they could face the possibility of dealing or receiving death with the enthusiasm of small boys for a piece of mischief.

Tanith felt herself excluded from this mysterious male camaraderie, and she was startled by the change which had come over Huy. Her gentle poet, her solemn scholar and shy lover was as inflamed as any of them. She recognized all the signs of his excitement in his fluttering hand gestures, the hectic spots of colour in his cheeks and the high-pitched giggle with which he greeted one of Bakmor's sallies.

'This is the day. Enough waiting,' Huy declared, as he stared upstream into the dawn gloom. There was a heavy mist upon the river, and the smoke from 10,000 campfires obscured the field. He paced restlessly. 'A curse upon this mist! I cannot see if they have strung their lines across the ford yet.'

'Shall I order one of the galleys upstream to investigate?' Mago asked.

'No,' Huy waved the suggestion aside. 'We will know soon enough, and I don't want to draw attention to the galleys yet.' Huy crossed to the parapet on which the food was spread. He poured a bowl of hot wine sweetened with honey and raised it to the company. 'A bright edge to your swords!'

Huy sang the greeting to Baal as the sun came up over a red and smoky horizon, and then standing bare-headed he drew the attention of the gods to the fact that he intended fighting a battle this day. In strong but respectful terms he pointed out that though the men he commanded were the finest, yet the odds were high, and he would need assistance if the day was to be carried. He relied on them for their co-operation. He made the sun sign, and then turned briskly to his staff.

'Very well, you know your stations and duties.' As they dispersed, Huy led Bakmor aside. 'You have a man to attend the priestess?'

Bakmor beckoned to a grizzled old infantry man who stood a short way off, and the man came forward.

'You know your duties?' Huy demanded, and the soldier nodded.

'I will remain with the priestess through the day.'

'Never let her out of your sight,' Huy cautioned him.

'Should the enemy triumph, and it seem that she will fall into their hands, I will—'

'Good,' Huy interrupted him gruffly. 'If it is necessary, make the stroke swift and sure.'

Huy could not look at Tanith; he turned away quickly and went down to where a small boat waited to row him out to the larger of the two galleys.

Huy stood on the castle of the galley and waited. The sun was well up now, and the mist was dispersed. The galley was singled up to a bow anchor, and she faced into the current. The rowers were at their benches, their shields and weapons laid at their feet, the oars feathered and ready.

The slave army was committed to its crossing. Twenty lines had been strung from the south bank to the mid-stream island, and now they were laying the lines from there to the north bank.

The ford was congested with a great struggling mass of humanity. Clinging to the bark ropes, they were wading steadily across towards the island. Only their heads showed, long lines of black dots around which the water swirled and creamed. Already there were fifteen or twenty thousand slaves in the water, and the number increased steadily as the horde on the south side filed down the bank and took to the ropes.

It was happening just the way that Huy had known it

would. The party on the south bank would dwindle to a size which would be a fair match for Bakmor's impatient warriors. Huy smiled as he imagined how Bakmor must be chafing at this delay. He had longer to wait, Huy decided, as he watched the first slaves emerge from the green waters and scramble thankfully out on to the island with their black skins shining wetly in the morning sunlight.

Their thankfulness was premature, Huy thought. There was still the north channel of the river between them and safety. They began filing off the island, while behind them the bark ropes bowed downstream with the weight of human bodies and the island itself swarmed with naked black flesh. It was an awesome spectacle, such a multitude strung across the river, and still a dense mass of black men upon the south bank.

If it is Timon, he will know enough to hold his best men in the rearguard. Huy peered at the men waiting to take their turns upon the ropes, and it seemed that they were steadier and better armed than those in the van. He must let their numbers reduce further before he could risk Bakmor's tiny force against them.

Huy turned his attention back to the ford, from the island the lines of heads were creeping slowly across towards the far bank. He could see now that he would have a difficult choice to make. If he delayed his attack much longer, then many of the fugitives would escape into the dense forests of the north, beyond the reach of his army for ever. However, if he struck before they escaped it would mean committing Bakmor to battle with vastly superior numbers. The choice was a delicate one, and Huy pondered it carefully. His decision was made when he thought suddenly of the day in the future when he would report to his king.

'Not one of them escaped, Majesty.' And he could almost hear the reply. 'I did not doubt it, my bird of the sun.'

Huy turned to the captain of the galley who stood beside him.

'Hoist the standard!' he said quietly, and immediately the order was shouted to the foredeck. The golden battle standard soared to the masthead.

As a hoarse cheer rose from the rowing decks of the galley, Huy saw the battle signal repeated in the other galley anchored on his starboard beam.

In the bows a sailor swung a battle-axe, severing the anchor cable and the galleys spread their wide wings of oars. They dipped and swung and rose, wet and gleaming golden and silver in the sunlight. Under Huy's feet the ship dashed forward against the current, so swiftly that he staggered before he caught his balance. The galleys flew in formation, their great wings beating, arrowing upstream on a diverging course that would carry one through each channel of the river.

'Steer for the centre of their line,' Huy ordered the galley captain, and the order was shouted to the helm.

They raced down on the crowded ropes, strung like black pearls with the heads of struggling men. Above the rush of water, and the creak and dip of oars, Huy heard a mounting hubbub of terror from the men who looked up at the deadly bows that towered above them.

He moved to the bulwark and looked down. He saw their faces turned up towards him, and their eyes showed white in the dark faces. He crushed down the stirrings of his pity, for these were not men. They were the enemy.

The archers in the bows were loosing their arrows into them now. Huy saw an arrow strike one of them squarely in the face and stand there as the man threw his arms high and was swept away by the current.

The galley cut into the heavily laden ropes, slowing slightly and lurching as the weight of them checked the forward dash, then they snapped and burst asunder beneath the iron-shod bows, and the current swept the lines of men away into deep water, washing them close under the walls of the garrison where Huy's archers waited to pick them like windfallen fruit.

The galleys drove through the shallows, scraping their keels against the rock bottom of the ford and then they were into the deep water beyond, and Huy ran to the stern and looked back. The river was filled from bank to bank with screaming, drowning men. Some of them clung to the branches of overhanging trees, others to slippery outcrops of rock, or to floating pieces of driftwood and mats of papyrus. The island was completely hidden by a solid blanket of wet and shivering humanity, and still others were trying to find a foothold upon it, floundering and struggling in the shallows.

There were so many of them that they reminded Huy of a migration of insects, rather than human beings. They were like ants, tens of thousands of ants. He held that thought as he steeled himself to give the next order.

The galley captain was watching him expectantly, he could see the sailors in the bows at the tubes. They were looking up at the castle, waiting for the order.

'Very well, Captain,' Huy said, remembering that they were ants and not men. Instantly the galley captain was shouting his orders, and the ship swung broadside to the current. The other galley conformed to this manoeuvre and from the bows of both of them the deadly jets of Opet's secret weapon, 'Baal's fire', were squirted.

It sprayed upon the surface of the river, spreading smoothly, the sunlight broke into rainbows of colour upon the floating liquid, and the stink of it was oily and rank.

Then magically it burst into flame, the entire surface of the river became a solid sheet of roaring orange flame from which banks of sooty black smoke billowed, and the heat of it was so intense that Huy drew back quickly as he felt his beard singe.

'In Baal's holy name,' Huy whispered, as he watched the

fire, named for the great god Baal, sweep majestically downstream, filling the great river from bank to bank, filling the sky with dark clouds. It flowed over the crowded island, and when it had passed, the blackened bodies lay in high smouldering heaps, while the driftwood and dried papyrus burned like a funeral pyre.

The wall of fire marched downstream, past the fortress walls, searing the vegetation along each bank, sweeping the river clear of life. In ten short minutes 20,000 souls had perished, and their charred bodies floated down towards the sea or washed up as flotsam along the sand banks and back eddies of the river.

After the flames passed, Timon stood appalled and stared at the devastation. He could not believe the dreadful destructive force he had just witnessed, he could not believe that more than half of his army had vanished so swiftly. He was left with a small portion of his original command.

Those left were his best men, but in truth he knew them to be no match for the cohorts that opposed him. Although he realized that he must make his dispositions for the attack which would now surely follow, yet he wasted a few seconds staring longingly across the river to the north where his own land lay. He was cut off from it now, perhaps for ever.

The galleys lay a hundred paces off the bank, with their bows pointed towards him. They were as menacing as two great reptilian monsters, and now he had seen them in action Timon felt fear's chilly breath on his neck when he looked at them.

Behind him rose the roar of challenge and counter-challenge and the clash of shields and weapons. Timon swung about. The second attack had come, as he feared. It had come with the precision and timing he had expected. It had come crashing into his rear at the exact moment when his men's stomachs were cold with the dreadful destruction they had witnessed in the van.

Timon felt his anger swell and buoy him upwards, his hatred rose with it. Anger and hatred, the forces upon which his whole existence depended. Anger that he must fight against men like these with such fragile weapons. Even as he turned to join the conflict he swore an oath that he had sworn a hundred times before. *I will build an army from my own people which will match these pale-skinned devils.*

Timon fought his way towards the rear through the press of his own men. The attack was driving them back steadily, jamming them against the river, packing them so densely that they could neither manoeuvre nor wield their weapons.

It was a nightmare sensation, attempting to find a way through this swaying, surging sea of black bodies. Desperately Timon bellowed his orders, trying to force them forward, trying to make them deploy outwards, but his voice was lost in the battle roar and even his great strength was helpless in this jam of black humanity.

Over the heads of his men he could see the enemy helmets and plumes ringing them. The sword and axe rose and fell to a solemn rhythm, and before them his men dropped their weapons, turned their backs and tried to burrow their way into the massed bodies of their companions. The pressure increased steadily, smothering the ranks behind and driving them steadily back towards the river.

Over the heads of the attackers the archers and javelin men hurled a rain of missiles into Timon's centre, and so densely was it packed that the dead men could not fall but were held upright by their neighbours' striving bodies.

Now the galleys stole in quietly towards the bank and

from the high castles the archers loosed their arrows into the van of Timon's army. The bank began to crumble away beneath the desperate feet, and living and dead slid and fell into the swift waters.

Soon the colour of the water changed from green to brown, and then to the bright scarlet of life blood.

'A river of blood, Holiness,' the galley commander remarked in conversational tones. 'I have heard it sung by the poets before, but this is the first time I have ever seen it.'

Huy nodded without answering. He could see the battle had reached a point of equilibrium. The pressure that Bakmor's cohorts, even strengthened with those of Mago, could exert was insufficient to drive the enemy back another yard. Soon that pressure must relax, for already the axemen were tiring. When that happened the slave army would explode outwards, like a released bowstring. It needed but an ounce more pressure to topple the slaves into the river, but that pressure must come within the next few minutes.

Huy muttered impatiently, 'Come, Bakmor, are you blinded by blood? Has battle-lust drowned your reason? Now is your moment, but it is passing!' And Huy began to pace the wooden deck anxiously. It was so clear to him what should be done, that it amazed him that others could not see it.

'Come, Bakmor, come!' he pleaded, and then he grunted his relief.

'Not a moment too soon!'

Bakmor had charged his war elephants into the massed remnant of Timon's army. Trumpeting and squealing, the huge animals waded through living bodies, crushing them underfoot, lifting men in their trunks and flinging them towards the sky. A terrified screeching of despair went up from 10,000 throats, and Timon's army turned to the water.

'Now!' shouted Huy, and the galleys shot in towards the

bank of the river. They ran aground together, and from them poured 400 heavy axemen, led by Huy Ben-Amon.

His men tried to keep with him. For in the sixth legion the place of honour in battle was at the side of the High Priest. But the vulture axe clave forward so swiftly that it took a good man to pace it.

'For Baal!' And they reaped the bloody harvest so the ground beneath their feet turned to red mud, and the river flowed brightly.

In the midst of it Huy saw Timon. The shock of it slowed his arm for a second, and a spear jabbed at him, scoring his ribs. Huy killed the spearman with a casual back-handed stroke, then cut his way through the press towards Timon. It was slow work, and Timon retreated ahead of him towards the river bank.

'Timon!' Huy shouted in desperation, and those terrible smoky yellow eyes turned to him and held his gaze. They were the eyes of a leopard in the trap, cruel and merciless.

'A challenge!' Huy called. 'Fight me!'

In reply Timon reared to his full height and hurled his spear at Huy. Huy ducked and the point glanced off his helmet and buried itself in the neck of the man beside Huy. The man cried out and fell.

Timon turned and with three strides he had reached the bank of the river. He leapt out into the red waters, and then struck out powerfully in the over-arm stroke that Huy had taught him.

Huy reached the edge of the bank and tore off his helmet and breastplate, he snapped the leather straps of his greaves and kicked off his sandals.

Naked, except for the belt which held his axe, Huy looked out across the river. Timon was out of range of the archers on the bank, he was half-way across to the island in the time which it had taken Huy to strip.

Huy dived cleanly from the bank, and struck the water flat on his belly. Then he was swimming, dragging himself through the bloody water with those long thick arms and churning the surface white with his powerful legs.

On the island Timon had found weapons. The throwing spears of the charred bodies that lay thick upon the ground.

As Huy found his footing and waded ashore, Timon hurled the first of them. Huy deflected the spear with a swing of his axe, catching the spear blade full on the great butterfly-shaped head, swatting the spear out of the air as though it were an insect.

Again Timon threw, and again – but now Huy was charging him across the rocky, corpse-strewn ground, and each thrown spear was caught neatly upon the head of the axe and sent spinning aside to fall harmlessly on the rocky earth.

In desperation Timon stooped and picked up one of the round river boulders as large as a man's head. He lifted it over his head with both hands, and stepped forward as he threw it. The rock caught Huy a glancing blow on his shoulder, and knocked him down on his back with the axe skidding away from his hand.

Timon charged at him, careless in his anger and hatred. Huy bounced off the earth, flipping him forward like a thrown javelin.

The top of Huy's head crashed into Timon's body just below the rib-cage and the air of his lungs rushed out of his throat in a gasp of agony. Timon doubled up and dropped to his knees, clutching at his chest with both hands.

Huy stood over him, and bunched his hand in the manner of the gladiators. He struck Timon with the bony hammer of his fist just below the ear, and Timon toppled forward senseless to the rocks.

'I cannot kill you, Timon,' Huy's voice came to him through the grey mist, and from a great distance. 'Though you deserve death as no one else has done before you. You have betrayed my trust. You have carried the sword against me and my king – you deserve to die.'

Huy's face came into focus, and Timon found himself lying on his back with arms out-stretched. He tried to move and found himself bound. Leather thongs were knotted tightly about his fingers and pegged down to the earth, holding him captive. He rolled his head and found himself on the north side of the island, hidden from watchers on the south bank and alone with Huy.

On the rocks beside him a small fire of driftwood burned. Huy had lit it from a smouldering remnant, and in it was heating a broad spearhead with its shaft snapped off short.

'There is little time. Soon my men will come to find me. And then it will be out of my hands,' Huy explained reasonably. 'I have made an oath to my gods, so I cannot give you the punishment which you have earned. Yet I have a duty to my king and my people. I cannot let you carry the sword against us again.

'The Romans had an answer for this, and though I hate all things of Rome, I must use their methods now.'

Huy stood up, and leaned over Timon.

'I made a mistake with you. No man can ever tame a wild leopard.' Huy held the vulture axe in his right hand. 'You were never Timon, you were always Manatassi. You are as different from me as the colour of my skin is different from yours. There was never a bond between us, it was illusion, for though our mouths speak the same language, our ears hear the sounds differently.

'Your destiny is to seek the destruction of all I hold dear, all that my people have built and tended. My destiny is to protect it, with my very life's blood.' Huy paused, and there was true regret in his heart as he went on. 'I cannot kill you, but I must make sure that you never carry the sword again.'

The vulture axe sang, and Timon screamed once, and then whimpered softly as his severed right hand twitched and trembled like a dying animal on the scorched earth of the island.

Huy fetched the heated spear blade from the fire and sealed off the pumping blood vessels of the stump in a hissing puff of stinking smoke. Then he cut the thongs that still bound Timon.

'Go,' he said. 'You must trust yourself to the river now. My men will come to search the island soon.'

Timon dragged himself down the beach, and at the water's edge he looked back at Huy. His huge black body was scarred and ravaged, and his eyes were terrible.

Slowly he lowered himself into the water, holding the raw stump of his arm across his chest. The current took him, and his head dwindled to a speck upon the wide river, until it was swept beyond the bend below the fort. Huy watched it out of sight, then he stooped and picked up the severed hand from the ground and dropped it onto the fire and piled dry driftwood upon it.

Bakmor had dug his cremation pits along the bank of the river, and he and Huy passed along the ranks of fallen warriors laid upon their last couch of wood. It was the ceremony of farewell, and Huy paused and looked down at old Mago. In death the garrison commander had a dignity which he had lacked in life.

'How sweet is the taste of glory now, Mago?' Huy asked him softly, and it seemed that Mago smiled in his sleep.

Huy sang the praise of Baal, and then he lit the funeral fires with his own hand.

Tanith was not upon the walls to welcome him when they marched back to the fortress of Sett, but Huy found her in her own chamber. She had been weeping and her face was pale, with dark blue smears beneath her eyes.

'I feared for you, my lord. My heart burned within me, but I did not weep. I was very brave through it all. Through all the horror of it. It was only when they told me that you were safe that I cried. Isn't that silly?'

Holding her close, Huy asked, 'Was it like the poets sang it? Was it glorious and heroic?'

'It was horrible,' Tanith whispered. 'Horrible beyond my dreams of horror. It was ugly, my lord, ugly enough to make me despair of beauty.' She was silent then, remembering it all again. 'You poets never tell of the blood, and the wounded screaming and – all the other things.'

'No,' Huy agreed. 'We never do.'

In the night Huy woke and found that Tanith was sitting beside him on the couch. The night lamp was trimmed low and her eyes were dark pools in her face.

'What troubles you?' Huy asked, and she was quiet a few seconds before she spoke.

'Holy Father, you are so gentle, so kind. How could you do what was done today?'

Huy pondered the reply a moment.

'It was my duty,' he explained at last.

'Your duty to slaughter those wretches?' Tanith asked incredulously.

'The law is death to rebel slaves.'

'The law is wrong then,' Tanith declared hotly.

'No.' Huy shook his head. 'The law is never wrong.'

'It is!' Tanith was close to tears again. 'It is!'

'The law is all we have that saves us from the void, Tanith. Obey the laws and the gods and you need never fear.'

'The laws should be changed.'

'Ah!' Huy smiled. 'Change them, by all means, but until they are changed, obey them.'

In the dawn of the next morning Lannon Hycanus arrived at Sett. He arrived at the head of two full legions in battle array, and fifty elephants of war.

'I fear I have been greedy, sire,' Huy told him at the

gates. 'I left you not a single one.' And Lannon shouted with laughter and embraced Huy, turning to his staff with an arm still about Huy's shoulders.

'Which of you was it said that Ben-Amon would not fight?'

That night while he was still sober Huy sang the ballad he had composed to commemorate the Battle of the River of Blood, and Lannon wept at the telling of it, and when it was done he cried out to his own staff.

'Three against 30,000 – it will always be our shame that we did not fight with Huy Ben-Amon that day at Sett.'

Lannon stood. 'I give you the new Commander-in-Chief of all the legions of Opet. I give you Huy Ben-Amon, Axeman of the Gods.'

Then king and priest got very drunk together.

G ondweni was one of the 200 tributary chiefs of the Vendi, and his territory bounded on the broken land of the Kal Gorge, the land of the outcasts. He was fat and prosperous, and because he was a prudent man he regularly left small gifts of salt and meat at a place in the hills where the outcasts came for it. Also because he was a prudent man he gave food and shelter to solitary travellers journeying to the hills or returning from them, and when they left his town the memory of their passing went with them.

Thus a tall gaunt stranger sat one night at his hearth and ate his food and drank his beer. Gondweni sensed power and purpose behind the impassive scarred visage with the fierce yellow eyes. He felt an unusual affinity for this man and he talked more freely than was his wont. Although he spoke the language of Vendi, the traveller seemed to know nothing of the politics and affairs of the tribe, not even the name of the paramount king who had succeeded Manatassi when he was carried off by the white devils from across the river.

'Of Manatassi's six brothers, five died swiftly and mysteriously after drinking of a special brewing of beer, prepared by the middle brother, Khani. Khani alone survived the feast.' And Gondweni chuckled and nodded and winked knowingly at the stranger.

'He is now our king, the Great Black Bull, the collector of the tribute, the Thunder of Heaven, the fat lecher of Vendi with his 500 wives and his 50 young boys.' Gondweni spat forcefully into the fire, and then drank from the beer pot before passing it to the stranger. When he took it Gondweni saw that the stranger's right hand was missing and he steadied the pot with the stump.

'What of Manatassi's counsellors, his war captains, his blood brothers?' the stranger asked. 'Where are they now?'

'Most of them are in the bellies of the birds.' And Gondweni drew a forefinger across his throat expressively.

'Most of them?'

'Some went over to Khani and ate his salt – others spread their wings and flew.' Gondweni pointed out into the hills which showed like the black teeth of an ancient shark against the moon sky. 'Some are my neighbours, chiefs of the outcasts, paying tribute to none, and waiting in the hills for they know not what.'

'Who are they?'

'Zingala.'

'Zingala, the ironsmith?' the stranger demanded eagerly, and Gondweni's expression changed. He turned on the stranger a hard stare.

'It seems to me you know more than is safe,' he said softly. 'Perhaps we should sleep now.' He stood up and pointed out a hut. 'There is a sleeping mat laid out for you, and I will send a young girl for your comfort.'

The stranger's need was like a raging storm on the girl's unresisting body, battering and driving, and Gondweni heard her crying out in pain and fear. He lay awake, troubled and restless, but in the dawn when he went to the stranger's hut the girl lay crumpled in exhausted sleep and the man was gone.

A deep gorge split the mountains, so deep that the path was dark and moss-covered and slippery underfoot. At the head of the gorge a fall of silver plunged down from the cliffs above, and the wind drove it in a fine cold mist into Manatassi's face as he climbed upwards.

At a level place he paused to rest, and the stump of his right arm ached cruelly in the cold. He ignored the pain, pushing it below the surface of his conscious mind, and he looked up the deep dark gut of the gorge.

High above him on the cliff top, outlined against the pale blue of the noon sky was the foreshortened figure of a man. The figure stood very still, and the stillness itself was menacing.

Manatassi ate a little cold millet cake, and drank from the stream of icy clear water, before beginning the climb again. Now there were other figures. They appeared silently and unexpectedly at steep or easily defended places on the trail and they watched him.

One of them stood atop a giant boulder, fully forty feet high, which all but blocked the gorge. He was a tall man, well muscled and heavily armed. Manatassi recognized him, the man had been a captain of one of his old regiments.

Manatassi stopped below the boulder, and let the cloak fall back from his head, exposing his face, but the man did not recognize him, could not see his king in this ravaged face from which pain and hatred had stripped the flesh and which the whip and the club had remoulded.

'Am I so altered?' Manatassi thought grimly. 'Will no man recognize me again?'

He and the man stared at each other for many seconds until Manatassi spoke.

'I seek Zingala, the ironsmith.'

He knew that even though Zingala had joined the outcasts, such a famous craftsman must still have many clients seek him out. He knew that alone and unarmed he would be allowed to pass on such business.

The sentry upon the boulder turned his head slightly and pointed with his chin up the gorge, and Manatassi went on.

There were narrow steps that climbed the black rock cliff beside the waterfall, and when Manatassi came out upon the summit there were armed and silent men waiting. They fell in behind and on each side of him as he strode out along the only path, through the thick forest which covered the crest of the mountain.

The smoke of the furnaces guided Manatassi, and he came at last to a natural amphitheatre of rock, a bowl one hundred paces across, where Zingala worked his art with iron.

The old master was at one of his furnaces, packing the ore into the belly of it, each lump carefully hand selected. His apprentices were gathered around respectfully, ready to add the layers of limestone and charcoal upon the ore.

Zingala straightened up from his task and held aching back muscles as he watched the tall stranger and his escort come down into the bowl. There was something familiar in the man's walk, in the way he carried his shoulders, the tilt of his head, and Zingala frowned. He dropped his hands to his sides, and shuffled uncertainly as the man's features touched a deep memory. The stranger stopped before him and stared into Zingala's face – those eyes, yellow and fierce and compelling. Quickly he looked down at the stranger's feet and he saw the deep cleft between the toes. Zingala wailed and dropped to his face upon the earth. He took one of Manatassi's deformed feet and placed it upon his own grey-frosted pate.

'Command me,' he cried. 'Command me, Manatassi, the great black beast, the Thunder of the Heavens.'

The others heard the name and they fell as though lightning had struck them down.

'Command us,' they cried. 'Command us, black bull of a thousand cows.'

Manatassi looked upon his band of outlaws as they grovelled about him, and he spoke softly but in a voice that cut to the heart of each of them.

'There is but one command I give you, and that is – OBEY!'

The furnace was shaped like the belly of a pregnant woman, and the entrance was slitted like her pudenda between spread thighs of moulded clay.

To fertilize the smelting ore, Zingala introduced the buck-horn nozzle of the bellows into the opening. The nozzle was shaped like a priapus, and the work was done in a strict ritualistic sequence while the apprentices sang the birth chant, and Zingala sweated and laboured like a midwife in his leather apron, pumping away at the leather bellows.

When at last the plug of clay was drawn and the molten metal ran in a fiery stream into the sand moulds there was a murmur of relief and congratulation from the watchers.

Using an anvil of ironstone and a set of special hammers Zingala forged the lion's paw with its five massive iron claws and its pad of solid metal. He filed and dressed and polished it, then he reheated it and tempered it in the blood of a leopard and the fat of a hippopotamus.

One of the skilled leather-workers built a socket of green elephant hide and shaped it to fit the stump of Manatassi's right arm. The iron claw was fixed securely into the leather socket and when it was strapped to Manatassi's stump it made a fearsome artificial limb.

Khani, the paramount ruler of Vendi and foppish half-brother of Manatassi, was with his women when the iron claw tore the top off his skull. The girl beneath him screamed and fainted with the shock of it.

S ondala, the king of Buthelezi, had many subjects, a multitude of cattle, a little grazing land and even less water to carry his people and his kine through a season of drought.

He was a small wiry man, with quick nervous eyes and a ready smile. Of all the tribes along the great river his was the latest to come out of the north, and he was crushed between the powerful Vendi tribe on the one hand and those white-robed, long-bearded, brown-skinned Dravs on the other. He was a desperate man, ready to listen with both ears to any proposition.

He sat in the firelight and grinned and darted quick eyes at the gaunt godlike figure across the hut from him – this king with the ruined face, and bird's feet and clawed hand of iron.

'You have 12 regiments, each of 2,000 men,' Manatassi told him. 'You have five flowerings of maidens each of 5,000. You have, at latest count, 127,000 cattle, bulls, cows, calves and oxen.'

Sondala grinned and wriggled uneasily, amazed at the accuracy of the Vendi king's intelligence.

'Where will you find food and grass and drink for such a multitude?' Manatassi asked, and Sondala smiled and listened.

'I will give you grazing, and land. I will give you a land rich with fruit and lush with grass, a land over which your people will march for ten generations without finding the limits of it.'

'What do you want of me?' Sondala whispered at last, still grinning and blinking his eyes quickly.

'I want your regiments to command. I want your spear in my hand, I want your shield to march beside me.'

'If I refuse?' Sondala asked.

'Then I will kill you,' said Manatassi. 'And take your regiments and all five flowerings of your maidens, and all your 127,000 cattle, except for ten which I will sacrifice upon your grave as a mark of respect to your ghost.' Manatassi grinned then also, and it was such a terrible baring of teeth in that battered face that Sondala's own smile froze.

'I am your dog,' he said hoarsely, and he knelt before Manatassi. 'Command me.'

'There is but one command,' said Manatassi softly. 'And that command is, OBEY!'

In the first year Manatassi made treaties with the Vingo, the Satassa and the Bey. He fought the Xhota in a single devastating battle, employing tactics so revolutionary and relentless that the Xhota king and his wives and courtiers and princes were taken twenty minutes after battle was joined. Instead of massacring the menfolk, and taking the women and cattle as was the custom, Manatassi had only the king and royal family strangled, then he assembled the defeated regiments, still intact and under their own commanders, and he made them swear their allegiance to him. They thundered it in massed voice that seemed to shake the leaves in the trees and rock the hills upon their foundations.

In the second year, after the rains had passed, Manatassi marched westwards as far as that desert coast on which a cold green surf raged eternally. He fought four great battles, strangled four kings – treated with two others, and added almost a hundred thousand warriors to his regiments.

Those close to the great black beast knew that he seldom slept. It seemed there was some driving force within him that denied him rest or pleasure. He ate food without tasting it, in the perfunctory manner in which a man might throw a log upon the fire merely to keep it burning. He never laughed, and smiled only when a task was performed to his satisfaction. He used women with a swift brutality that left them trembling and weeping, and he shared companionship with no man.

Only once did his lieutenants see him show the emotions of a man. They stood upon the tall yellow dunes at the western limit of the land. Manatassi was apart from them, draped in the leopard-skin of royalty and with the blue heron feathers of his head-dress fluttering in the cold breeze that came off the sea.

Suddenly one of the war captains exclaimed aloud and pointed out across the green waters. From out of the banks of silver sea fret, looming like a ghost ship through the mist, sped one of the galleys of Opet. With her single square sail bellied by the trade winds, and her banks of oars beating rhythmically, she sped in silence towards the north on her long voyage of trade to Cadiz.

Again a captain exclaimed, and they all looked towards the king. His face shone and dripped with sweat, and his jaws clenched and ground his teeth together with a sound like rock on rock. His eyes were burning mad as he watched the passage of the galley, and his body shook and shuddered with the strength of his hatred.

The captain ran to aid him, thinking him stricken with sudden fever. He touched the king's arm.

'High-born,' he started, and Manatassi turned upon him

in raging madness and struck him down with the iron claw, ripping half his face away.

'There,' he screamed, pointing with the claw at the disappearing galley. 'There is your enemy. Mark him well.'

Each day brought its own excitements, its secret delights and ventures – and its happiness. It did not seem five years since she and Huy had become lovers, so swiftly had the years sped. Yet it was so, for the Festival of the Fruitful Earth was almost come around once more.

Tanith laughed aloud at the memory of her seduction of Huy, and she made her plans to repeat the performance during the coming Festival. Beside her Aina mumbled a question, peering at her quizzically from the depths of her hood.

'Why do you laugh, child?'

'I laugh because I am happy, old mother.'

'Oh, to be young once again. You do not know what it is like to grow old.' Aina began one of her monologues, and Tanith led her through the bustle of the harbour area, past the low taverns and the taunting street girls to where steps were cut into the stone jetty. She danced down the steps and leapt lightly to the deck of the small sailing craft moored to one of the iron rings in the jetty.

Coming out of the tiny cabin, dressed in rough fisherman's clothes and with a scarf tied about his head, Huy was too late to help her aboard.

'You are late.'

'For your impertinence I shall punish you, just as soon as it is safe,' Tanith warned him.

'I look forward to it,' Huy grinned, and helped old Aina over the gunwale, while Tanith ran forward to cast off the head lines.

Huy was perched in the stern with the steering oar tucked under his arm, and Tanith sitting as close beside him as she could without touching. She had thrown off her cloak, and wore now a light cotton tunic edged with cloth thread and belted with a solid gold chain, a name-day gift from Huy.

Her hair billowed out behind her like black smoke, and her cheeks were flushed. Huy kept glancing at her, and each time she looked at him and laughed for no reason.

The wind was fine on their beam, and as they ran close-hauled for the islands the wind whipped droplets from the bow wave into their faces, and the water was cold in the warmth of the sun. Huy ran the vessel neatly through an almost invisible channel in the reeds, and they emerged into a quiet and sheltered lagoon whose surface was covered with the dark green pads of the water lilies and starred with the blue and gold of their blossoms. Water fowl paddled and dabbled and flighted over and upon the quiet waters.

They were out of the wind here and Huy took up a long pole from the deck and standing in the stern, he poled them across the lagoon to the beach of dazzling white sand. Jumping out into knee-deep water he hauled the vessel up onto the beach.

Amongst the polished black boulders above the beach Huy rigged a sun shelter with a strip of sail, and he helped Aina across the sand and installed her beneath the shelter.

'A bowl of wine, old mother,' he suggested solicitously.

'You are too kind, Holiness.'

They left her there, snoring quietly in the shade, and they walked hand in hand along the ribbon of beach, beyond the curve of the bay. Under the ivory palms Huy spread a cloak on the firm clean sand, and they rid themselves of their clothing and lay together talking and laughing and making love.

Then they bathed together in the clear warm lake water, and, as they lay in the shallows with the wavelets flopping lazily over them, shoals of silvery finger-long fish came to nibble at their naked skin. Tanith laughed and kicked at the tickle of their toothless mouths.

They went to lie in the sun and dry themselves, and Huy looked up at Tanith standing over him. Her hair was sodden and dangled in heavy black ropes down her back and breast. The sun had brought a glow to her shoulders, and there were water drops clinging in her eyelashes. She stood proudly under his scrutiny, and she cupped her breasts, one in each hand.

'Do you see aught different about me, Holy Father?' She asked in her teasing voice, so that Huy smiled and shook his head.

'Look closer,' she invited him, and it seemed then that her breasts were fatter and more pointed, he noticed also that they were marbled with bluish veins beneath the white skin.

'Yes?' Tanith asked, and ran her hands down her body to cradle her belly.

'And here?' she asked. 'Anything different here?' And she puffed out her stomach, laughing at him.

'You are getting fat,' Huy reprimanded her, giving her back her laughter. 'You eat too much.'

Tanith shook her head. 'What I have in here, Holy Father, certainly never went in through my mouth.'

Slowly the laughter dried up in the back of Huy's throat, and he gawked at her.

Huy lay in the darkness and he was still stunned and bemused. It still seemed impossible that some of the seed which he had sown so carelessly should have taken root; were not the priestesses of Astarte instructed in the secret ways of preventing just such an occurrence? This was really an event to rank with earthquake and storm and defeat in battle. Something would have to be done about it, something radical.

Lightly Huy's mind touched upon the thought of the grisly old hags who lived along the harbour front, whose job it was to rectify such blunders. Instantly he rejected the idea.

'No.' He spoke aloud, and then listened to the sound of Tanith's breathing, hoping he had not woken her. He began to moderate his plans; perhaps it was not necessary for such radical action, perhaps he could arrange for another shrine to be consecrated in a remote area of the kingdom, and there, away from prying eyes and busy tongues, she could bear his son. It would be simple enough to find a foster mother, someone he could trust. There were many of the veterans of his legion, men maimed in battle, now living the simple life on one of Huy's estates. Men with fruitful wives, whose breasts were fat and full enough to feed another little lodger.

There they could go as often as the opportunity arose to be with their son. He could imagine it already, the happiness and the laughter, and his son kicking and gurgling, fat-bellied in the sunlight.

Stealthily Huy reached beneath the bed covers, lightly his hand settled on Tanith's naked belly and he began to explore it.

'You cannot feel anything yet,' Tanith whispered, and turned to embrace him. Into his beard she whispered, 'I didn't do the things the priestess taught me. That was very wicked of me, wasn't it? Are you angry with me, my lord?'

'No,' said Huy. 'I am very pleased with you.'

'I thought you would be,' chuckled Tanith contentedly, and snuggled against him, and then she added drowsily, 'I mean, once you got used to the idea.'

The knocking and shouting woke them both and Huy bounded from the couch and snatched up the vulture axe before he was properly awake. Once the initial confusion had quieted, and the house slaves had satisfied themselves by shouted challenge and loud reply that the midnight callers were a contingent of the royal guard, Huy put aside the axe and lit another lamp.

'Holy Father.' One of the body slaves pounded on the door of the bed-chamber.

'What is it?'

'The king's guard. The Gry-Lion cannot sleep. He bids you take your lute and attend him.'

Huy sat on the edge of the couch and cursed softly but meaningfully, running his fingers through his beard and curls, trying to knuckle the sleep from his eyes.

'Did you hear me, Holiness?'

'I heard you,' growled Huy.

'The Gry-Lion said that they were to accept no excuse, and to wait while you dressed, and to escort you to the palace.'

Huy stood up and reached for his tunic, but held his hand as he saw Tanith watching him. Her eyes were enormous in the lamp light, and with her hair in cloudy disorder she looked like a child. Huy lifted the bed clothes and slipped in beside her.

'Tell the king that my picking finger is sore, my throat is raw, my lute strings are broken – and I am drunk,' he shouted, and took Tanith in his arms.

Sheikh Hassan rinsed his fingers in the silver bowl and dried them on a square of silk.

'He seeks to impress us with this show of strength,' Omar, his younger brother, murmured. Hassan glanced at him. His brother was a famous dandy. His beard was washed and perfumed and combed until it glistened, his robes were of the finest silk and his slippers and vest were heavy with embroidery of silk and gold thread. On his finger he wore a pigeon's blood ruby the size of the top joint of a man's thumb. He was misty-eyed from the bhang pipe beside him on the cushions. A dandy perhaps, and a pederast certainly, but nevertheless the possessor of a fine mind and an intuitive perception upon which Hassan relied heavily.

They sat together beneath the ancient fig tree with its widespread branches and its deep dark shade. The dhow that had brought them to this meeting was beached on the white sand of the island below them, and from their vantage point they could look across the channels and sandbanks and slow pools of the great river to the north bank.

There were troops of sea-cow lying on the sandbanks or half submerged in the shallows. Huge grey shapes, like river boulders upon which the white egrets perched unconcernedly.

On the north bank a thin ribbon of dark green vegetation grew along the river, but gave way immediately to the bare brown hills beyond. The country here had a blasted and desolate look to it. The hills were bleak and barren with rounded crests. The earth showed through the sparse dry grass, and the dead trees writhed and held their naked branches to the sky, trees drought-stricken and long dead.

However, as the sheikhs watched so the scene changed. Over the hills spread a dark shadow as though a storm cloud had blotted out the sun.

'Yes,' said Omar. 'This show is to open our ears to his words.'

Hassan spat a stream of bright red juice into the dust, and wiped his beard with silk as he watched the bare hills come to life, watched the dark shadow spread. He had never before seen such a vast concourse of humanity. The regiments and squadrons moved into orderly ranks until they covered the hills. Hassan was nervous, but his face was calm, his eyes grave and only the long brown fingers that fidgeted on the jewelled hilt of his dagger betrayed his disquiet. He had not expected anything like this. He had come to this place expecting to discuss trade and mutual boundaries with the new black emperor who had emerged out of that mysterious and little-known land beyond the river. Instead he had found himself confronted with one of the largest armies the world had ever seen assembled. He wondered if Alexander himself had ever commanded such a multitude.

Omar drew on his bhang pipe, held the smoke and then let it trickle thinly from his nostrils.

'He seeks to impress us,' he repeated, and Hassan's reply was brusque.

'If that is his intention, then he succeeds. I am impressed.'

Still the regiments came pouring over the sky-line in thick but orderly columns. They wheeled and fell into the pattern of the whole as though a single mind directed them, the way shoals of fish or flights of migrating birds react to unspoken commands. Indeed, this seemed to be not a gathering of individuals but a single organism, sprawling but well co-ordinated. Hassan watched it and shivered in the noon heat of the valley.

Upon the north bank all movement ceased, and a massive stillness settled over the serried ranks of black warriors. The stillness seemed more menacing than the preceding movement, and an expectant hush filled the valley, a sense of mounting tension which became unbearable, until Hassan swore and made a gesture as though to rise.

'I will not pander to the whims of a savage. This is an insult. We will go. He must come to us if he wishes to talk.' But the gesture never matured, and he sank back upon the cushions and fretted in silence until his brother spoke.

'It seems,' said Omar, 'that the world we know has changed, brother. What was true yesterday, is true no longer.'

'What is your advice?'

'Let us find the new truths, and examine them. It is possible that we shall still find something to our advantage in all of this.'

On the hills opposite them there was a disturbance, a stirring of the ranks, the way the tops of tall reeds move when a lion passes through. The sheikhs strained their eyes, calling out to their guards for advice of what was happening, but any reply was lost in an ocean of sound. The earth shook beneath the stamp of hundreds of thousands of feet, the air quivered with the drumming of spears on shields, and from the densely packed hills a single voice from the throats of that black multitude roared the royal salute to a king.

The storm of sound rolled across the valley, and died in echoes against the sky and the southern hills. Again the stillness and silence, then a large war canoe with fifty rowers a side was launched from the sandbank and shot across the green waters towards the island.

A man stepped out onto the white beach, and walked alone up the bank to where the sheikhs waited beneath the fig-tree. The very fact that he came without an escort was a mark of contempt, a sign of his strength and invulnerability.

He wore a cloak of leopard-skin and sandals upon his feet but he carried no ornament nor weapon. He stood tall and gaunt over the sheikhs, and they seemed to shrink in significance beside his bulk.

He looked at them with the fierce yellow eyes of a bird of prey, eyes that seemed to rake their souls.

'I am Manatassi,' he said in a soft deep rumble. 'I am the Black Beast.' They had known enough not to be surprised that he spoke their language fluently.

'I am Hassan, Sheikh of Sofala, Prince of Monomatapa and Viceroy of the Chan Emperor.'

'You love the yellow metal.' Manatassi said it like an accusation, and Hassan was taken off balance. He blinked and glanced at Omar.

'Yes,' said Omar. 'We love it.'

'I will give you enough to glut you,' said Manatassi.

Omar licked his lips, an unconscious expression of greed, and he smiled.

'You must have much of the precious stuff?' Hassan asked, this direct approach to trade was distasteful. This man was a savage, he did not understand the niceties of diplomacy. Yet gold was worth a little gaucherie, especially in the quantities this self-styled black beast hinted at. 'Where does it come from?'

'From the treasure house of Lannon Hycanus, Gry-Lion of Opet and king of the four kingdoms,' said Manatassi, and Hassan frowned quickly.

'I do not understand you?'

'Then you are stupid,' said Manatassi, and Hassan flushed dusky rose beneath his brown skin and a retort rose swiftly to his lips, but he felt his brother's cautionary fingers press his wrist.

'Explain it to me,' said Omar. 'Do you intend to war with Opet?'

'I will destroy them – destroy their people, their cities and their gods. I will leave not a trace of them, not a single living one.' The giant Negro began to tremble, a little white spittle wet his full purple lips and a light sheen of sweat greased his battered features.

Omar smiled delicately. 'We heard of a battle at a place named Sett.'

Manatassi roared, a sound of pain. He leaped towards the sheikh and from under his cloak he drew the clawed iron hand and held it in Omar's face. Omar scrambled backwards, and clung to his brother.

'Do not mock me, little brown man, do not mock me, or I will tear out your liver.'

Omar moaned with terror and sweat ran down into his beard.

'Peace,' Hassan intervened hurriedly. 'My brother meant only to remark that the legions of Opet will be difficult to destroy.'

Manatassi gulped for air, still shaking with his rage. He turned away and walked to the edge of the island and stared down into the water. His shoulders heaved, and his chest panted for air, but slowly he calmed himself and came back to them.

'Do you see them?' He pointed to his army that still darkened the hills.

'Numbers alone – will they be sufficient?' Hassan asked. 'You challenge a mighty foe.'

'I will show you,' said Manatassi, and he lifted the iron claw. Instantly one of his war captains ran from the canoe and knelt before him.

Manatassi spoke a few words in the Vendi language and pointed out at the river. The captain sprang to his feet with an expression of joy lighting his dark face. He saluted, went bounding away down the bank, leapt into the bows of the canoe and was sped swiftly across to the north bank.

The sheikhs watched with puzzled interest as a new movement began amongst the massed warriors on the far bank. They moved forward in two thick columns, swarming into the water, and Hassan exclaimed mildly. 'They carry no weapons.'

'They are naked,' added Omar, and his terror ebbed and was replaced by an erotic interest as he watched the black columns move out into the shallows. Like the horns of a buffalo they circled one of the sandbanks, and though the chest-deep water hampered them, yet the manoeuvre was completed before the old bull hippopotamus woke from his gargantuan slumber to find himself surrounded.

He lumbered to his feet and glared about him with his piggy pink eyes. Five tons of solid flesh, clad in a thick grey hide, splotched with pink upon the belly. His legs were short and thick and powerful, and when he opened his jaws to bellow he exposed great yellow fangs of ivory which could bite a war canoe in half.

He broke into a cumbersome gallop, leaving deep hoof-prints in the soft white sandbank, and he charged at the wall of black bodies that cut him off from the deep pool of the river. He entered the shallows, churning up a wake of foaming white water, while ahead of him the wall of black men solidified and thickened as the line bunched up to receive and absorb his charge.

The bull went into them at full gallop, and human bodies were flung about like chaff in the whirlwind. His jaws clashed as he chopped at them, and when he drove forward it seemed that nothing could stay such devastating power. He must burst through them and find safety in the deeps of the river. Yet they swarmed about him, from the sides and rear, and his charge slowed perceptibly, although his bellows seemed louder and the champing of ivory tusks cutting through living flesh carried clearly to the watchers on the island.

Manatassi stood quietly, leaning forward slightly, with a small frown upon his scar-riven brow, and his eyes were yellow and watchful.

In the river the water creamed and flashed and sparkled. The bull's bellows took on a new note, a hint of panic, and he was no longer visible beneath the swarming naked bodies. It was like a scorpion attacked by army ants, creatures only a small fraction of his size smothering him with their numbers. The sunlight glittered on the wet bodies, and the bull's forward progress was arrested. He was transformed into a struggling ball of human bodies, while around him the water turned dark brown with blood, and the mauled bodies fell away like poisoned black ticks from the body of an ox. They floated down on the sluggish current, while others swarmed forward eagerly to replace them.

Now, miraculously, the striving knot of men and beast began to move towards the island; leaving the debris of death behind them, they moved slowly through the shallows.

They reached the island, and came from the water – 1,000, perhaps 2,000 men, carrying the exhausted but still struggling hippopotamus bodily from the river and up the bank. The bull slashed viciously from side to side, and all within reach of his jaws died, while the bull's head and the inside of his mouth was clotted with the bright blood of his victims.

Leaving a thick trail of dead and terribly maimed men behind them, they carried the bull to where Manatassi stood waiting. The war captain came forward unsteadily. He was weak from loss of blood for he had lost one arm above the elbow, taken away by a single bite of those terrible jaws.

He handed a stabbing spear to his king. Manatassi walked forward, and while his men held down the terrified monster, he stabbed it in the throat, finding the jugular vein with the first thrust. The bull died in a burst of dark blood and a cry that rang against the hills.

Manatassi stepped back and watched impassively as his men despatched their wounded with swift mercy, and when the war captain came and knelt before him clutching the severed stump of an arm to his chest and begged for the honour at the hand of his king, a bright pride burned briefly in Manatassi's eyes. He made the mercy stroke, crushing the man's skull with a single blow of the iron claw, then he walked back, and smiled bleakly as he saw the sheikhs' amazement.

'That is my answer,' he said, and after a while Hassan asked, 'What do you want of us?'

'Two things,' Manatassi replied. 'An undefended passage of the river through your territory for my armies. You must forsake your pact of mutual defence with Opet – and I want iron weapons. My smiths will take another ten years to arm so many men. I want weapons from you.'

'In return you will deliver to us the gold of Opet, and the mines of the middle kingdom?'

'No!' Manatassi snarled angrily. 'You may take the gold. I have no use for it. It is a cursed metal, soft and useless. You may take all that Opet has, but,' and he paused, 'the mines of the middle kingdom will never be worked again. No more will men go down to die unnaturally in the earth.'

Hassan wanted to protest. Without the gold of the middle kingdom his own reason for existing would vanish. He could imagine the rage of the Chan Emperor denied his trade routes with the land of gold. Omar's fingers warned him gently, their soft insinuating touch speaking clearly.

'There will be another time to argue.' And Hassan heeded the warning, he choked back the protest and instead he smiled at Manatassi.

'You will have your weapons. I will see to it.'

'When?' demanded Manatassi.

'Soon,' promised Hassan, 'as soon as my ships can return from the land across the eastern seas.'

Lannon had aged these last few years, Huy thought. Yet the change was flattering, the new lines that care had chiselled dispelled the prettiness from his features and had given him dignity. Around the mouth there was the same petulance, the pout of the spoiled child, but one had to look closely to find it.

His body was as young and hard as it ever had been, however, and as he stood now, stark naked in the bows, in the attitude of the harpooner, every muscle in his back and shoulders stood out clearly beneath the oiled skin. The sun had gilded his body to a dark honey gold and only his buttocks were a creamed ivory where his breech clout had protected them. He was a beautiful creature, favoured beyond all others by the gods, and Huy compared this body to his own and felt a despair within him.

Words began to form in his mind, a song to Lannon, an ode to his beauty. As he poled the skiff silently and smoothly over the still waters of the lake the words tumbled about in his mind, like wind-blown leaves, then they began to fall into patterns and the song was born.

In the bows Lannon signalled with his free hand without looking around, still poised, staring down into the waters and Huy turned the skiff with an expert thrust of the pole. Suddenly Lannon's body unleashed its pent-up energy in a fluid explosive thrust, an uncoiling of tensed muscles as he hurled the long harpoon down through the surface. The water bulged and swirled, and the line coiled in the bottom of the skiff began tearing out over the side, hissing away into the water.

'Ha!' shouted Lannon. 'A fair thrust! Help me, Huy!' And together they jumped to the line, laughing with excitement and then swearing at the pain of scorched fingers as the line ran through them. Together they slowed the heavy run of the fish. The skiff was moving out into the lake as the fish sought the deep water, dragging them with it.

'In Baal's holy name, stop him, Huy,' Lannon panted. 'Don't let him get out there and sound on us, we'll lose him for a certainty.' And they threw their combined weight on the line. The muscles in Huy's arms and shoulders bunched and corded like a sack of pythons, and the fish turned.

They brought him up swirling and kicking in circles under the skiff and when his huge whiskered head broke the surface Lannon shouted, 'Hold him!' And Huy took a turn of the line about his wrist and braced his body against the weight, the skiff heeling dangerously as Lannon snatched up the killing club and aimed a blow at the glistening black head.

The surface exploded as the fish went into its death-throes, and water cascaded over them, drenching them both.

'Hit him!' yelled Huy. 'Kill him!' And half blinded with spray, Lannon hammered at the enormous snout. Some of the blows were wild, crunching against the side of the skiff and splintering the planking.

'Not the boat, you fool. Hit the fish!' shouted Huy, and at last the fish was dead, hanging in the water beside the boat.

Laughing and panting and cursing, they got a heavy line through its gills and dragged it aboard, slithering in over the gunwale, slimy and black with a belly of bright silver, and bulging eyes. The whiskers above its gaping mouth still twitched and quivered as it filled the bottom of the boat, twice as long as Huy and with a body too thick to encompass within the circle of his arms.

'It's a monster,' panted Huy. 'The biggest I have ever seen.'

'You called me a fool,' said Lannon.

'Nay, Majesty, I was talking to myself,' grinned Huy, and he unstoppered the amphora and poured wine for them.

Lannon lifted his bowl to Huy, and grinned at him over the rim.

'Fly for me, Bird of the Sun'.

'Roar for me, Gry-Lion.' And they drained the bowls at the same time, then laughed together like children.

'It has been too long, Huy,' Lannon told him. 'We must do this more often. We grow old too swiftly, you and I, our cares and duties envelop us and we are caught in a web of our own making.' A shadow passed across Lannon's eyes, and he sighed. 'I have been happy these last few days, truly happy for the first time in many years.' He looked up at Huy almost shyly. 'You are good for me, old friend.'

He reached out and clasped Huy's shoulder awkwardly. 'I do not know what I would do without you. Don't ever desert me, Huy.'

Huy flushed, clumsy in his embarrassment, this was a mood of Lannon's to which he was unaccustomed. 'Nay, Majesty,' he answered huskily, 'I will be with you always.' And Lannon dropped his hand and laughed, echoing Huy's embarrassment.

'Sweet Baal, but we grow sentimental as girls – is it old age do you think, Huy?' He rinsed his wine bowl over the side, making a great show of it, and avoiding Huy's eyes. 'There are still fish in the lake, and an hour or two of the day left, let us use it.'

In the dusk they returned to where their old shack stood, neglected and forlorn beneath the graceful ivory palms above the beach. As Huy poled the skiff around the point of the island, and they cleared the reed banks, they saw the galley lying at anchor in the bay. The royal standard of house Barca stood at her masthead, and there were lamps burning at stem and stern. The reflections of the lamps danced on the dark waters, and the sound of voices carried clearly to them.

Huy stopped the skiff and leaned on the pole, and in silence they stared at the long ship. Then Lannon spoke.

'The world has found us out, Huy.' And his voice was tired and resigned. 'Hail them for me.'

The lamp hanging in its chain from the roof of the stern cabin lit their faces unnaturally, highlighting cheeks and noses but leaving the eyes in shadow. Their faces were grim as they gathered about the table, and listened to the messenger from the north. Although he was young, an ensign in his first year of military service, yet he had the poise of high birth and he gave his report lucidly.

He described the ripples of unrest that had lapped along the northern borders in the last few weeks, small incidents, movements of large bodies of men seen at a distance, the smoke and fires of vast encampments. Spies reported rumours of strange occurrences, of a new god with the talons of an eagle and the claws of a lion, who would lead the tribes to a land of grass and water. Scouts had watched the sailing of many Drav vessels along the eastern reaches of the great river, an unusual coming and going, talk of secret meetings between nobody knew whom.

There was a restlessness, a vast stirring and muttering, a sense of pressures and tensions building, of secret affairs afoot. The itching of storm clouds gathering and lightning brewing. Things felt but not understood, signs pointing into the unknown.

Lannon listened quietly, frowning a little, his chin propped on his fist and his eyes in shadow.

'My commander bids me tell you of his fears that you might find all this fancy and starting at the hooting of owls.'

'No.' Lannon brushed aside the boy's plea for his report to be taken seriously. 'I know old Marmon better than that. He does not call out snake for an earthworm.'

'There is more,' said the boy, and he laid a leather bag upon the table. He loosed the draw-string and shook out a number of metal objects.

'One of the river patrols surprised a party of pagans attempting to cross in the night. They carried these, all of them.'

Lannon picked up one of the heavy spearheads, and examined it curiously. The shape and workmanship were distinctive and he glanced up at Huy.

'Well?' he asked and had his own opinions confirmed when Huy answered,

'Drav. No doubt of it.'

'Carried by the pagans?'

'Perhaps they were taken from dead Dravs, or stolen.'

'Perhaps,' Lannon nodded. He was silent a while longer then he looked up at the young officer. 'You have done well,' he said and the lad flushed with pleasure. Lannon turned next to Habbakuk Lal. 'Can you take us on another night run to Opet?' And the admiral smiled and nodded.

Lannon and Huy stood together at the stern rail and watched their island merge into the darkness as the galley drew swiftly away, leaving its wake shimmering in the light of the moon.

'I wonder when we will next return here, Huy,' Lannon asked softly, and Huy moved restlessly beside him but did not answer. 'I feel as though I am leaving something behind here. Something valuable which I will never find again,' Lannon went on. 'Do you feel it also, Huy?'

'Perhaps it is our youth, Lannon. Perhaps these last few days were the end of it.' They were silent then, swaying to the easy motion of the galley under oars. When the island was gone Lannon spoke again.

'I am sending you to the border, Huy. Be my eyes and ears, old friend.'

'It is not for long, my heart,' Huy apologized, although Tanith had said nothing, and was fully engaged in daintily devouring a bunch of purple grapes. 'I will be back before you know I have gone.'

Tanith pulled a face as though one of the grapes were sour, and Huy studied her face with exasperation. It was serene and lovely and as unyielding as that of the goddess herself.

Huy had come to know all of Tanith's moods, every expression or tilt of the head that heralded them. He had watched with fascination as she changed from child to full woman, from bud to ripe bloom, and he had studied her with the patience and dedication of love, but this was one mood he had not learned how to distract.

Tanith licked her long tapered thumb and forefinger with the tip of a pink tongue, then examined her hand with interest, twisting it from side to side to catch the light.

'There is nobody else that the king can trust to send on this mission. It is a matter of grave importance.'

'I am sure,' Tanith murmured, still examining her hand. 'Just as there was no other who could go with him to stick fish.'

'Now, Tanith,' Huy explained reasonably. 'Lannon and I have been companions since our childhood. We used to go out to the islands often in the old days. It was like a pilgrimage to revisit our youths.'

'While I sit here with a bellyful of your child, alone.'

'It was but five days,' Huy pointed out.

'But five days!' Tanith mimicked him with her cheeks flushing, signalling the change of her mood from ice to fire. 'I swear on my love of the goddess, that I do not understand you! You profess your love for me, yet when Lannon Hycanus crooks a finger you run to him, panting like a puppy dog and roll on your back that he may tickle your belly!'

'Tanith!' Huy began to grin. 'I swear you are jealous!'

'Jealous, is it!' Tanith cried, and snatched up the fruit bowl. 'I'll give you jealous!' She hurled the bowl, and while it was still in flight she was reaching for fresh missiles.

Old Aina, nodding in the sunlight at the end of the terrace, awoke in the midst of the storm and joined Huy in flight. They found shelter behind an angle of the wall, and from there Huy cautiously reconnoitred the field and found it deserted, but he could hear Tanith weeping somewhere in the house.

'Where is she?' quavered Aina.

'In the house,' answered Huy, combing fruit from his beard and mopping at wine stains on his tunic.

'What is she doing?'

'Weeping,' Huy said.

'Go to her,' commanded Aina.

'And if she attacks me again?' Huy answered nervously.

'Spank her,' instructed Aina. 'Then kiss her.' And she gave him a toothless but utterly knowing grin.

'Forgive me, Holy Father,' whispered Tanith and her tears were warm and wet upon Huy's neck. 'It was childish of me, I know, but every moment I spend away from you is a piece of my life wasted.'

Huy held her, stroking her hair, gentling her, and his chest felt congested and swollen with the strength of his love for her. He was close to tears himself as he listened to her voice.

'Is it not possible for me to go with you this time?' She made one last appeal. 'Please, Holy Father. Please, my love.'

Huy's response was regretful but firm. 'No. I go fast and hard, and you are already in your third month.'

She accepted it at last. She sat up on the couch and dried her eyes. Her smile was only a little lopsided as she asked, 'Won't you tell me again of the arrangements you have made for the baby?'

She sat beside him, soft and warm with her pale skin glowing over the faint bulge of her belly and the new heaviness of her breasts in the lamplight. Her eyes were intent as she listened, and she nodded and smiled and exclaimed as Huy told her how it would be – of the foster mother he had selected in the cool and healthy air of the hills, on the estate at Zeng. He told her how the child would grow healthy and strong, and how they would visit it there.

'It?' Tanith demanded playfully. 'Never *it*, my lord – her!'

'*Him!*' Huy corrected and they laughed. But beneath Tanith's laughter the sadness persisted. This was not the way it would be. She could not see this, she could not catch the happiness of it, could not hear the laughter of a child nor feel the warmth of its little body against her.

For a moment the dark curtains of time opened, and, as sometimes happened, she glimpsed the future, saw dark shapes and men and things that terrified her.

She clung to Huy and listened to his voice. It gave her comfort and strength, and at last she asked softly, 'If I fetch your lute, will you sing for me?'

And he sang the poem to Tanith, but there were new verses now. Every time he sang it, there were new verses.

Marmon was the captain of the north, governor of the northern kingdom and commander of the legions and forts that guarded the northern border.

He was an old friend of Huy's, thirty years his senior but with the bond of scholarship between them. Marmon was a keen military historian, and Huy was helping him with a manuscript history of the third war with Rome. He was a tall bony man with a fine mane of silver hair of which he was inordinately proud. He kept it shampooed and neatly clubbed. His skin was smooth as a girl's and firmly drawn over the prominent bones of his skull, but the shivering sickness had yellowed the tone of his complexion and yellowed the whites of his eyes also.

He was one of the empire's most trusted generals, and for two days he and Huy discussed the situation along the border, poring over a clay-box map of the territory so that Marmon could show Huy exactly where each piece of the puzzle fitted in. Marmon's fine-boned hands touched each of the counters, or drew out the lines and areas of disturbance and dispute, while Huy listened and asked his questions.

At the end of the second day they ate the evening meal together, sitting up on the ramparts of the fortress for the sake of the cool evening breeze. A slave girl anointed their limbs with perfumed oil to discourage the mosquitoes and Marmon filled Huy's wine bowl with his own hands, but did not drink himself. The shivering sickness damages a man's liver, and for him wine turns to poison.

Huy thanked Baal for the immunity that the gods had given him against the ravages of this disease which flourished in the hot lowlands of swamp and river. Huy's mind chased after the thought: Why did the disease kill some, cripple others and leave others untouched? Why did it strike only in the lowlands, and leave the cool uplands untainted? He must think about it more, try and find answers to these questions.

However, Marmon was talking again now and Huy stopped his mind from wandering, brought it back to the problem in hand.

'I am at last building up a system of spies upon which I can rely,' Marmon was saying. 'I have men with the tribes who report to me regularly.'

'I should like to meet some of them,' Huy intervened.

'I would rather that you did not, Holiness,' Marmon

535

began, then noticed Huy's expression and went on smoothly. 'I expect one of them to report within the next few days. He is my most reliable informant. A man named Storch, a Vendi, an ex-slave. Through him I am recruiting a body of spies across the river.'

'I will speak with him,' said Huy, and the conversation changed, Marmon asking advice of Huy about his manuscript. As old friends they talked on, until darkness had fallen and the servants lit torches for them. At last Marmon asked deferentially:

'My lord, I have been petitioned by my officers. Some of them have never heard you sing, and those who have wish to hear it again. They are importunate, Holiness, but I trust you will bear with them.'

'Send to my quarters for my lute.' Huy shrugged with resignation, and one of the young officers stepped forward with the lute.

'We have already presumed, Holy Father.'

Huy sang the songs of the legions, the drinking and marching songs, the bawdy songs and the songs of glory. They loved it. The officers crowded silently about Huy on the ramparts, and in the courtyard below the common soliders gathered with their faces upturned, ready to come crashing in with the chorus.

It was late when an aide pressed through the throng and spoke quietly to Marmon. He nodded and dismissed the aide before whispering to Huy, 'Holiness, the man I spoke of has come.'

Huy set aside the lute. 'Where is he?'

'In my quarters.'

'Let us go to him,' suggested Huy.

Storch was a tall man, with the distinctive willowy grace displayed by so many of the Vendi, but the smooth velvety black skin of his shoulders was marred by the thickened scars of the slave lash.

He noticed Huy's glance and adjusted his cloak to cover

the ugly cicatrice, and it seemed to Huy there was a flash of defiance in his eyes although his face was handsome and impassive.

'He speaks no Punic,' Marmon explained. 'But I know you speak the dialect.'

Huy nodded, and the spy looked at him a moment longer before he addressed Marmon. His voice was quiet, without either anger or accusation.

'It was in our agreement that no other should see my face,' he said.

'This is different,' Marmon explained quickly. 'This is no ordinary man, but the High Priest of Opet and the General of all the armies of the king.' Marmon paused. 'This is Huy Ben-Amon.'

The spy nodded, his face still showed no expression, not even when Huy spoke in Vendi.

They talked for an hour, and at the end of it Huy turned to Marmon, speaking in Punic.

'This disagrees with much else you have told me.' Huy frowned and knocked his knuckles irritably against the table top. 'This man has heard nothing of a god with lion claws, nor of regiments of trained warriors armed with the weapons of the Drav.'

'No,' Marmon agreed. 'This section of the river is quiet. Our reports come from further east.'

'You have spies there?' Huy asked.

'Some,' Marmon nodded, and Huy thought a moment.

'I will move eastward then,' Huy made up his mind. 'I will march at dawn.'

'The patrol galley will arrive in five days.'

'I will see nothing from the deck of a galley. I will go on foot.'

'I will have an escort waiting for you before the rise of the sun,' Marmon offered.

'No,' Huy rejected the offer. 'I will move faster, and draw less attention to myself if I travel alone.' He glanced again at Storch. 'This man can serve as a guide, if he is as reliable as you say.'

Marmon relayed Huy's order to the spy and ended, 'You may go now. Eat and rest, and be ready before the sun.'

When he was gone Huy looked after Storch for a long moment then asked, 'How much do you pay such a one?'

'Very little,' Marmon admitted. 'Salt, beads, a few copper ornaments.'

'I wonder why he does it,' said Huy softly. 'Why he works for us when the scars of the lash are fresh upon his body.'

'I am no longer amazed by the acts of men,' said Marmon. 'I have seen too much strange behaviour ever to question a man's motives.'

'I never cease to do so,' murmured Huy, still looking after the spy, troubled by the man's treachery which jarred so harshly on Huy's own sense of honour.

H uy's efforts to find out more about the spy over the next four days met with but small sucess. Storch was a silent man, speaking only when he was questioned directly, and then answering with words barely sufficient for the occasion. He never looked directly at Huy; his eyes focused to one side of Huy's face and he looked beyond.

Huy found him a disconcerting companion, though he clearly knew every bend of the river and every fold of the ground over which they travelled.

They called at two of the forts upon the south bank, and from the men who garrisoned them Huy gleaned much first-hand intelligence. Twice they found the sign where large parties of men had crossed the river on mysterious business, and there were other small indications of secret activity which heightened Huy's feelings of unrest.

It disturbed him that these signs were in contradiction of Storch's assurances of quiet and stable conditions beyond the river.

They travelled swiftly and silently, slipping like a pair of forest spirits through the dense valley bush. They travelled much in the cool of evening and night and rested in the hissing heat of noon. They ate little, husbanding the contents of the corn bag and not wasting time upon the hunt.

On the fourth day they reached the summit of a small granite hillock from which they could survey a huge area of the valley floor, a panorama that stretched from escarpment to escarpment and only shaded away into the blue haze of distance. Before them the river made a mighty bight towards the south, a wide glittering loop of many miles that twisted back upon itself.

Although the loop was some twenty or twenty-five miles around, yet across the neck was less than five and beyond it stood the squat solid block of another garrison. The smoke from the cooking fires rose in a pale blue feather into the still, hot air.

Huy looked at the twist of the river for a long time, seeing the choice as between a full day's hard slogging or a quick cut across the neck of the loop with its attendant risk.

'Storch,' he said, 'can we cross the river? Are there men of the tribes here?'

The spy looked away from Huy's scrutiny, hiding any expression. He sat very still, squatting upon the granite dome beside Huy – and Huy thought he had not understood the question.

'It would be shorter to cut across the bend. Is it safe?' he asked again, and Storch replied:

'I will find out. Wait here for me.'

He returned an hour before dark and led Huy down to the river bank. Hidden in the reeds was a narrow dugout canoe. The woodwork was rotten with worm, and it stank of old fish. Huy's suspicion flared.

'Where did you find this?'

'There is a family of fishermen camped downstream.'

'How many?'

'Four of them,' Storch replied.

'Vendi?'

'No, men of Sofala.'

'Warriors?'

'Fishermen. Old men with grey heads.'

'You told them about me?'

'No.'

Huy hesitated, peering into the blank stare of Storch's eyes, trying to find a hint of treachery there.

'No,' said Huy, 'we will not cross. We will go around the long way.' It was a test. He waited for Storch's reaction, waited for him to argue, to attempt to persuade Huy to make the crossing.

'It is for you to say,' Storch nodded, and began to cover the canoe with reeds.

'Very well,' Huy agreed, 'take me across.'

Storch used the current to angle the frail little craft across the river. Ahead of them the cormorants beat the water with their wings in their frenzied efforts to launch into flight, while the chocolate and white jacanas scurried across the lily pads and the sinister log-like shapes of the crocodiles slid down the bank into deep water.

They landed on a muddy beach heavily trodden by the hooves of the game that drank here, and Storch hid the canoe. He led Huy up the bank, and into a glade of bright poisonous green swamp grass. They waded waist-deep through the thick clutching stems, and the ground was soggy and yielding underfoot.

In the centre of the glade Storch stopped abruptly and motioned Huy to stand still. He cocked his head in a listening attitude. They stood frozen for a long time, then

Storch cautioned Huy to remain where he was and he moved forward.

A hundred paces from Huy, Storch stopped again, but now he turned and looked back at Huy.

For the first time his face showed expression, a wild exultation, a bright burst of triumph.

He lifted his right arm and pointed at Huy, a gesture of denunciation, and he shouted out in Vendi, 'There he is! Take him!'

The grass of the glade rustled and shook as though a high wind blew across it, and from their places of concealment rose rank upon rank of Vendi warriors. Their shields overlapped, their lines formed concentric circles about Huy, ringing him in completely, and the plumes of their head-dresses were the foaming crest of a menacing wave about him.

Like the tightening of a strangler's fist upon the throat, the ring of warriors closed in on Huy. Wildly he glared about him, seeking an avenue of escape. There was none, and he stripped the leather guard from the blade of the vulture axe and flew like a terrier at the throat of a black bull.

'For Baal!' he shouted his defiance as he charged into the solid mass of warriors.

'The air in here is foul,' Lannon complained, sniffing at it. 'Is there no way in which we can drive ventilation shafts to the surface?'

'Majesty!' Rib-Addi could not hide his horror. 'Think what that would mean. Workmen in here.' He made a wide gesture that took in the entire length of the treasury. 'Can you imagine what tales they would take with them to inflame the greed of every brigand in the four kingdoms?'

It was for this reason that the location and contents of the royal storehouse was such a closely guarded secret. The best-kept secret in the empire, known only to the king, the High Priest and Priestess, Rib-Addi and four other officials of the treasury.

'I would have them sent to the gods immediately they had completed the task,' Lannon explained reasonably.

Rib-Addi blinked with surprise. He had not envisaged such a sweeping solution to the problem. It took him a moment's beard-scratching and deep thought to unearth his next objection.

'A ventilation shaft would provide entry for thieves and rodents and damp. All these would damage and destroy.'

'Oh, very well.' Lannon dismissed the subject, knowing well that Rib-Addi resisted change merely because it was change. What had been good for the past two hundred years, must be good for the next two hundred.

Lannon watched as the latest shipment of finger ingots from the mines of the middle kingdom was reverently added to the piles of gold already laid down in the recess of the treasury. Rib-Addi noted the quantities meticulously in his scroll, and Lannon affirmed the entry by scrawling his personal sign beside the entry.

The four trusted officials filed out of the long chamber with its piles of treasure. While they climbed the flagged stairs, Rib-Addi sealed the iron gate. He pressed the Gry-Lion's mark into the clay tablet, then he and Lannon climbed the stairs and passed through the sun-door into the state archives. Lannon closed the door, and the massive slab swung into its seating with a solid clunk.

Lannon made the sun sign at the god's image upon the door, then with Rib-Addi beside him discoursing as ever on wealth in its many manifestations, he passed down the length of the archives. The shelves were loaded with the records of the kingdom, and there was little space left. Soon he must turn his mind to an extension of these catacombs, how to enlarge them without destroying or damaging the existing structure.

They went out through the main portals, with their heavy leather curtains, into the guards' ante-chamber where officers of the Sixth Legion guarded the entrance. At all times of the day and night two officers were here, and at their call a century of picked troopers of Legion Ben-Amon waited. The Sixth Legion had originally been formed as a guard to the temples and treasuries of the kingdom and these still formed an important part of its duties.

Within the maze of the temple of Astarte, Rib-Addi took obsequious leave of Lannon and with his four underlings backed away, bowing until he disappeared around the bend of the corridor.

Assisted by four priestesses, Lannon, naked and magnificent, took the ritual bath in the pool of Astarte and while they dressed him in the tunic of the supplicant, Lannon managed to insert a playful hand into the skirts of one of the novices without the others noticing. The novice's expression did not change, but she pressed eagerly onto Lannon's fingers for a moment before drawing away, and while Lannon strode down the passage to the audience chamber of the oracle he made the gesture of stroking his moustache to inhale the girl odour that lingered on his fingers.

They were all as hot as corn cakes sizzling on the griddle, these brides of the gods, having to rely as they did on the embraces of their own kind, or the furtive attentions of a priest or temple guard. Lannon grinned as he wondered how many of them took advantage of the licence of the Festival of the Fruitful Earth. How often had he committed the mortal sin of sacrilege with some heavy-cloaked and disguised priestess. The Festival was imminent, in two weeks it would begin, and as always he looked forward to it. Then with regret he remembered that Huy was unlikely to return from the north in time to join in the celebrations. It would detract from his own enjoyment. Lannon's moods were always mercurial and now within a dozen paces his good spirits evaporated. As he entered the audience chamber he was scowling heavily.

He looked up at the oracle on her throne, sitting like an ivory statue with her hands folded on her lap and her face painted with cosmetics to resemble a mask, forehead white with antimony powder, eyelids metallic shiny blue and the mouth a vivid slash of scarlet in the pale face. He found a focus for his bad temper.

As he made a perfunctory obeisance, he remembered how often this witch had thwarted and unsettled him. He detested these sessions of divination, and yet found that they exerted a weird fascination. He realized that much of her oracle was dross, probably inspired by the politically active priesthood. Yet there was also much shrewd comment and excellent counsel amongst it, and occasionally there were nuggets of purest gold to be gleaned from the witch's lips. During his regular visits he had tuned his ear to catch the nuances of the oracle's voice. As with Rib-Addi, the witch had shades of conviction or hesitation in the manner in which she delivered the oracle. Lannon was sensitive to these, but more particularly so to a rarer tone, a monotonous low-pitched voice which the witch used when she spoke the miraculous god-given truths of real prophecy.

Now he took up his stance before her, legs planted firmly astride and clenched fists on his hips. With the arrogance of royalty heightened by his temper he asked the question.

Tanith hated these sessions with the Gry-Lion. He awed and frightened her. It was like being caged with some beautiful but savage predator, with its restless energy and unpredictable moods. The pale steely blue of his eyes had a predator's cold killing lust, his features were chiselled perfect but cold also with the same relentless passion.

Usually she had the comfort of Huy's presence behind

the curtains to carry her through, but this morning she was alone – and sick.

The night had been hot and airless, and the child in her womb as heavy as a stone. She had risen listless and pale from her couch, her skin damp with night sweat and she had forced down the light morning meal Aina had prepared for her, only to vomit it up again in a dizzy attack of nausea.

The taste of acid-bitter bile was in the back of her throat now, and sweat poured down beneath her cloak, tickling as it slid over her flanks and fruitful belly. She felt herself stifling, her breathing hunting raggedly for air, her body limp and weak, while the king growled his questions.

She was unprepared, her answers were empty words given without conviction, and she struggled to concentrate, to remember what Huy had told her.

The king was becoming restless, he strode back and forth before her, wearying her with his energy. She felt sweat break out beneath her mask of cosmetics. Her skin felt itchy and swollen, the pores blocked with paints and she longed to wipe it away. She had a sudden wondrous image of cool water falling over moss-covered rocks, of plunging her naked body into the green water, of sinking into it with her hair spreading on the surface, like the tendrils of a water plant.

'Come, witch! Come, oh seer of the future. It is a simple question. Answer it!'

The king was stopped before her, one foot on the throne steps, shoulders drawn back and hips thrust forward in masculine hauteur, a sneer on his handsome face and mockery in his voice.

Tanith had not heard the question, she floundered for words, and another wave of nausea washed over her. She felt sweat break through the film of paint on her upper lip, and the nausea changed to dizziness.

Lannon's face receded, and blackness closed about her.

Her vision narrowed, and she looked down a long shaft of darkness at the end of which Lannon's face burned like a golden star. There was a roaring in her ears, the sound of the storm wind through the trees of the forest. Then the sound of the wind died away into silence, and a voice spoke. The voice was husky and low-pitched, even and monotonous, the voice of a deaf woman or one drugged by the smoke of the bhang pipe. With mild surprise Tanith realized that the voice issued from her own throat, and the words shocked her.

'Lannon Hycanus, last Gry-Lion of Opet, question not the future. The future for you is darkness and death.'

She saw her own shock repeated upon Lannon's face, saw the colour fly from his cheeks, and his lips turn to lines of pale marble.

'Lannon Hycanus, prisoner of time, pacing behind the bars of your cage. Blackness waits for you.'

Lannon was shaking his head, trying to deny the words. The golden locks of his hair, still damp from the ritual bath, danced upon his shoulders, and he held up both hands in the sun sign, trying to avert the words which struck his soul like war arrows flighted from the bow.

'Lannon Hycanus, your gods are passing, they fly upwards, and leave you to blackness.'

Lannon retreated from the throne, hands raised to shield his face, but the words sought him out relentlessly.

'Lannon Hycanus, you who seek to know the future, know then that it lies in wait for you as the lion awaits the unwary traveller.'

Lannon cried out, and his terror exploded into violence.

'Evil!' he screamed, and rushed at the oracle, bounding up the steps of the throne. 'Witchcraft!' He struck Tanith in the face with his open hands, knocking her head across and back with heavy blows. The hood of her cloak fell back and her dark hair tumbled loose. The blows rang loudly against her flesh, but Tanith made no sound. Her silence drove Lannon on to further violence.

He caught the front of her cloak and dragged her from the throne.

'Sorceress!' he screamed, and flung her down the steps. She fell heavily and rolled, trying to come to her feet, but Lannon's first kick caught her in the belly and she doubled up, clutching at her middle and groaning as his sandalled feet smashed into her.

Lannon was bellowing as he pursued her about the chamber; between kicks he was looking wildly about for a weapon, something to destroy the woman and the words she had spoken.

Then suddenly the chamber was filled with priestesses, and Lannon drew back panting heavily, the pale eyes bright with madness.

'Majesty!' The Reverend Mother came forward, and Lannon's madness faded, but he was still shaking and his lips were white and quivering.

He turned and strode from the chamber, leaving Tanith whimpering upon the flagged floor.

•

The Divine Council of Astarte met in the Reverend Mother's chamber, and when she read the Gry-Lion's demand to them they listened quietly, thinking their own thoughts. The Council consisted of the High Priestess and two advisers, both of them senior priestesses who stood in the direct line of succession to the Reverend Mother.

'How can we deliver one of the sisterhood to the temporal body of the Gry-Lion? What precedent would we set by doing so?' Sister Alma asked. She was small and wrinkled with a face like an inquisitive monkey. 'What crime is the child accused of? If she has erred then it is for us to judge and punish. We must protect our own, even if it means defying the king.'

'Can the sisterhood afford such a grand gesture?' asked Sister Haka; dark-skinned and pock-marked, with long raven hair streaked with iron grey, her face was strong-jawed and her voice deep as a man's. She was not yet forty years of age, and certain to outlive the Reverend Mother. Until recently it seemed she must succeed to the head of the sisterhood, a position for which she longed. However, since an oracle had emerged in Opet, her position was less secure. History had proved that every oracle, in time, became Reverend Mother over the claims of all others. In addition, this one had the unquestioned favour of the High Priest, an important consideration when it came to the filling of a vacant position at the head of the Divine Council. In Tanith she had a strong rival, but apart from the political considerations, Sister Haka had a more inti-mate score to reckon.

Even now as she remembered how her advances had been rejected, she felt hot anger flood her cheeks. She still longed for the girl, dreams of her still troubled her sleep, and often when she was with a young novice in the dark she would pretend that it was Tanith.

'Are we strong enough to resist the demands of the king?' She let the question hang, and looked at their faces. All of them knew what an impetuous, irresistible force ruled in Opet. All of them knew that no one, noble or priest, friend or enemy, had ever denied him his way.

The silence persisted, until Sister Alma coughed gusts of tortured sound, that crescendoed until she spluttered up a lump of bloody phlegm and wiped her lips with a damp cloth, her face strained and her eyes tired and dull.

'Not long for you, old woman,' thought Sister Haka with her grim satisfaction hidden behind a mask of concern.

Again they were silent, until the Reverend Mother

spoke hesitantly. 'Perhaps, if it could be shown that the girl has sinned, committed some crime.'

It was all that Sister Haka needed. Ruthlessly she took charge. 'Send for the girl,' she instructed. 'Let us question her.'

Aina helped Tanith into the chamber, both of them hobbling and doubled over, one with age and the other with pain. They clung to each other, and the ancient priestess was mumbling encouragement to the injured girl, but her face screwed up with anger when she saw the Council, and she screeched at them.

'The child is hurt. Have you no care? Why do you summon her thus?'

'Silence, old hag,' Sister Haka spoke without passion. She was looking at Tanith. Tanith's face was swollen and the bruises were purplish and livid. One eye was closed, the lid puffed and blue, and her lip was cut through and scabbed.

'Let her sit,' Aina demanded. 'She is weak, and sick.'

'Nobody sits before the Council,' said Sister Haka.

'In the name of the goddess.'

'Do not blaspheme here, old crow.'

'I speak not of blasphemy, but of ordinary mercy.'

'You talk too much,' Sister Haka warned her. 'Go! Leave the girl here.'

It seemed Aina might argue still, but Sister Haka rose to her feet and her face was furious and her voice harsh with anger.

'Go!' she repeated, and Aina shuffled out grumbling and whining, leaving Tanith swaying weakly on her feet before the Council. Sister Haka sank down onto her stool and looked at Tanith. She would take her time now, there was all day if she needed it, and besides she was enjoying herself.

Tanith stayed upright by an effort of her will alone, for her senses swam and floated on waves and washes of pain.

The leaden feeling in her legs and lower belly anchored her, but she could make little of the questions with which they pelted her. Sister Haka was leading her onto what it was that she had told the king to infuriate him, she was showing how Tanith had endangered the sisterhood by antagonizing him. She kept coming back to the question, 'What was it you told him?'

'I cannot remember, Sister. I cannot remember,' Tanith whispered.

'You want us to believe that words of such dire consequence can be so easily forgotten. Come, child, what were they?'

'They were not my words.'

'Whose then?' Sister Haka leaned forward attentively, her face blotched with brown speckles of the pox and the wings of grey glowing in her dark hair. 'Whose words were they if not your own? The goddess's?'

'I do not know,' breathed Tanith, and then she gasped as a fist of agony squeezed something within her lower belly.

'Do you speak with the voice of the goddess?' Sister Haka demanded in her hoarse voice, dark and cruel as a bird of prey. The hawk stooping on the sparrow.

'Oh please!' whispered Tanith, bowing slowly forward with both hands pressed to her stomach. 'Oh please, it hurts. Oh how it hurts!'

The three priestesses watching her saw the quick flood of liquid which drenched the front of Tanith's tunic skirts, and splattered in dark red drops upon the flagstones between her feet. With slow grace, Tanith folded and fell forward. She lay on her side with her knees drawn up and she moaned softly.

Sister Haka went quickly to her and stooped over her, drawing up Tanith's skirts and peering with tense lesbian interest as she pulled Tanith's knees roughly apart.

She was smiling as she straightened, and looked at the

other two. 'There is your sin, Holy Mother. There is your proof of crime.' She looked down at the huddled body at her feet. 'Sacrilege!' she accused harshly. 'Sacrilege! A crime against the goddess.'

'I will not answer,' said Tanith gently. The bruises had faded and the swelling abated a little, but there was still a plum-coloured smear under one eye and her lip was distorted and scarred. She had been bed-ridden for ten days and she was still weak. 'I will not tarnish something so dear to me with words. I will not tell you his name.'

'Child, you know this is a matter of mortal sin. Your life is at stake here,' said the Reverend Mother.

'You have taken life from me already. Have done then. Take it all.' Tanith looked directly at Sister Haka, and from her to Lannon Hycanus who stood by the casement of the chamber. 'It is your intention to kill me. Nothing I say will alter that. Very well then, I will cherish the name of my child's father. I shall not let you use this against him also.'

'You are being stupid and stubborn,' said Sister Haka. 'We will find out in the end.'

'Why is it important?' Tanith asked. 'All that matters is that I stand between you and your ambitions.' Tanith looked directly at Sister Haka, and saw her words had struck by the swarthy rose flushing of the priestess's scarred cheeks. Tanith smiled and turned to Lannon. 'All that matters is that I am the source of the prophecy. You seek to destroy that. You seek to have the gods revoke their sentence upon you. It is vain, Lannon Hycanus. The winds of destiny are blowing, the hounds of fate are already hunting.'

'Enough,' snapped Lannon, striding to the centre of the chamber. 'I have no more time to waste. No longer can I listen to your idiot chatter.' He looked at Sister Haka. 'Bring the old priestess, the witch's chaperone.'

When Aina stood blinking and bewildered before the king he looked at her without passion or anger. 'You had duties. You did not discharge them. Name the bull who mounted the goddess's heifer.'

Aina wailed protest, disclaimer, pleading her ignorance. She went down on creaking knees before Lannon, crawling to him, kissing the hem of his tunic, drooling with terror. Lannon pushed her away irritably with one foot and looked at Sister Haka.

'Unless I misjudge your worth, you will not shirk man's work. Have you the belly for it?' he asked, and Sister Haka nodded, licking her lips, her eyes lighting with cruel anticipation.

'Break her arms first,' commanded Lannon. 'And let the witch stand close by to watch it.'

Sister Haka pulled Aina to her feet, holding her easily with her strong brown hands on the back of which grew long silky black hairs. Aina flapped and squawked with terror, and Sister Haka turned and pinned her, twisting one arm backwards against the elbow joint. The arm was thin and white with thick blue cords of vein showing through the skin.

'Wait!' cried Tanith. 'Let her go!'

'Release her,' ordered Lannon.

Tanith went to the old priestess and kissed her gently on the forehead and cheek. Aina was sobbing.

'Forgive me, child. I am sorry. I would have told them. Forgive me.'

'Gently, old mother. Gently now.' Tanith led her to the doorway and pushed her tenderly out of the chamber. She went back to them and spoke to the king.

'I will tell you his name – but you alone.'

'Leave us,' commanded Lannon, and the Divine Council rose and filed from the chamber.

When they were alone Tanith said the name, proudly and defiantly, and she saw Lannon reel as though it had been a physical blow.

'How long has he been your lover?' he asked at last.

'Five years,' she answered.

'So,' he said, seeing the answer to many questions. 'It seems we shared his love then.'

'Nay, Majesty.' Tanith shook her head. 'I had all of it.'

'You are wise to speak of it as past,' Lannon told her. He turned away to stand by the casement, and looked out across the lake. Nothing must come between us, he thought, I need him. I need him.

'What will it be, Majesty? Poison or the secret dagger? How will you kill a priestess of Astarte? Have you forgotten that I belong to the goddess?'

'No,' said Lannon. 'I have not forgotten, and I will send you to her, on the tenth day of the Festival of the Fruitful Earth. You will go as the messenger of Opet to the Gods.'

'Huy will not allow it,' whispered Tanith in horror.

'Huy is in the north – a long way from the pool of Astarte.'

'He will hate you for it, always. You will lose him for ever,' Tanith warned him, but he shook his head.

'He will never know that I ordered it so. He will never know that you betrayed him, and told me his name.' He smiled then, a cold and golden smile. 'No, it is you that will lose him, and I that will have him. You see, I need him, and my need is more important than yours.'

He had been borne in a litter at first, while he was unconscious and then later when he was still too weak to march, so he did not know for how long and in what direction they had travelled.

Even later when he was forced to walk, they bound and blindfolded him, so that he was aware only of the press of their bodies about him and the stench of sweat and the rancid fat with which they smeared their skin. There was no answer when he spoke, and rough hands urged him forward, and a spear blade pricked him when he baulked.

He had been badly beaten and bruised, there were still lumps and gashes in his scalp, and his body was grazed and painfully wrenched, but he had taken no serious wounds, no deep spearthrust nor broken bones. It was as though they had carefully avoided dealing him a killing or crippling injury despite the fact that he had piled the corpses of their comrades in wind-rows about him, the vulture axe taking cruel toll before they overwhelmed him.

On the first night when they camped he began a tentative investigation of his position with escape in mind, but then when he tried to shift his blindfold enough to see out, a heavy blow in the face dissuaded him. They fed him a handful of boiled corn and a strip of badly cured meat, gamey and rank with bacon beetle. Huy ate it hungrily.

In the morning they were marching before the dawn, and when Huy felt the sun's warmth on his cheek and saw the light through his blindfold, he repeated the praise of Baal silently and asked the god for his help.

Later that day he was aware of the ground levelling beneath his feet as though they journeyed across an open plain, and there was the smell of cow dung and smoke and humanity. Over the thudding rhythm of his escorts' bare feet and the swish of their war-kilts he heard a vast susurration of voices and movement. Blending with this was the lowing of many cattle, the air quivered with sound and movement, a hive murmur which warned him of the presence of a great multitude.

At last they stopped him. He stood weary and thirsty in the hot sun with the raw-hide rope cutting into his wrists and his bruises and grazes aching. Time passed slowly in the silence of the waiting men.

At last a voice called out loudly, and Huy's nerves jumped. The voice was in Vendi demanding, 'Who seeks the lion-clawed, who seeks the bird-footed?'

Huy remained silent, waiting for some indication of how to behave, and to his surprise he felt the cool touch of iron at his wrists and a blade sawed through his bonds. He rubbed his fingers, wincing at the flow of blood. Then he lifted his hands to the blindfold, expecting another blow, but none came and he loosed the cloth and blinked uncertainly in the bright sunlight.

His eyes adjusted quickly, and he felt his heart lurch with shock at what he saw. Huy stood at the centre of a wide plain, a slightly concave bowl of land rimmed in with low hills.

Except for a circular open area a hundred paces across, at the centre of which Huy now stood, the land was black with warriors. Huy gazed in awe at this multitude, and he could not begin to reckon their numbers. He would never have believed that the land could support such numbers, it was unreal, completely nightmarish – and the quality of unreality was heightened by the menacing stillness of the black hordes. Only the feathers of their head-dresses stirred in the sluggish wash of heated noonday air.

The heat and the press of humanity threatened to suffocate him, and he looked about him desperately as though seeking an avenue of escape. Storch stood near him, and he carried the vulture axe on his shoulder. Huy felt a weak flutter of anger for the man's treachery, but somehow it seemed unimportant in the enormity of this fresh experience.

Storch was not looking at him, instead he was watching a group of Vendi war captains who stood about a low mound of earth at the end of the clearing. The mound was bare, but compelled the attention of them all, like an empty stage before the principals appear.

Again the voice demanded. 'Who seeks the Great Black Beast, who hunts the lion?'

The heated silence and stillness persisted, then suddenly the multitude stirred and sighed as a man stepped up onto the mound.

The tall crown of heron feathers on his head and the height of the mound upon which he stood made him god-like. His robes of leopard skin hung to the ground about him, and he stood as still as a tall tree in a rustling plain of grass as the royal salute shook the foundations of earth and sky.

Storch carried the vulture axe to the mound and laid it at the king's feet, then he backed away, and the king looked across the open ground at Huy.

Huy drew himself up, trying to ignore the aches of his body, trying not to limp as he approached the mound and looked up at Manatassi.

'I should have guessed,' he said in Punic.

'You should have killed me,' said Manatassi, and from the folds of his robes he lifted the iron claw. 'Instead of arming me with this.'

'You do not understand,' Huy said. 'Your life was not mine to take. I made an oath.'

'Still a man who lives on his word,' Manatassi said, yet Huy looked in vain for the traces of mockery in his voice.

'There is no other way to live.' Huy felt tired now; he faced his certain death with resignation. He did not really have the energy to debate it.

Manatassi made a gesture with the claw, indicating the massed ranks of his army.

'You see what a spear I have forged?'

'Yes,' Huy nodded.

'Who can stand against me?' Manatassi asked.

'Many will try,' said Huy.

'You amongst them?'

And Huy smiled. 'I do not think I will have the chance to do so.'

Manatassi looked down at the little hunchback in his tattered tunic, his beard matted and the bruises on his face and arms, soiled and beaten, but not humble as he discussed his own fate.

'Not one of my men understands us,' Manatassi told Huy. 'We can speak freely.'

Huy nodded, puzzled, but interested in this change of mood.

'I offer you life, Huy Ben-Amon. Come to me, give me the love and duty you have given to the Gry-Lion of Opet and you will live to be an old man.'

'Why do you choose me?' Huy asked.

'I have waited for you. I knew you would come. My spies have watched for you, but it was fate that delivered you so neatly into my hands.'

'Why me?' Huy repeated.

'I need you,' Manatassi said simply. 'I need your learning, I need your understanding, and your humanity.'

'You forgive me the taking of your hand?' Huy asked.

'You could have taken my life,' Manatassi answered.

'You forgive the slave ash and the mines of Hulya?'

'Those I will never forgive,' Manatassi snarled, his face twitching and the eyes glaring smoky yellow. 'But they were not your doing.'

'You forgive the massacre at Sett?' Huy persisted.

'You are a soldier, you could do nothing else.'

Manatassi was still trembling, and Huy sensed how narrowly he skirted the abyss, but he felt compelled to explore this man's strength – and weakness.

'What would you have of me, then?' Huy asked.

557

'March beside me,' said Manatassi.

'Against?'

'Against Opet and its monstrous cruelties and terrible gods,' Manatassi urged him. 'With you beside me and this army at my back I will rule the world.'

'I cannot do that.' Huy shook his head.

'Why not? Tell me why. It is evil, it must be destroyed.'

'It is mine,' said Huy. 'My land, my people, my gods – therefore they cannot be evil.'

'I thought you were a man of reason,' Manatassi snarled.

'Reason can carry a man just so far, and then he must trust to his heart,' said Huy.

'You refuse me, then?'

'Yes.'

'You know that you choose death?'

'Yes.'

Manatassi raised his hand, the iron claw glowing in the sunlight, and Huy knew that when the hand fell he would die. He steeled himself to meet it as calmly as he had dealt it.

Manatassi turned away. Then after a moment he sighed, and his shoulders beneath the thick scars heaved.

'You spared me,' said Manatassi. 'I shall spare you.'

Huy felt weak with relief. He had not wanted to die, and he allowed himself at last to think of Tanith and the child. Now he would still see his son, and his heart soared.

'Go back to Opet. Go back to your king. Tell him that Manatassi, the Great Black Beast, marches out of the north to destroy him.'

'Should you warn an enemy?' Huy asked. 'Did I teach you that?'

Manatassi smiled. 'A warning will not help him,' he said. 'Tell him what you saw here. Tell him of this army – and let it chill his guts. Tell him I come for him, and I will spare none nor leave a memory of him to taint this land. Tell him I come, and I come swiftly.'

Manatassi picked up the vulture axe and handed it to Huy.

'Go!' he said. 'All debts between us have been paid. You have no call on me, and I have no call upon you. When I meet you again I shall kill you.'

They stared at each other, standing close enough to touch, but separated by a distance wider than the span of the oceans or the vastness of the land.

Huy turned and limped away down the corridor of warriors that opened for him, and no man barred his way.

'Old mother, you must not distress yourself so,' Tanith whispered. 'It was not your fault.'

'I would have told them,' Aina mumbled. 'I know I would have told them. That Sister Haka, she terrifies me.'

'You did not tell,' Tanith comforted her. 'You kept our secret well – even we ourselves did not know you had found out.'

Aina set down the food bowl beside Tanith's bed, and she smiled reflectively. 'You were so happy, the two of you. It made me feel good just to see you. He is a good person, despite his poor crooked back, he is gentle and kind.'

Tanith moved across on the couch, making room for Aina to sit. 'Sit by me for a while, old mother. I am so lonely here, it makes the waiting so much harder.'

Aina glanced fearfully across the narrow chamber at the barred doorway.

'They do not like me to stay too long.'

'Please,' Tanith entreated. 'There is so little time left.' And Aina nodded and gathered up her skirts to sit, creaking at her knee-joints, upon the couch. Tanith leaned close to her, and she whispered eagerly, 'Did you send messengers, did you find someone to go?'

'I sent two young ensigns from Legion Ben-Amon. They worship the Holy Father as though he were himself a god. I told them that you were in mortal danger, and that the Holy Father must return with all speed.'

'Do you think they will find him?'

'There are a hundred roads that he might take, and the land is wide. I would not lie to you, my child. The chance is not good.'

'I know,' said Tanith. 'And if they find him, can he return in time, and if he does, is there aught he can do to dissuade the Gry-Lion?'

'If he returns in time, then you are safe. I know the man.'

'Wait for him, Aina. If he returns, go to him secretly and tell him that the king knows about us. You must warn him of that, for he is also in danger.'

'I will warn him,' promised Aina.

'Oh, I pray to all the gods that he returns swiftly to Opet. I do not want to die, old mother. There is so much I would yet have from life, but the days run out now. It is already the sixth day of the Festival. Unless Huy comes there are but four days of my life left.'

'Gently, child,' Aina crooned and put an arm about Tanith to pat and cuddle her. 'Be brave,' she crooned, 'be brave, child.'

'It is not so easy,' Tanith told her, 'but I will try.' And she pulled away from Aina's embrace and sat up straight. 'You must go now, old mother – or Haka will beat you again.'

On the walls of the fortress at Zanat, south of the great river, a sentry held a javelin lightly in his right hand, concealing it below the level of the parapet, and he looked down on the strange wild figure below him. The man's hair was filthy and matted, he wore no armour, his tunic hung in tatters, and his face was bruised and badly swollen. He seemed to be wounded for he was doubled up painfully in an unnatural posture, bowed beneath the weight of the huge battle-axe he carried.

'What is your name, and what your business?' the sentry hailed, and the traveller looked up at him.

'I am Ben-Amon, High Priest of Baal and warrior of Opet. My business is the king's.'

The sentry started, and thrust the javelin back into its rack. He realized how close he had come to making a fool of himself. The crooked back and the axe were famous throughout the four kingdoms, he should have recognized them immediately, and he berated himself as he ran down into the courtyard shouting for the officer of the guard, warning him of their distinguished caller.

Huy came in through the side gate the moment it swung open, and he cut short the military salutes with a curt, 'Enough of that nonsense.'

The officer of the guard was startled at having the legion's beloved ceremonial dismissed in such a cavalier fashion, and he smothered a grin. Coupled with his appearance and his beggar's garb this story would go to swell the body of legend that already existed about this remarkable little man.

Huy was striding past the hastily assembled guard, demanding of the officer as he passed, 'Where is the general? Is he here?'

'Yes, my lord – Holiness. He is in his quarters.'

'Praise to Baal!' Huy grunted with relief.

Huy wolfed a thick cut of cold meat folded between two corn cakes, and he washed it down with a bowl of red wine, speaking through and around each mouthful of food as he issued his orders.

Marmon's scribe dashed off each article, racing to keep up with the flow of Huy's words. Marmon sat on his stool in the corner, his head of silver hair shining like a summer thunder cloud and his handsome face anxious and worried.

He could hardly believe what he was hearing, yet he knew better than to doubt the word of Huy Ben-Amon. He realized that he was culpable, that he should have been the one to discover this deadly threat that had grown up so swiftly on their borders. Perhaps he had spent too much of his time dreaming over his ancient histories, perhaps he had grown old and feeble without realizing it. He wondered what retribution there would be from Huy Ben-Amon and the Gry-Lion of Opet. Neither of them were men who let failure pass unnoticed.

He listened as Huy issued the orders which would place every garrison and every unit on the alert, would mobilize every disbanded legion, would send messengers racing across the land carrying the scrolls that would place the entire empire on a war footing. Marmon wondered at the courage of a man who could make this battle decision alone, a decision for which he would have to answer to the king and the council of nobles. He might be held responsible for all the losses and damages that would arise when the entire industry and commerce of the nation were suspended. It was a decision upon which his own life might hang, as well as that of Opet.

As he watched Huy signing the orders he doubted that he would have had that much certainty of the rightness of his own actions. He knew he would have sent to Opet for orders, and probably have jeopardized whatever chance there was of survival. For, from what Huy had told him, it was a matter of survival. They were confronted by an enemy so vastly superior in numbers that success lay with the gods.

Huy was finished. He signed the last scroll and the fire went out in him. It was only then that Marmon realized that the man was exhausted. He staggered slightly, his whole body slumping and he seemed to shrivel in size under the burden of his weariness.

Marmon jumped up from his stool and went to him. Huy brushed off the helping arm and tried to gather his strength in hand again.

'I must leave for Opet,' he said, slurring like a drunkard and steadying himself against a corner of the table. 'What day is it, Marmon? I seem to have lost count of the days.'

'It is the seventh day of the Festival, Holiness.'

'The Festival?' Huy looked at him stupidly.

'The Fruitful Earth,' Marmon reminded him.

'Ah!' Huy nodded. 'I did not think it was that late. Have you a war-elephant to carry me to Opet?'

'Nay, Holiness,' Marmon told him regretfully. 'There are no elephant here.'

'Then I must march.' Huy resigned himself.

'You must rest first.'

'Yes,' Huy agreed. 'I must rest.' And he let Marmon lead him to the bed-chamber. As he fell across the couch he asked, 'How long will it take to reach Opet from here, Marmon?'

'If you move fast, six days. Five, if you fly.'

'I shall fly,' said Huy. 'Wake me at dusk.' And he fell asleep.

Looking down on the sleeping figure, Marmon felt the familiar stirring of his affections. He felt his admiration for the great heart of this little fighting man, felt envy for the thrust and drive which always carried him ahead of the pack, and he was glad that Huy Ben-Amon led them at a time of such crisis.

It was then he remembered the messenger from Opet, the young ensign of Legion Ben-Amon who had passed through the garrison the previous day carrying an urgent message for the High Priest. He debated with himself for a moment, then decided not to disturb Huy's rest. He would tell him when he woke at dusk.

At dusk Huy woke, ate a light meal and oiled his body. Twenty minutes later he ran out into the cool of evening through the garrison gate with fifteen legionaries as escort, and it was only after they had disappeared into the dark and silent forests of the south that Marmon again remembered the message that the young ensign had given him.

He thought to send a messenger after Huy, but he knew that no runner of his could hope to catch the priest after he had such a head start. The speed of Huy's long legs was part of the legend.

Marmon thought comfortably, 'He will be in Opet soon enough.' And he paced along the parapet until he reached the far side of the fortress. He stayed there until after darkness had fallen, staring into the turbulent north and wondering how soon they would come.

The Divine Council came to Tanith's cell on the morning of the ninth day of the Festival of the Fruitful Earth. They were led by the Reverend Mother, frail and uncertain, shifty-eyed with guilt.

'We have joyous news for you, my child,' she told Tanith, and Tanith sat up quickly on her couch – her heart leaping within her. The Gry-Lion had changed his mind perhaps.

'Oh, Reverend Mother!' she whispered, feeling the tears of relief at the back of her eyelids. She was still shaky and weak from the loss of the child, and it took little to make her weep now.

The Reverend Mother was gabbling on, not looking at Tanith, unable to meet her eyes, and for a while Tanith was puzzled. She could not understand this talk of precedent and ecclesiastical law, until she glanced at Sister Haka's face and saw how gloating and lustful were the dark features and how brightly the cruel eyes shone.

Then suddenly she realized that this was no reprieve.

'And so in his wisdom the king has chosen you, has given to you the great honour of carrying the message of Opet to the goddess.'

They had not come to release her, but to seal her fate. Sister Haka was smiling.

'You must give thanks, my child. The king has given you life eternal. You will live in glory at the side of the goddess, hers for ever,' said the Reverend Mother, and the priestesses chorused, 'Praise to Astarte. Praise to Baal.'

The Reverend Mother went on, 'You must prepare yourself. I will send Aina to help you. She knows the path of the messenger well, for she has attended many of the chosen ones. Remember to pray, my child. Pray that the goddess will find you acceptable.'

Tanith stared at them, white-faced and afraid. She did not want to die. She wanted to cry out, 'Spare me. I am too young. I want just a little more happiness, just a little more love before I die.'

The Divine Council filed from the chamber, leaving her alone. Now at last the tears flooded her eyes, and she cried out aloud.

'Huy, come to me! Please, come to me.'

Huy struggled up through the glutinous dark swamp of exhausted sleep with the nightmare cry still echoing in his ears. It took him a while to remember where he was and to realize that he had dreamed the horror that had woken him.

He lay in the sparse shade of the wild fig, and through the branches he saw the altitude of the sun and knew that they had slept for only an hour. His legs still felt leaden, his body torpid and completely enervated by two days of hard travel.

He should sleep again for another three or four hours at the least, but the nightmare stayed with him, denying him rest.

He pulled himself up on an elbow, surprised at the effort it required, but then remembering that he had run over two hundred Roman miles in two days. He looked at the remains of his escort, three of them, haggard-faced and finely drawn from their exertions, sleeping like dead men in the attitudes in which they had fallen. The other twelve had dropped along the way, unable to match the blistering pace which Huy had set.

Huy heaved himself to his feet. He could not sleep, could not rest, while dread haunted him and the safety of his king and his land was in jeopardy.

He limped stiffly down to the bed of the small stream, and knelt in the sugary white sand. He splashed his face and body with the clear water, soaking his tunic and beard, then he climbed the bank and looked at his sleeping men. He felt pity for them, pity that did not prevent him calling out, 'Up! On your feet! We march for Opet.'

One of them could not wake, though Huy kicked his ribs and slapped his cheeks with an open hand. They left him lying, whimpering in his sleep.

The other two dragged themselves up, groaning, moving with stiff sore legs, and the glazed expressions of fatigue.

Huy walked the first half-mile to loosen aching muscles, with the escort staggering after him.

Then he went up onto his toes, changed the vulture axe from one shoulder to the other, and went away at a run, bouncing long-legged on a springy stride that covered the ground like the trot of an eland bull.

One of the legionaries cried out as his leg collapsed under him and he went down sprawling in the dust. He was finished, and he lay there groaning with mortification and the pain of cramped and torn muscles.

The other followed Huy, his steps firming as his legs loosened and charged with new blood.

They ran the sun to its zenith, spurning the pitiless heat of the noonday, and they ran on into the afternoon.

Ahead of them, low on the horizon, stood the perpetual bank of cloud which marked the Lake of Opet, a beacon of hope, and Huy ran with his face lifted to it, instinct guiding his feet and his will feeding his exhausted body, allowing him to run on when all physical strength was burned up.

In the last low rays of the sun the walls and towers of Opet glowed with a warm rose colour and the surface of the lake was flaming gold that pained the eye.

Huy plunged on down the caravan road, racing past other dusty travellers who pulled to the side of the track, calling after him as they recognized him.

'Pray for us, Holy Father.'

'Baal's blessing on you, Holiness.'

Half-way down the pass of the cliffs that led to the lake shore and the city, the legionary who followed Huy shouted in a clear strong voice, 'Forgive me, Holy Father, I can go no further.' And his knees buckled under him, he lost direction, blundering to the side of the track; his face contorted at the agony of his bursting heart, he went down face first and lay without movement, dead before he struck the ground.

Huy Ben-Amon ran on alone, and the guard upon the palace gate of Opet saw him afar off, and they swung the gates open to welcome him.

Tanith woke with gentle hands shaking her. There was a lamp burning beside her couch, and Aina leaned over her. Tanith saw that the old face was screwed up into a toothless grin, the monkey eyes twinkling in their web of ancient wrinkles.

'Child, are you awake?'

'What is it, Aina?' Tanith sat up quickly, her spirits leaping upwards like sparks from the bonfire of hope when she saw Aina's smile.

'He has come!' Aina told her jubilantly.

'Huy?'

'Yes, the Holy Father has come.'

'Are you sure?' Tanith demanded.

'I have heard it shouted in the streets. The whole city is agog. They say he ran from Zanat to Opet in three days, they say he killed fifteen men who tried to run with him. He broke their hearts and left them lying on the road.'

'Oh, Aina.' Tanith embraced the old priestess, hugging her to her breast. 'If he came so fast, it must be because he knows.'

'Yes, child. Of course he knows. Why else would he come with such speed? One of the ensigns would have reached him with my message. He knows all right.' Aina drooled and nodded her conviction. 'He knows!'

'Where is he now?' Tanith was laughing with her excitement. 'Do you know where he is?'

'With the king. He went straight to the palace.'

'Oh, praise the goddess and all the gods,' breathed Tanith. 'He has gone to use his influence with the Gry-Lion. Do you think he will succeed, Aina? Will the king change his mind?'

'Of course, child. Do you doubt it? If Huy Ben-Amon set his mind to it, he would make Baal himself change his mind.'

'Oh, I am so happy, old mother.' Tanith clung to Aina,

568

and they comforted each other in the night. Until at last Tanith drew away.

'Go to him, Aina. Wait for him outside the palace. Tell him everything, and come back to me with his message.'

As Aina was about to leave the chamber Tanith called after her, 'Tell him I love him. Tell him I love him better than life – and all the gods.'

'Hush,' said Aina, 'hush, child. Someone may hear you.'

Alone, Tanith lay back on her couch and smiled.

'I don't care,' she whispered. 'Huy is here, and nothing else matters.'

Lannon listened to Huy in rising consternation. His first thought when Huy had arrived unheralded and unexpected in the night was that he had somehow learned of the sacrifice at tomorrow's ceremony. He had considered refusing Huy an audience, considered all manner of evasion, but while he was considering it Huy had barged his way into Lannon's bed-chamber past the startled and protesting guards.

Lannon had risen naked from the side of his youngest wife, angry words shrivelled on his lips when he saw the state to which Huy was reduced.

'Forgive me, Majesty. I carry dreadful tidings.'

Lannon stared at him, saw the filthy and dusty tunic, the unkempt hair and beard, the skull-like face from which the flesh had wasted, and the wild eyes in their bruised and sunken sockets.

'What is it, Huy?' He went quickly to the priest, and steadied him with a brotherly arm.

The Council of Nine, all the noble families of Opet, met in night session and they heard the report of Huy Ben-Amon in horrified silence. Only when he had croaked out the last of it and slumped wearily on his stool did the babble of fault-finding, and blame-laying, and self-pity and doubt begin.

'We were told he was destroyed at Sett!'

Huy said, 'You were told only that I slew 30,000 at Sett. I did not name them.'

'How could such an army be recruited without our knowledge? Who is to blame?'

Huy answered, 'It was recruited beyond our borders. No one is to blame.'

'What of the mines – we must protect them.'

Huy smiled wearily. 'That is what we intend.'

'Why is there only one legion on the border?'

Huy answered them grimly, 'Because you refused to vote the money for more.'

They turned on him then, their words hammering through the fog of weariness.

'How did you pass unscathed through enemy lines?'

'Was not this Timon once your protégé?'

'You know him well, you taught him, did you not?' And Huy looked at Lannon.

'Enough!' Lannon's voice cut through the tirade. 'His Holiness has called the nation to war. He has shown me copies of the scrolls, and I am about to sign them in ratification.'

'Should we not wait a while?' That was Philo, naturally, 'Are we not being too hasty?'

'What will you wait for?' Huy demanded. 'Until they open your bowels with a spear blade and cut off your testicles?'

Lannon signed the war orders a little before dawn, and he dismissed the Council of Nine with the words:

'We will meet again at noon, after the final ceremony of the Fruitful Earth. See to your arms and take leave of your families.'

To Huy he spoke kindly when they were alone. 'Sleep here. There is nothing more you can do now.'

He was too late. Huy was already asleep, slumped forward on the table with his head on his arms. Lannon picked him up from his stool, and carried him like a sleeping child to a guest chamber.

He placed a sentry at the door.

'No one must wake the Holy Father,' he instructed. 'No one! Do you understand.'

It was almost dawn. The sacrifice would take place in a very few hours, and he knew that Huy was in a kind of death sleep that might last for many days. He left him, and went to bathe and dress for the procession.

Aina lifted the hood of her cloak over her head, covering her face. She thrust her bony old hands into the wide sleeves, and leaned forward to blow out the lamp.

She stood in the darkness, considering what she must do. She would not wait for the High Priest to leave the palace. Aina had access to the palace kitchens. The major domo there was the grandson of her youngest sister, and she often went to eat there as a change from the temple fare. All the palace slaves knew her. It would be a simple matter to find out from one of them whereabouts in the rambling mud-walled building the High Priest was, an even simpler matter to get word to him.

Quietly she drew the curtains of her cell aside, and peered out. There was a single torch guttering in its bracket at the end of the passage, but it threw only a feeble light and Aina did not see the dark figure waiting for her in a shadowy angle of the corridor until it came gliding towards her.

'Not yet asleep, old woman?' a deep, almost masculine voice asked softly, and a strong hand closed on Aina's wrist.

'Are you going visiting so late at night? Is it that you have heard of Huy Ben-Amon's return to Opet?'

'No,' whimpered Aina. 'I swear it.' And she struggled feebly. With her free hand Sister Haka pushed the old priestess's hood back from her face and peered into her eyes.

'You were going to Ben-Amon, were you not?'

'No. I swear it.' Aina saw death in Sister Haka's expression, and she began to scream. It was a thin passionless sound like the sound of the wind, and it was cut off abruptly as Sister Haka's powerful hand whipped over her mouth.

From a doorway opposite a frightened face peered out, and Sister Haka snapped, 'Go back to your couch.' And the young novice obeyed quickly.

Sister Haka forced Aina's frail body back through the curtains and onto her couch. She held her hand over mouth and nostrils, holding Aina down with an arm across her chest.

Aina's struggles exploded feverishly, her heels drummed and kicked against the wall and her arms flapped and clawed at Sister Haka's face. Then swiftly it was over and she subsided and lay still. Sister Haka held her mouth and nostrils closed for a long time after she was quiet, then with one hand she felt the scrawny old chest with its empty pendulant dugs for a heartbeat.

Finding none she nodded with satisfaction, arranged the careless limbs tidily, and left the cell. Through the single window slit the first light of dawn lit Aina's face. Her mouth hung open, her eyes were startled and a wisp of silky silver hair floated on her forehead.

L annon was conscious of the need to carry through the final ritual of the Festival meticulously. It was apparent that he faced a national emergency of vast proportions, that Opet was opposed by an enemy more powerful and relentless than any in her long history. The oracle had spoken against him, perhaps he or his kingdom had incurred the wrath of the gods.

Lannon knew that the fate of nations hangs not entirely on the actions of men, battles are not won by swords alone. He knew there were influences beyond, sometimes malignant and sometimes benign, which dictated the outcome of earthly affairs. He knew it was possible to placate an angry god, and to enlist the goodwill of one that was kindly disposed.

As the Reverend Mother led him through the catechism beside the pool of Astarte, he paid special concern to the correctness of his responses, and there was no mistaking the sincerity of his voice as he made his pledge to the goddess.

The priestesses closed in about him and light hands helped him shed his robes of purple silk. Currents of cool air stroked his naked body as he strode forward to the edge of the pool, went down the stone steps and lowered himself into the clear green waters.

His body shone white below the surface, and his long golden tresses and beard glistened with water as the priestesses beside him scooped up water in the conch shells and poured it over his head.

They emerged from the pool, and Lannon felt a sense of spiritual cleansing, as though the sacred waters had washed away his cares and armed him against the dangers that lay ahead. He was not a man of deep religious faith, and yet in this moment he felt uplifted. He was happy then that he had chosen such an important messenger for the goddess.

His own petty and personal motives no longer counted. He was sending a priestess of the blood, a god-touched oracle, a person of value and weight. Surely the goddess must find her acceptable, surely Astarte would now turn her countenance upon the children of Opet, spread her wings across the nation in this time of trial and danger.

They dried off his skin, and the muscle was firm and beautifully shaped in leg and arm and wide shoulders. Two priestesses came forward and lifted a white silk robe over his head, the colour of joy and rejoicing. The Reverend Mother placed a garland of flowers about his neck, crimson cave lilies whose scent was sweet and heavy in the hushed cavern.

It was the moment when the praise of the goddess must be sung, and then the offertory. The silence persisted a moment longer and then a voice rang through the cavern.

The voice startled Lannon, and he turned his head searching for the singer. There was no mistaking that voice, the sweet shimmering power of it, the depth and timbre that made the hair on Lannon's forearms come erect and set the echoes flying about the temple, seeming almost to ruffle the quiet surface of the green pool.

Lannon gaped at Huy. He had stepped out of the ranks of nobles and officers and as he sang he paced slowly towards Lannon. His arms spread in the sun sign, his mouth wide open showing the strong white teeth and that achingly beautiful voice pouring from his throat. The praise song ended, and Huy stood close beside the king, looking up at him. His face was still raddled with fatigue, the dark eyes still underscored by bluish purple smears, the skin pale and drawn, but he was smiling at Lannon with an expression of loyal affection.

'Huy!' Lannon whispered in horror. 'Why are you here? I left you resting with orders not to disturb you.'

'At this time my place was with you.'

'You should not have come,' Lannon protested. This was beyond his planning. It was not part of it that Huy should witness the death of the witch. He had not intended torturing him with the deed. Wildly Lannon considered halting the ritual, withdrawing the sacrifice, ordering Huy to leave the temple.

Yet Lannon realized that the safety of the empire might be resolved in these next few moments. Could he halt the sacrifice, dare he risk antagonizing the goddess, was his duty to Huy greater than his duty to Opet, was it not already too late, had he not committed himself long ago to this path? Were the gods and demons mocking him now, could he not hear their hellish laughter echoing in the deserts of his soul?

Bewildered and appalled he stared at Huy. He took a step towards him, reaching out one hand in entreaty as though asking for understanding and forgiveness.

'I need you,' he said hoarsely, and Huy, not understanding, took the hand, thinking it the hand of friendship; proudly he smiled at his king and friend as he began to sing the offertory to the goddess.

His voice rose on eagle's wings, flying up to the sacrificial platform in the roof of the cavern high above them. All the eyes in the temple turned upwards also and a tense expectant hush gripped the throng of worshippers.

Tanith could not believe it was happening to her. When they had come to her cell in the dawn she thought it must be Huy come to fetch her away. She had leapt from her couch and run to meet him.

It was not Huy but Sister Haka. They had taken her from the temple up the secret steps to the top of the cliffs above Opet. There in a stone building with a roof of thatch beside the sacrificial platform over the gaping hole above the pool of Astarte, they had dressed her in the rich embroidered robes of the sacrifice and put flowers in her hair.

Then they had draped her with the heavy gold chains, and bracelets, and leg bangles until Tanith felt she must collapse beneath the weight of them. She knew that this treasure formed part of the sacrifice, and that it was also intended to weight her down swiftly into the green depths of the pool. The pool which had no bottom to it, the pool which would carry her to the bosom of the goddess.

Solemnly and in silence she was seated at the small banquet table, and her sister priestesses waited upon her, pressing her with choice foods and wines. It was the feast of farewell, the feast to someone who goes upon a journey. Tanith sipped a little of the wine, hoping that it might warm her icy spirit.

'Huy,' she thought. 'Where are you, my love?'

At last a priestess came to the door and nodded to the others. There were fifteen of them, all strong young women, more than enough of them to overwhelm any resistance.

They closed in about where Tanith sat, not yet menacing but utterly determined. They looked down on her expressionlessly, their faces closed against pity or regret.

'Come,' said one of them, and Tanith stood up. They led her through the doorway into the sunlight, and ahead of her she saw the carved stone platform jutting out over the dark and gaping hole in the earth.

The path to the sacrificial platform was strewn with blossoms of the yellow mimosa tree, a flower sacred to the goddess. The scent was light and nostalgic on the warm still air, and the blossoms crushed beneath Tanith's bare feet as she passed over them weighted down by her chains of gold, and the heaviness of her dread.

Suddenly she stopped, frozen at the sound of the voice issuing from the pit before her, a voice faint with distance and echoing strangely from the cavern walls; but the voice of such purity and beauty that she could not help but recognize it.

'Huy!' she whispered. 'My lord!' But the upward flight

of her spirits was short-lived, for the voice of Huy Ben-Amon was uplifted in the offertory of the sacrifice.

It was Huy who was sending her to the goddess, and in that moment a vision of hell and desolation opened before her. She found herself caught in the web of some monstrous conspiracy, not understanding it clearly, knowing only that Huy had deserted her. He was against her also. He was the one offering her to the goddess.

There was nothing to live for now. It was easy to take those last few steps up onto the platform.

As she paused on the brink she spread her arms in the sun sign and looked down into the gloom of the cavern. The waters of the pool were still and dark, and beside them stood the king and the priest.

They were looking up at her, but it was too far for her to judge their expressions. All she knew was that Huy's voice was still raised in prayer, offering her to the goddess.

She felt hatred and anger replacing desolation, and she did not want to die with those emotions in her heart. To forestall them she swayed forward over the drop, over the deep green pool, and as she felt her balance go Huy's voice stopped abruptly, cut off in the middle of a word.

Slowly she leaned out over the drop, and then suddenly she was in the air, plunging downwards, hurtling towards the pool by the weight of gold she carried. As her stomach swooped within her she heard Huy's voice again, raised in a shriek of despair as he called her name.

'Tanith!'

She struck the surface of the pool with such force that all life was crushed from her, and the heavy ornaments plucked her beneath the limpid waters so swiftly that Huy saw only the brief gleam of gold deep down as though a great fish had turned upon its side to feed.

Manatassi crossed the great river in the winter of the Opet year 543. He used the cooler weather to carry his armies through the valley where the water was at its lowest levels. He crossed with three armies of varying sizes. The smallest, a mere 70,000 warriors, crossed in the west and overwhelmed the garrisons there. They drove swiftly for the western shores of the lake of Opet where the narrow waterway drained the lake and gave access to the ocean for the galleys of Opet. It was called the River of Life, the artery that fed the heart of Opet.

Manatassi's impis severed the artery, freed the slaves employed at dredging the channel and slaughtered the garrison and slave-masters. Most of Habbakuk Lal's fleet was drawn up on the beach, careened for cleansing of the hulls. The galleys were burned where they lay and the sailors thrown alive on the fires.

Then Manatassi's war captain blocked the channel. His warriors, and the tens of thousands of freed slaves tore down a small granite hill which stood beside the River of Life, and dumped it into the narrowest stretch of the river, rendering it impassable to any vessel larger than a canoe. This was a labour comparable with the construction of the great pyramid of Cheops, and it effectively sealed off the city and population of Opet from the outside world.

At the same time a second larger army crossed in the east, swept unhindered through the territory of the Dravs and burst like a black storm on the hills of Zeng.

The third and largest army, nearly three-quarters of a million strong, surged across the river at Sett. Manatassi commanded them in person and he chose the crossing place as a gesture.

Marmon hurried to oppose him with his single legion of 6,000 men and was crushed in a swift and bloody battle. Marmon fled the field and died on his own sword amidst the burning ruins of Zanat.

Manatassi placed his centre across the road to Opet and rolled along it. His front was three miles wide and twenty deep, a multitude whose own bulk reduced the march to a stately progress.

Manatassi swept the land. He took no prisoner, neither man nor woman nor child. He took no loot, burning cloth and book and leather, smashing pot and cup, throwing it all upon the funeral pyre of a nation. The buildings he burned, and then threw down and scattered the hot stone slabs.

As his hatred fed upon this destruction so it seemed to grow, like the very flames he lit, it burned higher the more was heaped upon it.

The total fighting strength of Opet was nine legions. Of these one had died with Marmon in the north, and two others were hacked to pieces upon the terraces of Zeng, the survivors holding out in a dozen besieged fortresses upon the crest of the hills.

With the remaining six legions Lannon Hycanus marched from Opet to meet Manatassi. They came together 150 miles north-east of Opet, and Lannon won a victory which gained him two miles of territory and one day's respite – but which cost him 4,000 dead and wounded.

Bakmor, who commanded Legion Ben-Amon in the absence of the High Priest, came to Lannon's tent upon the battlefield when the sky still glowed like a furnace from the cremation fires, and the stench of scorching flesh spoiled what little appetite for food that battle fatigue had left.

'The enemy left 48,000 dead upon the field,' Bakmor reported exultantly, and Lannon saw he was a young man no longer. How the years had sped away. 'We took twelve for each of ours,' Bakmor went on.

Lannon looked up at him, sitting on his couch while a physician dressed a minor wound in his arm, and he saw that dried sweat and blood had stiffened Bakmor's hair and beard and that there were new lines and shadows in the handsome face.

'How soon can you fight again?' Lannon asked, and the shadows around Bakmor's eyes deepened.

'It was a hard day,' he said. Legion Ben-Amon had held the centre firm during those desperate hours when it seemed the line must sunder at the pressure of black bodies and darting steel.

'How soon?' Lannon repeated.

'In four or five days,' Bakmor told him. 'My men are weary.'

'It will be sooner than that,' Lannon warned him.

They fought again the following day, a battle as desperate and as costly as the other. Again Lannon won a heavy victory, but he could not hold the field and he must leave over a thousand of his wounded to the hyena and jackal while he fell back to a new defensive line of hills.

They fought again five days later, and five times more in the next seventy days. At the end of that time they were encamped twenty Roman miles from Opet, and Lannon's six fine legions had shrunk to three.

It mattered not that they had won eight great battles, and that they had slain almost 200,000 of the enemy. For Zeng had fallen, only a handful of warriors winning through to describe its fate. The towns were burned and razed to the ground, the gardens cut down and burned also. The mines of the middle kingdom were destroyed, the slaves freed to join Manatassi's horde and the shafts blocked with earth and rock.

The channel of the River of Life was choked with rock, there was no escape upon Habbakuk Lal's galleys now, and from east and west new armies marched to reinforce Manatassi's drive on Opet.

Despite the toll that Lannon had taken from the armies of Manatassi, they seemed unaffected in number or determination. Each time Lannon planted his standards and stood to dispute Manatassi's advance, fresh hordes poured forward to attack him. Though he cut them down by the tens of thousands, they bled his own legions and left them each time more exhausted and with despair more deeply corroding their fighting spirit.

On the seventy-first day one full legion, 6,000 men, stabbed their officers in the night and scattered away into the darkness in small groups. Stopping only to pick up their women from the villages around Opet, they disappeared into the south.

Bakmor pursued them a short distance and dragged a hundred of them back in chains to face Lannon's wrath. They were all men of mixed Yuye blood, one class above that of freed slave, the lowest type of citizen allowed the privilege of bearing arms for the king. It seemed they did not count the privilege dear. Made bold by the certainty of execution, their spokesman told the king:

'If you had given us something to fight for, some station above that of dog, we might have stayed with you.'

Lannon had the man scalded to death with boiling water for his insolence, and retired his two remaining legions on the city.

They camped upon the lake shore without the city wall and Lannon looked to the north in the night and saw the bivouac fires of Manatassi's army spread like a field of yellow Namaqua daisies upon the hills. Manatassi was pressing him hard.

Bakmor found the king on the outskirts of the camp, watching the enemy positions. He approached Lannon eagerly, bearing the first good news they had received in many long days.

'There is word of Huy Ben-Amon, Majesty.' And Lannon felt a lift of his spirits.

'Where is he? Is he alive? Has he returned?' Lannon demanded. It was only now he admitted to himself how he had missed the little priest. He had not seen him since Huy had run out of the cavern of Astarte in the midst of the ceremony of the Fruitful Earth.

Although Lannon had conducted a diligent search, even offering a reward of 100 gold fingers for information about him, Huy had disappeared.

'Has he returned?' How many times in the long nights since then had Lannon longed for his companionship, his counsel and his comfort.

How often in the din of the battle had he listened for Huy's cry, 'For Baal!' and the song of the great axe.

How often had he wished that he could stiffen a crumbling centre or check a pivoting flank with the priest's presence.

'Where is he?' demanded Lannon.

'A fisherman saw him. He is out on the island,' said Bakmor.

The days had drifted past in a haze of grief. Huy had lost count of them, one slid so easily into the next. Most of the time he spent working on the scrolls. He had brought all five of the golden books with him and when he was not in the hut he kept them buried beneath his sleeping mat.

He wrote exclusively of Tanith, of his love for her and her death. In the beginning he worked through the nights as well as the days, but then he used up the last of the oil for the lamp and he spent his nights wandering along the beach and listening to the low surf hiss and growl upon the sands, and the wind across the lake rattle the palm fronds.

He lived on the fresh-water clams and a few fish that he took in the shallows, and he grew lean and unkempt; his beard and hair tangled and uncared for.

His grief showed in his eyes, making them wild and haunted, half mad and uncaring for anything but his own loss. Many of these hopeless days passed before anger and resentment began to work within him. From deep within him rose thoughts dark and dangerous as the shapes of killer sharks rising to the smell of blood.

Brooding over a smoky cooking fire he thought about his land and his gods. It seemed to him that both of them were cruel and greedy. A land devoted to the accumulation of wealth, counting not the toll in human suffering. Frivolous gods demanding the sacrifice, both of them greedy and devouring.

Huy left the fire and went down to the lake shore. He sat in the sand and the water ran up and tugged at his ankles before sliding back. The dark thoughts persisted, and mingled with them were the memories of Tanith.

He pondered the gods who would choose for the sacrifice the beloved of their faithful servant. What more did they demand of him, he wondered. He had given them everything he held dear, and still they wanted more.

How cruel that they should choose Lannon as the instrument to strip him of his love. He wished now that he could have told Lannon about Tanith. If Lannon had known of their love he would have protected her, Huy was sure of this. In the beginning he had hated Lannon, for it was he who had named Tanith as the sacrifice. Then reason had prevailed with Huy. He realized now that Lannon had acted in good faith. He had known nothing of Huy's and Tanith's relationship. He had known only that the nation was in dire danger and a valuable messenger was needed. Tanith was a natural choice then, reluctantly Huy saw that this was so, and knew that he would have done the same.

He no longer hated Lannon, but suddenly he found himself hating those who had forced him to it. The gods – the merciless gods.

Out of the lake great Baal rose in all his splendour of glittering gold and red, and across the waters he could see the rosy cliffs and towers of Opet glowing on the horizon.

From life-long habit Huy rose to his feet and spread his arms in the sun sign, and he opened his mouth to sing the praise of Baal.

Suddenly he was shaking with anger. He felt fiery gusts of it rising through his soul, setting his hatred alight, the funeral fire on which his faith perished.

'Damn you!' he shouted. 'What more do you want of me, you eater of flesh? How much longer must I be your plaything?'

Now his fists were clenched as he shook them in defiance at the rising sun, his face contorted and his tears streaming down into the wild bush of his beard. He walked forward into the lake.

'How much longer must I feed your cruel appetite, man-killer? How many more innocents before you quench your monstrous lust for blood?'

He dropped to his knees in the wet sand, and the running water surged about his waist.

'I reject you!' he shouted. 'You and your bloodless mate. I want no more of you – I hate you. Do you hear me, I hate you!'

Then he fell silent, and bowed his head. The water surged softly about him and after a while he scooped handfuls of it and washed his face. Then he rose and walked back to the hut above the beach. He felt a sense of fateful release, the peace which follows an irrevocable decision. He was priest no longer.

He ate a piece of smoked fish and drank a bowl of lake water, before he began work on the scrolls.

Again he wrote of Tanith, trying to recall every tone of her voice, every smile and frown, the way she laughed, and the way she held her head – as though he could give her immortality in words, as though he could give her life for the next 1,000 years in words cut into a sheet of imperishable gold.

Once he looked up from the scroll with peering short-sighted eyes and saw that the day was passing, and the long shadows of the palms cast tiger-stripes upon the yellow sands of the beach. He stooped again to the scroll and worked on.

There was the crunch of a footstep in the sand outside the hut, and a dark shape blocked out the light.

Again Huy looked up, and Lannon Hycanus stood in the doorway.

'I need you,' he said.

Huy did not reply. He sat hunched over the scroll blinking up at Lannon.

'It was on this island that you promised me you would never desert me,' Lannon went on softly. 'Do you remember?'

Huy stared at him. He saw the deep lines of care and suffering cut into Lannon's flesh, the dark shadowed eye-sockets in the gaunt face. He saw the greyish tone of the skin and the silver glint of old man's hair in the beard and at the temples.

He saw the wounds half healed, and freshly weeping through the linen bindings. He saw a man who was extended to the limits of his strength and determination, and in whose throat was the bitter taste of defeat.

'Yes,' said Huy. 'I remember.' He stood up and went to Lannon.

They came back to Opet in the early morning. All night they had sat together beside the fire in Huy's hut and they had talked.

Lannon told him of the course of the campaign, and the state of the nation. He told him of each battle, every strategy the enemy had deployed.

'I had placed much reliance upon the war-elephants. That trust was ill-founded. We lost most of them in the very first encounter. They used spears dipped in the poison taken from countless bees. I learned from a prisoner how they had smoked out hundreds of hives and laboriously squeezed out the poison sac from each sting. The burning pain of the wounds drove my elephants insane. They raged through our lines, and we had to use spikes on them.

'Also they had trained athletes who could vault onto the elephants' backs. They half leapt and were half thrown by their companions, flipped through the air like professional tumblers to kill the drivers and then stab the beasts in the back of the neck.'

'I was to blame for that,' said Huy. 'I told him of those tactics that the Romans used against Hannibal's elephants. He has not forgotten a single word of my teaching.'

Lannon went on to tell Huy of each battle which, though victorious, left Opet weakened, of the slow retreat before the black hordes, of the mounting despair amongst the legions, of the desertions and mutinies, of the destruction of the greater part of the fleet upon the beaches and the blocking of the channel.

'How many ships remain?'

'Nine galleys,' Lannon replied, 'and an assortment of fishing craft.'

'Enough to carry all of us across the lake, to the southern shores?'

'No,' Lannon shook his head. 'Not nearly enough.'

They talked on through the night, and in the dark hour before the first glimmer of dawn Lannon asked the question that had hovered on his lips all evening. He knew Huy would expect it.

'Why did you desert me, Huy?' Lannon asked softly. If Huy were to believe that Lannon knew nothing of his relationship with the witch, if he were to believe that Lannon's choice of sacrifice was accidental, then Lannon must pretend ignorance.

Huy looked up at the question and the firelight lit his face from below, leaving his eyes as dark pits.

'You do not know?' he asked, watching Lannon intently.

'I know only that you called out the witch's name, and then you were gone.'

Huy went on studying Lannon's face in the firelight, searching for some sign of guilt, some flicker of deceit. There was none. Lannon's face was tired and strained, but the pale blue eyes were direct and steadfast.

'What was it, Huy?' he insisted. 'I have puzzled over it so often now. What drove you from the temple?'

'Tanith. I loved her,' said Huy, and Lannon's expression changed. He stared at Huy for long seconds, appalled and stricken.

'Oh, my friend, what have I done to you? I did not know, Huy, I did not know.'

Huy dropped his gaze to the fire, and he sighed.

'I believe you,' he said.

'Pray Baal's forgiveness for me, Huy,' whispered Lannon and leaned across to grip Huy's shoulder, 'that I should ever have given you grief.'

'No, Lannon,' Huy answered. 'I shall never pray again. I have lost my love, and denied my gods. Now I have nothing.'

'You still have me, old friend,' said Lannon, and Huy smiled shyly at him.

'Yes,' he agreed, 'I still have you.'

They carried the golden scrolls and the vulture axe down to the beach where Bakmor and the crew of the fishing-boat waited patiently, and they came to Opet in the early morning.

The legions cheered them, king and priest, as they moved through the encampment and Huy felt tears scalding his eyelids.

'I do not deserve this,' he whispered. 'I deserted them. I should have been with them.'

Although the two legions were reconstituted from the shattered remnants of the original nine, yet it seemed to Huy they were built around the foundations of Legion Ben-Amon. Everywhere he saw familiar faces, grinning affectionately at him out of the ranks. He stopped to talk with them, trying to keep his tone cheerful as he noted the dented armour and the roughly bound wounds, half healing or suppurating.

He saw how exhausted they were, an exhaustion of the soul as well as the body. The smiles were short-blooming and the cheers were forced from reluctant throats – yet they were in hand, and there was fight left in them. They were lucky that none of the fevers that so often attended an encamped army had not yet weakened them further. It was strange how when they moved regularly, not staying at any one place long enough to foul the water supply or to allow their dung heaps to fester, then the fevers often did not appear.

There were 26,000 men encamped upon the lake shore, and they made a brave show. Huy felt small flames of confidence and hope warming his belly as he passed amongst them. Perhaps there was still something that could be done with this force.

Lannon and Huy ate the noon meal with their officers. There was no shortage of corn or meat or wine so close to the granaries of Opet, and they feasted and toasted each other while their men enjoyed the double wine ration that Lannon had ordered. In the afternoon Lannon allowed the wives into the camp. This was a privilege usually granted only after a great victory, not before a battle. They came streaming out of the city in their thousands, many of them wives for a day – to more than one husband.

'Let them enjoy it,' Lannon remarked with a little regret in his voice, as they strode through the camp with an escort of officers and picked legionaries. 'The gods know well that it may be the last time any of them do so.' Then his voice hardened. 'But see to it that none of the women remain after sundown.'

There was a desperate quality to the mass matings, as though life was trying to ensure its survival on the eve of extinction. As though in the motions of love the morrow's slaughter might be discounted.

Lannon left them to their frenzy and led his party out of the camp at a trot, the easy ground-devouring gait of a legion in forced march. Lannon led them to a spur of high ground which jutted out from the cliffs to overlook the lake shore for twenty miles in each direction. They stayed for many hours, watching Manatassi's hordes debouch from the passes of the cliffs onto the gently sloping lake shore. They watched mainly in silence, for it was a sight to strike ice into the souls of the bravest men.

It was as though a nest of black pythons were uncoiling, flowing outwards in long thick columns. It seemed endless, this massing of men; this stretching and bunching of primeval forces. It seemed as inevitable and undeviating as the tides of the sea, or the march of black storm clouds across a summer sky, and in the face of it they were silent and subdued.

Manatassi went into camp upon the lake shore with his vanguard only five miles from Lannon's own camp. However, the rear of his army had not yet emerged from the hills, and the plain between was thick with his regiments. There was no end to his numbers, no chance of counting them, for they knew not where his columns ended.

Lannon and Huy went down from the high ground in

the dusk. The star of Astarte was a bright prick of light in the indigo sky above Opet. Huy averted his eyes from it.

They went to the harbour and watched the embarkation of the women and children upon the remaining galleys of Habbakuk Lal. They would lie off-shore during the night, and the following day until the battle was decided. If the day went against Opet, as Huy knew it must, then they would be taken across the lake and would strike southwards in an attempt to stay ahead of Manatassi. The men who survived would follow as best they might.

There was not room for all of them aboard the galleys, so the royal and noble women went first, followed by the priestesses and the merchant families. At one stage there was an ugly and fierce moment when a mob of the Yuye women and classless ones tried to rush the harbour and find seats aboard the ferries. They were clubbed down and driven back by Habbakuk Lal's sailors. Huy felt a deep pity for them as they screamed and covered their heads with their hands against the spear butts. One of them, a young Yuye girl, sat dazed upon the flags of the wharf with her head bowed over the baby in her lap and the blood flowing down the ropes of her long black hair to form a dark shadow on the stone.

Lannon took leave of his wives and the children on the deck of Habbakuk Lal's flagship. He was remote and dignified as each woman came to kneel briefly before him. The children followed their mothers, and Lannon barely glanced down at them.

The twins had grown into marriageable young women now. Pretty and vital with long blonde hair plaited and roped. They came to kiss Huy for the last time, and his voice was husky as he said his farewells. The younger children were unaware of the gravity of the moment, and they were tired and petulant, squabbling amongst themselves or squalling in their nurses' arms.

Lannon and Huy were rowed back across the black

waters on which the reflected fire-flies of torchlight danced. The crowds upon the wharf were massed and silent, opening reluctantly to give them passage through, and Huy detected a sullenness close to open hostility. The escort closed in about them and they hurried through the streets of the city towards the encampment.

There were bonfires burning in the streets and about them drunkenness and revelry as the lowly citizens of Opet snatched a few last hours of pleasure before the dreaded morrow. The revels were more wild and grotesque than even those of the religious festivals. Men and women danced naked in the leaping firelight, or lay in puddles of their own vomit besotted with drink, while others rutted unashamedly in open view.

Huy saw a woman reeling drunkenly past them with her tunic torn and stained with red wine hanging in tatters from pale shoulders, and one breast protruding, round and fat with a big copper-coloured nipple. She tripped and fell into one of the fires, her hair exploding in a flare of orange flame.

In the shadows and dark lanes scurried other shapes, bowed under heavy burdens, and Huy knew that the looters were already at work, plundering the empty homes of the rich. Huy knew that his own slaves would still be protecting his house, but none the less he felt a pang of alarm as he remembered the golden books.

'Majesty, grant me an hour,' he said as they came abreast of the turning that led down to his house beside the lake.

'What is it, Huy?' Lannon demanded irritably. 'There is still much to do, and we must rest. What is it that demands your time?'

'I must take leave of my household. My slaves must be released from their duties and my valuables hidden, especially the scrolls – the golden scrolls.'

'As you will,' Lannon conceded bad-temperedly. 'But do not waste time. Return as soon as you can.'

The old slaves could not understand Huy's dismissal.

'This is our home,' they pleaded. 'Do not drive us out.' And Huy could not explain. He left them there sitting huddled together in the kitchens, bewildered and afraid.

With one of the younger slaves to help him, both of them bowed under the immense weight of the scrolls, Huy crossed the temple of Baal and went through the cleft into the cavern of Astarte. It was silent and deserted. The priestesses were all aboard the galleys in the harbour. Huy paused beside the pool and looked down into its depths.

'Wait for me, my love,' he said. 'I will follow close behind you. Keep a place for me at your side.'

He crossed the audience hall of the oracle and found the officers of the temple guards in the chamber beyond. They greeted him joyfully.

'We had heard you were dead, Holiness.'

'Is our duty still at this post, Holy Father?'

'Release us from the temple, Holiness. Let us fight at your side.'

They helped him place the scrolls in the pottery jars and seal them with the golden tablets. Then they carried them through into the archives and placed them upon the stone shelves, hidden by a row of the larger jars.

Huy led the four officers and one hundred men of Legion Ben-Amon back through the city to the camp of the army, leaving the temple unguarded, and Lannon greeted him with relief.

'I doubted you would return, Huy. I thought the fates might keep us apart once more.'

'I gave you a promise, Majesty,' Huy reassured him. 'See what I have for you.' And he led him from the tent to show him the temple guard. One hundred of the finest warriors of Opet, worth as much as a cohort of Yuye troops. Lannon laughed.

'Huy, my worker of miracles.' Then he turned to the

men and looked at them. They were fresh, their armour burnished and bright, and there was a fierce wolfish quality about them which contrasted with the battle weariness of the rest of Lannon's army.

Lannon spoke to their officers. 'You are mine own guard. When the battle begins, stay with me, close with me and Huy Ben-Amon.' Then he dismissed them to eat and rest.

In the big leather tent Lannon and Huy planned the battle, deciding what formations to employ, working out the evolutions for every eventuality, while scribes wrote out the orders.

They were interrupted continually by officers and aides asking for orders, or reporting the movements of the enemy.

Rib-Addi came into the tent begging audience, dry-washing his hands, tugging nervously at his beard and whispering in his secretive book-keeper's voice.

'The treasury, Majesty. Should we not move it to a place of safety?'

'Tell me what place is safe,' Lannon snarled at him, looking up from the clay box in which he and Huy were studying the dispositions. 'Nobody out there knows about the sun door. Leave the treasure where it is, it will remain there until we come for it.'

'The guards have been withdrawn,' Rib-Addi persisted. 'It is not right—'

'Listen to me, old man. It would require 1,000 men and ten days to remove that treasure. I have neither the men nor the time to spare. Go, leave us alone. We have more important matters to employ us now.'

Rib-Addi went, looking very distressed. What more important matters were there than gold and treasure?

Before midnight Lannon straightened up and ran his hands through his thick golden curls, now laced with silver. He sighed, and he looked ill and tired.

'That is all we can do now, Huy. The rest is in the

hands of the gods.' He placed an arm about Huy's shoulders and led him to the flap of the tent. 'A bowl of wine, a breath of lake air – then sleep.'

They stood outside the tent, drinking together and a cool breeze came off the lake, fluttering the tassels upon the golden battle standards.

Something which Huy thought for a moment was a big brown dog sleeping curled against the side of the tent stirred at their voices. Then Huy saw it was the little bushman huntmaster Xhai, faithful as ever, sleeping at the opening of his master's tent. He shook himself awake, grinned when he saw Lannon and Huy, and came to squat beside Lannon.

'I have tried to send him away,' said Lannon. 'He does not understand. He will not leave.' Lannon sighed. 'It seems unnecessary that he should die also, but how can I force him to go.'

'Send him on an errand,' suggested Huy and Lannon glanced at him thoughtfully.

'What errand?'

'Send him to search for sign of the gry-lion upon the southern shores. He will believe that.'

'Yes, he will believe that,' Lannon agreed. 'Tell him, Huy.'

In his own language Huy explained to the little yellow man that the king wanted to hunt the gry-lion once more. Xhai's slanted yellow eyes crinkled and he grinned and nodded with delight, pleased to be of service to the man he considered a god.

'You must go at once,' Huy told him. 'It is an urgent matter.'

Xhai clasped Lannon's knees, bobbing his head, and then he rolled up his sleeping mat and vanished amongst the shadows of the camp. Once he had gone they were silent for a while until Lannon said, 'Do you recall the prophecy, Huy?'

And Huy nodded, remembering it upon Tanith's lips.

'Who shall reign in Opet after me?'

'He who slays the gry-lion.'

He remembered also the prophecy that followed.

'What must I fear?'

'Blackness.'

Huy turned and looked to the north where the great black beast crouched, ready to spring. Lannon's thoughts paralleled his own.

'Yes, Huy,' he murmured. 'Blackness!' And then he drained his wine bowl and hurled it upon the watch fire. A spout of sparks flew upwards.

'At the hand of a friend,' he said, remembering the final prophecy. 'We shall see,' he said. 'We shall see.' Then he glanced at Huy and saw his face.

'Oh, forgive me, old friend. I did not mean to add fuel to the fires of your sorrow. I should not have reminded you of the girl.'

Huy drank the last of his wine and threw the bowl upon the fire. He did not need to be reminded of Tanith, she was ever in his thoughts.

'Let us rest now,' Huy said, but his face was ravished with grief.

The shouting and the trumpets woke Huy, and his first thought was of a night attack upon the camp. He threw on his armour and snatched up the vulture axe, stumbling out of the tent still fumbling with the straps of his breastplate.

The night sky was aglow with a light like that of the dawn, but it was rising from the wrong direction, coming up out of the lake, lighting the towers and walls of Opet.

Lannon joined him, still half-asleep, cursing as he struggled with his armour and helmet.

'What is it, Huy?' he demanded.

'I do not know,' Huy admitted, and they stood staring at the strange light which grew brighter, until they could clearly see each other's features.

'The harbour,' said Huy, understanding at last. 'The fleet. The women.'

'Merciful Baal,' gasped Lannon. 'Come!' And they ran together.

Manatassi had taken the tubes from the beached galleys before he burned them. A little experimentation had shown him how they worked. It was a simple procedure, dependent mostly upon current and wind direction. He had carried the tubes overland, and installed them in the bows of a pair of captured fishing-boats, whose slave crew were skilled seamen and eager to join Manatassi.

The on-shore wind had suited his purpose ideally and carried the boats silently into the mouth of the harbour of Opet. He had personally gone aboard one of the boats and he stood now in the stern wrapped in a leopard-skin robe, watching with fierce and hungry eyes as the jets squirted upon the surface of the wind-chopped water and burst into flame.

Carried on the wind the flame swept into the harbour in a solid wall, roaring like a waterfall and lighting the sky with a false dawn.

Huy stood beside Lannon upon the wharf. The entire basin of the harbour was filled with tall yellow flame, roaring hungrily, the black smoke clouds blocking out the starry sky and rolling in thick evil-smelling billows across the city.

The galleys of Habbakuk Lal stood like islands in a sea of fire. The decks were crowded with the women and children of all the noble families of Opet, and their screams carried over the dull furnace roar of flame.

The watchers upon the shore were unable to offer any escape to them, they looked on helplessly while from the alleyways the lowly ones who had been denied passage hooted and screeched with laughter.

The flames caught upon the wooden hulls and the mooring lines, racing upwards to the crowded decks.

Like ants upon a piece of rotten firewood, they scrambled and milled aimlessly, until the circle of flame tightened about them and shrivelled them.

One of the galleys began drifting in towards the shore. Its anchor lines were burned through, and the wind pushed it so it turned and swung gently, its mast and rigging traced in outlines of yellow fire. Upon the high castle at the stern, clinging together with their blonde hair shining in the firelight, stood Helancá and Imilce, the twin daughters of Lannon Hycanus.

Before the galley touched the stone wall of the quayside, the flames had smothered it, and the girls were gone.

Manatassi watched intently, the firelight glinting on those fierce yellow eyes. When the last flames had died and only the burnt-out hulks of the galleys still smouldered, he lifted his iron hand in command. The two fishing-boats hoisted sail and bore out, close on the wind, northwards to where Manatassi's army was stirring like an awakening monster in the dawn.

This was the mood in which to fight the last battle, this fine blend of sadness and anger, Huy thought as he strode with Lannon along the ranks.

The sun was up, throwing long shadows on the pale brown grass of the plain. On their left stretched the cheerful azure of the lake, flecked with crests of white by the morning breeze. The water fowl flew low in loose V-formations, white against the cloudless blue of the high heavens. On their left rose the rugged rampart of the cliffs, touched with subtle shades of rose and pink and capped with dark green vegetation.

Huy, looking at lake and cliff, saw them only as points on which to anchor his flanks.

Ahead, in front of the walls, the land was open, with

low scrub and a very few big shady trees; it sloped gently from cliff to lake shore, a Roman mile wide. It was a clear front from which no surprise could spring, although it undulated in a series of low rises like the swell of a sleepy ocean.

In their rear were the buildings and streets of the lower city, a maze of low clay walls and flat roofs, while further back rose the massive stone walls of the temple, and above them showed the tops of the sun towers.

This then was a good place in which to fight the last battle, this attenuated front with firm flanks and an open line of retreat.

Lannon strode along the ranks. There was a spring and purpose in his step that belied his tired eyes and grief-sick face; the face of a man who had seen his family burn to death while he stood by. Huy followed a pace behind him, walking with the long-legged crabbing gait which was so familiar to them all. The axe was on his shoulder, and the armour shaped to his bowed back was highly polished and sparkled in the sunlight. Bakmor and a group of officers followed him.

The legions were drawn up into their battle formations, and Huy could find no fault with the placing. The light infantry thrown out in a screen, each man armed with a bundle of javelins as well as his side arms. Behind them were placed the heavy infantry, big men armed with axe and war-spear, carrying a great weight of armour, these men were the backbones of the legions. When hard-pressed, the light infantry could retire through their ranks, and let the enemy spend themselves upon this solid reef of armour.

In the rear were the archers. Drawn up in neat blocks from which they could deliver massed flights of arrows over the heads of the infantry.

Behind them again were the baggage boys, ready with the bundles of fresh javelins and arrows, bags of cold meat and corn cakes, amphorae of water and wine, spare helmets, swords and axes, and those other items which the battle would expend or destroy.

At first Lannon's procession along the ranks was in silence. The men at ease, resting on their weapons, many with their helmets removed, some of them munching a last mouthful of food, all of them with that surface calm of the veteran who has walked many times with old Dame Death, who knows well her whore's face and the smell of her breath. Many of them still showed the recent marks of her claws upon their bodies, but there was no sign of fear on their faces, no shadows in their eyes.

Huy felt a humbleness when he met their steady gaze, a pride when one of them grinned and called out, 'We've missed you, Holiness.'

'It's good to be back,' Huy told him, and there was a growl of assent from those who heard him. Huy passed on, a ripple of animation followed him now.

Quick banter, in which Lannon and the officers joined.

'Leave a few for us, Sunbird,' a grizzled old centurion shouted.

'I think there will be enough for all of us,' Huy grinned at him.

'Too many?' another voice called out.

'Not enough,' Lannon answered. 'For none of those who oppose us is named Ben-Amon.'

They cheered then lustily, and it was taken up all along the line from cliff to lake. New waves of sound and shouting followed them as they went to take their place at the centre of the line upon a rise of higher ground where they could see over the whole field.

Above their heads the standards stood, gaudy with gleaming gold and silken multi-coloured tassels, and at their backs the hundred men of the temple guard. Huy looked over the precisely laid-out cohorts with the sun sparkling on their helmets and weapons, and thought that these were good men with which to fight the last battle, good men in whose company to die.

He loosened his helmet and lifted it from his head, holding it in the crook of his arm.

'Wine here!' he called, and baggage boys came scampering to them with bowls and amphorae. It was the best of Huy's own stocks, rich and red as the blood which would soon soak this field.

Huy saluted his officers with a raised bowl, then turned to Lannon. They looked at each other for a long moment.

'Fly for me, Bird of the Sun,' said Lannon softly.

'Roar for me today, Lion of Opet,' Huy answered him and they drank and broke the bowls and laughed together for the last time. The men about them heard them laugh, and taking courage from it they looked to the north.

Manatassi came in the middle of the bright hot morning. He came on a front that filled the plain from lake shore to cliff foot. He came singing with 500,000 throats, and the rhythmic slapping of bare feet and war rattles which rolled across the sky like the thunder of the heavens. He came in orderly ranks, spaced to give each man fighting space, but the rank behind pressed hard upon that ahead, ready to close any gap in the line, to show a solid unbroken front.

He came in rank upon countless rank, so there was no end to his advance, and the singing was deep and murmurous.

He came like the shadow of storm clouds moving stately and slow across the land, he came dark as night and numerous as the grass of the fields, and the singing took on a harsher more menacing sound.

Huy settled his helmet and tightened the strap. He untied the leather sheath from the vulture axe and watched Manatassi advance on a million moving legs like a single vast black animal topped with a froth of feather headdresses, and the spear blades sparkled like multiple insect eyes in the blackness.

He had never in all his life seen a sight to compare with Manatassi in his full power. This is a worthy foe with whom to fight the last battle, he thought, for there will be no dishonour in defeat by such a one.

Manatassi rolled on deliberately past the markers which Huy had placed on his front to measure the range; 200 paces, 150 – and the dust from a million stamping feet rose as a bank of fire-golden smoke over the horde, blanketing them so that they seemed to appear endlessly out of the moving shifting loom of it.

Huy felt his mouth drying out, and the tingle of his blood as it sped through his tensed body. He lifted the vulture axe high, and glanced left and right to make certain that each commander of the archery had seen the signal.

One hundred and fifty paces, the black tide washed towards him and the singing changed again, rising, shrilling into the blood trill, the high ululation as chilling as any sound Huy had ever heard. He felt the hair on his forearms and at the back of his neck come erect, and his bowels seemed to drop out of his body.

They came on still, trilling, stamping, drumming with spear on shield, head-dresses dipping and tossing, and Huy stood with his axe held aloft.

One hundred paces, and Huy brought down the axe and instantly the air was filled with the soft fluting, the whistle of the wings of wild duck at dusk.

The arrows rose and arched over and fell into them in thick dark flights like that of the locust, and a growl came out of the blackness, the growl of the beast, but it came on steadily into the javelins, seeming to pass through them unscathed for the gaps in the front were instantly filled and the fallen were hidden by the dense mass of bodies passing over them.

Huy's light infantry melted away before this massive advance, falling back through the heavies behind them, and Manatassi rolled weightily into Huy's front.

It seemed as though nothing could check it, it was too heavy, too wide and deep and strong. It must burst through this line of bright helmets.

Then unbelievably the blackness was no longer moving forward, but piling up on itself like a log jam in a river. The ranks pressing forward violated the fighting space of those in the van, catching them in a struggling mass, throwing them onto the prickly metal hedge that was Huy's front line.

Suddenly it was drawing back, sucked away like the wave of the sea from a steep beach.

Immediately the javelin men advanced through the heavies to harass the retreat, while the cry of the centurions carried clearly to Huy as they repaired their line.

'Close up here!'

'Javelins here!'

'Fill that gap!'

'Men here! Men here!'

Manatassi drew back, and bunched, gathered himself like a humping wave and surged forward again, struck and pressed hard, gained a yard of ground and drew back again, gathered himself, started forward gaining momentum and crashing into Huy's front once more.

At noon Lannon and Huy were forced from their vantage point, as the fighting surged about their feet. The standards moved back.

An hour after noon, Huy ordered the last of his reserves into the line, holding only the temple guard under his own hand in a bunch around the battle standards. Still the black waves burst upon the line with a terrible unvarying rhythm, like the ground swell of the ocean.

Huy gave them ground slowly, drawing back each time just enough to reaffirm his line. It was stretched so finely now, that it seemed each new rush of blackness must rip through it, but still it held.

Then they were into the lower city, fighting back along

the streets, and Huy was cut off from visual contact with the battle as a whole. It was merely a narrow street plugged with a knot of legionaries, holding back a steady rush of black warriors.

For the first time that day Huy was drawn into the fighting. A small group of wild-eyed black men burst through the rank ahead of him; they were shiny with sweat and grease, their faces painted with stripes of white ochre, making them appear monstrous and unreal.

Huy cut them down quickly, and ordered a squad of the temple guard into the gap they had opened.

He knew then that the battle was out of his control. He and Lannon were isolated in a cell of fighting men, able only to direct those of their men within sound of their voices.

From some distant part of the field came an animal roar of triumph, and Lannon caught Huy's shoulder and shouted into his ear, 'I think they have broken through.' And Huy nodded.

The set battle was over now. Huy knew that through many gaps in his shattered line the enemy was pouring. It would become a rout now. The miracle had not taken place – the last battle was lost.

'Fall back on the temple?' Lannon shouted the question and again Huy nodded. The army of Opet was no more, it was reduced to hundreds of isolated groups of desperate men locked shoulder to shoulder and back to back in their last fight, a fight from which there would be no surrender, from which death was the only surcease.

They gathered the temple guard about them, and moved back along the street, keeping a steady pace, close up and in hand, offering a solid carapace of shields to the enemy.

Manatassi's hordes were in their rear now, between them and the temple. They had put fire into the lower city, and the flames were taking a swift grip. The streets through which Huy marched were choked with terrified citizens and groups of wild blood-spattered warriors. Huy drove through all of them, his shields locked in the testudo formation, immune to the press of black men at the rear and the greasy billows of black smoke which spread over him.

The main temple gate was open and undefended. The guards had fled, the temple enclosure was empty and silent. Huy and ten men held the steps, while Lannon had the gates swung closed, and at the last instant Huy raced back with his men through the closing gap.

They were resting on the bloody weapons, loosening helmets, wiping the sweat out of their eyes.

'The east gate?' Huy demanded of Lannon. 'It is held? Did you send men to close it?'

Lannon stared at him with dismay, his silence answering Huy's question eloquently.

'You men!' Huy picked a group with a quick wave of his arm. 'Follow me.' But it was too late. Across the temple enclosure black warriors were streaming through the smaller gate.

'Testudo!' shouted Huy. 'Back to the cavern.' They formed the tortoise again, and moved like an armadillo with metal scales across the enclosure while the warriors swarmed about them, unable to pierce the shell. Smoke from the burning city eddied about them, choking them, blinding them.

Suddenly the man beside Huy cried out and grabbed at his groin. Blood spurted out between his fingers and he dropped to his knees. The ground over which they were advancing was strewn with dead warriors cut down by the head of the tortoise. They had to step over them. Dozens of these bodies who had been feigning death came suddenly to life, rolling quickly onto their backs and stabbing up under the skirts of the men above them.

Huy shouted a warning, but it was in vain. The enemy were inside the body of the tortoise, leaping to their feet, thrusting and hacking about them, forcing Huy's men to turn and defend themselves, exposing their backs to the warriors on the outside.

The tortoise disintegrated into a mob of individuals, and the black swarm poured over them as hiving bees.

'With me!' Huy gathered Lannon, Bakmor and a few others about him and they broke out of the mob in a tight bunch and raced for the cleft of the cavern. The smoke was thick and oily, choking them so they coughed as they ran. Huy swung the axe, cutting a path for them and five of them reached the entrance to the cavern but Bakmor had taken a thrust through the ribs. He pressed one fist to it, trying to staunch the flow of life blood. Huy changed the axe to his other hand, and helped Bakmor up the steps into the mouth of the cleft. His blood ran down Huy's side, it felt hot and gelatinous. On the top step Bakmor stumbled to his knees.

'It is finished, Huy,' he choked, but Huy picked him up bodily and carried him into the entrance. He propped him against the wall of the cavern.

'Bakmor,' he panted, and pushed his head back to look into his face. Bakmor's eyes looked back at him without seeing, dead and glazed. Huy let the handsome head drop forward, and stood up.

'Here they come,' shouted Lannon, and Huy hefted the axe and leapt to Lannon's side to meet the first dark rush of bodies into the passage. The four of them – Lannon, Huy and two legionaries – held the entrance long enough to clog it with piles of dead warriors.

Then the archers came up and the first volley of arrows swept the passage. One of them struck a legionary in the throat, and he fell with a dark gush of blood from the mouth.

'No cover in here,' Huy shouted. 'Back to the temple.' They raced back along the passage, and the next volley whistled amongst them. One struck Huy's helmet and glanced away to light sparks off the wall beside him, another found the seam in the last legionary's breastplate and lodged in the bone of his spinal column. His legs collapsed under him. Desperately he clawed his way after Huy, dragging his crippled body by the sheer strength of his arms alone.

'Your favour, my lord,' he screamed, in terror of the castrating blade, the ripping of his bowels while he still lived. 'Don't leave me for them, Holiness.'

Huy checked his run, and shouted, 'Go on, Lannon. I'll follow you.' He went back, and the legionary saw him coming.

'Baal's blessing on you, Holiness,' he cried, and tore his helmet loose, bowing his head forward to expose the neck.

'Find peace!' Huy told him, and cut his head from the trunk with a single stroke of the axe, turning to run again as he did so. An arrow hit Huy in the face below the eye, glancing off the bone and sliced him open to the ear, dangling there by the barb in the fleshy skin.

Huy tore it loose as he ran after Lannon.

Together they crossed the cavern of Astarte, their footsteps echoing from the domed walls; skirting the still green pool, they reached the door of the temple as the next flight of arrows hummed around them. Lannon stumbled slightly, and then they were into the temple.

'Can we hold them here?' Lannon gasped.

'No.' Huy stopped to catch his breath. 'The archives!' Then he looked at Lannon. 'What is it, Majesty?'

'I also am hit, Huy.' The arrow stood out of the joint of his armour near the left armpit. The angle of penetration was such that Huy felt a cold gust of despair. The arrowhead must lie close to the heart. It was mortal, no man could recover from a wound of that nature.

'How is it?' Lannon demanded. 'There is no pain, Huy. It cannot be too bad.'

'You're lucky,' said Huy, and snapped off the shaft, leaving a short stub protruding from the wound.

'Come,' he said, and with a gentle hand on Lannon's arm led him back through the temple into the archives.

'The sun door?' Lannon asked.

'Only at the very end,' said Huy. 'Only when all else fails.' And he steered Lannon into one of the stone recesses.

'Your face.' Lannon stared at Huy in the uncertain light of the torches, as though he had noticed the gaping slash across his cheek for the first time.

'No doubt it's an improvement,' Huy grunted as he tore a strip from his tunic and knotted it into a crude sling for Lannon's left arm.

'Can you use it?' he asked and Lannon worked his fingers, opening and closing them.

'Good,' Huy nodded, and placed the tang of Lannon's shield in his left hand. The sling would help support the weight of it.

Huy cocked his head, listening to the stealthy footsteps, the whispered voices and the clink of weapons within the temple of Astarte.

'They are coming,' he said. 'It will not take them long to find the passage.'

As he spoke the first of them stepped through the entrance from the guard room, and peered into the archives. The wavering light of the smoky torches in their wall brackets emphasized the man's size. He was huge and black, shiny with grease and paint, and Huy smelled him, a warm musky smell like that of a predatory cat.

Huy stepped out of the recess into the light, and in Vendi shouted a challenge at him. The warrior came bounding down the passage at Huy, and their shields came together with a clash that echoed through the temple.

Huy felt the spear blade sting his side, but the lance on the tip of the vulture axe bit in deep, touching bone, and the warrior slid down off the steel.

Lannon limped out of the recess and took his place on Huy's left hand, they stepped over the shivering twitching corpse and went down the passage side by side to meet the rush of dark bodies that came at them.

Manatassi stood in the temple of Astarte. It was after midnight but there were many torches burning and the halls were crowded with warriors, so many that Manatassi had ordered the interior walls torn out of the building to give them access to the mouth of the tunnel.

The dark, evil-looking stone mouth which had already swallowed up so many of his men, was where the two fighting devils of Opet still held out, defying all his efforts to dislodge them. Even now they were dragging dead and badly wounded from the entrance. One of them had his right arm lopped off above the elbow. He made no sound as he clutched at the stump, but his eyes were huge and white in the torchlight.

Manatassi knew what weapon had inflicted that wound, and his anger and his hatred smouldered hotly, warring with the superstitious dread that gripped him.

He had learned enough about the gods of Opet while he was a slave to know their vast powers, their strengths and cruelties. He feared them, and he knew that he stood now in the stronghold of these terrible gods, in their holy place.

He remembered now hearing of this underground place beyond the temple of Astarte, he knew that a death curse guarded it.

Clearly this was the reason why they had taken sanctuary here, in this dark hole.

His anger cooled, chilled by religious awe. He knew the white gods were watching him. He wanted to end it now, destroy this place and go – however, two doomed but stubborn men defied him.

'Fire!' he said. 'Smoke them from their den like wild dogs.'

They built the fire in the entrance of the tunnel, and fed it with green branches, and dense acrid smoke filled the temple and the tunnel. They ringed the tunnel entrance, coughing and choking in the smoke, and they held their weapons ready, knowing that no man could live in there. This must bring them out, surely – but an hour passed with no movement through the smoke.

The fire burned down into a smouldering pile of logs, and the smoke cleared gradually. Manatassi ordered it quenched with water from the pool, and once again they stared into the dark passage from which wisps and streamers of smoke still drifted.

The floor of the passage was still carpeted with the dead, but there was no sign of life.

Manatassi subdued his religious awe, and abruptly snatched a torch from the hand of one of his warriors. Holding it high above his head, he stepped over the hot and sizzling logs and into the passage.

He picked his way amongst the dead, and the floor was puddled and sticky with blood that clung to his bare feet. The torch threw yellow light into each of the stone recesses with their burdened shelves. Manatassi knew what the earthenware pots contained. He had assisted Huy often enough with the scrolls.

He looked for sign of him now, but there was none. Only the black bodies, and the empty recesses.

He reached the end of the passage and the torch lit the engraved image. Manatassi recognized it as the symbol of the sun god, and his courage melted at this tangible evidence of divine influence.

On the floor below the image something caught his eye, sparkling in the torch light.

He suppressed a gasp. It was the vulture axe, laid like an offering before the god image – and the place was empty.

They had gone to their gods. They had cheated him of his revenge, and led him into deadly peril, into a direct confrontation with supernatural forces.

Manatassi backed away, until the god image merged into the darkness and he turned and ran from the place into the hall of the temple of Astarte. There he looked back at the mouth of the tunnel.

'Bring me masons from amongst the freed slaves. Seal off that entrance. It is evil. Seal it.'

They ran to obey, and Manatassi's courage – his anger and his hatred – returned to him.

'I will destroy this evil. I place a curse upon this place, upon these cliffs. A curse that will last for ever.' His voice rose into a scream. 'Burn it. Burn it all. Destroy it. It is an evil to be cleaned from the earth and from the minds of men, for ever.'

So the masons sealed off the entrance to the tomb of the kings. They worked with all the skill that the men of Opet had taught them, and when they were finished the entrance had vanished.

Then Manatassi destroyed the city. He slew every single living thing and threw them on the fires which raged through the lower city for many days. Then he looked at the walls and the towers, and he pointed with his iron claw. They tore it down block by massive block. The walls and the sun towers and the beautiful temple of Astarte. They went down to the very foundations. They lifted the flagged pavings. They tore out the stone wharves of the harbour. Working like a million ants they razed the city until no trace of it remained. They carried each block of masonry up to the cavern and dropped it into the bottom-less green pool. They took the entire city and gave it to the goddess, and the pool was so deep – or the goddess so eternally greedy – that it was swallowed without a trace and the level of the green clear waters rose not a finger's width.

When Manatassi marched from Opet, eastwards to complete the destruction of the empire, he left nothing behind him but piles of loose ash which the wind was already scattering in pale runs of dust.

Manatassi spread his regiments like a net across the four kingdoms, with the command to destroy all trace of the cities and the mines and the gardens built by the men of Opet. But his hatred had burned low now, like a forest fire when the trees are gone. The hatred had left him hollow and blackened and dying, his huge battered frame a husk, even the smoky yellow eyes dull and uncaring.

He came to Zimbao, the great walled city of the middle kingdom, and the men of Opet were dead. The city like his own body was untenanted, empty and deserted.

Manatassi wrapped himself in a fur kaross and lay down beside the watch fire, and in the morning his body was stiff and cold.

They buried him outside the walls, and then they quarrelled and fought, for Manatassi had named no successor. Each war captain named himself, and the army of Manatassi split into a hundred tribes.

In time Manatassi and the city of Opet faded from the memory of men.

Whrn Xhai the bushman was an old man and he knew he was dying, he came back to Opet.

The lake had vanished, its shores were twenty miles from the red cliffs and the waters were brackish and shallow and sunwarmed.

Xhai walked over the spot on which the temple of Baal had stood without recognizing it, until he saw the cleft in the red rock leading to the cavern of Astarte.

He camped beside the pool, building a small fire and sitting over it mumbling to himself in the manner of old men. When his memories paraded before him they were magnified and magnificent, and he sought to capture and fix them.

He picked up his belt on which were strung the little horn pots of pigment, each plugged with a piece of wood, and he went to the wall at the rear of the cavern.

He made the outline of the figure in charcoal upon the smoothest place of the wall. He worked slowly and carefully, with great love.

Then he mixed his pigment and began to paint the proud god-like figure with its white face, red-gold beard and majestic vaunting manhood, and as he worked it seemed as though ghost voices whispered deep in the rock, down in the vault of the kings.

'Huy, I am cold. Favour me, old friend. Give me the hand of friendship that the oracle foresaw.'

'I cannot, Lannon. I cannot do it.'

'I am cold and in pain, Huy. If you love me, you will do it.'

'I love you.'

'Fly for me, Bird of the Sun.'

As the old man worked, the wind whispered and sighed along the cliffs, and the sigh was that which a man might make when he has lost his love and his land, has denied his gods and has given mercy to his friend. He might sigh like that as he takes the sword still dulled with his friend's blood and sets the hilt firmly in a niche of the stone floor and places the point up under his ribs, and falls forward on it.

* * *

THE RAND DAILY MAIL
27th May

Death of Multi-Millionaire Financier
Louren Sturvesant Dies of Mystery Disease

BOTSWANA, SATURDAY. The well-known millionaire financier and sportsman, Mr Louren Sturvesant of Kleine Schuur, Sandown, Johannesburg, died here yesterday after a brief illness.

Mr Sturvesant was visiting the site of the recently discovered ancient Carthaginian city in Botswana. The leader of the expedition, Dr Benjamin Kazin, has also contracted the disease which is believed to be infectious.

Dr Kazin has been flown to Johannesburg where a hospital spokesman stated that his condition was critical.

THE FINANCIAL GAZETTE
28th May

Stop Press

Anglo-Sturvesant Crashes 97 Points
Panic on Exchange

HOLLARD STR. MONDAY. Following reports of the death of Mr Louren Sturvesant, Chairman of Anglo-Sturvesant, quoted prices of the Sturvesant Group of Companies fell sharply on the Johannesburg Stock Exchange today.

THE STAR
3rd June

Famous Archaeologist Regains Consciousness

JOHANNESBURG, FRIDAY. After ten days in coma, Dr Benjamin Kazin today regained consciousness, according to a hospital spokesman.

Dr Kazin is the Director of the Institute of Anthropology and African Prehistory, and the discoverer of the ancient Carthaginian city of Opet. He was suffering from a rare fungus infection contracted while working on the site of his recent find.

Today Dr Kazin was visited by his assistant, Dr Sally Benator, who said afterwards that Dr Kazin was 'very much better but still terribly upset by the death of Mr Sturvesant'.

THE STAR
6th September

Well-known Archaeologists Marry

CAPE TOWN, FRIDAY. The discoverer of the city of Opet, Dr Benjamin Kazin, was married to his long-time assistant, Dr Sally Benator, in a brief civil ceremony here today. The bride said that she planned a working honeymoon at the site of the ancient city of Opet.

THE TIMES
20th April

Archaeologist Honoured

LONDON, SATURDAY. At the Royal Geographical Society, an Extraordinary General Meeting of the Society was held today during which Dr Benjamin Kazin was awarded the Society's much-prized Founder's and Patron's Medal.

After the meeting there was a short ceremony at which a portrait of Dr Kazin by the well-known artist Pietro Annigoni was hung in the Society.

Dr Kazin was accompanied by his wife, Dr Sally Kazin, formerly Benator, who is also a well-known figure in archaeological circles. The couple will spend two weeks holidaying in Britain and on the continent before returning to Africa.